THE WHEEL OF TIME ®
by Robert Jordan

*Forthcoming

THE FIRES OF HEAVEN

Book Five

of

THE WHEEL OF TIME

Robert Jordan

TOR ®
fantasy

A TOM DOHERTY ASSOCIATES BOOK
NEW YORK

This is a work of fiction. All the characters and events portrayed in this book are fictitious, and any resemblance to real people or events is purely coincidental.

THE FIRES OF HEAVEN

Copyright © 1993 by The Bandersnatch Group, Inc.

The phrases "The Wheel of Time®" and "The Dragon Reborn™" and the snake-wheel symbol are trademarks of Robert Jordan.

All rights reserved.

Cover art by Darrell K. Sweet
Maps by Thomas Canty and Ellisa Mitchell
Interior illustrations by Matthew C. Nielsen and Ellisa Mitchell

A Tor Book
Published by Tom Doherty Associates, LLC
175 Fifth Avenue
New York, NY 10010

www.tor-forge.com

Tor® is a registered trademark of Tom Doherty Associates, LLC.

ISBN 978-0-8125-5030-6

First Edition: November 1993
First International Mass Market Edition: March 1994
First U.S. Mass Market Edition: October 1994

Printed in the United States of America

20   19   18   17

For Harriet

The light of her eyes is my Light.

CONTENTS

With his coming are the dread fires born again. The hills burn, and the land turns sere. The tides of men run out, and the hours dwindle. The wall is pierced, and the veil of parting raised. Storms rumble beyond the horizon, and the fires of heaven purge the earth. There is no salvation without destruction, no hope this side of death.

—fragment from *The Prophecies of the Dragon*
    believed translated by N'Delia Basolaine
    First Maid and Swordfast to Raidhen of Hol Cuchone
    (circa 400 AB)

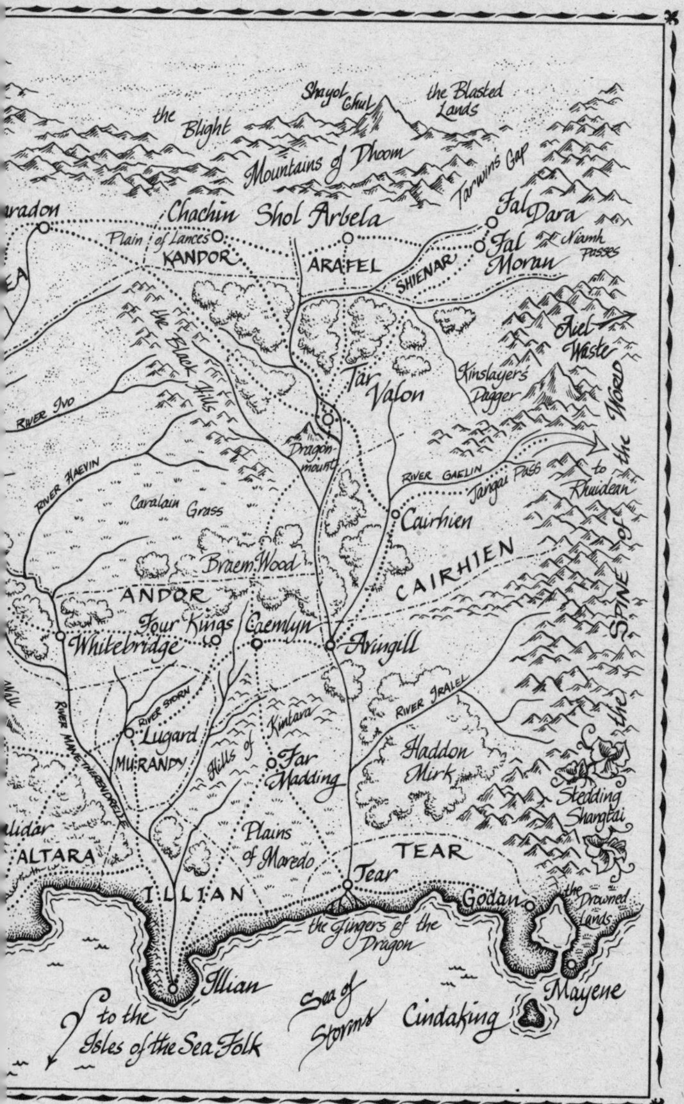

Shayol Ghul
the Blasted Lands
the Blight
Mountains of Dhoom
Tarwin's Gap
Chachin
Shol Arbela
Fal Dara
Fal Moran
Niamh Passes
Plain of Lances
KANDOR
ARAFEL
SHIENAR
Aiel Waste
the Black Hills
Kinslayer's Dagger
Tar Valon
RIVER IVO
Dragonmount
RIVER HAEVIN
RIVER GAELIN
Jangai Pass
to Rhuidean
Caralain Grass
Cairhien
CAIRHIEN
Braem Wood
ANDOR
Four Kings
Caemlyn
Aringill
Whitebridge
the Spine of the World
RIVER IRALELL
RIVER STORN
Lugard
MURANDY
Hills of Kintara
Far Madding
Haddon Mirk
RIVER MANETHERENDRELLE
Stedding Shangtai
Plains of Maredo
TEAR
Tear
ALTARA
ILLIAN
Godan
the Drowned Lands
the Fingers of the Dragon
Illian
Mayene
Sea of Storms
Cindaking
to the Isles of the Sea Folk

PROLOGUE

The First Sparks Fall

Elaida do Avriny a'Roihan absently fingered the long, seven-striped stole about her shoulders, the stole of the Amyrlin Seat, as she sat behind her wide writing table. Many would have accounted her beautiful, at first glance, but a second look made it clear that the severity of her ageless, Aes Sedai face was not a momentary matter. Today there was something more, a light of anger in her dark eyes. If anyone had noticed.

She barely listened to the women arrayed on stools before her. Their dresses were every color from white to the darkest red, in silk or wool as each woman's taste dictated, yet all but one wore their formal shawls, embroidered White Flame of Tar Valon centered on their backs, colored fringe proclaiming their Ajahs, as though this were a meeting of the Hall of the Tower. They discussed reports and rumors of events in the world, trying to sift fact from fancy, trying to decide the Tower's course of action, but they seldom even glanced at the woman behind the table, the woman they had sworn to obey. Elaida could not keep her full attention on them. They did not know what was really important. Or rather, they knew and feared to speak of it.

"There is apparently something happening in Shienar." That was Danelle, slight and often seemingly lost in a dream, the only Brown sister present. Green and Yellow also had only one sister apiece, and none of the three Ajahs was pleased about that. There were no Blues. Now Danelle's big blue eyes looked thoughtfully inward; an unnoticed ink smudge stained her cheek, and her dark gray wool dress was rumpled. "There are rumors of skirmishes. Not with Trollocs, and not Aiel, though raids through the Niamh Passes appear to have increased. Between Shienarans. Unusual for the Borderlands. They seldom fight each other."

"If they intend to have a civil war, they have chosen the proper time for it," Alviarin said coolly. Tall and slim and all in white silk, she was the one without a shawl. The stole of the Keeper around her shoulders was white also, to show she had been raised from the White Ajah, Elaida's former Ajah, as tradition held. Not Red, Elaida's former Ajah, as tradition held. Whites were always cool. "The Trollocs might as well have vanished. The entire Blight seems quiet enough for two farmers and a novice to guard."

Teslyn's bony fingers shuffled papers on her lap, though she did not look at them. One of four Red sisters there—more than any other Ajah—she ran Elaida a close second for severity, though no one had ever thought her beautiful. "Better perhaps if it did no be so quiet," Teslyn said, her Illianer accent strong. "I did receive a message this morning that the Marshal-General of Saldaea does have an army on the move. No toward the Blight, but in the opposite direction. South and east. He would no ever have done that if the Blight did no seem to be asleep."

"Then word of Mazrim Taim is seeping out." Alviarin could have been discussing the weather or the price of carpets instead of a potential disaster. Much effort had gone into capturing Taim, and as much into hiding his escape. No good to the Tower if the world learned they could not hold on to a false Dragon once he was taken. "And it seems that Queen Tenobia, or Davram Bashere, or both, thinks we cannot be trusted to deal with him again."

Dead quiet fell at the mention of Taim. The man could channel—he had been on his way to Tar Valon to be gentled, cut off from the One Power forever, when he was broken free—yet that was not what curbed tongues. Once the existence of a man able to channel the One Power had been the deepest anathema; hunting such men down was the main reason of existence for the Red, and every Ajah helped as it could. But now most of the women beyond the table shifted on their stools, refusing to meet each other's eyes, because speaking of Taim brought them too close to another subject they did not want to speak aloud. Even Elaida felt bile rise in her stomach.

Apparently Alviarin experienced no such reluctance. One corner of her mouth quirked momentarily in what might have been smile or grimace. "I will redouble our efforts to retake Taim. And I suggest that a sister be dispatched to counsel Tenobia. Someone used to overcoming the sort of stubborn resistance that young woman will put up."

Others rushed to help fill the silence.

Joline shifted her green-fringed shawl on slender shoulders and smiled, though it seemed a bit forced. "Yes. She needs an Aes Sedai at her shoulder. Someone able to handle Bashere. He has excessive influence with Tenobia. He must move his army back where it can be used if the Blight wakes up." Too much bosom showed in the gap of her shawl, and her pale green silk was too snug, too clinging. And she smiled too much for Elaida's liking. Especially at men. Greens always did.

"The last thing we need now is another army on the march," Shemerin, the Yellow sister, said quickly. A slightly plump woman, she had somehow never really managed the outward calm of Aes Sedai; there was often a strain of anxiety around her eyes, and more so of late.

"And someone to Shienar," added Javindhra, another Red. Despite smooth cheeks, her angular face was hard enough to hammer nails. Her voice was harsh. "I don't like trouble of this sort in the Borderlands. The last thing we need is Shienar weakening itself to the point where a Trolloc army could break through."

"Perhaps." Alviarin nodded, considering. "But there are agents in Shienar—Red, I am sure, and perhaps others?—" The four Red sisters nodded tightly, reluctantly; no one else did. "—who can warn us if these small clashes become anything to worry us."

It was an open secret that every Ajah except the White, devoted to logic and philosophy as it was, had watchers and listeners scattered through the nations to varying degrees, though the Yellow network was believed to be a pitiful thing. There was nothing of sickness or Healing they could learn from those who could not channel. Some individual sisters had their own eyes-and-ears, though perhaps even more closely guarded than agents of the Ajahs. The Blues had had the most extensive, both Ajah and personal.

"As for Tenobia and Davram Bashere," Alviarin went on, "are we agreed that they must be dealt with by sisters?" She hardly waited for heads to nod. "Good. It is done. Memara will do nicely; she will take no nonsense from Tenobia, while never letting her see the leash. Now. Does anyone have fresh word out of Arad Doman or Tarabon? If we do not do something there soon, we may find that Pedron Niall and the Whitecloaks have sway from Bandar Eban to the Shadow Coast. Evanellein, you have something?" Arad Doman and Tarabon were racked by civil wars, and worse. There was no order anywhere. Elaida was surprised they would bring it up.

"Only a rumor," the Gray sister replied. Her silk dress, matching the fringe on her shawl, was finely cut and scooped low at the neck. Often Elaida thought the woman should have been Green, so concerned was she with her looks and clothes. "Almost everyone in those poor lands is a refugee, including those who might send news. The Panarch Amathera has apparently vanished, and it seems an Aes Sedai may have been involved. . . ."

Elaida's hand tightened on her stole. Nothing touched her face, but her eyes smoldered. The matter of the Saldaean army was done. At least Memara was Red; that was a surprise. But they had not even asked her opinion. It was done. The startling possibility that an Aes Sedai was involved in the disappearance of the Panarch—if this was not another of the thousand improbable tales that drifted from the western coast—could not take Elaida's mind from that. There were Aes Sedai scattered from the Aryth Ocean to the Spine of the World, and the Blues at least might do anything. Less than two months since they had all knelt to swear fealty to her as the embodiment of the White Tower, and now the decision was made without so much as a glance in her direction.

The Amyrlin's study sat only a few levels up in the White Tower, yet this room was the heart of the Tower as surely as the Tower itself, the color of bleached bone, was the heart of the great island city of Tar Valon, cradled in the River Erinin. And Tar Valon was, or should be, the heart of the world. The room spoke of the power wielded by the long line of women who had occupied it, floor of polished redstone from the Mountains of Mist, tall fireplace of golden Kandori marble, walls paneled in pale, oddly striped wood marvelously carved with unknown birds and beasts more than a thousand years ago. Stone like glittering pearls framed the tall, arched windows that let onto the balcony overlooking the Amyrlin's private garden, the only stone like it known, salvaged from a nameless city swallowed by the Sea of Storms during the Breaking of the World. A room of power, a reflection of Amyrlins who had made thrones dance to their calling for nearly three thousand years. And they did not even ask her opinion.

It happened too often, this slighting. Worst—most bitter of all, perhaps—they usurped her authority without even thinking of it. They knew how she had come to the stole, knew their aid had put it on her shoulders. She herself had been too much aware of that. But they presumed too far. It would soon be time to do something about that. But not quite yet.

She had put her own stamp on the room, as much as possible, with a writing table ornately carved in triple-linked rings and a heavy chair that raised an inlaid ivory Flame of Tar Valon above her dark hair like a large snowy teardrop. Three boxes of Altaran lacquerwork were arranged on the table, precisely equidistant from each other; one held the finest of her collection of carved miniatures. A white vase on a simple plinth against one wall held red roses that filled the room with sweet fragrance. There had been no rain since she was raised, but fine blossoms were always available with the Power; she had always liked flowers. They could be so easily pruned and trained to produce beauty.

Two paintings hung where, seated, she could see them merely by lifting her head. The others avoided looking at them; among all the Aes Sedai who came to Elaida's study, only Alviarin ever so much as glanced at them.

"Is there any news of Elayne?" Andaya asked diffidently. A thin, birdlike little woman, outwardly timid despite Aes Sedai features, the second Gray looked an unlikely mediator, but was in fact one of the best. There were still faint traces of Tarabon in her voice. "Or Galad? If Morgase discovers that we have lost her stepson, she may begin to ask more questions concerning the whereabouts of her daughter, yes? And if she learns we have lost the Daughter-Heir, Andor may become as closed to us as Amadicia."

A few women shook their heads—there was no news, and Javindhra said, "A Red sister is in place in the Royal Palace. Newly raised, so she can easily pass for other than Aes Sedai." She meant that the woman had not yet taken on the agelessness that came with long use of the Power. Someone trying to guess the age of any woman in the study would have fumbled over a range of twenty years, and in some cases would be off by twice that. "She is well trained, though, quite strong, and a good observer. Morgase is absorbed in putting forward her claim to the Cairhienin throne." Several women shifted on their stools, and as if realizing she had stepped close to dangerous ground, Javindhra hurried on. "And her new lover, Lord Gaebril, seems to be keeping her occupied otherwise." Her thin mouth narrowed even further. "She is completely besotted with the man."

"He keeps her concentrated on Cairhien," Alviarin said. "The situation there is nearly as bad as in Tarabon and Arad Doman, with every House contending for the Sun Throne, and famine everywhere. Morgase will reestablish order, but it will take time for her to have the throne secure. Until that is done, she will have little energy left to worry about other matters, even the Daughter-Heir. And I set a clerk the task of sending occasional letters; the woman does a good imitation of Elayne's hand. Morgase will keep until we can secure proper control of her again."

"At least we still have her son in hand." Joline smiled.

"Gawyn do hardly be in hand," Teslyn said sharply. "Those Younglings of his do skirmish with Whitecloaks on both sides of the river. He does act on his own as much as at our direction."

"He will be brought under control," Alviarin said. Elaida was beginning to find that constant cool composure hateful.

"Speaking of the Whitecloaks," Danelle put in, "it appears that Pedron Niall is conducting secret negotiations, trying to convince Altara and Murandy to cede land to Illian, and thus keep the Council of Nine from invading one or both."

Safely back from the precipice, the women on the other side of the table nattered on, deciding whether the Lord Captain Commander's negotiations might gain too much influence for the Children of the Light. Perhaps they should be disrupted so the Tower could step in and replace him.

Elaida's mouth twisted. The Tower had often in its history been cautious of necessity—too many feared them, too many distrusted them—but it had never *feared* anything or anyone. Now, it feared.

She raised her eyes to the paintings. One consisted of three wooden panels depicting Bonwhin, the last Red to have been raised to the Amyrlin Seat, a thousand years before, and the reason no Red had worn the stole since. Until Elaida. Bonwhin, tall and proud, ordering Aes Sedai in their manipulations of Artur Hawkwing; Bonwhin, defiant, on the white walls of Tar Valon, under siege by Hawkwing's forces; and Bonwhin, kneeling and humbled, before the Hall of the Tower as they stripped her of stole and staff for nearly destroying the Tower.

Many wondered why Elaida had had the triptych retrieved from the storerooms where it had lain covered in dust; if none spoke openly, she had still heard the whispers. They did not understand that constant reminder of the price of failure was necessary.

The second painting was in the new fashion, on
stretched canvas, a copy of a street artist's sketch from
the distant west. That one caused even more unease
among the Aes Sedai who saw it. Two men fought among
clouds, seemingly in the sky, wielding lightning for
weapons. One had a face of fire. The other was tall and
young, with reddish hair. It was the youth who caused
the fear, who made even Elaida's teeth clench. She was
not sure if it was in anger, or to keep them from
chattering. But fear could and must be controlled. Control was all.

"We are done, then," Alviarin said, rising smoothly
from her stool. The others copied her, adjusting skirts
and shawls in preparation for leaving. "In three days, I
will expect—"

"Have I given you leave to go, daughters?" Those were
the first words Elaida had spoken since telling them to be
seated. They looked at her in surprise. Surprise! Some
moved back toward the stools, but not with any haste.
And not a word of apology. She had let this go on much
too long. "Since you are standing, you will remain so
until I am done." A moment of confusion caught those
half-seated, and she continued as they straightened again
uncertainly. "I have heard no mention of the search for
that woman and her companions."

No need to name *that woman,* Elaida's predecessor.
They knew who she meant, and Elaida found it harder
every day even to think the former Amyrlin's name. All
of her current problems—all!—could be laid at *that
woman*'s feet.

"It is difficult," Alviarin said evenly, "since we have
bolstered the rumors that she was executed." The woman had ice for blood. Elaida met her eyes firmly until she
added a belated "Mother," but it too was placid, even
casual.

Elaida swung her gaze to the others, made her voice
steel. "Joline, you have charge of that search, and of the
investigation of her escape. In both cases I hear of
nothing but difficulties. Perhaps a daily penance will
help you increase your diligence, daughter. Write out
what you think suitable and submit it to me. Should I

find it—less than suitable, I will triple it."

Joline's ever-present smile faded in satisfactory fashion. She opened her mouth, then closed it again under Elaida's steady stare. Finally, she curtsied deeply. "As you command, Mother." The words were tight, the meekness forced, but it would do. For now.

"And what of trying to bring back those who fled?" If anything, Elaida's tone was even harder. The return of the Aes Sedai who had run away when *that woman* was deposed meant the return of Blues to the Tower. She was not sure she could ever trust any Blue. But then, she was not sure she could ever bring herself to trust any who had fled instead of hailing her ascension. Yet the Tower must be whole again.

Javindhra was overseeing that task. "Again, there are difficulties." Her features remained as severe as ever, but she licked her lips quickly at the storm that swept silently across Elaida's face. "Mother."

Elaida shook her head. "I will not hear of difficulties, daughter. Tomorrow you will place before me a list of everything you have done, including all measures taken to see the world does not learn of any dissension in the Tower." That was deadly important; there was a new Amyrlin, but the world must see the Tower as united and strong as ever. "If you do not have enough time for the work I give you, perhaps you should give up your place as Sitter for the Red in the Hall. I must consider it."

"That will not be necessary, Mother," the hard-faced woman said hurriedly. "You will have the report you require tomorrow. I am sure many will start returning soon."

Elaida was not so certain, however much she wanted it—the Tower must be strong; it *must*!—but her point was made. Troubled thoughtfulness marked every eye but Alviarin's. If Elaida was ready to come down on one of her own former Ajah, and even harder on a Green who had been with her from the first day, perhaps they had made a mistake in treating her as a ceremonial effigy. Perhaps *they* had put her on the Amyrlin Seat, but now *she* was the Amyrlin. A few more examples in the coming days should drive it home. If necessary, she would have every woman here doing penance till they begged mercy.

"There are Tairen soldiers in Cairhien, as well as Andoran," she went on, ignoring averted eyes. "Tairen soldiers sent by the man who took the Stone of Tear." Shemerin clasped her plump hands tight, and Teslyn flinched. Only Alviarin remained unruffled as a frozen pond. Elaida flung out her hand and pointed to the painting of two men fighting with lightning. "Look at it. Look! Or I will have every last one of you on hands and knees scrubbing floors! If you have not the backbone even to look at a painting, what courage can you have for what is to come? Cowards are no use to the Tower!"

Slowly they raised their eyes, shuffling feet like nervous girls instead of Aes Sedai. Only Alviarin merely looked, and only she appeared untouched. Shemerin wrung her hands, and tears actually welled in her eyes. Something would have to be done about Shemerin.

"Rand al'Thor. A man who can channel." The words left Elaida's mouth like a whip. They made her own stomach knot up till she feared she might vomit. Somehow she kept her face smooth and pressed on, pushed the words out, stones from a sling. "A man fated to go mad and wreak horror with the Power before he dies. But more than that. Arad Doman and Tarabon and everything between is a ruin of rebellion because of him. If the war and famine in Cairhien cannot be tied to him of a certainty, he surely precipitates a greater war there, between Tear and Andor, when the Tower needs peace! In Ghealdan, some mad Shienaran preaches of him to crowds too great for Alliandre's army to contain. The greatest danger the Tower has ever faced, the greatest threat the world has ever faced, and you cannot make yourselves speak of him? You cannot gaze at his image?"

Silence answered her. All save Alviarin looked as though their tongues were frozen. Most stared at the young man in the painting, birds hypnotized by a snake.

"Rand al'Thor." The name tasted bitter on Elaida's lips. Once she had had that young man, so innocent in appearance, within arm's reach. And she had not seen what he was. Her predecessor had known—had known for the Light alone knew how long, and had left him to run wild. *That woman* had told her a great deal before escaping, had said things, when put hard to the question, that Elaida would not let herself believe—if the Forsaken were truly free, all might be lost—but somehow she had managed to refuse some answers. And then escaped before she could be put to the question again. *That woman* and Moiraine. *That woman* and the Blue had known all along. Elaida intended to have them both back in the Tower. They would tell every last scrap of what they knew. They would plead on their knees for death before she was done.

She forced herself to go on, though the words curdled in her mouth. "Rand al'Thor is the Dragon Reborn, daughters." Shemerin's knees gave way, and she sat down hard on the floor. Some of the others appeared to have weak knees as well. Elaida's eyes flogged them with scorn. "There can be no doubt of it. He is the one spoken of in the Prophecies. The Dark One is breaking free of his prison, the Last Battle is coming, and the Dragon Reborn must be there to face him or the world is doomed to fire and destruction so long as the Wheel of Time turns. And he runs free, daughters. We do not know where he is. We know a dozen places he is not. He is no longer in Tear. He is not here in the Tower, safely shielded, as he should be. He brings the whirlwind down on the world, and we must stop it if there is to be any hope of surviving Tarmon Gai'don. We must have him in hand to see he fights in the Last Battle. Or do any of you believe he will go willingly to his prophesied death to save the world? A man who must be going mad already? We must have him in control!"

"Mother," Alviarin began with that irritating lack of emotion, but Elaida stopped her with a glare.

"Putting our hands on Rand al'Thor is more important by far than skirmishes in Shienar or whether the Blight is quiet, more important than finding Elayne or Galad, more important even than Mazrim Taim. You will find him. You *will*! When next I see you, each of you will be ready to tell me in detail what you have done to make it so. Now you may leave me, daughters."

A ripple of unsteady curtsies, breathy murmurs of "As you command, Mother," and they came close to running, Joline helping Shemerin wobbling to her feet. The Yellow sister would do nicely for the next example; some would be necessary, to make sure none of them slid back, and she was too weak to be allowed in this council. Of course, this council would not be allowed to continue much longer in any case. The Hall would hear her words, and leap.

All save Alviarin went.

For a long moment after the door had closed behind the others, the two women met each other's eyes. Alviarin had been the first, the very first, to hear and agree with the charges against Elaida's predecessor. And Alviarin knew full well why she wore the Keeper's stole instead of someone from the Red. The Red Ajah had favored Elaida unanimously, but the White had not done so, and without wholehearted support from the White, many others might not have come round, in which case Elaida would have been in a cell instead of sitting on the Amyrlin Seat. That is, if the remains of her head were not decorating a spike for the ravens to play with. Alviarin would not be so easily intimidated as the others. If she could be intimidated at all. There was a disturbing feel of equal-to-equal in Alviarin's unwavering gaze.

A tap at the door sounded loud in the quiet.

"Come!" Elaida snapped.

One of the Accepted, a pale, slender girl, stepped hesitantly into the room and immediately dropped a curtsy so low her white skirt with its seven bands of color at the hem made a wide pool around her on the floor. From the wideness of her blue eyes and the way she kept them on the floor, she had caught the mood of the women leaving. Where Aes Sedai left shaking, an Accepted went at great peril. "M-Mother, Master F-Fain is here. He said you w-would see him at th-this hour." The girl swayed in her crouch, on the point of falling over from stark fear.

"Then send him in, girl, instead of keeping him waiting," Elaida growled, but she would have had the girl's hide if she had not kept the man outside. The anger she held back from Alviarin—she would not let herself think that she did not dare show it—that anger welled up. "And if you cannot learn to speak properly, perhaps the kitchens are a better place for you than the Amyrlin's anteroom. Well? Are you going to do as you were told? Move, girl! And tell the Mistress of Novices you need to be taught to obey with alacrity!"

The girl squeaked something that might have been a correct response and darted out.

With an effort, Elaida got hold of herself. It did not concern her whether Silviana, the new Mistress of Novices, beat the girl to incoherence or let her off with a lecture. She barely saw novices or Accepted unless they intruded on her, and cared less. It was Alviarin she wanted humbled and on her knees.

But Fain, now. She tapped one finger against her lips. A bony little man with a big nose, who had appeared at the Tower only days earlier in dirty, once-fine clothes too big for him, arrogant and cringing by turns, seeking audience with the Amyrlin. Except for those who served the Tower, men came there only under duress or in great need, and none asked to speak to the Amyrlin. A fool, in some ways, or conceivably a half-wit; he claimed to be from Lugard, in Murandy, but spoke in various accents, sometimes slipping from one to another in midsentence. Yet it seemed he might be useful.

Alviarin was still looking at her, so icily complacent, just a hint in her eyes of the questions she must have about Fain. Elaida's face hardened. Almost she reached for *saidar,* the female half of the True Source, to teach the woman her place with the Power. But that was not the way. Alviarin might even resist, and fighting like a farmgirl in a stableyard was no method for the Amyrlin to make her authority plain. Yet Alviarin would learn to yield to her as surely as the others would. The first step would be leaving Alviarin in the dark concerning Master Fain, or whatever his real name was.

Padan Fain put the frantic young Accepted out of his mind as he stepped into the Amyrlin's study; she was a toothsome bit, and he liked them fluttering like birds in the hand, but there were more important matters to concentrate on now. Dry-washing his hands, he ducked his head suitably low, suitably humbly, but the two awaiting him seemed unaware of his presence at first, locked eye-to-eye as they were. It was all he could do not to stretch out a hand to caress the tension between them. Tension and division wove everywhere through the White Tower. All to the good. Tension could be tweaked, division exploited, as need be.

He had been surprised to find Elaida on the Amyrlin Seat. Better than what he had expected, though. In many ways she was not so tough, as he had heard, as the woman who had worn the stole before her. Harder, yes, and more cruel, but more brittle, too. More difficult to bend, likely, but easier to break. If either became necessary. Still, one Aes Sedai, one Amyrlin even, was much like another to him. Fools. Dangerous fools, true, but useful dupes at times.

Finally they realized he was there, the Amyrlin frowning slightly at being taken by surprise, the Keeper of the Chronicles unchanging. "You may go now, daughter," Elaida said firmly, a slight but definite emphasis on "now." Oh, yes. The tensions, the cracks in power. Cracks where seeds could be planted. Fain caught himself on the point of giggling.

Alviarin hesitated before giving the briefest of curtsies. As she swept out of the room, her eyes brushed across him, expressionless yet disconcerting. Unconsciously he huddled, hunching his shoulders protectively; his upper lip fluttered in a half-snarl at her slim back. On occasion he had the feeling, just for an instant, that she knew too much about him, but he could not have said why. Her cool face, cool eyes, they never changed. At those times he wanted to make them change. Fear. Agony. Pleading. He nearly laughed at the thought. No point, of course. She could know nothing. Patience, and he could be done with her and her never-changing eyes.

The Tower held things worth a little patience in its strongrooms. The Horn of Valere was there, the fabled Horn made to call dead heroes back from the grave for the Last Battle. Even most of the Aes Sedai were ignorant of that, but he knew how to sniff out things. The dagger was there. He felt its pull where he stood. He could have pointed to it. It was his, a part of him, stolen and mired away here by these Aes Sedai. Having the dagger would

make up for so much lost; he was not sure how, but he
was sure it would. For Aridhol lost. Too dangerous to
return to Aridhol, perchance to be trapped there again.
He shivered. So long trapped. Not again.

Of course, no one called it Aridhol any longer, but
Shadar Logoth. Where the Shadow Waits. An apt name.
So much had changed. Even himself. Padan Fain.
Mordeth. Ordeith. Sometimes he was uncertain which
name was really his, who he really was. One thing was
sure. He was not what anyone thought. Those who
believed they knew him were badly mistaken. He was
transfigured, now. A force unto himself, and beyond any
other power. They would all learn, eventually.

Suddenly he realized with a start that the Amyrlin had
said something. Casting about in his mind, he found it.
"Yes, Mother, the coat suits me very well." He ran a
hand down the black velvet to show how fine he found it,
as if garments mattered. "'Tis a very good coat. I am
thanking you kindly, Mother." He was prepared to suffer
more of her trying to make him feel at ease, ready to
kneel and kiss her ring, but this time she went straight to
the heart.

"Tell me more of what you know of Rand al'Thor,
Master Fain."

Fain's eyes went to the painting of the two men, and as
he gazed at it, his back straightened. Al'Thor's portrait
tugged at him almost as much as the man would, sent
rage and hate roiling along his veins. Because of that
young man he had suffered pain beyond remembering,
pain he did not let himself remember, suffered far worse
than pain. He had been broken and remade because of
al'Thor. Of course, that remaking gave him the means of
revenge, but that was beside the point. Beside his desire
for al'Thor's destruction, everything else dimmed from
sight.

When he turned back to the Amyrlin, he did not
realize his manner was as commanding as hers, meeting
her stare for stare. "Rand al'Thor is devious and sly,
uncaring of anyone or anything but his own power." Fool
woman. "He's never a one to do what you expect." But if
she could put al'Thor in his hands. . . . "He is difficult to

lead—very difficult—but I believe it can be done. First you must tie a string to one of the few he trusts. . . ." If she gave him al'Thor, he might leave her alive when he finally went, even if she was Aes Sedai.

Lounging in a gilded chair in his shirtsleeves, one booted leg over the padded arm, Rahvin smiled as the woman standing before the fireplace repeated what he had told her. There was a slight glaze in her large, brown eyes. A young, pretty woman, even in the plain gray woolens she had adopted for disguise, but that was not what interested him about her.

No breath of air stirred through the room's tall windows. Sweat rolled down the woman's face as she spoke, and beaded on the narrow face of the other man present. For all of that man's fine red silk coat with its golden embroidery, he stood as stiffly as a servant, which he was in a way, if of his own free will, unlike the woman. Of course, he was deaf and blind for the moment.

Rahvin handled the flows of Spirit he had woven around the pair delicately. There was no need to damage valuable servants.

He did not sweat, of course. He did not let the summer's lingering heat touch him. He was a tall man, large, dark and handsome despite the white streaking his temples. Compulsion had presented no difficulties with this woman.

A scowl twisted his face. It did with some. A few—a very few—had a strength of self so firm that their minds searched, even if unaware for crevices through which to slide away. It was his bad luck that he still had some small need for one such. She could be handled, but she kept trying to find escape without knowing she was trapped. Eventually that one would no longer be needed, of course; he would have to decide whether to send her on her way or be rid of her more permanently. Dangers lay either way. Nothing that could threaten him, of course, but he was a careful man, meticulous. Small dangers had a way of growing if ignored, and he always chose his risks with a measure of prudence. To kill her, or keep her?

The cessation of the woman's speech pulled him from his reverie. "When you leave here," he told her, "you will remember nothing of this visit. You will remember only taking your usual morning walk." She nodded, eager to please him, and he tied off the strands of Spirit lightly, so they would evaporate from her mind shortly after she reached the street. Repeated use of compulsion made obedience easier even when it was not in use, but while it was, there was always a danger it might be detected.

That done, he released Elegar's mind as well. Lord Elegar. A minor noble, but faithful to his vows. He licked his thin lips nervously and glanced at the woman, then went immediately to one knee before Rahvin. Friends of the Dark—Darkfriends they were called, now—had begun learning just how strictly they would be kept to their vows now that Rahvin and the others were freed.

"Take her to the street by back ways," Rahvin said, "and leave her there. She is not to be seen."

"It will be as you say, Great Master," Elegar said, bowing where he knelt. Rising, he backed from Rahvin's presence, bowing and pulling the woman along by one arm. She went docilely, of course, her eyes still fogged. Elegar would ask her no questions. He knew enough to be well aware that there were things he did not want to know.

"One of your play pretties?" a woman's voice said behind him as the carved door closed. "Have you taken to dressing them like that?"

Snatching at *saidin,* he filled himself with the Power, the taint on the male half of the True Source rolling off the protection of his bonds and oaths, the ties to what he knew as a greater power than the Light, or even the Creator.

In the middle of the chamber a gateway stood above the red-and-gold carpet, an opening to somewhere else. He had a brief view of a chamber lined with snowy silken hangings before it vanished, leaving a woman, clad in white and belted in woven silver. The slight tingle in his skin, like a faint chill, was all that told him she had channeled. Tall and slender, she was as beautiful as he was handsome, her dark eyes bottomless pools, her hair, decorated with silver stars and crescents, falling in perfect black waves to her shoulders. Most men would have felt their mouths go dry with desire.

"What do you mean to come sneaking up on me, Lanfear?" he demanded roughly. He did not let go of the Power, but rather prepared several nasty surprises in case he had need. "If you want to speak with me, send an emissary, and I will decide when and where. And if."

Lanfear smiled that sweet, treacherous smile. "You were always a pig, Rahvin, but seldom a fool. That woman is Aes Sedai. What if they miss her? Do you also send out heralds to announce where you are?"

"Channel?" he sneered. "She is not strong enough to be allowed outdoors without a keeper. They call untutored children Aes Sedai when half what they know is self-taught tricks and the other half barely scratches the surface."

"Would you still be so complacent if those untutored children put a circle of thirteen around you?" The cool mockery in her voice stabbed him, but he did not let it show.

"I take my precautions, Lanfear. Rather than one of my 'play pretties,' as you call them, she is the Tower's spy here. Now she reports exactly what I want her to, and she is eager to do so. Those who serve the Chosen in the Tower told me right where to find her." The day would come soon when the world gave up the name Forsaken and knelt to the Chosen. It had been promised, so very long ago. "Why have you come, Lanfear? Surely not in aid of defenseless women."

She merely shrugged. "You can play with your toys as much as you wish, so far as I am concerned. You offer little in the way of hospitality, Rahvin, so you will forgive me if . . ." A silver pitcher rose from a small table by Rahvin's bed and tilted to pour dark wine into a gold-chased goblet. As the pitcher settled, the goblet floated to Lanfear's hand. He felt nothing beyond a slight tingle, of course, saw no flows being woven; he had never liked that. That she would be able to see as little of his weaving was only a slight redressing of the balance.

"Why?" he demanded again.

She sipped calmly before speaking. "Since you avoid the rest of us, a few of the Chosen will be coming here. I came first so you would know it was not an attack."

"Others? Some plan of yours? What need have I of someone else's designs?" Suddenly he laughed, a deep, rich sound. "So it is no attack, is it? You were never one for attacking openly, were you? Not as bad as Moghedien, perhaps, but you did always favor the flanks and the rear. I will trust you this time, enough to hear you out. As long as you are under my eye." Who trusted Lanfear behind him deserved the knife he might well find in his back. Not that she was so very trustworthy even when watched; her temper was uncertain at best. "Who else is supposed to be part of this?"

He had clearer warning this time—it was male work —as another gateway opened, showing marble arches open onto wide stone balconies, and gulls wheeling and crying in a cloudless blue sky. Finally a man appeared and stepped through, the way closing behind him.

Sammael was compact, solid and larger-seeming than he truly was, his stride quick and active, his manner abrupt. Blue-eyed and golden-haired, with a neat square-trimmed beard, he would perhaps have been above the ordinary in looks except for a slanting scar, as if a red-hot poker had been dragged across his face from hairline to jaw. He could have had it removed as soon as it was made, all those long years ago, but he had elected not to.

Linked to *saidin* as tightly as Rahvin—this close Rahvin could feel it, dimly—Sammael eyed him warily. "I expected serving maids and dancing girls, Rahvin. Have you finally wearied of your sport after all these years?" Lanfear laughed softly into her wine.

"Did someone mention sport?"

Rahvin had not even noticed the opening of a third gateway, showing a large room full of pools and fluted columns, nearly nude acrobats and attendants wearing less. Oddly, a lean old man in a wrinkled coat sat disconsolately among the performers. Two servants in filmy bits of nothing much, a well-muscled man bearing a wrought-gold tray and a beautiful, voluptuous woman anxiously pouring wine from a cut-crystal flagon into a matching goblet on the tray, followed the true arrival before the opening winked out.

In any other company but Lanfear's, Graendal would have been accounted a stunningly beautiful woman, lush and ripe. Her gown was green silk, cut low. A ruby the size of a hen's egg nestled between her breasts, and a coronet encrusted with more rested on her long, sun-colored hair. Beside Lanfear she was merely plumply pretty. If the inevitable comparison bothered her, her amused smile gave no sign of it.

Golden bracelets clattered as she waved a heavily beringed hand generally behind her; the female servant quickly slipped the goblet into her grasp with a fawning smile mirrored by the man. Graendal took no notice. "So," she said gaily. "Nearly half the surviving Chosen in one place. And no one trying to kill anyone. Who would have expected it before the Great Lord of the Dark returns? Ishamael did manage to keep us from one another's throats for a time, but this . . ."

"Do you always speak so freely in front of your servants?" Sammael asked with a grimace.

Graendal blinked, glanced back at the pair as if she had forgotten them. "They won't speak out of turn. They worship me. Don't you?" The two fell to their knees, practically babbling their fervent love of her. It was real; they actually did love her. Now. After a moment, she frowned slightly, and the servants froze, mouths open in midword. "They do go on. Still, they won't bother you now, will they?"

Rahvin shook his head, wondering who they were, or had been. Physical beauty was not enough for Graendal's servants; they had to have power or position as well. A former lord for a footman, a lady to draw her bath; that was Graendal's taste. Indulging herself was one thing, but she was wasteful. This pair might have been of use, properly manipulated, but the level of compulsion Graendal employed surely left them good for little more than decoration. The woman had no true finesse.

"Should I expect more, Lanfear?" he growled. "Have you convinced Demandred to stop thinking he is all but the Great Lord's heir?"

"I doubt he is arrogant enough for that," Lanfear replied smoothly. "He can see where it took Ishamael. And that is the point. A point Graendal raised. Once we were thirteen, immortal. Now four are dead, and one has betrayed us. We four are all who meet here today, and enough."

"Are you certain Asmodean went over?" Sammael demanded. "He never had the courage to take a chance before. Where did he find the heart to join a lost cause?"

Lanfear's brief smile was amused. "He had the courage for an ambush he thought would set him above the rest of us. And when his choice became death or a doomed cause, it took little courage for him to choose."

"And little time, I'll wager." The scar made Sammael's sneer even more biting. "If you were close enough to him to know all of this, why did you leave him alive? You could have killed him before he knew you were there."

"I am not as quick to kill as you. It is final, with no going back, and there are usually other, more profitable ways. Besides, to put it in terms you would understand, I did not want to launch a frontal assault against superior forces."

"Is he really so strong?" Rahvin asked quietly. "This Rand al'Thor. Could he have overwhelmed you, face-to-face?" Not that he himself could not, if it came to it, or Sammael, though Graendal would likely link with Lanfear if either of the men tried. For that matter, both women were probably filled to bursting with the Power right that moment, ready to strike at the slightest suspicion of either man. Or of each other. But this farmboy. An untrained shepherd! Untrained unless Asmodean was trying.

"He is Lews Therin Telamon reborn," Lanfear said just as softly, "and Lews Therin was as strong as any." Sammael absently rubbed the scar across his face; it had been Lews Therin who gave it to him. Three thousand years ago and more, well before the Breaking of the World, before the Great Lord was imprisoned, before so much, but Sammael never forgot.

"Well," Graendal put in, "have we come around at last to what we are here to discuss?"

Rahvin gave a displeased start. The two servants were

frozen still—or again, rather. Sammael muttered in his beard.

"If this Rand al'Thor really is Lews Therin Telamon reborn," Graendal went on, settling herself on the man's back where he crouched on all fours, "I am surprised you haven't tried to snuggle him into your bed, Lanfear. Or would it be so easy? I seem to remember Lews Therin led you by the nose, not the other way around. Squelched your little tantrums. Sent you running to fetch his wine, in a manner of speaking." She set her own wine on the tray, held out rigidly by the sightlessly kneeling woman. "You were so obsessed with him you'd have stretched out at his feet if he said 'rug.'"

Lanfear's dark eyes glittered for a moment before she regained control of herself. "He may be Lews Therin reborn, but he is not Lews Therin himself."

"How do you know?" Graendal asked, smiling as if it were all a joke. "It may well be that, as many believe, all are born and reborn as the Wheel turns, but nothing like this has ever happened that I have read. A specific man reborn according to prophecy. Who knows what he is?"

Lanfear gave a disparaging smirk. "I have observed him closely. He is no more than the shepherd he seems, still more naive than not." Scorn faded to seriousness. "But now he has Asmodean, weak ally as he is. And even before Asmodean, four of the Chosen have died confronting him."

"Let him whittle away the dead wood," Sammael said gruffly. He wove flows of Air to drag a chair across the carpet and sprawled with his boots crossed at the ankle and one arm over the low, carved back. Anyone who believed he was at ease was a fool; Sammael had always liked to dupe his enemies into thinking they could take him by surprise. "More for the rest of us on the Day of Return. Or do you think he might win Tarmon Gai'don, Lanfear? Even if he stiffens Asmodean's backbone, he has no Hundred Companions this time. With Asmodean or alone, the Great Lord will extinguish him like a broken sar-light."

The look Lanfear gave him bristled with contempt. "How many of us will be alive when the Great Lord is freed at last? Four gone already. Will he come after you next, Sammael? You might like that. You could finally get rid of that scar if you defeated him. But I forget. How many times did you face him in the War of Power? Did you ever win? I cannot seem to remember." Without pause she rounded on Graendal. "Or it might be you. He is reluctant to hurt women for some reason, but you won't even be able to make Asmodean's choice. You cannot teach him any more than a stone could. Unless he decides to keep you as a pet. That would be a change for you, would it not? Instead of deciding which of your pretties pleases you best, you could learn to please."

Graendal's face contorted, and Rahvin prepared to shield himself against whatever the two women might hurl at one another, prepared to Travel at even a whiff of balefire. Then he sensed Sammael gathering the Power, sensed a difference in it—Sammael would call it seizing a tactical advantage—and bent to grab the other man's arm. Sammael shook him off angrily, but the moment had passed. The two women were looking at them now, not each other. Neither could know what had almost happened, but clearly something had passed between Rahvin and Sammael, and suspicion lit their eyes.

"I want to hear what Lanfear has to say." He did not look at Sammael, but meant it for him. "There must be more to this than a foolish attempt to frighten us." Sammael jerked his head in what might have been a nod or merely disgruntlement. It would have to do.

"Oh, there is, though a little fright could not hurt." Lanfear's dark eyes still held distrust, but her voice was as clear as still water. "Ishamael tried to control him and failed, tried to kill him in the end and failed, but Ishamael tried bullying and fear, and bullying does not work with Rand al'Thor."

"Ishamael was more than half-mad," Sammael muttered, "and less than half-human."

"Is that what we are?" Graendal arched an eyebrow. "Merely human? Surely we are something more. This is human." She stroked a finger down the cheek of the woman kneeling beside her. "A new word will have to be created to describe us."

"Whatever we are," Lanfear said, "we can succeed where Ishamael failed." She was leaning slightly forward, as if to force the words on them. Lanfear seldom showed tension. Why now?

"Why only we four?" Rahvin asked. The other "why" would have to wait.

"Why more?" was Lanfear's reply. "If we can present the Dragon Reborn kneeling to the Great Lord on the Day of Return, why share the honor—and the rewards —further than need be? And perhaps he can even be used to—how did you put it, Sammael?—whittle away the dead wood."

It was the sort of answer Rahvin could understand. Not that he trusted her, of course, or any of the others, but he understood ambition. The Chosen had plotted among themselves for position up to the day Lews Therin had imprisoned them in sealing up the Great Lord's prison, and they had begun again the day they were freed. He just had to be sure Lanfear's plot did not disrupt his own plans. "Speak on," he told her.

"First, someone else is trying to control him. Perhaps to kill. I suspect Moghedien or Demandred. Moghedien has always tried to work from the shadows, and Demandred always did hate Lews Therin." Sammael smiled, or perhaps grimaced, but his hatred was a pale thing beside Demandred's, though for better cause.

"How do you know it is not one of us here?" Graendal asked glibly.

Lanfear's smile showed as many teeth as the other woman's, and as little warmth. "Because you three choose to carve out niches for yourselves and secure your power while the rest slash at each other. And other reasons. I told you I keep a close watch on Rand al'Thor."

It was true, what she said of them. Rahvin himself preferred diplomacy and manipulation to open conflict, though he would not shy from it if needed. Sammael's way had always been armies and conquest; he would not go near Lews Therin, even reborn as a shepherd, until he was sure of victory. Graendal, too, followed conquest, though her methods did not involve soldiers; for all her concern with her toys, she took one solid step at a time. Openly to be sure, as the Chosen reckoned such things, but never stretching too far at any step.

"You know I can keep an eye on him unseen," Lanfear continued, "but the rest of you must stay clear or run the risk of detection. We must draw him back. . . ."

Graendal leaned forward, interested, and Sammael began to nod as she went on. Rahvin reserved judgment. It might well work. And if not . . . If not, he saw several ways to shape events to his advantage. This might work out very well indeed.

CHAPTER
1

Fanning the Sparks

The Wheel of Time turns, and Ages come and pass, leaving memories that become legend. Legend fades to myth, and even myth is long forgotten when the Age that gave it birth comes again. In one Age, called the Third Age by some, an Age yet to come, an Age long past, a wind rose in the great forest called Braem Wood. The wind was not the beginning. There are neither beginnings nor endings to the turning of the Wheel of Time. But it was *a* beginning.

South and west it blew, dry, beneath a sun of molten gold. There had been no rain for long weeks in the land below, and the late-summer heat grew day by day. Brown leaves come early dotted some trees, and naked stones baked where small streams had run. In an open place where grass had vanished and only thin, withered brush held the soil with its roots, the wind began uncovering long-buried stones. They were weathered and worn, and no human eye would have recognized them for the remains of a city remembered in story yet otherwise forgotten.

Scattered villages appeared before the wind crossed

the border of Andor, and fields where worried farmers trudged arid furrows. The forest had long since thinned to thickets by the time the wind swept dust down the lone street of a village called Kore Springs. The springs were beginning to run low this summer. A few dogs lay panting in the swelter, and two shirtless boys ran, beating a stuffed bladder along the ground with sticks. Nothing else stirred, save the wind and the dust and the creaking sign above the door of the inn, red brick and thatch-roofed like every other building along the street. At two stories, it was the tallest and largest structure in Kore Springs, a neat and orderly little town. The saddled horses hitched in front of the inn barely twitched their tails. The inn's carved sign proclaimed the Good Queen's Justice.

Blinking against the dust, Min kept an eye pressed to the crack in the shed's rough wall. She could just make out one shoulder of the guard on the shed door, but her attention was all for the inn further on. She wished the name were less ominously apt. Their judge, the local lord, had apparently arrived some time ago, but she had missed seeing him. No doubt he was hearing the farmer's charges; Admer Nem, along with his brothers and cousins and all their wives, had seemed in favor of an immediate hanging before one of the lord's retainers happened by. She wondered what the penalty was here for burning up a man's barn, and his milkcows with it. By accident, of course, but she did not think that would count for much when it all began with trespass.

Logain had gotten away in the confusion, abandoning them—he would, burn him!—and she did not know whether to be happy about that or not. It was he who had knocked Nem down when they were discovered just before dawn, sending the man's lantern flying into the straw. The blame was his, if anyone's. Only sometimes he had trouble watching what he said. Perhaps as well he was gone.

Twisting to lean back against the wall, she wiped sweat from her brow, though it only sprang out again. The inside of the shed was stifling, but her two companions did not appear to notice. Siuan lay stretched out on her back in a dark woolen riding dress much like Min's, staring at the shed roof, idly tapping her chin with a straw. Coppery-skinned Leane, willowy and as tall as most men, sat cross-legged in her pale shift, working on her dress with needle and thread. They had been allowed to keep their saddlebags, after they were searched for swords or axes or anything else that might help them escape.

"What's the penalty for burning down a barn in Andor?" Min asked.

"If we are lucky," Siuan replied without moving, "a strapping in the village square. Not so lucky, and it will be a flogging."

"Light!" Min breathed. "How can you call that *luck*?"

Siuan rolled onto her side and propped herself up on an elbow. She was a sturdy woman, short of beautiful though beyond handsome, and looked no more than a few years older than Min, but those sharp blue eyes had a commanding presence that did not belong on a young woman awaiting trial in a backcountry shed. Sometimes Siuan was as bad as Logain about forgetting herself; maybe worse. "When a strapping is done," she said in a brook-no-nonsense, do-not-be-foolish tone, "it is done, and we can be on our way. It wastes less of our time than any other penalty I can think of. Considerably less than hanging, say. Though I don't think it will come to that, from what I remember of Andoran law."

Wheezing laughter shook Min for a moment; it was that or cry. "Time? The way we are going, we've nothing but time. I swear we have been through every village between here and Tar Valon, and found nothing. Not a glimmer, not a whisper. I don't think there *is* any gathering. And we are on foot, now. From what I overheard, Logain took the horses with him. Afoot and locked in a shed awaiting the Light knows what!"

"Watch names," Siuan whispered sharply, shooting a meaning glance at the rough door with the guard on the other side. "A flapping tongue can put you in the net instead of the fish."

Min grimaced, partly because she was growing tired of

Siuan's Tairen fisherman's sayings, and partly because the other woman was right. So far they had outrun awkward news—deadly was a better word than awkward —but some news had a way of leaping a hundred miles in a day. Siuan had been traveling as Mara, Leane as Amaena, and Logain had taken the name Dalyn, after Siuan convinced him Guaire was a fool's choice. Min still did not think anyone would recognize her own name, but Siuan insisted on calling her Serenla. Even Logain did not know their true names.

The real trouble was that Siuan was not going to give up. Weeks of utter failure, and now this, yet any mention of heading for Tear, which was sensible, set off a tempest that quailed even Logain. The longer they had searched without finding what Siuan sought, the more temper she had developed. *Not that she couldn't crack rocks with it before.* Min was wise enough to keep that particular thought to herself.

Leane finally finished with her dress and tugged it on over her head, doubling her arms behind her to do up the buttons. Min could not see why she had gone to the trouble; she herself hated needlework of any sort. The neckline was a little lower now, showing a bit of Leane's bosom, and it fit in a snugger way there and perhaps around the hips. But what was the point, here? No one was going to ask her to dance in this roasting shed.

Digging into Min's saddlebags, Leane pulled out the wooden box of paints and powders and whatnots that Laras had forced on Min before they set out. Min had kept meaning to throw it away, but somehow she had never gotten around to it. There was a small mirror inside the hinged lid of the box, and in moments Leane was at work on her face with small rabbit-fur brushes. She had never shown any particular interest in the things before. Now she appeared vexed that there was only a blackwood hairbrush and a small ivory comb to use on her hair. She even muttered about the lack of a way to heat the curling iron! Her dark hair had grown since they began Siuan's search, but it still came well short of her shoulders.

After watching a bit, Min asked, "What are you up to,

'Le—Amaena?" She avoided looking at Siuan. She *could* guard her tongue; it was just being cooped up and baked alive, that on top of the coming trial. A hanging or a public strapping. What a choice! "Have you decided to take up flirting?" It was meant for a joke—Leane was all business and efficiency—something to lighten the moment, but the other woman surprised her.

"Yes," Leane said briskly, peering wide-eyed into the mirror while she carefully did something to her eyelashes. "And if I flirt with the right man, perhaps we will not need to worry about strappings or anything else. At the least, I might get us lighter sentences."

Hand half-raised to wipe her face again, Min gasped—it was like an owl announcing it meant to become a hummingbird—but Siuan merely sat up facing Leane with a level "What brought this on?"

Had Siuan directed that gaze at her, Min suspected she would have confessed to things she had forgotten. When Siuan concentrated on you like that, you found yourself curtsying and leaping to do as you were told before you realized it. Even Logain did, most of the time. Except for the curtsy.

Leane calmly stroked a tiny brush along her cheekbones and examined the result in the small mirror. She did glance at Siuan, but whatever she saw, she answered in the same crisp tones she always used. "My mother was a merchant, you know, in furs and timber mainly. I once saw her fog a Saldaean lord's mind till he consigned his entire year's timber harvest to her for half the amount he wanted, and I doubt he realized what had happened until he was nearly back home. If then. He sent her a moonstone bracelet, later. Domani women don't deserve the whole reputation they have—stiff-necked prigs going by hearsay built most of it—but we have earned some. My mother and my aunts taught me along with my sisters and cousins, of course."

Looking down at herself, she shook her head, then returned to her ministrations with a sigh. "But I fear I was as tall as I am today on my fourteenth naming day. All knees and elbows, like a colt that grew too fast. And not long after I could walk across a room without tripping twice, I learned—" She drew a deep breath. "—learned my life would take me another way than being a merchant. And now that is gone, too. About time I put to use what I was taught all those years ago. Under the circumstances, I can't think of a better time or place."

Siuan studied her shrewdly a moment more. "That isn't the reason. Not the whole reason. Out with it."

Hurling a small brush into the box, Leane blazed up in a fury. "The whole reason? I do not know the whole reason. I only know I need something in my life to replace—what is gone. You yourself told me that is the only hope of surviving. Revenge falls short, for me. I know your cause is necessary, and perhaps even right, but the Light help me, that is not enough either; I can't make myself be as involved as you. Maybe I came too late to it. I will stay with you, but it isn't enough."

Anger faded as she began resealing pots and vials and replacing them, though she used more force than was strictly necessary. There was the merest hint of rose scent about her. "I know flirting isn't something to fill up the emptiness, but it is enough to fill an idle moment. Maybe being who I was born to be will suffice. I just do not know. This isn't a new idea; I always wanted to be like my mother and my aunts, daydreamed of it sometimes after I was grown."

Leane's face became pensive, and the last things went into the box more gently. "I think perhaps I've always felt I was masquerading as someone else, building up a mask until it became second nature. There was serious work to be done, more serious than merchanting, and by the time I realized there was another way I could have gone even so, I had the mask on too firmly to take off. Well, that is done with, now, and the mask *is* coming off. I even considered beginning with Logain a week ago, for practice. But I *am* out of practice, and I think he is the kind of man who might hear more promises than you meant to offer, and expect to have them fulfilled." A small smile suddenly appeared on her lips. "My mother always said if that happened, you had miscalculated badly; if there was no back way out, you had to either abandon dignity and run, or pay the price and consider it a lesson." The smile took on a roguish cast. "My Aunt Resara said you paid the price and enjoyed it."

Min could only shake her head. It was as if Leane had become a different woman. Talking that way about . . . ! Even hearing it, she could hardly believe. Come to that, Leane actually looked different. For all of the work with brushes, there was not a hint of paint or powder on her face that Min could see, yet her lips seemed fuller, her cheekbones higher, her eyes larger. She was a more than pretty woman at any time, but now her beauty was magnified fivefold.

Siuan was not quite finished, though. "And if this country lord is one like Logain?" she said softly. "What will you do then?"

Leane drew herself up stiff-backed on her knees and swallowed hard before answering, but her voice was perfectly level. "Given the alternatives, what choice would you make?"

Neither blinked, and the silence stretched.

Before Siuan could answer—if she meant to; Min would have given a pretty to hear it—the chain and lock rattled on the other side of the door.

The other two women got slowly to their feet, gathering their saddlebags in calm preparation, but Min leaped up wishing she had her belt knife. *Fool thing to wish for,* she thought. *Just get me in worse trouble. I'm no bloody hero in a story. Even if I jumped the guard—*

The door opened, and a man with a long leather jerkin over his shirt filled the doorway. Not a fellow to be attacked by a young woman, even with a knife. Maybe not even with an axe. Wide was the word for him, and thick. The few hairs remaining on his head were more white than not, but he looked hard as an old oak stump. "Time for you girls to stand before the lord," he said gruffly. "Will you walk, or must we haul you like grain sacks? You go, either way, but I'd as soon not have to carry you in this heat."

Peeking past him, Min saw two more men waiting, gray-haired but just as hard, if not quite so big.

"We will walk," Siuan told him dryly.

"Good. Come, then. Step along. Lord Gareth won't like being kept waiting."

Promise to walk or no, each man took one of them firmly by the arm as they started up the dusty dirt street. The balding man's hand encircled Min's arm like a manacle. *So much for running for it,* she thought bitterly. She considered kicking his booted ankle to see if that would loosen his grip, but he looked so solid she suspected all it would earn her was a sore toe and being dragged the rest of the way.

Leane appeared lost in thought; she half-made small gestures with her free hand, and her lips moved silently as though reviewing what she meant to say, but she kept shaking her head and starting over again. Introspection wrapped Siuan, too, but she wore an openly worried frown, even chewing her underlip; Siuan *never* showed that much unease. All in all, the pair of them did nothing for Min's confidence.

The beam-ceilinged common room of the Good Queen's Justice did less. Lank-haired Admer Nem, a yellowed bruise around his swollen eye, stood to one side with half a dozen equally stout brothers and cousins and their wives, all in their best coats or aprons. The farmers eyed the three prisoners with a mixture of anger and satisfaction that made Min's stomach sink. If anything, the farmwives' glares were worse, pure hate. The rest of the walls were lined six deep with villagers, all garbed for the work they had interrupted for this. The blacksmith still wore his leather apron, and a number of women had sleeves rolled up, arms dusted with flour. The room buzzed with their murmuring among themselves, the elders as much as the few children, and their eyes latched onto the three women as avidly as the Nems' did. Min thought this must be as much excitement as Kore Springs had ever witnessed. She had seen a crowd with this mood once—at an execution.

The tables had been removed, except for one placed in front of the long brick fireplace. A bluff-faced, stocky man, his hair thick with gray, sat facing them in a well-cut coat of dark green silk, hands folded in front of him on the tabletop. A slim woman who showed as much age stood beside the table in a fine, gray wool dress embroidered with white flowers around the neck. The local lord, Min supposed, and his lady; country nobility little better informed of the world than their tenants and crofters.

The guards situated them in front of the lord's table and melted into the watchers. The woman in gray stepped forward, and the murmurs died.

"All here attend and give ear," the woman announced, "for justice will be meted today by Lord Gareth Bryne. Prisoners, you are called before the judgment of Lord Bryne." Not the lord's lady, then; an official of some sort. Gareth Bryne? The last Min remembered, he was Captain-General of the Queen's Guards, in Caemlyn. If it was the same man. She glanced at Siuan, but Siuan had her eyes locked on the wide floorboards in front of her feet. Whoever he was, this Bryne looked weary.

"You are charged," the woman in gray went on, "with trespass by night, arson and destruction of a building and its contents, the killing of valuable livestock, assault on the person of Admer Nem, and the theft of a purse said to contain gold and silver. It is understood that the assault and theft were the work of your companion, who escaped, but you three are equally culpable under the law."

She paused to let it sink in, and Min exchanged rueful glances with Leane. Logain *would* have to add theft to the stew. He was probably halfway to Murandy by now, if not more distant yet.

After a moment the woman began again. "Your accusers are here to face you." She gestured to the cluster of Nems. "Admer Nem, you will give your testimony."

The stout man eased forward in a blend of self-importance and self-consciousness, tugging at his coat where the wooden buttons strained over his middle, running his hands through thinning hair that kept dropping into his face. "Like I said, Lord Gareth, it was like this. . . ."

He gave a fairly straightforward account of discovering them in the hayloft and ordering them out, though he made Logain near a foot taller and turned the man's single blow into a fight where Nem gave as good as he got. The lantern fell, the hay went up, and the rest of the family came spilling out of the farmhouse into the predawn; the prisoners were seized and the barn burned to the ground, and then the loss of the purse from the house was discovered. He did slight the part where Lord Bryne's retainer rode by as some of the family were bringing out ropes and eyeing tree limbs.

When he started on the "fight" again—this time he seemed to be winning—Bryne cut him off. "That will be enough, Master Nem. You may step back."

Instead, a round-faced one of the Nem women, of an age to be Admer's wife, joined him. Round-faced, but not soft; round like a frying pan or a river rock. And flushed with something more than anger. "You whip these hussies good, Lord Gareth, hear? Whip them good, and ride them to Jornhill on a rail!"

"No one called on you to speak, Maigan," the slim woman in gray said sharply. "This is a trial, not a petition meeting. You and Admer step back. Now." They obeyed, Admer with a shade more alacrity than Maigan. The gray-clad woman turned to Min and her companions. "If you wish to offer testimony, in defense or mitigation, you may now give it." There was no sympathy in her voice, nor anything else for that matter.

Min expected Siuan to speak—she always took the lead, did the talking—but Siuan never stirred or raised her eyes. Instead, it was Leane who moved toward the table, her eyes on the man behind it.

She stood as straight as ever, but her usual walk—a graceful stride, but a stride—had become a sort of glide, with just a hint of willowy sway to it. Somehow her hips and bosom seemed more obvious. Not that she flaunted anything; the way she moved just made you aware. "My Lord, we are three helpless women, refugees from the storms that sweep the world." Her usually brisk tones were gone, changed to a velvety soft caress. There was a light in her dark eyes, a sort of smoldering challenge. "Penniless and lost, we took shelter in Master Nem's barn. It was wrong, I know, but we were afraid of the night." A small gesture, hands half-raised, the insides of her wrists to Bryne, made her seem for a moment utterly helpless. Only for that moment, though. "The man Dalyn was a stranger to us really, a man who offered us his protection. In these days, women alone must have a protector, my Lord, yet I fear we made a poor choice." A widening of the eyes, an entreating look, said he could make a better for them. "It was indeed he who attacked Master Nem, my Lord; we would have fled, or worked to repay our night's lodging." Stepping around the side of the table, she knelt gracefully beside Bryne's chair and gently rested the fingers of one hand on his wrist as she gazed up into his eyes. A tremble touched her voice, but her slight smile was enough to set any man's heart racing. It—suggested. "My Lord, we are guilty of some small crime, yet not so much as we are charged with. We throw ourselves on your mercy. I beg you, my Lord, have pity on us, and protect us."

For a long moment, Bryne stared back into her eyes. Then, clearing his throat roughly, he scraped back his chair, rose, and walked around the opposite end of the table from her. There was a stir among the villagers and farmers, men clearing their throats as their lord had done, women muttering under their breath. Bryne stopped in front of Min. "What is your name, girl?"

"Min, my Lord." She caught a muffled grunt from Siuan and hastily added, "Serenla Min. Everyone calls me Serenla, my Lord."

"Your mother must have had a premonition," he murmured with a smile. He was not the first to react to the name in a like way. "Do you have any statement to make, Serenla?"

"Only that I am very sorry, my Lord, and it really wasn't our fault. Dalyn did it all. I ask for mercy, my Lord." That did not seem much alongside Leane's plea—anything at all would seem insignificant beside Leane's performance—but it was the best she could find. Her mouth was as dry as the street outside. What if he did decide to hang them?

Nodding, he moved over to Siuan, who was still studying the floor. Cupping a hand under her chin, he raised her eyes to his. "And what is your name, girl?"

With a jerk of her head, Siuan pulled her chin free and took a step back. "Mara, my Lord," she whispered. "Mara Tomanes."

Min groaned softly. Siuan was plainly frightened, yet at the same time she stared at the man defiantly. Min more than half-expected her to demand Bryne let them walk away on the instant. He asked her if she wished to make a statement, and she denied it in another unsteady whisper, but all the while looking at him as though she were the one in charge. She might be controlling her tongue, but certainly not her eyes.

After a time, Bryne turned away. "Take your place with your friends, girl," he told Leane as he returned to his chair. She joined them with a look of open frustration, and what in anyone else Min would have called a touch of petulance.

"I have reached my decision," Bryne said to the room at large. "The crimes are serious, and nothing I have heard alters the facts. If three men sneak into another's house to steal his candlesticks and one of them attacks the owner, all three are equally guilty. There must be recompense. Master Nem, I will give you the cost of rebuilding your barn, plus the price of six milkcows." The stout farmer's eyes brightened, until Bryne added, "Caralin will disburse the coin to you when she is content as to costs and prices. Some of your cows were going dry, I hear." The slim woman in gray nodded in satisfaction. "For the bump on your head, I award you one silver mark. Don't complain," he said firmly as Nem opened his mouth. "Maigan has given you worse for drinking too much." A ripple of laughter among the onlookers greeted that, not diminished at all by Nem's half-abashed glares, and perhaps spurred by the tight-lipped look Maigan gave her husband. "I will also replace the amount of the stolen purse. Once Caralin has satisfied herself as to how much was in it." Nem and his wife appeared equally disgruntled, but they held their tongues; it was plain he had given them what he would. Min began to feel hope.

Leaning his elbows on the table, Bryne turned his attention to her and the other two. His slow words tied her stomach into a knot. "You three will work for me, at the normal wages for whatever tasks you are given, until the coin I've paid out is repaid to me. Do not think I am being lenient. If you swear an oath that satisfies me you don't have to be guarded, you can work in my manor. If not, it means the fields, where you can be under someone's eyes every minute. Wages are lower in the fields, but it is your decision."

Frantically she racked her brain for the weakest oath that might satisfy. She did not like breaking her word in any circumstances, but she meant to be gone as soon as a chance presented, and she did not want too heavy an oathbreaking on her conscience.

Leane seemed to be searching, too, but Siuan barely hesitated before kneeling and folding her hands over her heart. Her eyes seemed fastened to Bryne's, and the challenge had not faded one bit. "By the Light and my hope of salvation and rebirth, I swear to serve you in whatever way you require for as long as you require, or may the Creator's face turn from me forever and darkness consume my soul." She delivered the words in a breathy whisper, but they created a dead silence. There was no oath stronger, unless it was the one a woman took on being made Aes Sedai, and the Oath Rod bound her to that as surely as to a part of her flesh.

Leane stared at Siuan; then she was on her knees, too. "By the Light and my hope of salvation and rebirth . . ."

Min floundered desperately, searching for some way out. Swearing a lesser oath than they did meant the fields for certain, and someone watching her every instant, but this oath. . . . By what she had been taught, breaking it would be not much less than murder, maybe no less. Only there *was* no way out. The oath, or who knew how many years laboring in a field all day and probably locked up at night. Sinking down beside the other two women, she muttered the words, but inside she was howling. *Siuan, you utter fool! What have you gotten me into now? I can't stay here! I have to go to Rand! Oh, Light, help me!*

"Well," Bryne breathed when the last word was spoken, "I did not expect that. But it does suffice. Caralin, would you take Master Nem somewhere and find out what he thinks his losses amount to? And clear everyone else but these three out of here, too. And make arrangements to transport them to the manor. Under the circumstances, I don't think guards will be necessary."

The slim woman gave him a harassed look, but in short order she had everyone moving out in a milling throng. Admer Nem and his male kin stuck close to her, his face especially painted with avarice. The Nem women looked scarcely less greedy, but they still spared a few hard glowers for Min and the other two, who remained kneeling as the room emptied out. For herself, Min did not believe her legs could hold her up. The same phrases repeated over and over in her mind. *Oh, Siuan, why? I can't stay here. I can't!*

"We have had a few refugees through here," Bryne said when the last of the villagers had gone. He leaned back in his chair, studying them. "But never as odd a threesome as you. A Domani. A Tairen?" Siuan nodded curtly. She and Leane stood up, the slender, coppery-skinned woman delicately brushing her knees, Siuan simply standing. Min managed to join them, on wobbly legs. "And you, Serenla." Once more he gave the ghost of a smile at the name. "Somewhere in the west of Andor, unless I mistake your accent."

"Baerlon," she muttered, then bit her tongue too late. Someone might know Min was from Baerlon.

"I've heard of nothing in the west to make refugees," he said in a questioning tone. When she remained silent, he did not press it. "After you have worked off your debt, you will be welcome to remain in my service. Life can be hard for those who've lost their homes, and even a maid's cot is better than sleeping under a bush."

"Thank you, my Lord," Leane said caressingly, making a curtsy so graceful that even in her rough riding dress it looked part of a dance. Min's echo was leaden, and she did not trust her knees for a curtsy. Siuan simply stood there staring at him and said nothing at all.

"A pity your companion took your horses. Four horses would reduce your debt by some."

"He was a stranger, and a rogue," Leane told him, in a voice suitable for something far more intimate. "I for one am more than happy to exchange his protection for yours, my Lord."

Bryne eyed her—appreciatively, Min thought—but all he said was "At least you will be safely away from the Nems at the manor."

There was no reply for that. Min supposed scrubbing floors in Bryne's manor would not be much different from scrubbing floors in the Nem farmhouse. *How do I get out of this? Light, how?*

The silence went on, except for Bryne drumming his fingers on the table. Min would have thought he was at a loss for what to say next, but she did not think this man was ever off balance. More likely he was irritated that only Leane appeared to be showing any gratitude; she supposed their sentence could have been much worse, from his point of view. Perhaps Leane's heated glances and stroking tones had worked after a fashion, but Min found herself wishing the woman had remained the way she was. Being hung up by the wrists in the village square would be better than this.

Finally Caralin returned, muttering to herself. She sounded prickly, reporting to Bryne. "It will take days to get straight answers from those Nems, Lord Gareth. Admer would have five new barns and fifty cows, if I let him. At least I believe there really was a purse, but as to how much was in it . . ." She shook her head and sighed. "I will find out, eventually. Joni is ready to take these girls to the manor, if you are done with them."

"Take them away, Caralin," Bryne said, rising. "When you've sent them off, join me at the brickyard." He sounded weary again. "Thad Haren says he needs more water if he's to keep making bricks, and the Light alone knows where I will find it for him." He strode out of the common room as if he had forgotten all about the three women who had just sworn to serve him.

Joni turned out to be the wide, balding man who had come for them in the shed, waiting now in front of the inn beside a high-wheeled cart enclosed by a round canvas cover, with a lean brown horse in the shafts. A few of the villagers stood about to watch their departure, but most seemed to have gone back to their homes and out of the heat. Gareth Bryne was already far down the dirt street.

"Joni will see you safely to the manor," Caralin said. "Do as you are told, and you will not find the life hard." For a moment she considered them, dark eyes nearly as sharp as Siuan's; then she nodded to herself as if satisfied and hurried off after Bryne.

Joni held the curtains open for them at the back of the cart, but let them clamber up unaided and find places to sit on the cart bed. There was not so much as a handful of straw for padding, and the heavy covering trapped the heat. He said not a word. The cart rocked as he climbed up on the driver's seat, hidden by the canvas. Min heard him cluck to the horse, and the cart lurched off, wheels creaking slightly, bumping over occasional potholes.

There was just enough of a crack in the covering at the back for Min to watch the village dwindle behind them and vanish, replaced alternately by long thickets and rail-fenced fields. She felt too stunned to speak. Siuan's grand cause was to end scrubbing pots and floors. She should never have helped the woman, never stayed with her. She should have ridden for Tear at the first opportunity.

"Well," Leane said suddenly, "that worked out not badly at all." She was back to her usual brisk voice again, but there was a flush of excitement—excitement!—in it, and a high color in her cheeks. "It could have been better, but practice will take care of that." Her low laugh was almost a giggle. "I never realized how much fun it would be. When I actually felt his pulse racing . . ." For a moment she held out her hand the way she had placed it on Bryne's wrist. "I don't think I ever felt so alive, so aware. Aunt Resara used to say men were better sport than hawks, but I never really understood until today."

Holding herself against the sway of the cart, Min goggled at her. "You have gone mad," she said finally. "How many years have we sworn away? Two? Five? I suppose you hope Gareth Bryne will spend them dandling you on his knee! Well, I hope he turns you over it. Every day!" The startled look on Leane's face did nothing for Min's temper. Did she expect Min to take it as calmly as she appeared to? But it was not Leane that Min was really angry with. She twisted around to glare at Siuan. "And you! When you decide to give up, you don't do it small. You just surrender like a lamb at slaughter. Why did you choose *that* oath? Light, why?"

"Because," Siuan replied, "it was the one oath I could be sure would keep him from setting people to watch us night and day, manor house or not." Lying half stretched out on the rough planks of the cart, she made it sound the most obvious thing in the world. And Leane appeared to agree with her.

"You mean to break it," Min said after a moment. It came out in a shocked whisper, but even so she glanced worriedly at the canvas curtains that hid Joni. She did not think he could have heard.

"I mean to do what I must," Siuan said firmly, but just as softly. "In two or three days, when I can be sure they really aren't watching us especially, we will leave. I fear we must take horses, since ours are gone. Bryne must have good stables. I will regret that." And Leane just sat there like a cat with cream on her whiskers. She must have realized from the first; that was why she had not hesitated in swearing.

"You will regret stealing horses?" Min said hoarsely. "You plan to break an oath anyone but a Darkfriend would keep, and you regret stealing horses? I can't believe either of you. I don't *know* either of you."

"Do you really mean to stay and scrub pots," Leane asked, her voice just as low as theirs, "when Rand is out there with your heart in his pocket?"

Min glowered silently. She wished they had never learned she was in love with Rand al'Thor. Sometimes she wished she had never learned it. A man who barely knew she was alive, a man like that. What he was no longer seemed as important as the fact that he had never looked at her twice, but it was all of a piece, really. She wanted to say she would keep her oath, forget about Rand for however long it took her to work off her debt. Only, she could not open her mouth. *Burn him! If I'd never met him, I wouldn't be in this pickle!*

When the silence between them had gone on far too

long for Min's liking, broken only by the rhythmic creak of the wheels and the soft thud of the horse's hooves, Siuan spoke. "I mean to do as I swore to do. When I have finished what I *must* do first. I did not swear to serve him immediately; I was careful not to even imply it, strictly speaking. A fine point, I know, and one Gareth Bryne might not appreciate, but true all the same."

Min sagged in amazement, letting herself lurch with the cart's slow motion. "You intend to run away, then come back in a few years and hand yourselves over to Bryne? The man will sell your hides to a tannery. *Our* hides." Not until she said that did she realize she had accepted Siuan's solution. Run away, then come back and . . . *I can't! I love Rand. And he wouldn't notice if Gareth Bryne made me work in his kitchens the rest of my life!*

"Not a man to cross, I agree," Siuan sighed. "I met him once—before. I was terrified he might recognize my voice today. Faces may change, but voices don't." She touched her own face wonderingly, as she sometimes did, apparently unaware of doing so. "Faces do change," she murmured. Then her tone firmed. "I've paid heavy prices already for what I had to do, and I will pay this one. Eventually. If you must drown or ride a lionfish, you ride and hope for the best. That is all there is to it, Serenla."

"Being a servant is far from the future I would choose," Leane said, "but it *is* in the future, and who knows what may happen before? I can remember too well when I thought I had no future." A small smile appeared on her lips, her eyes half-closed dreamily, and her voice became velvet. "Besides, I don't think he will sell our hides at all. Give me a few years of practice, and then a few minutes with Lord Gareth Bryne, and he will greet us with open arms and put us up in his best rooms. He'll deck us with silks, and offer his carriage to carry us wherever we want to go."

Min left her wrapped in her fantasy. Sometimes she thought the other two both lived in dreamworlds. Something else occurred to her. A small thing, but it was beginning to irritate. "Ah, Mara, tell me something. I've noticed some people smile when you call me by name. Serenla. Bryne did, and he said something about my mother having a premonition. Why?"

"In the Old Tongue," Siuan replied, "it means 'stubborn daughter.' You did have a stubborn streak when we first met. A mile wide and a mile deep." Siuan said that! Siuan, the most stubborn woman in the whole world! Her smile was as wide as her face. "Of course, you do seem to be coming along. At the next village, you might use Chalinda. That means 'sweet girl.' Or maybe—"

Suddenly the cart gave a harder lurch than any before, then picked up speed as if the horse were reaching for a gallop. Bumping around like grain on a chaffing sieve, the three women stared at one another in surprise. Then Siuan levered herself up and pulled aside the canvas hiding the driver's seat. Joni was gone. Throwing herself across the wooden seat, Siuan grabbed the reins and reared back, hauling the horse to a halt. Min threw open the back curtains, searching.

The road ran through a thicket here, nearly a small forest of oak and elm, pine and leatherleaf. The dust of their short dash was still settling, some of it on Joni, where he lay sprawled by the side of the hard-packed dirt road sixty or so paces back.

Instinctively Min leaped down and ran back to kneel beside the big man. He was still breathing, but his eyes were closed and a bloody gash on the side of his head was coming up in a purple lump.

Leane pushed her aside and felt Joni's head with sure fingers. "He will live," she said crisply. "Nothing seems broken, but he will have a headache for days after he wakes." Sitting back on her heels, she folded her hands, and her voice saddened. "There is nothing I can do for him in any case. Burn me, I promised myself I would not cry over it again."

"The question—" Min swallowed and started again. "The question is, do we load him in the back of the cart and take him on to the manor, or do we—go?" *Light, I'm no better than Siuan!*

"We could carry him as far as the next farm," Leane said slowly.

Siuan came up to them, leading the cart horse as if afraid the placid animal might bite. One glance at the man on the ground, and she frowned. "He never had that falling off the cart. I don't see root or rock here to cause it." She started studying the wood around them, and a man rode out of the trees on a tall black stallion, leading three mares, one shaggy and two hands shorter than the others.

He was a tall man in a blue silk coat, with a sword at his side, his hair curling to broad shoulders, darkly handsome despite a hardening as though misfortune had marked him deeply. And he was the last man Min expected to see.

"Is this your work?" Siuan demanded of him.

Logain smiled as he reined in beside the cart, though there was little amusement in it. "A sling is a useful thing, Mara. You are lucky I am here. I didn't expect you to leave the village for some hours yet, and barely able to walk then. The local lord was indulgent, it seems." Abruptly his face went even darker, and his voice was rough stone. "Did you think I would leave you to your fate? Maybe I should have. You made promises to me, Mara. I want the revenge you promised. I've followed you halfway to the Sea of Storms on this search, though you won't tell me what for. I've asked no questions as to how you plan to give me what you promised. But I will tell you this now. Your time is growing short. End your search soon, and deliver your promises, or I will leave you to find your own way. You'll quickly find most villages offer small sympathy to penniless strangers. Three pretty women alone? The sight of this," he touched the sword at his hip, "has kept you safe more times than you can know. Find what you are seeking soon, Mara."

He had not been so arrogant at the beginning of their journey. Then he had been humbly thankful for *their* help—as humbly as a man like Logain could manage, anyway. It seemed that time—and a lack of results—had withered his gratitude.

Siuan did not flinch away from his stare. "I hope to," she said firmly. "But if you want to go, then leave our horses and go! If you won't row, get out of the boat and swim by yourself! See how far you get with your revenge alone."

Logain's big hands tightened on his reins until Min heard his knuckles crack. He shivered with emotions in strong check. "I will stay a while longer, Mara," he said finally. "A little while longer."

For an instant, to Min's eyes, a halo flared around his head, a radiant crown of gold and blue. Siuan and Leane saw nothing, of course, though they knew what she could do. Sometimes she saw things about people—viewings, she called them—images or auras. Sometimes she knew what they meant. That woman would marry. That man would die. Small matters or grand events, joyous or bleak, there was never any rhyme or reason to who or where or when. Aes Sedai and Warders always had auras; most people never did. It was not always pleasant, knowing.

She had seen Logain's halo before, and she knew what it meant. Glory to come. But for him, perhaps above all men, surely that made no sense at all. His horse and his sword and his coat had come from playing at dice, though Min was not certain how fair the games had been. He had nothing else, and no prospects except Siuan's promises, and how could Siuan ever keep them? His very name was likely a death sentence. It just made no sense.

Logain's humor returned as suddenly as it had gone. Pulling a fat, roughly woven purse from his belt, he jangled it at them. "I've come by a few coins. We won't have to sleep in another barn for a while."

"We heard of it," Siuan said dryly. "I suppose I should have expected no better from you."

"Think of it as a contribution to your search." She stretched out her hand, but he tied the purse back to his belt with a faintly mocking grin. "I would not want to taint your hand with stolen coin, Mara. Besides, this way perhaps I can be sure *you* won't run off and leave *me*." Siuan looked as if she could have bitten a nail in two, but she said nothing. Standing in his stirrups, Logain peered down the road toward Kore Springs. "I see a flock of sheep coming this way, and a pair of boys. Time for us to

ride. They'll carry word of this as fast as they can run."
Settling back down, he glanced at Joni, still lying there
unconscious. "And they'll fetch help for that fellow. I
don't think I hit him hard enough to hurt him badly."

Min shook her head; the man continually surprised
her. She would not have thought he would spare a second
thought for a man whose head he had just cracked.

Siuan and Leane wasted no time scrambling into their
high-cantled saddles, Leane onto the gray mare she
called Moonflower, Siuan onto Bela, the short, shaggy
mare. It was more of a scramble for Siuan. She was no
horsewoman; after weeks in the saddle she still treated
sedate Bela like a fiery-eyed warhorse. Leane handled
Moonflower with effortless ease. Min knew she was
somewhere in between; she climbed onto Wildrose, her
bay, with considerably more grace than Siuan, considerably less than Leane.

"Do you think he will come after us?" Min asked as
they started south, away from Kore Springs, at a trot. She
meant the question for Siuan, but it was Logain who
answered.

"The local lord? I doubt he thinks you important
enough. Of course, he may send a man, and he'll
certainly spread your descriptions. We will ride as far as
we can manage before stopping, and again tomorrow." It
seemed he was taking charge.

"We *aren't* important enough," Siuan said, bouncing
awkwardly in her saddle. She might have been wary of
Bela, but the look she directed at Logain's back said his
challenge to her authority would not last long.

For herself, Min hoped Bryne considered them unimportant. He probably did. As long as he never learned
their real names. Logain quickened the stallion's pace,
and she heeled Wildrose to keep up, putting her thoughts
ahead, not behind.

Tucking his leather gauntlets behind his sword belt,
Gareth Bryne picked up the curl-brimmed velvet hat
from his writing table. The hat was the latest fashion
from Caemlyn. Caralin had seen to that; he had no care
for fashion, but she thought he should dress suitably for

his position, and it was the silks and velvets she laid out for him in the mornings.

As he set the high-crowned hat on his head, he caught sight of his shadowy reflection in one of the study windows. Fitting that it was so wavery and thin. Squint as much as he would, his gray hat and gray silk coat, embroidered with silver scrolls down the sleeves and collar, looked nothing like the helmet and armor he was used to. That was over and done. And this . . . This was something to fill empty hours. That was all.

"Are you certain you want to do this, Lord Gareth?"

He turned from the window to where Caralin stood beside her own writing table, across the room from his. Hers was piled with the estate account books. She had run his estates all the years he had been gone, and without doubt she still made a better job of it than he did.

"If you had set them to work for Admer Nem, as the law required," she went on, "this would be none of your affair at all."

"But I did not," he told her. "And would not if I had it to do again. You know as well as I do, Nem and his male kin would be trying to corner those girls day and night. And Maigan and the rest of the women would make their lives the Pit of Doom, that is if all three girls didn't accidentally fall down a well and drown."

"Even Maigan would not use a well," Caralin said dryly, "not with the weather we've been having. Still, I take your point, Lord Gareth. But they have had most of a day and a night to run in any direction. You will locate them as soon by sending out word of them. If they can be found."

"Thad can find them." Thad was over seventy, but he could still track yesterday's wind across stone by moonlight, and he had been more than happy to turn the brickyard over to his son.

"If you say so, Lord Gareth." She and Thad did not get on. "Well, when you bring them back, I can certainly use them in the house."

Something in her voice, casual as it was, pricked his attention. A touch of satisfaction. Practically from the day he arrived home Caralin had introduced a succession of pretty maids and farmgirls into the manor house, all willing and eager to help the lord forget his miseries. "They are oathbreakers, Caralin. I fear it's the fields for them."

A brief, exasperated tightening of her lips confirmed his suspicions, but she kept her tone indifferent. "The other two perhaps, Lord Gareth, but the Domani girl's grace would be wasted in the fields, and would suit serving at table very well. A remarkably pretty young woman. Still, it will be as you wish, of course."

So that was the one Caralin had picked out. A remarkably pretty young woman indeed. Though oddly different from the Domani women he had met. A touch hesitant here, a touch too fast there. Almost as if she were just now trying out her arts for the first time. That was impossible, of course. Domani women trained their daughters to twine men around their fingers almost from the cradle. Not that she had been ineffective, he admitted. If Caralin had sprung her on him among the farmgirls . . . Remarkably pretty.

So why was it not her face that kept filling his mind? Why did he find himself thinking of a pair of blue eyes? Challenging him as though wishing she had a sword, afraid and refusing to yield to fear. Mara Tomanes. He had been sure she was one to keep her word, even without oaths. "I will bring her back," he muttered to himself. "I will know why she broke oath."

"As you say, my Lord," Caralin said. "I thought she might do for your bedchamber maid. Sela is getting a bit old to be running up and down the stairs to fetch for you at night."

Bryne blinked at her. What? Oh. The Domani girl. He shook his head at Caralin's foolishness. But was he being any less foolish? He was the lord here; he should remain here to take care of his people. Yet Caralin had taken better care than he knew how, all the years he was gone. He knew camps and soldiers and campaigns, and maybe a bit of how to maneuver in court intrigues. She was right. He should take off his sword and this fool hat, and have Caralin write out their descriptions, and . . .

Instead, he said, "Keep a close eye on Admer Nem and his kin. They'll try to cheat you as much as they can."

"As you say, my Lord." The words were perfectly respectful; the tone told him to go teach his grandfather to shear sheep. Chuckling to himself, he went outside.

The manor house was really little more than a tremendously overgrown farmhouse, two rambling stories of brick and stone under a slate roof, added to again and again by generations of Brynes. House Bryne had owned this land—or it had owned them—since Andor was wrought from the wreckage of Artur Hawkwing's empire a thousand years before, and for all that time it had sent its sons off to fight Andor's wars. He would fight no more wars, but it was too late for House Bryne. There had been too many wars, too many battles. He was the last of the blood. No wife, no son, no daughter. The line ended with him. All things had to end; the Wheel of Time turned.

Twenty men waited beside saddled horses on the stone-paved yard in front of the manor house. Men even grayer than he, mostly, if they had hair. Experienced soldiers all, former squadmen, squadron leaders and bannermen who had served with him at one time or another in his career. Joni Shagrin, who had been Senior Bannerman of the Guards, was right at the front with a bandage around his temples, though Bryne knew for a fact his daughters had set their children to keep him in his bed. He was one of the few who had any family, here or anywhere else. Most had chosen to come serve Gareth Bryne again rather than drink away their pensions over reminiscences no one but another old soldier wanted to hear.

All wore swords belted over their coats, and a few carried long, steel-tipped lances that had hung for years on a wall until this morning. Every saddle had a fat blanket roll behind, and bulging saddlebags, plus a pot or kettle and full water bags, just as if they were riding out on campaign instead of a week's jaunt to chase down three women who set fire to a barn. Here was a chance to relive old days, or pretend to.

He wondered if that was what was rousting him out.

He was certainly too old to go riding off after a set of pretty eyes on a woman young enough to be his daughter. Maybe his granddaughter. *I am not that big a fool,* he told himself firmly. Caralin could manage things better with him not getting in the way.

A lanky bay gelding came galloping up the oak lane that led down to the road, and the rider threw himself out of the saddle before the animal came to a full stop; the man half-stumbled but still managed to put fist to heart in a proper salute. Barim Halle, who served under him as a senior squadman years ago, was hard and wiry, with a leather egg for a head and white eyebrows that seemed to be trying to make up for the lack of other hair. "You been recalled to Caemlyn, my Captain-General?" he panted.

"No," Bryne said, too sharply. "What do you mean riding in here as though you had Cairhienin cavalry on your tail?" Some of the other horses were frisking, catching the bay's mood.

"Never rode that hard unless we was chasing them, my Lord." Barim's grin faded when the man saw he was not laughing. "Well, my Lord, I seen the horses, and I reckoned—" The man took another look at his face and cut off that line. "Well, actually, I got some news, too. I been over to New Braem to see my sister, and I heard plenty."

New Braem was older than Andor—"old" Braem had been destroyed in the Trolloc Wars, a thousand years before Artur Hawkwing—and it was a good place for news. A middling-sized border town well to the east of his estates, on the road from Caemlyn to Tar Valon. Even with Morgase's current attitude, the merchants would keep that road busy. "Well, out with it, man. If there's news, what is it?"

"Uh, just trying to figure where to start, my Lord." Barim straightened unconsciously, as though making a report. "Most important, I reckon, they say Tear has fallen. Aielmen took the Stone itself, and the Sword That Cannot Be Touched has flat been touched. Somebody drew it, they say."

"An Aielman drew it?" Bryne said incredulously. An

Aiel would die before he touched a sword; he had seen it happen, in the Aiel War. Though it was said *Callandor* was not really a sword at all. Whatever that meant.

"They didn't say, my Lord. I heard names; Ren somebody or other most often. But they was talking it like fact, not rumor. Like everybody knew."

Bryne's forehead creased in a frown. Worse than troubling, if true. If *Callandor* had been drawn, then the Dragon was Reborn. According to the Prophecies, that meant the Last Battle was coming, the Dark One breaking free. The Dragon Reborn would save the world, so the Prophecies said. And destroy it. This was news enough by itself to have set Halle galloping, if he had thought twice.

But the leathery fellow was not finished. "Word come down from Tar Valon is near as big, my Lord. They say there's a new Amyrlin Seat. Elaida, my Lord, who was the Queen's advisor." Blinking suddenly, Halle hurried on; Morgase was forbidden ground, and every man on the estate knew it, though Bryne had never said so. "They say the old Amyrlin, Siuan Sanche, was stilled and executed. And Logain died, too. That false Dragon they caught and gentled last year. They talked it like it was true, my Lord. Some of them claimed they was in Tar Valon when it all happened."

Logain was no great news, even if he had started a war in Ghealdan by claiming to be the Dragon Reborn. There had been several false Dragons the last few years. He could channel, though; that was a fact. Until the Aes Sedai gentled him. Well, he was not the first man to be caught and gentled, cut off from the Power so he could never channel again. They said men like that, whether false Dragons or just poor fools the Red Ajah took against, never lived long. It was said they gave up wanting to live.

Siuan Sanche, though, that was news. He had met her once, nearly three years ago. A woman who demanded obedience and gave no reasons. Tough as an old boot, with a tongue like a file and a temper like that of a bear with a sore tooth. He would have expected her to tear any upstart claimant limb from limb with her bare hands.

Stilling was the same as gentling for a man, but more rare by far. Especially for an Amyrlin Seat. Only two Amyrlins in three thousand years had suffered that fate, so far as the Tower admitted, though it was possible they could have hidden two dozen more; the Tower was very good at hiding what they wanted hidden. But an execution on top of stilling seemed unnecessary. It was said women survived stilling no better than men did gentling.

It all stank of trouble. Everyone knew the Tower had secret alliances, strings tied to thrones and powerful lords and ladies. With a new Amyrlin raised in this fashion, some would surely try to test whether the Aes Sedai still watched as closely. And once this fellow in Tear quelled any opposition—not that there was likely to be much if he really did have the Stone—he would move, against Illian or Cairhien. The question was, how quickly could he move? Would forces be gathered against him, or for him? He had to be the true Dragon Reborn, but the Houses would go both ways, and the people, too. And if petty squabbles broke out because the Tower—

"Old fool," he muttered. Seeing Barim give a start, he added, "Not you. Another old fool." None of this was his affair any longer. Except to decide which way House Bryne went, when the time came. Not that anyone would care, except to know whether or not to attack him. Bryne had never been a powerful House, or large.

"Uh, my Lord?" Barim glanced at the men waiting with their horses. "Do you think you might need me, my Lord?"

Without even asking where or why. He was not the only one bored with country life. "Catch up to us when you have your gear together. We'll be heading south on the Four Kings Road to start." Barim saluted and dashed away, dragging his horse behind him.

Climbing into his saddle, Bryne swung his arm forward without a word, and the men fell into a column of twos behind him as they headed down the oak lane. He meant to have answers. If he had to take this Mara by the scruff of the neck and shake her, he would have answers.

* * *

The High Lady Alteima relaxed as the gates of the Royal Palace of Andor swung open and her carriage rolled in. She had not been certain they would open. It had surely taken long enough to get a note taken in, and longer still to have a reply. Her maid, a thin girl acquired here in Caemlyn, goggled and all but bounced on the seat across from her at the excitement of actually entering the palace.

Snapping open her lace fan, Alteima tried to cool herself. It was still well short of midday; the heat would grow worse yet. To think she had always thought of Andor as cool. Hastily she reviewed what she meant to say one last time. She was a pretty woman—she knew exactly how pretty—with large brown eyes that made some mistakenly think her innocent, even harmless. She knew she was neither, but it suited her very well to have others believe her so. Especially here, today. This carriage had taken almost the last of the gold she had managed to carry away when she fled Tear. If she was to reestablish herself, she needed powerful friends, and there was none more powerful in Andor than the woman she had come to see.

The carriage halted near a fountain in a column-ringed courtyard, and a servant in red-and-white livery rushed to open the door. Alteima barely glanced at the courtyard or the serving man; her mind was all on the meeting ahead. Black hair spilled to the middle of her back from beneath a close-fitting cap of seed pearls, and more pearls lined the tiny pleats of her high-necked gown of watery green silk. She had met Morgase once, briefly, five years ago during a state visit; a woman who radiated power, as reserved and stately as one should expect of a queen, and also proper, in the Andoran way. Which meant prim. The rumors in the city that she had a lover—a man not much liked, it seemed—did not fit that very well, of course. But from what Alteima remembered, the formality of the gown—and the high neck— should please Morgase.

As soon as Alteima's slippers were firmly on the paving stones, the maid, Cara, leaped down and began fussing over the fall of the pleats. Until Alteima snapped her fan

shut and slapped the girl's wrist with it; a courtyard was
no place for that. Cara—such a foolish name—flinched
back, clutching her wrist with a wounded look and the
beginnings of tears.

Alteima compressed her lips in irritation. The girl did
not even know how to take mild reproof. She had been
fooling herself: the girl would not do; she was too
obviously untrained. But a lady had to have a maid,
especially if she was to differentiate herself from the
mass of refugees in Andor. She had seen men and women
laboring in the sun, even begging in the streets, while
wearing the remnants of Cairhienin nobles' garb. She
thought she had recognized one or two. Perhaps she
should take one of them in service; who could know the
duties of a lady's maid better than a lady? And if they
were reduced to working with their hands, they should
leap at the chance. It might be amusing to have a former
"friend" for a maid. Too late for today, though. And an
untrained maid, a local girl, said a little too clearly that
Alteima was at the edge of her resources, only one step
removed from those beggars herself.

She put on a look of concerned gentleness. "Did I hurt
you, Cara?" she said sweetly. "Remain here in the
carriage and soothe your wrist. I am certain someone
will bring you cool water to drink." The mindless
gratitude on the girl's face was stupefying.

The liveried men, well trained, stood looking at nothing at all. Still, word of Alteima's kindness would spread,
if she knew anything about servants.

A tall young man appeared before her in the white-
collared red coat and burnished breastplate of the
Queen's Guard, bowing with a hand to his sword hilt. "I
am Guardsman-Lieutenant Tallanvor, High Lady. If you
will come with me, I will escort you to Queen Morgase."
He offered an arm, which she took, but otherwise she was
scarcely aware of him. She had no interest in soldiers
unless generals and lords.

As he attended her down broad corridors seemingly
full of scurrying men and women in livery—they took
care not to impede her way, of course—she subtly
examined the fine wall hangings, the ivory-inlaid chests

and highchests, the bowls and vases of chased gold or silver, or thin Sea Folk porcelain. The Royal Palace did not display as much wealth as the Stone of Tear, but Andor was still a wealthy land, perhaps even as wealthy as Tear. An older lord would do nicely, malleable for a woman still young, perhaps a touch feeble and infirm. With vast estates. That would be a beginning, while she found out exactly where the strings of power lay in Andor. A few words exchanged with Morgase some years ago were not much of an introduction, but she had that which a powerful queen must want and need. Information.

Finally Tallanvor ushered her into a large sitting room with a high ceiling painted in birds and clouds and open sky, where ornately carved and gilded chairs stood before a polished white marble fireplace. A part of Alteima's mind noted with amusement that the wide red-and-gold carpet was Tairen work. The young man went to one knee. "My Queen," he said in a suddenly rough voice, "as you have commanded, I bring you the High Lady Alteima, of Tear."

Morgase waved him away. "You are welcome, Alteima. It is good to see you again. Sit, and we will talk."

Alteima managed a curtsy and murmured thanks before taking a chair. Envy curdled inside her. She had remembered Morgase as a beautiful woman, but the golden-haired reality told her how pale that memory had grown. Morgase was a rose in full bloom, ready to overshadow every other flower. Alteima did not blame the young soldier for stumbling on his way out. She was just glad he was gone, so she would not have to be aware of him looking at the two of them, comparing.

Yet, there were changes, too. Vast changes. Morgase, by the Grace of the Light, Queen of Andor, Defender of the Realm, Protector of the People, High Seat of House Trakand, so very reserved and stately and proper, wore a gown of shimmering white silk that showed enough bosom to shock a tavern maid in the Maule. It clung to hip and thigh close enough to suit a Taraboner jade. The rumors were clearly true. Morgase had a lover. And for her to have altered so much, it was equally clear that she tried to please this Gaebril, not make him please her. Morgase still radiated power and a presence that filled the room, but that dress transformed both to something less.

Alteima was doubly glad she had worn a high neck. A woman that deep in a man's thrall could lash out in a jealous rage on the smallest provocation or none at all. If she met Gaebril, she would present him as near indifference as civility would allow. Even being suspected of *thinking* of poaching Morgase's lover could get her a hangman's noose instead of a rich husband on his last legs. She herself would have done the same.

A woman in red-and-white livery brought wine, an excellent Murandian, and poured it into crystal goblets deeply engraved with the rearing Lion of Andor. As Morgase took a goblet, Alteima noticed her ring, a golden serpent eating its own tail. The Great Serpent ring was worn by some women who had trained in the White Tower, as Morgase had, without becoming Aes Sedai, as well as by Aes Sedai themselves. It was a thousand-year tradition for the Queens of Andor to be Tower trained. But rumors were on every lip of a break between Morgase and Tar Valon, and the anti-Aes Sedai sentiment in the streets could have been quashed quickly had Morgase wanted to. Why was she still wearing the ring? Alteima would be careful of her words until she knew the answer.

The liveried woman withdrew to the far end of the room, out of earshot but close enough to see when the wine needed replenishing.

Taking a sip, Morgase said, "It is long since we met. Is your husband well? Is he in Caemlyn with you?"

Hastily Alteima shuffled her plans. She had not thought Morgase knew she had a husband, but she had always been able to think on the run. "Tedosian was well when I last saw him." The Light send he died soon. As well to get on with it. "He was of some question about serving this Rand al'Thor, and that is a dangerous chasm to straddle. Why, lords have been hung as if they were common criminals."

"Rand al'Thor," Morgase mused softly. "I met him once. He did not look like one who would name himself the Dragon Reborn. A frightened shepherd boy, trying not to show it. Yet thinking back, he seemed to be looking for some—escape." Her blue eyes looked inward. "Elaida warned me of him." She seemed unaware of having spoken those last words.

"Elaida was your advisor then?" Alteima said cautiously. She knew it was so, and it made the rumors of a break all the more difficult to believe. She had to know if it was true. "You have replaced her, now that she is Amyrlin?"

Morgase's eyes snapped back into focus. "I have not!" The next instant her voice softened again. "My daughter, Elayne, is training in the Tower. She has already been raised to the Accepted."

Alteima fluttered her fan, hoping sweat was not breaking out on her forehead. If Morgase did not know her own feelings toward the Tower, there was no way to speak safely. Her plans teetered on the edge of a precipice.

Then Morgase rescued them, and her. "You say your husband was of two minds about Rand al'Thor. And you?"

She nearly sighed with relief. Morgase might be behaving like an untutored farmgirl over this Gaebril, but she still had her sense when it came to power and possible dangers to her realm. "I observed him closely, of course, in the Stone." That should plant the seed, if it needed planting. "He can channel, and a man who can channel is always to be feared. Yet he is the Dragon Reborn. There is no doubt. The Stone fell, and *Callandor* was in his hand when it did. The Prophecies . . . I fear I must leave decisions of what to do about the Dragon Reborn to those who are wiser than I. I only know that I am afraid to remain where he rules. Even a High Lady of Tear cannot match the courage of the Queen of Andor."

The golden-haired woman gave her a shrewd look that made her afraid she had overdone the flattery. Some did not like it too open. But Morgase merely leaned back in her chair and sipped her wine. "Tell me about him, this man who is supposed to save us, and destroy us doing it."

Success. Or at least, the beginnings of it. "He is a dangerous man beyond any question of the Power. A lion seems lazy, half-asleep, until suddenly he charges; then he is all speed and power. Rand al'Thor seems innocent, not lazy, and naive, not asleep, but when he charges . . . He has no proper respect for person or position at all. I did not exaggerate when I said he has hanged lords. He is a breeder of anarchy. In Tear under his new laws, even a High Lord or Lady can be called before a magistrate, to be fined or worse, on the charges of the meanest peasant or fisherman. He . . ."

She kept strictly to the truth as she saw it; she could tell the truth as quickly as a lie when it was necessary. Morgase sipped her wine and listened; Alteima might have thought her lounging indolently, except that her eyes showed she was taking in every word and storing it. "You must understand," Alteima finished, "that I have only touched the surface. Rand al'Thor and what he has done in Tear are subjects for hours."

"You will have them," Morgase said, and in her mind Alteima smiled. Success. "Is it true," the Queen went on, "that he brought Aiel with him to the Stone?"

"Oh, yes. Great savages with their faces hidden half the time, and even the women ready to kill as soon as look. They followed him like dogs, terrorizing everyone, and took whatever they wanted from the Stone."

"I had thought it must be the wildest rumor," Morgase reflected. "There have been rumors this past year, but they have not come out of the Waste in twenty years, not since the Aiel War. The world certainly does not need this Rand al'Thor bringing the Aiel down on us again." Her look sharpened again. "You said 'followed.' They have gone?"

Alteima nodded. "Just before I left Tear. And he went with them."

"With them!" Morgase exclaimed. "I feared he was in Cairhien right this—"

"You have a guest, Morgase? I should have been told, so I could greet her."

A big man strode into the room, tall, his gold-embroidered red silk coat fitting massive shoulders and a deep chest. Alteima did not need to see the radiant look on Morgase's face to name him as Lord Gaebril; the assurance with which he had interrupted the Queen did that. He lifted a finger, and the serving woman curtsied and left quickly; he did not ask Morgase's permission to dismiss her servants from her presence, either. He was darkly handsome, incredibly so, with wings of white at his temples.

Composing her face to commonplace, Alteima put on a marginally welcoming smile, suitable for an elderly uncle with neither power, wealth nor influence. He might be gorgeous, but even if he did not belong to Morgase, he was not a man she would try manipulating unless she absolutely had to. There was perhaps even more of an air of power about him than about Morgase.

Gaebril stopped by Morgase and put his hand on her bare shoulder in a very familiar way. She clearly came close to resting her cheek on the back of his hand, but his eyes were on Alteima. She was used to men looking at her, but these eyes made her shift uneasily; they were far too penetrating, saw far too much.

"You come from Tear?" The sound of his deep voice sent a tingle through her; her skin, even her bones, felt as though she had been dipped in icy water, but oddly her momentary anxiety melted.

It was Morgase who answered; Alteima could not seem to find her tongue with him watching her. "This is the High Lady Alteima, Gaebril. She has been telling me all about the Dragon Reborn. She was in the Stone of Tear when it fell. Gaebril, there really were Aiel—" The pressure of his hand cut her off. Irritation flashed across her face, but then it was gone, replaced by a smile beaming up at him.

His eyes, still on Alteima, sent that shiver through her again, and this time she gasped aloud. "So much talking must have fatigued you, Morgase," he said without shifting his gaze. "You do too much. Go to your bedchamber and sleep. Go now. I will wake you when you have rested enough."

Morgase stood immediately, still smiling at him devotedly. Her eyes seemed slightly glazed. "Yes, I am tired. I will take a nap now, Gaebril."

She glided from the room with never a glance at Alteima, but Alteima's attention was all on Gaebril. Her heart beat faster; her breath quickened. He was surely the handsomest man she had ever seen. The grandest, the strongest, the most powerful. . . . Superlatives rolled through her mind like a flood.

Gaebril paid no more attention to Morgase's leaving than she did. Taking the chair the Queen had vacated, he leaned back with his boots stretched out in front of him. "Tell me why you came to Caemlyn, Alteima." Again the chill ran through her. "The absolute truth, but keep it brief. You can give me details later if I want them."

She did not hesitate. "I tried to poison my husband and had to flee before Tedosian and that trull Estanda could kill me instead, or worse. Rand al'Thor meant to let them do it, as an example." Telling made her cringe. Not because it was a truth she had kept hidden so much as because she found she wanted to please him more than anything else in the world, and she feared that he might send her away. But he wanted the truth. "I chose Caemlyn because I could not bear Illian and though Andor is little better, Cairhien is in near ruins. In Caemlyn, I can find a wealthy husband, or one who thinks he is my protector if need be, and use his power to—"

He stopped her with a wave of his hand, chuckling. "A vicious little cat, though pretty. Perhaps pretty enough to keep, with your teeth and claws drawn." Suddenly his face became more intent. "Tell me what you know of Rand al'Thor, and especially his friends, if he has any, his companions, his allies."

She told him, talking until her mouth and throat went dry, and her voice cracked and rasped. She never raised her goblet until he told her to drink; then she gulped the wine down and spoke on. She could please him. She could please him better than Morgase could think of.

* * *

The maids working in Morgase's bedchamber dropped hasty curtsies, surprised to see her there in the middle of the morning. Waving them out of the room, she climbed onto her bed still in her dress. For a time she lay staring at the gilded carvings of the bedposts. No Lions of Andor here, but roses. For the Rose Crown of Andor, but roses suited her better than lions.

Stop being stubborn, she chided herself, then wondered why. She had told Gaebril she was tired, and . . . Or had he told her? Impossible. She was the Queen of Andor, and no man told her to do anything. *Gareth.* Now why had she thought of Gareth Bryne? He had certainly never told her to do anything; the Captain-General of the Queen's Guards obeyed the Queen, not the other way around. But he had been stubborn, entirely capable of digging in his heels until she came around to his way. *Why am I thinking of him? I wish he were here.* That was ridiculous. She had sent him away for opposing her; about what no longer seemed quite clear, but that was not important. He had opposed her. She could remember the feelings she had had for him only dimly, as though he had been gone for years. Surely it had not been so long? *Stop being stubborn!*

Her eyes closed, and she fell immediately into sleep, a sleep troubled by restless dreams of running from something she could not see.

CHAPTER
2

Rhuidean

High in the city of Rhuidean, Rand al'Thor looked out from a tall window; whatever glass might have once been in it was long since gone. The shadows below slanted sharply east. A bard-harp played softly in the room behind him. Sweat evaporated from his face almost as soon as it appeared; his red silk coat, damp between the shoulders, hung open in a fruitless bid for air, and his shirt was unlaced half down his chest. Night in the Aiel Waste would bring freezing cold, but during daylight even a breeze was never cool.

With his hands above his head on the smooth stone window frame, his coatsleeves fell down to reveal the front part of the figure wrapped around each forearm: a golden-maned, serpentine creature with eyes like the sun, scaled in scarlet and gold, each foot tipped with five golden claws. Part of his skin, they were, not tattoos; they glittered like precious metals and polished gems, seemed almost alive in the late-afternoon sunlight.

Those marked him, to the people on this side of the mountain range variously called the Dragonwall or the Spine of the World, as He Who Comes With the Dawn.

And like the herons branded into his palms, they marked him for those beyond the Dragonwall, too, according to the Prophecies, as the Dragon Reborn. In both cases prophesied to unite, save—and destroy.

They were names he would have avoided if he could, but that time was long past if it had ever existed, and he no longer thought of it. Or if he did, on rare occasion, it was with the faint regret of a man recalling a foolish dream of his boyhood. As if he were not close enough to boyhood to remember every minute. Instead, he tried to think only of what he had to do. Fate and duty held him on the path like a rider's reins, but he had often been called stubborn. The end of the road must be reached, but if it could be attained by a different way, maybe it need not be the end. Small chance. No chance, almost certainly. The Prophecies demanded his blood.

Rhuidean stretched below him, seared by a sun still pitiless as it sank toward craggy mountains, bleak, with barely a sign of vegetation. This rugged, broken land, where men had killed or died over a pool of water they could step across, was the last place on earth anyone would think to find a great city. Its long-ago builders had never finished their work. Impossibly tall buildings dotted the city, stepped and slab-sided palaces that sometimes ended after eight or even ten stories not with a roof but with the ragged masonry of another half-built floor. The towers soared higher yet, but stopped in jagged abruptness as often as not. Now a good quarter of the great structures, with their massive columns and immense windows of colored glass, lay strewn as rubble across wide avenues with broad strips of bare dirt down their centers, dirt that had never held the trees they were planned for. The marvelous fountains stood dry as they had for hundreds upon hundreds of years. All that futile labor, the builders finally dying with their work undone; yet at times Rand thought that maybe the city had only been begun so he could find it.

Too proud, he thought. *A man would have to be half-mad at least to be so proud.* He could not help chuckling dryly. There had been Aes Sedai with the men and women who had come here so long ago, and they had known *The Karaethon Cycle,* the Prophecies of the Dragon. Or perhaps they had written the Prophecies. *Too proud by tenfold.*

Directly below him lay a vast plaza, half-covered in stretching shadow, littered with a jumble of statues and crystal chairs, oddities and peculiar shapes of metal or glass or stone, things he could put no name to, scattered about in tangled heaps as if deposited by a storm. Even the shadows were cool only by comparison. Rough-clothed men—not Aiel—sweated to load wagons with items chosen by a short, slender woman in pristine blue silk, straight-backed and gliding from place to place as though the heat did not press down on her as hard as on the others. Still, she wore a damp white cloth tied around her temples; she just did not let herself show the effects of the sun. Rand would have wagered she did not even perspire.

The workmen's leader was a dark, bulky man named Hadnan Kadere, a supposed merchant dressed all in cream-colored silk that was sweat-sodden today. He mopped his face continually with a large handkerchief, shouting curses at the men—his wagon drivers and guards—but he leaped as quickly as they to haul at whatever the slim woman pointed out, big or small. Aes Sedai had no need of size to impose their will, but Rand thought Moiraine would have done as well if she had never been near the White Tower.

Two of the men were trying to move what appeared to be an oddly twisted redstone doorframe; the corners did not meet properly, and the eye did not want to follow the straight pieces. It stayed upright, turning freely but refusing to tip over however they manhandled it. Then one slipped and fell, through the doorway up to his waist. Rand tensed. For a moment, the fellow seemed not to exist above the waist; his legs kicked wildly in panic. Until Lan, a tall man in drab shades of green, strode over and hauled him out again by his belt. Lan was Moiraine's Warder, bonded to her in some way Rand did not understand, and a hard man who moved like the Aiel, like a hunting wolf; the sword at his hip did not seem part of him, it was part of him. He dropped the workman on the paving stones on the seat of his breeches and left him there; the fellow's terrified cries rose thinly to Rand, and his companion looked ready to run. Several of Kadere's men who had been close enough to see were looking at one another and at the mountains around the city, plainly assessing their chances.

Moiraine appeared among them so quickly it seemed by the Power, moving smoothly from man to man. Her manner made Rand almost hear the cool, imperious instructions coming from her lips, so full of certainty that they would be obeyed that not obeying would seem foolish. In short order she overrode resistance, stamped firmly on objections, chivvied them every one back to work. The pair with the doorframe were soon dragging and shoving as hard as ever, if with frequent looks at Moiraine when they thought she would not see. In her own way, she was even harder than Lan.

As far as Rand knew, all of those things down there were *angreal* or *sa'angreal* or *ter'angreal,* made before the Breaking of the World to magnify the One Power or use it in various ways. Made with the Power certainly, though not even Aes Sedai knew how to construct such things now. He more than suspected the use of the twisted doorframe—a doorway to another world—but for the rest, he had no idea. No one did. That was why Moiraine worked so hard, to have as many as she could carted to the Tower for study. It was possible that even the Tower did not contain as many objects of the Power as lay about this square, though supposedly the Tower held the largest collection in the world. Even there, the Tower only knew the uses of some.

What was in the wagons or tossed about on the pavement did not interest Rand; he had already taken what he needed from down there. Had already taken more than he wanted, in some ways.

In the center of the plaza, near the burned remains of a great tree a hundred feet high, stood a small forest of tall glass columns, each nearly as tall as the tree and so slender it seemed the first stormwind must bring them all crashing down. Even with an edge of shadow touching them, the columns caught and refracted the sunlight in glitters and sparkles. For countless years Aiel men had entered that array and returned marked as Rand was, but on only one arm, marked as clan chiefs. They came out marked or did not come out. Aiel women had come to this city as well, on the path toward becoming Wise Ones. No one else, not and live. *A man may go to Rhuidean once, a woman twice; more means death.* That was what the Wise Ones had said, and it had been truth, then. Now anyone could enter Rhuidean.

Hundreds of Aiel walked the streets, and increasing numbers actually dwelled in the buildings; each day more of the dirt strips down the streets showed beans or squash or *zemai,* arduously watered from clay pots hauled from the huge new lake that filled the south end of the valley, the only such body of water in the entire land. Thousands made their camps in the surrounding mountains, even on Chaendaer itself, where before they had come only with ceremony, to send a single man or woman at a time into Rhuidean.

Wherever he went, Rand brought change and destruction. This time, he hoped against hope that the change was for the good. It might yet be so. The burned tree mocked him. *Avendesora,* the legendary Tree of Life; the stories never said where it was, and it had been a surprise to find it here. Moiraine said it still lived, that it would put out shoots again, but so far he saw only blackened bark and bare branches.

With a sigh, he turned from the window into a big room, though not the biggest in Rhuidean, with tall windows on two sides, its domed ceiling worked in a fanciful mosaic of winged people and animals. Most of the furniture left in the city had long since rotted away even in the dryness, and much of the little that remained was riddled with beetles and worms. But on the far side of the room stood one high-backed chair, solid, and its gilding largely intact, but mismatched with its table, a wide thing with legs and edges thickly carved in flowers. Someone had polished the wood with beeswax till it shone dully despite its age. The Aiel had found them for him, though they shook their heads at such things; there were few trees in the Waste that could have produced wood straight and long enough to make that chair, and none to make the table.

That was all the furniture, as he thought of it. A fine silk Illianer carpet in blue and gold, booty in some long-ago battle, covered the middle of the dark red floor tiles. Cushions lay scattered about, in bright silks, and tasseled. Those were what Aiel used instead of chairs, when they did not merely sit on their heels, as comfortable as he would be in a padded chair.

Six men reclined against cushions on the carpet. Six clan chiefs, representing the clans that had so far come to follow Rand. Or rather, to follow He Who Comes With the Dawn. Not always eagerly. He thought Rhuarc, a broad-shouldered, blue-eyed man with heavy streaks of gray in his dark red hair, might have some friendship for him, but not the rest. Only six of the twelve.

Ignoring the chair, Rand sat down cross-legged, facing the Aiel. Outside of Rhuidean, the only chairs in the Waste were chief's chairs, used only by the chief and only for three reasons: to be acclaimed as clan chief, to accept the submission of an enemy with honor, or to pass judgment. Taking the chair with these men now would imply that he meant to do one of those.

They wore the *cadin'sor,* coats and breeches in shades of brown and gray that would fade into the ground, and soft boots that laced to the knee. Even here, meeting with the man they had proclaimed the *Car'a'carn,* the chief of chiefs, each had a heavy-bladed knife at his belt and the gray-brown *shoufa* draped like a wide scarf around his neck; if any man covered his face with the black veil that was part of the *shoufa,* he would be ready to kill. It was not beyond possibility. These men had fought one another in a never-ending cycle of clan raids and battles and feuds. They watched him, waited for him, but an Aiel's waiting always spoke of a readiness to move, suddenly and violently.

Bael, the tallest man Rand had ever seen, and Jheran, blade-slender and whip-quick, lay as far from one another as they could manage and still be on the carpet. There was blood feud between Bael's Goshien and Jheran's Shaarad, suppressed for He Who Comes With the Dawn but not forgotten. And perhaps the Peace of Rhuidean still held, despite all that had happened. Still, the tranquil sounds of the harp made a sharp contrast with the hard refusal of Bael and Jheran to look at one another. Six sets of eyes, blue or green or gray, in sun-dark faces; Aiel could make hawks look tame.

"What must I do to bring the Reyn to me?" he said. "You were sure they would come, Rhuarc."

The chief of the Taardad looked at him calmly; his face could have been carved stone for all its expression. "Wait. Only that. Dhearic will bring them. Eventually."

White-haired Han, lying next to Rhuarc, twisted his mouth as if about to spit. His leathery face wore a sour look, as usual. "Dhearic has seen too many men and Maidens sit staring for days, then throw down their spears. Throw them down!"

"And run away," Bael added quietly. "I have seen them myself, among the Goshien, even from my own sept, running. And you, Han, among the Tomanelle. We all have. I do not think they know where they are running to, only what they are running from."

"Cowardly snakes," Jheran barked. Gray streaked his light brown hair; there were no young men among Aiel clan chiefs. "Stinkadders, wriggling away from their own shadows." A slight shift of his blue eyes toward the far side of the carpet made it clear he meant it for a description of the Goshien, not just those who had thrown down their spears.

Bael made as if to rise, his face hardening further, if that was possible, but the man next to him put a quieting hand on his arm. Bruan, of the Nakai, was big enough and strong enough for two blacksmiths, but he had a placid nature that seemed odd for an Aiel. "All of us have seen men and Maidens run." He sounded almost lazy, and his gray eyes looked so, yet Rand knew otherwise; even Rhuarc considered Bruan a deadly fighter and a devious tactician. Luckily, not even Rhuarc was stronger for Rand than Bruan. But he had come to follow He Who Comes With the Dawn; he did not know Rand al'Thor. "As you have, Jheran. You know how hard it was to face what they face. If you cannot name coward those who died because they could not face it, can you name coward those who run for the same reason?"

"They should never have learned," Han muttered, kneading his red-tasseled blue cushion like an enemy's throat. "It was for those who could enter Rhuidean and live."

He spoke the words to no one in particular, but they had to be for Rand's ears. It was Rand who had revealed to everyone what a man learned amid the glass columns in the plaza, revealed enough that the chiefs and Wise Ones could not turn aside when asked the rest. If there was an Aiel in the Waste who did not know the truth now, he had not spoken to anyone in a month.

Far from the glorious heritage of battle most believed in, the Aiel had begun as helpless refugees from the Breaking of the World. Everyone who survived had been refugees then, of course, but the Aiel had never seen themselves as helpless. Worse, they had been followers of the Way of the Leaf, refusing to do violence even in defense of their lives. Aiel meant "dedicated" in the Old Tongue, and it had been to peace that they were dedicated. Those who called themselves Aiel today were the descendants of those who had broken a pledge of untold generations. Only one remnant of that belief remained: an Aiel would die before taking up a sword. They had always believed it a part of their pride, of their separateness from those who lived outside the Waste.

He had heard Aiel say that they had committed some sin to be placed in the desolate Waste. Now they knew what it was. The men and women who had built Rhuidean and died here—those called the Jenn Aiel, the clan that was not, on the few occasions they were spoken of—had been the ones who kept faith with the Aes Sedai of the time before the Breaking. It was hard to face the knowledge that what you had always believed was a lie.

"It had to be told," Rand said. *They had a right to know. A man shouldn't have to live a lie. Their own prophecy said I would break them. And I couldn't have done differently.* The past was past and done; he should be worrying about the future. *Some of these men dislike me, and some hate me for not being born among them, but they follow. I need them all.* "What of the Miagoma?"

Erim, lying between Rhuarc and Han, shook his head.

His once bright red hair was half white, but his green eyes were as strong as any younger man's. His big hands, wide and long and hard, said his arms were as strong, too. "Timolan does not let his feet know which way he will jump until after he has leaped."

"When Timolan was young as a chief," Jheran said, "he tried to unite the clans and failed. It will not sit well with him that at last one has come to succeed where he failed."

"He will come," Rhuarc said. "Timolan never believed himself He Who Comes With the Dawn. And Janwin will bring the Shiande. But they will wait. They must settle matters in their own minds first."

"They must settle He Who Comes With the Dawn being a wetlander," Han barked. "I mean no offense, *Car'a'carn.*" There was no obsequiousness in his voice; a chief was not a king, and neither was the chief of chiefs. At best he was first among equals.

"The Daryne and the Codarra will come eventually, as well, I think," Bruan said calmly. And quickly, lest silence should grow to a reason for dancing the spears. First among equals at best. "They have lost more than any other clans to the bleakness." That was what the Aiel had taken to calling the long period of staring before someone tried to run away from being Aiel. "For the moment, Mandelain and Indirian are concerned with holding their clans together, and both will want to see the Dragons on your arms for themselves, but they will come."

That left only one clan to be discussed, the one none of the chiefs wanted to mention. "What news of Couladin and the Shaido?" Rand asked.

Silence answered him, broken only by the softly serene sounds of the harp in the background, each man waiting for another to speak, all coming as close as Aiel could to showing discomfort. Jheran frowned at his thumbnail, and Bruan toyed with one of the silvery tassels on his green cushion. Even Rhuarc studied the carpet.

Graceful, white-robed men and women moved into the hush, pouring worked silver goblets of wine to set beside each man, bringing small silver plates with olives, rare in the Waste, and white ewe's-milk cheese, and the pale, wrinkled nuts the Aiel called *pecara*. The Aiel faces looking out of those pale cowls had downcast eyes and an unfamiliar meekness on their features.

Whether captured in battle or on a raid, the *gai'shain* were sworn to serve obediently for one year and a day, touching no weapon, doing no violence, at the end returning to their own clan and sept as if nothing had happened. A strange echo of the Way of the Leaf. *Ji'e'toh*, honor and obligation, required it, and breaking *ji'e'toh* was nearly the worst thing an Aiel could do. Perhaps *the* worst. It was possible that some of these men and women were serving their own clan chief, but neither would acknowledge it by the blink of an eye so long as the period of *gai'shain* held, not even for a son or daughter.

It struck Rand suddenly that this was the real reason that some Aiel took what he had revealed so hard. To those, it must seem that their ancestors had sworn *gai'shain*, not only for themselves but for all succeeding generations. And those generations—all, down to the present day—had broken *ji'e'toh* by taking up the spear. Had the men in front of him ever worried along those lines? *Ji'e'toh* was very serious business to an Aiel.

The *gai'shain* departed on soft slippered feet, barely making a sound. None of the clan chiefs touched their wine, or the food.

"Is there any hope that Couladin will meet with me?" Rand knew there was not; he had stopped sending requests for a meeting once he learned Couladin was having the messengers skinned alive. But it was a way to start the others talking.

Han snorted. "The only word we have had from him is that he means to flay *you* when next he sees you. Does that sound as if he will talk?"

"Can I break the Shaido away from him?"

"They follow him," Rhuarc said. "He is not a chief at all, but they believe he is." Couladin had never entered those glass columns; he might even still believe as he claimed, that everything Rand had said was a lie. "He says that he is the *Car'a'carn,* and they believe that as well. The Shaido Maidens who came, came for their society, and that because *Far Dareis. Mai* carried your honor. None else will."

"We send scouts to watch them," Bruan said, "and the Shaido kill them when they can—Couladin builds the makings of half a dozen feuds—but so far he shows no signs of attacking us here. I have heard that he claims we have defiled Rhuidean, and that attacking us here would only deepen the desecration."

Erim grunted and shifted on his cushion. "He means there are enough spears here to kill every Shaido twice over and to spare." He popped a piece of white cheese into his mouth, growling around it. "The Shaido were ever cowards and thieves."

"Honorless dogs," Bael and Jheran said together, then stared at one another as though each thought the other had tricked him into something.

"Honorless or not," Bruan said quietly, "Couladin's numbers are growing." Calm as he sounded, he still took a deep drink from his goblet before going on. "You all know what I am speaking of. Some of those who run, after the bleakness, do not throw away their spears. Instead they join with their societies among the Shaido."

"No Tomanelle has ever broken clan," Han barked.

Bruan looked past Rhuarc and Erim at the Tomanelle chief and said deliberately, "It has happened in every clan." Without waiting for another challenge to his word, he settled back on his cushion. "It cannot be called breaking clan. They join their societies. Like the Shaido Maidens who have come to their Roof here."

There were a few mutters, but no one disputed him this time. The rules governing Aiel warrior societies were complex, and in some ways their members felt as closely bound to society as to clan. For instance, members of the same society would not fight each other even if their clans were in blood feud. Some men would not marry a woman too closely related to a member of their own society, just as if that made her their own close blood kin. The ways of *Far Dareis Mai*, the Maidens of the Spear, Rand did not even want to think about.

"I need to know what Couladin intends," he told them. Couladin was a bull with a bee in his ear; he might charge in any direction. Rand hesitated. "Would it violate honor to send people to join their societies among the Shaido?" He did not need to describe what he meant any further. To a man, they stiffened where they lay, even Rhuarc, eyes cold enough to banish the heat from the room.

"To spy in that manner"—Erim twisted his mouth around "spy" as if the word tasted foul—"would be like spying on your own sept. No one of honor would do such a thing."

Rand refrained from asking whether they might find someone with a slightly less prickly honor. The Aiel sense of humor was a strange thing, often cruel, but about some matters they had none at all.

To change the subject, he asked, "Is there any word from across the Dragonwall?" He knew the answer; that sort of news spread quickly even among as many Aiel as were gathered around Rhuidean.

"None worth the telling," Rhuarc replied. "With the troubles among the treekillers, few peddlers come into the Three-fold Land." That was the Aiel name for the Waste; a punishment for their sin, a testing ground for their courage, an anvil to shape them. "Treekillers" was what they called Cairhienin. "The Dragon banner still flies over the Stone of Tear. Tairens have moved north into Cairhien as you ordered, to distribute food among the treekillers. Nothing more."

"You should have let the treekillers starve," Bael muttered, and Jheran closed his mouth with a snap. Rand suspected he had been about to say much the same.

"Treekillers are fit for nothing except to be killed or sold as animals in Shara," Erim said grimly. Those were two of the things Aiel did to those who came into the Waste uninvited; only gleeman, peddlers, and Tinkers had safe passage, though Aiel avoided the Tinkers as if they carried fever. Shara was the name of the lands beyond the Waste; not even the Aiel knew much about them.

From the corner of his eye, Rand saw two women standing expectantly just inside the tall, arched doorway. Someone had hung strings of colored beads there, red and blue, to replace the missing doors. One of the women was Moiraine. For a moment he considered making them wait; Moiraine had that irritatingly commanding look on her face, clearly expecting them to break off everything for her. Only, there was really nothing left to discuss, and he could tell from the men's eyes that they did not want to make conversation. Not so soon after speaking of the bleakness, and the Shaido.

Sighing, he stood, and the clan chiefs imitated him. All except Han were as tall as he or taller. Where Rand had grown up, Han would have been considered of average height or better; among Aiel, he was accounted short. "You know what must be done. Bring in the rest of the clans, and keep an eye on the Shaido." He paused a moment, then added, "It will end well. As well for the Aiel as I can manage."

"The prophecy said you would break us," Han said sourly, "and you have made a good beginning. But we will follow you. Till shade is gone," he recited, "till water is gone, into the Shadow with teeth bared, screaming defiance with the last breath, to spit in Sightblinder's eye on the Last Day." Sightblinder was one of the Aiel names for the Dark One.

There was nothing for Rand except to make the proper response. Once he had not known it. "By my honor and the Light, my life will be a dagger for Sightblinder's heart."

"Until the Last Day," the Aiel finished, "to Shayol Ghul itself." The harper played on pacifically.

The chiefs filed out past the two women, eyeing Moiraine respectfully. There was nothing of fear in them. Rand wished he could be as sure of himself. Moiraine had too many plans for him, too many ways of pulling strings he did not know she had tied to him.

The two women came in as soon as the chiefs were gone, Moiraine as cool and elegant as ever. A small, pretty woman, with or without those Aes Sedai features he could never put an age to, she had abandoned the damp, cooling cloth for her temples. In its place, a small blue stone hung suspended on her forehead from a fine golden chain in her dark hair. It would not have mattered if she had kept it; nothing could diminish her queenly carriage. She usually seemed to own a foot more height than she actually had, and her eyes were all confidence and command.

The other woman was taller, though still short of his shoulder, and young, not ageless. Egwene, whom he had grown up with. Now, except for her big dark eyes, she could almost have passed as an Aiel woman, and not only for her tanned face and hands. She wore a full Aiel skirt of brown wool and a loose white blouse of a plant fiber called *algode. Algode* was softer than even the finest-woven wool; it would do very well for trade, if he ever convinced the Aiel. A gray shawl hung around Egwene's shoulders, and a folded gray scarf made a wide band to hold back the dark hair that fell below her shoulders. Unlike most Aiel women, she wore only one bracelet, ivory carved into a circle of flames, and a single necklace of gold and ivory beads. And one more thing. A Great Serpent ring on her left hand.

Egwene had been studying with some of the Aiel Wise Ones—exactly what, Rand did not know, though he more than suspected something to do with dreams; Egwene and the Aiel women were closemouthed—but she had studied in the White Tower, too. She was one of the Accepted, on the way to becoming Aes Sedai. And passing herself off, here and in Tear at least, as full Aes Sedai already. Sometimes he teased her about that; she did not take his japes very well, though.

"The wagons will be ready to leave for Tar Valon soon," Moiraine said. Her voice was musical, crystalline.

"Send a strong guard," Rand said, "or Kadere may not take them where you want." He turned for the windows again, wanting to look out and think, about Kadere. "You've not needed me to hold your hand or give you permission before."

Abruptly something seemed to strike him across the shoulders, for all the world like a thick hickory stick; only the slight feel of goose bumps on his skin, not likely in this heat, told him that one of the women had channeled.

Spinning back to face them, he reached out to *saidin*, filled himself with the One Power. The Power felt like life itself swelling inside him, as if he were ten times, a hundred times as alive; the Dark One's taint filled him, too, death and corruption, like maggots crawling in his mouth. It was a torrent that threatened to sweep him away, a raging flood he had to fight every moment. He was almost used to it now, and at the same time he would never be used to it. He wanted to hold on to the sweetness of *saidin* forever, and he wanted to vomit. And all the while the deluge tried to scour him to the bone and burn his bones to ash.

The taint would drive him mad eventually, if the Power did not kill him first; it was a race between the two. Madness had been the fate of every man who had channeled since the Breaking of the World began, since that day when Lews Therin Telamon, the Dragon, and his Hundred Companions had sealed up the Dark One's prison at Shayol Ghul. The last backblast from that sealing had tainted the male half of the True Source, and men who could channel, madmen who could channel, had torn the world apart.

He filled himself with the Power. . . . And he could not tell which woman had done it. They both looked at him as if butter would not melt in their mouths, each with an eyebrow arched almost identically in slightly amused questioning. Either or both could be embracing the female half of the Source right that instant, and he would never know.

Of course, a stick across the shoulders was not Moiraine's way; she found other means of chastising, more subtle, usually more painful in the end. Yet even sure that it must have been Egwene, he did nothing. *Proof.* Thought slid along the outside of the Void; he floated within, in emptiness, thought and emotion, even his anger, distant. *I will do nothing without proof. I will not be goaded, this time.* She was not the Egwene he had grown up with; she had become part of the Tower since Moiraine sent her there. Moiraine again. Always Moiraine. Sometimes he wished he were rid of Moiraine. *Only sometimes?*

He concentrated on her. "What do you want of me?" His voice sounded flat and cold to his own ears. The Power stormed inside him. Egwene had told him that for a woman, touching *saidar,* the female half of the Source, was an embrace; for a man, always, it was a war without mercy. "And don't mention wagons again, little sister. I usually find out what you mean to do long after it is done."

The Aes Sedai frowned at him, and no wonder. She was surely not used to being addressed so, not by any man, even the Dragon Reborn. He had no idea himself where "little sister" had come from; sometimes of late words seemed to pop into his head. A touch of madness, perhaps. Some nights he lay awake till the small hours, worrying about that. Inside the Void, it seemed someone else's worry.

"We should speak alone." She gave the harper a cool glance.

Jasin Natael, as he called himself here, lay half-sprawled on cushions against one of the windowless walls, softly playing the harp perched on his knee, its upper arm carved and gilded to resemble the creatures on Rand's forearms. Dragons, the Aiel called them. Rand had only suspicions where Natael had gotten the thing. He was a dark-haired man, who would have been accounted taller than most elsewhere than the Aiel Waste, in his middle years. His coat and breeches were dark blue silk suitable for a royal court, elaborately embroidered with thread-of-gold on collar and cuffs, everything buttoned up or laced despite the heat. The fine clothes were at odds with his gleeman's cloak spread out beside him. A perfectly sound cloak, but covered completely with hundreds of patches in nearly as many colors, all sewn so as to flutter at the slightest breeze, it signified a country entertainer, a juggler and tumbler, musician and storyteller who wandered from village to village. Certainly not a man to wear silk. The man had his conceits. He appeared completely immersed in his music.

"You can say what you wish in front of Natael," Rand said. "He is gleeman to the Dragon Reborn, after all." If keeping the matter secret was important enough, she would press it, and he would send Natael away, though he did not like the man to be out of his sight.

Egwene sniffed loudly and shifted her shawl on her shoulders. "Your head is swelled up like an overripe melon, Rand al'Thor." She said it flatly, as a statement of fact.

Anger bubbled outside the Void. Not at what she had said; she had been in the habit of trying to take him down a rung even when they were children, usually whether he deserved it or not. But of late it seemed to him she had taken to working with Moiraine, trying to put him off balance so the Aes Sedai could push him where she wanted. When they were younger, before they learned what he was, he and Egwene had thought they would marry one day. And now she sided with Moiraine against him.

Face hard, he spoke more roughly than he intended. "Tell me what you want, Moiraine. Tell me here and now, or let it wait until I can find time for you. I'm very busy." That was an outright lie. Most of his time was spent practicing the sword with Lan, or the spears with Rhuarc, or learning to fight with hands and feet from both. But if there was any bullying to be done here today, he would do it. Natael could hear anything. Almost anything. So long as Rand knew where he was at all times.

Moiraine and Egwene both frowned, but the real Aes Sedai at least seemed to see he would not be budged this time. She glanced at Natael, her mouth tightening—the man still seemed deep in his music—then took a thick wad of gray silk from her pouch.

Unfolding it, she laid what it had contained on the table, a disc the size of a man's hand, half dead black, half purest white, the two colors meeting in a sinuous line to form two joined teardrops. That had been the symbol of Aes Sedai, before the Breaking, but this disc was more. Only seven like it had ever been made, the seals on the Dark One's prison. Or rather, each was a focus for one of those seals. Drawing her belt knife, its hilt wrapped in silver wire, Moiraine scraped delicately at the edge of the disc. And a tiny flake of solid black fell away.

Even encased in the Void, Rand gasped. The emptiness itself quivered, and for an instant the Power threatened to overwhelm him. "Is this a copy? A fake?"

"I found this in the square below," Moiraine said. "It is real, though. The one I brought with me from Tear is the same." She could have been saying she wanted pea soup for the midday meal. Egwene, on the other hand, clutched her shawl around her as if cold.

Rand felt the stirrings of fright himself, oozing across the surface of the Void. It was an effort to let go of *saidin,* but he forced himself. If he lost concentration, the Power could destroy him where he stood, and he wanted all his attention on the matter at hand. Even so, even with the taint, it was a loss.

That flake lying on the table was impossible. Those discs were made of *cuendillar,* heartstone, and nothing made of *cuendillar* could be broken, not even by the One Power. Whatever force was used against it only made it stronger. The making of heartstone had been lost in the Breaking of the World, but whatever had been made of it during the Age of Legends still existed, even the most fragile vase, even if the Breaking had sunk it to the bottom of the ocean or buried it beneath a mountain. Of course, three of the seven discs were broken already, but it had taken a good deal more than a knife.

Come to think of it, though, he did not know how those three really had been broken. If no force short of the Creator could break heartstone, then that should be that.

"How?" he asked, surprised that his voice was still as steady as when the Void had surrounded him.

"I do not know," Moiraine replied, just as calm outwardly. "But you do see the problem? A fall from the table could break this. If the others, wherever they may be, are like this, four men with hammers could break open that hole in the Dark One's prison again. Who can even say how effective one is, in this condition?"

Rand saw. *I'm not ready yet.* He was not sure he ever would be ready, but he surely was not yet. Egwene looked as though she were staring into her own open grave.

Rewrapping the disc, Moiraine replaced it in her pouch. "Perhaps I will think of a possibility before I carry this to Tar Valon. If we know why, perhaps something can be done about it."

He was caught by the image of the Dark One reaching out from Shayol Ghul once more, eventually breaking free completely; fires and darkness covered the world in his mind, flames that consumed and gave no light, blackness solid as stone squeezing the air. With that filling his head, what Moiraine had just said took a moment to penetrate. "You intend to go yourself?" He had thought she meant to stick to him like moss to a rock. *Isn't this what you want?*

"Eventually," Moiraine replied quietly. "Eventually I will—have to leave you, after all. What will be, must be." Rand thought she shivered, but it was so quick it could have been his imagination, and the next instant she was all composure and self-control once more. "You must be ready." The reminder of his doubts came unpleasantly. "We should discuss your plans. You cannot sit here much longer. Even if the Forsaken are not planning to come after you, they are out there, spreading their power. Gathering the Aiel will do no good if you find that everything beyond the Spine of the World is in their hands."

Chuckling, Rand leaned back against the table. So this was just another ploy; if he was anxious about her leaving, perhaps he would be more willing to listen, more amenable to being guided. She could not lie, of course, not right out. One of the vaunted Three Oaths took care of that: to speak no word that was not true. He had learned that it left a barn-width of wriggle room. She would leave him alone eventually. After he was dead, no doubt.

"You want to discuss my plans," he said dryly. Pulling a short-stemmed pipe and a leather tabac pouch from his coat pocket, he thumbed the bowl full and briefly touched *saidin* to channel a flame dancing above the tabac. "Why? They are my plans." Puffing slowly, he waited, ignoring Egwene's glower.

The Aes Sedai's face never changed, but her large, dark eyes seemed to blaze. "What have you done when you refused to be guided by me?" Her voice was as cool as her features, yet the words still seemed to come like whip-cracks. "Wherever you have gone, you have left death, destruction and war behind you."

"Not in Tear," he said, too quickly. And too defensively. He must not let her put him off balance. Determinedly, he took spaced, deliberate puffs at his pipe.

"No," she agreed, "not in Tear. For once you had a nation behind you, a people, and what did you do with it? Bringing justice to Tear was commendable. Establishing order in Cairhien, feeding the hungry, is laudable. Another time I would praise you for it." She herself was Cairhienin. "But it does not help you toward the day you face Tarmon Gai'don." A single-minded woman, and cold when it came to anything else, even her own land. But should he not be just as single-minded?

"What would you have me do? Hunt down the Forsaken one by one?" Again he forced himself to draw more slowly on the pipe; it was an effort. "Do you even know where they are? Oh, Sammael is in Illian—you know that—but the rest? What if I go after Sammael as you wish, and find two or three or four of them? Or all nine?"

"You could have faced three or four, perhaps all nine surviving," she said icily, "had you not left *Callandor* in Tear. The truth is, you are running. You do not really have a plan, not a plan to ready you for the Last Battle. You run from place to place, hoping that in some way everything will come out for the best. Hoping, because you do not know what else to do. If you would take my advice, at least you—" He cut her off, gesturing sharply with his pipe, with never a care for the glares the two women gave him.

"I do have a plan." If they wanted to know, let them know, and he would be burned if he changed a word. "First, I mean to put an end to the wars and killing, whether I started them or not. If men have to kill, let them kill Trollocs, not each other. In the Aiel War, four clans crossed the Dragonwall, and had their way for better than two years. They looted and burned Cairhien, defeated every army sent against them. They could have taken Tar Valon, had they wanted. The Tower couldn't have stopped them, because of your Three Oaths." Not to use the Power as a weapon except against Shadowspawn or Darkfriends, or in defense of their own lives, that was another of the Oaths, and the Aiel had not threatened the Tower itself. Anger had him in its grip now. Running and hoping, was he? "Four clans did that. What will happen when I lead eleven across the Spine of the World?" It would have to be eleven; small hope of bringing in the Shaido. "By the time the nations even think of uniting, it will be too late. They'll accept my peace, or I'll be buried in the Can Breat." A discordant plunk rose from the harp, and Natael bent over the instrument, shaking his head. In a moment the soothing sounds came again.

"A melon couldn't be swollen enough for your head," Egwene muttered, folding her arms beneath her breasts. "And a stone couldn't be as stubborn! Moiraine is only trying to help you. Why won't you see that?"

The Aes Sedai smoothed her silk skirts, though they did not need it. "Taking the Aiel across the Dragonwall might be the worst thing you could possibly do." There was an edge to her voice, anger or frustration. At least he was getting across to her that he was no puppet. "By this time, the Amyrlin Seat will be approaching the rulers of every nation that still has a ruler, laying the proofs before them that you are the Dragon Reborn. They know the Prophecies; they know what you were born to do. Once they are convinced of who and what you are, they will accept you because they must. The Last Battle is coming, and you are their only hope, humankind's only hope."

Rand laughed out loud. It was a bitter laugh. Sticking his pipe between his teeth, he hoisted himself to sit cross-legged atop the table, staring at them. "So you and Siuan Sanche still think you know everything there is to know." The Light willing, they did not know near everything about him, and would never find out. "You're both fools."

"Show some respect!" Egwene growled, but Rand went on over her words.

"The Tairen High Lords know the Prophecies, too, and they knew me, once they saw the Sword That Cannot Be Touched clutched in my fist. Half of them expect me to bring them power or glory or both. The other half would as soon slip a knife in my back and try to forget the Dragon Reborn was ever in Tear. That is how the nations will greet the Dragon Reborn. Unless I quell them first, the same way I did the Tairens. Do you know why I left *Callandor* in Tear? To remind them of me. Every day they know it is there, driven into the Heart of the Stone, and they know I'll come back for it. That is what holds them to me." That was one reason he had left the Sword That Is Not a Sword behind. He did not like even to think of the other.

"Be very careful," Moiraine said after a moment. Just that, in a voice all frozen calm. He heard stark warning in the words. Once he had heard her say in much the same tone that she would see him dead before letting the Shadow have him. A hard woman.

For a long moment she gazed at him, her eyes dark pools that threatened to swallow him. Then she made a perfect curtsy. "By your leave, my Lord Dragon, I will see to letting Master Kadere know where I expect him to work tomorrow."

No one could have seen or heard the faintest mockery in action or words, but Rand felt it. Anything that might put him off balance, make him more biddable by guilt or shame or uncertainty or whatever, she would try. He stared after her until the clicking beads in the doorway obscured her.

"There is no need you scowling like that, Rand al'Thor." Egwene's voice was low, her eyes irate; she held on to her shawl as if she wanted to strangle him with it. "Lord Dragon, indeed! Whatever you are, you're a rude, ill-mannered lout. You deserve more than you got. It would not kill you to be civil!"

"So it *was* you," he snapped, but to his surprise she half-shook her head before catching herself. It had been Moiraine after all. If the Aes Sedai was showing that much temper, something must be wearing at her terribly. Him, no doubt. Perhaps he should apologize. *I suppose it wouldn't hurt to be civil.* Though he could not see why he was supposed to be mannerly to the Aes Sedai while she tried to lead him on a leash.

But if he was thinking of trying to be polite, Egwene was not. If glowing coals were dark brown, they would have been exactly like her eyes. "You are a wool-headed fool, Rand al'Thor, and I should never have told Elayne you were good enough for her. You aren't good enough for a weasel! Bring your nose down. I remember you sweating, trying to talk your way out of some trouble Mat had gotten you into. I can remember Nynaeve switching you till you howled, and you needing a cushion to sit on the rest of the day. Not that many years gone, either. I ought to tell Elayne to forget you. If she knew half what you've turned into . . ."

He gaped at her as the tirade went on, with her more furious than at any time since first coming through the bead curtain. Then it hit him. That little near shake of her head that she had not meant to give, letting him know it had been Moiraine who struck him with the Power. Egwene worked very hard at doing what she was about in proper fashion. Studying with the Wise Ones, she wore Aiel clothes; she might even be trying to adopt Aiel customs, for all he knew. It would be like her. But she worked hard at being a proper Aes Sedai all the time, even if she *was* only one of the Accepted. Aes Sedai usually kept a rein on their tempers, but they never ever gave anything away that they wanted to hide.

Ilyena never flashed her temper at me when she was angry with herself. When she gave me the rough side of her tongue, it was because she . . . His mind froze for an instant. He had never met a woman named Ilyena in his life. But he could summon up a face for the name, dimly; a pretty face, skin like cream, golden hair exactly the shade of Elayne's. This had to be the madness. Remembering an imaginary woman. Perhaps one day he would find himself having conversations with people who were not there.

Egwene's harangue shut off with a concerned look.

"Are you all right, Rand?" The anger was gone from her voice as if it had never been. "Is something wrong? Should I fetch Moiraine back to—"

"No!" he said, and just as quickly softened his own tone. "She can't Heal. . . . " Even an Aes Sedai could not Heal madness; none of them could Heal any of what ailed him. "Is Elayne well?"

"She is well." Despite what Egwene had said, there was a hint of sympathy in her voice. That was all he really expected. Beyond what he had known when Elayne left Tear, what she was up to was an Aes Sedai concern and none of his; so Egwene had told him more than once, and Moiraine echoed her. The three Wise Ones who could dreamwalk, those Egwene was studying with, had been even less informative; they had their own reasons not to be pleased with him.

"I had best go, too," Egwene went on, settling her shawl over her arms. "You are tired." Frowning slightly, she said, "Rand, what does it mean to be buried in the Can Breat?"

He started to ask what under the Light she was talking about. Then he remembered using that phrase. "Just something I heard once," he lied. He had no more idea what it meant than where it had come from.

"You rest, Rand," she said, sounding twenty years older rather than two younger. "Promise me you will. You need it." He nodded. She studied his face for a moment as though searching for the truth, then started for the door.

Rand's silver goblet of wine floated up from the carpet and drifted to him. He hastily snatched it out of the air just before Egwene looked back over her shoulder.

"Perhaps I shouldn't tell you this," she said. "Elayne didn't give it to me as a message for you, but . . . She said she loves you. Perhaps you know already, but if you don't, you should think about it." With that she was gone, the beads clicking together behind her.

Leaping from the table, Rand hurled the goblet away, splashing wine across the floor tiles as he rounded on Jasin Natael in a fury.

CHAPTER
3

Pale Shadows

Seizing *saidin,* Rand channeled, wove flows of Air that snatched Natael up from the cushions; the gilded harp tumbled to the dark red tiles as the man was pinned against the wall, immobile from neck to ankles and his feet half a pace above the floor. "I've warned you! *Never* channel when anyone else is around. Never!"

Natael tilted his head in that peculiar way he had, as if trying to look at Rand sideways, or watch without being noticed. "If she had seen, she would have thought it was you." There was no apology in his voice, no diffidence, but no challenge either; he seemed to think he was offering a reasonable explanation. "Besides, you looked thirsty. A court-bard should look after his lord's needs." That was one of the small conceits he surrounded himself with; if Rand was the Lord Dragon, then he himself must be a court-bard, not a simple gleeman.

Feeling disgusted with himself as much as angry at the man, Rand unraveled the weave and let him drop. Manhandling him was like picking a fight with a boy of ten. He could not see the shield that constricted the other man's access to *saidin*—it was female work—but he knew it was there. Moving a goblet was about the extent of Natael's ability, now. Luckily the shield had been hidden from female eyes, too. Natael called the trick "inverting"; he did not seem able to explain it, though. "And if she'd seen my face and was suspicious? I was as startled as if that goblet had flown at me by itself!" He stuck his pipe back between his teeth and sent up furious streams of smoke.

"She still wouldn't suspect." Settling back onto the cushions, the other man took up the harp again, strumming a line of music that had a devious sound. "How could anyone suspect? I do not entirely believe the situation myself." If there was even a touch of bitterness in his voice, Rand could not detect it.

He was not entirely sure he believed it either, though he had worked hard enough for it. The man in front of him, Jasin Natael, had another name. Asmodean.

Idly playing the harp, Asmodean did not look like one of the dreaded Forsaken. He was even moderately handsome; Rand supposed he would be attractive to women. It often seemed strange that evil had left no outward mark. He was one of the Forsaken, and far from trying to kill him, Rand hid what he was from Moiraine and everyone else. He needed a teacher.

If what was true for the women Aes Sedai called "wilders" also held for men, he had only one chance in four of surviving the attempt to learn to use the Power on his own. That was discounting the madness. His teacher had to be a man; Moiraine and others had told him often enough that a bird could not teach a fish to fly, nor a fish a bird to swim. And his teacher had to be someone experienced, someone who already knew all the things he needed to learn. With Aes Sedai gentling men who could channel as soon as they were found—and fewer were found every year—that left small choices. A man who had simply discovered he could channel would know no more than he did. A false Dragon who could channel—if Rand could find one not already caught and gentled—would not be likely to give up his own dreams of glory for another claiming to be the Dragon Reborn.

What remained, what Rand had lured to him, was one of the Forsaken.

Asmodean plucked random chords as Rand took a seat on a cushion facing him. It was well to remember that the man had not changed, not inside, from the day so long ago when he had pledged his soul to the Shadow. What he did now, he did under duress; he had not come to the Light. "Do you ever think of turning back, Natael?" He was always careful of the name; one breath of "Asmodean," and Moiraine would be sure he had gone over to the Shadow. Moiraine and maybe others. Neither he nor Asmodean might survive that.

The man's hands froze on the strings, his face utterly blank. "Turn back? Demandred, Rahvin, any of them would kill me on sight, now. If I was lucky. Except Lanfear perhaps, and you will understand if I don't want to put her to the test. Semirhage could make a boulder beg for mercy and thank her for death. And as for the Great Lord—"

"The Dark One," Rand broke in sharply around his pipestem. The Great Lord of the Dark was what Darkfriends called the Dark One. Darkfriends and the Forsaken.

Asmodean bowed his head briefly in acquiescence. "When the Dark One breaks free . . ." If his face had been expressionless before, now it was bleak in every line. "Suffice it to say that I will find Semirhage and give myself to her before I'll face the—the Dark One's punishment for betrayal."

"As well you are here to teach me, then."

Mournful music began to flow from the harp, speaking of loss and tears. "'The March of Death,'" Asmodean said over the music, "the final movement of *The Grand Passions Cycle,* composed some three hundred years before the War of Power by—"

Rand cut him off. "You are not teaching me very well."

"As well as may be expected, under the circumstances. You can grasp *saidin* every time you try, now, and tell one flow from another. You can shield yourself, and the Power does what you want it to." He stopped playing and frowned, not looking at Rand. "Do you think Lanfear really intended me to teach you everything? If she had wanted that, she would have contrived to stay close so she could link us. She wants you to live, Lews Therin, but this time she means to be stronger than you."

"Don't call me that!" Rand snapped, but Asmodean did not seem to hear.

"If you planned this between you—trapping me—" Rand sensed a surge in Asmodean, as if the Forsaken were testing the shield Lanfear had woven around him; women who could channel saw a glow surrounding another woman who had embraced *saidar* and felt her channeling clearly, but he never saw anything around Asmodean and felt little. "If you worked it out together, then you let her outfox you on more levels than one. I've told you I am not a very good teacher, especially without a link. You did plan it between you, didn't you?" He did look at Rand then, sidelong but still intent. "How much do you remember? Of being Lews Therin, I mean. She said you recalled nothing at all, but she could lie to the Gr—the Dark One himself."

"This time she spoke the truth." Seating himself on one of the cushions, Rand channeled one of the clan chiefs' untouched silver goblets to him. Even such a brief touch of *saidin* was exhilarating—and fouling. And hard to release. He did not want to talk about Lews Therin; he was tired of people thinking he *was* Lews Therin. The bowl of his pipe had grown hot with all the puffing, so he held it by the stem and gestured with it. "If linking will help you teach me, why don't we link?"

Asmodean looked at him as if he had asked why they did not eat rocks, then shook his head. "I continually forget how much you don't know. You and I cannot. Not without a woman to join us. You could ask Moiraine, I suppose, or the girl Egwene. One of them might be able to reason out the method. So long as you don't mind them finding out who I am."

"Don't lie to me, Natael," Rand growled. Well before meeting Natael he had learned that a man's channeling and a woman's were as different as men and women themselves, but he took little the man said on trust. "I've heard Egwene and others talk about Aes Sedai linking their powers. If they can do it, why not you and I?"

"Because we can't." Exasperation filled Asmodean's tone. "Ask a philosopher if you want to know why. Why can't dogs fly? Perhaps in the grand scheme of the Pattern, it's a balance for men being stronger. We cannot link without them, but they can without us. Up to thirteen of them can, anyway, a small mercy; after that, they need men to make the circle larger."

Rand was sure he had caught a lie, this time. Moiraine said that in the Age of Legends men and women had been equally strong in the Power, and she could not lie. He said as much, adding, "The Five Powers are equal."

"Earth, Fire, Air, Water, and Spirit." Natael strummed a chord for each. "They are equal, true, and it is also true that what a man can do with one, a woman can also. In kind, at least. But that has nothing to do with men being stronger. What Moiraine believes to be truth, she tells as truth whether or not it is; one of a thousand weaknesses in those fool Oaths." He played a bit of something that did indeed sound foolish. "Some women have stronger arms than some men, but in general it is the other way around. The same holds with strength in the Power, and in about the same proportion."

Rand nodded slowly. It did make a kind of sense. Elayne and Egwene were considered two of the strongest women to train in the Tower for a thousand years or more, but he had tested himself against them once, and later Elayne had confessed that she felt like a kitten seized by a mastiff.

Asmodean was not finished. "If two women link, they do not double their strength—linking is not as simple as adding together the power of each—but if they are strong enough, they can match a man. And when they take the circle to thirteen, then you must be wary. Thirteen women who can barely channel could overpower most men, linked. The thirteen weakest women in the Tower could overpower you or any man, and barely breathe hard. I came across a saying in Arad Doman. 'The more women there are about, the softer a wise man steps.' It would not be bad to remember it."

Rand shivered, thinking of a time when he had been among many more than thirteen Aes Sedai. Of course, most of them had not known who he was. If they had . . . *If Egwene and Moiraine linked* . . . He did not want to believe Egwene had gone that far toward the Tower and away from their friendship. *Whatever she does, she does with her whole heart, and she's becoming Aes Sedai. So is Elayne.*

Swallowing half his wine did not completely wash the thought away. "What more can you tell me about the Forsaken?" It was a question he was sure he had asked a hundred times, but he always hoped there was a scrap more to dig out. Better than thinking about Moiraine and Egwene linking to . . .

"I have told everything I know." Asmodean sighed heavily. "We were hardly close friends at the best. Do you believe I am holding back something? I don't know where the others are, if that is what you want. Except Sammael, and you knew he'd taken Illian for his kingdom before I told you. Graendal was in Arad Doman for a time, but I expect she has gone now; she likes her comforts too well. I suspect Moghedien is or was in the west somewhere as well, but no one ever finds the Spider unless she wants to be found. Rahvin has a queen for one of his pets, but your guess is as good as mine as to what country she rules for him. And that is all I know that might help locate them."

Rand had heard all that before; it seemed he had heard all Asmodean had to say of the Forsaken fifty times already. So often that at moments it seemed he had always known what the man was telling him. Some of it he almost wished he had never learned—what Semirhage found amusing, for instance—and some made no sense. Demandred had gone over to the Shadow because he envied Lews Therin Telamon? Rand could not imagine envying someone enough to do anything because of it, and surely not that. Asmodean claimed it had been the thought of immortality, of endless Ages of music, that seduced him; he claimed to have been a noted composer of music, before. Senseless. Yet in that mass of often blood-chilling knowledge might lie keys to surviving Tarmon Gai'don. Whatever he told Moiraine, he knew he would have to face them then, if not before. Emptying the goblet, he set it on the floor tiles. Wine would not wash out facts.

The bead curtain rattled, and he looked over his shoulder as *gai'shain* entered, white-robed and silent. While some began gathering up the food and drink that had been laid out for him and the chiefs, another, a man, carried a large silver tray to the table. On it were covered dishes, a silver cup, and two large, green-striped pottery pitchers. One would hold wine, the other water. A *gai'shain* woman brought in a gilded lamp, already lit, and set it beside the tray. Through the windows, the sky was beginning to take on the yellow-red of sunset; in the brief time between baking and freezing, the air actually felt comfortable.

Rand stood as the *gai'shain* departed, but did not follow immediately. "What do you think of my chances when the Last Battle comes, Natael?"

Asmodean hesitated in pulling red-and-blue striped wool blankets from behind his cushions and looked up at him, head tilted in that sideways manner of his. "You found . . . something . . . in the square the day we met here."

"Forget that," Rand said harshly. There had been two, not one. "I destroyed it, in any case." He thought Asmodean's shoulders slumped a trifle.

"Then the—Dark One—will consume you alive. As for me, I intend to open my veins the hour I know he is free. If I get the chance. A quick death is better than what I'll find elsewhere." He tossed the blankets aside and sat staring glumly at nothing. "Better than going mad, certainly. I'm as subject to that as you, now. You broke the bonds that protected me." There was no bitterness in his voice; only hopelessness.

"What if there was another way to shield against the taint?" Rand demanded. "What if it could be removed somehow? Would you still kill yourself then?"

Asmodean's barked laugh was utterly acid. "The Shadow take me, you must be beginning to think you really are the bloody Creator! We are dead. Both of us. Dead!

Are you too blind with pride to see it? Or just too thick-witted, you hopeless shepherd?"

Rand refused to be drawn. "Then why not go ahead and end it?" he asked in a tight voice. *I wasn't too blind to see what you and Lanfear were up to. I wasn't too thick-witted to fool her and trap you.* "If there's no hope, no chance, not the smallest shred . . . then why are you still alive?"

Still not looking at him, Asmodean rubbed the side of his nose. "I once saw a man hanging from a cliff," he said slowly. "The brink was crumbling under his fingers, and the only thing near enough to grasp was a tuft of grass, a few long blades with roots barely clinging to the rock. The only chance he had of climbing back up on the cliff. So he grabbed it." His abrupt chuckle held no mirth. "He had to know it would pull free."

"Did you save him?" Rand asked, but Asmodean did not answer.

As Rand started for the doorway, the sounds of "The March of Death" began again behind him.

The strings of beads fell together behind him, and the five Maidens who had been waiting in the wide, empty hall flowed easily to their feet from where they had been squatting on the pale blue tiles. They were all but one tall for women, though not for Aiel women. Their leader, Adelin, lacked little more than a hand of being able to look him in the eyes. The exception, a fiery redhead named Enaila, was no taller than Egwene, and extremely touchy about being so short. Like the clan chiefs', their eyes were all blue or gray or green, and their hair, light brown or yellow or red, was cut short except for a tail at the nape of the neck. Full quivers balanced the long-bladed knives at their belts, and they wore cased horn bows on their backs. Each carried three or four short, long-bladed spears and a round, bull-hide buckler. Aiel women who did not want hearth and children had their own warrior society, *Far Dareis Mai,* the Maidens of the Spear.

He acknowledged them with a small bow, which made them smile; it was not an Aiel custom, at least not the way he had been taught to do it. "I see you, Adelin," he said. "Where is Joinde? I thought she was with you earlier. Has she taken ill?"

"I see you, Rand al'Thor," she replied. Her pale yellow hair seemed paler framing her sun-dark face, which had a fine white scar across one cheek. "In a way she has. She had been talking to herself all day, and not an hour ago, she went off to lay a bridal wreath at the feet of Garan, of the Jhirad Goshien." Some of the others shook their heads; marrying meant giving up the spear. "Tomorrow is his last day as her *gai'shain.* Joinde is Black Rock Shaarad," she added significantly. It was significant; marriages came frequently with men or women taken *gai'shain,* but very seldom between clans with blood feud, even blood feud in abeyance.

"It is an illness that spreads," Enaila said heatedly. Her voice was usually as hot as her hair. "One or two Maidens make their bridal wreaths every day since we came to Rhuidean."

Rand nodded with what he hoped they took for sympathy. It was his fault. If he told them, he wondered how many would still risk staying near him. All, probably; honor would hold them, and they had no more fear than the clan chiefs. At least it was only marriages, so far; even Maidens would think marrying better than what some had experienced. Maybe they would. "I will be ready to go in a moment," he told them.

"We will wait with patience," Adelin said. It hardly seemed patience; standing there, they all appeared poised on the edge of sudden movement.

It really did take him only a moment to do what he wanted, weave flows of Spirit and Fire into a box around the room and tie them so the weave held on its own. Anyone could go in or out—except a man who could channel. For himself—or Asmodean—walking through that doorway would be like walking through a wall of solid flame. He had discovered the weave—and that Asmodean, blocked, was too weak to channel through it—by accident. No one was likely to question the doings of a gleeman, but if someone did, Jasin Natael had simply chosen to sleep as far from Aiel as he could manage in Rhuidean. That was a choice that Hadnan Kadere's drivers and guards, at least, could sympathize with. And this way Rand knew exactly where the man was of a night. The Maidens asked him no questions.

He turned away. The Maidens followed him, spread out and wary as if they expected an attack right there. Asmodean was still playing the lament.

Arms outstretched to either side, Mat Cauthon walked the wide white coping of the dry fountain, singing to the men who watched him in the fading light.

> *"We'll drink the wine till the cup is dry,*
> *and kiss the girls so they'll not cry,*
> *and toss the dice until we fly*
> *to dance with Jak o' the Shadows."*

The air felt cool after the day's heat, and he thought briefly of buttoning up his fine green silk coat with the golden embroidery, but the drink the Aiel called *oosquai* had put a buzz in his head like giant flies, and the thought flittered away. The white stone figures of three women stood on a platform in the dusty basin, twenty feet tall and unclothed. Each had been made with one hand upraised, the other holding a huge stone jar tilted over her shoulder for water to pour from, but one was missing her head and upraised hand, and on another the jar was a shattered ruin.

> *"We'll dance all night while the moon runs free,*
> *and dandle the lasses upon our knee,*
> *and then you'll ride along with me,*
> *to dance with Jak o' the Shadows."*

"A fine song to be singing about death," one of the wagon drivers shouted in a heavy Lugarder accent. Kadere's men kept themselves in a tight knot apart from the Aielmen around the fountain; they were all tough, hard-faced men, but every one was sure any Aiel would slit his throat for a wrong glance. They were not far wrong. "I heard my old grandmother talk about Jak o' the Shadows," the big-eared Lugarder went on. "'Tisn't right to sing about death that way."

Mat muzzily considered the song he had been singing

and grimaced. No one had heard "Dance with Jak o' the Shadows" since Aldeshar fell; in his head, he could still hear the defiant song rising as the Golden Lions launched their last, futile charge at Artur Hawkwing's encircling army. At least he had not been babbling it in the Old Tongue. He was not as juicy as he looked by half, but there had indeed been too many cups of *oosquai*. The stuff looked and tasted like brown water, but it hit your head like a mule's kick. *Moiraine will pack me off to the Tower yet, if I'm not careful. At least it would get me out of the Waste and away from Rand.* Maybe he was drunker than he thought, if he considered that a fair trade. He shifted to "Tinker in the Kitchen."

"Tinker in the kitchen, with a job of work to do.
Mistress up above, slipping on a robe of blue.
She dances down the staircase, her fancy all so free,
crying, Tinker, oh, dear Tinker, won't you mend a pot
for me?"

Some of Kadere's men joined in the song as he danced back to where he had begun. The Aiel did not; among them, men did not sing except for battle chants or laments for the slain, and neither did Maidens, except among themselves.

Two Aielmen were squatting on the coping, showing none of the effects of the *oosquai* they had consumed, unless their eyes were the faintest bit glassy. He would be glad to get back where light-colored eyes were a rarity; growing up, he had not seen anything but brown or black except on Rand.

A few pieces of wood—wormholed arms and legs from chairs—lay on the broad paving stones, in the area left open by the watchers. An empty red pottery crock lay beside the coping, as did another that still held *oosquai*, and a silver cup. The game was to take a drink, then try to hit a target thrown into the air with a knife. None of Kadere's men and few of the Aiel would dice with him, not when he won as often as he did, and they did not play at cards. Knife throwing was supposed to be different, especially with *oosquai* added in. He had not won as often as he did with dice, but half a dozen worked gold cups and two bowls lay inside the basin beneath him, along with bracelets and necklaces set with rubies or moonstones or sapphires, and a scattering of coins as well. His flat-crowned hat and an odd spear with a black haft rested beside his winnings. Some of it was even Aiel made. They were more likely to pay for something with a piece of loot than with a coin.

Corman, one of the Aiel on the coping, looked up at him as he cut off singing. A white scar slanted across his nose. "You are nearly as good with knives as you are with dice, Matrim Cauthon. Shall we call it an end? The light is failing."

"There's plenty of light." Mat squinted at the sky; pale shadows covered everything here in the valley of Rhuidean, but the sky was still light enough to see against, at least. "My grandmother could make the throw in this. I could make it blindfolded."

Jenric, the other squatting Aiel, peered around the onlookers. "Are there women here?" Built like a bear, he considered himself a wit. "The only time a man talks like that is when there are women to impress." The Maidens scattered through the crowd laughed as hard as anyone else, and maybe harder.

"You think I can't?" Mat muttered, ripping off the dark scarf he wore around his neck to hide the scar where he had once been hung. "Just you shout 'now' when you throw it up, Corman." Hastily he tied the scarf around his eyes and drew one of his knives from his sleeve. The loudest sound was the watchers breathing. *Not drunk? I'm juicier than a fiddler's whelp.* And yet, he suddenly felt his luck, felt that surge the way he did when he knew which spots would show before the dice stopped tumbling. It seemed to clear his head a little. "Throw it," he murmured calmly.

"Now," Corman called, and Mat's arm whipped back, then forward.

In the stillness, the *thunk* of steel stabbing wood was as loud as the clatter of the target on the pavement.

No one said a word as he pulled the scarf back down

around his neck. A piece of a chair arm no bigger than
his hand lay in the open space, his blade stuck firmly in
the middle. Corman had tried to shave the odds, it
appeared. Well, he had never specified the target. He
suddenly realized he had not even made a wager.

Finally one of Kadere's men half-shouted, "The Dark
One's own luck, that!"

"Luck is a horse to ride like any other," Mat said to
himself. No matter where it came from. Not that he
knew where his luck came from; he only tried to ride it as
best he could.

As quietly as he had spoken, Jenric frowned up at him.
"What was that you said, Matrim Cauthon?"

Mat opened his mouth to repeat himself, then closed it
again as the words came clear in his mind. *Sene sovya
caba'donde ain dovienya.* The Old Tongue. "Nothing,"
he muttered. "Just talking to myself." The onlookers
were beginning to drift away. "I guess the light really is
fading too much to go on."

Corman put a foot on the piece of wood to wrench
Mat's knife free and brought it back to him. "Some time
again maybe, Matrim Cauthon, some day." That was the
Aiel way of saying "never" when they did not want to say
it right out.

Mat nodded as he slipped the blade back into one of
the sheaths inside his sleeve; it was the same as the time
he had rolled six sixes twenty-three times in a row. He
could hardly blame them. Being lucky was not all it was
made out to be. He noted with a bit of envy that neither Aiel
staggered in the slightest as they joined the departing
crowd.

Scrubbing a hand through his hair, Mat sat down
heavily on the coping. The memories that had once
cluttered his head like raisins in a cake now blended with
his own. In one part of his mind he knew he had been
born in the Two Rivers twenty years before, but he could
remember clearly leading the flanking attack that turned
the Trollocs at Maighande, and dancing in the court of
Tarmandewin, and a hundred other things, a thousand.
Mostly battles. He remembered dying more times than
he wanted to think of. No seams between lives anymore;

he could not tell his memories from the others unless he concentrated.

Reaching behind him, he set his wide-brimmed hat on his head and fished the odd spear across his knees. Instead of an ordinary spearhead, it had what looked like a two-foot sword blade, marked with a pair of ravens. Lan said that that blade had been made with the One Power during the War of the Shadow, the War of the Power; the Warder claimed it would never need sharpening and never break. Mat thought he would not trust that unless he had to. It might have lasted three thousand years, but he had little trust of the Power. Cursive script ran along the black haft, punctuated at either end with another raven, inlaid in some metal even darker than the wood. In the Old Tongue, but he could read it now, of course.

Thus is our treaty written; thus is agreement made.
Thought is the arrow of time; memory never fades.
What was asked is given. The price is paid.

One way down the wide street, half a mile off, was a square that would have been called large in most cities. The Aiel traders were gone for the night, but their pavilions still stood, made of the same grayish brown wool used for Aiel tents. Hundreds of traders had come to Rhuidean from every part of the Waste, for the biggest fair the Aiel had ever seen, and more arrived every day. The traders had been among the first to actually start living in the city.

Mat did not really want to look the other way, toward the great plaza. He could make out the shapes of Kadere's wagons, awaiting more loading tomorrow. What appeared to be a twisted redstone doorframe had been heaved into one that afternoon; Moiraine had taken particular care to see it lashed firmly in place just as she wanted.

He did not know what she knew of it—and he was not about to ask; better if she forgot he was alive, though small chance of that—but whatever she knew, he was sure he knew more. He had stepped through it, a fool looking for answers. What he had gotten instead was a head full of other men's memories. That, and dead. He tucked the scarf closer around his neck. And two other things. A silver foxhead medallion that he wore under his shirt, and the weapon across his knees. Small recompense. He ran his fingers lightly down the script. *Memory never fades.* They had a sense of humor fit for Aiel, those folk on the other side of that doorway.

"Can you do that every time?"

He jerked his head around to stare at the Maiden who had just sat down beside him. Tall even for an Aiel, maybe taller than he was, she had hair like spun gold and eyes the color of a clear morning sky. She was older than he, maybe by ten years, but that had never put him off. Then again, she was *Far Dareis Mai.*

"I am Melindhra," she went on, "of the Jumai sept. Can you do that every time?"

She meant the knife throwing, he realized. She gave her sept, but no clan. Aiel never did that. Unless . . . She had to be one of the Shaido Maidens who had come to join Rand. He did not really understand all this about societies, but as for Shaido, he remembered them trying to stick spears in him too well. Couladin did not like anyone associated with Rand, and what Couladin hated, the Shaido hated. On the other hand, Melindhra had come here to Rhuidean. A Maiden. But she wore a small smile; her gaze held an inviting light.

"Most of the time," he said truthfully. Even when he did not feel it, his luck was good; when he did, it was perfect. She chuckled, her smile widening, as if she thought he was boasting. Women seemed to make up their minds whether you were lying without looking at the evidence. On the other hand, if they liked you, they either did not care or else decided even the most outrageous lie was true.

Maidens could be dangerous, whatever their clan— any woman could; he had learned that on his own—but Melindhra's eyes were definitely not just looking at him.

Dipping into his winnings, he pulled up a necklace of gold spirals, each centered on a deep blue sapphire, the largest as big as the joint of his thumb. He could remember a time—his own memory—when the smallest of those stones would have made him sweat.

"They'll look pretty with your eyes," he said, laying the heavy strand in her hands. He had never seen a Maiden wear baubles of any sort, but in his experience, every woman liked jewelry. Strangely, they liked flowers nearly as well. He did not understand it, but then, he was willing to admit that he understood women less than he did his luck, or what had happened on the other side of that twisted doorway.

"Very fine work," she said, holding it up. "I accept your offer." The necklace disappeared into her belt pouch, and she leaned over to push his hat back on his head. "Your eyes are pretty. Like dark polished catseye." She twisted around to pull her feet up onto the coping and sat with her arms wrapped around her knees, studying him intently. "My spear sisters have told me about you."

Mat pulled his hat back into place and watched her warily from under the brim. What had they told her? And what "offer"? It was only a necklace. The invitation was gone from her eyes; she looked like a cat studying a mouse. That was the trouble with Maidens of the Spear. Sometimes it was hard to tell whether they wanted to dance with you, kiss you, or kill you.

The street was emptying, the shadows deepening, but he recognized Rand slanting across down the way, pipe clenched between his teeth. He was the only man in Rhuidean likely to be walking with a fistful of *Far Dareis Mai. They're always around him,* Mat thought. *Guarding him like a pack of she-wolves, leaping to do whatever he says.* Some men might have envied him that much, at least. Not Mat. Not most of the time. If it had been a pack of girls like Isendre, now . . .

"Excuse me for a moment," he told Melindhra hurriedly. Leaning his spear against the low wall around the fountain, he leaped up already running. His head still buzzed, but not so loudly as before, and he did not stagger. He had no worries about his winnings. The Aiel had very definite views of what was allowed: taking in a raid was one thing, theft another. Kadere's men had learned to keep their hands in their pockets after one of them had been caught stealing. After a beating that left him striped from shoulders to heels, he had been sent away. The one water bag he had been allowed would not have been nearly enough for him to reach the Dragonwall, even if he had had any clothes on. Now Kadere's men would not pick up a copper they found lying in the street.

"Rand?" The other man walked on with his encircling escort. "Rand?" Rand was not even ten paces away, but he did not waver. Some of the Maidens looked back, but not Rand. Mat felt cold suddenly, and it had nothing to do with the onset of night. He wet his lips and spoke again, not a shout. "Lews Therin." And Rand turned around. Mat almost wished he had not.

For a time they only looked at one another in the twilight. Mat hesitated about going closer. He tried telling himself it was because of the Maidens. Adelin had been one of those who taught him a so-called game, Maidens' Kiss, that he was never likely to forget; or play again, if he had any say in it. And he could feel Enaila's gaze like an auger boring into his skull. Who would have expected a woman to go up like oil thrown on a fire just because you told her she was the prettiest little flower you had ever seen?

Rand, now. He and Rand had grown up together. They and Perrin, the blacksmith's apprentice back in Emond's Field, had hunted together, fished together, tramped through the Sand Hills to the edge of the Mountains of Mist, camped under the stars. Rand was his friend. Only now he was the kind of friend who might bash your head in without meaning to. Perrin could be dead, because of Rand.

He made himself walk to arm's reach of the other man. Rand was nearly a head taller, and in the early-evening gloom he seemed taller yet. Colder than he had been. "I've been thinking, Rand." Mat wished he did not sound hoarse. He hoped Rand would answer to his right name this time. "I've been away from home a long time."

"We both have," Rand said softly. "A long time." Suddenly he gave a laugh, not loud, but almost like the old Rand. "Are you beginning to miss milking your father's cows?"

Mat scratched his ear, grinning a bit. "Not that, exactly." If he never saw the inside of another barn it would be too soon. "But I was thinking that when Kadere's wagons go, I might go with them."

Rand was silent. When he spoke again, the brief flash of mirth was gone. "All the way to Tar Valon?"

It was Mat's turn to hesitate. *He wouldn't give me away to Moiraine. Would he?* "Maybe," he said casually. "I don't know. That's where Moiraine will want me. Maybe I'll find a chance to get back to the Two Rivers. See if everything's all right at home." *See if Perrin's alive. See if my sisters are, and Mother and Da.*

"We all have to do what we must, Mat. Not what we want to, very often. What we must."

It sounded like an excuse, to Mat, as if Rand was asking him to understand. Only, he had done what he had to himself a few times. *I can't blame Perrin on him, not by himself. Nobody bloody forced me to follow after Rand like some bloody heelhound!* Only that was not true, either. He had been forced. Just not by Rand. "You won't—stop me leaving?"

"I don't try to tell you to come or go, Mat," Rand said wearily. "The Wheel weaves the Pattern, not me, and the Wheel weaves as the Wheel wills." *For all the world like a bloody Aes Sedai!* Half turning to go, Rand added, "Don't trust Kadere, Mat. In some ways he's about as dangerous a man as you ever met. Don't trust him an inch, or you might get your throat slit, and you and I wouldn't be the only ones to regret that." Then he was gone, down the street in the deepening dusk, with the Maidens around him like slinking wolves.

Mat stared after him. Trust the merchant? *I wouldn't trust Kadere if he was tied in a sack.* So Rand did not weave the Pattern? He came close! Before ever any of them learned that the Prophecies had anything to do with them, they had learned that Rand was *ta'veren,* one of those rare individuals who, instead of being woven willy-nilly into the Pattern, instead forced the Pattern to shape itself around them. Mat knew about being *ta'veren;* he was one himself, though not as strong as Rand. Sometimes Rand could affect people's lives, change the course of them, just by being in the same town. Perrin was *ta'veren* as well—or maybe had been. Moiraine had thought it was significant, finding three young men who grew up in the same village, all destined to be *ta'veren.* She meant to fit them all into her plans, whatever they were.

It was supposed to be a grand thing; all the *ta'veren* Mat had been able to learn about had been men like Artur Hawkwing, or women like Mabriam en Shereed, who stories said had founded the Compact of the Ten Nations after the Breaking. But none of the stories told what happened when one *ta'veren* was close to another as strong as Rand. It was like being a leaf in a whirlpool.

Melindhra stopped beside him and handed him his spear and a heavy, coarse-woven sack that clinked. "I put your winnings in this for you." She *was* taller than he was, by a good two inches. She glanced after Rand. "I had heard you were near-brother to Rand al'Thor."

"In a manner of speaking," he said dryly.

"It does not matter," she said dismissively, and concentrated her gaze on him, fists on her hips. "You attracted my interest, Mat Cauthon, before you gave me a regard-gift. Not that I will give up the spear for you, of course, but I have had my eye on you for days. You have a smile like a boy about to do mischief. I like that. And those eyes." In the failing light her grin was slow and wide. And warm. "I do like your eyes."

Mat tugged his hat straight, though it had not been crooked. From pursuer to pursued, in the blink of an eye. It could happen like that, with Aiel women. Especially Maidens. "Does 'Daughter of the Nine Moons' mean anything to you?" It was a question he asked women sometimes. The wrong answer would send him out of Rhuidean tonight if he had to try walking out of the Waste.

"Nothing," she said. "But there are things I like to do by moonlight." Putting an arm around his shoulder, she took off his hat and began to whisper in his ear. In no time at all he was grinning even more widely than she.

CHAPTER
4

Twilight

With his *Far Dareis Mai* escort, Rand approached the Rhuidean Roof of the Maidens. White stairs as wide as the tall building, each step a stride deep, ran up to thick columns twenty paces high, black-seeming in the twilight but bright blue by day, and fluted in spirals. The outside of the building was a patterned mosaic of glazed tiles, white and blue in spirals that appeared endless to the eye, and a huge window of colored glass directly above the columns showed a black-haired woman fifteen feet tall, in complicated blue robes, right hand upraised, either to bless or command a halt. Her face was serene and stern at the same time. Whoever she had been, she was surely no Aiel, not with that pale skin and those dark eyes. An Aes Sedai, perhaps. He tapped his pipe out on his bootheel and stuffed it into his coat pocket before starting up the steps.

Except for *gai'shain,* men were not allowed beneath a Roof of the Maidens, not any man, not in any hold in the Waste. A chief or a Maiden's blood kin could die trying, though in fact no Aielman would ever think of it. It was the same for any society; only members and the *gai'shain* were allowed inside.

The two Maidens standing guard at the tall bronze doors flashed Maiden handtalk at one another, cutting their eyes in his direction as he came through the columns, then shared a small grin. He wished he knew what they had said. Even in as dry a land as the Waste, bronze would tarnish with enough time, but *gai'shain* had polished these doors until they looked new-made. They stood wide open, and the pair of guards made no move to hinder him as he walked through, Adelin and the others on his heels.

The wide, white-tiled corridors and great rooms inside were full of Maidens, sitting about on bright cushions, talking, tending to weapons, playing cat's cradle, or stones, or Thousand Flowers, an Aiel game that involved laying out patterns of flat bits of stone carved with what seemed a hundred different symbols. Of course, a profusion of *gai'shain* moved smoothly about their chores, cleaning, serving, mending, seeing to oil lamps that ranged from simple glazed pottery to gilded loot from somewhere to the tall stand-lamps that had been found in the city. In most rooms, colorful carpets and bright tapestries covered the floors and walls, in nearly as many patterns and styles as there *were* carpets and tapestries. The walls and ceilings themselves were detailed mosaics, of forests and rivers and skies that had never been seen in the Waste.

Young or old, the Maidens smiled when they saw him, and some nodded familiarly or even patted his shoulder. Others called out, asking how he was, had he eaten, would he like the *gai'shain* to bring him wine or water? He responded briefly, though with answering smiles. He was well, and neither hungry nor thirsty. He kept walking, not even slowing when he spoke. Slowing would lead inevitably to stopping, and he was not up to that tonight.

Far Dareis Mai had adopted him, after a fashion. Some treated him as a son, others as a brother. Age seemed not to come into it; women with white in their hair might talk to him as a brother over tea, while Maidens no more than a year older than he tried to make sure he wore the proper clothes for the heat. There was no avoiding the mothering; they simply did it, and he could not see how to make them stop, short of using the Power against the whole lot of them.

He had thought of trying to have another society provide his guards—*Shae'en M'taal,* the Stone Dogs, perhaps, or *Aethan Dor,* the Red Shields; Rhuarc had been a Red Shield before becoming chief—only, what reason could he possibly give? Not the truth, certainly. Just thinking about explaining that to Rhuarc and the others made him uncomfortable; Aiel humor being what it was, even sour old Han would likely break his ribs laughing. Any reason at all would probably offend the honor of every last Maiden. At least they rarely mothered him except under the Roof, where there was no one to see but themselves, and *gai'shain* who knew better than to speak of anything that happened there. "The Maidens," he had once said, "carry my honor." Everyone remembered that, and the Maidens were as proud of it as if he had given them all thrones. But it had turned out that they carried it in a manner they chose.

Adelin and the other four left him to join their friends, but he was hardly alone as he climbed higher in the building, along curving flights of wide white stairs. He had to answer the same questions at practically every step. No, he was not hungry. Yes, he knew he was not used to the heat yet, and no, he had not spent too much time in the sun. He bore it all patiently, but he did heave a sigh of relief when he reached the second story above the huge window. Here there were no Maidens and no *gai'shain* in the broad hallways or on the stairs that led on upward. The bare walls and empty chambers emphasized the absence of people, but after traversing the floors below, he found solitude a blessing.

His bedroom was a windowless chamber near the center of the building, one of the few that was not huge, though its ceiling still reached high enough to make height the room's longest dimension. What it had been meant for originally, he had no idea; a mosaic of vines around the small fireplace was the only ornamentation. A servant's room, he would have said, but servants' rooms did not have a door sheathed in bronze, however plain, that he pushed most of the way shut. *Gai'shain* had polished the metal to a dull gleam. A few tasseled cushions lay scattered on the blue floor tiles for sitting, and a thick pallet, atop bright layered rugs, for sleeping. A simple blue-glazed pitcher of water and a dark green cup sat on the floor near the "bed." That was it, except for two three-pronged stand-lamps, already lit, and a pace-high pile of books in one corner. With a tired sigh, he lay down on the pallet still in his coat and boots; no matter how he shifted it was not much softer than sleeping on the bare floor.

The night's chill was already seeping into the room, but he did not bother to light the dried cow dung on the hearth; he was readier to face the cold than the smell. Asmodean had tried to show him a simple way to keep the room warm; simple, but something the man did not have enough strength to do himself. The one time Rand had tried it, he had awakened in the middle of the night, gasping for breath while the edges of the rugs smoldered from the heat of the floor. He had not made another attempt.

He had chosen this building for his quarters because it was whole and near to the plaza; its great high ceilings gave a semblance of coolness even to the hottest part of the day, and its thick walls kept out the worst of the cold at night. It had not been the Roof of the Maidens then, of course. One morning he simply awakened to find it so, Maidens in every room on the first two floors and their guards on the doors. It had taken him a while to realize that they intended the building for their society's Roof in Rhuidean, yet expected him to continue to stay in it. In fact, they were ready to move the Roof wherever he went. That was why he had to meet the clan chiefs elsewhere. The best he had been able to manage was to make the Maidens agree to stay below the floor where he slept; that had amused them all no end. *Even the* Car'a'carn *is not a king,* he reminded himself wryly. Twice already he had moved upward as the numbers of Maidens increased. Idly he tried to calculate how many more could come in before he was sleeping on the roof.

That was better than remembering how he had let Moiraine get under his skin. He had not meant her to learn his plans until the day the Aiel moved. She knew exactly how to manipulate his emotions, how to make him so angry that he said more than he wanted to. *I never used to get so angry. Why is it so hard to hold on to my temper?* Well, there was nothing she could do to stop him. He did not think there was. He had to remember to be careful around her. His increasing abilities occasionally made him careless toward her, but if he was far stronger, she still knew more than he, even with Asmodean's teaching.

In a way, letting Asmodean know his plans was less important than revealing his intentions to the Aes Sedai. *To Moiraine I'm still just a shepherd she can use for the Tower's ends, but to Asmodean I'm the only branch he can hold on to in a flood.* Strange to think he could probably trust one of the Forsaken more than he could Moiraine. Not that he could trust either very far. Asmodean. If his bonds to the Dark One had shielded him from the taint on *saidin,* there had to be another way to do it. Or to cleanse it.

The trouble was that before they went over to the Shadow, the Forsaken had been among the most powerful Aes Sedai in the Age of Legends, when things the White Tower never dreamed of were commonplace. If Asmodean did not know a way, it probably did not exist. *It has to. There has to be something. I'm not going to just sit until I go mad and die.*

That was plain foolish. Prophecy had made a rendezvous for him at Shayol Ghul. When, he did not know; but afterward, he would not have to worry about going mad any longer. He shivered and thought about unfolding his blankets.

The faint sound of soft-soled footsteps in the hall snapped him upright. *I told them! If they can't . . . !* The woman who pushed open the door, her arms full of thick wool blankets, was not anyone he expected.

Aviendha paused just inside the room to regard him with cool, blue-green eyes. A more than pretty woman, of an age with him, she had been a Maiden until she gave up the spear to become a Wise One, not very long ago. Her dark reddish hair still came well short of her shoulders and hardly needed the folded brown scarf to keep it out of her face. She seemed a bit awkward with her brown shawl, a bit impatient with her full gray skirts.

He felt a stab of jealousy at the silver necklace she wore, an elaborate string of intricately worked discs, each different. *Who gave her that?* She would not have chosen it herself; she did not seem to like jewelry. The only other piece she wore was a wide ivory bracelet, carved in finely detailed roses. He had given her that, and he was not sure she had forgiven him for it yet. It was foolish of him to be jealous in any case.

"I haven't seen you in ten days," he said. "I thought the Wise Ones would have tied you to my arm once they found out I'd blocked them out of my dreams." Asmodean had been amused at the first thing he wanted to learn, and then frustrated at how long Rand took to learn it.

"I have my training to do, Rand al'Thor." She would be one of the few Wise Ones who could channel; that was part of what she was being taught. "I am not one of your wetlander women, to stand about so you can look at me whenever you wish." Despite knowing Egwene, and Elayne for that matter, she had an oddly wrongheaded view of what she called wetlander women, and of wetlanders in general. "They are not pleased at what you have done." She meant Amys, Bair and Melaine, the three Wise One dreamwalkers who were teaching her, and trying to watch him. Aviendha shook her head ruefully. "They were especially not pleased that I had let you know they were walking your dreams."

He stared at her. "You told them? But you didn't really say anything. I figured it out myself, and I would have eventually even if you hadn't let a hint slip out. Aviendha, they *told* me they could speak to people in their dreams. It was only a step from that."

"Would you have had me dishonor myself further?" Her voice was level enough, but her eyes could have started the fire laid on the hearth. "I will not dishonor myself for you or any man! I gave you the trail to follow, and I will not deny my shame. I should have let you freeze." She threw the blankets right on top of his head.

He pulled them off and laid them beside him on the pallet while trying to think of what to say. It was *ji'e'toh* again. The woman was as prickly as a thornbush. Supposedly she had been given the task of teaching him Aiel customs, but he knew her true job, to spy on him for the Wise Ones. Whatever dishonor was attached to spying among Aiel, apparently it did not extend to the Wise Ones. They knew he knew, but for some reason it did not seem to concern them, and as long as they were willing to let matters remain as they were, so was he. For one thing, Aviendha was not a very good spy; she almost never tried to find anything out, and her own temper got in the way of making him angry or guilty the way Moiraine did. For another, she was actually pleasant company sometimes, when she forgot to keep her thorns out. At least he knew who it was that Amys and the others had set to watch him; if it was not she, it would be someone else, and he would be constantly wondering who. Besides, she was never wary around him.

Mat, Egwene, even Moiraine sometimes looked at him with eyes that saw the Dragon Reborn, or at least the danger of a man who could channel. The clan chiefs and the Wise Ones saw He Who Comes With the Dawn, the man prophesied to break the Aiel like dried twigs; if they did not fear him, they still sometimes treated him like a red adder they had to live with. Whatever Aviendha saw, it never stopped her being scathing whenever she chose, which was most of the time.

An odd sort of comfort, but compared to the rest, it was a comfort nonetheless. He had missed her. He had even picked flowers from some of the spiny plants around Rhuidean—bloodying his fingers until he realized he could use the Power—and sent them to her, half a dozen times; the Maidens had carried the blossoms themselves, instead of sending *gai'shain*. She had never acknowledged them, of course.

"Thank you," he said finally, touching the blankets. They seemed a safe enough subject. "I suppose you can't have too many in the nights here."

"Enaila asked me to bring them to you when she found out I was here to see you." Her lips twitched in the beginnings of an amused smile. "A number of the spear-sisters were worried that you might not be warm enough. I am to see that you light your fire tonight; you didn't last night."

Rand felt his cheeks coloring. She knew. *Well, she would, wouldn't she? The bloody Maidens may not tell her everything anymore, but they don't bother to keep anything from her, either.* "Why did you want to see me?"

To his surprise, she folded her arms beneath her breasts and paced the short length of the room twice before stopping to glare at him. "This was not a regard-gift," she said accusingly, shaking the bracelet at him. "You admitted as much." True, though he thought she might have put a knife in his ribs had he not conceded it. "It was simply a fool gift from a man who did not know or care what my—what the spear-sisters might think. Well, this has no meaning either." She pulled something from her pouch and tossed it onto the pallet beside him. "It cancels debt between us."

Rand picked up what she had thrown and turned it over in his hands. A belt buckle in the shape of a dragon, ornately made in good steel and inlaid with gold. "Thank you. It's beautiful. Aviendha, there is no debt to cancel."

"If you will not take it against my debt," she said firmly, "then throw it away. I will find something else to repay you. It is only a trinket."

"Hardly a trinket. You must have had this made."

"Do not think that means anything, Rand al'Thor. When I . . . gave up the spear, my spears, my knife"—unconsciously her hand brushed her belt, where that long-bladed knife used to hang—"even the points of my arrows were taken from me and handed to a smith to make simple things to give away. Most I gave to friends, but the Wise Ones had me name the three men and three women I most hate, and I was told to give each of them a gift made from my weapons, with my own hands. Bair says it teaches humility." Straight-backed and glaring, biting off each word, she looked and sounded anything but humble. "So you will not think that means anything."

"It means nothing," he said, nodding sadly. Not that he wanted it to mean anything, really, but it would have been pleasing to think she might be beginning to see him as a friend. It was plain foolish to feel jealousy over her. *I wonder who gave it to her?* "Aviendha? Was I one of those you hate so much?"

"Yes, Rand al'Thor." She suddenly sounded hoarse. For a moment she turned her face away, eyes shut and quivering. "I hate you with all of my heart. I do. And I always will."

He did not bother to ask why. Once he had asked her why she disliked him and practically had his nose snapped off. She had not told him, though. But this was more than a dislike she sometimes seemed to forget. "If you really hate me," he said reluctantly, "I will ask the Wise Ones to send someone else to teach me."

"No!"

"But if you—"

"No!" If anything, her denial was even more fierce this time. She planted her fists on her hips and lectured as if she meant to drive every word home in his heart. "Even if the Wise Ones allowed me to stop, I have *toh*, obligation and duty, to my near-sister Elayne, to watch you for her. You belong to her, Rand al'Thor. To her and no other woman. Remember that."

He felt like throwing up his hands. At least this time she was not describing to him how Elayne looked without any clothes; some Aiel customs took even more getting used to than others. He sometimes wondered if she and Elayne had agreed on this "watching" between them. He could not believe it, but then again, even women who were not Aiel were odd as often as not. More than that, he wondered who Aviendha was supposed to be protecting him from. Except for the Maidens and the Wise Ones, Aiel women seemed to look at him half as prophecy made flesh, and thus not really flesh at all, and half as a blood snake loose among children. The Wise Ones were nearly as bad as Moiraine when it came to trying to make him do what they wanted, and the Maidens he did not want to think about. The whole thing made him furious.

"Now, you listen to me. I kissed Elayne a few times, and I think she enjoyed it as much as I did, but I am not promised to anyone. I'm not even sure she wants that much from me anymore." In the space of a few hours she had written him two letters; one called him the dearest light of her heart before going on to make his ears burn, while the other named him a coldhearted wretch she never wanted to see again and then proceeded to rip him up one side and down the other, better than Aviendha ever had. Women were definitely odd. "I don't have time to think about women anyway. The only thing on my mind is uniting the Aiel, even the Shaido if I can. I—" He cut off with a groan as the very last woman he could have hoped for swayed into the room in a clatter of jewelry, carrying a silver tray with a blown-glass flagon of wine and two silver cups.

A diaphanous red silk scarf wrapped around Isendre's head did nothing to hide her palely beautiful, heart-shaped face. Her long dark hair and dark eyes never belonged to any Aiel. Her full, pouting lips were curved enticingly—until she saw Aviendha. Then the smile faded to a sickly thing. Aside from the scarf she had on a dozen or more necklaces of gold and ivory, some set with pearls or polished gems. As many bracelets weighted each wrist, and even more bunched around her ankles. That was it; she wore not another thing. He made himself keep his eyes strictly on her face, but even so his cheeks felt hot.

Aviendha looked like a thunderhead about to spit lightning, Isendre like a woman who had just learned she was to be boiled alive. Rand wished he were in the Pit of Doom, or anywhere but there. Still, he got to his feet; he would have more authority looking down on them than the other way around. "Aviendha," he began, but she ignored him.

"Did someone send you with that?" she asked coldly.

Isendre opened her mouth, the intended lie plain on her face, then gulped and whispered, "No."

"You have been warned about this, *sorda*." A *sorda* was a kind of rat, especially sly according to the Aiel, and good for absolutely nothing; its flesh was so rank that even cats seldom ate the ones they killed. "Adelin thought the last time would have taught you."

Isendre flinched, and swayed as if about to faint.

Rand gathered himself. "Aviendha, whether she was sent or not doesn't matter. I am a little thirsty, and if she was kind enough to bring me wine, she should be thanked for it." Aviendha glanced coolly at the two cups and raised her eyebrows. He took a deep breath. "She should not be punished just for bringing me something to drink." He was careful not to look at the tray himself. "Half the Maidens under the Roof must have asked if I—"

"She was taken by the Maidens for theft from Maidens, Rand al'Thor." Aviendha's voice was even colder than it had been for the other woman. "You have meddled too much already in the business of *Far Dareis Mai,* more than you should have been allowed. Not even the *Car'a'carn* can thwart justice; this is no concern of yours."

He grimaced—and let it go. Whatever the Maidens did to her, Isendre certainly had coming. Just not for this. She had entered the Waste with Hadnan Kadere, but Kadere had not cracked his teeth when the Maidens took her for stealing the jewelry that was now all they let her wear. It had been all Rand could do to keep her from being sent off to Shara tethered like a goat, or else dispatched naked toward the Dragonwall with one water bag; watching her plead for mercy once she realized what the Maidens intended, he had not been able to make himself stay out of it. Once he had killed a woman; a woman who meant to kill him, but the memory still burned. He did not think he would ever be able to do it again, even with his life in the balance. A foolish thing, with female Forsaken likely seeking his blood or worse, but there it was. And if he could not kill a woman, how could he stand by and let a woman die? Even if she deserved it?

That was the rub. In any land west of the Dragonwall,

Isendre would face the gallows or the headsman's block for what he knew about her. About her, and Kadere, and probably most of the merchant's men if not all. They were Darkfriends. And he could not expose them. Not even they were aware that he knew.

If any one of them was revealed as a Darkfriend . . . Isendre endured as best she could, because even being a servant and kept naked was better than being tied hand and foot and left for the sun, but none would keep silent once Moiraine had her hands on them. Aes Sedai had no more mercy for Darkfriends than for anyone else; she would loosen their tongues in short order. And Asmodean had come into the Waste with the merchant's wagons, too, just another Darkfriend so far as Kadere and the others knew, though one with authority. No doubt they thought he had taken service with the Dragon Reborn on orders from some still higher power. To keep his teacher, to keep Moiraine from trying to kill both of them very probably, Rand had to keep their secret.

Luckily, no one questioned why the Aiel kept such a close watch on the merchant and his men. Moiraine thought it was the usual Aiel suspicion of outsiders in the Waste, magnified by them being in Rhuidean; she had had to use all of her persuasion to make the Aiel let Kadere and his wagons into the city. The suspicion was there; Rhuarc and the other chiefs likely would have set guards even if Rand had not asked. And Kadere just seemed happy he did not have a spear through his ribs.

Rand had no idea how he was going to resolve the situation. Or if he could. It was a fine mess. In gleemen's stories, only villains got caught in a cleft stick like this.

Once she was sure that he was not going to try to interfere further, Aviendha turned her attention back to the other woman. "You may leave the wine."

Isendre half-knelt gracefully to set the tray beside his pallet, a peculiar grimace on her face. It took Rand a moment to recognize an attempt to smile at him without letting the Aiel woman see.

"And now you will run to the first Maiden you can find," Aviendha went on, "and tell her what you have done. Run, *sorda*!" Moaning and wringing her hands,

Isendre ran in a great rattle of jewelry. As soon as she was out of the room, Aviendha rounded on him. "You belong to Elayne! You have no right to try luring any woman, but especially not that one!"

"Her?" Rand gasped. "You think I—? Believe me, Aviendha, if she were the last woman on earth, I'd still stay as far from her as I could run."

"So you say." She sniffed. "She has been switched seven times—seven!—for trying to sneak to your bed. She would not persist like that without some encouragement. She faces *Far Dareis Mai* justice, and she is no concern of even the *Car'a'carn.* Take that as your lesson for today on our customs. And remember that you belong to my near-sister!" Without letting him get a word in, she stalked out wearing such a look that he thought Isendre might not survive if Aviendha caught up to her.

Letting out a long breath, he got up long enough to put the tray and its wine in a corner of the room. He was not about to drink anything Isendre brought him.

Seven times she's tried to reach me? She must have learned that he interceded for her; no doubt to her way of thinking, if he was willing to do that for a smoky look and a smile, what might he do for more? He shivered at the thought as much as the increasing cold. He would rather have a scorpion in his bed. If the Maidens failed to convince her, he might tell her what he knew about her; that should put an end to any schemes.

Snuffing the lamps, he crawled onto his pallet in the dark, still booted and fully dressed, and fumbled around until he had pulled all of the blankets over him. Without the fire, he suspected he really would be grateful to Aviendha before morning. Setting the wards of Spirit that shielded his dreams from intrusion was almost automatic to him now, but even as he did it, he chuckled to himself. He could have gotten into bed and *then* put out the lamps, with the Power. It was the simple things that he never thought of doing with the Power.

For a time he lay waiting for his body's heat to warm the inside of the blankets. How the same place could be so hot by day and so cold by night was beyond him.

Sticking one hand under his coat, he fingered the half-healed scar on his side. That wound, the one that Moiraine could never completely Heal, was what would kill him, eventually. He was sure of it. His blood on the rocks of Shayol Ghul. That was what the Prophecies said.

Not tonight. I won't think of that tonight. I have a little time yet. But if the seals can be shaved with a knife, now, do they still hold as strongly . . . ? No. Not tonight.

The inside of the blankets was becoming a little warmer, and he shifted around, trying and failing to find a comfortable way to lie. *I should have washed,* he thought drowsily. Egwene was probably in a warm sweat tent right that minute. Half the time he used one, a fistful of Maidens tried to come in with him—and nearly rolled on the ground laughing when he insisted on them staying outside. It was bad enough having to undress and dress in the steam.

Sleep finally came, and with it, safely protected dreams, safe from the Wise Ones or anyone else. Not protected from his own thoughts, though. Three women invaded them continually. Not Isendre, except in a brief nightmare that nearly woke him. By turns he dreamed of Elayne, and Min, and Aviendha, by turns and together. Only Elayne had ever looked at him as a man, but all three saw him as who he was, not what he was. Aside from the nightmare, they were all pleasant dreams.

CHAPTER

5

Among the Wise Ones

Standing as close as she could to the small fire in the middle of the tent, Egwene still shivered as she poured water from the generous teakettle into a wide, blue-striped bowl. She had lowered the sides of the tent, but cold seeped through the colorful layered rugs covering the ground, and all the fire's heat seemed to rush up and out of the smoke hole in the middle of the tent roof, leaving only the smell of the burning cow dung. Her teeth wanted to chatter.

Already the steam from the water was beginning to fade; she embraced *saidar* for a moment and channeled Fire to heat it more. Amys or Bair would probably have washed in it cold, though in fact they always took sweat baths. *So I'm not as tough as they are. I did not grow up in the Waste. I don't have to freeze to death and wash in cold water if I don't want to.* She still felt guilty as she lathered a cloth with a piece of lavender-scented soap bought from Hadnan Kadere. The Wise Ones had never asked her to do differently, but it still felt like cheating.

Letting go of the True Source made her sigh with

remorse. Even trembling with cold, she laughed softly at her own foolishness. The wonder of being filled with the Power, the wondrous rush of life and awareness, was its own danger. The more you drew on *saidar,* the more you wanted to draw, and without self-discipline you eventually drew more than you could handle and either died or stilled yourself. And that was nothing to laugh at.

That's one of your biggest faults, she lectured herself firmly. *You always want to do more than you're supposed to. You ought to wash in cold water; that would teach you self-discipline.* Only there was so much to learn, and it sometimes seemed a lifetime would be too short to learn it. Her teachers were always so cautious, whether Wise Ones or Aes Sedai in the Tower; it was hard to hold back when she knew that in so many ways she already outstripped them. *I can do more than they realize.*

A blast of freezing air hit her, swirling smoke from the fire about the tent, and a woman's voice said, "If it pleases you—"

Egwene jumped, yelping shrilly before managing to get out, "Shut that!" She hugged herself to stop from capering. "Get in or get out, but shut it!" All that effort to be warm, and now she was icy goose bumps from head to toe!

The white-robed woman shuffled into the tent on her knees and let the tent flap drop. She kept her eyes downcast, her hands folded meekly; she would have done the same if Egwene had hit her instead of just shouting. "If it pleases you," she said softly, "the Wise One Amys sent me to bring you to the sweat tent."

Wishing she could stand on top of the fire, Egwene groaned. *The Light burn Bair and her stubbornness!* If not for the white-haired old Wise One, they could be in rooms in the city instead of tents on the edge of it. *I could have a room with a proper fireplace. And a door.* She was willing to bet that Rand did not have to put up with people wandering in on him whenever they wanted. *Rand bloody Dragon al'Thor snaps his fingers, and the Maidens jump like serving girls. I'll wager they've found him a real bed, instead of a pallet on the ground.* She was sure that he got a hot bath every night. *The Maidens probably haul buckets of hot water up to his rooms. I'll bet they even found him a proper copper bathtub.*

Amys, and even Melaine, had been amenable to Egwene's suggestion, but Bair had put her foot down, and they acquiesced like *gai'shain*. Egwene supposed that with Rand bringing so much change, Bair wanted to hold on to as much of the old ways as she could, but she wished the woman could have chosen something else to be intractable over.

There was no thought of refusing. She had promised the Wise Ones to forget that she was Aes Sedai—the easy part, since she was not—and do exactly as she was told. That was the hard part; she had been away from the Tower long enough to become her own mistress again. But Amys had told her flatly that dreamwalking was dangerous even after you knew what you were about and far more so until then. If she would not obey in the waking world, they could not trust her to obey in the dream, and they would not take the responsibility. So she did chores right along with Aviendha, accepted chastisement with as good a grace as she could muster, and hopped whenever Amys or Melaine or Bair said frog. In a manner of speaking. None of them had ever seen a frog. *Not that they'll want anything but for me to hand them their tea.* No, it would be Aviendha's turn to do that tonight.

For a moment she considered donning stockings, but finally just bent to slip on her shoes. Sturdy shoes, suitable for the Waste; she rather regretted the silk slippers she had worn in Tear. "What is your name?" she asked, trying to be companionable.

"Cowinde" was the docile reply.

Egwene sighed. She kept trying to be friends with the *gai'shain,* but they never responded. Servants were one thing she had not had a chance to get used to, though of course *gai'shain* were not precisely servants. "You were a Maiden?"

A quick, fierce flash of deep blue eyes told her that her guess was correct, but just as quickly they lowered again. "I am *gai'shain*. Before and after are not now, and only now exists."

"What is your sept and clan?" Usually there was no need to ask, not even with *gai'shain*.

"I serve the Wise One Melaine of the Jhirad sept, of the Goshien Aiel."

Trying to choose between two cloaks, a stout brown woolen and a blue quilted silk she had purchased from Kadere—the merchant had sold everything in his wagons to make room for Moiraine's freight, and at very good prices—Egwene paused to frown at the woman. That was no proper response. She had heard that a form of the bleakness had taken some *gai'shain*; when their year and a day was done, they simply refused to put off the robe. "When is your time up?" she asked.

Cowinde crouched lower, almost huddling over her knees. "I am *gai'shain*."

"But when will you be able to return to your sept, to your own hold?"

"I am *gai'shain*," the woman hoarsely told the rugs in front of her face. "If the answer displeases, punish me, but I can give no other."

"Don't be silly," Egwene said sharply. "And straighten up. You aren't a toad."

The white-robed woman obeyed immediately and sat there on her heels, submissively awaiting another command. That brief flare of spirit might as well never have been.

Egwene took a deep breath. The woman had made her own accommodation with the bleakness. A foolish one, but nothing she could say would change it. Anyway, she was supposed to be on her way to the sweat tent, not talking with Cowinde.

Remembering that cold draft, she hesitated. The icy gust had made two large white blossoms, resting in a shallow bowl, curl partway closed. They came from a plant called a *segade*, a fat, leafless, leathery thing that bristled with spines. She had come on Aviendha looking at them in her hands that morning; the Aiel woman had given a start when she saw her, then pushed them into Egwene's hands, saying she had picked them for her. She supposed there was enough of the Maiden left in Aviendha that she did not want to admit liking flowers.

Though come to think of it, she had seen the occasional Maiden wearing a blossom in her hair or on her coat.

You are just trying to put it off, Egwene al'Vere. Now stop being a silly woolhead! You are being as foolish as Cowinde. "Lead the way," she said, and just had time to swing the woolen cloak around her nakedness before the woman swept open the tent flap for her, and for the bone-chilling night.

Overhead, the stars were crisp points in the darkness, and the three-quarter moon was bright. The Wise Ones' camp was a cluster of two dozen low mounds, not a hundred paces from where one of Rhuidean's paved streets ended in hard, cracked clay and stones. Moonshadows turned the city into strange cliffs and crags. Every tent had its flaps down, and the smells of fires and cooking blended to fill the air.

The other Wise Ones came here for almost daily gatherings, but they spent nights with their own septs. Several even slept in Rhuidean now. But not Bair. This was as close to the city as Bair had been willing to come; if Rand had not been there, doubtless she would have insisted on making camp in the mountains.

Egwene held the cloak tight with both hands and walked as fast as she could. Icy tendrils curled under the cloak's bottom, swept in every time her bare legs kicked a gap open. Cowinde had to pull her white robes to her knees in order to keep ahead. Egwene did not need the *gai'shain*'s guidance, but since the woman had been sent to bring her, she would be shamed and maybe offended if not allowed to. Clenching her teeth to keep them from chattering, Egwene wished the woman would run.

The sweat tent looked like any other, low and wide, with the flaps lowered all around, except that the smoke hole had been covered. Nearby a fire had burned down to glowing embers scattered over a few rocks the size of a man's head. There was not enough light to define the much smaller shadowed mound beside the tent entrance, but she knew it was neatly folded women's clothes.

Taking one deep, chilling breath, she hurriedly scuffed off her shoes, let her cloak drop, and all but dove into the tent. An instant of shuddering cold before the flap fell shut behind her, then steamy heat clamped down, squeezing out sweat that covered her in an instant sheen while she was still gasping and shaking.

The three Wise Ones who were teaching her about dreamwalking sat sweating unconcernedly, their waist-length hair hanging damply. Bair was talking to Melaine, whose green-eyed beauty and red-gold hair made a sharp contrast to the older woman's leathery face and long white tresses. Amys was white-haired, too—or perhaps it was just so pale a yellow that it seemed white—but she did not look old. She and Melaine could both channel—not many Wise Ones could—and she had something of the Aes Sedai look of agelessness about her. Moiraine, seeming slight and small beside the others, also looked unruffled, although sweat rolled down her pale nudity and slicked her dark hair to her scalp, with a regal refusal to acknowledge that she had no clothes on. The Wise Ones were using slim, curved pieces of bronze, called *staera*, to scrape off sweat and the day's dirt.

Aviendha was squatting sweatily beside the big black kettle of hot, sooty rocks in the middle of the tent, carefully using a pair of tongs to move a last stone from a smaller kettle to the larger. That done, she sprinkled water onto the rocks from a gourd, adding to the steam. If she let the steam fall too far, she would be spoken to sharply at the very least. The next time the Wise Ones met in the sweat tent, it would be Egwene's turn to tend the rocks.

Egwene cautiously sat down cross-legged next to Bair —instead of layered rugs, there was only rocky ground, unpleasantly hot, lumpy and damp—and realized with a shock that Aviendha had been switched, and recently. When the Aiel woman gingerly took her own place, beside Egwene, she did so with a face as stony as the ground, but a face that could not hide her flinch.

This was something Egwene did not expect. The Wise Ones exacted a hard discipline—harder even than the Tower, which took some doing—but Aviendha worked at learning to channel with a grim determination. She could not dreamwalk, but she surely put as much effort into absorbing every art of a Wise One as she could ever have put into learning her weapons as a Maiden. Of

course, after she confessed to letting Rand know about
the Wise Ones watching his dreams, they had made her
spend three days digging shoulder-deep holes and filling
them in again, but that was one of the few times
Aviendha had ever seemed to put a foot wrong. Amys
and the other two had held her up to Egwene so often as a
model of meek obedience and proper fortitude that
sometimes Egwene wanted to shriek, even if Aviendha
was a friend.

"You took long enough in coming," Bair said grumpily, while Egwene was still gingerly searching for a comfortable seat. Her voice was thin and reedy, but a reed of
iron. She continued to scrape her arms with a *staera*.

"I am sorry," Egwene said. There; that should be meek
enough.

Bair sniffed. "You are Aes Sedai beyond the
Dragonwall, but here you are yet a pupil, and a pupil
does not dally. When I send for Aviendha, or send her for
something, she runs, even if all I want is a pin. You could
do much worse than to pattern yourself after her."

Flushing, Egwene tried to make her voice humble. "I
will try, Bair." This was the first time a Wise One had
made the comparison in front of others. She sneaked a
glance at Aviendha and was surprised to find her looking
thoughtful. Sometimes she wished her "near-sister" were
not always such a good example.

"The girl will learn, Bair, or she will not," Melaine
said irritably. "Instruct her in promptness later, if she
still needs it." No more than ten or twelve years older
than Aviendha, she usually sounded as if she had a burr
under her skirts. Maybe she was sitting on a sharp rock.
She would not move if she was; she would expect the
rock to move. "I tell you again, Moiraine Sedai, the Aiel
follow He Who Comes With the Dawn, not the White
Tower."

Obviously, Egwene was meant to pick up what they
were talking about as they went on.

"It may be," Amys said in a level voice, "that the Aiel
will serve the Aes Sedai again, but that time has not
come yet, Moiraine Sedai." Her scraping barely paused
as she eyed the Aes Sedai calmly.

It would come, Egwene knew, now that Moiraine was

aware that some of the Wise Ones could channel. Aes Sedai would be journeying into the Waste to find girls who could be taught, and would almost certainly be trying to take any Wise One with the ability back to the Tower, too. Once she had worried about the Wise Ones being browbeaten and dominated, hauled away whenever they wanted; Aes Sedai never let any woman who could channel run free of the Tower for long. She did not worry anymore, though the Wise Ones themselves seemed to. Amys and Melaine could match any Aes Sedai will for will, as they showed every day with Moiraine. Bair could very likely make even Siuan Sanche jump through hoops, and Bair could not even channel.

For that matter, Bair was not the strongest-willed Wise One. That honor went to an even older woman, Sorilea, of the Jarra sept of the Chareen Aiel. The Wise One of Shende Hold could channel less than most novices, but she was as likely to send another Wise One on an errand as a *gai'shain*. And they went. No, there was no reason to distress herself over Wise Ones being bullied.

"It is understandable that you wish to spare your lands," Bair put in, "but Rand al'Thor obviously does not mean to lead us to punish. No one who submits to He Who Comes With the Dawn, and the Aiel, will be harmed." So that was it. Of course.

"It is not only sparing lives or lands that concerns me." Moiraine made wiping sweat from her brow with one finger into a queenly gesture, but her voice sounded nearly as tight as Melaine's. "If you allow this, it will be disastrous. Years of planning are coming to fruition, and he means to ruin it all."

"Plans of the White Tower," Amys said, so smoothly she might have been agreeing. "Those plans have nothing to do with us. We, and the other Wise Ones, must consider what is right for the Aiel. We will see that the Aiel do what is best for the Aiel."

Egwene wondered what the clan chiefs would say about that. Of course, they frequently complained that the Wise Ones meddled in matters that were not theirs, so perhaps it would not come as a surprise. The chiefs all seemed to be hard-willed, intelligent men, but she believed they had as much chance against the combined Wise Ones as the Village Council back home did against the Women's Circle.

This time, though, Moiraine was right.

"If Rand—" she began, but Bair stepped on her firmly.

"We will hear what you have to say later, girl. Your knowledge of Rand al'Thor is valuable, but you will hold your peace and listen until you are bidden to speak. And stop looking sullen, or I will dose you with bluespine tea."

Egwene grimaced. Respect for the Aes Sedai, though a respect between equals, included but little for the pupil, even one they believed *was* Aes Sedai. She kept her tongue still, in any case. Bair was capable of sending her to fetch her herb pouches and telling her to brew the incredibly bitter tea herself; it had no purpose at all except to cure sullenness or sulkiness or whatever else a Wise One might find disfavor with, which it did by taste alone. Aviendha gave her a comforting pat on the arm.

"You believe it will not be a catastrophe for the Aiel as well?" It must have been difficult to sound as cool as a winter stream when you glistened from head to foot with condensed steam and your own sweat, but Moiraine apparently had no difficulty. "It will be the Aiel War all over again. You will kill and burn and loot towns as you did then, until you have turned every man and woman against you."

"The fifth is our due, Aes Sedai," Melaine said, throwing her long hair back over her shoulder so she could work a *staera* across a smooth shoulder. Even heavy and damp with the steam, her hair glistened like silk. "We took no more even from the treekillers." Her glance at Moiraine was too bland not to be significant; they knew she was Cairhienin. "Your kings and queens take as much in their taxes."

"And when the nations turn against you?" Moiraine persisted. "In the Aiel War, the nations united turned you back. That can and will happen again, with great loss of life on both sides."

"None of us fears death, Aes Sedai," Amys told her,

smiling gently as if explaining something to a child. "Life is a dream from which we all must wake before we can dream again. Besides, only four clans crossed the Dragonwall under Janduin. Six are here already, and you say Rand al'Thor means to take all of the clans."

"The Prophecy of Rhuidean says he will break us." The spark in Melaine's green eyes could have been for Moiraine or because she was not as resigned as she sounded. "What does it matter whether it is here or beyond the Dragonwall?"

"You will lose him the support of every nation west of the Dragonwall," Moiraine said. She looked as calm as ever, but an edge in her voice said she was ready to chew rocks. "He must have their support!"

"He has the support of the Aiel nation," Bair told her in that fragile, unyielding voice. She emphasized her words by gesturing with the slim metal blade. "The clans have never been a nation, but now he makes us one."

"We will not help you turn him in this, Moiraine Sedai," Amys added just as firmly.

"You may leave us now, Aes Sedai, if it pleases you," Bair said. "We have discussed what you wished to discuss as much as we will tonight." It was politely said, but a dismissal all the same.

"I will leave you," Moiraine replied, once again all serenity. She sounded as though it were her suggestion, her decision. By this time she was used to the Wise Ones making it clear they were not under the Tower's authority. "I have other matters to see to."

That much had to be the truth, of course. Very likely something concerning Rand. Egwene knew better than to ask; if Moiraine wanted her to know, she would tell her, and if not . . . If not, she would be handed some slippery bit of Aes Sedai avoidance of a lie, or else be told bluntly that it was none of her business. Moiraine knew that "Egwene Sedai of the Green Ajah" was a fraud. She tolerated the lie in public, but otherwise she let Egwene know her proper place whenever it suited her.

As soon as Moiraine had gone, in a burst of cold air, Amys said, "Aviendha, pour the tea."

The young Aiel woman gave a startled jerk, and her

mouth opened twice before she said faintly, "I must brew it yet." With that she scurried out of the tent on all fours. The second blast from outside dimmed the steam.

The Wise Ones exchanged looks that were almost as surprised as Aviendha's. And Egwene's; Aviendha always did even the most onerous chores efficiently, if not always with a good grace. Something must be troubling her greatly, to make her forget a thing like making tea. The Wise Ones always wanted tea.

"More steam, girl," Melaine said.

That was her, Egwene realized, with Aviendha gone. Hurriedly splashing more water on the rocks, she channeled to heat the stones further, and the kettle, until she heard stones cracking and the kettle itself radiated heat like a furnace. The Aiel might be used to leaping from roasting in their own juices to freezing, but she was not. Hot, thick clouds rolled up to fill the tent. Amys nodded approvingly; she and Melaine could see the glow of *saidar* surrounding her, of course, though she herself could not. Melaine merely went on scraping with her *staera*.

Letting go of the True Source, she sat back and leaned close to Bair to whisper, "Has Aviendha done something very wrong?" She did not know how Aviendha would feel about it, but she saw no reason to embarrass her, even behind her back.

Bair had no such compunctions. "You mean her stripes?" she said in a normal voice. "She came to me and said she had lied twice today, though she would not say to whom or about what. It was her own affair, of course, so long as she did not lie to a Wise One, but she claimed her honor required that a *toh* must be met."

"She *asked* you to . . ." Egwene gasped, but could not finish.

Bair nodded as if it were not very much out of the ordinary at all. "I gave her a few extra for troubling me with it. If *ji* was involved, her obligation is not to me. Very likely her so-called lies were nothing anyone but a *Far Dareis Mai* would worry about. Maidens, even former Maidens, are sometimes as fussy as men." Amys gave her a flat look that was plain even in the thick steam.

Like Aviendha, Amys had been *Far Dareis Mai* before becoming a Wise One.

Egwene had never met an Aiel who was not fussy about *ji'e'toh,* the way she saw it. But this! Aiel were all mad as loons.

Apparently, Bair had already put the matter out of her mind. "There are more Lost Ones in the Three-fold Land than I can ever remember before," she said to the tent at large. That was what the Aiel had always called the Tinkers, the Tuatha'an.

"They flee the troubles beyond the Dragonwall." The sneer in Melaine's voice was clear.

"I have heard," Amys said slowly, "that some of those who run after the bleakness have gone to the Lost Ones and asked to be taken in." A long silence followed. They knew now that the Tuatha'an had the same descent as themselves, that they had broken away before the Aiel crossed the Spine of the World into the Waste, but if anything the knowledge had only deepened their aversion.

"He brings change," Melaine whispered harshly into the steam.

"I thought you were reconciled to the changes he brings," Egwene said, sympathy welling up in her voice. It must be very hard to have your whole life stood on end. She half-expected to be told to hold her tongue again, but no one did.

"Reconciled," Bair said, as though tasting the word. "Better to say we endure them, as best we can."

"He transforms everything." Amys sounded troubled. "Rhuidean. The Lost Ones. The bleakness, and telling what should not have been told." The Wise Ones—all the Aiel, for that matter—still had difficulty speaking of that.

"The Maidens cluster about him as though they owe more to him than to their own clans," Bair added. "For the first time ever, they have allowed a man beneath a Roof of the Maidens." For a moment Amys looked about to say something, but whatever she knew about the inner workings of *Far Dareis Mai* she shared with no one but those who were or had been Maidens of the Spear.

"The chiefs no longer listen to us as they did," Melaine muttered. "Oh, they ask our advice as always—they have not become complete fools—but Bael will no longer tell me what he has said to Rand al'Thor, or Rand al'Thor to him. He says I must ask Rand al'Thor, who tells me to ask Bael. The *Car'a'carn,* I can do nothing about, but Bael . . . He has always been a stubborn, infuriating man, yet now he is beyond all bounds. Sometimes I want to thump his head with a stick." Amys and Bair chuckled as if that were a fine joke. Or perhaps they just wanted to laugh to forget the changes for a time.

"There are only three things you can do with a man like that," Bair chortled. "Stay away from him, kill him, or marry him."

Melaine stiffened, her sun-dark face going red. For a moment Egwene thought the golden-haired Wise One was about to let fly words hotter than her face. Then a biting gust announced Aviendha's return carrying a worked silver tray holding a yellow-glazed teapot, delicate cups of golden Sea Folk porcelain, and a stone jar of honey.

She shivered as she poured—no doubt she had not bothered to wrap anything around herself out there—and hurriedly passed around the cups and the honey. She did not fill cups for herself and Egwene until Amys told her she could, of course.

"More steam," Melaine said; the chill air seemed to have cooled her temper. Aviendha set down her cup untouched and scrambled for the gourd, plainly trying to make up for her lapse with the tea.

"Egwene," Amys said, sipping her tea, "how would Rand al'Thor take it if Aviendha asked to sleep in his sleeping chamber?" Aviendha froze with the gourd in her hands.

"In his—?" Egwene gasped. "You cannot ask her to do such a thing! You cannot!"

"Fool girl," Bair muttered. "We do not ask her to share his blankets. But will he think that is what she asks? Will he even allow it? Men are strange creatures at the best, and he was not raised among us, so he is stranger still."

"He certainly would not think any such thing,"

Egwene spluttered, then more slowly, "I don't think he would. But it isn't proper. It just isn't!"

"I ask that you not require this of me," Aviendha said, sounding more humble than Egwene would have believed she could. She was sprinkling water in jerky motions, sending up increasing clouds of steam. "I have been learning a great deal the past days, not having to spend time with him. Since you have allowed Egwene and Moiraine Sedai to help me with channeling, I learn even faster. Not that they teach any better than you, of course," she added hastily, "but I want very much to learn."

"You will still learn," Melaine told her. "You will not have to stay every hour with him. As long as you apply yourself, your lessons will not be much slowed. You do not study while you sleep."

"I cannot," Aviendha mumbled, head down over the water gourd. More loudly, and more firmly, she added, "I will not." Her head came up, and her eyes were blue-green fire. "I will not be there when he summons that flipskirt Isendre to his blankets again!"

Egwene gaped at her. "Isendre!" She had seen—and heartily disapproved of—the scandalous way the Maidens kept the woman naked, but this! "You can't really mean he—"

"Be silent!" Bair snapped like a whip. Her blue-eyed stare could have chipped stone. "Both of you! You are both young, but even the Maidens should know men can be fools, especially when they are not attached to a woman who can guide them."

"I am glad," Amys said dryly, "to see you no longer hold your emotions so tightly, Aviendha. Maidens are as foolish as men when it comes to that; I remember it well, and it embarrasses me still. Letting emotions go clouds judgment for a moment, but holding them in clouds it always. Just be sure you do not release them too often, or when it is best to keep control of them."

Melaine leaned forward on her hands, until it seemed the sweat dripping from her face must fall on the hot kettle. "You know your fate, Aviendha. You will be a Wise One of great strength and great authority, and more besides. You already have a strength in you. It saw you through your first test, and it will see you through this."

"My honor," Aviendha said hoarsely, then swallowed, unable to go on. She crouched there, huddling around the gourd as if it contained the honor she wanted to protect.

"The Pattern does not see *ji'e'toh,*" Bair told her, with only a hint of sympathy, if that. "Only what must and will be. Men and Maidens struggle against fate even when it is clear the Pattern weaves on despite their struggles, but you are no longer *Far Dareis Mai.* You must learn to ride fate. Only by surrendering to the Pattern can you begin to have some control over the course of your own life. If you fight, the Pattern will still force you, and you will find only misery where you might have found contentment instead."

To Egwene, that sounded very much like what she had been taught concerning the One Power. To control *saidar,* you first had to surrender to it. Fight, and it would come wildly, or overwhelm you; surrender and guide it gently, and it did as you wished. But that did not explain why they wanted Aviendha to do this thing. She asked as much, adding again, "It is not proper."

Instead of answering, Amys said, "Will Rand al'Thor refuse to allow her? We cannot force him." Bair and Melaine were looking at Egwene as intently as Amys.

They were not going to tell her why. It was easier to make a stone talk than to get something out of a Wise One against her will. Aviendha was studying her toes in sulky resignation; she knew the Wise Ones would get what they wanted, one way or another.

"I don't know," Egwene said slowly. "I do not know him as well as I used to." She regretted that, but so much had happened, quite aside from her realizing that she did not love him as more than a brother. Her training, in the Tower as well as here, had changed things just as much as him being who he had become. "If you give him a good reason, perhaps. I think he likes Aviendha." The young Aiel woman heaved a heavy sigh without looking up.

"A good reason," Bair snorted. "When I was a girl, any man would have been overjoyed to have a young woman show that much interest in him. He would have gone to pick the flowers for her bridal wreath himself." Aviendha started, and glared at the Wise Ones with some of her old spirit. "Well, we will find a reason even someone raised in the wetlands can accept."

"It is several nights before your agreed meeting in *Tel'aran'rhiod,"* Amys said. "With Nynaeve, this time."

"That one could learn much," Bair put in, "if she were not so stubborn."

"Your nights are free until then," Melaine said. "That is, unless you have been entering *Tel'aran'rhiod* without us."

Egwene suspected what was coming. "Of course not," she told them. It had only been a little. Any more than a little, and they would find out for sure.

"Have you succeeded in finding either Nynaeve's or Elayne's dreams?" Amys asked. Casually, as if it were nothing.

"No, Amys."

Finding someone else's dreams was a lot harder than stepping into *Tel'aran'rhiod,* the World of Dreams, especially if they were any distance away. It was easier both the closer they were and the better you knew them. The Wise Ones still demanded that she not enter *Tel'aran'rhiod* without at least one of them along, but someone else's dream was maybe just as dangerous in its own way. In *Tel'aran'rhiod* she was in control of herself and of things around her to a large degree, unless one of the Wise Ones decided to take over; her command of *Tel'aran'rhiod* was increasing, but she still could not match any of them, with their long experience. In another's dream, though, you were a part of that dream; it took all you could muster not to behave as the dreamer wanted, be as their dream took you, and still sometimes it did not work. The Wise Ones had been very careful when watching Rand's dreams never to enter fully. Even so they insisted she learn. If they were to teach dreamwalking, they meant to teach all that they knew of it.

She was not reluctant, exactly, but the few times they had let her practice, with themselves and once with

Rhuarc, had been chastening experiences. The Wise Ones had some considerable mastery over their own dreams, so what had happened there—to show her the dangers, they said—had all been their doing, but it had been a shock to learn that Rhuarc saw her as a little more than a child, like his youngest daughters. And her own control had wavered for one fatal moment. After that she had *been* little more than a child; she still could not look at the man without remembering being given a doll for studying hard. And being as pleased with the gift as with his approval. Amys had had to come and take her away from happy play with it. Amys knowing was bad enough, but she suspected that Rhuarc remembered some of it, too.

"You must keep trying," Amys said. "You have the strength to reach them, even as far as they are. And it will do you no harm to learn how they see you."

She was not so sure of that herself. Elayne was a friend, but Nynaeve had been Wisdom of Emond's Field for most of her growing up. She suspected Nynaeve's dreams would be worse than Rhuarc's.

"Tonight I will sleep away from the tents," Amys went on. "Not far. You should be able to find me easily, if you try. If I do not dream of you, we will speak of it in the morning."

Egwene suppressed a groan. Amys had guided her to Rhuarc's dreams—she herself had remained only an instant, barely long enough to reveal that Rhuarc still saw her, unchanged, as the young woman he had married —and the Wise Ones had always been in the same tent before when she tried.

"Well," Bair said, rubbing her hands, "we have heard what needed to be heard. The rest of you can remain if you wish, but I feel clean enough to go to my blankets. I am not so young as the rest of you." Young or not, she could probably run any of them into the ground, then carry them the rest of the way.

As Bair was getting to her feet, Melaine spoke, and strangely for her, she was hesitant. "I need . . . I must ask your help, Bair. And you, Amys." The older woman settled back, and both she and Amys looked at Melaine expectantly. "I . . . would ask you to approach Dorindha for me." The last words came out in a rush. Amys smiled widely, and Bair cackled aloud. Aviendha seemed to understand, too, and be startled, but Egwene was lost.

Then Bair laughed. "You always said you did not need a husband and did not want one. I have buried three, and would not mind another. They are very useful when the night is cold."

"A woman can change her mind." Melaine's voice was firm enough, but belied by the deep flush in her cheeks. "I cannot stay away from Bael, and I cannot kill him. If Dorindha will accept me as her sister-wife, I will make my bridal wreath to lay at Bael's feet."

"What if he steps on it instead of picking it up?" Bair wanted to know. Amys fell back, laughing and slapping her thighs.

Egwene did not think there was much danger of that, not the way Aiel customs ran. If Dorindha decided she wanted Melaine for sister-wife, Bael would not have much say in the matter. It no longer shocked her, precisely, that a man could have two wives. Not exactly. *Different lands mean different customs,* she reminded herself firmly. She had never been able to bring herself to ask, but for all she knew, there might be Aiel women with two husbands. They were very strange people.

"I ask you to act as my first-sisters in this. I think that Dorindha likes me well enough."

As soon as Melaine spoke those words, the other women's hilarity changed to something else. They still laughed, but they hugged her and told her how happy they were for her, and how well she would do with Bael. Amys and Bair, at least, took Dorindha's acceptance for granted. The three of them departed all but arm-in-arm, still laughing and giggling like girls. Not before telling Egwene and Aviendha to straighten the tent, though.

"Egwene, could a woman of your land accept a sister-wife?" Aviendha asked, using a stick to push the cover off the smoke hole.

Egwene wished she had left that duty till last; the heat began to dissipate immediately. "I don't know," she said, quickly gathering the cups and the honey jar. The *staera* went onto the tray, too. "I don't think so. Maybe if it was a close friend," she added hurriedly; there was no point in seeming to denigrate Aiel ways.

Aviendha only grunted and began pushing up the side flaps.

Teeth chattering as loudly as the rattle of teacups and bronze blades on the tray, Egwene scurried outside. The Wise Ones were dressing unhurriedly, as though this were a balmy night and they in sleeping chambers in some hold. A white-robed figure, pale in the moonlight, took the tray from her, and she quickly began searching for her cloak and shoes. They were nowhere among the remaining garments on the ground.

"I had your things taken to your tent," Bair said, tying the laces of her blouse. "You will not need them yet."

Egwene's stomach sank into her feet. Hopping in place, she flapped her arms in a futile effort for warmth; at least they did not tell her to stop. Abruptly she realized the snowy-robed figure bearing the tray away was too tall for even an Aiel woman. Gritting her teeth, she glared at the Wise Ones, who seemed not to care if she froze to death jumping up and down. To the Aiel women it might not matter that a man had seen them with no clothes on, at least if he was *gai'shain,* but it did to her!

In a moment, Aviendha joined them and, seeing her leaping about, merely stood there without any effort to find her own garments. She showed no more effect of the cold than the Wise Ones.

"Now," Bair said, settling her shawl on her shoulders. "You, Aviendha, are not only stubborn as a man, you cannot remember a simple task you have done many times. You, Egwene, are just as stubborn, and you still think you can linger in your tent when you are summoned. Let us hope running fifty times around the camp will temper your stubbornness, clear your minds, and remind you of how to answer a summons or do a chore. Off with you."

Without a word, Aviendha immediately began loping toward the edge of the camp, easily dodging dark-shrouded tent ropes. Egwene hesitated only a moment before following. The Aiel woman kept her pace down so she could catch up. The night air froze her, and the cracked stony clay underfoot was just as cold, and tried to catch her toes besides. Aviendha ran with effortless ease.

As they reached the last tent and turned southward, Aviendha said, "Do you know why I study so hard?" Neither the cold nor running had made an impression on her voice.

Egwene was shivering so hard she could barely speak. "No. Why?"

"Because Bair and the others always point to you, and tell me how easily you learn, how you never have to have something explained twice. They say I ought to be more like you." She gave Egwene a sidelong glance, and Egwene found herself sharing a giggle as they ran. "That is part of the reason. The things I am learning to do . . ." Aviendha shook her head, wonderment plain even by moonlight. "And the Power itself. I have never felt like that. So alive. I can smell the faintest scent, feel the slightest stir in the air."

"It is dangerous to hold on too long or too much," Egwene said. Running did seem to warm her a little, though now and again a shudder ran through her. "I've told you that, and I know the Wise Ones have, too."

Aviendha merely sniffed. "Do you think I would stab my own foot with a spear?"

For a time they ran in silence.

"Did Rand really . . . ?" Egwene said finally. The cold had nothing to do with her difficulty getting the words out; in fact, she was beginning to sweat again. "I mean . . . Isendre?" She could not make herself say it clearer than that.

At last Aviendha said slowly, "I do not think that he did." She sounded angry. "But why would she ignore switchings if he has shown no interest in her? She is a milk-hearted wetlander who waits for men to come to her. I saw how he looked at her, though he tried to hide it. He enjoyed looking at her."

Egwene wondered if her friend ever thought of her as a milk-hearted wetlander. Probably not, or they would not be friends. But Aviendha had never learned to worry if what she said might hurt someone; she would probably be surprised to learn that Egwene could even think of being hurt.

"The way the Maidens make her dress," Egwene admitted reluctantly, "any man would look." Reminded that she herself was in the open without any clothes, she stumbled and almost fell as she looked around anxiously. The night was empty as far as she could make out. Even the Wise Ones were already back in their tents. Warm in their blankets. She was sweating, but the beads seemed to want to freeze as soon as they appeared.

"He belongs to Elayne," Aviendha said fiercely.

"I admit I don't know your customs fully, but ours are not the same as yours. He is not betrothed to Elayne." *Why am I defending him? He's the one who ought to be switched!* But honesty made her go on. "Even your Aiel men have the right to say no, if they're asked."

"You and she are near-sisters, as you and I are," Aviendha protested, slowing a step before picking it up again. "Did you not ask me to look after him for her? Do you not want her to have him?"

"Of course I do. If he wants her." That was not exactly true. She wanted Elayne to have what happiness she could, in love with the Dragon Reborn as she was, and she would do everything short of tying Rand hand and foot to see that Elayne got what she wanted. Maybe not far short, at that, if need be. Admitting it was another thing. Aiel women were far more forward than she could ever make herself be. "It would not be right, otherwise."

"He belongs to her," Aviendha said determinedly.

Egwene sighed. Aviendha simply did not want to understand any customs but her own. The Aiel woman was still shocked that Elayne would not ask Rand to marry her, that a man could ask that question. "I'm sure the Wise Ones will listen to reason tomorrow. They can't make you sleep in a man's bedchamber."

The other woman looked at her in clear surprise. For a moment her grace left her, and she stubbed a toe on the uneven ground; the mishap brought a few curses that would have made even Kadere's wagon drivers listen with interest—and made Bair reach for the bluespine—

but she did not stop running. "I do not understand why that upsets you so," she said when the last curse died. "I have slept next to a man many times on raids, even sharing blankets for warmth if the night was very cold, but it disturbs you that I will sleep within ten feet of him. Is this part of your customs? I have noticed you will not bathe in the sweat tent with men. Do you not trust Rand al'Thor? Or is it me you do not trust?" Her voice had sunk to a concerned whisper by the end.

"Of course I trust you," Egwene protested heatedly. "And him. It's just that . . ." She trailed off, uncertain how to go on. Aiel notions of propriety were sometimes stricter than what she had grown up with, but in other ways they would have had the Women's Circle back home trying to decide whether to faint or reach for a stout stick. "Aviendha, if your honor is involved somehow . . ." This was touchy ground. "Surely if you explain to the Wise Ones, they will not make you go against your honor."

"There is nothing to explain," the other woman said flatly.

"I know I don't understand *ji'e'toh* . . ." Egwene began, and Aviendha laughed.

"You say you do not understand, Aes Sedai, yet you show that you live by it." Egwene regretted maintaining that lie with her—it had been hard work to get Aviendha to call her simply Egwene, and sometimes she slipped back—but it had to be kept with everyone if it was to hold with anyone. "You are Aes Sedai, and strong enough in the Power to overcome Amys and Melaine together," Aviendha continued, "but you said that you would obey, so you scrub pots when they say scrub pots, and you run when they say run. You may not know *ji'e'toh,* but you follow it."

It was not the same thing at all, of course. She gritted her teeth and did as she was told because that was the only way to learn dreamwalking, and she wanted to learn, to learn everything, more than anything else she could imagine. To even think that she could live by this foolish *ji'e'toh* was simply silly. She did what she had to do, and only when and because she had to.

They were coming back to where they had begun. As her foot hit the spot, Egwene said, "That's one," and ran on through the darkness with no one to see but Aviendha, no one to say whether she went back to her tent right then. Aviendha would not have told, but it never occurred to Egwene to stop short of the fifty.

CHAPTER

6

Gateways

Rand woke in total darkness and lay there beneath his blankets trying to think of what had wakened him. It had been something. Not the dream; he had been teaching Aviendha how to swim, in a pond in the Waterwood back home in the Two Rivers. Something else. Then it came again, like a faint whiff of a foul miasma creeping under the door. Not a smell at all, really; a sense of otherness, but that was how it felt. Rank, like something dead a week in stagnant water. It faded again, but not all the way this time.

Tossing aside his blankets, he stood up, wrapping himself in *saidin*. Inside the Void, filled with the Power, he could feel his body shiver, but the cold seemed in another place from where he was. Cautiously he pulled open the door and stepped out. Arched windows at either end of the corridor let in falls of moonlight. After the pitch black of his room, it was nearly like day. Nothing moved, but he could feel . . . something . . . coming closer. Something evil. It felt like the taint that roared through him on the Power.

One hand went to his coat pocket, to the small carved figure of a round little man holding a sword across his knees. An *angreal*; with that he could channel more of the Power than even he could safely handle unaided. He thought it would not be necessary. Whoever had sent this attack against him did not know who they were dealing with, now. They should never have let him wake.

For a moment, he hesitated. He could take the fight to whatever had been sent against him, but he thought it was still below him. Down where the Maidens were still sleeping, by the silence. With luck, it would not bother them, unless he rushed down to battle it in their midst. That would surely wake them, and they would not stand by and watch. Lan said that you should choose your ground, if you could, and make your enemy come to you.

Smiling, he raced the thud of his boots up the nearest curving stairway, on upward, until he reached the top floor. The highest level of the building was one large chamber with a slightly domed ceiling and scattered thin columns fluted in spirals. Glassless arched windows all around flooded every corner with moonlight. The dust and grit and sand on the floor still faintly showed his own footprints, from the one time he had come up here, and no other mark. It was perfect.

Striding to the center of the room, he planted himself atop the mosaic there, the ancient symbol of the Aes Sedai, ten feet across. It was an apt place. "Under this sign will he conquer." That was what the Prophecy of Rhuidean said of him. He stood straddling the sinuous dividing line, one boot on the black teardrop that was now called the Dragon's Fang and used to represent evil, the other on the white now called the Flame of Tar Valon. Some men said it stood for the Light. An appropriate place to meet this attack, between Light and darkness.

The fetid feel grew stronger, and a burned sulphur smell filled the air. Suddenly things moved, slinking away from the stairs like moonshadows, along the outside of the room. Slowly they resolved into three black dogs, darker than night and big as ponies. Eyes shining silver, they circled him warily. With the Power in him, he could hear their hearts beat, like deep drums pounding. He could not hear them breathe, though; perhaps they did not.

He channeled, and a sword was in his hands, its slightly curving, heron-marked blade seeming hammered out of fire. He had expected Myrddraal, or something even worse than the Eyeless, but for dogs, even Shadowspawn dogs, the sword would be enough. Whoever had sent them did not know him. Lan said he had very nearly reached the level of a blademaster, now, and the Warder was sparing enough with praise to make him think he might have passed onto that level already.

With snarls like bones being ground to dust, the dogs hurtled at him from three sides, faster than galloping horses.

He did not move until they were almost on him; then he flowed, one with the sword, move to move, as though dancing. In the blink of an eye the sword form called Whirlwind on the Mountain became The Wind Blows Over the Wall became Unfolding the Fan. Great black heads flew apart from black bodies, their dripping teeth, like burnished steel, still bared as they bounced across the floor. He was already stepping from the mosaic as the dark forms collapsed in twitching, bleeding heaps.

Laughing to himself, he let the sword go, though he held on to *saidin,* to the raging Power, the sweetness and the taint. Contempt slid along the outside of the Void. Dogs. Shadowspawn, certainly, but still just . . . Laughter died.

Slowly, the dead dogs and their heads were melting, settling into pools of liquid shadow that quivered slightly, as if alive. Their blood, fanned across the floor, trembled. Suddenly the smaller pools flowed across the floor in viscous streams to merge with the larger, which oozed away from the mosaic to mound higher and higher, until the three huge black dogs stood there once more, slavering and snarling as they gathered massive haunches under them.

He did not know why he felt surprise, dim outside the emptiness. Dogs, yes, but Shadowspawn. Whoever had sent them had not been as careless as he had thought. But they still did not know him.

Instead of reaching for the sword again, he channeled as he remembered doing once long ago. Howling, the huge dogs leaped, and a thick shaft of white light shot from his hands, like molten steel, like liquid fire. He swept it across the springing creatures; for an instant they became strange shadows of themselves, all colors reversed, and then they were made of sparkling motes that broke apart, smaller and smaller, until there was nothing.

He let go of the thing he had made, with a grim smile. A purple bar of light still seemed to cross his vision in afterimage.

Across the great chamber a piece of one of the columns crashed to the floor tiles. Where that bar of light—or whatever it had been; not light, exactly—had swung, neat slices were gone from the columns. A gaping swath cut half the width of the wall behind them.

"Did any of them bite you, or bleed on you?"

He spun at the sound of Moiraine's voice; absorbed in what he had done, he had not heard her come up the stairs. She stood clutching her skirts with both hands, peering at him, face lost in moonshadow. She would have sensed the things the same way he did, but to be here so quickly she must have run. "The Maidens let you pass? Have you become *Far Dareis Mai*, Moiraine?"

"They grant me some privileges of a Wise One," she said in a rush, impatience raw in her usually melodious voice. "I told the guards I had to speak with you urgently. Now, answer me! Did the Darkhounds bite you, or bleed on you? Did their saliva touch you?"

"No," he answered slowly. Darkhounds. The little he knew he had gotten from old stories, the sort used to frighten children in the southlands. Some grown-ups believed, too. "Why should a bite worry you? You could Heal it. Does this mean the Dark One is free?" Enclosed in the Void as he was, even fear was distant.

The tales he had heard said the Darkhounds ran the night in the Wild Hunt, with the Dark One himself the hunter; they left no print on even the softest dirt, only on stone, and they would not stop until you faced and defeated them or put running water between you. Crossroads were supposed to be particularly dangerous places to meet them, and the time just after sunset or just before sunrise. He had seen enough old stories walking by now to believe that any of it could be true.

"No, not that, Rand." She seemed to be regaining her self-control; her voice was silver chimes again, calm and cool. "They are only another kind of Shadowspawn, something that should never have been made. But their bite is death as surely as a dagger in the heart, and I do not think I could have Healed such a wound before it killed you. Their blood, even their saliva, is poison. A drop on the skin can kill, slowly, with great pain at the end. You are lucky there were only three. Unless you killed more before I arrived? Their packs are usually larger, as many as ten or twelve, or so say the scraps left from the War of the Shadow."

Larger packs. He was not the only target in Rhuidean for one of the Forsaken. . . .

"We must speak of what you used to kill them," Moiraine began, but he was already running as hard as he could, ignoring her cries to know where he was going and why.

Down flights of stairs, through darkened corridors where sleepy Maidens, roused by the pounding boots, peered at him in consternation from moonlit rooms. Through the front doors, where Lan stood restlessly with the two women on guard, his color-shifting Warder's cloak about his shoulders, making parts of him seem to blend into the night.

"Where is Moiraine?" he shouted as Rand dashed by, but Rand leaped down the broad steps two at a time without replying.

The half-healed wound in his side clenched like a fist, pain he was only vaguely aware of inside the Void, by the time he reached the building he sought. It stood at the very edge of Rhuidean, far from the plaza, as far from the camp Moiraine shared with the Wise Ones as it was possible to be and remain in the city. The upper floors had collapsed in a mound of rubble that fanned out onto the cracked earth beyond the pavement. Only the bottom two floors remained whole. Refusing his body's efforts to hunch over around the pain, he went in, still at a dead run.

Once the great antechamber, encircled by a stone balcony, had been tall; now it was taller, open to the night sky, its pale stone floor strewn with rubble from the collapse. In the moonshadows beneath the balcony, three Darkhounds were up on their hind legs, clawing and chewing at a bronze-clad door that shivered under their assault. The smell of burned sulphur hung strong in the air.

Remembering what had happened before, Rand darted to one side as he channeled, the shaft of liquid white fire streaking by the door as it destroyed the Shadowspawn. He had tried to make it less this time, to confine the destruction to the Darkhounds, but the thick wall at the far end of the chamber had a shadowed hole in it. Not all the way through, he thought—it was hard to tell by moonlight—but he would have to fine his control of this weapon.

The bronze sheathing on the door was tattered and torn as though the teeth and toenails of the Darkhounds really had been steel; lamplight shone through a number of small holes. There were pawprints in the floorstones, but surprisingly few. Releasing *saidin,* he found a place where he would not cut his hand to shreds and pounded on the door. Suddenly the pain in his side was very real and present; he took a deep breath and tried to thrust it away. "Mat? It's me, Rand! Open up, Mat!"

After a moment, the door opened a crack, letting out a spill of lamplight; Mat peered through doubtfully, then pulled the door wider, leaning against it as if he had run ten miles carrying a sack of rocks. Except for a silver foxhead medallion hanging around his neck, its eye shaped and shaded like the ancient Aes Sedai symbol, he was naked. The way Mat felt about Aes Sedai, Rand was surprised he had not sold the thing long since. Deeper in the room, a tall, golden-haired woman was calmly wrapping a blanket around herself. A Maiden, by the spears and buckler lying at her feet.

Rand hastily averted his eyes and cleared his throat. "I just wanted to make sure you were all right."

"We're fine." Uneasily, Mat looked around the antechamber. "Now we are. You killed it, or something? I don't want to know what it was, as long as it's gone. It's bloody hard on a man sometimes, being your friend."

Not only a friend. Another *ta'veren,* and perhaps a key to victory in Tarmon Gai'don; anyone who wanted to strike at Rand had reason to strike at Mat, as well. But Mat always tried to deny both things. "They're gone, Mat. Darkhounds. Three of them."

"I told you I didn't want to know," Mat groaned. "Darkhounds now. I can't say it isn't always something new around you. A man wouldn't get bored; not until the day he died. If I hadn't been on my feet for a drink of wine when the door started to open . . ." He trailed off, shivering, and scratched a red place on his right arm as he studied the ravaged metal sheathing. "You know, it's funny how the mind plays tricks. When I was putting everything I had into holding this door shut, I could have sworn one of them had chewed a hole right through it. I could see its bloody head. And its teeth. Melindhra's spear didn't even faze it."

Moiraine's arrival was more spectacular this time, running in, skirts held up, panting and fuming. Lan was at her heels with his sword in hand and thunderclouds on his stone face, and right behind, a throng of *Far Dareis Mai* that spilled out into the street. Some of the Maidens wore no more than smallclothes, but every one held her spears alertly and had her *shoufa* wrapped around her head, black veil hiding all but her eyes, ready to kill. Moiraine and Lan, at least, looked relieved to see him standing there calmly talking to Mat, though the Aes Sedai also looked as if she meant to have strong words with him. With the veils, it was impossible to tell what the Aiel thought.

Letting out a loud yelp, Mat darted back into his room and began hastily tugging on a pair of breeches, his capering impeded by the way he kept trying to haul at the breeches and scratch his arm at the same time. The golden-haired Maiden watched with a broad grin that threatened to break into laughter.

"What's the matter with your arm?" Rand asked.

"I told you the mind plays funny tricks," Mat said, still trying to scratch and pull at the same time. "When I thought that thing chewed through the door, I thought it slobbered all over my arm, too, and now it bloody itches like fire. Even looks like a burn there."

Rand opened his mouth, but Moiraine was already pushing past him. Staring at her, Mat fell down while frantically dragging his breeches on the rest of the way, but she knelt beside him, ignoring his protests, clasping his head in her hands. Rand had been Healed before, and seen it done, but instead of what he expected, Mat only gave a shiver and lifted up the medallion by its leather thong so that it hung against his hand.

"Bloody thing is colder than ice all of a sudden," he muttered. "What are you doing, Moiraine? If you want to do something, Heal this itch; it has my whole arm now." His right arm was red from wrist to shoulder, and had begun to look puffy.

Moiraine stared at him with the most startled expression Rand had ever seen on her face. Maybe the only one. "I will," she said slowly. "If the medallion is cold, take it off."

Mat frowned at her, then finally pulled it over his head and laid it beside him. She took his head again, and he gave a shout as if he had been ducked headfirst into ice; his legs stiffened and his back arched; his eyes stared at nothing, as wide as they would go. When Moiraine took her hands away, he slumped, gulping air. The redness and swelling were gone. It took three tries before he could speak. "Blood and ashes! Does it have to be that flaming way every flaming time? It was just a bloody itch!"

"You watch your tongue with me," Moiraine told him, getting up, "or I will find Nynaeve and put her in charge of you." But her heart was not in it; she could have been talking in her sleep. She was trying not to stare at the foxhead as Mat hung it back around his neck. "You will need rest," she said absently. "Stay in bed tomorrow, if you feel like it."

The Maiden in the blanket—Melindhra?—knelt behind Mat and put her hands on his shoulders, looking up at Moiraine over his head. "I will see that he does as you say, Aes Sedai." With a sudden grin, she ruffled his hair.

"He is my little mischief maker, now." From the horrified look on Mat's face, he was gathering his strength to run.

Rand became aware of soft, amused chuckles behind him. The Maidens, *shoufas* and veils around their shoulders now, had crowded around and were peering into the room.

"Teach him to sing, spear-sister," Adelin said, and the other Maidens crowed with laughter.

Rand rounded on them firmly. "Let the man rest. Don't some of you have to put on clothes?" They gave way reluctantly, still trying to peer into the room, until Moiraine came out.

"Will you leave us, please?" the Aes Sedai said as the mangled door banged shut behind her. She half looked back with a vexed tightening of her mouth. "I must speak with Rand al'Thor alone." Nodding, the Aiel women started for the door, some still jesting about whether Melindhra—a Shaido, it seemed; Rand wondered if Mat knew that—would teach Mat to sing. Whatever that meant.

Rand stopped Adelin with a hand on her bare arm; others who noticed stopped as well, so he spoke to them all. "If you will not go when I tell you to, what will you do if I have to use you in battle?" He did not intend to if he could help it; he knew they were fierce warriors, but he had been raised to believe it was a man's place to die if necessary before a woman had to. Logic might say it was foolish, especially with women like this, but that was how he felt. He knew better than to tell them that, however. "Will you think it a joke, or decide to go in your own good time?"

They looked at him with the consternation of those listening to someone who had revealed his ignorance of the simplest facts. "In the dance of spears," Adelin told him, "we will go as you direct, but this is not the dance. Besides, you did not tell us to go."

"Even the *Car'a'carn* is not a wetlander king," a gray-haired Maiden added. Sinewy and hard despite her age, she wore only a short shift and her *shoufa*. He was getting tired of that phrase.

The Maidens resumed their joking as they left him alone with Moiraine and Lan. The Warder had finally put up his sword, and looked as at ease as he ever did. Which was to say as still and calm as his face, all stony planes and angles in the moonlight, and with an air of being on the brink of sudden movement that made the Aiel appear placid in comparison. A braided leather cord held Lan's hair, graying at the temples, back from his face. His gaze could have come from a blue-eyed hawk.

"I must speak with you about—" Moiraine began.

"We can talk tomorrow," Rand said, cutting her off. Lan's face hardened further, if such was possible; Warders were far more protective of their Aes Sedai, of their position as well as their persons, than they were of themselves. Rand ignored Lan. His side still wanted to hunch him over, but he managed to keep erect; he was not about to show her any weakness. "If you think I'll help you get that foxhead away from Mat, you can think again." Somehow that medallion had stopped her channeling. Or at least it had stopped her channeling from affecting Mat while he touched it. "He paid a hard price for it, Moiraine, and it is his." Thinking of how she had thumped his shoulders with the Power, he added dryly, "Maybe I'll ask if I can borrow it from him." He turned away from her. There was still one he had to check on, though one way or another the urgency was gone; the Darkhounds would have done what they intended by now.

"Please, Rand," Moiraine said, and the open pleading in her voice halted him in his tracks. He had never heard anything like that from her before.

The tone seemed to offend Lan. "I thought you had become a man," the Warder said harshly. "Is this how a man behaves? You act like an arrogant boy." Lan practiced the sword with him—and liked him, Rand thought—but if Moiraine said the right word, the Warder would do his best to kill him.

"I will not be with you forever," Moiraine said urgently. Her hands gripped her skirts so hard that they trembled. "I might die in the next attack. I could fall from my horse and break my neck, or take a Darkfriend's arrow through my heart, and death cannot be Healed. I have given my entire life to the search for you, to find you and help you. You still do not know your own strength; you cannot know half of what you do. I—apologize— most humbly for any offense I have given you." Those words—words he had never thought to hear from her— came out as if dragged, but they came; and she could not lie. "Let me help you as much as I can, while I can. Please."

"It's hard to trust you, Moiraine." He disregarded Lan, shifting in the moonlight; his attention was all on her. "You have handled me like a puppet, made me dance the way you wanted, from the day we met. The only times I've been free of you were either when you were far away or when I ignored you. And you make even that hard."

Her laugh was as silvery as the moon above, but bitterness tinged it. "It has been more like wrestling with a bear than pulling strings on a puppet. Do you want an oath not to try manipulating you? I give it." Her voice hardened to crystal. "I even swear to obey you like one of the Maidens—like one of the *gai'shain,* if you require— but you must—" Taking a deep breath, she began again, more softly. "I *ask* you, humbly, to allow me to help you."

Lan was staring at her, and Rand thought his own eyes must be popping out of his head. "I will accept your help," he said slowly. "And I apologize, too. For all the rudeness I've shown." He had the feeling he was still being manipulated—he had had good cause to be rude, when he was—but she could not lie.

Tension drained from her visibly. She stepped closer to look up at him. "What you used to kill the Darkhounds is called balefire. I can still sense the residue of it here." He could, too, like the fading smell remaining after a pie was carried out of the room, or the memory of something just snatched out of sight. "Since before the Breaking of the World, the use of balefire has been forbidden. The White Tower forbids us even to learn it. In the War of Power, the Forsaken and the Shadowsworn themselves used it only reluctantly."

"Forbidden?" Rand said, frowning. "I saw you use it once." He could not be sure in the pale light of the moon, but he thought color flamed in her cheeks. For this once, perhaps she was the one off balance.

"Sometimes it is necessary to do that which is forbidden." If she was flustered, it did not show in her voice. "When anything is destroyed with balefire, it ceases to exist *before* the moment of its destruction, like a thread that burns away from where the flame touched it. The greater the power of the balefire, the further back in time it ceases to exist. The strongest I can manage will remove only a few seconds from the Pattern. You are much stronger. Very much so."

"But if it doesn't exist *before* you destroy it . . ." Rand raked fingers through his hair in confusion.

"You begin to see the problems, the dangers? Mat remembers seeing one of the Darkhounds chew through the door, but there is no opening, now. If it had slavered on him as much as he remembers, he would have been dead before I could reach him. For as far back as you destroyed the creature, whatever it did during that time *no longer happened.* Only the memories remain, for those who saw or experienced it. Only what it did before is real, now. A few tooth holes in the door, and one drop of saliva on Mat's arm."

"That sounds just fine to me," he told her. "Mat's alive because of it."

"It is terrible, Rand." An urgent note entered her voice. "Why do you think even the Forsaken feared to use it? Think of the effect on the Pattern of a single thread, one man, removed from hours, or days, that have already been woven, like one thread picked partly out of a piece of cloth. Fragments of manuscripts remaining from the War of Power say several entire cities were destroyed with balefire before both sides realized the dangers. Hundreds of thousands of threads pulled from the Pattern, gone for days already past; whatever those people had done, now no longer had been done, and neither had what others had done because of their actions. The memories remained, but not the actions. The ripples were incalculable. The Pattern itself nearly unraveled. It could have been the destruction of everything. World, time, Creation itself."

Rand shivered, nothing to do with the cold cutting through his coat. "I can't promise not to use it again, Moiraine. You yourself said there are times when it's necessary to do what's forbidden."

"I did not think that you would," she said coolly. Her agitation was vanishing, her balance restored. "But you must be careful." She was back to "must" again. "With a sa'angreal like Callandor, you could annihilate a city with balefire. The Pattern could be disrupted for years to come. Who can say that the weave would even remain centered on you, ta'veren as you are, until it settled down? Being ta'veren, and so strongly so, may be your margin of victory, even in the Last Battle."

"Perhaps it will," he said bleakly. In tale after heroic tale, the protagonist proclaimed he would have victory or death. It seemed that the best he could hope for was victory and death. "I have to check on someone," he went on quietly. "I will see you in the morning." Gathering the Power into him, life and death in swirling layers, he made a hole in the air taller than he was, opening into blackness that made the moonlight seem day. A gateway, Asmodean called it.

"What is that?" Moiraine gasped.

"Once I've done something, I remember how. Most of the time." That was no answer, but it was time to test Moiraine's vows. She could not lie, but Aes Sedai could find loopholes in a stone. "You are to leave Mat alone tonight. And you won't try to take that medallion away from him."

"It belongs in the Tower for study, Rand. It must be a ter'angreal, but none has ever been found that—"

"Whatever it is," he said firmly, "it is his. You will leave it with him."

For a moment she seemed to struggle with herself, back stiffening and head coming up as she stared at him. She could not be used to taking orders from anyone except Siuan Sanche, and Rand was willing to wager she had never done that without a tussle. Finally she nodded, and even made the suggestion of a curtsy. "As you say,

Rand. It is his. Please be careful, Rand. Learning a thing like balefire by yourself can be suicide, and death cannot be Healed." This time there was no mockery. "Until the morning." Lan followed her as she left, the Warder giving Rand an unreadable expression; he would not be pleased by this turn of events.

Rand stepped through the gateway, and it vanished.

He was standing on a disc, a six-foot copy of the ancient Aes Sedai symbol. Even the black half of it seemed lighter against the endless darkness that surrounded him, above and below; he was sure that if he fell off, he would fall forever. Asmodean claimed there was a faster method, called Traveling, for using a gateway, but he had not been able to teach it, partly because he did not have the strength to make a gateway while wearing Lanfear's shield. In any case, Traveling required that you know your starting point very well. It seemed more logical to him that you should have to know where you were heading well, but Asmodean seemed to think that that was like asking why air was not water. There was a great deal that Asmodean took for granted. Anyway, Skimming was fast enough.

As soon as he planted his boots on it, the disc lurched what seemed to be a foot and stopped, another gateway appearing in front of it. Fast enough, especially over this short distance. Rand stepped into the hallway outside the room where Asmodean was.

The moon through the windows at the ends of the corridor gave the only light; Asmodean's lamp was out. The flows he had woven around the room were still in place, still firmly tied. Nothing moved, but there was still a faint smell of burned sulphur.

Moving close to the bead curtain, he peered through the doorway. Moonshadows filled the room, but one of them was Asmodean, tossing in his blankets. Wrapped in the Void, Rand could hear his heartbeat, smell the sweat of troubled dreams. He bent to examine the pale blue floor tiles, and the prints impressed in them.

He had learned to track as a boy, and reading them was no difficulty. Three or four Darkhounds had been there. They had approached the doorway one by one, it seemed, each stepping almost in the others' footprints. Had the net woven around the room stopped them there? Or had they merely been sent to look, and report? Troubling, to think of even Shadowspawn dogs having that much intelligence. But then, Myrddraal used ravens and rats for spies, too, and other animals closely linked to death. Shadoweyes, the Aiel called them.

Channeling fine flows of Earth, he smoothed out the floor tiles, lifting up the compressions until he was out in the empty, night-cloaked street and a hundred paces from the tall building. In the morning, anyone would be able to see the trail ending there, but none would suspect that the Darkhounds had gone anywhere near Asmodean. Darkhounds could have no interest in Jasin Natael the gleeman.

Every Maiden in the city was likely awake by this time; certainly none would still be asleep under the Roof of the Maidens. Making another gateway there in the street, a deeper blackness against the night, he let the disc carry him back to his own room. He wondered why he had chosen the ancient symbol—it was his choice, if unconscious; other times it had been a stairstep or a piece of floor. The Darkhounds had oozed away from that sign before re-forming. *Under this sign will he conquer.*

Standing in his pitch-black bedchamber, he channeled the lamps alight, but he did not let go of *saidin.* Instead he channeled again, careful not to spring any of his own traps, and a piece of the wall vanished, revealing a niche he had carved there himself.

In the little alcove stood two figurines a foot tall, a man and a woman, each in flowing robes and serene of face, each holding a crystal globe aloft in one hand. He had lied to Asmodean about them.

There were *angreal,* like the round little man in Rand's coat pocket, and *sa'angreal,* like *Callandor,* that increased the amount of the Power that could be safely handled as much over *angreal* as *angreal* did over channeling unaided. Both were very rare, and prized by Aes Sedai, though they could only recognize those attuned to women and *saidar.* These two figures were something else, not so rare, but just as highly valued.

Ter'angreal had been made to use the Power not magnify it, but to use it in specific ways. The Aes Sedai did not know the intended purpose even of most *ter'angreal* they had in the White Tower; some they used, but without knowing whether the use they put them to was anything like the function they had been made for. Rand knew the function of these two.

The male figure could link him to a huge replica of itself, the most powerful male *sa'angreal* ever made, even if he were on the other side of the Aryth Ocean from it. It had only been finished after the Dark One's prison was resealed—*How do I know that?*—and hidden before any of the male Aes Sedai going mad could find it. The female figure could do the same for a woman, joining her to the female equivalent of the great statue he hoped was still almost completely buried in Cairhien. With that much power . . . Moiraine had said death could not be Healed.

Unbidden, unwanted, memory returned of the next-to-last time he had dared let himself hold *Callandor*, images floating beyond the Void.

The body of the dark-haired girl, little more than a child, lay sprawled with eyes wide and fixed on the ceiling, blood blackening the bosom of her dress where a Trolloc had run her through.

The Power was in him. Callandor *blazed, and he was the Power. He channeled, directing flows into the child's body, searching, trying, fumbling; she lurched to her feet, arms and legs unnaturally rigid and jerky.*

"Rand, you cannot do this," Moiraine cried. "Not this!"

Breathe. She had to breathe. The girl's chest rose and fell. Heart. Had to beat. Blood already thick and dark oozed from the wound in her chest. Live, burn you! his mind howled. I didn't mean to be too late! Her eyes stared at him, filmed, heedless of all the Power in him. Lifeless. Tears trickled unheeded down his cheeks.

He forced the memory away roughly; even encased in the Void, it hurt. With this much Power . . . With this much Power, he could not be trusted. "You are not the Creator," Moiraine had told him as he stood over that child. But with that male figure, with only half of its power, he had made the mountains move, once. With far less, with only *Callandor,* he had been sure he could turn back the Wheel, make a dead child live. Not only the One Power was seductive; the power of it was, too. He should destroy them both. Instead he rewove the flows, reset the traps.

"What are you doing there?" a woman's voice said as the wall became apparently whole again.

Tying off the flows hastily—and the knot with its own deadly surprises—he pulled the Power into him and turned.

Beside Lanfear, in her white and silver, Elayne or Min or Aviendha would look almost ordinary. Her dark eyes alone were enough to make a man give up his soul. At the sight of her, his stomach clenched until he wanted to vomit.

"What do you want?" he demanded. Once he had blocked Egwene and Elayne both from the True Source, but he could not remember how. So long as Lanfear could touch the Source, he had more chance of catching the wind in his hands than of holding her prisoner. *One flash of balefire, and . . .* He could not do it. She was one of the Forsaken, but the memory of a woman's head rolling on the ground stopped him dead.

"You have two of them," she said finally. "I thought I glimpsed . . . One is a woman, isn't it?" Her smile could have halted a man's heart and made him grateful. "You are beginning to consider my plan, aren't you? With those, together, the other Chosen will kneel at our feet. We can supplant the Great Lord himself, challenge the Creator. We—"

"You were always ambitous, Mierin." His voice grated in his ears. "Why do you think I turned away from you? It wasn't Ilyena, whatever you like to think. You were out of my heart long before ever I met her. Ambition is all there is to you. Power is all you ever wanted. You disgust me!"

She stared at him, both hands pressed hard against her stomach, her dark eyes even larger than usual. "Graendal said . . ." she began faintly. Swallowing, she began again. "Lews Therin? I love you, Lews Therin. I have always loved you, and I always will. You know that. You must!"

Rand's face was like rock; he hoped it hid his shock. He had no idea where his words had come from, but it seemed he could remember her. A dim memory, from before. *I am not Lews Therin Telamon!* "I am Rand al'Thor!" he said harshly.

"Of course you are." Studying him, she nodded slowly to herself. That cool composure returned. "Of course. Asmodean has been telling you things, about the War of Power, and me. He lies. You did love me. Until that yellow-haired trollop Ilyena stole you." For an instant, rage made her face a contorted mask; he did not think she was even aware of it. "Did you know that Asmodean severed his own mother? What they call stilling, now. Severed her, and let Myrddraal drag her away screaming. Can you trust a man like that?"

Rand laughed aloud. "After I caught him, you helped trap him so he had to teach me. And now you say I cannot trust him?"

"For teaching." She sniffed dismissively. "He will do that because he knows his lot is cast with you for good. Even if he managed to convince the others that he has been a prisoner, they would still tear him apart, and he knows it. The weakest dog in the pack often suffers that fate. Besides, I watch his dreams on occasion. He dreams of you triumphing over the Great Lord and putting him up beside you on high. Sometimes he dreams of me." Her smile said those dreams were pleasant for her, but not so for Asmodean. "But he will try to turn you against me."

"Why are you here?" he demanded. Turn against her? No doubt she was full of the Power right that moment, ready to shield him if she even suspected he meant to try anything. She had done it before, with humiliating ease.

"I like you like this. Arrogant and proud, full of your own strength."

Once she had said that she liked him unsure, that Lews Therin had been too arrogant. "Why are you here?"

"Rahvin sent the Darkhounds after you tonight," she

said calmly, folding her hands at her waist. "I would have come sooner, to help you, but I cannot let the others know I am on your side yet."

On his side. One of the Forsaken loved him, or rather the man he had been three thousand years ago, and all she wanted was for him to give his soul to the Shadow and rule the world with her. Or a step below her, at least. That, and try to replace both the Dark One and the Creator. Was she completely mad? Or could the power of those two huge *sa'angreal* really be as great as she claimed? That was a direction he did not want his thoughts to take.

"Why would Rahvin choose now to attack me? Asmodean says he looks to his own interests, that he'll sit to one side even in the Last Battle, if he can, and wait for the Dark One to destroy me. Why not Sammael, or Demandred? Asmodean says they hate me." *Not me. They hate Lews Therin.* But to the Forsaken, that was the same thing. *Please, Light, I am Rand al'Thor.* He pushed away a sudden memory of this woman in his arms, both of them young and just learning what they could do with the Power. *I am Rand al'Thor!* "Why not Semirhage, or Moghedien, or Graen—?"

"But you *are* impinging on his interests now." She laughed. "Don't you know where he is? In Andor, in Caemlyn itself. He rules there in all but name. Morgase simpers and dances for him, her and half a dozen others." Her lip curled in disgust. "He has men scouring town and countryside to find new pretties for him."

For a moment shock held him. Elayne's mother in the hands of one of the Forsaken. Yet he dared not show concern. Lanfear had displayed her jealousy more than once; she was capable of hunting Elayne down and killing her, if she even thought he had feelings for her. *What* do *I feel for her?* Aside from that, one hard fact floated beyond the Void, cold and cruel in its truth. He would not run off to attack Rahvin even if what Lanfear said was true. *Forgive me, Elayne, but I can't.* She might well be lying—she would weep no tears for any of the other Forsaken he killed; they all stood in the way of her own plans—but in any event, he was done with reacting to what others did. If he reacted, they could reason out what he would do. Let them react to him, and be as surprised as Lanfear and Asmodean had been.

"Does Rahvin think I'll rush to defend Morgase?" he said. "I have seen her once in my life. The Two Rivers is part of Andor on a map, but I never saw a Queen's Guardsman there. No one has in generations. Tell a Two Rivers man Morgase is his queen, and he'll probably think you're crazy."

"I doubt Rahvin expects you to run to defend your homeland," Lanfear said wryly, "but he will expect you to defend your ambitions. He means to sit Morgase on the Sun Throne, too, and use her like a puppet until the time he can come into the open. More Andoran soldiers move into Cairhien every day. And you sent Tairen soldiers north, to secure your own hold on the land. No wonder that he attacked you as soon as he found you."

Rand shook his head. It had not been that way at all, sending the Tairens, but he did not expect her to understand. Or believe him if he told her, for that matter. "I thank you for the warning." Politeness to one of the Forsaken! Of course, there was nothing he could do except hope that some of what she told him was truth. *A good reason not to kill her. She'll tell you more than she thinks, if you listen carefully.* He hoped that was his own thought, chill and cynical as it was.

"You ward your dreams against me."

"Against everyone." That was simple truth, though she was at least as prominent in the list as the Wise Ones.

"Dreams are mine. You and your dreams are mine especially." Her face remained smooth, but her voice hardened. "I can break through your warding. You would not like it."

To show his unconcern, he sat down on the foot of his pallet, legs folded and hands on his knees. He thought his face was as calm as hers. Inside him, the Power swelled. He had flows of Air ready to bind her, and flows of Spirit. That was what wove a shield against the True Source. The racking of his brain for the how of it seemed far off, but he could not remember anyway. Without that, the other was useless. She could pick apart or slice through anything he wove, even if she could not see it. Asmodean was trying to teach him that trick, but it was hard going without a woman's weaving to practice on.

Lanfear eyed him in a disconcerted fashion, a slight frown marring her beauty. "I have examined the Aiel women's dreams. These so-called Wise Ones. They do not know how to shield themselves very well. I could frighten them till they never dream again, never even think of invading yours surely."

"I thought you would not help me openly." He did not dare tell her to leave the Wise Ones alone; she might well do something to spite him. She had made it plain from the start, if not in words, that she meant to have the upper hand between them. "Wouldn't that risk another of the Forsaken finding out? You aren't the only one who knows how to enter people's dreams."

"The Chosen," she said absently. For a moment she chewed a full underlip. "I have watched the girl's dreams, too. Egwene. Once I thought you had feelings for her. Do you know who she dreams of? Morgase's son and stepson. The son, Gawyn, most often." Smiling, she put on a tone of mock shock. "You would not believe a simple country girl could have such dreams."

She was trying to test his jealousy, he realized. She really thought he warded his dreams to hide thoughts of another woman! "The Maidens guard me closely," he said dryly. "If you want to know how close, look at Isendre's dreams."

Spots of color flared in her cheeks. Of course. He was not supposed to see what she was trying. Confusion rolled outside the Void. Or did she think . . . ? Isendre? Lanfear knew she was a Darkfriend. Lanfear had brought Kadere and the woman to the Waste in the first place. And planted most of the jewelry Isendre was accused of stealing; Lanfear's spite was cruel even when petty. Still, if she thought he could love her, Isendre being a Darkfriend was probably no obstacle in her eyes.

"I should have let them send her off to try reaching the Dragonwall," he went on casually, "but who knows what she might have said to save herself? I must protect her and Kadere to some extent in order to protect Asmodean."

The color faded, but as she opened her mouth again, a knock came at the door. Rand bounded to his feet. No one would recognize Lanfear, yet if a woman were discovered in his room, a woman whom none of the Maidens below had seen enter, questions would be asked and he had no answers.

But Lanfear already had a gateway open, to somewhere full of white silk hangings and silver. "Remember that I am your only hope of surviving, my love." It was a very cool voice in which to call someone that. "Beside me, you need fear nothing. Beside me, you can rule—everything that is or will be." Lifting her snowy skirts, she stepped through, and the gateway winked shut.

The knock sounded again before he could make himself push away *saidin* and haul open the door.

Enaila peered past him suspiciously, muttering, "I thought perhaps Isendre. . . ." She gave him an accusing look. "Spear-sisters are searching everywhere for you. No one saw you return." With a shake of her head, she straightened; she always tried to stand as tall as possible. "The chiefs have come to speak with the *Car'a'carn*," she said formally. "They wait below."

They waited on the columned portico, as it turned out, being men. The sky was still dark, but the first glimmers of dawn lined the mountains to the east. If they felt any impatience with the two Maidens who stood between them and the tall doors, it did not show on their shadowed faces.

"The Shaido are moving," Han barked as soon as Rand appeared. "And the Reyn, the Miagoma, the Shiande. . . . Every clan!"

"Joining Couladin, or me?" Rand demanded.

"The Shaido are moving toward the Jangai Pass," Rhuarc said. "For the others, it is too early to tell. But they are on the march with every spear not needed to defend the holds, herds and flocks."

Rand only nodded. All of his determination not to let anyone else dictate what he would do, and now this.

Whatever the other clans intended, Couladin had to plan a crossing into Cairhien. So much for his grand schemes of imposing peace, if the Shaido ravaged Cairhien even further while he sat in Rhuidean waiting for the other clans.

"Then we move for the Jangai, too," he said finally.

"We cannot catch him if he means to cross," Erim cautioned, and Han added sourly, "If any of the others are joining him, we will be caught strung out like blindworms in the sun."

"I won't sit here until I find out," Rand said. "If I can't catch Couladin, I mean to be right behind him into Cairhien. Rouse the spears. We leave as soon after first light as you can manage."

Giving him that odd Aiel bow used only on the most formal occasions, one foot forward and one hand extended, the chiefs departed. Only Han said anything. "To Shayol Ghul itself."

CHAPTER

7

A Departure

Yawning in the early-morning grayness, Egwene pulled herself up onto her fog-colored mare, then had to handle her reins smartly as Mist frisked about. The animal had not been ridden in weeks. Aiel not only preferred their own legs, they avoided riding almost completely, though they did use packhorses and pack mules. Even if there had been enough wood to build wagons, the terrain in the Waste was not hospitable to wheels, as more than one peddler had learned to his or her sorrow.

She was not looking forward to the long journey west. The mountains hid the sun now, but the heat would grow by the hour once it climbed clear, and there would be no convenient tent to duck into at nightfall. She was not certain that Aiel garb was suitable for riding, either. The shawl, worn over her head, always did a surprisingly good job of keeping the sun off, but those bulky skirts would bare her legs to the thigh if she was not careful. Blisters worried her as much as modesty. *The sun on one side, and . . .* A month out of the saddle should not have softened her that much. She hoped it had not, or this would be a *very* long journey.

Once she had settled Mist down, Egwene found Amys looking at her, and shared a smile with the Wise One. All of that running the night before was not the reason she was still sleepy; if anything, it had helped her sleep even more soundly. She *had* found the other woman's dreams last night, and in celebration they had sipped tea in the dream, in Cold Rocks Hold, early on an evening when children were playing among the crop-planted terraces and a pleasant breeze blew down the valley as the sun sank.

Of course, that would not have been enough to steal her rest, but she had been so exultant that when she left Amys' dreams, she did not stop; she could not, not then, no matter what Amys would have said. There had been dreams all around, though with most she had no idea whose they were. With most, not all. Melaine had been dreaming of suckling a babe at her breast, and Bair of one of her dead husbands, both of them young and yellow-haired. She had been especially careful not to enter those; the Wise Ones would have known an intruder in an instant, and she shuddered to think of what they would have done before letting her go.

Rand's dreams had been a challenge, of course, one she could not fail to face. Now that she could flit from dream to dream, how could she not try where the Wise Ones failed? Only, attempting to enter his dreams had been like running headlong into an invisible stone wall. She knew that his dreams lay on the other side, and she was sure she could find a way through, but there had been nothing to work on, nothing to pry at. A wall of nothing. It was a problem she meant to worry at until she solved it. Once she put her mind on something, she could be as persistent as a badger.

All around her *gai'shain* were bustling about, loading the Wise Ones' camp onto mules. Before long, only an Aiel or someone just as skilled at tracking would be able to tell there had ever been tents on that patch of hard clay. The same activity covered the surrounding mountain slopes, and the hubbub extended into the city, as well. Not everyone would be going, but thousands would. Aiel thronged the streets, and Master Kadere's train of wagons stood strung out across the great plaza, laden with Moiraine's selections, the three white-painted water wagons at the end of the line like huge barrels on wheels behind twenty-mule teams. Kadere's own wagon, at the head of the column, was a little white house on wheels, with steps at the back and a metal stovepipe sticking out of the flat roof. The thick, hawk-nosed merchant, all in ivory-colored silk today, swept off his incongruously battered hat as she rode past, his dark, tilted eyes not sharing in the wide smile he flashed at her.

She ignored him frostily. His dreams had been decidedly dark and unpleasant, where they were not lewd as well. *He ought to have his head dunked in a* cask *of bluespine tea,* she thought grimly.

Approaching the Roof of the Maidens, she threaded her way through scurrying *gai'shain* and patiently standing mules. To her surprise, one of those loading the Maidens' things wore a black robe, not white. A woman, by the size of her, and staggering under the weight of a cord-tied bundle on her back. Bending as she guided Mist past, to get a look inside the woman's cowl, Egwene saw Isendre's haggard face, sweat already rolling down her cheeks. She was glad the Maidens had stopped letting the woman go outside—or sending her out—more naked than not, but it did seem needlessly cruel to robe her in black. If she was sweating so hard already, she would nearly die once the day's heat took hold.

Still, *Far Dareis Mai* business was none of hers. Aviendha had told her so gently but firmly. Adelin and Enaila had been little short of rude about it, and a wiry, white-haired Maiden named Sulin had actually threatened to haul her back to the Wise Ones by her ear. Despite her efforts to persuade Aviendha to stop addressing her as "Aes Sedai," it had been irritating to find that after walking a fine line of uncertainty toward her, the rest of the Maidens had come down on the side of her being just another pupil of the Wise Ones. Why, they would not even let her past the door of the Roof unless she claimed to be on an errand.

The quickness with which she heeled Mist on through

the crowd had nothing to do with acceptance of *Far Dareis Mai* justice, or her uncomfortable awareness that some of the Maidens were eyeing her, no doubt ready to lecture if they thought she intended to interfere. It even had little to do with her dislike of Isendre. She did not want to think about her glimpse of the woman's dreams, just before Cowinde had come to rouse her. They had been nightmares of torture, of things being done to the woman that sent Egwene fleeing in horror, and with something dark and evil laughing as it watched her run. No wonder Isendre looked haggard. Egwene had started up out of her sleep so quickly that Cowinde had jumped back from laying a hand on her shoulder.

Rand was in the street in front of the Maidens' Roof, wearing a *shoufa* against the coming sun and a blue silk coat with enough gold embroidery to befit a palace, though it hung open halfway down the front. His belt had a new buckle, an elaborate thing shaped like a Dragon. He really was beginning to think a great deal of himself, that was clear. Standing beside Jeade'en, his dappled stallion, he was talking with the clan chiefs and some of the Aiel traders who would be staying in Rhuidean.

Jasin Natael, nearly at Rand's heels, with his harp on his back and holding the reins of a saddled mule bought from Master Kadere, was even more elaborately dressed, with silver embroidery nearly hiding his black coat, and spills of white lace at his neck and cuffs. Even his boots were worked in silver where they turned down at the knee. The gleeman's cloak with its patches did spoil the effect, but gleemen were odd folk.

The male traders wore the *cadin'sor,* and though their belt knives were smaller than those of warriors, Egwene knew they could all handle a spear if called to; they had something, if not all, of the deadly grace of their brothers who carried the spear. The women traders, in loose white *algode* blouses and full woolen skirts, head scarves and shawls, were more easily distinguishable. Except for Maidens and *gai'shain*—and Aviendha—Aiel women all wore multiple bracelets and necklaces of gold and ivory, silver and gemstones, some of Aiel make, some traded for, and some looted. Among Aiel traders, though, the women displayed twice as many, if not more.

She caught part of what Rand was telling the traders. ". . . give the Ogier stonemasons a free hand on some of what they build, at least. On as much as you can make yourselves. There's no point in just trying to remake the past."

So he was having them send to the *stedding* for Ogier to rebuild Rhuidean. That was good. Much of Tar Valon was Ogier work, and where they were left to their own devices their buildings were enough to take the breath away.

Mat was already up on his gelding, Pips, with his wide-brimmed hat pulled down and the butt of that odd spear resting on his stirrup. As usual, his high-collared green coat looked slept in. She had avoided his dreams. One of the Maidens, a very tall golden-haired woman, gave Mat a roguish grin that seemed to embarrass him. And well it should; she was much too old for him. Egwene sniffed. *I know very well what* he *was dreaming about, thank you very much!* She only reined in beside him to look around for Aviendha.

"He told her to be quiet, and she did," he said as she halted Mist. He nodded toward Moiraine and Lan, she in pale blue silk, gripping the reins of her white mare, and he in his Warder's cloak, holding his great black warhorse. Lan was watching Moiraine intently, expressionless as always, while she looked ready to burst with impatience as she glared at Rand. "She started telling him why this is the wrong thing to do—sounded to me like she was saying it for the hundredth time—and he said, 'I've decided, Moiraine. Stand over there and be quiet till I have time for you.' Like he expected her to do as she was told. And she did. Is that steam coming out of her ears?"

His chortle was so pleased, so amused at his own wit, that she nearly embraced *saidar* and taught him a lesson right there in front of everybody. Instead she sniffed again, loudly enough to let him know it was for him and his wit and his amusement. He gave her a wry, sidelong look, and chuckled again, which did nothing for her temper.

For a moment she stared at Moiraine, perplexed. The Aes Sedai had done as Rand told her? Without protest?

That was like one of the Wise Ones obeying, or the sun rising at midnight. She had heard about the attack, of course; rumors about giant dogs that left footprints on stone had been all over this morning. She could not see what that could have to do with this, but aside from the news of the Shaido it was the only new thing she knew of, and not enough to produce this reaction. *Nothing* could produce it, that she could think of. Doubtless Moiraine would tell her it was none of her concern, but one way or another she would worry it out. She did not like not understanding things.

Spotting Aviendha, standing on the bottom step of the Roof, she guided Mist around to the other side of the crowd near Rand. The Aiel woman was staring at him as hard as the Aes Sedai did, but with absolutely no expression. She kept turning the ivory bracelet on her wrist over and over, apparently without realizing it. Somehow or other that bracelet was part of the difficulty the woman was having with him. Egwene did not understand; Aviendha refused to talk about it, and she could not just ask someone else, not when it might embarrass her friend. Her own flame-carved ivory bracelet was a gift from Aviendha, to seal them as near-sisters; her return gift had been the silver necklace the other woman wore, which Master Kadere claimed was a Kandori pattern called snowflakes. She had had to ask Moiraine for enough money, but it had seemed appropriate for a woman who would never see snow. Or would not have if she was not leaving the Waste; small chance that she could return before winter. Whatever that bracelet meant, Egwene was confident she could puzzle it out eventually.

"Are you all right?" she asked. As she leaned out of her high-cantled saddle, her skirts shifted till her legs showed, but she was concerned enough with her friend to hardly notice.

She had to repeat the question before Aviendha gave a start and stared up at her. "All right? Of course I am."

"Let me speak to the Wise Ones, Aviendha. I'm sure I can convince them that they cannot just make you . . ."

She could not make herself say it, not out here where anyone in the crowd might hear.

"Does *that* still worry you?" Aviendha shifted her gray shawl and gave a small shake of her head. "Your customs are still very strange to me." Her eyes drifted back to Rand like iron filings drawn to a lodestone.

"You do not have to be afraid of him."

"I am not afraid of any man," the other woman snapped, eyes flashing blue-green fire. "I want no trouble between us, Egwene, but you should not say such things."

Egwene sighed. Friend or not, Aviendha was quite capable of trying to box her ears when offended enough. In any case, she was not sure she would have admitted it, either. Aviendha's dream had been too painful to watch for long. Naked but for that ivory bracelet, and that seeming to drag at her as if it weighed a hundred pounds, Aviendha had been running as hard as she could across a cracked clay flat. And behind her, Rand came, a giant twice the size of an Ogier on a huge Jeade'en, slowly but inexorably catching up.

But you could not simply tell a friend that she was lying. Egwene's face reddened slightly. Especially not when you would have to tell her how you knew. *She would box my ears, then. I won't do it again. Go rummaging about in people's dreams. Not in Aviendha's dreams, anyway.* It was not right to spy on a friend's dreams. Not that it was spying, exactly, but still . . .

The crowd around Rand was beginning to break up. He swung into his saddle easily, imitated promptly by Natael. One of the traders, a broad-faced, flame-haired woman wearing a small fortune in worked gold, cut gems and carved ivory, lingered, though. "*Car'a'carn,* do you mean to leave the Three-fold Land forever? You have spoken as if you will never return."

The others stopped at that and turned back. Silence spread on an expanding ripple of murmurs telling what had been asked.

For a moment Rand was silent as well, looking around at the faces turned to him. At last he said, "I hope to return, but who can say what will happen? The Wheel weaves as the Wheel wills." He hesitated, with every eye on him. "But I will leave you something to remember me by," he added, sticking a hand in his coat pocket.

Abruptly a fountain near the Roof burst to life, water gushing from the mouths of incongruous porpoises standing on their tails. Beyond that, a statue of a young man with a horn raised to the sky suddenly was putting up a spreading fan, and then two stone women farther on were casting sprays of water from their hands. In stunned stillness the Aiel watched as all the fountains of Rhuidean flowed once more.

"I should have done that long since." Rand's mutter was no doubt meant for himself, but in the hush Egwene could hear him quite clearly. The splash of hundreds of fountains was the only other sound. Natael shrugged as if he had expected no less.

It was at Rand that Egwene stared, not the fountains. A man who could channel. *Rand. He's still Rand, despite everything.* But each time she saw him do it was like learning that he could all over again. Growing up, she had been taught that only the Dark One was more to be feared than a man who could channel. *Maybe Aviendha's right to be afraid of him.*

But when she looked down at Aviendha, open wonder shone on her face; so much water delighted the Aiel woman as the finest silk dress might have Egwene, or a garden full of flowers.

"It is time to march," Rand announced, reining the dapple westward. "Anyone who isn't ready will have to catch up." Natael followed close behind on the mule. Why did Rand let such a bootlicker stay near him?

The clan chiefs immediately began passing orders, and the bustle increased tenfold. Maidens and Water Seekers darted ahead, and more *Far Dareis Mai* closed around Rand as a guard of honor, incidentally enclosing Natael. Aviendha strode beside Jeade'en, right at Rand's stirrup, easily matching the stallion stride for stride even in her bulky skirts.

Falling in beside Mat, behind Rand and his escort, Egwene frowned. Her friend wore that look of grim determination again, as if she had to put her arm into a viper den. *I have to do something to help her.* Egwene did not give up on a problem once she had her teeth into it.

Settling herself in her saddle, Moiraine patted Aldieb's arched neck with a gloved hand, but she did not immediately follow Rand. Hadnan Kadere was bringing his wagons up the street, driving the lead wagon himself. She should have made him tear that wagon down to carry cargo as she had the other like it; the man was frightened enough of her, of Aes Sedai, to have done it. The doorframe *ter'angreal* was lashed firmly in the wagon behind Kadere, canvas tied over it tightly so no one could fall through by accident again. A long line of Aiel—*Seia Doon,* Black Eyes—strode along on either side of the wagon train.

Kadere bowed to her from the driver's seat, but her gaze swept on down to the line of wagons, all the way to the great square surrounding the forest of slim glass columns, already sparkling in the morning light. She would have taken everything in the plaza if she could, rather than the small fraction that would fit into the wagons. Some were too large. Like the three dull gray metal rings, each more than two paces across, standing on edge and joined at the middle. A braided leather rope had been strung around that one, to warn all from entering without the Wise Ones' permission. Not that anyone was likely to, of course. Only the clan chiefs and the Wise Ones entered that square with any sense of ease; only the Wise Ones touched anything, and they with something approaching proper reticence.

For countless years the second test faced by an Aiel woman who wanted to be a Wise One had been to enter the array of glittering glass columns, seeing exactly what the men saw. More women survived it than men—Bair said it was because women were tougher, Amys that those too weak to survive were winnowed out before reaching that point—but it was not a certainty. Those who did survive were not marked. The Wise Ones claimed that only men needed visible signs; for a woman, to be alive was enough.

The first test, the first winnowing, before any training

even, was to step through one of those three rings. Which one did not matter, or perhaps the choice was a matter of fate. That step seemingly took her through her life again and again, her future spread out before her, all of the possible futures based on every decision she might make for the rest of her life. Death was possible in those, too; some women could not face the future any more than others could face the past. All possible futures were too many for a mind to retain, of course. They jumbled together and faded away for the most part, but a woman gained a sense of things that would happen in her life, that must happen, that might happen. Usually even that was hidden until the moment was on her. Not always, though. Moiraine had been through those rings.

A spoonful of hope and a cup of despair, she thought.

"I do not like seeing you like this," Lan said. From Mandarb's back and his own height, he looked down on her, disquiet creasing the corners of his eyes. For him that was near tears of frustration from another man.

Aiel streamed by on both sides of their horses, and *gai'shain* with pack animals. Moiraine was startled to realize that Kadere's water wagons had already gone by; she had not realized she had been staring at the plaza for so long.

"Like what?" she asked, turning her mare to join the throng. Rand and his escort were already out of the city.

"Worried," he said bluntly, no readable expression on that stone-carved face now. "Afraid. I've never seen you afraid, not when we had Trollocs and Myrddraal swarming over us, not even when you learned the Forsaken were loose and Sammael was sitting almost on top of us. Is the end coming?"

She gave a start, and immediately wished she had not. He was looking straight ahead over his stallion's ears, but the man never missed anything. Sometimes she thought he could see a leaf fall behind his back. "Do you mean Tarmon Gai'don? A redbird in Seleisin knows as well as I. The Light send, not so long as any of the seals remain unbroken." The pair she had were on one of Kadere's wagons, too, each packed by itself in a cask stuffed with wool. A different wagon than the redstone doorframe; she had made sure of that.

"What else could I mean?" he asked slowly, still not looking at her, and making her wish she had bitten her tongue. "You have become—impatient. I can remember when you could wait weeks for one tiny scrap of information, one word, without twitching a finger, but now—" He did look at her then, a blue-eyed gaze that would have intimidated most women. And most men as well. "The oath you gave to the boy, Moiraine. Whatever under the Light possessed you?"

"He has been drawing further and further away from me, Lan, and I must be close to him. He needs whatever guidance I can give, and I will do everything short of sharing his bed to see that he gets it." The rings had told her that that would be disaster. Not that she had ever considered it—the very idea still shocked her!—but in the rings it was something she would or could have considered in the future. It was a measure of her growing desperation, no doubt, and in the rings she had seen that it would bring ruination on everything. She wished she could remember how—there were keys to Rand al'Thor in anything she could learn about him—but only the simple fact of calamity remained in her mind.

"Perhaps it will help your humility grow, if he tells you to fetch his slippers and light his pipe."

She stared at him. Could that be a joke? If so, it was not amusing. She had never found that humility served very well in any situation. Siuan claimed that growing up in the Sun Palace in Cairhien had put arrogance deeply into Moiraine's bones, where she could not even see it—something she firmly denied—but for all that Siuan was a Tairen fisherman's daughter, she could match any queen stare for stare, and to her arrogance meant opposition to her own plans.

If Lan was attempting jokes, however feeble and wrongheaded, he was changing. For nearly twenty years he had followed her, and saved her life more times than she cared to count, often at great risk to his own. Always he had accounted his life a small thing, valuable only for her need of it; some said he wooed death the way a bridegroom wooed his bride. She had never held his heart, and never felt jealousy toward the women who seemed to throw themselves at his feet. He had long claimed that he had no heart. But he had found one this past year, found it when a woman tied it on a string to hang around her neck.

He denied her, of course. Not his love for Nynaeve al'Meara, once a Wisdom in the Two Rivers and now an Accepted of the White Tower, but that he could ever have her. He had two things, he said, a sword that would not break and a war that could not end; he would never gift a bride with those. That, at least, Moiraine had taken care of, though he would not know how until it was done. If he did, he would very probably try to change matters, stubborn fool man that he could be.

"This arid land seems to have withered your own humility, al'Lan Mandragoran. I shall have to find some water to make it grow again."

"My humility is honed to razor sharpness," he told her dryly. "You never let it grow too dull." Wetting a white scarf from his leather water bottle, he handed her the sodden cloth. She tied it around her temples without comment. The sun was beginning to rise above the mountains behind them, a searing ball of molten gold.

The thick column snaked up the barren side of Chaendaer, its tail still in Rhuidean when its head had crested the slope, then down onto rough, hilly flats dotted with rock spires and flat-topped buttes, some streaked with red or ocher through the gray or brown. The air was so clear that Moiraine could see for miles, even after they were down off Chaendaer. Great natural arches reared, and in every direction jagged mountains clawed at the sky. Dry gullies and hollows split a land sparsely dotted with low, thorny bushes and leafless spiny plants. The rare tree, gnarled and stunted, usually bore spines or thorns as well. The sun made it an oven. A hard land that had shaped a hard people. But Lan was not the only one changing, or being changed. She wished she could see what Rand would make of the Aiel in the end. There was a long journey ahead for everyone.

CHAPTER
8

Over the Border

Clinging to her perch at the rear of the jouncing wagon, Nynaeve used one hand for herself and one for her straw hat as she peered back at the furious dust storm dwindling behind them in the distance. The broad brim shaded her face in the morning heat, but the breeze generated by the wagon's rumbling speed was enough to snatch it from her head despite the dark red scarf tied under her chin. Low-hilled grassland with occasional thickets rolled by, the grass sere and thin in the late-summer heat; dust churned up by the wagon wheels obscured her vision somewhat, and made her cough besides. The white clouds in the sky lied. There had been no rain since before they left Tanchico, weeks earlier, and it had been some time since the wide road had borne the traffic of wagons that once kept it hard-packed.

No one appeared riding out of that seemingly solid wall of brown, which was just as well. She had lost her anger at brigands trying to stop them this close to escaping the madness of Tarabon, and unless she was angry, she could not sense the True Source, much less channel. Even angry, she had been surprised at being able to raise such a storm; once whipped up, full of her fury, it held a life of its own. Elayne had been startled at the size of it, too, though thankfully she had not let on to Thom or Juilin. But even if her strength was increasing —her teachers in the Tower had said that it would, and certainly none of them was strong enough to best one of the Forsaken as she had—even with that, she still had that limitation. Had any of the bandits appeared, Elayne would have had to deal with them alone, and she did not want that. Her earlier anger was gone, but she was making fine for another crop.

Awkwardly climbing up over the canvas lashed across the load of casks, she reached down to one of the water barrels fastened along the sides of the wagon together with the chests of their possessions and supplies. Immediately her hat was on the back of her head, held only by the scarf. Her fingers could just touch the lid of the barrel, unless she released the rope that she was gripping with her other hand, and the way the wagon was lurching along, that would probably send her off onto her nose.

Juilin Sandar guided the lanky brown gelding he was riding—Skulker was the improbable name he had put on the animal—close to the wagon, and reached over to hand her one of the leather water bottles slung about his saddle. She drank gratefully, though not gracefully. Hanging there like a bunch of grapes on a windblown vine, she spilled nearly as much water down the front of her good gray dress as she did down her throat.

It was a suitable dress for a merchant, high-necked, finely woven and well-cut, but still plain. The pin on her breast, a small circle of dark garnets in gold, was perhaps too much for a merchant, but it had been a gift from the panarch of Tarabon, along with other jewelry, much richer, hidden in a compartment beneath the wagon driver's seat. She wore it to remind herself that even women who sat on thrones sometimes needed to be taken by the scruff of the neck and shaken. She had a little more sympathy for the Tower's manipulations of kings and queens now that she had dealt with Amathera. She suspected that Amathera had meant her gifts as a bribe to make them depart Tanchico. The woman had been willing to buy a ship so that they would not remain an hour more than necessary, but no one had been willing to sell. The few vessels remaining in Tanchico Harbor that were suitable for more than coasting had been jammed with refugees. Besides, a ship was the obvious way, the fastest way, to leave, and the Black Ajah might well be watching for her and Elayne, after what had happened. They had been sent to hunt Aes Sedai who were Darkfriends, not to be ambushed by them. Thus the wagon and the long trek across a land torn by civil war and anarchy. She was beginning to wish she had not insisted on avoiding the ships. Not that she would ever admit it to the others.

When she tried to hand the water bottle back to Juilin, he waved it away. A tough man, seemingly carved from some dark wood, he was not very comfortable on the back of a horse. He looked ridiculous, to her; not because of his obvious ill ease in the saddle, but for the silly red Taraboner hat that he had taken to wearing on his flat, black hair, a brimless, conical thing, tall and flat-topped. It did not go well with his dark Tairen coat, tight to the waist, then flaring. She did not think it would go well with anything. In her opinion, he looked as if he were wearing a cake on his head.

It was clumsy scrambling the rest of the way forward with the leather bottle in one hand and her hat flapping, and she did it muttering imprecations for the Tairen thief-catcher—*Never thief-taker, not him!*—for Thom Merrilin—*Puffed-up gleeman!*—and for Elayne of House Trakand, Daughter-Heir of Andor, who ought to be shaken by the scruff of the neck herself!

She meant to slide onto the wooden driver's seat between Thom and Elayne, but the golden-haired girl was pressed tightly against Thom, her own straw hat hanging on her back. She was clutching the white-mustached old fool's arm as if afraid of falling off. Tight-mouthed, Nynaeve had to settle for Elayne's other side. She was glad she had her hair in one proper braid again, wrist-thick and hanging down to her waist; she could give it a tug instead of thumping Elayne's ear for her. The girl had used to seem reasonably sensible, but something seemed to have addled her wits in Tanchico.

"They aren't following us anymore," Nynaeve announced, pulling her hat back into place. "You can slow this thing down now, Thom." She could have shouted that from the back and not needed to clamber over the casks, but the image of herself bouncing about and calling for them to slow had stopped her. She did not like making a fool of herself, and liked even less others seeing her in a foolish light. "Put your hat on," she told Elayne. "That fair skin of yours will not appreciate this sun for long."

As she had half-expected, the girl ignored her friendly advice. "You drive so wonderfully," Elayne gushed as Thom drew back on the reins, pulling the four-horse team to a walk. "You were in control every minute."

The tall, wiry man glanced down at her, bushy white eyebrows twitching, but all he said was, "We have more company ahead, child." Well, maybe he was not such a fool.

Nynaeve looked, and saw the snowy-cloaked mounted column approaching them over the next low rise, perhaps half a hundred men in burnished mail and shining conical helmets, escorting as many heavily laden wagons. Children of the Light. She was suddenly very conscious of the leather thong hanging around her neck beneath her dress, and the two rings dangling between her breasts. Lan's heavy gold signet ring, the ring of the Kings of lost Malkier, would mean nothing to the Whitecloaks, but if they saw the Great Serpent ring . . .

Fool woman! They aren't likely to, unless you decide to undress!

Hastily she ran an eye over her companions. Elayne could not stop being beautiful, and now that she had let go of Thom and was retying the green scarf that held her hat, her manner looked more suited to a throne room than a merchant's wagon, but aside from being blue, her dress was no different from Nynaeve's. She wore no jewelry; she had called Amathera's gifts "gaudy." She would pass; she had done so fifty times since Tanchico. Barely. Only, this was the first meeting with Whitecloaks. Thom, in stout brown wool, could have been any of a thousand gnarled, white-haired men who worked wagons. And Juilin was Juilin. He knew how to behave, though he looked as though he wished he were sure footed on the ground, with his staff or the slotted sword-breaker he wore at his belt, rather than on a horse.

Thom drew the team over to one side of the road and halted as several Whitecloaks broke away from the head of the column. Nynaeve put on a welcoming smile. She hoped they had not decided that they needed another wagon.

"The Light illumine you, Captain," she said to the narrow-faced man who was obviously the leader, the only one not carrying a steel-tipped lance. She had no idea what rank the two golden knots signified on the breast of his cloak, right below the flaring sunburst they all wore, but in her experience men would accept any flattery. "We are very glad to see you. Bandits tried to rob us a few miles back, but a dust storm appeared like a miracle. We barely esc—"

"You are a merchant? Few merchants have come out of Tarabon in some time." The man's voice was as harsh as his face, and that looked as though all joy had been boiled out of it before he left the cradle. Suspicion filled his dark, deep-set eyes; Nynaeve did not doubt that was permanent, too. "Bound to where, with what?"

"I carry dyes, Captain." She worked to maintain her smile under that steady, unblinking stare; it was a relief when he shifted it to the others briefly. Thom was making a good job of appearing bored, just a wagon driver who would be paid stopped or moving, and if Juilin had not snatched off that ridiculous hat as he once would have, at least he seemed no more than idly interested, a hired man with nothing to hide. When the Whitecloak's gaze dropped to Elayne, Nynaeve felt the other woman stiffen, and hurried on. "Taraboner dyes. The finest in the world. I can get a good price for them in Andor."

At a signal from the captain—or whatever he was—one of the other Whitecloaks heeled his horse to the back of the wagon. Slicing one of the ropes with his dagger, he jerked some of the canvas loose, enough to expose three or four casks. "They're branded 'Tanchico,' Lieutenant. This one says 'crimson.' Do you want me to break open a few?"

Nynaeve hoped the Whitecloak officer took the anxiety on her face the right way. Even without looking at her, she could all but feel Elayne wanting to call the soldier down for his manners, but any real merchant would be worried at having dyes exposed to the elements. "If you will show me the ones you want opened, Captain, I will be more than happy to do it myself." The man showed no response at all, to flattery or offers of cooperation. "The casks were sealed to keep out dust and water, you see. If the cask head is broken, I'll never be able to cover it over with wax again here."

The rest of the column reached them and began to pass in a cloud of dust; the wagon drivers were roughly dressed, nondescript men, but the soldiers rode stiffly erect, their long steel lance points all slanted at exactly the same angle. Even sweaty-faced and coated with dust, they looked hard men. Only the drivers glanced at Nynaeve and the others.

The Whitecloak lieutenant waved dust away from his face with one gauntleted hand, then motioned the man back from the wagon. His eyes never left Nynaeve. "You come from Tanchico?"

Nynaeve nodded, a picture of cooperation and openness. "Yes, Captain. Tanchico."

"What word have you of the city? There have been rumors."

"Rumors, Captain? When we left, there was little order remaining. The city was full of refugees, and the countryside of rebels and bandits. Trade hardly exists." That was the truth, pure and simple. "That's why these dyes will fetch particularly good prices. There will be no more Taraboner dyes available for a long while, I think."

"I do not care about refugees, trade or dyes, merchant," the officer said in flat tones. "Was Andric still on the throne?"

"Yes, Captain." Obviously, rumor said someone had taken Tanchico and supplanted the King, and perhaps someone had. But who—one of the rebel lords who fought each other as hard as they did Andric, or the Dragonsworn who had pledged themselves to the Dragon Reborn without ever seeing him? "Andric was still King, and Amathera still Panarch, when we left."

His eyes said she could be lying. "It is said the Tar Valon witches were involved. Did you see any Aes Sedai, or hear of them?"

"No, Captain," she said quickly. The Great Serpent ring seemed hot against her skin. Fifty Whitecloaks, close at hand. A dust storm would not help this time, and anyway, though she tried to deny it, she was more scared than angry. "Plain merchants don't mingle with that sort." He nodded, and she risked adding a question. Anything to change the subject. "If you please, Captain, have we entered Amadicia yet?"

"The border is five miles east," he pronounced. "For the time being. The first village you come to will be Mardecin. Obey the law, and you will be well. There is a garrison of the Children there." He sounded as if the garrison would spend all of its time making sure they did obey the law.

"Have you come to move the border?" Elayne asked suddenly and coolly. Nynaeve could have strangled her.

The deep-set, suspicious eyes shifted to Elayne, and Nynaeve said hastily, "Forgive her, my Lord Captain. My eldest sister's girl. She thinks she should have been born a lady, and she can't keep away from the boys besides. That's why her mother sent her to me." Elayne's indignant gasp was perfect. It was also probably quite real. Nynaeve supposed she had not needed to add that about boys, but it seemed to fit.

The Whitecloak stared at them a moment longer, then said, "The Lord Captain Commander sends food into Tarabon. Otherwise, we would have Taraboner vermin over the border and stealing anything they could chew. Walk in the Light," he added before swinging his horse to gallop back to the head of the column. It was neither suggestion nor blessing.

Thom got the wagon moving as soon as the officer left, but everyone sat silent, except for coughing, until they were well beyond the last soldier and out of the other wagons' dust.

Swallowing a little water to wet her throat, Nynaeve pushed the water bottle at Elayne. "What did you mean back there?" she demanded. "We aren't in your mother's throne room, and your mother would not stand for it anyway!"

Elayne emptied the rest of the leather bottle before deigning to reply. "You were crawling, Nynaeve." She pitched her voice high, in a mock servility. "I am very good and obedient, Captain. May I kiss your boots, Captain?"

"We are supposed to be merchants, not queens in disguise!"

"Merchants do not have to be lickspittles! You are lucky he didn't think we were trying to hide something, acting so servile!"

"They don't stare down their noses at Whitecloaks with fifty lances, either! Or did you think we could overwhelm them all with the Power, if need be?"

"Why did you tell him I could not keep away from boys? There was no need for that, Nynaeve!"

"I was ready to tell him anything that would make him go away and leave us alone! And you—!"

"Both of you shut up," Thom barked suddenly, "before they come back to see which of you is murdering the other!"

Nynaeve actually twisted around on the wooden seat to look back before she realized the Whitecloaks were too far off to hear even if they had been shouting. Well, maybe they had been. It did not help that Elayne did the same.

Nynaeve took a firm hold on her braid and glared at Thom, but Elayne snuggled herself against his arm and practically cooed, "You are right, Thom. I am sorry I raised my voice." Juilin was watching them sideways, pretending not to, but he was wise enough not to bring his horse close enough to become part of it.

Letting go of her braid before she pulled it out by the roots, Nynaeve adjusted her hat and sat staring straight ahead over the horses. Whatever had gotten into the girl, it was high time to get it out again.

Only a tall stone pillar to each side of the road marked the border between Tarabon and Amadicia. There was no traffic on the road but them. The hills gradually became a little higher, but otherwise the land remained much the same, brown grass and thickets with few green leaves except on pine or leatherleaf or other evergreens. Stone-fenced fields and thatch-roofed stone farmhouses dotted the slopes and dells, but they had a look of abandonment. No smoke rising from chimneys, no men working crops, no sheep or cows. Sometimes a few chickens scratched in a farmyard near the road, but they scurried away, gone feral, at the wagon's approach. Whitecloak garrison or no, apparently no one was willing to risk Taraboner brigands this close to the border.

When Mardecin appeared, from the top of a rise, the sun still had a long way to climb to its zenith. The town ahead looked too big for the name of village, nearly a mile across, straddling a small bridged stream between two hills, with as many slate roofs as thatched, and considerable bustle in the wide streets.

"We need to buy supplies," Nynaeve said, "but we want to be quick about it. We can cover a lot of ground yet before nightfall."

"We are wearing out, Nynaeve," Thom said. "First light to last light every day for nearly a month. One day resting will not make much difference in reaching Tar Valon." He did not sound tired. More likely he was looking forward to playing his harp or his flute in one of the taverns and getting men to buy him wine.

Juilin had finally brought his mount close to the wagon, and he added, "I could do with a day on my feet. I do not know whether this saddle or that wagon seat is worse."

"I think we should find an inn," Elayne said, looking up at Thom. "I have had quite enough of sleeping under this wagon, and I would like to listen to you tell stories in the common room."

"One-wagon merchants are little more than peddlers,"

Nynaeve said sharply. "They cannot afford inns in a town like this."

She did not know whether that was true or not, but despite her own desire for a bath and clean sheets, she was not going to let the girl get away with directing the suggestion at Thom. It was not until the words were out of her mouth that she realized that she had given in to Thom and Juilin. *One day won't hurt. It's a long way to Tar Valon yet.*

She wished she had insisted on a ship. With a fast ship, a Sea Folk raker, they could have gotten to Tear in a third of what it had taken them to cross Tarabon, as long as they had good winds, and with the right Atha'an Miere Windfinder that would have been no problem; she or Elayne could have handled it, for that matter. The Tairens knew that she and Elayne were friends of Rand's, and she expected that they still sweated buckets for fear of offending the Dragon Reborn; they would have provided a carriage and escort for the journey up to Tar Valon.

"Find us a place to camp," she said reluctantly. She should have insisted on a ship. They might have been back in the Tower by now.

CHAPTER

9

A Signal

Nynaeve had to admit that Thom and Juilin between them had chosen a good campsite, in a sparse thicket growing on an eastern slope, covered with dead leaves, a scant mile from Mardecin. Scattered sourgums and some sort of small, droopy-branched willow screened the wagon from the road and the town, and a two-foot-wide rivulet ran from a stone outcrop near the top of the rise, down a bed of dried mud twice as broad. Enough water for their purposes. It was even a little cooler under the trees, with a small and welcome breeze.

Once the two men had watered the team and hobbled them where the horses could feed on the sparse grass upslope, they tossed a coin to decide which should take the lanky gelding into Mardecin to purchase what they needed. The coin flipping was a ritual that they had developed. Thom, whose nimble fingers were used to performing sleight-of-hand, never lost when he flipped the coin, so Juilin always did it now.

Thom won anyway, and while he was stripping the saddle from Skulker, Nynaeve put her head under the wagon seat and levered up a floorboard with her belt knife. Besides two small gilded coffers containing Amathera's presents of jewelry, several leather purses bulging with coin lay in the recess. The panarch had been more than generous in her desire to see their backs. The other things looked trifling by comparison; a small dark wooden box, polished but plain and uncarved, and a washleather purse lying flat and showing the impression of a disc inside. The box held the two *ter'angreal* they had recovered from the Black Ajah, both linked to dreams, and the purse . . . That was their prize from Tanchico. One of the seals on the Dark One's prison.

As much as she wanted to find out where Siuan Sanche wanted them to chase the Black Ajah next, the seal was the source of her haste to reach Tar Valon. Digging coins from one of the fat purses, she avoided touching the flat purse; the longer it remained in her possession, the more she wanted to hand it to the Amyrlin and be done with it. Sometimes she thought she could feel the Dark One, trying to break through, when she was near the thing.

She saw Thom off with a pocketful of silver and a strong admonition to search out some fruit and green vegetables; either man was likely as not to buy nothing but meat and beans, left to himself. Thom's limp as he led the horse off toward the road made her grimace; an old injury, and nothing to be done for it now, so Moiraine said. That rankled as much as the limp itself. Nothing to be done.

When she had left the Two Rivers, it had been to protect young people from her village, snatched away in the night by an Aes Sedai. She had gone to the Tower still with the hope that she could somehow shelter them, and the added ambition of bringing down Moiraine for what she had done. The world had changed since then. Or maybe she only saw the world differently. *No, it is not me that's changed. I'm the same; it is everything else that's different.*

Now it was all she could do to protect herself. Rand was what he was, and no turning back, and Egwene eagerly went her own way, not letting anyone or anything hold her back even if her way led over a cliff, and Mat had learned to think of nothing but women, carousing

and gambling. She even found herself sympathizing with
Moiraine sometimes, to her disgust. At least Perrin had
gone back home, or so she had heard through Egwene,
secondhand from Rand; perhaps Perrin was safe.

Hunting the Black Ajah was good and right and
satisfying—and also terrifying, though she tried to hide
that part; she was a grown woman, not a girl who needed
to hide in her mother's apron—yet that was not the
main reason she was willing to keep on bashing her head
against a wall, keep on trying to learn to use the Power
when most of the time she could not channel any more
than Thom. That reason was the Talent called Healing.
As Wisdom of Emond's Field it had been gratifying to
bring the Women's Circle around to her way of thinking
—especially since most were old enough to be her
mother; with not many years on Elayne, she had been the
youngest Wisdom ever in the Two Rivers—and even
more so to see that the Village Council did what they
should, stubborn men that they were. The most satisfaction, though, had always come from finding the right
combination of herbs to cure an illness. To Heal with the
One Power . . . She had done it, fumbling, curing what
her other skills never could. The joy of it was enough to
bring tears. One day she meant to Heal Thom and watch
him dance. One day she would even Heal that wound in
Rand's side. Surely there was nothing that could not be
Healed, not if the woman wielding the Power was
determined enough.

When she turned from watching Thom go, she found
that Elayne had filled the bucket that normally hung
beneath the wagon and was kneeling to wash her hands
and face, a towel around her shoulders to keep her dress
dry. That was something she particularly wanted to do
herself. In this heat it was pleasant sometimes to wash in
water cool from a stream. Often enough there had been
no water but what was in the barrels strapped to the
wagon, and that was needed for drinking and cooking
more than washing.

Juilin was sitting with his back against one of the
wagon wheels, his thumb-thick staff of pale ridged wood
leaning next to him. His head was down, that silly hat
tipped precariously over his eyes, but she was not willing

to bet on even a man sleeping at this time of the morning. There were things he and Thom did not know, things it was best they did not know.

The thick carpet of dead sourgum leaves crackled as she seated herself near Elayne. "Do you think Tanchico really has fallen?" Rubbing a soapy cloth slowly across her face, the other woman did not reply. She tried again. "I think that Whitecloak's 'Aes Sedai' were us."

"Perhaps." Elayne's voice was cool, a pronouncement from the throne. Her eyes were blue ice. She did not look at Nynaeve. "And perhaps reports of what we did got tangled with other rumors. Tarabon could have a new king, and a new panarch, very easily."

Nynaeve kept her temper in check and her hands away from her braid. They clutched her knees instead. *You are trying to put her at ease with you. Watch your tongue.* "Amathera was difficult, but I do not wish her any harm. Do you?"

"A pretty woman," Juilin said, "especially in one of those Taraboner serving girl's dresses, with a pretty smile. I thought she—" He saw Elayne and her looking at him and quickly pulled his hat back down, pretending to sleep again. She and Elayne shared a glance, and she knew the other's thought was the same as hers. *Men.*

"Whatever has happened to Amathera, Nynaeve, she is behind us, now." Elayne sounded more normal. Her washcloth slowed. "I wish her well, but mainly I hope the Black Ajah is not behind us. Not following, I mean."

Juilin stirred uneasily without raising his head; he was still uncomfortable with the knowledge that Black Aes Sedai were real and not simply a tale in the streets.

He should be happy he doesn't have our knowledge. Nynaeve had to admit that the thought was not entirely logical, but if he had known about the Forsaken being loose, even Rand's foolish instruction to *look after* her and Elayne would not have kept him from running. Still, he was useful at times. He and Thom both. It had been Moiraine who had fastened Thom to them, and the man knew a great deal about the world for an ordinary gleeman.

"If they were following, they'd have caught up by

now." That was surely true, considering the usual lumbering speed of the wagon. "With any luck, they still do not know who we are."

Elayne nodded, grim but her old self again, and began rinsing her face. She could be almost as determined as a Two Rivers woman. "Liandrin and most of her cronies surely escaped from Tanchico. Maybe all of them. And we still don't know who is giving orders for the Black Ajah in the Tower. As Rand would say, we still have it to do, Nynaeve."

Despite herself, Nynaeve winced. True, they had a list of eleven names, but once they were back in the Tower, almost any Aes Sedai they spoke to might be Black Ajah. Or any women they encountered on the road. For that matter, anyone they met *might* be a Darkfriend, but that was hardly the same thing, not by a wide degree.

"More than the Black Ajah," Elayne continued, "I worry about Mo—" Nynaeve put a quick hand on her arm and nodded slightly toward Juilin. Elayne coughed and went on as though that was what had stopped her. "About mother. She has no reason to like you, Nynaeve. Quite the opposite."

"She is far away from here." Nynaeve was glad her voice was steady. They were not talking about Elayne's mother, but the Forsaken she had defeated. Part of her hoped fervently that Moghedien was far away. Very far.

"But if she was not?"

"She is," Nynaeve said firmly, but she still hitched her shoulders uncomfortably. A part of her remembered humiliations suffered at Moghedien's hands and desired nothing more than to face the woman again, to defeat her again, for good this time. Only, what if Moghedien took her by surprise, came at her when she was not angry enough to channel? The same was true of any of the Forsaken, of course, or of any Black sister for that matter, but after her rout in Tanchico, Moghedien had reason to hate her personally. Not pleasant at all to think that one of the Forsaken knew your name and likely wanted your head. *That is just rank cowardice,* she told herself sharply. *You are not a coward, and you will not be!* That did not stop the itch between her shoulder blades every time Moghedien came to mind, as if the woman was staring at her back.

"I suppose looking over my shoulder for bandits has made me nervous," Elayne said casually, patting her face with the towel. "Why, sometimes when I dream of late, I have the feeling that someone is watching me."

Nynaeve gave a start at what seemed an echo of her own thoughts, but then she realized there had been a slight emphasis on "dream." Not any dreams, but *Tel'aran'rhiod.* Another thing the men did not know about. She had had the same sensation, but then there was often a feel of unseen eyes in the World of Dreams. It could be uncomfortable, but they had discussed the sensation before.

She made her voice light. "Well, your mother is not in our dreams, Elayne, or she would probably snatch us both up by an ear." Moghedien would probably torture them until they begged for death. Or arrange a circle of thirteen Black sisters and thirteen Myrddraal; they could turn you to the Shadow against your will that way, bind you to the Dark One. Maybe Moghedien could even do it by herself. . . . *Don't be ridiculous, woman! If she could have, she would have. You beat her, remember?*

"I do hope not," the other woman replied soberly.

"Do you mean to give me a chance to wash?" Nynaeve asked irritably. Putting the girl at ease was all very well, but she could do with less talk of Moghedien. The Forsaken had to be somewhere distant; she would not have let them come this far peacefully if she knew where they were. *Light send that that's true!*

Elayne emptied and refilled the bucket herself. She was a very nice girl usually, when she remembered that she was not in the Royal Palace in Caemlyn. And when she was not acting the fool. That, Nynaeve would take care of when Thom came back.

Once Nynaeve had enjoyed a slow, cooling wash of face and hands, she set about making the camp ready, and put Juilin to breaking dead branches from the trees for a fire. By the time Thom returned with two wicker hampers slung across the gelding's back, her and Elayne's blankets were laid out under the wagon and the two men's under the hanging branches of one of the twenty-foot willows, a good supply of firewood had been stacked, the teakettle stood cooling beside the ashes of a fire in a circle cleared of leaves, and the thick pottery cups had been washed. Juilin was grumbling to himself as he caught water in the tiny stream to refill the water barrels. From the snatches Nynaeve heard, she was glad he kept most of it to an inaudible mutter. From her perch on one of the wagon shafts, Elayne hardly tried to hide her interested attempt to make out what he was saying. Both she and Nynaeve had put on clean dresses on the other side of the wagon, switching colors as it happened.

After fastening hobbles between the gelding's forelegs, Thom lifted the heavy hampers down easily and began unpacking them. "Mardecin's not as prosperous as it looks from a distance." He set a net bag of small apples on the ground, and another of some dark green leafy vegetable. "With no trade into Tarabon, the town is withering." The rest seemed to be all sacks of dried beans and turnips, plus pepper-cured beef and salt-cured hams. And a gray pottery bottle sealed with wax that Nynaeve was sure held brandy; both men had complained of not having a bit of something with their pipes of an evening. "You can hardly take six steps without seeing a Whitecloak or two. The garrison is about fifty men or so, with barracks over the hill from the town on the far side of the bridge. It was considerably larger, but it seems Pedron Niall is pulling Whitecloaks from everywhere into Amador." Knuckling his long mustaches, he looked thoughtful for a moment. "I cannot see what he is up to." Thom was not a man who liked that; usually a few hours in a place was enough for him to begin ferreting out the currents between noble and merchant Houses, the alliances and schemes and counterplots that made up the so-called Game of Houses. "The rumors are all about Niall trying to stop a war between Illian and Altara, or maybe Illian and Murandy. No reason there for him to be gathering in soldiers. I'll tell you one thing, though. Whatever that lieutenant said, it is a King's Tax that buys the food being sent into Tarabon, and the people are not happy with it. Not to feed Taraboners."

"King Ailron and the Lord Captain Commander are not our concern," Nynaeve said, studying what he had brought. *Three* salted hams! "We will pass through Amadicia as quickly and unobtrusively as we can. Perhaps Elayne and I will have more luck finding vegetables than you did. Would you care for a walk, Elayne?"

Elayne got up immediately, smoothing her gray skirts and lifting her hat from the wagon. "That would be very nice, after that wagon seat. It might be different if Thom and Juilin let me take a turn riding Skulker more often." For once she did not give the old gleeman a coquettish look, which was something.

Thom and Juilin exchanged glances, and the Tairen thief-catcher pulled a coin from his coat pocket, but Nynaeve gave him no chance to flip it. "We will be quite all right by ourselves. We could hardly expect trouble of any sort with so many Whitecloaks to keep order." Planting her hat on her head, she tied the scarf under her chin and gave them a firm look. "Besides, all those things Thom bought need to be put away." Both men nodded; slowly, reluctantly, but they did it. Sometimes they took their roles as supposed protectors entirely too seriously.

She and Elayne had reached the empty road and were walking down the verge, on the thin grass so as not to kick up dust, before she had it settled in her mind how to bring up what she wanted to say. Before she could speak, though, Elayne said, "You obviously want to talk to me alone, Nynaeve. Is it about Moghedien?"

Nynaeve blinked, and looked at the other woman sideways. It was well to remember that Elayne was no fool. She had only been acting like one. Nynaeve resolved to keep a tight hold on her temper; this was going to be difficult enough without letting it dissolve into a shouting match. "Not that, Elayne." The girl thought they should add Moghedien to their hunt; she could not seem to realize the difference between one of the Forsaken and, say, Liandrin, or Chesmal. "I thought we should discuss how you've been behaving toward Thom."

"I do not know what you mean," Elayne said, staring straight ahead toward the town, but sudden spots of color in her cheeks gave her the lie.

"Not only is he old enough to be your father twice over, but—"

"He is *not* my father!" Elayne snapped. "My father was Taringail Damodred, a Prince of Cairhien and First Prince of the Sword of Andor!" Straightening her hat needlessly, she went on in a milder tone, though not by much. "I am sorry, Nynaeve. I did not mean to shout."

Temper, Nynaeve reminded herself. "I thought you were in love with Rand," she said, making her voice gentle. It was not easy. "The messages you have me give to Egwene for him certainly say so. I expect you tell her the same."

The color in the other woman's face heightened. "I do love him, but . . . He is very far away, Nynaeve. In the Waste, surrounded by a thousand Maidens of the Spear who jump to do his bidding. I cannot see him, or speak to him, or touch him." She was whispering by the end.

"You can't think he'll turn to a Maiden," Nynaeve said incredulously. "He is a man, but he isn't as fickle as that, and besides, one of them would put a spear in him if he looked at her crossways, even if he is this Dawn whatever. Anyway, Egwene says Aviendha is keeping an eye on him for you."

"I know, but . . . I should have made *sure* that he knew I love him." Elayne's voice was determined. And worried. "I should have told him so."

Nynaeve had hardly looked at a man before Lan, at least not seriously, but she had seen and learned much as Wisdom; from her observations, there was no quicker way to send a man running for his life, unless he said it first.

"I think Min had a viewing," Elayne went on. "About me, and about Rand. She always used to joke about having to share him, but I think it wasn't a joke and she could not bring herself to say what it really was."

"That is ridiculous." It certainly was. Though in Tear, Aviendha had told her of a vile Aiel custom. . . . *You share Lan with Moiraine,* a small voice whispered. *That isn't the same thing at all!* she told it briskly. "Are you certain Min had one of her visions?"

"Yes. I wasn't at first, but the more I think on it, the

more sure I become. She joked about it too often to mean anything else."

Well, whatever Min had seen, Rand was no Aiel. Oh, his blood might be Aiel as the Wise Ones claimed, but he had grown up in the Two Rivers, and she would not stand by and let him take up wicked Aiel ways. She doubted very much that Elayne would, either. "Is that why you've been—" She would not say *throwing yourself at* "—teasing Thom?"

Elayne gave her a sidelong glance, the crimson back in her cheeks. "There are a thousand leagues between us, Nynaeve. Do you think Rand is refraining from looking at other women? 'A man is a man, on a throne or in a pigsty.'" She had a stock of homely sayings from her childhood nurse, a clearheaded woman named Lini whom Nynaeve wished she would meet one day.

"Well, I don't see why you have to flirt just because you think Rand might." She refrained from bringing up Thom's age again. *Lan is old enough to be your father,* that small voice murmured. *I love Lan. If I can only reason out how to get him free of Moiraine. . . . That is not the matter at hand!* "Thom is a man with secrets, Elayne. Remember that Moiraine sent him with us. Whatever he is, he is no simple country gleeman."

"He was a great man," Elayne said softly. "He could have been greater, except for love."

With that, Nynaeve's temper snapped. She rounded on the other woman, seizing her by the shoulders. "The man doesn't know whether to turn you over his knee or . . . or . . . climb a tree!"

"I know." Elayne gave a frustrated sigh. "But I do not know what else to do."

Nynaeve ground her teeth in the effort not to shake her until her skull rattled. "If your mother heard of this, she'd send Lini to haul you back to the nursery!"

"I am not a child any longer, Nynaeve." Elayne's voice was strained, and now the flush in her cheeks was not embarrassment. "I am as much a woman as my mother is."

Nynaeve stalked on toward Mardecin, gripping her braid so hard that her knuckles hurt.

After a few strides, Elayne caught up. "Are we really going to buy vegetables?" Her face was composed, her tone light.

"Did you see what Thom brought back?" Nynaeve said tightly.

Elayne shuddered elaborately. "Three hams. And that awful peppered beef! Do men ever eat anything but meat if it isn't set before them?"

Nynaeve's temper faded as they walked on talking about the foibles of the weaker sex—men, of course—and such simple matters as that. Not completely away, of course. She liked Elayne, and enjoyed her company; at times it seemed as if the girl really was Egwene's sister, as they sometimes called each other. When Elayne was not acting the twitchskirt. Thom could put a stop to it, of course, but the old fool indulged Elayne like a fond father with his favorite daughter, even when he did not know whether to say boo or faint. One way or another, she meant to get to the bottom of it. Not for Rand's sake, but because Elayne was better than this. It was as if she had contracted a strange fever. Nynaeve intended to cure it.

Granite slabs paved the streets of Mardecin, worn by generations of feet and wagon wheels, and the buildings were all brick or stone. A number of them were empty though, both shops and houses, sometimes with the front door standing open so Nynaeve could see the bare interior. She saw three blacksmith's shops, two abandoned, and in the third the smith was halfheartedly rubbing his tools with oil and the forges were cold. One slate-roofed inn, with men sitting morosely on benches out front, had a number of broken windows, and at another the adjoining stable had its doors half-off the hinges and a dusty coach squatting in the stableyard, one forlorn hen nesting on the driver's high seat. Somebody in that one was playing the bittern; "Heron on the Wing," it sounded like, but the tune was dispirited. The door of a third inn was barred by two splintery planks nailed across it.

People thronged the streets, but they moved lethargically, weighted down by the heat; dull faces said they had no real reason to stir at all, beyond habit. Many women, in large deep bonnets that almost hid their faces, had on dresses worn at the hem, and more than one man had a frayed collar or cuffs on his knee-length coat.

There were indeed Whitecloaks scattered through the streets; if not so many as Thom had made out, still enough. Nynaeve's breath caught every time she saw a man in a pristine cloak and shining armor look at her. She knew she had not worked with the Power nearly long enough to take on Aes Sedai agelessness, but those men might well try to kill her—a Tar Valon witch, and outlawed in Amadicia—if they even suspected a connection to the White Tower. They strode through the crowds, seemingly oblivious of the apparent poverty around them. People moved out of their way respectfully, receiving perhaps a nod, if that, and often a sternly pious "Walk in the Light."

Ignoring the Children of the Light as best she could, she set herself to finding fresh vegetables, but by the time the sun reached its peak, a blazing ball of gold that burned through the thin clouds, she and Elayne had wandered both sides of the low bridge and between them had managed to garner one small bunch of honeypeas, some tiny radishes, a few hard pears, and a basket to carry them in. Perhaps Thom really had looked. This time of year, the barrows and stalls should have been full of the summer's produce, but most of what they saw was heaped potatoes and turnips that had known better days. Thinking of all those empty farms approaching the town, Nynaeve wondered how these people were going to make it through the winter. She walked on.

Hanging upside down beside the door of a thatch-roofed seamstress' shop was a bunch of what looked almost like broomweed, with tiny yellow flowers, the stalks wrapped their whole length in a white ribbon, then tied with a dangling yellow one. It might have been some woman's feeble attempt at a festive decoration in the midst of hard times. But she was sure it was not.

Stopping beside an empty shop with a carving knife incised on the sign still hanging over the door, she pretended to search for a stone in her shoe while furtively studying the seamstress' shop. The door was open, and colorful bolts of cloth stood in the small-paned windows, but no one went in or out.

"Can you not find it, Nynaeve? Take off your shoe."

Nynaeve's head jerked; she had almost forgotten that Elayne was there. No one else was paying any attention to them, and no one looked close enough to overhear. She still lowered her voice. "That bunch of broomweed by that shop door. It is a Yellow Ajah signal, an emergency signal from one of the Yellow's eyes-and-ears."

She did not have to tell Elayne not to stare; the girl's eyes barely moved toward the shop. "Are you certain?" she asked quietly. "And how do you know?"

"Of course I am certain. It's exact; the hanging bit of yellow ribbon is even split in three." She paused to take a deep breath. Unless she was completely mistaken, that insignificant fistful of weeds held a dire meaning. If she *was* wrong, she was making a fool of herself, and she did hate to do that. "I spent a good deal of time talking with Yellows in the Tower." Healing was the main purpose of the Yellows; they did not care much for her herbs, but you did not need herbs when you could Heal with the Power. "One of them told me. She did not think it too great a transgression, since she was sure I'll choose Yellow. Besides, it has not been used in nearly three hundred years. Elayne, only a few women in each Ajah actually know who the Ajah's eyes-and-ears are, but a bunch of yellow flowers tied and hung like that tells any Yellow sister that here one is, and with a message urgent enough to risk uncovering herself."

"How are we going to find out what it is?"

Nynaeve liked that. Not "What are we going to do?" The girl had backbone.

"Follow my lead," she said, gripping the basket tighter as she straightened. She hoped she remembered everything Shemerin had told her. She hoped Shemerin had told her everything. The plump Yellow could be fluttery for an Aes Sedai.

The interior of the shop was not large, and every scrap of wall was taken up by shelves holding bolts of silk or finely woven wool, spools of piping and binding, and ribbon and lace of every width and description. Dress-maker's dummies stood about the floor wearing garments ranging from half-made to complete, from something suitable for a dance in embroidered green wool to a pearly gray silk gown that could have done very well at court. At first glance the shop had a look of prosperity and activity, but Nynaeve's sharp eye caught a hint of dust in one high neck of frothy Solinde lace, and on a large black velvet bow at the waist of another gown.

There were two dark-haired women in the shop. One, young and thin and trying to wipe her nose surreptitiously with the back of her hand, held a bolt of pale red silk clutched anxiously to her bosom. Her hair was a mass of long curls to her shoulders, in the Amadician fashion, but it seemed a tangle beside the other woman's neat array. The other, handsome and in her middle years, was assuredly the seamstress, as proclaimed by the large bristling pincushion fastened to her wrist. Her dress was of a good green wool, well cut and well made to show her skill, but only lightly worked with white flowers around the high neck so as not to overshadow her patrons.

When Nynaeve and Elayne walked in, both women gaped as if none had entered in a year. The seamstress recovered first, regarding them with careful dignity as she made a slight curtsy. "May I serve you? I am Ronde Macura. My shop is yours."

"I want a dress embroidered with yellow roses on the bodice," Nynaeve told her. "But no thorns, mind," she added with a laugh. "I don't heal very fast." What she said did not matter, so long as she included "yellow" and "heal" in it. Now, if only that bunch of flowers was not happenstance. If that was the case, she would have to find some reason not to buy a dress with roses. And a way to keep Elayne from recounting the whole miserable experience to Thom and Juilin.

Mistress Macura stared at her for a moment with dark eyes, then turned to the thin girl, pushing her toward the back of the shop. "Go on to the kitchen, Luci, and make a pot of tea for these good ladies. From the blue canister. The water's hot, thank the Light. Go on, girl. Put that down and stop gawking. Quickly, quickly. The blue canister, mind. My best tea," she said, turning back to Nynaeve as the girl vanished through a door at the rear. "I live over the shop, you see, and my kitchen is in the back." She was smoothing her skirts nervously, thumb and forefinger of her right hand forming a circle. For the Great Serpent ring. There would be no need for an excuse about the dress, it seemed.

Nynaeve repeated the sign, and after a moment Elayne did, too. "I am Nynaeve, and this is Elayne. We saw your signal."

The woman fluttered as if she might fly away. "The signal? Ah. Yes. Of course."

"Well?" Nynaeve said. "What is the urgent message?"

"We should not talk about that out here . . . uh . . . Mistress Nynaeve. Anyone might walk in." Nynaeve doubted that. "I will tell you over a nice cup of tea. My best tea, did I say?"

Nynaeve exchanged looks with Elayne. If Mistress Macura was this reluctant to speak her news, it must be appalling indeed.

"If we may just step into the back," Elayne said, "no one will hear but us." Her regal tone made the seamstress stare. For a moment, Nynaeve thought it might cut through her nervousness, but the next instant the fool woman was babbling again.

"The tea will be ready in a moment. The water's already hot. We used to get Taraboner tea through here. That is why I am here, I suppose. Not the tea, of course. All the trade that used to be, and all the news that came both ways with the wagons. They—you are mainly interested in outbreaks of disease, or a new kind of illness, but I find that interesting myself. I dabble a little with—" She coughed and rushed on; if she smoothed her dress any harder, she would wear a hole in it. "Some about the Children, of course, but they—you—are not much interested in them, really."

"The kitchen, Mistress Macura," Nynaeve said firmly as soon as the other woman paused for breath. If the woman's news made her this afraid, Nynaeve would brook no more delay in hearing it.

The door at the back opened enough to admit Luci's

anxious head. "It's ready, Mistress," she announced breathlessly.

"This way, Mistress Nynaeve," the seamstress said, still rubbing the front of her dress. "Mistress Elayne."

A short hallway led past narrow stairs to a snug, beam-ceilinged kitchen, with a steaming kettle sitting on the hearth and tall cupboards everywhere. Copper pots hung between the back door and a window that looked out into a small yard with a high wooden fence. The small table in the middle of the floor held a brilliant yellow teapot, a green honey jar, three mismatched cups in as many colors, and a squat blue pottery canister with the lid beside it. Mistress Macura snatched the canister, lidded it, and hastily put it into a cupboard that held more in two dozen shades and hues.

"Sit, please," she said, filling the cups. "Please."

Nynaeve took a ladder-back chair next to Elayne, and the seamstress set cups in front of them, flitting to one of the cupboards for pewter spoons.

"The message?" Nynaeve said as the woman sat down across from them. Mistress Macura was too nervous to touch her own teacup, so Nynaeve stirred a little honey into hers and took a sip; it was hot, but had a cool, minty aftertaste. Hot tea might settle the woman's nerves, if she could be made to drink.

"A pleasant taste," Elayne murmured over the edge of her cup. "What sort of tea is it?"

Good girl, Nynaeve thought.

But the seamstress' hands only fluttered beside her cup. "A Taraboner tea. From near the Shadow Coast."

Sighing, Nynaeve took another swallow to settle her own stomach. "The message," she said insistently. "You did not hang that signal to invite us for tea. What is your urgent news?"

"Ah. Yes." Mistress Macura licked her lips, eyed them both, then said slowly, "It came near a month ago, with orders that any sister passing through heard it at all costs." She wet her lips again. "All sisters are welcome to return to the White Tower. The Tower must be whole and strong."

Nynaeve waited for the rest, but the other woman fell

silent. *This* was the dire message? She looked at Elayne, but the heat seemed to be catching up to the girl; drooping in her chair, she was staring at her hands on the table. "Is that all of it?" Nynaeve demanded, and surprised herself by yawning. The heat must be reaching her, too.

The seamstress only watched her, intently.

"I said," Nynaeve began, but suddenly her head felt too heavy for her neck. Elayne had slumped onto the table, she realized, eyes closed and arms hanging limply. Nynaeve stared at the cup in her hands with horror. "What did you give us?" she said thickly; that minty taste was still there, but her tongue felt swollen. "Tell me!" Letting the cup fall, she levered herself up against the table, knees wobbling. "The Light burn you, what?"

Mistress Macura scraped back her chair and stepped out of reach, but her earlier nervousness was now a look of quiet satisfaction.

Blackness rolled in on Nynaeve; the last thing she heard was the seamstress' voice. "Catch her, Luci!"

CHAPTER
10

Figs and Mice

Elayne realized that she was being carried upstairs by her shoulders and ankles. Her eyes opened, she could see, but the rest of her body might as well have belonged to someone else for all the control she had over it. Even blinking was slow. Her brain felt crammed full of feathers.

"She's awake, Mistress!" Luci shrilled, nearly dropping her feet. "She's looking at me!"

"I told you not to worry." Mistress Macura's voice came from above her head. "She cannot channel, or twitch a muscle, not with forkroot tea in her. I discovered that by accident, but it has certainly come in handy."

It was true. Elayne sagged between them like a doll with half the stuffing gone, bumping her bottom along the steps, and she could as well have run as channel. She could sense the True Source, but trying to embrace it was like trying to pick up a needle on a mirror with cold-numbed fingers. Panic welled up, and a tear slid down her cheek.

Perhaps these women meant to turn her over to the Whitecloaks for execution, but she could not make herself believe that the Whitecloaks had women setting traps in the hope that an Aes Sedai might wander in. That left Darkfriends, and almost certainly serving the Black Ajah right along with the Yellow. She would surely be put in the hands of the Black Ajah unless Nynaeve had escaped. But if she was to escape, she could not count on anyone else. And she could neither move nor channel. Suddenly she realized that she was trying to scream, and producing only a thin, gurgling mewl. Halting it took all the strength she had left.

Nynaeve knew all about herbs, or claimed she did; why had she not recognized whatever that tea was? *Stop this whining!* The small, firm voice in the back of her head sounded remarkably like Lini. *A shoat squealing under a fence just attracts the fox, when it should be trying to run.* Desperately, she set herself to the simple task of embracing *saidar*. It *had* been a simple task, but now she might as well have been attempting to reach *saidin*. She kept on, though; it was the only thing she could do.

Mistress Macura, at least, seemed to have no worry. As soon as they had dropped Elayne onto a narrow bed in a small, close room with one window, she hustled Luci right out again with not even a backward glance. Elayne's head had fallen so she could see another cramped bed, and a highchest with tarnished brass pulls on the drawers. She could move her eyes, but shifting her head was beyond her.

In a few minutes the two women returned, puffing, with Nynaeve slung between them, and heaved her onto the other bed. Her face was slack, and glistening with tears, but her dark eyes . . . Fury filled them, and fear, too. Elayne hoped anger was uppermost; Nynaeve was stronger than she, when she *could* channel; perhaps Nynaeve could manage where she was failing miserably, time after time. Those had to be tears of rage.

Telling the thin girl to stay there, Mistress Macura hurried out once more, this time coming back with a tray that she placed atop the highchest. It held the yellow teapot, one cup, a funnel and a tall hourglass. "Now Luci, mind you pour a good two ounces into each of them as soon as that hourglass empties. As soon, mind!"

"Why don't we give it to them now, Mistress?" the girl

moaned, wringing her hands. "I want them to go back to sleep. I don't like them looking at me."

"They would sleep like the dead, girl, and this way we can let them rouse just enough to walk when we need them to. I will dose them more properly when it's time to send them off. They'll have headaches and stomach cramps to pay for it, but no more than they deserve, I suppose."

"But what if they *can* channel, Mistress? What if they do? They're looking at me."

"Stop blathering, girl," the older woman said briskly. "If they could, don't you think they would have by now? They are helpless as kittens in a sack. And they will stay that way as long you keep a good dose in them. Now, you do as I told you, understand? I must go tell old Avi to send off one of his pigeons, and make a few arrangements, but I will be back as soon as I can. You had better brew another pot of forkroot just in case. I'll go out the back. Close up the shop. Someone might wander in, and that would never do."

After Mistress Macura left, Luci stood staring at them for a while, still wringing her hands, then finally scurried out herself. Her sniffling faded down the stairs.

Elayne could see sweat beading on Nynaeve's brow; she hoped it was effort, not the heat. *Try, Nynaeve.* She herself reached for the True Source, fumbling clumsily through the wads of wool that seemed to pack her head, failed, tried again and failed, tried again. . . . *Oh, Light, try Nynaeve! Try!*

The hourglass filled her eyes; she could not look at anything else. Sand pouring down, each grain marking another failure on her part. The last grain dropped. And Luci did not come.

Elayne strained harder, for the Source, to move. After a bit the fingers of her left hand twitched. *Yes!* A few minutes more, and she could lift her hand; only a feeble inch before it fell again, but it had lifted. With an effort, she could turn her head.

"Fight it," Nynaeve mumbled thickly, barely intelligible. Her hands were gripping the coverlet under her tightly; she seemed to be trying to sit up. Not even her head lifted, but she was trying.

"I am," Elayne tried to say; it sounded more like a grunt to her ears.

Slowly she managed to raise her hand to where she could see it, and hold it there. A thrill of triumph shot through her. *Stay afraid of us, Luci. Stay down there in the kitchen a little while longer, and . . .*

The door banged open, and sobs of frustration racked her as Luci dashed in. She had been so close. The girl took one look at them and with a yelp of pure terror darted for the highchest.

Elayne tried to fight her, but thin as she was, Luci batted her floundering hands away effortlessly, forced the funnel between her teeth just as easily. The girl panted as if running. Cold, bitter tea filled Elayne's mouth. She stared up at the girl in a panic that Luci's face shared. But Luci held Elayne's mouth shut and stroked her throat with a grim if fearful determination until she swallowed. As darkness overwhelmed Elayne, she could hear liquid sounds of protest coming from Nynaeve.

When her eyes opened again, Luci was gone, and the sands trickled through the glass again. Nynaeve's dark eyes were bulging, whether in fear or anger, Elayne could not have said. No, Nynaeve would not give in. That was one of the things she admired in the other woman. Nynaeve's head could have been on the chopping block and she would not give up. *Our heads* are *on the block!*

It made her ashamed that she was so much weaker than Nynaeve. She was supposed to be Queen of Andor one day, and she wanted to howl with terror. She did not, even in her head—doggedly she went back to trying to force her limbs to move, to trying to touch *saidar*—but she wanted to. How could she ever be a queen, when she was so weak? Again she reached for the Source. Again. Again. Racing the grains of sand. Again.

Once more the glass emptied itself without Luci. Ever so slowly, she reached the point where she could raise her hand again. And then her head! Even if it did flop back immediately. She could hear Nynaeve muttering to herself, and she could actually understand most of the words.

The door crashed open once more. Elayne lifted her

head to stare at it despairingly—and gaped. Thom Merrilin stood there like the hero of one of his own tales, one hand firmly gripping the neck of a Luci near fainting, the other holding a knife ready to throw. Elayne laughed delightedly, though it came out more like a croak.

Roughly, he shoved the girl into a corner. "You stay there, or I'll strop this blade on your hide!" In two steps he was at Elayne's side, smoothing her hair back, worry painting his leathery face. "What did you give them, girl? Tell me, or—!"

"Not her," Nynaeve muttered. "Other one. Went away. Help me up. Have to walk."

Thom left her reluctantly, Elayne thought. He showed Luci his knife again threateningly—she cowered as if she never meant to move again—then made it disappear up his sleeve in a twinkling. Hauling Nynaeve to her feet, he began walking her up and down the few paces the room allowed. She sagged against him limply, shuffling.

"I am glad to hear this frightened little cat didn't trap you," he said. "If she had been the one . . ." He shook his head. No doubt he would think just as little of them if Nynaeve told him the truth; Elayne certainly did not intend to. "I found her rushing up the stairs, so panicked she did not even hear me behind her. I am not so glad that another one got away without Juilin seeing her. Is she likely to bring others back?"

Elayne rolled over onto her side. "I do not think so, Thom," she mumbled. "She can't let—too many people —know about herself." In another minute she might be able to sit up. She was looking right at Luci; the girl flinched and tried to shrink through the wall. "The Whitecloaks—would take her as—quickly as they would us."

"Juilin?" Nynaeve said. Her head wavered as she glared up at the gleeman. She had no trouble speaking, though. "I told the pair of you to stay with the wagon."

Thom blew out his mustaches irritably. "You told us to put up the supplies, which did not take two men. Juilin followed you, and when none of you came back, I went looking for him." He snorted again. "For all he knew, there were a dozen men in here, but he was ready to come in after you alone. He is tying Skulker in the back. A good thing I decided to ride in. I think we'll need the horse to get you two out of here."

Elayne found that she could sit up, barely, pulling herself hand over hand along the coverlet, but an effort to stand nearly put her flat again. *Saidar* was as unobtainable as ever; her head still felt like a goose-down pillow. Nynaeve was beginning to hold herself a little straighter, to lift her feet, but she still hung on Thom.

Minutes later Juilin arrived, pushing Mistress Macura ahead of him with his belt knife. "She came through a gate in the back fence. Thought I was a thief. It seemed best to bring her on in."

The seamstress' face had gone so pale at the sight of them that her eyes seemed darker, and about to come out of her head besides. She licked her lips and smoothed her skirt incessantly, and cast quick little glances at Juilin's knife as if wondering whether it might not be best to run anyway. For the most part, though, she stared at Elayne and Nynaeve; Elayne thought it an even chance whether she would burst into tears or swoon.

"Put her over there," Nynaeve said, nodding to where Luci still shivered in the corner with her arms wrapped around her knees, "and help Elayne. I never heard of forkroot, but walking seems to help the effects pass. You can walk most things off."

Juilin pointed to the corner with his knife, and Mistress Macura scurried to it and sat herself down beside Luci, still wetting her lips fearfully. "I—would not have done—what I did—only, I had orders. You must understand that. I had orders."

Gently helping Elayne to her feet, Juilin supported her in walking the few steps available, crisscrossing the other pair. She wished it were Thom. Juilin's arm around her waist was much too familiar.

"Orders from whom?" Nynaeve barked. "Who do you report to in the Tower?"

The seamstress looked sick, but she clamped her mouth shut determinedly.

"If you don't talk," Nynaeve told her, scowling, "I'll let Juilin have you. He's a Tairen thief-catcher, and he knows how to bring out a confession as quickly as any Whitecloak Questioner. Don't you, Juilin?"

"Some rope to tie her," he said, grinning a grin so villainous that Elayne almost tried to step away from him, "some rags to gag her until she is ready to talk, some cooking oil and salt. . . ." His chuckle curdled Elayne's blood. "She will talk." Mistress Macura held herself rigidly against the wall, staring at him, eyes as wide as they would go. Luci looked at him as if he had just turned into a Trolloc, eight feet tall and complete with horns.

"Very well," Nynaeve said after a moment. "You should find everything you need in the kitchen, Juilin." Elayne shifted a startled look from her to the thief-catcher and back. Surely they did not really mean to . . . ? Not Nynaeve!

"Narenwin Barda," the seamstress gasped suddenly. Words tripped over one another spilling out of her. "I send my reports to Narenwin Barda, at an inn in Tar Valon called The Upriver Run. Avi Shendar keeps pigeons for me on the edge of town. He doesn't know who I send messages to or who I get them from, and he does not care. His wife had the falling sickness, and . . ." She trailed off, shuddering and watching Juilin.

Elayne knew Narenwin, or at least had seen her in the Tower. A thin little woman you could forget was there, she was so quiet. And kind, too; one day a week, she let children bring their pets to the Tower grounds for her to Heal. Hardly the sort of woman to be Black Ajah. On the other hand, one of the Black Ajah names they knew was Marillin Gemalphin; she liked cats, and went out of her way to look after strays.

"Narenwin Barda," Nynaeve said grimly. "I want more names, inside the Tower or out."

"I—don't have any more," Mistress Macura said faintly.

"We will see about that. How long have you been a Darkfriend? How long have you served the Black Ajah?"

An indignant squall erupted from Luci. "We aren't Darkfriends!" She glanced at Mistress Macura and sidled away from her. "At least, I'm not! I walk in the Light! I do!"

The other woman's reaction was no less strong. If her eyes had bulged before, they popped now. "The Black—! You mean it really exists? But the Tower has always denied— Why, I asked Narenwin, the day she chose me for the Yellow's eyes-and-ears, and it was the next morning before I could stop weeping and crawl out of my bed. I am not—not!—a Darkfriend! *Never!* I serve the Yellow Ajah! The *Yellow!*"

Still hanging on to Juilin's arm, Elayne exchanged puzzled looks with Nynaeve. Any Darkfriend would deny it, of course, but there seemed a ring of truth in the women's voices. Their outrage at the accusation was nearly enough to overcome their fear. From the way Nynaeve hesitated, she heard the same thing.

"If you serve the Yellow," she said slowly, "why did you drug us?"

"It was her," the seamstress replied, nodding at Elayne. "I was sent her description a month since, right down to that way she holds her chin sometimes so she seems to be looking down at you. Narenwin said she might use the name Elayne, and even claim to be of a noble House." Word by word, her anger over being called a Darkfriend seemed to bubble higher. "Maybe you are a Yellow sister, but she's no Aes Sedai, just a runaway Accepted. Narenwin said I was to report her presence, and that of anyone with her. And to delay her, if I could. Or even capture her. And anyone with her. How they expected me to capture an Accepted, I do not know—I don't think even Narenwin knows about my forkroot tea!—but that is what my orders said! They said I should risk exposure even—here, where it'd be my death!—if I had to! You just wait until the Amyrlin puts her hands on you, young woman! On all of you!"

"The Amyrlin!" Elayne exclaimed. "What does she have to do with this?"

"It was on her orders. By order of the Amyrlin Seat, it said. It said the Amyrlin herself said I could use any means short of killing you. You will wish you *were* dead when the Amyrlin gets hold of you!" Her sharp nod was full of furious satisfaction.

"Remember that we are not in anyone's hands yet," Nynaeve said dryly. "You are in ours." Her eyes looked as shocked as Elayne felt, though. "Was any reason given?"

The reminder that she was the captive sapped the brief burst of spirit from the woman. She sagged listlessly against Luci, each keeping the other from falling over. "No. Sometimes Narenwin gives a reason, but not this time."

"Did you intend to just keep us here, drugged, until someone came for us?"

"I was going to send you off by cart, dressed in some old clothes." Not even a shred of resistance remained in the woman's voice. "I sent a pigeon to tell Narenwin you were here, and what I was doing. Therin Lugay owes me a strong favor, and I meant to give him enough forkroot to last all the way to Tar Valon, if Narenwin didn't send sisters to meet you sooner. He thinks you are ill, and the tea is the only thing keeping you alive until an Aes Sedai can Heal you. A woman has to be careful, dealing in remedies in Amadicia. Cure too many, or too well, somebody whispers Aes Sedai, and the next you know your house is burning down. Or worse. Therin knows to hold his tongue about what he . . ."

Nynaeve made Thom help her closer, where she could stare down at the seamstress. "And the message? The real message? You did not put that signal out in the hope of luring us in."

"I gave you the real message," the woman said wearily. "I did not think it could do any harm. I don't understand it, and I— please—" Suddenly she was sobbing, clinging to Luci as hard as the younger woman did to her, both of them wailing and babbling. "Please, don't let him use the salt on me! Please! Not the salt! Oh, please!"

"Tie them up," Nynaeve said disgustedly after a moment, "and we will go downstairs where we can talk." Thom helped her to sit on the edge of the nearest bed, then quickly cut strips from the other coverlet.

In short order both women were bound, back to back,

the hands of one to the feet of the other, with wadded bits of coverlet tied in for gags. The pair were still weeping when Thom assisted Nynaeve from the room.

Elayne wished she could walk as well as the other woman, but she still needed Juilin's support not to go tumbling down the stairs. She felt a small stab of jealousy watching Thom with his arm around Nynaeve. *You are a foolish little girl,* Lini's voice said sharply. *I am a grown woman,* she told it with a firmness she would not have dared with her old nurse even today. *I do love Rand, but he is far away, and Thom is sophisticated and intelligent and . . .* It sounded too much like excuses, even to her. Lini would have given the snort that meant she was about to stop tolerating foolishness.

"Juilin," she asked hesitantly, "what were you going to do with the salt and cooking oil? Not exactly," she added more quickly. "Just a general idea."

He looked at her for a moment. "I do not know. But they did not, either. That is the trick of it; their minds made up worse than I ever could. I have seen a tough man break when I sent for a basket of figs and some mice. You have to be careful, though. Some will confess anything, true or not, just to escape what they imagine. I do not think those two did, though."

She did not either. She could not repress a shiver, however. *What* would *somebody do with figs and mice?* She hoped she stopped wondering before she gave herself nightmares.

By the time they reached the kitchen, Nynaeve was tottering about without help, poking into the cupboard full of colorful canisters. Elayne needed one of the chairs. The blue canister sat on the table, and a full green teapot, but she tried not to look at them. She still could not channel. She could embrace *saidar,* yet it slipped away as soon as she did. At least she was confident now that the Power would return to her. The alternative was too horrible to contemplate, and she had not let herself until this moment.

"Thom," Nynaeve said, lifting the lids on various containers and peering in. "Juilin." She paused, took a deep breath, and, still not looking at the two men, said,

"Thank you. I begin to see why Aes Sedai have Warders. Thank you very much."

Not all Aes Sedai did. Reds considered all men tainted because of what men who could channel did, and a few never bothered because they did not leave the Tower or simply did not replace a Warder who died. The Greens were the only Ajah to allow bonding with more than one Warder. Elayne wanted to be a Green. Not for that reason, of course, but because the Greens called themselves the Battle Ajah. Where Browns searched for lost knowledge and Blues involved themselves in causes, Green sisters held themselves ready for the Last Battle, when they would go forth, as they had in the Trolloc Wars, to face new Dreadlords.

The two men stared at one another in open amazement. They had surely been ready for the usual rough side of Nynaeve's tongue. Elayne was almost as shocked. Nynaeve liked having to be helped as much as she liked being wrong; either made her as prickly as a briar, though of course she always claimed to be a picture of sweet reason and sense.

"A Wisdom." Nynaeve took a pinch of powder from one of the canisters and sniffed it, touched it to the tip of her tongue. "Or whatever they call it here."

"They don't·have a name for it here," Thom said. "Not many women follow your old craft in Amadicia. Too dangerous. For most of those it's only a sideline."

Pulling a leather scrip from the bottom of the cupboard, Nynaeve began making up small bundles from some of the containers. "And who do they go to when they're ill? A hedge-doctor?"

"Yes," Elayne said. It always pleased her to show Thom that she knew things about the world, too. "In Amadicia, it is men who study herbs."

Nynaeve frowned scornfully. "What could a man ever know about curing anything? I'd as soon ask a farrier to make a dress."

Abruptly Elayne realized that she had been thinking of anything and everything except what Mistress Macura had said. *Not thinking about a thorn doesn't make it hurt your foot less.* One of Lini's favorites. "Nynaeve, what do you think that message means? All sisters are welcome to return to the Tower? It makes no sense." That was not what she wanted to say, but at least she was closing in on it.

"The Tower has its own rules," Thom said. "What Aes Sedai do, they do for reasons of their own, and often not for those they give. If they give reasons at all." He and Juilin knew they were only Accepted, of course; that was at least part of why neither man did as he was told nearly as well as he might.

The struggle was plain on Nynaeve's face. She did not like being interrupted, or people answering for her. There was quite a list of things Nynaeve did not like. But it was only a moment since she had thanked Thom; it could not be easy to call down a man who had just saved you from being hauled off like a cabbage. "Very little in the Tower makes sense most of the time," she said sourly. Elayne suspected that the tartness was as much for Thom as the Tower.

"Do you believe what she said?" Elayne took a deep breath. "About the Amyrlin saying I was to be brought back by any means."

The brief look Nynaeve gave her was touched with sympathy. "I don't know, Elayne."

"She was telling the truth." Juilin turned one of the chairs around and straddled it, leaning his staff against the back. "I've questioned enough thieves and murderers to know truth when I hear it. Part of the time she was too frightened to lie, and the rest too angry."

"The pair of you—" Taking a deep breath, Nynaeve tossed the scrip onto the table and folded her arms as if to trap her hands away from her braid. "I am afraid Juilin is probably right, Elayne."

"But the Amyrlin knows what we are doing. She sent us out of the Tower in the first place."

Nynaeve sniffed loudly. "I can believe anything of Siuan Sanche. I would like to have her for one hour where she could not channel. We would see how tough she is then."

Elayne did not think that would make any difference. Remembering that commanding blue gaze, she suspected Nynaeve would earn a fine lot of bruises in the unlikely event that she ever got her wish. "But what are we going to do about it? The Ajahs have eyes-and-ears everywhere, it seems. And the Amyrlin herself. We could have women trying to slip things into our food all the way to Tar Valon."

"Not if we do not look like what they expect." Lifting a yellow jug out of the cupboard, Nynaeve set it on the table beside the teapot. "This is white henpepper. It will soothe a toothache, but it will also turn your hair black as night." Elayne put a hand to her red-gold tresses—*her* hair, not Nynaeve's, she would wager!—but as much as she hated the idea, it was a good one. "A little needle-work on some of those dresses in the front, and we are not merchants anymore, but two ladies traveling with their servants."

"Riding on a wagonload of dye?" Juilin said.

Her level look said gratitude for saving her extended only so far. "There is a coach in a stableyard on the other side of the bridge. I think the owner will sell it. If you go back to the wagon before somebody steals it—I do not know what got into you two, just leaving it for whoever came along!—if it is still there, you can take one of the purses. . . ."

A few people goggled when Noy Torvald's coach pulled up in front of Ronde Macura's shop, drawn by a team of four, with chests strapped to the roof and a saddled horse tied on behind. Noy had lost everything when the trade with Tarabon collapsed; he was scraping a living doing odd jobs for Widow Teran, now. No one in the street had ever seen the coachman before, a tall leathery fellow with long white mustaches and cold, imperious eyes, or the dark, hard-faced footman in a Taraboner hat who jumped down nimbly to open the coach door. The goggling turned to murmurs when two women swept out of the shop with bundles in their arms; one wore a green silk gown, the other plain blue wool, but each had a scarf wrapped around her head so that not so much as a hint of her hair was visible. They all but leaped into the coach.

Two of the Children began sauntering over to inquire

who the strangers were, but while the footman was still scrambling up to the driver's seat, the coachman cracked his long whip, shouting something about making way for a lady. Her name was lost as the Children threw themselves out of the way, tumbling in the dusty street, and the coach rumbled away at a gallop toward the Amador Road.

The onlookers walked away talking among themselves; a mysterious lady, obviously, with her maid, making purchases from Ronde Macura and rushing away from the Children. Little enough happened in Mardecin of late, and this would provide days of conversation. The Children of the Light brushed themselves off furiously, but finally decided that reporting the incident would make them look foolish. Besides, their captain did not like nobles; he would probably send them to bring the coach back, a long ride in the heat for no more than an arrogant young sprig of one House or another. If no charges could be brought—always tricky with the nobility—it would not be the captain who took the blame. Hoping that word of their humiliation did not spread, they certainly never thought of questioning Ronde Macura.

A short time later, Therin Lugay led his cart into the yard behind the shop, provisions for the long journey ahead already packed away under the round canvas top. Indeed, Ronde Macura had cured him of a fever that had taken twenty-three the winter before, but it was a nagging wife and a shrewish mother-in-law that made him glad of a journey all the way to where the witches lived. Ronde had said someone might meet him, though not who, but he hoped to make it to Tar Valon.

He tapped on the kitchen door six times before going in, but it was not until he climbed the stairs that he found anyone. In the back bedroom, Ronde and Luci lay stretched out on the beds, sound asleep and fully clothed, if rather rumpled, with the sun still in the sky. Neither woman roused when he shook them. He did not understand that, or why one of the coverlets was lying on the floor cut into knotted strips, or why there were two empty teapots in the room but only one cup, or why a funnel was lying on Ronde's pillow. But he had always known that there was a great deal in the world he did not understand. Returning to his cart, he thought about the supplies Ronde's money had purchased, thought of his wife and her mother, and when he led the cart horse off, it was with the intention of seeing what Altara was like, or maybe Murandy.

One way and another, it was quite a time before a disheveled Ronde Macura tottered up to Avi Shendar's house and sent off a pigeon, a thin bone tube tied to its leg. The bird launched itself north and east, straight as an arrow toward Tar Valon. After a moment's thought, Ronde prepared another copy on another narrow strip of thin parchment, and fastened it to a bird from another coop. That one headed west for she had promised to send duplicates of all of her messages. In these hard times, a woman had to make out as best she could, and there could be no harm in it, not the sort of reports she made to Narenwin. Wondering if she could ever get the taste of forkroot out of her mouth, she would not have minded if the report brought just a little harm to the one who called herself Nynaeve.

Hoeing in his garden patch as usual, Avi paid no attention to what Ronde did. And as usual, as soon as she was gone, he washed his hands and went inside. She had placed a larger sheet of parchment underneath the strips to cushion the nib of the pen. When he held it up to the afternoon light, he could make out what she had written. Soon a third pigeon was on its way, heading in still another direction.

CHAPTER
11

The Nine Horse Hitch

A wide straw hat shaded Siuan's face as she let Logain lead the way through Lugard's Shilene Gate under the late-afternoon sun. The city's tall gray outer walls were in some disrepair; in two places she could see, tumbled stone lowered the wall to no more than a tall fence. Min and Leane rode close behind her, both tired from the pace the man had set over the weeks since Kore Springs. He wanted to be in charge, and it took little enough to convince him that he was. If he said when they started of a morning, when and where they stopped of a night, if he kept the money, even if he expected them to serve his meals as well as cook them, it was of little account to her. All in all, she felt sorry for him. He had no idea what she planned for him. *A big fish on the hook to catch a bigger,* she thought grimly.

In name, Lugard was the capital of Murandy, the seat of King Roedran, but lords in Murandy spoke the words of fealty, then refused to pay their taxes, or do much of anything else that Roedran wanted, and the people did the same. Murandy was a nation in name only, the people barely held together by supposed allegiance to the king or queen—the throne changed hands at sometimes short intervals—and fear that Andor or Illian might snap them up if they did not hold together in some fashion.

Stone walls crisscrossed the city, most in a worse state than the outer bastions, for Lugard had grown haphazardly over the centuries, and more than once had actually been divided among feuding nobles. It was a dirty city, many of the broad streets unpaved and all of them dusty. Men in high-crowned hats and aproned women in skirts that showed their ankles dodged between merchants' lumbering trains, while children played in wagon ruts. Trade kept Lugard alive, trade up from Illian and Ebou Dar, from Ghealdan to the west and Andor to the north. Large bare patches of ground through the city held wagons parked wheel-to-wheel, many heavy-laden under strapped-down canvas covers, others empty and awaiting freight. Inns lined the main streets, along with horse lots and stables, nearly outnumbering the gray stone houses or shops, all roofed with tiles in blue or red or purple or green. Dust and noise filled the air, clanging from the smithies, the rumble of wagons and curses of the drivers, boisterous laughter from the inns. The sun baked Lugard as it slid toward the horizon, and the air felt as though it might never rain again.

When Logain finally turned in to a stableyard and dismounted behind a green-roofed inn called The Nine Horse Hitch, Siuan clambered down from Bela gratefully and gave the shaggy mare a doubtful pat on the nose, wary of teeth. In her view, sitting on the back of an animal was no way to travel. A boat went as you turned the rudder; a horse might decide to think for itself. Boats never bit, either; Bela had not so far, but she could. At least those awful first days of stiffness were gone, when she was sure Leane and Min were grinning behind her back as she hobbled about in the evening camp. After a day in the saddle she still felt as if she had been thoroughly beaten, but she managed to hide it.

As soon as Logain began bargaining with the stableman, a lanky, freckled old fellow in a leather vest and no shirt, Siuan sidled close to Leane. "If you want to practice your wiles," she said softly, "practice them on

Dalyn the next hour." Leane gave her a dubious look—she had dabbled in smiles and glances at some of the villages since Kore Springs, but Logain had gotten no more than a flat look—then sighed and nodded. Taking a deep breath, she glided forward in that startling sinuous way, leading her arch-necked gray and already smiling at Logain. Siuan could not see how she did that; it was as if some of her bones were no longer rigid.

Moving over to Min, she spoke just as quietly again. "The instant Dalyn is done with the stableman, tell him you are going to join me inside. Then hurry ahead, and stay away from him and Amaena until I come back." From the noise roaring out of the inn, the crowd inside was big enough to hide an army. Surely big enough to hide the absence of one woman. Min got that mulish look about her eyes and opened her mouth, no doubt to demand why. Siuan forestalled her. "Just do it, Serenla. Or I'll let you add cleaning his boots to handing him his plate." The stubborn look remained, but Min gave a sullen nod.

Pushing Bela's reins into the other woman's hands, Siuan hurried out of the stableyard and started down the street in what she hoped was the right direction. She did not want to have to search the entire city, not in this heat and dust.

Heavy wagons behind teams of six or eight or even ten filled the streets, drivers cracking long whips and cursing equally at the horses and at the people who darted between the wagons. Roughly dressed men mingling through the crowds in long wagondrivers' coats sometimes directed laughing invitations at women who passed them. The women who wore colorful aprons, sometimes striped, their heads wrapped in bright scarves, walked on with eyes straight ahead, as though they did not hear. Women without aprons, hair hanging loose around their shoulders and skirts sometimes ending a foot or more clear of the ground, often shouted back even ruder replies.

Siuan gave a start when she realized that some of the men's suggestions were aimed at her. They did not make her angry—she really could not apply them to herself in her own mind—only startled. She was still not used to the changes in herself. That men might find her attractive. . . . Her reflection in the filthy window of a tailor's shop caught her eye, not much more than a murky image of a fair-skinned girl under a straw hat. She was young; not just young-appearing, as far as she could tell, but young. Not much older than Min. A girl in truth, from the vantage of the years she had actually lived.

An advantage to having been stilled, she told herself. She had met women who would pay any price to lose fifteen or twenty years; some might even consider her price a fair bargain. She often found herself listing such advantages, perhaps trying to convince herself they were real. Freed from the Three Oaths, she could lie at need, for one thing. And her own father would not have recognized her. She did not really look as she had as a young woman; the changes maturity had made were still there, but softened into youth. Coldly objective, she thought she might be somewhat prettier than she had been as a girl; pretty was the best that had ever been said of her. Handsome had been the more usual compliment. She could not connect that face to her, to Siuan Sanche. Only inside was she still the same; her mind yet held all its knowledge. There, in her head, she was still herself.

Some of the inns and taverns in Lugard had names like The Farrier's Hammer, or The Dancing Bear, or The Silver Pig, often with garish signs painted to match. Others had names that should not have been allowed, the mildest of that sort being The Domani Wench's Kiss, with a painting of a coppery-skinned woman—bare to the waist!—with her lips puckered. Siuan wondered what Leane would make of that, but the way the woman was now, it might only give her notions.

At last, on a side street just as wide as the main, just beyond a gateless opening in one of the collapsing inner walls, she found the inn she wanted, three stories of rough gray stone topped with purple roof tiles. The sign over the door had an improbably voluptuous woman wearing only her hair, arranged to hide as little as possible, astride a barebacked horse, and a name that she skipped over as soon as she recognized it.

Inside, the common room was blue with pipesmoke, packed with raucous men drinking and laughing, trying to pinch serving maids, who dodged as best they could with long-suffering smiles. Barely audible over the babble, a zither and a flute accompanied a young woman singing and dancing on a table at one end of the long room. Occasionally the singer swirled her skirts high enough to show nearly the whole length of her bare legs; what Siuan could catch of her song made her want to wash out the girl's mouth. Why would a woman go walking with no clothes on? Why would a woman sing about it to a lot of drunken louts? It was not a sort of place she had ever been into before. She intended to make this visit as brief as possible.

There was no mistaking the inn's owner, a tall, heavy-set woman encased in a red silk dress that practically glowed; elaborate, dyed curls—nature had never produced that shade of red, surely never with such dark eyes—framed a thrusting chin and a hard mouth. In between shouting orders to the serving girls, she stopped at this table or that to speak a few words or slap a back and laugh with her patrons.

Siuan held herself stiffly and tried to ignore the considering looks men gave her as she approached the crimson-haired woman. "Mistress Tharne?" She had to repeat the name three times, each louder than the last, before the inn's owner looked at her. "Mistress Tharne, I want a job singing. I can sing—"

"You can, can you now?" The big woman laughed. "Well, I have a singer, but I can always use another to give her a rest. Let me be seeing your legs."

"I can sing 'The Song of the Three Fishes,'" Siuan said loudly. This had to be the right woman. Surely two women in one city could not have hair like that, not and answer to the right name at the right inn.

Mistress Tharne laughed harder still and slapped one of the men at the nearest table on the shoulder, jolting him half off his bench. "Not much call for that one here, eh, Pel?" Gap-toothed Pel, a wagon driver's whip curled around his shoulder, cackled with her.

"And I can sing 'Blue Sky Dawning.'"

The woman shook, scrubbing at her eyes as though she had laughed herself to tears. "Can you, now? Ah, I'm sure the lads will love that. Now let me see your legs. Your legs, girl, or get out!"

Siuan hesitated, but Mistress Tharne only stared at her. And an increasing number of the men did, too. This *had* to be the right woman. Slowly, she pulled her skirt up to her knees. The tall woman gestured impatiently. Closing her eyes, Siuan gathered more and more of her skirt in her hands. She felt her face growing redder by the inch.

"A modest one," Mistress Tharne chortled. "Well, if those songs are the extent of your knowledge, you'd better have legs to make a man fall on his face. Can't tell till we get those woolen stockings off her, eh, Pel? Well, come on with me. Maybe you have a voice, anyway, but I can't hear it in here. Come on, girl! Hustle your rump!"

Siuan's eyes snapped open, blazing, but the big woman was already striding toward the back of the common room. Backbone like an iron rod, Siuan let her skirts fall and followed, trying to ignore the guffaws and lewd suggestions directed at her. Her face was stone, but inside, worry warred with anger.

Before being raised to the Amyrlin Seat, she had run the Blue Ajah's network of eyes-and-ears; some had also been her own personal listeners both then and later. She might no longer be Amyrlin, or even Aes Sedai, but she still knew all of those agents. Duranda Tharne had already been serving the Blue when she took over the network, a woman whose information was always timely. Eyes-and-ears were not to be found everywhere, and their reliability varied—there had been only one that she trusted enough to approach between Tar Valon and here, at Four Kings, in Andor, and she had vanished—but a vast amount of news and rumor passed through Lugard with the merchants' wagon trains. There might be eyes-and-ears for other Ajahs here; it would be well to remember that. *Caution gets the boat home,* she reminded herself.

This woman fit the description of Duranda Tharne perfectly, and surely no other inn could have a name so vile, but why had she responded as she did when Siuan identified herself as another agent of the Blue? She had to risk it; Min and Leane, in their own fashion, were growing as impatient as Logain. Caution got the boat home, but sometimes boldness brought back a full hold. At the worst, she could knock the woman over the head with something and escape out the back. Eyeing the woman's width and height, and the firmness of her thick arms, she hoped that she could.

A plain door in the corridor that led to the kitchens opened into a sparsely furnished room, a desk and one chair on a scrap of blue carpet, a large mirror on one wall, and surprisingly, a short shelf with a few books. As soon as the door was shut behind them, diminishing if not cutting off the noise of the common room, the big woman rounded on Siuan, fists planted on ample hips. "Now, then. What do you want with me? Don't bother giving me a name; I don't want to know, whether it's yours or not."

A little of the tension oozed out of Siuan. Not the anger, though. "You had no right to treat me in that manner out there! What did you mean forcing me to—!"

"I had every right," Mistress Tharne snapped, "and every necessity. If you'd come at opening or closing, as you're supposed to, I could have hustled you in here and none the wiser. Do you think some of those men wouldn't be wondering if I escorted you back here like a long-lost friend? I can't afford to have anyone wondering about me. You're lucky I didn't make you take Susu's place on the table for a song or two. And you watch your manner with me." She raised a wide, hard hand threateningly. "I've married daughters older than you, and when I visit them, they step right and talk proper. You come Mistress Snip with me, and you'll be learning why. Nobody out there will even hear you yelp, and if they did, they wouldn't interfere." With a sharp nod, as if that were settled, she put fists on hips again. "Now, what do you want?"

Several times during the onslaught Siuan had tried to speak, but the woman rolled over her like a tidal wave. That was not something she was accustomed to. By the time Mistress Tharne was done, she quivered with anger; both hands held her skirts in a white-knuckled grip. She held on to her temper every bit as hard. *I am supposed to be just another agent,* she reminded herself firmly. *Not the Amyrlin anymore, just another agent.* Besides, she suspected that the woman might carry out her threat. This was something else still new to her, having to be wary of someone under her eye just because they were larger and stronger.

"I was given a message to deliver to a gathering of those we serve." She hoped Mistress Tharne took the strain in her voice for being cowed; the woman might be more helpful if she thought Siuan properly intimidated. "They were not where I was told to find them. I can only hope you know something to help me find them."

Folding her arms under a massive bosom, Mistress Tharne studied her. "Know how to hold your temper when it suits, eh? Good. What's happened in the Tower? And don't try denying you come from there, my fine haughty wench. Your message has courier writ large all over it, and you never got that snooty manner in a village."

Siuan drew a deep breath before answering. "Siuan Sanche has been stilled." Her voice did not even tremble; she was proud of that. "Elaida a'Roihan is the new Amyrlin." She could not keep a hint of bite out of that, however.

Mistress Tharne's face showed no reaction. "Well, that explains some of the orders I've gotten. Some of them, maybe. Stilled her, did they? I thought she'd be Amyrlin forever. I saw her once, a few years ago in Caemlyn. At a distance. She looked like she could chew harness straps for breakfast." Those impossible scarlet curls swung as she shook her head. "Well, done's done. The Ajahs have split, haven't they? Only thing that fits; my orders, and the old buzzard stilled. The Tower's broken, and the Blues are running."

Siuan ground her teeth. She tried telling herself the woman was loyal to the Blue Ajah, not to her personally, but it did not help. *Old buzzard? She's old enough to be my mother. And if she was, I'd drown myself.* With an effort, she made her voice meek. "My message is important. I must be on my way as soon as possible. Can you help me?"

"Important, is it? Well, I'm doubting it. Trouble is, I can give you something, but it's up to you to cipher it out. Do you want it?" The woman refused to make this any easier.

"Yes, please."

"Sallie Daera. I don't know who she is or was, but I was told to give her name to any Blue who came around looking lost, so to speak. You may not be one of the sisters, but you carry your nose high enough for one, so there it is. Sallie Daera. Make of it what you will."

Siuan suppressed a thrill of excitement and made her face dejected. "I never heard of her, either. I'll just have to go on looking."

"If you find them, you tell Aeldene Sedai I'm still loyal, whatever's happened. I've worked for the Blues so long, I wouldn't know what to do with myself else."

"I will tell her," Siuan said. She had not known that Aeldene was her replacement controlling the Blues' eyes-and-ears; the Amyrlin, whatever Ajah she came from, was of all but part of none. "I suppose you need some reason for not hiring me. I really cannot sing; that should do."

"As if it mattered to that lot out there." The big woman quirked an eyebrow and grinned in a way Siuan did not like. "I'll think of something, wench. And I'll give you a bit of advice. If you don't climb down a rung or two, some Aes Sedai will take you down the whole ladder. I'm surprised it hasn't been done already. Now go on. Get out of here."

Hateful woman, Siuan growled in her head. *If there was a way to manage it, I'd have her doing penance till her eyes popped.* The woman thought she deserved more respect, did she? "Thank you for your help," she said coolly, making a curtsy that would have graced any court. "You have been too kind."

She was three steps into the common room when Mistress Tharne appeared behind her, raising her voice in a laughing shout that cut through the noise. "A shy maiden, that one! Legs white and slender enough to set you all drooling, and she bawled like a baby when I told her she'd have to show them to you! Just sat right down on the floor and cried! Hips round enough for any taste, and she . . . !"

Siuan stumbled as the tide of laughter rose, never quite drowning out the woman's recitation. She managed another three steps, face red as a beet, then fled at a run.

In the street, she paused to get her breath back and let her heart stop pounding. *That horrible old harridan! I should . . . !* It did not matter what she should do; that disgusting woman had told her what she needed. Not Sallie Daera; not a woman at all. Only a Blue would know, or even suspect. Salidar. Birthplace of Deane Aryman, the Blue sister who had become Amyrlin after Bonwhin and had rescued the Tower from the ruin Bonwhin had poised it for. Salidar. One of the last places anyone would look for Aes Sedai, short of Amadicia itself.

Two men in snowy cloaks and brightly burnished mail were riding down the street toward her, reluctantly moving their horses aside for wagons. Children of the Light. They could be found everywhere these days. Tipping her head down, watching the Whitecloaks cautiously from beneath the brim of her hat, Siuan moved closer to the blue-and-green front of the inn. They glanced at her as they rode by—hard faces beneath shining conical helmets—and passed on.

Siuan bit her lip in vexation. She had probably called their attention to her by shrinking back. And if they had seen her face . . . ? Nothing, of course. Whitecloaks might try to kill an Aes Sedai they found alone, but hers was an Aes Sedai face no longer. Only, they had seen her try to hide from them. If Duranda Tharne had not upset her so, she would not have made such a foolish error. She could remember when a little thing like Mistress Tharne's remarks would not have made her stride waver in the least, when that overgrown dyed fishwife would not have dared say a word of it. *If that termagant doesn't like my manner, I'll* . . . What she would do was continue about the business she was on before Mistress Tharne pummeled her so she could not sit a saddle. Sometimes it was hard remembering that the days were gone when she could call kings or queens and have them come.

Striding down the street, she glared so hard that some of the wagon drivers bit back the comments they had been going to make to a pretty young woman alone. Some of them did.

Min sat on a bench against the wall of the crowded common room in The Nine Horse Hitch, watching a table surrounded by standing men, some with coiled driver's whips, others wearing the swords that marked them merchants' guards. Six more sat shoulder to shoulder around the table. She could just make out Logain and Leane, sitting on the far side. He wore a disgruntled frown; the other men hung on Leane's every smiling word.

The air was thick with pipesmoke, and full of chatter that nearly drowned the music of flute and tambour and the singing of a girl dancing on a table between the stone fireplaces. Her song had to do with a woman convincing six men that each was the only man in her life; Min found it interesting even when it made her blush. The singer darted jealous glances at the crowded table from time to time. Or rather at Leane.

The tall Domani woman had already been leading Logain by the nose when they entered the inn, and she had attracted more men like flies to honey with that swaying walk and the smoldering light in her eyes. There had very nearly been a riot, Logain and the merchants' guards with hands on swords, knives being drawn, the stout proprietor and two heavily muscled fellows rushing in with cudgels. And Leane had doused the flames much as she had ignited them, with a smile here, a few words there, a pat on the cheek. Even the innkeeper had lingered awhile, grinning like a fool, until his custom called him away. And Leane thought she needed practice. It hardly seemed fair.

If I could do that to one particular man, I'd be more than satisfied. Maybe she'd teach me— Light, what am I thinking? She had always been herself, and everyone else could accept her as she was or not. Now she was thinking about changing what she was, for a man. It was bad enough that she had to hide herself in a dress, instead of the coat and breeches she had always worn. *He'd look at you in a dress with neckline cut low. You've more to show than Leane does, and she— Stop that!*

"We have to go south," Siuan said at her shoulder, and Min gave a start. She had not seen the other woman come in. "Now." From the shine in Siuan's blue eyes, she had learned something. Whether she would share it was another matter. The woman seemed to think she was still Amyrlin, most of the time.

"We cannot reach anywhere else with an inn before nightfall," Min said. "We might as well take rooms here for the night." It was pleasant to sleep in a bed again instead of under hedges and in haystacks, even if she did usually have to share it with Leane and Siuan. Logain was willing to rent them all rooms, but Siuan was tight with their coin even when Logain was doling it out.

Siuan looked around, but whoever in the common room was not staring at Leane was listening to the singer. "That isn't possible. I—I think some Whitecloaks may be asking questions about me."

Min whistled softly. "Dalyn won't like that."

"Then do not tell him." Siuan shook her head at the gathering about Leane. "Just tell Amaena that we have to go. He'll follow. Let us just hope the rest don't as well."

Min grinned wryly. Siuan might claim that she did not care that Logain—Dalyn—had taken charge, mostly by just ignoring her whenever she tried to make him do anything, but she was still determined to bring him to heel again.

"What *is* a Nine Horse Hitch, anyway?" she asked, getting to her feet. She had gone out front hoping for a hint, but the sign over the door bore only the name. "I have seen eight, and ten, but never nine."

"In this town," Siuan said primly, "it is better not to ask." Sudden spots of color in her cheeks made Min think that she knew very well. "Go fetch them. We've a long way to go, and no time to waste. And don't let anyone overhear you."

Min snorted softly. With that small smile on Leane's face, none of those men would even see her. She wished she knew how Siuan had brought herself to the Whitecloaks' attention. That was the last thing they needed, and it was not like Siuan to make mistakes. She wished she knew how to make Rand look at her like those men were looking at Leane. If they were going to be riding all night—and she suspected they were—maybe Leane *would* be willing to give her a few tips.

CHAPTER
12

An Old Pipe

A gust of wind swirling dust down the Lugard street caught Gareth Bryne's velvet hat, sweeping it from his head directly under one of the lumbering wagons. An iron-rimmed wheel ground the hat into the hard clay of the street, leaving a flattened ruin behind. For a moment he stared at it, then walked on. *It was showing travel stains anyway,* he told himself. His silk coat had been dusty before reaching Murandy, too; brushing no longer did much good, when he even took the trouble. It looked more brown than gray, now. He should find something plainer; he was not on his way to a ball.

Dodging between wagons rumbling down the rutted street, he ignored the drivers' curses that followed him—any decent squadman could give better in his sleep—and ducked into a red-roofed inn called The Wagon Seat. The painting on the sign gave the name an explicit interpretation.

The common room was like every common room he had seen in Lugard, wagon drivers and merchants' guards packed in with stablemen, farriers, laborers, every sort of man, all talking or laughing as loud as they could while drinking as much as they could, one hand for the cup and one to fondle the serving girls. For that matter, it was not all that much different from common rooms and taverns in many other towns, though most were considerably milder. A buxom young woman, in a blouse that seemed about to fall off, capered and sang atop a table at one side of the room, to the supposed music of two flutes and a twelve-string bittern.

He had little ear for music, but he paused a moment to appreciate her song; she would have gone over well in any soldiers' camp he had ever seen. But then, she would have been as popular if she could not sing a note. Wearing that blouse, she would have found a husband in short order.

Joni and Barim were already there, Joni's size enough to grant them a table by themselves despite his thin hair and the bandage he still wore around his temples. They were listening to the girl sing. Or at least staring at her. He touched each man on the shoulder and nodded toward the side door that led to the stableyard, where a sullen groom with a squint delivered their horses for three silver pennies. A year or so earlier Bryne could have bought a fair horse for no more. The troubles to the west and in Cairhien were playing havoc with trade and prices.

No one spoke until they passed the city gates and were on a seldom-traveled road winding north toward the River Storn, little more than a wide dirt track. Then Barim said, "They was here yesterday, my Lord."

Bryne had learned that much himself. Three pretty young women together, obvious outlanders, could not pass through a city like Lugard without being remarked. By men, anyway.

"Them and a fellow with shoulders," Barim went on. "Sounds maybe like that Dalyn was with them when they burned down Nem's barn. Anyway, whoever he is, they was at The Nine Horse Hitch for a bit, but all they did was drink some and leave. That Domani girl the lads was telling me about, she nearly kicked up a fuss flashing her smile and swaying about, but then she calmed everything down again the same way. Burn me, but I'd like to meet me a Domani woman."

"Did you hear which way they went, Barim?" Bryne asked patiently. He had not been able to learn that.

"Uh, no, my Lord. But I heard there's been plenty of Whitecloaks passing through, all heading west. You think maybe old Pedron Niall's planning something? Maybe in Altara?"

"That's not our business anymore, Barim." Bryne knew his patience sounded a little frayed this time, but Barim was an old enough campaigner to stick to the matter at hand.

"I know where they went, my Lord," Joni said. "West, on the Jehannah Road, and pushing hard by what I heard." He sounded troubled. "My Lord, I found two merchant's guards, lads who used to be in the Guards, and had a drink with them. Happens they were in a stew called The Good Night's Ride when that girl Mara came in and asked for a job singing. She didn't get it—didn't want to show her legs the way the singers in most of these places do, as who can blame her?—and she left. From what Barim told me, it was right after that they all set off west. I don't like it, my Lord. She isn't the kind of girl to want a job in a place like that. I think she's trying to get away from that Dalyn fellow."

Strangely, despite the lump on his head, Joni had no animosity toward the three young women. It was his opinion, often expressed since leaving the manor, that the girls were in some sort of predicament and needed to be rescued. Bryne suspected that if he did catch up to the young women and take them back to his estate, Joni would be after him to turn them over to Joni's daughters to mother.

Barim had no such feelings. "Ghealdan." He scowled. "Or maybe Altara, or Amadicia. We'll kiss the Dark One getting them back. Hardly seems worth the annoyance for a barn and some cows."

Bryne said nothing. They had followed the girl this far, and Murandy was a bad place for Andormen; too many border troubles over too many years. Only a fool would chase into Murandy after an oathbreaker's eyes. How much bigger a fool to follow halfway across the world?

"Those lads I talked to," Joni said diffidently. "My Lord, it seems a lot of the old lads who—who served under you are being sent off." Emboldened by Bryne's silence, he went on. "Lots of new fellows in. Lots. Those lads said at least four or five for everyone told he wasn't wanted anymore. The sort that like to cause trouble more than stop it. There's some calling themselves the White Lions who only answer to this Gaebril"—he spat to show what he thought of that—"and a bunch more not part of the Guards at all. Not House levies. Near as they could say, Gaebril's got ten times as many men under arms as there are Guards, and they've all sworn to the throne of Andor, but not to the Queen."

"That's no longer our business, either," Bryne said curtly. Barim had his tongue stuffed into his cheek, the way he always did when he knew something he either did not want to tell or was not sure was important enough. "What is it, Barim? Out with it, man."

The leather-faced fellow stared at him in amazement. Barim had never figured out how Bryne knew he was holding back. "Well, my Lord, some of the folks I talked to said some of those Whitecloaks yesterday was asking questions. About a girl sounds like that Mara. Wanted to know who she was, where she went. Like that. I heard they got real interested when they learned she was gone. If they're after her, she could be hanged before we ever find her. If they have to go to the trouble of chasing her down, they might not ask too many questions about whether she's really a Darkfriend. Or whatever it is they're after her for."

Bryne frowned. Whitecloaks? What would the Children of the Light want with Mara? He would never believe she was a Darkfriend. But then, he had seen a baby-faced young fellow hanged in Caemlyn, a Darkfriend who had been teaching children in the streets about the glories of the Dark One—the Great Lord of the Dark, he had called him. The lad had killed nine of them in three years, as near as could be discovered, when they looked like turning him in. *No. That girl is no Darkfriend, and I'll stake my life on it.* Whitecloaks were suspicious of everyone. And if they took it into their heads that she had fled Lugard to avoid them . . .

He booted Traveler to a canter. The big-nosed bay gelding was not flashy, but he had endurance, and courage. The other two caught up soon enough, and they kept their mouths shut, seeing the mood he was in.

Two miles or so from Lugard, he turned off into a thicket of oak and leatherleaf. The rest of his men had made a temporary camp here, in a clear space under thick, spreading oak limbs. Several small, smokeless fires were burning; they would take any opportunity to brew up some tea. Some were dozing; sleep was another thing an old soldier never missed a chance to snatch.

Those awake kicked the rest out of their naps, and they all looked up at him. For a moment he sat his saddle studying them. Gray hair and bald heads and age-creased faces. Still hard and fit, but even so . . . He had been a fool to risk bringing them into Murandy just because he had to know why a woman had broken an oath. And maybe with Whitecloaks after them. No telling how far or how long from home before it was done. If he turned back now, they would have been gone more than a month before they saw Kore Springs again. If he went on, there was no guarantee the chase would stop short of the Aryth Ocean. He should be taking these men, and himself, home. He should. He had no call to ask them to try snatching those girls out of Whitecloak hands. He could leave Mara to Whitecloak justice.

"We will be heading west," he announced, and immediately there was a scramble of dousing fires with the tea and fastening pots to saddles. "We will have to press hard. I mean to catch them in Altara, if I can, but if not, there's no telling where they'll lead us. You could see Jehannah or Amador or Ebou Dar before we're done." He affected a laugh. "You'll find out how tough you are if we reach Ebou Dar. They've taverns there where the barmaids skin Illianers for dinner and spit Whitecloaks for sport."

They laughed harder than the jest was worth.

"We won't worry with you along, my Lord," Thad cackled, stuffing his tin cup into his saddlebags. His face was wrinkled like crumpled leather. "Why, I hear you had a run-in with the Amyrlin herself once, and—" Jar Silvin kicked him on the ankle, and he rounded on the younger man—gray-haired, but still younger—with a clenched fist. "Why'd you do that, Silvin? You want a broke head, you just— What?" The meaningful glares Silvin and some of the others were giving him finally sank in. "Oh. Oh, yes." He buried himself in checking the girth straps on his saddle, but no one was laughing anymore.

Bryne forced his face to relax from stoniness. It was time he put the past in the past. Just because a woman whose bed he had shared—and more, he had thought— just because that woman looked at him as though she had never known him was no reason to stop speaking her name. Just because she had exiled him from Caemlyn, on pain of death, for giving her the advice he had sworn to give. . . . If she came a cropper with this Lord Gaebril who had suddenly appeared in Caemlyn, it was no longer any concern of his. She had told him, in a voice as flat and cold as smooth ice, that his name would never be spoken in the palace again, that only his long service kept her from sending him to the headsman for treason. Treason! He needed to keep spirits up, especially if this turned into a long chase.

Hooking a knee around the high cantle of his saddle, he took out his pipe and pouch and filled his pipe with tabac. The bowl was carved with a wild bull collared with the Rose Crown of Andor. For a thousand years that had been the sign of House Bryne; strength and courage in service of the queen. He needed a new pipe; this one was old.

"I didn't come out of that as well as you might have heard." He leaned down for one of the men to hand him a twig still glowing from one of the spent fires, then straightened to puff his pipe alight. "It was some three years ago. The Amyrlin was making a progression. Cairhien, Tear, Illian, and finishing up in Caemlyn before returning to Tar Valon. At that time we were having problems with Murandian border lords—as usual." Laughter rippled; they had all served on the Murandian border at one time or another. "I had sent some of the Guards down to set the Murandians straight on who owned the sheep and cattle on our side of the border. I never expected the Amyrlin to take an interest." He certainly had their attention; preparations to leave were still going on, but more slowly.

"Siuan Sanche and Elaida closeted themselves with Morgase—" There; he had said her name again, and it did not even smart. "—and when they came out, Morgase was half thunderhead, with lightning shooting out of her eyes, and half ten-year-old who'd been hauled up by her mother for stealing honeycakes. She's a tough woman, but caught between Elaida and the Amyrlin Seat . . ." He shook his head, and they chuckled; Aes Sedai attentions were one thing none of them envied lords and rulers. "She ordered me to remove all troops from the border with Murandy immediately. I asked her to discuss it with me in private, and Siuan Sanche jumped all over me. In front of half the court, she chewed me up one side and down the other like a raw recruit. Said if I couldn't do as I was told, she'd use me for fishbait." He had had to beg her pardon before it was done—in front of everyone, for trying to do as he had been sworn to do—but there was no need to add that. Even at the end he had not been sure that she would not make Morgase behead him, or have it done herself.

"Must have meant to catch herself a mighty big fish," someone laughed, and others joined in.

"The upshot was," Bryne went on, "my hide got singed, and the Guards were ordered back from the border. So if you're looking to me to protect you in Ebou Dar, just remember it's my opinion those barmaids would hang the Amyrlin out to dry along with the rest of us." They roared with mirth.

"Did you ever find out what it was about, my Lord?" Joni wanted to know.

Bryne shook his head. "Aes Sedai business of some sort, I expect. They don't tell the likes of you and me what they are up to." That earned a few chuckles as well.

They mounted up with an alacrity that belied their ages. *Some of them are no older than me,* he thought wryly. Too old to go chasing after a pretty pair of eyes young enough to be his daughter's if not his granddaughter's. *I only want to know why she broke oath,* he told himself firmly. *Only that.*

Raising his hand, he signaled forward, and they headed west, leaving a trail of dust. It would take hard riding to catch up. But he meant to. In Ebou Dar or the Pit of Doom, he would find them.

CHAPTER

13

A Small Room in Sienda

Elayne held herself against the swaying of the coach on its leather hinges, trying to ignore Nynaeve's sour face across from her. The curtains were drawn back despite a sprinkling of dust that sometimes whipped through the windows; the breeze blew away some of the late-afternoon heat. Rolling, forested hills streamed past, the woods occasionally broken by short stretches of farmland. A lord's manor, in the fashion of Amadicia, topped one of the hills a few miles from the road, a huge stone foundation fifty feet high with an elaborate wooden structure atop that, all ornate balconies and red-tiled roofs. Once it all would have been stone, but many years had passed since a lord needed a fortress in Amadicia, and the king's law now required the wooden construction. No rebel lord would be able to hold out against the king for long. Of course, the Children of the Light were exempted from that law; they were immune to a number of Amadician laws. She had had to learn something of the laws and customs of other countries from the time she was a child.

Cleared fields dotted the distant hills, too, like brown

patches on a mostly green cloth, the men working them seeming ants. Everything looked dry; one bolt of lightning would set a fire that could burn for leagues. But lightning meant rain, and the few clouds in the sky were too high and thin for that. Idly she wondered whether she could make it rain. She had learned considerable control over weather. Still, it was very difficult if you had to begin with nothing.

"Is my Lady bored?" Nynaeve asked acidly. "The way my Lady is staring at the countryside—down my Lady's nose—I think my Lady must want to travel faster." Reaching back over her head, she pushed open a small flap and shouted, "More speed, Thom. Don't argue with me! You hold your tongue, too, Juilin Thief-catcher! I said more speed!"

The wooden flap banged down, but Elayne could still hear Thom muttering loudly. Cursing, very likely; Nynaeve had been barking at the men all day. A moment later his whip cracked, and the coach racketed ahead even faster, rocking so hard that both women bounced on the golden-colored silk seats. The silk had been thoroughly dusted when Thom bought the vehicle, but the padding had long since gone hard. Yet jounced about as she was, the set of Nynaeve's jaw said she would not ask Thom to slow again right after ordering him to go faster.

"Please, Nynaeve," Elayne said. "I—" The other woman cut her off.

"Is my Lady uncomfortable? I know ladies are used to comfort, the sort of thing a poor maid wouldn't know about, but surely my Lady wants to make the next town before dark? So my Lady's maid can serve my Lady's supper and turn down my Lady's bed?" Her teeth clicked shut as the seat coming up met her coming down, and she glowered at Elayne as though it were her fault.

Elayne sighed heavily. Nynaeve had seen the point, back in Mardecin. A lady never traveled without a maid, and two ladies would probably have a pair. Unless they put Thom or Juilin in a dress, that meant one of them. Nynaeve *had* seen that Elayne knew more of how ladies behaved; she had put it very gently, and Nynaeve usually knew sense when she heard it. Usually. But that was back in Mistress Macura's shop, after they had filled the two women with their own horrible concoction.

Leaving Mardecin, they had traveled hard until midnight to reach a small village with an inn, where they had roused the innkeeper from his bed to rent two cramped rooms with narrow beds, waking before first light yesterday to push on, skirting around Amador by a few miles. Neither of them would be taken for anything but what they claimed, on sight, but neither felt comfortable about passing through a great city full of Whitecloaks. The Fortress of the Light was in Amador. Elayne had heard it said that the king reigned in Amador, but Pedron Niall ruled.

The trouble had started last night, at a place called Bellon, on a muddy stream grandly named the Gaean River, some twenty miles or so beyond the capital. The Bellon Ford Inn was larger than the first, and Mistress Alfara, the innkeeper, offered the Lady Morelin a private dining room, which Elayne could not very well refuse. Mistress Alfara had been sure that only the Lady Morelin's maid, Nana, would know how to serve her properly; ladies did require everything just so, the woman said, as well they should, and her girls were simply not used to ladies. Nana would know exactly how the Lady Morelin wanted her bed turned down, and would prepare her a nice bath after a hot day of travel. The list of things that Nana would do exactly right for her mistress had been endless.

Elayne was not sure whether Amadician nobility expected such or Mistress Alfara was just getting work out of an outlander's servant. She had tried to spare Nynaeve, but the woman had been as full of "as you wish" and "my Lady is most particular" as the innkeeper. She would have seemed a fool, or at least odd, to press it. They were trying to avoid attracting undue attention.

As long as they had been in Bellon, Nynaeve had acted the perfect lady's maid in public. In private was another matter. Elayne wished the woman would just revert to herself instead of bludgeoning her with a lady's maid from the Blight. Apologies had been met with "my Lady is too kind" or simply ignored. *I will not apologize again,* she thought for the fiftieth time. *Not for what was not my fault.*

"I have been thinking, Nynaeve." Gripping a hanging strap, she felt like the ball in the children's game called Bounce in Andor, where you tried to keep a colorful wooden ball bouncing up and down on a paddle. She would not ask for the coach to be slowed, though. She could stand it as long as Nynaeve did. The woman was so stubborn! "I want to reach Tar Valon and find out what is going on, but—"

"My Lady has been thinking? My Lady must have a headache from all that effort. I will make my Lady a nice tea of sheepstongue root and red daisy as soon as—"

"Be quiet, Nana," Elayne said, calmly but firmly; it was her very best imitation of her mother. Nynaeve's jaw dropped. "If you pull that braid at me, you can ride on the roof with the baggage." Nynaeve made a strangled sound, trying so hard to talk that nothing came out. Quite satisfactory. "Sometimes you seem to think I am still a child, but you are the one behaving like a child. I did not ask you to wash my back, but I would have had to wrestle to stop you. I did offer to scrub yours in turn, remember. And I offered to sleep in the trundle bed. But you climbed in and wouldn't get out. Stop sulking. If you like, I will be the maid at the next inn." It would probably be a disaster. Nynaeve would shout at Thom in public, or box someone's ears. But anything for a little peace. "We can stop right now and change in the trees."

"We chose the gowns to fit you," the other woman muttered after a moment. Pushing the flap open again, she shouted, "Slow down! Are you trying to kill us? Fool men!"

There was dead silence from above as the coach's speed diminished to something much more reasonable, but Elayne would have wagered the two men were talking. She straightened her hair as best she could without a mirror. It was still startling to see those glistening black tresses when she did look in one. The green silk was going to need a thorough brushing itself.

"What was it you were thinking, Elayne?" Nynaeve

asked. Crimson stained her cheeks. At least she knew that Elayne was right, but backing down was very likely as much apology as she would ever give.

"We are rushing back to Tar Valon, but do we really have any idea what awaits us in the Tower? If the Amyrlin truly did give those orders . . . I do not really believe it, and I cannot understand it, but I do not intend to walk into the Tower until I do. 'A fool puts her hand into a hollow tree without finding out what's inside first.'"

"A wise woman, Lini," Nynaeve said. "We may learn more if I see another bunch of yellow flowers hanging upside down, but until then I think we should behave as though the Black Ajah itself has control of the Tower."

"Mistress Macura will have sent off another pigeon to Narenwin by now. With descriptions of this coach, and the dresses we took, and most likely Thom and Juilin, too."

"It cannot be helped. This would not have happened if we hadn't dawdled across Tarabon. We should have taken ship." Elayne gaped at her accusatory tone, and Nynaeve had the grace to blush again. "Well, done is done. Moiraine knows Siuan Sanche. Perhaps Egwene can ask her if—"

Abruptly the coach lurched to a halt, throwing Elayne forward on top of Nynaeve. She could hear horses screaming and thrashing as she frantically untangled herself, Nynaeve pushing her off as well.

Embracing *saidar,* she put her head out of the window —and released it again in relief. Here was something of a sort that she had seen pass through Caemlyn more than once. A traveling menagerie was camped amid afternoon shadows in a large clearing by the side of the road. A great, black-maned lion lay half-asleep in one cage that took up the entire back of a wagon, while his two consorts paced in the confines of another. A third cage stood open; in front of it a woman was making two black bears with white faces balance themselves on big red balls. Another cage held what appeared to be a large, hairy boar, except that its snout was too pointed and it had toes with claws; that came from the Aiel Waste, she knew, and was called a *capar*. Other cages held other animals, and brightly colored birds, but unlike any menagerie she had ever seen, this one traveled with human performers: two men were juggling ribbon-twined hoops between them, four acrobats were practicing standing on one another's shoulders in a tall column, and a woman was feeding a dozen dogs that walked on their hind legs and did backflips for her. In the background, some other men were putting up two tall poles; she had no idea what they were for.

None of that was what had the horses rearing in their harness and rolling their eyes, though, despite all that Thom could do with the reins. She could smell the lions herself, but it was at three huge, wrinkled gray animals that the horses gazed, wild-eyed. Two were as tall as the coach, with big ears and great curving tusks beside a long nose that dangled to the ground. The third, shorter than the horses if likely as heavy, had no tusks. A baby, she supposed. A woman with pale yellow hair was scratching that one behind the ear with a heavy, hooked goad. Elayne had seen creatures like this before, too. And had never expected to see them again.

A tall, dark-haired man strode out of the camp, of all things in this heat wearing a red silk cloak that he flourished as he made an elegant bow. He was good-looking, with a well-turned leg, and very much aware of both things. "Forgive me, my Lady, if the giant boar-horses frightened your animals." As he straightened, he beckoned two of his men to help quiet the horses, then paused, staring at her, and murmured, "Be still, my heart." It was just loud enough for Elayne to be sure she was supposed to hear. "I am Valan Luca, my Lady, showman extraordinary. Your presence overwhelms me." He made another bow, even more elaborate than the first.

Elayne shared a look with Nynaeve, catching the same amused smile that she knew she herself wore. A man very full of himself, this Valan Luca. His men did seem to be very good at soothing the horses; they still snorted and stamped, but their eyes were not so wide as they had been. Thom and Juilin were staring at the strange animals almost as hard as the horses were.

"Boar-horses, Master Luca?" Elayne said. "Where do they come from?"

"*Giant* boar-horses, my Lady" was the ready reply, "from fabled Shara, where I myself led an expedition into a wilderness full of strange civilizations and stranger sights to trap them. It would fascinate me to tell you of them. Gigantic people twice the size of Ogier." He made grand gestures to illustrate. "Beings with no heads. Birds big enough to carry off a full-grown bull. Snakes that can swallow a man. Cities made of solid gold. Descend, my Lady, and let me tell you."

Elayne had no doubt that Luca would fascinate himself with his own tales, but she certainly doubted that those animals came from Shara. For one thing, even the Sea Folk saw no more of Shara than the walled ports they were confined to; any who went beyond the walls were never seen again. The Aiel knew little more. For another, she and Nynaeve had both seen creatures like these in Falme, during the Seanchan invasion. The Seanchan used them for work animals, and for war.

"I think not, Master Luca," she told him.

"Then let us perform for you," he said quickly. "As you can see, this is no ordinary wandering menagerie, but something entirely new. A private performance. Tumblers, jugglers, trained animals, the strongest man in the world. Even fireworks. We have an Illuminator with us. We are on our way to Ghealdan, and tomorrow we will be gone on the wind. But for a pittance—"

"My mistress said she thinks not," Nynaeve broke in. "She has better things to spend her money on than looking at animals." In fact, she herself kept a tight fist on all their coin, reluctantly doling out what they needed. She seemed to think everything should cost what it had back in her Two Rivers.

"Why would you want to go to Ghealdan, Master Luca?" Elayne asked. The other woman did make rough spots and leave them to her to smooth over. "I hear there is a great deal of trouble there. I hear the army has not been able to suppress this man called the Prophet, with his preaching of the Dragon Reborn. Surely you do not want to travel into riots."

"Greatly exaggerated, my Lady. Greatly exaggerated. Where there are crowds, people want to be entertained. And where people want to be entertained, my show is always welcome." Luca hesitated, then stepped closer to the coach. An embarrassed look crossed his face as he gazed up into Elayne's eyes. "My Lady, the truth of the matter is that you would do me a very great favor by allowing me to perform for you. The fact is that one of the boar-horses caused a little trouble in the next town up the road. It was an accident," he added hastily, "I assure you. They are gentle creatures. Not dangerous at all. But not only are the people of Sienda unwilling to let me put on a show, or even come to one here . . . Well, it took all of my coin to pay for the damages, and the fines." He winced. "Especially the fines. If you allowed me to entertain you—for a trifle, truly—I would name you as patroness of my show wherever we go across the world, spreading the fame of your generosity, my Lady . . . ?"

"Morelin," she said. "The Lady Morelin of House Samared." With her new hair, she could pass for Cairhienin. She had no time to see his show, as much as she would have enjoyed it another time, and she told him so, adding, "But I will help you a little, if you have no money. Give him something, Nana, to help him on his way to Ghealdan." The last thing she wanted was him "spreading her fame," but helping the poor and those in distress was a duty she would not slight when she had the means, even in a foreign land.

Grumbling, Nynaeve dug a purse out of her belt pouch and dipped into it. She leaned out of the coach enough to press Luca's hand around what she gave him. He looked startled as she said, "If you took a decent job of work, you would not have to beg. Drive on, Thom!"

Thom's whip cracked, and Elayne was thrown back into her seat. "You did not have to be rude," she said. "Or so abrupt. What did you give him?"

"A silver penny," Nynaeve replied calmly, putting the

purse back into her pouch. "And more than he deserved."

"Nynaeve," Elayne groaned. "The man probably thinks we were making sport of him."

Nynaeve sniffed. "With those shoulders, a good day's work would not kill him."

Elayne kept silent, though she did not agree. Not exactly. Certainly work would not harm the man, but she did not think there was much available. *Not that I think Master Luca would accept work that didn't allow him to wear that cape.* If she brought it up, though, Nynaeve would probably argue—when she gently pointed out things that Nyaneve did not know, the woman was quite capable of accusing her of having an arrogant manner, or of lecturing—and Valan Luca was hardly worth another altercation so soon after smoothing over the last.

The shadows were lengthening by the time they reached Sienda, a sizable village of stone and thatch with two inns. The first, The King's Lancer, had a gaping hole where the front door had been, and a crowd was watching workmen make repairs. Perhaps Master Luca's "boar-horse" had not liked the sign, propped up beside the hole now, a charging soldier with lance lowered. It seemed to have been ripped down somehow.

Surprisingly, there were even more Whitecloaks in the crowded dirt streets than back in Mardecin, far more, and other soldiers besides, men in mail and conical steel caps whose blue cloaks bore the Star and Thistle of Amadicia. There must be garrisons nearby. The King's men and the Whitecloaks did not seem to like each other at all. They either brushed by as if the man wearing the wrong color did not exist, or else with challenging stares little short of drawn swords. Some of the white-cloaked men had red shepherd's crooks behind the sunbursts on their cloaks. The Hand of the Light, those named themselves, the Hand that seeks out truth, but everyone else called them Questioners. Even the other Whitecloaks kept clear of them.

All in all, it was enough to make Elayne's stomach clench. But there was no more than another hour's sunlight left, if that, and that was taking into account the late-summer sunsets. Even driving half the night again would not guarantee another inn ahead, and driving on this late might call attention. Besides, they had reason to halt early today.

She exchanged looks with Nynaeve, and after a moment the other woman nodded and said, "We have to stop."

When the coach drew up in front of The Light of Truth, Juilin hopped down to open the door, and Nynaeve waited with a deferential look on her face for him to hand Elayne down. She did flash Elayne a smile, though; she would not slide back into sulks. The leather scrip she slung from her shoulder appeared a bit incongruous, but not too much so, Elayne hoped. Now that Nynaeve had acquired a stock of herbs and ointments again, she did not mean to let them out of her sight.

From her first sight of the inn's sign—a flaring golden sun like that the Children wore on their cloaks—she wished the "boar-horse" had taken exception to this place instead of the other. At least there was no shepherd's crook behind it. Half the men filling the common room wore snowy white cloaks, their helmets set on the tables in front of them. She took a deep breath and a firm hold on herself not to spin on her heel and leave.

Aside from the soldiers, it was a pleasant inn, with high-beamed ceilings and dark polished paneling. Cut green branches decorated the cold hearths of two large fireplaces, and good cooking smells wafted from the kitchens. The white-aproned serving maids all seemed cheerful as they scurried among the tables with trays of wine and ale and food.

The arrival of a lady created little stir, this close to the capital. Or perhaps it was because of that lord's manor. A few men looked at her; more eyed her "maid" with interest, though Nynaeve's stern frown, when she realized they were staring at her, quickly turned them back to their wine. Nynaeve seemed to think a man looking was a crime, even if he said nothing and did not leer. Given that, sometimes Elayne wondered why she did not wear less becoming clothes. She had had to work very hard to make sure that simple gray dress fit the other woman properly. Nynaeve was hopeless with a needle when it came to fine work.

The innkeeper, Mistress Jharen, was a plump woman with long gray curls, a warm smile, and searching dark eyes. Elayne suspected she could spot a worn hem or a flat purse at ten paces. They obviously passed muster, for she made a deep curtsy, spreading her gray skirts wide, and made effusive welcome, inquiring whether the Lady was on her way to or from Amador.

"From," Elayne replied with a languid hauteur. "The city's balls were most enjoyable, and King Ailron is quite as handsome as they say, which is not always so for kings, but I must return to my estates. I require a room for myself and Nana, and something for my footman and driver." Thinking of Nynaeve and the trundle, she added, "I must have two full beds. I need Nana close, and if she has only a trundle, she will keep me awake with her snoring." Nynaeve's respectful face slipped— just a fraction, thankfully—but it was quite true. She had snored terribly.

"Of course, my Lady," the plump innkeeper said. "I have just the thing. But your men will have to bed down in the stable, in the hayloft. I am quite crowded, as you can see. A troupe of vagabonds brought some horrible great animals into the village yesterday and one of them quite destroyed The King's Lancer. Poor Sim has lost half his custom or more, and they've all come here." Mistress Jharen's smile was more satisfaction than commiseration. "I do have one room left, however."

"I am sure it will do very well. If you will send up a light repast and some washwater, I think I shall retire early." There was still sunlight showing in the windows, but she put a hand delicately over her mouth as if stifling a yawn.

"Of course, my Lady. As you wish. This way."

Mistress Jharen seemed to think she had to keep Elayne entertained as she showed them to the second floor. She went on the whole way about the crowding at the inn and how it was a miracle that she had a room left, about the vagrants with their animals and how they had been chased out of town and good riddance to rubbish, about all the nobles who had stayed at her establishment over the years, even the Lord Captain Commander of the Children, once. Why, a Hunter of the Horn had come through just the day before, on his way to Tear, where they said the Stone of Tear had fallen into the hands of some false Dragon, and was it not horrible wickedness that men could do such things? "I hope they never find it." The innkeeper's gray curls swung as she shook her head.

"The Horn of Valere?" Elayne said. "Why ever not?"

"Why, my Lady, if they find it, it means the Last Battle is coming. The Dark One breaking free." Mistress Jharen shivered. "The Light send the Horn is never found. That way, the Last Battle cannot happen, can it?" There did not seem to be much answer to such curious logic.

The bedchamber was snug, if not *exactly* cramped. Two narrow beds with striped coverlets stood to either side of a window looking out onto the street, and little more than walking room separating them from each other or the white-plastered walls. A small table holding a lamp and tinderbox between the beds, a tiny, flowered rug, and a washstand with a small mirror above it completed the furnishings. Everything was clean and well polished, at least.

The innkeeper plumped the pillows and smoothed the coverlets and said the mattresses were the best goose down and the Lady's men would be bringing her chests up by the back stairs and everything would be very cozy, there was a good breeze at night if the Lady opened the window and left the door cracked. As though she would sleep with her door open to a public hallway. Two aproned girls arrived with a large blue pitcher of steaming water and a large lacquered tray covered with a white cloth before Elayne managed to get Mistress Jharen out. The shape of a wine pitcher and two cups mounded up one side of the cloth.

"I think she believed we might go to The King's Lancer even with a hole in it," she said, once the door was firmly shut. Looking around the room, she grimaced. There would barely be room for them and the chests. "I am not certain we shouldn't."

"I do not snore," Nynaeve said in a tight voice.

"Of course you do not. I had to say something, though."

Nynaeve gave a loud harrumph, but all she said was "I am glad I am tired enough to go to sleep. Aside from that forkroot, I did not recognize anything to aid sleep in what that Macura woman had."

It took Thom and Juilin three trips to bring the iron-bound wooden chests up, grumbling all the while, the way men did, about having to haul them up the narrow stairs at the rear of the inn. They were muttering about being made to sleep in the stables, too, when they brought in the first one between them—it had leaf-shaped hinges; the bulk of their money and valuables were in the bottom of that, including the recovered *ter'angreal*—but one glance at the room and they shared a look and shut their mouths. About that, at least.

"We're going to see what we can learn in the common room," Thom said once the last chest was jammed in. Barely enough space remained to reach the washstand.

"And maybe take a walk around the village," Juilin added. "Men talk when there's as much dislike as I saw in the street."

"That will be very good," Elayne said. They did so want to think they had more to do than haul and carry. It had been so in Tanchico—and Mardecin, of course—and might well be again, but hardly here. "Do be careful not to get into any trouble with the Whitecloaks, now." A long-suffering look passed between them, just as if she had not seen both with bruised and bleeding faces after jaunts for information, but she forgave them, and smiled at Thom. "I cannot wait to hear what you learn."

"In the morning," Nynaeve said firmly. She was looking away from Elayne so hard that she might as well have been glowering at her. "If you disturb us before then for less than Trollocs, you'll learn the reason why."

The glance that passed between the two men spoke volumes—it made Nynaeve's eyebrows rise sharply—

but once she had reluctantly handed over a few coins, they left agreeing to let the women sleep untroubled.

"If I cannot even speak to Thom," Elayne began when they were gone, but Nynaeve cut her off.

"I am not having them walk in on me asleep in my shift." She was awkwardly undoing the buttons down the back of her dress. Elayne went to help her, and she said, "I can manage. You get the ring out for me."

With a sniff, Elayne pulled up her skirt to reach the small pocket she had sewn to the underside. If Nynaeve wanted to be peevish, let her; she would not respond even if Nynaeve began ranting again. There were two rings in the pocket. She left the golden Great Serpent she had been given on being raised to Accepted, and took out the stone ring.

All flecks and stripes of red and blue and brown, it was just too large to fit a finger, and flattened and twisted besides. Odd as it seemed, the ring had only one edge; a finger drawn along that edge would circle inside and out before coming back to where it began. It was a *ter'angreal,* and what it did was allow access to *Tel'aran'rhiod,* even for someone who did not have the Talent that Egwene and the Aiel dreamwalkers shared. All that was needed was to sleep with it next to your skin. Unlike the two *ter'angreal* they had recovered from the Black Ajah, it did not require channeling. For all Elayne knew, even a man might be able to use it.

Clad only in her linen shift, Nynaeve threaded the ring onto the leather thong with Lan's signet and her own Great Serpent, then reknotted and hung it back around her neck before lying down atop one of the beds. Carefully tucking the rings in next to her skin, she settled her head on the pillows.

"Is there time before Egwene and the Wise Ones get there?" Elayne asked. "I can never reason out what hour it is in the Waste."

"There is time unless she comes early, which she won't. The Wise Ones keep her on a very short leash. It will do her good, in the long run. She was always headstrong." Nynaeve opened her eyes, looking right at her—at her!—as if that could stand for her as well.

"Remember to tell Egwene to let Rand know that I am thinking of him." She was *not* going to let the woman start a row. "Tell her to . . . tell him that I love him, and only him." There. She had it out.

Nynaeve rolled her eyes in what was really a most offensive way. "If you wish me to," she said dryly, snuggling herself into the pillows.

As the other woman's breathing began to slow, Elayne pushed one of the chests against the door and sat on it to wait. She always hated waiting. It would serve Nynaeve right if she went down to the common room. Thom would probably still be there, and . . . And nothing. He was supposed to be her coachman. She wondered whether Nynaeve had thought of that before agreeing to be the maid. With a sigh, she leaned back against the door. She *did* hate waiting.

CHAPTER

14

Meetings

The effects of the ring *ter'angreal* did not startle Nynaeve anymore. She was in the place she had been thinking of when sleep closed in, the great chamber in Tear called the Heart of the Stone, within the massive fortress called the Stone of Tear. The gilded stand-lamps were unlit, but pale light seemed to come from everywhere and nowhere, to simply be, all around her, fading into dim shadows in the distance. At least it was not hot; it never seemed hot or cold in *Tel'aran'rhiod.*

Huge redstone columns ran off in every direction, the vaulted dome far above lost in dim shadows along with more golden lamps hanging on golden chains. The pale floorstones beneath her feet were worn; the High Lords of Tear had come to this chamber—in the waking world, of course—only when their law and custom demanded, but they had come ever since the Breaking of the World. Centered beneath the dome was *Callandor,* apparently a glittering sword made of crystal, driven half its length into the stone of the floor. Just as Rand had left it.

She did not go near *Callandor.* Rand claimed to have

woven traps around it with *saidin,* traps that no woman could see. She expected they would be nasty—the best of men could be vicious when they tried to be devious—nasty and just as primed for a woman as for the men who might use that *sa'angreal.* He had meant to guard it against those in the Tower as much as the Forsaken. Aside from Rand himself, the one who touched *Callandor* might die or worse.

That was a fact of *Tel'aran'rhiod.* What was in the waking world was here, too, although the reverse was not always so. The World of Dreams, the Unseen World, reflected the waking world, if sometimes in odd ways, and perhaps other worlds as well. Verin Sedai had told Egwene that there was a pattern woven of worlds, of the reality here and others, just as the weaving of people's lives made up the Pattern of the Ages. *Tel'aran'rhiod* touched them all, yet few could enter except accidentally, for unknowing moments, during their own mundane dreams. Dangerous moments for those dreamers, though they never knew it unless they were very unlucky. Another fact of *Tel'aran'rhiod* was that what happened to the dreamer here happened in the waking world, too. To die in the World of Dreams was to die in fact.

She had the sensation of being watched from the dimnesses between the columns, but it did not trouble her. It was *not* Moghedien. *Imaginary eyes; there* are *no watchers. I told Elayne to ignore them, and here I . . .* Moghedien would certainly do more than look. Even so, she wished she were angry enough to channel. Not that she was frightened, of course. Only not angry. Not frightened at all.

The twisted stone ring felt light, as if it were trying to drift up out of her shift, reminding her that she was wearing only that. As soon as she thought of clothing herself, she was in a dress. It was a trick of *Tel'aran'rhiod* that she liked; in some ways channeling was unnecessary, for here she could do things that she doubted any Aes Sedai had ever done with the Power. It was not the dress she had expected, though; not good stout Two Rivers wool. The high neck trimmed in Jaerecruz lace came right up under her chin, but pale yellow silk draped her in folds that clung revealingly. How many times had she called Taraboner gowns like this indecent when she had worn them to blend into Tanchico? It seemed that she had grown more used to them than she knew.

Giving her braid a sharp pull for the waywardness of her own mind, she left the dress as it was. The gown might not be as she wanted, but she was no flighty girl to go leaping and squealing over it. *A dress is a dress.* She would wear it when Egwene arrived, with whichever of the Wise Ones accompanied her this time, and if any of them said a word . . . *I did not come early to blather at myself about dresses!*

"Birgitte?" Silence answered her, and she raised her voice, though it should not have been necessary. In this place, this particular woman could hear her own name spoken on the other side of the world. "Birgitte?"

A woman stepped out from among the columns, blue eyes calm and proudly confident, her golden hair in a long braid more intricate than Nynaeve's own. Her short white coat and voluminous yellow silk trousers, gathered at the ankles above short boots with raised heels, were garments of more than two thousand years ago that she had taken a liking to. The arrows in the quiver at her side appeared to be silver, and so did the bow she carried.

"Is Gaidal about?" Nynaeve asked. He was usually close by Birgitte, and he made Nynaeve nervous, refusing to acknowledge her existence, scowling when Birgitte spoke to her. It had been something of a shock at first to find Gaidal Cain and Birgitte—long-dead heroes linked in so many stories and legends—in *Tel'aran'rhiod.* But, as Birgitte herself had said, where better for heroes bound to the Wheel of Time to await rebirth than in a dream? A dream that had existed as long as the Wheel. It was they, Birgitte and Gaidal Cain and Rogosh Eagle-eye and Artur Hawkwing and all the others, that the Horn of Valere would summon back to fight at Tarmon Gai'don.

Birgitte's braid swung as she shook her head. "I have not seen him for some time. I think the Wheel has spun him out again. It always happens so." Expectation and concern both touched her voice.

If Birgitte was right, then somewhere in the world a

boychild had been born, a mewling babe with no knowledge of who he was, yet destined for adventures that would make new legends. The Wheel wove the heroes into the Pattern as they were needed, to shape the Pattern, and when they died they returned here to wait again. That was what it meant to be bound to the Wheel. New heroes could find themselves bound so as well, men and women whose bravery and accomplishments raised them far above the ordinary, but once bound, it was forever.

"How long do you have?" Nynaeve asked. "Years yet, surely." Birgitte was always tied to Gaidal, had been tied in story after story, in Age after Age, of adventure and a romance that even the Wheel of Time did not break. She was always born after Gaidal; a year, or five, or ten, but after.

"I do not know, Nynaeve. Time here is not like time in the waking world. I met you here last ten days gone, as it seems to me, and Elayne only a day before. What was it for you?"

"Four days and three," Nynaeve muttered. She and Elayne had been coming to speak with Birgitte as often as they could, though too frequently it had not been possible with Thom and Juilin sharing the camp and standing night guard. Birgitte actually remembered the War of Power, one lifetime of it anyway, and the Forsaken. Her past lives were like books fondly remembered from long ago, the more distant dimmer than the nearer, but the Forsaken stood out. Especially Moghedien.

"You see, Nynaeve? The flow of time here can shift in larger ways, too. It might be months before I am born again, or days. Here, for me. In the waking world it could be years yet before my birth."

With an effort Nynaeve suppressed her vexation. "Then we mustn't waste what time we have. Have you seen any of them since we last met?" There was no need to say who.

"Too many. Lanfear is often in *Tel'aran'rhiod*, of course, but I have seen Rahvin and Sammael and Graendal. Demandred. And Semirhage." Birgitte's voice tightened at the last name; even Moghedien, who hated her, did not frighten her visibly, but Semirhage was another matter.

Nynaeve shivered as well—the golden-haired woman had told her too much of that one—and realized she was wearing a thick wool cloak, with a deep hood pulled up to hide her face; flushing, she made it disappear.

"None of them have seen you?" she asked anxiously. Birgitte was more vulnerable than herself in many ways, despite her knowledge of *Tel'aran'rhiod.* She had never been able to channel; any of the Forsaken could destroy her as if crushing an ant, without breaking stride. And if she were destroyed here, there would be no rebirth for her ever again.

"I am not so unskilled—or so foolish—as to allow that." Birgitte leaned on her silver bow; legend said she never missed with that bow and her silver arrows. "They are concerned with each other, not anyone else. I have seen Rahvin and Sammael, Graendal and Lanfear, each stalking the others unseen. And Demandred and Semirhage each shadowing them as well. I have not seen so much of them here since they were freed."

"They are up to something." Nynaeve bit her lip in vexed frustration. "But what?"

"I cannot say yet, Nynaeve. In the War of the Shadow, they were always plotting, against each other as often as not, but their work has never boded well for the world, waking or dreaming."

"Try to find out, Birgitte; as much as you can safely, at any rate. Do not take any risks." The other woman's face did not change, but Nynaeve thought she was amused; the fool woman thought as little of danger as did Lan. She wished she could ask about the White Tower, about what Siuan might be scheming, but Birgitte could neither see nor touch the waking world unless she was called there by the Horn. *You are just trying to avoid what you really want to ask!* "Have you seen Moghedien?"

"No," Birgitte sighed, "but not for lack of trying. In the usual course I can find anyone who knows they are in the World of Dreams; there is a feel, like ripples spreading through the air from them. Or perhaps from their awareness; I do not know, really. I am a soldier, not a scholar. Either she has not come into *Tel'aran'rhiod* since you defeated her, or . . ." She hesitated, and Nynaeve wanted to stop her from saying what she knew would come next, but Birgitte was too strong to dodge unpalatable possibilities. "Or else she knows I have been looking for her. She can hide, that one. She is not called the Spider for nothing." That was what a *moghedien* had been, in the Age of Legends; a tiny spider that spun its webs in secret places, its bite poisonous enough to kill in heartbeats.

Suddenly very much aware of feeling unseen eyes, Nynaeve shivered heavily. It was not trembling. Just a shiver, not trembling. Still, she kept the sleek Taraboner gown firmly in mind lest she abruptly find herself wearing armor. It was embarrassing enough if that sort of thing happened when she was alone, even more under the cool blue gaze of a woman valiant enough to be a match for Gaidal Cain.

"Can you find her even when she wants to remain hidden, Birgitte?" It was a very great deal to ask, if Moghedien knew she was being hunted; like searching for a lion in high grass armed only with a stick.

The other woman did not hesitate. "Perhaps. I will try." Hefting her bow, she added, "I must go, now. I do not want to risk being seen by the others when they come."

Nynaeve put a hand on her arm to stop her. "It would be a help if you let me tell them. That way I could share what you've told me about the Forsaken with Egwene and the Wise Ones, and they could tell Rand. Birgitte, he needs to know—"

"You promised, Nynaeve." Those bright blue eyes were unyielding as ice. "The prescripts say that we must not let anyone know that we reside in *Tel'aran'rhiod*. I have broken many by speaking to you, much more by giving aid, because I cannot stand by and watch you battle the Shadow—I have fought that battle in more lifetimes than I can remember—but I *will* keep as many of the prescripts as I can. You must hold to your promise."

"Of course I will," she said indignantly, "unless you release me from it. And I *do* ask you to—"

"No."

And Birgitte was gone. One moment Nynaeve's hand rested on a white coatsleeve, the next on empty air. In her mind she ran through a few curses she had overheard from Thom and Juilin, the sort she would have scolded Elayne for listening to, much less using. There was no point calling Birgitte's name again. She probably would not come. Nynaeve only hoped she responded the next time she or Elayne called. "Birgitte! I will keep my promise, Birgitte!"

She would have heard that. Perhaps by their next meeting she would know something of Moghedien's activities. Nynaeve almost hoped she would not. If she did, it meant that Moghedien really was stalking *Tel'aran'rhiod.*

Fool woman! "If you don't look for snakes, you cannot complain when one bites you." She really did want to meet Elayne's Lini one day.

The emptiness of the vast chamber oppressed her, all those great polished columns and that sense of being watched from the dimness between. *If there really was anybody there, Birgitte would have known.*

She realized that she was smoothing the silk gown over her hips, and, to take her mind off eyes that were not there, she concentrated on the dress. It had been in good Two Rivers woolens that Lan had first seen her, and a simple embroidered dress that she had been wearing when he professed his love, but she wanted him to see her in gowns like this. It would not be indecent if he was the one seeing her.

A tall standing mirror appeared, casting her reflection as she turned this way and that, even peering back over her shoulder. The yellow folds sheathed her closely, suggesting everything they hid. The Women's Circle in Emond's Field would have hauled her off for a good talking to in private, Wisdom or no Wisdom. Yet it was quite beautiful. Here, alone, she could admit that she had a bit more than gotten used to wearing something like this in public. *You enjoyed it,* she scolded herself. *You are every bit as much a hussy as Elayne seems to be turning into!* But it was beautiful. And maybe not as immodest as she had always said. Not a neckline cut halfway to her knees, like the First of Mayene, for instance. Well, perhaps Berelain's were not that low, but they were still far deeper than respectability required.

She had heard about what Domani women often wore; even Taraboners called *those* indecent. With the thought, the yellow silk folds became rippling flows, with a narrow belt of woven gold. And thin. Her face colored. Very thin. Barely opaque at all, in fact. The gown certainly did more than suggest. If Lan saw her in that, he would not gabble that his love for her was hopeless and that he would not give her widow's weeds for a bridal gift. One glimpse, and his blood would catch fire. He would—

"What under the Light is that you have on, Nynaeve?" Egwene asked in scandalized tones.

Nynaeve leaped straight up, spinning, and when she came down facing Egwene and Melaine—it *would* be Melaine, though none of the Wise Ones would have been any better—the mirror was gone and she was wearing a dark woolen Two Rivers dress thick enough for the depths of winter. Mortified at being startled as much as anything else—it *was* mainly at being startled—she changed the dress instantly, without thinking, flashing back into the gossamer Domani and just as quickly to the yellow Taraboner folds.

Her face flamed. They probably thought her a complete fool. And in front of Melaine, at that. The Wise One was beautiful, with her long red-gold hair and clear green eyes. Not that she cared a whit how the woman looked. But Melaine had been at her last meeting here with Egwene, too, and taunted her about Lan. Nynaeve had lost her temper over it. Egwene claimed they were not taunts, not among Aiel women, but Melaine had complimented Lan's shoulders, and his hands, and his eyes. What right did that green-eyed cat have to look at Lan's shoulders? Not that she had any doubts of his faithfulness. But he was a man, and far away from her, and Melaine was right there, and . . . Firmly, she put a stop to that line of reasoning.

"Is Lan—?" She thought her face was going to burn off. *Can't you control your own tongue, woman?* But she would not—could not—back away, not with Melaine there. Egwene's bemused smile was bad enough, but Melaine dared to put on a look of understanding. "Is he well?" She tried for cool composure, but it came out strained.

"He is well," Egwene said. "He worries about whether you are safe."

Nynaeve let out a breath she had not realized she was holding. The Waste was a dangerous place even without the likes of Couladin and the Shaido, and the man did not know the meaning of caution. He was worried about her safety? Did the fool man think she could not take care of herself?

"We've finally reached Amadicia," she said quickly, hoping to cover herself. *A flapping tongue, and then sighs! The man has stolen my wits!* There was no telling from the others' faces whether she was succeeding. "A village called Sienda, east of Amador. Whitecloaks everywhere, but they don't look at us twice. It is others we have to worry about." In front of Melaine, she had to be careful—to bend the truth a little, in fact, here and there—but she told them of Ronde Macura and her odd message, and her trying to drug them. Trying, because she could not make herself admit in front of Melaine that the woman had succeeded. *Light, what am I doing? I've never lied to Egwene before in my life!*

The supposed reason—the return of a runaway Accepted—certainly could not be mentioned, not in front of one of the Wise Ones. They thought that she and Elayne were full Aes Sedai. But she had to let Egwene know the truth of that somehow. "It might have to do with some plot concerning Andor, but Elayne and you and I have things in common, Egwene, and I think we should be just as careful as Elayne." The girl nodded slowly; she looked stunned, as well she might, but she seemed to understand. "A good thing the taste of that tea made me suspicious. Imagine trying to feed forkroot to someone who knows herbs as well as I do."

"Schemes within schemes," Melaine murmured. "The Great Serpent is a good sign for you Aes Sedai, I think. Someday you may swallow yourselves by accident."

"We have news ourselves," Egwene said.

Nynaeve could see no reason for the girl's haste. *I am certainly not going to let the woman bait me into losing my temper. And I certainly wouldn't get angry over her insulting the Tower.* She took her hand away from her braid. What Egwene had to say put temper right out of her head.

Couladin crossing the Spine of the World was surely grave, and Rand following scarcely less so; he was pushing hard for the Jangai Pass, marching from first light until after dusk, and Melaine said they would soon reach it. Conditions in Cairhien were harsh enough without a war between Aiel on its territory. And a new Aiel War to come, surely, if he tried to carry out his mad plan. Mad. Not yet, surely. He had to hang on to sanity, somehow.

How long since I was worrying how to protect him? she thought bitterly. *And now I just want him to stay sane to fight the Last Battle.* Not only for that reason, but for that one, too. He was what he was. *The Light burn me, I'm as bad as Siuan Sanche or any of them!*

It was what Egwene had to say about Moiraine that shocked her. "She *obeys* him?" she said incredulously.

Egwene gave a vigorous nod, in that ridiculous Aiel scarf. "Last night they had an argument—she's still trying to convince him not to cross the Dragonwall—and finally he told her to stand outside until she cooled down; she looked about to swallow her tongue, but she did it. She stayed out in the night for an hour, anyway."

"It is not proper," Melaine said, resettling her shawl firmly. "Men have no more business ordering Aes Sedai about than they do Wise Ones. Even the *Car'a'carn*."

"They certainly do not," Nynaeve agreed, then had to clamp her mouth shut to keep from gaping at herself. *What do I care if he makes her dance to his tune? She has made all of us dance to hers often enough.* But it was not proper. *I do not want to be Aes Sedai, just to learn more about Healing. I want to stay who I am. Let him order her about!* Still, it was not proper.

"At least he talks with her, now," Egwene said. "Before, he turned to acid if she came within ten feet of him. Nynaeve, his head swells bigger every day."

"Back when I thought you'd follow me as Wisdom," Nynaeve told her wryly, "I taught you how to take swelling down. Best for him if you do it, even if he has turned into the king bull in the pasture. Maybe most because he is. It seems to me that kings—and queens—can be fools when they forget what they are and act like who they are, but they're worse when they only remember what they are and forget who. Most could do with someone whose only job is to remind them that they eat and sweat and cry the same as any farmer."

Melaine folded her shawl around her, seeming unsure whether to agree or not, but Egwene said, "I try, but sometimes he doesn't seem like himself at all, and even when he is, his arrogance is usually too thick a bubble to prick."

"Do the best you can. Helping him hold on to himself may be the best thing that anyone could do. For him, and the rest of the world."

That produced a silence. She and Egwene certainly did not like to talk about the eventuality of Rand going mad, and Melaine could not like it any better.

"I have something else important to tell you," she went on after a moment. "I think the Forsaken are planning something." It was not the same as telling them about Birgitte. She made it seem that she herself had seen Lanfear and the others. In truth, Moghedien was the only one she could recognize at sight, and maybe Asmodean, though she had only seen him once, and at a distance. She hoped neither of them thought to ask how she knew who was who, or why she thought Moghedien might be skulking about. In actuality, the problem did not arise from that at all.

"Have you been wandering the World of Dreams?" Melaine's eyes were green ice.

Nynaeve met her level stare for level stare, despite Egwene's rueful headshaking. "I could hardly see Rahvin and the rest without it, now could I?"

"Aes Sedai, you know little, and you try too much. You should not have been taught the few pieces that you have. For myself, I sometimes regret that we agreed even to these meetings. Unschooled women should not be allowed in *Tel'aran'rhiod*."

"I have schooled myself in more than you ever taught me." Nynaeve kept her voice cool with an effort. "I learned to channel on my own, and I do not see why *Tel'aran'rhiod* should be any different." It was only stubborn anger that made her say that. She had taught herself to channel, true, but without knowing what it was that she was doing and only after a fashion. Before the White Tower, she had Healed sometimes, but unaware, until Moiraine proved it to her. Her teachers in the Tower had said that was why she needed to be angry in order to channel; she had hidden her ability from herself, afraid of it, and only fury could break through that long-buried fear.

"So you are one of those the Aes Sedai call wilders." There was a hint of something in the last word, but whether scorn or pity, Nynaeve did not like it. The term was seldom complimentary, in the Tower. Of course, there were no wilders among the Aiel. The Wise Ones who could channel found every last girl with the spark born in her, those who would develop the ability to channel sooner or later even if they did not try to learn. They claimed also to find every girl without the spark who could learn if instructed. No Aiel girl died trying to learn by herself. "You know the dangers of learning the Power without guidance, Aes Sedai. Do not think the dangers of the dream are less. They are just as great, perhaps more for those who venture without knowledge."

"I am careful," Nynaeve said in a tight voice. She had not come to be lectured by this sun-haired vixen of an Aiel. "I know what I am doing, Melaine."

"You know nothing. You are as headstrong as this one was when she came to us." The Wise One gave Egwene a smile that actually seemed affectionate. "We tamed her excessive exuberance, and now she learns swiftly. Though she does have many faults, still." Egwene's pleased grin faded; Nynaeve suspected that grin was why Melaine had added the last. "If you wish to wander the dream," the Aiel woman went on, "come to us. We will tame your zeal, as well, and teach you."

"I do not need taming, thank you very much," Nynaeve said with a polite smile.

"Aan'allein will die on the day he learns that you are dead."

Ice stabbed into Nynaeve's heart. *Aan'allein* was what the Aiel called Lan. One Man, it meant in the Old Tongue, or Man Alone, or the Man Who Is an Entire People; exact translations from the Old Tongue were often difficult. The Aiel had a great deal of respect for Lan, the man who would not give up his war with the Shadow, the enemy that had destroyed his nation. "You are a dirty fighter," she muttered.

Melaine quirked an eyebrow. "Do we fight? If we do, then know that in battle there is only winning and losing. Rules against hurting are for games. I want your promise that you will do nothing in the dream without first asking one of us. I know Aes Sedai cannot lie, so I would hear you say it.

Nynaeve gritted her teeth. The words would be easy to say. She did not have to hold to them; she was not bound by the Three Oaths. But it would be admitting that Melaine was right. She did not believe it, and she would not say it.

"She'll not promise, Melaine," Egwene said finally. "When she gets that muley look, she wouldn't come out of the house if you showed her the roof on fire."

Nynaeve spared a piece of glare for her. Muley, indeed! When all she did was refuse to be pushed about like a rag doll.

After a long moment, Melaine sighed. "Very well. But it would be well to remember, Aes Sedai, that you are but a child in *Tel'aran'rhiod*. Come, Egwene. We must go." An amused wince crossed Egwene's face as the two faded away.

Abruptly Nynaeve realized that her clothes had changed. Had been changed; the Wise Ones knew enough of *Tel'aran'rhiod* to alter things about others as well as themselves. She wore a white blouse and a dark skirt, but unlike those of the women who had just gone, this stopped well short of her knees. Her shoes and stockings were gone, and her hair was divided into two braids, one over each ear, woven with yellow ribbons. A rag doll with a carved and painted face sat beside her bare feet. She could hear her teeth grinding. This had happened once before, and she had pried out of Egwene that this was how the Aiel dressed little girls.

In a fury she switched back to the yellow Taraboner silk—this time it adhered even more closely—and kicked the doll. It sailed away, vanishing in midair. That Melaine probably had her eye on Lan; the Aiel all seemed to think he was some sort of hero. The high neck became a tall lace collar, and the deep narrow neckline showed her cleavage. If that woman so much as smiled at him . . . ! If he . . . ! Suddenly she became aware of her fast-sinking, rapidly widening neckline and hastily brought it back up; not all the way, but enough that she did not have to blush. The dress had grown so tight that she could not move; she took care of that, too.

So she was supposed to *ask permission,* was she? Go begging the Wise Ones before doing anything? Had she not defeated Moghedien? They had been properly impressed at the time, but they seemed to have forgotten.

If she could not use Birgitte to find out what was going on in the Tower, perhaps there was a way she could do it herself.

CHAPTER
15

What Can Be Learned in Dreams

Carefully Nynaeve formed an image in her mind of the Amyrlin's study, just as she had envisioned the Heart of the Stone on going to sleep. Nothing happened, and she frowned. She should have been taken to the White Tower, to the room she had visualized. Trying again, she imagined a room there that she had visited much more often, if more unhappily.

The Heart of the Stone became the study of the Mistress of Novices, a compact, dark-paneled room full of plain, sturdy furnishings that had been used by generations of women who had held that office. When a novice's transgressions were such that extra hours of scrubbing floors or raking paths would not atone, it was here that she was sent. For an Accepted to receive that summons took a greater transgression, but still she went, on leaden feet, knowing the outcome would be just as painful, perhaps more so.

Nynaeve did not want to look at the room—Sheriam had called her willfully stubborn on her numerous visits—but found herself staring into the mirror on the wall, where novices and Accepted had to look at their own weeping faces while listening to Sheriam lecture about obeying the rules or showing proper respect or whatever. Obeying others' rules and showing required respect had always tripped up Nynaeve. The faint remnants of gilt on the carved frame said it had been there since the War of the Hundred Years, if not the Breaking.

The Taraboner dress was beautiful, but anyone who saw her in it would be suspicious. Even Domani women usually dressed circumspectly when they visited the Tower, and she could not imagine anybody dreaming of herself in the Tower except on her best behavior. Not that she was likely to meet anyone, except perhaps someone who had dreamed herself into *Tel'aran'rhiod* for a few moments; before Egwene, there had not been a woman in the Tower who could enter the World of Dreams unaided since Corianin Nedeal, over four hundred years ago. On the other hand, among the *ter'angreal* stolen from the Tower that were still in the hands of Liandrin and her confederates, eleven had last been studied by Corianin. The two others of Corianin's study, the two that she and Elayne had in hand, both gave access to *Tel'aran'rhiod*; it was best to assume that the rest did, too. There was small chance that Liandrin or any of the others would dream themselves back to the Tower they had fled, but even that chance was too big to risk when it might mean being waylaid. For that matter, she could not really be sure that the stolen *ter'angreal* were all that Corianin had investigated. The records were often murky about *ter'angreal* no one understood, and others could very well be in the hands of Black sisters still in the Tower.

The dress changed completely, became white wool, soft but not of a particularly fine quality, and banded at the hem with seven colored stripes, one for each Ajah. If she saw anyone who did not vanish after a few moments, she would take herself back to Sienda, and they would think she was only one of the Accepted, touching *Tel'aran'rhiod* in her dreams. No. Not the inn, but Sheriam's study. Anyone like that would have to be

Black Ajah, and after all, she was supposed to be hunting them.

Completing her disguise, she gripped her suddenly red-gold braid and grimaced at Melaine's face in the mirror. Now, there was a woman she would like to hand over to Sheriam.

The study of the Mistress of Novices was near the novices' quarters, and the wide, tiled hallways flickered with occasional motion past elaborate wall hangings and unlit stand-lamps; flashes of frightened girls all in novice white. A good many novice nightmares would contain Sheriam. She ignored them as she hurried by; they were not in the World of Dreams long enough to see her, or if they did they would simply think her part of their own dream.

It was only a short climb up broad stairs to the Amyrlin's study. As she approached, suddenly Elaida was in front of her, sweaty-faced in a blood-red gown, the stole of the Amyrlin Seat around her shoulders. Or almost the Amyrlin's stole; it had no blue stripe.

Those stern dark eyes focused on Nynaeve. "I am the Amyrlin Seat, girl! Do you not know how to show respect? I will have yo—" In midword, she was gone.

Nynaeve exhaled raggedly. Elaida as Amyrlin; that was a nightmare for certain. *Probably her fondest dream,* she thought wryly. *It will snow in Tear before* she *ever rises that high.*

The anteroom was much as she remembered it, with one wide table and a chair behind it for the Keeper of the Chronicles. A few chairs sat against the wall for Aes Sedai waiting to speak with the Amyrlin; novices and Accepted stood. The neat array of papers on the table, bound scrolls and large parchments with seals and letters, seemed unlike Leane, though. Not that she was untidy, quite the reverse, yet Nynaeve had always thought she would put everything away at night.

She pushed open the door to the inner room, but her step slowed as she entered. No wonder she had not been able to dream herself here; the room was nothing like what she remembered. That heavily carved table and tall, thronelike chair. The vine-carved stools arranged in a perfect curve in front of the table, not one so much as an inch out of place. Siuan Sanche affected simple furnishings, as if pretending she was still only a fisherman's daughter, and she kept only one extra chair, which she did not always let visitors use. And that white vase full of red roses, rigidly arranged on a pedestal like a monument. Siuan enjoyed flowers, but she preferred a bouquet of colors, like a field of wildflowers in miniature. Above the fireplace had hung a simple drawing of fishing boats in tall reeds. Now there were two paintings, one of which Nynaeve recognized. Rand, battling the Forsaken who had called himself Ba'alzamon, in the clouds above Falme. The other, on three wooden panels, portrayed scenes that linked to nothing she could pull out of her memory.

The door opened, and Nynaeve's heart leaped into her throat. A red-haired Accepted she had never seen before stepped into the room and stared at her. She did not wink out of existence. Just as Nynaeve was preparing to leap back to Sheriam's study, the red-haired woman said, "Nynaeve, if Melaine knew you were using her face, she'd do more than put you in a child's dress." And just that suddenly she was Egwene, in her Aiel garb.

"You nearly frightened ten years out of me," Nynaeve muttered. "So the Wise Ones have finally decided to let you come and go as you please? Or is Melaine behind—"

"You should be frightened," Egwene snapped, color rising in her cheeks. "You are a fool, Nynaeve. A child playing in the barn with a candle."

Nynaeve gaped. *Egwene* berating *her?* "You listen to me, Egwene al'Vere. I'll not take that from Melaine, and I won't take it—"

"You had best take it from someone, before you get yourself killed."

"I—"

"I ought to take that stone ring away from you. I should have given it to Elayne and told her not to let you use it at all."

"Told her not—!"

"Do you think Melaine was exaggerating?" Egwene

said sternly, shaking her finger almost exactly like Melaine. "She was not, Nynaeve. The Wise Ones have told you the simple truth about *Tel'aran'rhiod* time and again, but you seem to think they're fools whistling in a high wind. You are supposed to be a grown woman, not a silly little child. I vow, whatever sense you once had in your head seems to have vanished like a puff of smoke. Well, find it, Nynaeve!" She sniffed loudly, rearranging the shawl on her shoulders. "Right now you are trying to play with the pretty flames in the fireplace, too foolish to realize you might fall in."

Nynaeve stared in amazement. They argued often enough, but Egwene had never ever tried to dress her down like a girl caught with her fingers in the honeyjar. Never! The dress. It was the Accepted's dress she was wearing, and someone else's face. She changed herself back to herself, in a good blue wool that she had often worn for Circle meetings and to put the Council straight. She felt robed in all her old authority as Wisdom. "I am well aware of how much I don't know," she said levelly, "but those Aiel—"

"Do you realize you could dream yourself into something you could not get out of? Dreams are real here. If you let yourself drift into a fond dream, it could trap you. You'd trap yourself. Until you died."

"Will you—?"

"There are nightmares walking *Tel'aran'rhiod*, Nynaeve."

"Will you let me speak?" Nyaneve barked. Or rather, she tried to bark it; there was rather too much frustrated pleading in there to suit her. Any at all would have been too much.

"No, I will not," Egwene said firmly. "Not until you want to say something worth listening to. I said nightmares, and I meant nightmares, Nynaeve. When someone has a nightmare while in *Tel'aran'rhiod*, it is real too. And sometimes it survives after the dreamer has gone. You just don't realize, do you?"

Suddenly rough hands enveloped Nynaeve's arms. Her head whipped from side to side, eyes bulging. Two huge, ragged men lifted her into the air, faces half-melted ruins of coarse flesh, drooling mouths full of sharp, yellowed teeth. She tried to make them vanish—if a Wise One dreamwalker could, so could she—and one of them ripped her dress open down the front like parchment. The other seized her chin in a horny, callused hand and twisted her face toward him; his head bent toward her, mouth opening. Whether to kiss or bite, she did not know, but she would rather die than allow either. She flailed for *saidar* and found nothing; it was horror filling her, not anger. Thick fingernails dug into her cheeks, holding her head steady. Egwene had done this, some-how. Egwene. "Please, Egwene!" It was a squeal, and she was too terrified to care. "Please!"

The men—creatures—vanished, and her feet thud-ded to the floor. For a moment all she could do was shudder and weep. Hastily she repaired the damage to her dress, but the scratches from long fingernails re-mained on her neck and chest. Clothing could be mended easily in *Tel'aran'rhiod,* but whatever happened to a human . . . Her knees shook so badly that it was all she could do to stay upright.

She half-expected Egwene to comfort her, and for once she would have accepted it gladly. But the other woman only said, "There are worse things here, but nightmares are bad enough. I made these, and unmade them, but even I have trouble with those I just find. And I did not try to hold them, Nynaeve. If you knew how to unmake them, you could have."

Nynaeve tossed her head angrily, refusing to scrub the tears from her cheeks. "I could have dreamed myself away. To Sheriam's study, or back to my bed." She did not sound sulky. Of course she did not.

"If you had not been too scared spitless to think of it," Egwene said dryly. "Oh, take that sullen look off your face. It looks silly on you."

She glared at the other woman, but it did not work as it usually did. Instead of flaring into argument, Egwene merely arched an eyebrow at her. "None of this looks like Siuan Sanche," Nynaeve said to change the subject. What had gotten into the girl?

"It doesn't," Egwene agreed, looking around the

room. "I see why I had to come by way of my old room in the novices' quarters. But I suppose people do decide to try something new sometimes."

"That is what I mean," Nynaeve told her patiently. She had not sounded sulky, and she had not looked sullen. It was ridiculous. "The woman who furnished this room doesn't look at the world the same as the woman who chose what used to be here. Look at those paintings. I don't know what the triple thing is, but you can recognize the other as well as I." They had both seen it happen.

"Bonwhin, I should say," Egwene said thoughtfully. "You never did listen to the lectures as you should. It is a triptych."

"Whatever it is, it's the other that's important." She had listened to the Yellows well enough. The rest was a pack of useless nonsense often as not. "It seems to me that the woman who hung it wants to be reminded how dangerous Rand is. If Siuan Sanche has turned against Rand for some reason . . . Egwene, this could be far worse than just her wanting Elayne back in the Tower."

"Perhaps," Egwene said judiciously. "Maybe the papers will tell us something. You search in here. When I finish with Leane's desk, I will help you."

Nynaeve stared indignantly at Egwene's back as she left. *You search in here, indeed!* Egwene had no right to give her orders. She ought to march right after her and tell her so in no uncertain terms. *Then why are you standing here like a lump?* she asked herself angrily. Searching the papers was a good idea, and she might as well do so in here as out there. In fact, the Amyrlin's desk was more likely to hold something important. Grumbling to herself about what she would do to set Egwene straight, she stalked to the thickly carved table, kicking her skirts with every step.

There was nothing on the table except three ornately lacquered boxes, arrayed with painful precision. Remembering the sorts of traps that could be set by someone wanting to insure privacy, she made a long stick to push open the hinged lid of the first, a gold and green thing decorated with wading herons. It was a writing case, with pens and ink and sand. The largest box, with red roses twining through golden scrolls, held twenty or more delicate carvings of ivory and turquoise, animals and people, all laid out on pale gray velvet.

As she pushed up the lid of the third box—golden hawks fighting among white clouds in a blue sky—she noticed that the first two were closed again. Things like that happened here; everything seemed to want to remain as it was in the waking world, and on top of that, if you took your eyes away for a moment, details could be different when you looked back.

The third box did hold documents. The stick vanished, and she gingerly lifted out the top sheet of parchment. Formally signed "Joline Aes Sedai," it was a humble request to serve a set of penances that made Nynaeve wince just scanning them rapidly. Nothing there that mattered, except to Joline. A scrawl at the bottom said "approved" in angular script. As she reached to put the parchment down, it faded away; the box was closed, too.

Sighing, she opened it again. The papers inside looked different. Holding the lid, she lifted them out one by one and read quickly. Or tried to read. Sometimes the letters and reports vanished while she was still picking them up, sometimes when she was no more than halfway down a page. If they had a salutation, it was simply, "Mother, with respect." Some were signed by Aes Sedai, others by women with other titles, nobles, or no honorific at all. None of it seemed to bear on the matter at hand. The Marshal General of Saldaea and his army could not be found, and Queen Tenobia was refusing to cooperate; she managed to finish that report, but it assumed that the reader knew why the man was not in Saldaea and what the queen was supposed to be cooperating about. No report had come from any Ajah's eyes-and-ears in Tanchico for three weeks; but she got no further than that one fact. Some trouble between Illian on one side and Murandy on the other was abating, and Pedron Niall was claiming credit; even in the few lines she got she could see the writer's teeth gnashing. The letters were all no doubt very important, those she was able to hurry through and those that faded away under her eyes, but of no use to her at all. She had just begun what seemed to be a report on a suspected—that was the word used— gathering of Blue sisters, when a wretched cry of "Oh, Light, no!" came from the outer room.

Darting for the door, she made a stout wooden club appear in her hands, its head bristling with spikes. But when she dashed in expecting to find Egwene defending herself, the woman was standing behind the Keeper's table staring at nothing. With a look of horror on her face, to be sure, but still unharmed and unthreatened that Nynaeve could see.

Egwene gave a start at the sight of her, then gathered herself visibly. "Nynaeve, Elaida is Amyrlin Seat."

"Don't be a goose," Nynaeve scoffed. Yet the other room, so unlike Siuan Sanche . . . "You're imagining things. You must be."

"I had a parchment in my hands, Nynaeve, signed 'Elaida do Avriny a'Roihan, Watcher of the Seals, Flame of Tar Valon, The Amyrlin Seat,' and sealed with the Amyrlin's seal."

Nynaeve's stomach tried to flutter up into her chest. "But how? What has happened to Siuan? Egwene, the Tower doesn't depose an Amyrlin except for something serious. Only two in nearly three thousand years."

"Maybe Rand was serious enough." Egwene's voice was steady, though her eyes were still too wide. "Maybe she became ill with something the Yellows couldn't Heal, or fell down the stairs and broke her neck. What matters is that Elaida is Amyrlin. I don't think she will support Rand as Siuan did."

"Moiraine," Nynaeve muttered. "So sure that Siuan would put the Tower behind him." She could not imagine Siuan Sanche dead. She had hated the woman often, been the slightest bit afraid of her on occasion—she could admit that now, to herself anyway—yet she had respected her, too. She had thought that Siuan would last forever. "Elaida. Light! She's as mean as a snake and as cruel as a cat. There's no telling what she might do."

"I am afraid I have a clue." Egwene pressed both hands to her stomach as though to quell flutters of her own. "It was a very short document. I managed to read it all. 'All loyal sisters are required to report the presence of the woman Moiraine Damodred. She is to be detained if possible, by whatever means are necessary, and returned to the White Tower for trial on charge of treason.' The same sort of language that was apparently used about Elayne."

"If Elaida wants Moiraine arrested, it must mean she knows Moiraine has been helping Rand, and she does not like it." Talking was good. Talking kept her from sicking up. Treason. They stilled women for that. She had wanted to bring Moiraine down. Now Elaida was going to do it for her. "She certainly won't support Rand."

"Exactly."

"Loyal sisters. Egwene, that fits with the Macura woman's message. Whatever happened to Siuan, the Ajahs have split over Elaida as Amyrlin. It must be."

"Yes, of course. Very good, Nynaeve. I did not see that."

Her smile was so pleased that Nynaeve smiled back. "There's a report on Siu— on the Amyrlin's writing table about a gathering of Blues. I was just reading it when you shouted. I'll wager the Blues didn't support Elaida." The Blue and Red Ajahs had a sort of armed truce at the best of times, and came near going for each other's throats at the worst.

But when they went back into the inner room, the report was not to be found. There were plenty of documents—Joline's letter had reappeared; a brief reading made Egwene's eyebrows climb nearly to her hair— but not the one that they wanted.

"Can you remember what it said?" Egwene asked.

"I had just gotten a few lines when you shouted, and . . . I just can't remember."

"Try, Nynaeve. Try very hard."

"I am, Egwene, but it will not come. I *am* trying."

What she was doing hit Nynaeve like a sudden hammer between the eyes. Excusing herself. To Egwene, a girl whose bottom she had switched for throwing a tantrum not more than two years ago. And a moment earlier she had been proud as a hen with a new egg because Egwene was pleased with her. She remembered quite clearly the day when the balance between them had shifted, when they ceased being the Wisdom and the girl who fetched when the Wisdom said fetch, becoming instead just two women far from home. It seemed that balance had shifted further, and she did not like it. She was going to have to do something to move it back where it belonged.

The lie. She had deliberately lied to Egwene for the first time ever today. That was why her moral authority had vanished, why she was floundering around, unable to assert herself properly. "I drank the tea, Egwene." She forced each word deliberately. She had to force them. "The Macura woman's forkroot tea. She and Luci hauled us upstairs like sacks of feathers. That is about how much strength we had between us. If Thom and Juilin hadn't come to pull us out by the scruffs of our necks, we would probably be there still. Or else on our way to the Tower, so full of forkroot we wouldn't wake up until we got here." Taking a deep breath, she tried for a tone of righteous firmness, but it was difficult when you had just confessed to having been an utter fool. What came out sounded much more tentative than she liked. "If you tell the Wise Ones about this—especially that Melaine—I'll box your ears."

Something in that should have sparked Egwene's ire. It seemed odd to want to start a row—usually their quarrels were over Egwene refusing to see reason, and they seldom ended pleasantly, since the girl had formed the habit of continuing to refuse—but that was certainly better than this. Yet Egwene only smiled at her. An amused smile. A *condescending* amused smile.

"I more than suspected as much, Nynaeve. You used to drone on about herbs day and night, but you never mentioned any plant called forkroot. I was sure you'd never heard of it until that woman mentioned it. You've always tried to put the best face on things. If you fell head first into a pigsty, you'd try to convince everybody you did it on purpose. Now, what we have to decide—"

"I do no such thing," Nynaeve spluttered.

"You certainly do. Facts are facts. You might as well stop whining about it and help me decide—"

Whining! This was not going at all the way she wanted. "They are no such thing. Not facts, I mean. I have never done what you said."

For a moment Egwene stared at her silently. "You will not let go of this, will you? Very well. You lied to me . . ."

"It was not a lie," she muttered. "Not exactly."

The other woman ignored her interruption. ". . . And you lie to yourself. Do you remember what you made me drink the last time I lied to you?" Suddenly a cup was in her hand, full of viscous sickly green liquid; it looked as if it had been scooped from a scummy stagnant pond. "The *only* time I ever lied to you. The memory of that taste was an effective discouragement. If you cannot tell the truth even to yourself . . ."

Nynaeve took a step back before she could stop herself. Boiled catfern and powdered mavinsleaf; her tongue writhed at just the thought. "I did not *really* lie, actually." Why was she making excuses? "I just didn't tell the whole truth." *I am the Wisdom! I was the Wisdom; that ought to count for something still.* "You cannot really think . . ." *Just tell her. You're not the child here, and you certainly are not going to drink.* "Egwene, I—" Egwene pushed the cup nearly under her nose; she could smell the acrid tang. "All right," she said hastily. *This can't be happening!* But she could not take her eyes off that brimming cup, and she could not stop the words tumbling out. "Sometimes I try to make things look better for myself than they were. Sometimes. But never anything important. I've never—lied—about anything important. Never, I swear. Only small things." The cup vanished, and Nynaeve heaved a sigh of relief. *Fool, fool woman! She couldn't have made you drink it! What is wrong with you?*

"What we have to decide," Egwene said as if nothing at all had happened, "is who to tell. Moiraine certainly has to know, and Rand, but if everyone hears of it . . . The Aiel are peculiar, about Aes Sedai no less than anything else. I think they'll follow Rand as He Who

Comes With the Dawn in spite of anything, but once they learn the White Tower is against him, maybe they won't be so fervent."

"They'll learn sooner or later," Nynaeve muttered. *She could not have made me drink it!*

"Later better than sooner, Nynaeve. So don't you go bursting out in a temper and telling the Wise Ones about this at our next meeting. In fact, it would be best if you didn't mention this visit to the Tower at all. That way maybe you can keep it secret."

"I am not a fool," Nynaeve said stiffly, and felt a slow burn when Egwene quirked that eyebrow at her again. She was not about to bring the visit up with the Wise Ones. Not because it was easier defying them behind their backs. Nothing like that. And she was *not* trying to put a good face on things. It was not fair that Egwene could leap about *Tel'aran'rhiod* however she wanted, while she had to put up with lectures and bullying.

"I know you are not," Egwene said. "Unless you let your temper get the better of you. You need to hold your temper and keep your wits about you if you're right about the Forsaken, especially Moghedien." Nynaeve glowered at her, opening her mouth to say that she could too keep her temper and she would smack Egwene's ears if she thought differently, but the other woman gave her no chance. "We must find that gathering of Blue sisters, Nynaeve. If they oppose Elaida, maybe—just maybe— they will support Rand the way Siuan did. Was a town mentioned, or a village? A country, even?"

"I think . . . I cannot remember." She struggled to take the defensive note out of her voice. *Light, I confessed everything, made a fool of myself, and it's only made things worse!* "I will keep trying."

"Good. We must find them, Nynaeve." For a moment Egwene studied her, while she refused to repeat herself. "Nynaeve, take care concerning Moghedien. Do not go rushing off like a bear in spring just because she got away from you in Tanchico."

"I am not a fool, Egwene," Nynaeve said carefully. It was frustrating having to hold her temper, but if all Egwene would do was ignore it or scold her, there was nothing to be gained beyond looking a bigger ninnyhead than she did already.

"I know. You said that. Just be sure you remember it. Be careful." Egwene did not fade away this time; she vanished, as suddenly as Birgitte.

Nynaeve stared at the spot where she had been, running through her head all the things she should have said. Finally she realized that she could stand there all night; she was repeating herself, and the time for saying anything was past. Grumbling under her breath, she stepped out of *Tel'aran'rhiod,* back to her bed in Sienda.

Egwene's eyes popped open in near total darkness, broken only by a little moonlight streaming in through the smoke hole. She was glad to be under a pile of blankets; the fire was out, and freezing cold filled the tent. Her breath turned to mist in front of her face. Without raising her head, she scanned the interior. No Wise Ones. She was still alone.

That was her biggest fear on these solitary excursions into *Tel'aran'rhiod*: returning to find Amys or one of the others waiting for her. Well, maybe not her biggest fear—the dangers in the World of Dreams were every bit as great as she had told Nynaeve—but a big one none-theless. It was not punishment that frightened her, not the sort that Bair doled out. Had she wakened to find a Wise One staring at her, she would have accepted such gladly, but Amys had told her near the beginning that if she entered *Tel'aran'rhiod* without one of them accom-panying her, they would send her away, refuse to teach her any longer. That made her quail far more than anything else they could do. But even so, she had to push ahead. As rapidly as they taught, they were not rapid enough. She wanted to know now, to know everything.

Channeling, she lit her lamp and put flames in the firepit; nothing remained for them to burn, but she tied the weave off. She lay there, watching her breath mist in front of her mouth, and waited for warmth enough to dress. It was late, but perhaps Moiraine would still be awake.

What had happened with Nynaeve still amazed her. *I*

think she'd actually have drunk, if I had pressed her. She had been so afraid that Nynaeve would learn that she certainly did not have the Wise Ones' permission to jaunt about in the World of Dreams alone, so sure that the flush of embarrassment had given her away, that all she could think of was keeping Nynaeve from speaking, keeping her from winkling out the truth. And she had been so sure that Nynaeve would find out anyway—the woman was quite capable of turning her in and saying it was for her own good—that all she could do was talk, try to keep the focus on whatever Nynaeve was doing wrong. No matter how angry Nynaeve made her, she could not seem to bring up a shout. And with all of that, somehow, she had gained the upper hand.

Come to think of it, Moiraine seldom raised her voice, and when she did she was least effective in having what she wanted done. It had been so even before she began behaving so strangely with Rand. The Wise Ones never yelled at anyone, either—except each other, sometimes —and for all their grumping about the chiefs no longer listening, they still seemed to get their way much more often than not. There was an old saying that she had never really understood before: "He strains to hear a whisper who refuses to hear a shout." She would not shout at Rand again. A quiet, firm, womanly voice, that was the thing. For that matter, she ought not to shout at Nynaeve, either; she *was* a woman, not a girl throwing tantrums.

She found herself giggling. She especially ought not to raise her voice with Nynaeve when speaking calmly produced such results.

The tent finally seemed warm enough, and she scampered out, dressing quickly. She still had to break ice in her water pitcher before she could wash the sleep out of her mouth. Tossing the dark woolen cloak about her shoulders, she untied the strands of Fire—Fire by itself was dangerous to leave tied—and as the flames vanished, ducked out of the tent. Cold closed on her like an icy vise as she hurried through the camp.

Only the nearest tents were really visible to her, low, shadowed shapes that could have been part of the rugged earth, save that the camp extended for miles into the mountainous land to either side. These tall jagged peaks were not the Spine of the World; that was much higher, and lay days to the west yet.

She approached Rand's tent hesitantly. A sliver of light showed along the tent flap. A Maiden seemed to rise out of the ground as she came closer, horn bow on her back, quiver at her waist and spears and buckler in hand. Egwene could not make out any others in the darkness, but she knew they were there, even here surrounded by six clans all claiming loyalty to the *Car'a'carn*. The Miagoma were somewhere to the north, paralleling their march; Timolan would not say what his intentions were. Where the other clans were, Rand did not seem to care. His attention was all on the race for Jangai Pass.

"Is he awake, Enaila?" she asked.

Moonshadows shifted on the Maiden's face as she nodded. "He does not sleep enough. A man cannot go without rest." She sounded for all the world like a mother fretting over her son.

A shadow beside the tent stirred, became Aviendha with her shawl wrapped around her. She did not seem to feel the cool, only the hour. "I would sing him a lullaby, if I thought it might work. I have heard of women being kept awake all night by an infant, but a grown man should know that others would like to have their blankets." She and Enaila shared a quiet chuckle.

Shaking her head over Aiel strangeness, Egwene bent to peer through the crack. Several lamps lit the interior. He was not alone. Natael's dark eyes looked haggard, and he stifled a yawn. He at least wanted sleep. Rand lay sprawled close by one of the gilded oil lamps, reading a battered leather-bound book. One translation or another of the Prophecies of the Dragon, if she knew him at all.

Abruptly he flipped back through the pages, read, then laughed. She tried to tell herself there was nothing of madness in that laugh, only bitterness. "A fine joke," he told Natael, snapping the book shut and tossing it to him. "Read page two hundred eighty-seven and page four hundred, and tell me if you don't agree."

Egwene's mouth tightened as she straightened. He

really should be more careful with a book. She could not speak to him, not in front of the gleeman. It was a shame that he had to use a man he barely knew for company. No. He had Aviendha, and the chiefs often enough, and Lan every day, and Mat sometimes. "Why don't you join them, Aviendha? If you were there, maybe he'd want to talk of something besides that book."

"He wanted to talk with the gleeman, Egwene, and he seldom does that in front of me or anyone. Had I not left, he and Natael would have."

"Children are a great worry, I have heard." Enaila laughed. "And sons the worst. You may find out the truth of this for me, now that you have given up the spear." Aviendha gave her a moonlit frown and stalked back to her place against the side of the tent like an offended cat. Enaila seemed to think that funny, too; she clutched her sides laughing.

Muttering to herself about Aiel humor—she almost never understood it—Egwene made her way to Moiraine's tent, not far from Rand's. Here, too, there was a sliver of light, and she knew that the Aes Sedai was awake. Moiraine was channeling; only tiny amounts of the Power, but still enough for Egwene to sense. Lan lay sleeping nearby, wrapped in his Warder's cloak; except for his head and boots, the rest of him seemed part of the night. Gathering her cloak, she held her skirts up and tiptoed so as not to wake him.

His breathing did not change, but something made her look at him again. Moonlight glinted on his eyes, open and watching her. Even as she turned her head, they closed again. Not another muscle stirred; he might never have wakened at all. Sometimes the man unnerved her. Whatever Nynaeve saw in him, she could not see.

Kneeling beside the tent flap, she peered in. Moiraine sat surrounded by the glow of *saidar,* the small blue stone that usually hung on her forehead dangling from her fingers in front of her face. It shone, adding a bit to the light of a single lamp. The firepit held only ashes; even the smell was gone.

"May I come in?"

She had to repeat herself before Moiraine answered.

"Of course." The light of *saidar* faded away, and the Aes Sedai began fastening the fine golden chain back into her hair.

"You were eavesdropping on Rand?" Egwene settled herself beside the other woman. It was as cold in the tent as it was outside. She channeled flames atop the ashes in the firepit and tied the flow. "You said you would not do it again."

"I said that since the Wise Ones could watch his dreams, we should allow him some privacy. They have not asked again since he shut them out, and I have not offered. Remember that they have their own goals, which may not be those of the Tower."

As quickly as that, they had come to it. Egwene was still not sure how to tell what she knew without betraying herself to the Wise Ones, but perhaps the only method was to just tell it and then feel her way. "Elaida is Amyrlin, Moiraine. I do not know what has happened to Siuan."

"How do you know?" Moiraine said quietly. "Did you learn something dreamwalking? Or has your Talent as a Dreamer finally manifested itself?"

That was her way out. Some of the Aes Sedai in the Tower thought that she might be a Dreamer, a woman whose dreams foretold the future. She did have dreams that she knew were significant, but learning to interpret them was another matter. The Wise Ones said the knowledge had to come from within, and none of the Aes Sedai had been any more help. Rand sitting down in a chair, and somehow she knew that the chair's owner would be murderously angry at having her chair taken; that the owner was a woman was as much as she could pick out of that, and not a thing more. Sometimes the dreams were complex. Perrin, lounging with Faile on his lap, kissing her while she played with the short-cut beard that he wore in the dream. Behind them two banners waved, a red wolf's head and a crimson eagle. A man in a bright yellow coat stood near to Perrin's shoulder, a sword strapped to his back; in some way she knew that he was a Tinker, though no Tinker would even touch a sword. And every bit of it except the beard seemed important. The banners, Faile kissing Perrin, even the Tinker. Every time he moved closer to Perrin it was as if a chill of doom shot through everything. Another dream. Mat throwing dice with blood streaming down his face, the wide brim of his hat pulled low so she could not see his wound, while Thom Merrilin put his hand into a fire to draw out the small blue stone that now dangled on Moiraine's forehead. Or a dream of a storm, great dark clouds rolling without wind or rain while forked lightning bolts, every one identical, rent the earth. She had the dreams, but as a Dreamer she was a failure so far.

"I saw an arrest warrant for you, Moiraine, signed by Elaida as Amyrlin. And it was no ordinary dream." All true. Just not all of the truth. She was suddenly glad that Nynaeve was not there. *I'd be the one staring at a cup, if she was.*

"The Wheel weaves as the Wheel wills. Perhaps it will not matter so much if Rand takes the Aiel across the Dragonwall. I doubt that Elaida has continued to approach rulers, even if she knows that Siuan was doing so."

"Is that all you can say? I think Siuan was your friend once, Moiraine. Can't you shed a tear for her?"

The Aes Sedai looked at her, and that cool, serene gaze told her how far she had to go before she could use that title herself. Sitting, Egwene was nearly a head taller, and she was stronger in the Power besides, but there was more to being Aes Sedai than strength. "I have no time for tears, Egwene. The Dragonwall is not many days distant now, and the Alguenya. . . . Siuan and I were friends, once. In a few months it will be twenty-one years since we began the search for the Dragon Reborn. Only the two of us, newly raised Aes Sedai. Sierin Vayu was raised Amyrlin shortly after, a Gray with more than a touch of Red in her. Had she learned what we intended, we would have spent the rest of our lives doing penance with Red sisters watching us even while we slept. There is a saying in Cairhien, though I have heard it as far away as Tarabon and Saldaea. 'Take what you want, and pay for it.' Siuan and I took the path we wanted, and we knew we would have to pay for it eventually."

"I do not see how you can be so calm. Siuan could be dead, or even stilled. Elaida will either oppose Rand altogether or try to hold him somewhere until Tarmon Gai'don; you know she'll never let a man who can channel run free. At least not everyone is behind Elaida. Some of the Blue Ajah are gathering somewhere—I don't know where yet—and I think others have left the Tower, too. Nynaeve said that she was given a message about all sisters being welcome to return to the Tower by an eyes-and-ears of the Yellow. If Blues and Yellows have both gone, others must have. And if they oppose Elaida, they may support Rand."

Moiraine sighed, a soft sound. "Do you expect me to be happy that the White Tower has split apart? I am Aes Sedai, Egwene. I gave my life to the Tower long before I ever suspected the Dragon would be Reborn in my lifetime. The Tower has been a bulwark against the Shadow for three thousand years. It has guided rulers to wise decisions, stopped wars before they began, halted wars that did begin. That humankind even remembers that the Dark One waits to escape, that the Last Battle will come, is because of the Tower. The Tower, whole and united. I could almost wish that every sister had sworn to Elaida, whatever happened to Siuan."

"And Rand?" Egwene kept her voice just as steady, just as smooth. The flames were beginning to put a little warmth into the air, but Moiraine had just added her own chill. "The Dragon Reborn. You yourself said that he cannot be ready for Tarmon Gai'don unless he is allowed his freedom, both to learn and to affect the world. The Tower united could take him prisoner despite all the Aiel in the Waste."

Moiraine smiled a small smile. "You learn. Cool reason is always better than hot words. But you forget that only thirteen sisters linked can shield any man from *saidin,* and even if they do not know the trick of tying flows, fewer can hold that shield."

"I know you are not giving up, Moiraine. What do you mean to do?"

"I mean to deal with the world as I find the world, for as long as I can. At least Rand will be—easier to be around—now that I no longer need try to turn him from what he wants. I suppose I should be happy that he does not make me fetch his wine. He does listen most of the time, even if he seldom gives any sign what he thinks of what I tell him."

"I will leave you to tell him about Siuan and the Tower." That would avoid awkward questions; with Rand as bigheaded as he was, he might want to know more about her Dreaming than she could invent. "There's something else. Nynaeve has seen Forsaken in *Tel'aran'rhiod*. She mentioned every last one still alive except Asmodean and Moghedien. Including Lanfear. She thinks they are plotting something, perhaps together."

"Lanfear," Moiraine said after a moment.

They both knew that Lanfear had visited Rand in Tear, and maybe other times that he had not told them of. No one had much knowledge of the Forsaken except the Forsaken themselves—only fragments of fragments remained in the Tower—but it was known that Lanfear had loved Lews Therin Telamon. They two, and Rand, knew that she still did.

"With luck," the Aes Sedai went on, "we will not have to worry about Lanfear. The others Nynaeve saw are another matter. You and I must keep as close a watch as we can. I wish more of the Wise Ones could channel." She gave a small laugh. "But I might as well wish they were all Tower trained while I am about it, or to live forever. They may be strong in many ways, but they are sadly lacking in others."

"A watch is all very well, but what else? If six Forsaken come at him together, he will need every bit of help we can give him."

Moiraine leaned over to put a hand on her arm, a look of affection on her face. "We cannot hold his hand forever, Egwene. He has learned to walk. He is learning to run. We can only hope he learns before his enemies catch him. And, of course, continue to advise him. To guide him when we can." Straightening, she stretched, and stifled a small yawn behind her hand. "It is late, Egwene. And I expect that Rand will have us breaking camp in a very few hours now, even if he gets no sleep at all. I, however, would like to take what rest I can before facing my saddle."

Egwene made ready to go, but first she had a question. "Moiraine, why have you started doing everything Rand tells you to? Even Nynaeve doesn't think it is right."

"She does not, does she?" Moiraine murmured. "She will be Aes Sedai yet, whatever she wishes. Why? Because I remembered how to control *saidar*."

After a moment, Egwene nodded. To control *saidar*, first you had to surrender to it.

It was not until she was shivering her way back to her own tent that she realized Moiraine had spoken to her the whole time as an equal. Perhaps she was closer to being ready to choose her Ajah than she thought.

CHAPTER
16

An Unexpected Offer

Sunlight creeping through the window woke Nynaeve. For a moment she lay sprawled atop the striped coverlet. Elayne lay sleeping in the other bed. The early morning was already warm, and the night had not been much better, but that was not the reason Nynaeve's shift was twisted and sweaty. Her dreams after discussing what she had seen with Elayne had not been good. In most she had been back in the Tower, being dragged before the Amyrlin, who was sometimes Elaida and sometimes Moghedien. In some Rand had been lying beside the Amyrlin's writing table like a dog, collared and leashed and muzzled. The dreams about Egwene had been as bad in a way; boiled catfern and powdered mavinsleaf tasted just as bad in a dream as they did awake.

Making her way to the washstand, she cleansed her face, and scrubbed her teeth with salt and soda. The water was not hot, but it could not be called cool either. The sodden shift she stripped off, and dug a fresh one from one of the chests, along with a hairbrush and mirror. Peering at her own image, she regretted undoing her braid for comfort. It had not helped, and now her hair hung in a tangle to her waist. Sitting down on the chest, she laboriously worked the knots out, then began giving her hair its hundred strokes.

Three scratches ran down her neck and disappeared beneath her shift. They were not as red as they might have been, thanks to an ointment of healall taken from the Macura woman. She had told Elayne they came from brambles. Foolish—she suspected that Elayne knew it was not true, despite her tale of looking about the Tower grounds after Egwene left—but she had been too upset to think straight. She had snapped at the other woman several times, for no reason except that she was thinking about her unfair treatment by Melaine and Egwene. *Not that it doesn't do her good to be reminded she's not the Daughter-Heir here.* Still, it was none of the girl's fault; she would have to make it up to her.

In the mirror she saw Elayne rise and begin washing. "I still think my plan is best," the girl said, scrubbing her face. Her raven-dyed hair did not seem to have one snarl, despite her curls. "We could be in Tear much more quickly my way."

Her plan was to abandon the coach once they reached the Eldar, at some small village where there would not likely be many Whitecloaks, and just as important, no eyes-and-ears for the Tower. There they were to take a riverboat down to Ebou Dar, where they could find a ship for Tear. That they had to go to Tear was no longer in doubt. Tar Valon they would avoid at all cost.

"How long before a boat stops where we are?" Nynaeve said patiently. She had thought this was all settled before they went to sleep. It had been, to her mind. "You yourself said that every boat might not stop. And how long do we wait in Ebou Dar before we find a ship for Tear?" Putting the brush down, she began remaking her braid.

"The villagers hang out a flag if they want a boat to put in, and most will. And there are always ships for any-where in a seaport the size of Ebou Dar."

As if the girl had ever been in a seaport of any size before leaving the Tower with Nynaeve. Elayne always thought that whatever she had not learned of the world as Daughter-Heir of Andor, she had learned in the Tower, even after plenty of proof to the contrary. And how dare she put on that forbearing tone with her! "We are not likely to find that gathering of Blues on a ship, Elayne."

Her own plan was to stick with the coach, cross the rest of Amadicia, then Altara and Murandy, to Far Madding in the Hills of Kintara, and over the Plains of Maredo to Tear. It would certainly take longer, but aside from the chance of finding that gathering somehow, coaches very rarely sank. She could swim, but she was not comfortable with land completely out of sight.

Patting her face dry, Elayne changed her shift and came to help with doing the braid. Nynaeve was not fooled; she would hear about boats again. Her stomach did not like boats. Not that that had influenced her decision, of course. If she could bring Aes Sedai to Rand's aid, it would be well worth the longer travel time.

"Have you recalled the name?" Elayne asked, weaving the strands of hair.

"At least I remembered there *was* a name. Light, give me time." She was sure there had been a name. A town, it would have to be, or a city. She could not have seen the name of a country and forgotten it. Drawing a long breath, she took a hold on her temper, and went on in a milder tone. "I will remember it, Elayne. Just give me time."

Elayne made a noncommittal sound and continued braiding. After a bit, she said, "Was it really wise to send Birgitte looking for Moghedien?"

Nynaeve shot the young woman a sidelong frown, but it rolled off her like water off oiled silk. As a change of subject, this was not the one she would have chosen. "Better we find her than she finds us."

"I suppose so. But what will we do when we find her?"

She had no answer for that. But it was better to be the hunter than the hunted, however roughly it went. The Black Ajah had taught her that.

The common room was not crowded when they went down, yet even at that early hour there was a sprinkling of pale cloaks among the patrons, mostly on older men, all with officers' rank. No doubt they preferred to eat from the inn's kitchens rather than what Whitecloak cooks dished up in the garrison. Nynaeve would almost rather have eaten on a tray again, but that little room was like a box. All of these men were intent on their food, the Whitecloaks no less than the others. Surely it was quite safe. Cooking smells filled the air; apparently these men wanted beef or mutton even first thing in the morning.

No sooner did Elayne's foot leave the last step than Mistress Jharen bustled up to offer them, or "the Lady Morelin" rather, a private dining room. Nynaeve never shifted her eyes toward Elayne, but the other woman said, "I think we will eat here. I seldom have the opportunity to eat in a common room, and I quite enjoy it, really. Have one of your girls bring us something cooling. If the day is like this already, I fear I'll swelter before we reach the next stop."

It was a constant wonder to Nynaeve that that haughty manner never got them thrown bodily into the street. She had met enough lords and ladies by now to know that nearly all behaved in that fashion, but still. She would not have put up with it for a minute. The innkeeper, though, bobbed a curtsy, smiling and drywashing her hands, then showed them to a table near a window looking onto the street and scurried away to do Elayne's bidding. Perhaps that was her way of getting back at the girl. They were off by themselves, well away from the men already at other tables, but anyone walking by could stare in at them, and if any of their food was hot—which she hoped it was not—they were as far from the kitchens as it was possible to be.

When it came, breakfast consisted of spicy muffins—wrapped in a white cloth and still warm, and pleasant even so—yellow pears, blue grapes that looked a bit wizened, and some sort of red things that the serving girl called strawberries, though they looked like no berry that Nynaeve had ever seen. They certainly did not taste anything like straw, especially with clotted cream spooned on top. Elayne claimed to have heard of them, but then she would. With a lightly spiced wine supposedly cooled in the springhouse—one sip told her that the spring was not very cool, if there was one—it made a refreshing morning meal.

The nearest man was three tables away, and he wore a dark blue woolen coat, a prosperous tradesman perhaps, but they did not talk. Plenty of time for that when they were on the road again, and could be sure that there was no danger of sharp ears. Nynaeve finished her food well before Elayne. The way the girl took her time quartering a pear, you would think they had all day to sit at table.

Suddenly Elayne's eyes went wide with shock, and the short knife clattered to the table. Nynaeve's head whipped around to find a man taking the bench on the other side of the table.

"I thought it was you, Elayne, but the hair put me off at first."

Nynaeve stared at Galad, Elayne's half-brother. Stared was the word, of course. Tall and steely slender, dark of hair and eye, he was the most handsome man she had ever seen. Handsome was not enough; he was gorgeous. She had seen women cluster around him in the Tower, even Aes Sedai, all of them smiling like fools. She wiped the smile from her own face. But she could do nothing about her racing heart, nor make herself breathe properly. She did not feel anything for him; it was just that he was beautiful. *Take hold of yourself, woman!*

"What are you doing here?" She was pleased that she did not sound strangled. It was not fair for a man to look like that.

"And what are you doing wearing *that*?" Elayne's voice was low, but it still held a snap.

Nynaeve blinked, and realized he wore a shirt of shining mail and a white cloak with two golden knots of rank beneath a flaring sun. She felt color rising in her cheeks. Staring at a man's face so hard that she had not even seen what he was wearing! She wanted to hide her own face from humiliation.

He smiled, and Nynaeve had to take a deep breath. "I am here because I was one of the Children recalled from the north. And I am a Child of the Light because it seemed the right thing to do. Elayne, when you two and

Egwene vanished, it did not take long for Gawyn and me to find out that you were not doing penance on a farm, whatever we were told. They had no right to involve you in their plots, Elayne. Any of you."

"You seem to have attained rank very quickly," Nynaeve said. Did the fool man not realize that talking of Aes Sedai plots here was a good way to get them both killed?

"Eamon Valda seemed to think my experience warranted it, wherever gained." His shrug dismissed rank as unimportant. It was not modesty, precisely, but not pretense either. The finest swordsman among those who came to study with the Warders in the Tower, he had also stood high in the classes on strategy and tactics, but Nynaeve could not remember him boasting about his prowess, even in jest. Accomplishments meant nothing to him, perhaps because they came so easily.

"Does Mother know of this?" Elayne demanded, still in that quiet voice. Her scowl would have frightened a wild boar, though.

Galad shifted just a hair, uneasily. "There has been no good time to write her. But do not be so sure she will disapprove, Elayne. She is not so friendly with the north as she was. I hear a ban may be made law."

"I sent her a letter, explaining." Elayne's glare had transformed to puzzlement. "She must understand. She trained in the Tower, too."

"Keep your voice down," he said, low and hard. "Remember where you are." Elayne flushed a deep red, but whether in anger or embarrassment, Nynaeve could not say.

Abruptly she realized that he had been speaking as quietly as they, and carefully, too. He had not mentioned the Tower once, or Aes Sedai.

"Is Egwene with you?" he went on.

"No," she replied, and he sighed deeply.

"I had hoped . . . Gawyn was nearly unhinged with worry when she disappeared. He cares for her, too. Will you tell me where she is?"

Nynaeve took note of that "too." The man had

become a Whitecloak, yet he "cared for" a woman who wanted to be Aes Sedai. Men were so strange they were hardly human sometimes.

"We will not," Elayne said firmly, the crimson receding from her cheeks. "Is Gawyn here, too? I will not believe he has become a—" She had the wit to lower her voice further, but she still said, "A Whitecloak!"

"He remains in the north, Elayne." Nynaeve supposed that he meant Tar Valon, but surely Gawyn had gone from there. Surely he could not support Elaida. "You cannot know what has happened there, Elayne," he continued. "All the corruption and vileness in that place bubbled to the top, as it had to. The woman who sent you away has been deposed." He looked around and dropped his voice to a momentary whisper, despite no one being close enough to overhear. "Stilled and executed." Taking a deep breath, he made a disgusted sound. "It was never a place for you. Or for Egwene. I have not been long with the Children, but I am certain my captain will give me leave to escort my sister home. That is where you should be, with Mother. Tell me where Egwene is, and I will see that she is brought to Caemlyn, too. You will both be safe there."

Nynaeve's face felt numb. Stilled. And executed. Not an accidental death, or illness. That she had considered the possibility did not make the fact less shocking. Rand had to be the reason. If there had ever been any small hope that the Tower might not oppose him, it was gone. Elayne showed no expression at all, her eyes staring at the distance.

"I see my news shocks you," he said in a low voice. "I do not know how deeply that woman meshed you in her plot, but you are free of her now. Let me see you safely to Caemlyn. No one need know you had any more contact with her than the other girls who went there to learn. Either of you."

Nynaeve showed him her teeth, in what she hoped looked like a smile. It was nice to be included, finally. She could have smacked him. If only he were not so good-looking.

"I will think on it," Elayne said slowly. "What you say makes sense, but you must give me time to think. I must think."

Nynaeve stared at her. It made sense? The girl was blathering.

"I can give you a little time," he said, "but I do not have much if I am to ask leave. We may be ordered—"

Suddenly there was a square-faced, black-haired Whitecloak clapping Galad on the shoulder and grinning widely. Older, he wore the same two knots of rank on his cloak. "Well, young Galad, you can't keep all the pretty women for yourself. Every girl in town sighs when you walk by, and most of their mothers as well. Introduce me."

Galad scraped back his bench to stand. "I . . . thought I knew them when they came downstairs, Trom. But whatever charm you think I possess, it does not work on this lady. She does not like me, and I think she will not like any friend of mine. If you practice the sword with me this afternoon, perhaps you can attract one or two."

"Never with you around," Trom grumped good-naturedly. "And I'd sooner let the farrier pound my head with his hammer than practice against you." But he let Galad start him for the door with only a regretful look at the two women. As they left, Galad shot a glance back at the table, full of frustration and indecision.

No sooner were they out of sight than Elayne stood. "Nana, I need you upstairs." Mistress Jharen materialized at her side, inquiring if she had enjoyed her repast, and Elayne said, "I require my driver and footman immediately. Nana will settle the bill." She was moving for the stairs before she finished speaking.

Nynaeve stared after her, then dug out her purse and paid the woman, making assurances that everything had been to her mistress's liking and trying not to wince at the price. Once rid of the woman, she hurried upstairs. Elayne was stuffing their things into the chests any which way, including the sweaty shifts they had hung on the ends of the beds to dry.

"Elayne, what's the matter?"

"We must leave immediately, Nynaeve. At once." She

did not look up until the last article was crammed in. "Right this minute, wherever he is, Galad is puzzling over something he may never have faced before. Two things that are right, but opposite. To his mind it is right to tie me to a packhorse if necessary and haul me to Mother, to salve her worries and *save* me from becoming Aes Sedai, whatever I want. And it is also right to turn us in, to the Whitecloaks or the army or both. That is the law in Amadicia, and Whitecloak law, too. Aes Sedai are outlawed here, and so is any woman who has ever trained in the Tower. Mother met Ailron once to sign a trade treaty, and they had to do it in Altara because Mother could not legally enter Amadicia. I embraced *saidar* the moment I saw him, and I won't let it go until we are far from him."

"Surely you exaggerate, Elayne. He is your brother."

"He is *not* my brother!" Elayne drew a deep breath and let it out slowly. "We had the same father," she said in a calmer voice, "but he is not my brother. I will not have him. Nynaeve, I've told you time and again, but you will not take it in. Galad does what is right. Always. He never lies. Did you hear what he said to that Trom fellow? He didn't say he did not know who we are. Every word he said was the truth. He does what is *right*, no matter who is hurt by it, even himself. Or me. He used to tell on Gawyn and me for everything, and on himself, too. If he decides the wrong way, we will have Whitecloaks lying in ambush for us before we reach the edge of the village."

A tap sounded at the door, and Nynaeve's breath caught in her throat. Surely Galad would not really . . . Elayne's face was set, ready to fight.

Hesitantly, Nynaeve cracked the door. It was Thom, and Juilin with that fool hat in his hand. "My Lady wants us?" Thom asked, with a touch of servility for anyone who might overhear.

Able to breathe again, not caring who was listening, she snatched the door the rest of the way open. "Get in here, you two!" She was growing tired of them looking at one another every time she spoke.

Before she had the door shut again, Elayne said, "Thom, we must leave right away." The determined look had left her face, and anxiety filled her voice. "Galad is here. You must remember what a monster he was as a child. Well, he is no better grown, and he is a Whitecloak besides. He could—" The words seemed to catch in her throat. She stared at Thom, mouth working soundlessly, but no more wide-eyed than he stared at her.

He sat down heavily on one of the chests, never taking his eyes from Elayne's. "I—" Clearing his throat roughly, he went on. "I thought I saw him, watching the inn. A Whitecloak. But he looked the man the boy would grow into. I suppose it shouldn't be a surprise he grew into a Whitecloak at that."

Nynaeve went to the window; Elayne and Thom hardly seemed to notice her passage between them. Traffic was beginning to pick up in the street, farmers and farm carts and villagers mingling with Whitecloaks and soldiers. Across the way, one Whitecloak was sitting on an upended barrel, that perfect face unmistakable.

"Did he—?" Elayne swallowed. "Did he recognize you?"

"No. Fifteen years changes a man more than it does a boy. Elayne, I thought you had forgotten."

"I remembered in Tanchico, Thom." With a wavering smile, Elayne reached out and tugged one of his long mustaches. Thom smiled back almost as unsteadily; he looked as if he was contemplating a leap from the window.

Juilin was scratching his head, and Nynaeve wished she had some idea what they were talking about, too, but there were more important matters at hand. "We still have to leave before he brings the entire garrison down on us. With him watching, it won't be easy. I haven't seen another patron who looks like they have a coach."

"Ours is the only one in the stableyard," Juilin said. Thom and Elayne were still staring at one another, plainly not hearing a word.

Driving off with the curtains down was no protection, then. Nynaeve was willing to bet that Galad had already learned exactly how they had come to Sienda. "Is there a back way from the stableyard?"

"A gate wide enough for one of us at a time," Juilin

said dryly. "And what's on the other side is little more than an alley, anyway. There aren't more than two or three streets in this village wide enough for the coach." He studied that cylindrical hat, turning it in his hands. "I could get close enough to crack his head. If you were ready, you could drive off during the confusion. I could catch you up on the road."

Nynaeve sniffed loudly. "How? Gallop after on Skulker? Even if you didn't fall out of the saddle inside a mile, do you think you would even reach a horse if you attacked a Whitecloak in that street?" Galad was still there across the street, and Trom had joined him, the pair apparently chatting idly. She leaned over and yanked Thom's nearest mustache. "Do you have anything to add? Any brilliant plans? Did all your listening to gossip yield anything that might help?"

He clapped a hand to his face and gave her an offended look. "Not unless you think there's help in Ailron laying claim to some border villages in Altara. A strip the whole length of the border, from Salidar to So Eban to Mosra. Is there any help in that, Nynaeve? Is there? Try to pull a man's mustache out of his face. Somebody ought to box your ears, for once."

"What would Ailron want with a strip along the border, Thom?" Elayne asked. Perhaps she was interested—she seemed interested in every fool twist and turn of politics and diplomacy—or perhaps she was just trying to stop an argument. She used to try smoothing over things all the time, before she became wrapped up in flirting with Thom.

"It isn't the King, child." His voice softened, for her. "It's Pedron Niall. Ailron does what he is told usually, though he and Niall make out that it isn't so. Most of those villages have been empty since the Whitecloak War, what the Children call the Troubles. Niall was the general in the field then, and I doubt he's ever given up wanting Altara. If he controls both banks of the Eldar, he can squeeze the river trade to Ebou Dar, and if he can crack Ebou Dar, the rest of Altara will trickle into his hands like grain flowing from a hole in a sack."

"That is all very well," Nynaeve said firmly before he

or the girl could speak again. There had been something in what he had said that tickled her memory, but she could not say what or why. In any case, they had no time for lectures on relations between Amadicia and Altara, not with Galad and Trom watching the front of the inn. She said as much, adding, "What about you, Juilin? You consort with low types." The thief-catcher always sought out the cutpurses and burglars and footpads in a town; he claimed they knew more of what was really going on than any official. "Are there smugglers we can bribe to sneak us out, or . . . or . . . You know the sort of thing we need, man."

"I heard little. Thieves keep low in Amadicia, Nynaeve. First offense is branding, second is loss of your right hand, and third is hanging, whether it's the King's crown or a loaf of bread. There aren't many thieves in a town this size, not who do it for a living"—he was contemptuous of amateur thieves—"and for the most part they only wanted to talk about two things. Whether the Prophet is really coming to Amadicia, the way rumor says he is, and whether the town fathers might relent and let that traveling menagerie put on a show. Sienda is too far from the borders for smugglers to—"

She cut him off with peremptory satisfaction. "That is it! The menagerie." They all looked at her as if she had gone mad.

"Of course," Thom said, much too mildly. "We can get Luca to bring the boar-horses back, and make off while they destroy some more of the town. I don't know what you gave him, Nynaeve, but he threw a rock at us as we were driving off."

For once Nynaeve forgave him his sarcasm, feeble as it was. And his lack of wit to see what she saw. "That's as may be, Thom Merrilin, but Master Luca wants a patron, and Elayne and I are going to be his patrons. We still have to abandon the coach and team—" That smarted; she could have built a snug house in the Two Rivers for what they had cost. "—And sneak out that back way." Tossing open the chest with the leaf-shaped hinges, she rooted through clothes and blankets and pots and everything that she had not wanted to leave behind with the wagon full of dyes—she had made sure that the men packed everything except the harness—until she came to the gilded caskets and the purses. "Thom, you and Juilin go out by that back gate, and find a wagon and team of some sort. Buy some supplies and meet us on the road back to Luca's camp." Regretfully, she filled Thom's hand with gold, not even bothering to count; there was no telling what things would cost, and she did not want him wasting time bargaining.

"That is a wonderful idea," Elayne said, grinning. "Galad will be looking for two women, not a troupe of animals and jugglers. And he will never think we would head for Ghealdan."

Nynaeve had not thought of that. She had intended making Luca head straight for Tear. A menagerie such as he had put together, with tumblers and jugglers in addition to animals, could earn its way almost anywhere, she was sure. But if Galad did come looking for them, or send someone, it would be to the east. And he might be smart enough to look even in a menagerie; men did show brains sometimes, usually when you least expected it. "That was the first thing I thought of, Elayne." She ignored the sudden faint taste in her mouth, the acrid memory of boiled catfern and powered mavinsleaf.

Thom and Juilin protested, of course. Not the idea as such, but they seemed to think that one of them remaining behind could protect her and Elayne against Galad and any number of Whitecloaks. They did not seem to realize that if it came to that, channeling would do more than the pair of them and ten more besides. They still seemed troubled, but she managed to push them both out with the stern injunction "And don't you dare come back here. We will meet you on the road."

"If it comes to channeling," Elayne quietly said once the door was shut, "we will quickly find ourselves facing the whole Whitecloak garrison, and probably the army garrison as well. The Power doesn't make us invincible. All it will take is two arrows."

"We will worry about that when it comes," Nynaeve told her. She hoped the men had not thought of that. If they had, likely one of them would lurk about, and probably rouse Galad's suspicions if he was not careful. She was ready to accept their help when it was needed—Ronde Macura had taught her that, though having to be rescued like a kitten down a well still galled—but it would be when she thought it necessary, not they.

A quick trip downstairs found Mistress Jharen. Her lady had changed her mind; she did not think she could face the heat and dust of travel again so quickly; she intended to nap, and did not want to be disturbed until a late supper that she would send down for. Here was the coin for another night's lodging. The innkeeper was very understanding of a noble lady's delicacy, and how inconstant their desires. Nynaeve thought Mistress Jharen would be understanding of anything short of murder, so long as the reckoning was paid.

Leaving the plump woman, Nynaeve cornered one of the serving girls for a moment. A few silver pennies changed hands, and the girl darted off in her apron to find two of the deep bonnets that Nynaeve said looked so shady and cool; not the sort of thing her lady would wear, of course, but they would do nicely for her.

When she got back to the room, Elayne had the gilded caskets on a blanket with the dark polished box holding the recovered *ter'angreal* and the washleather purse that held the seal. The fat purses of coin lay beside Nynaeve's scrip on the other bed. Folding the blanket, Elayne tied the bundle with some stout cord from one of their chests. Nynaeve had saved *everything*.

She regretted leaving it all behind now. It was not just the expense. Not only that. You never knew when something was going to come in handy. Take the two woolen dresses that Elayne had laid out on her bed. They were not fine enough for a lady, and too fine for a lady's maid, but if they had left them in Mardecin as Elayne had wanted, they would be in a fine fix for clothing now.

Kneeling, Nynaeve rummaged in another chest. A few shifts, two more wool dresses for changes. The pair of cast-iron frying pans in a canvas bag were perfectly good, but too heavy, and the men would certainly not forget replacements for those. The sewing kit, in its neat bone-inlaid box; they would never think to buy so much as a pin. Her mind was only partly on her selections, though.

"You knew Thom before?" she asked in what she hoped was a casual tone. She watched Elayne from the corner of her eye while pretending to concentrate on rolling stockings.

The girl had begun pulling out clothes of her own, sighing over the silks before putting them aside. She froze with her hands deep in one of the chests, and she did not look at Nynaeve. "He was Court-bard in Caemlyn when I was little," she said quietly.

"I see." She did not see at all. How did a man go from a court-bard, entertaining royalty, the next thing to a noble, to a gleeman wandering from village to village?

"He was Mother's lover after Father died." Elayne had gone back to choosing, and she said it so matter-of-factly that Nynaeve gaped.

"Your mother's—!"

The other woman still was not looking at her, though. "I did not remember him until Tanchico. I was very small. It was his mustaches, and standing close enough to look up at his face, and hearing him recite part of *The Great Hunt of the Horn.* He thought I'd forgotten again." Her face colored slightly. "I—drank too much wine, and the next day I made out that I could not remember anything."

Nynaeve could only shake her head. She remembered the night the girl had filled her fool self with wine. At least she had never done that again; her head the next morning had seemed an effective cure. Now she knew why the girl behaved as she did with Thom. She had seen the same back in the Two Rivers a few times. A girl just old enough to really think of herself as a woman. Who else would she measure herself against except her mother? And sometimes, who better to compete against, to prove that she was a woman? Usually it led to no more than trying to be better at everything from cooking to sewing, or maybe some harmless flirting with her father, but in the case of one widow, Nynaeve had seen the woman's nearly grown daughter make a complete fool of herself trying to capture the man her mother intended to marry. The trouble was, Nynaeve had no idea what to do about this silliness in Elayne. Despite severe lectures and more from her and the Women's Circle, Sari Ayellin had not settled down until her mother was married again and she herself had found a husband too.

"I suppose he must have been like a second father to you," Nynaeve said carefully. She pretended to concentrate on her own packing. Thom had certainly been looking at the girl that way. It explained so much.

"I hardly think of him so." Elayne appeared intent on deciding how many silk shifts to take, but her eyes saddened. "I cannot really remember my father; I was only a baby when he died. Gawyn says he spent all of his time with Galad. Lini tried to make the best of it, but I know he never came to see Gawyn or me in the nursery. He would have, I know, once we were old enough to teach things, like Galad. But he died."

Nynaeve tried again. "At least Thom is fit for a man of his age. We'd be in a fine fix if he suffered from stiff joints. Old men often do."

"He could still do backflips if not for his limp. And I don't care if he does limp. He is intelligent and knowledgeable about the world. He is gentle, and yet I feel quite safe with him. I don't think I should tell him that. He tries to protect me enough as it is."

With a sigh, Nynaeve gave up. For now, at least. Thom might look on Elayne as a daughter, but if the girl kept this up he just might remember that she was not, and then Elayne would find herself in the pickling kettle. "Thom is very fond of you, Elayne." Time to shift to some other subject. "Are you sure about Galad? Elayne? Are you sure Galad could turn us in, Elayne?"

The other woman gave a start, wiping a small frown from her face.

"What? Galad? I'm *certain,* Nynaeve. And if we refuse to let him take us to Caemlyn, that will only make the decision for him."

Muttering to herself, Nynaeve pulled a silk riding dress out of her chest. Sometimes she thought the Creator had only made men to cause trouble for women.

CHAPTER
17

Heading West

Wwhen the serving girl came with the bonnets, Elayne was stretched out on one of the beds in a white silk shift, a damp cloth over her eyes, and Nynaeve was pretending to mend the hem of the pale green dress that Elayne had been wearing. As often as not she stuck her thumb; she would never have admitted it to anyone, but she was not very good at needlework. She wore her dress, of course—maids did not loll about like ladies—but she did have her hair hanging loose. Clearly she had no intention of leaving the room any time soon. She thanked the girl in a whisper, so as not to wake her lady, and pressed another silver penny on her, with the repeated injunction that her lady was not to be disturbed on any account.

As soon as the door clicked shut, Elayne bounded to her feet and began pulling their bundles out from under the beds. Nynaeve tossed the silk gown down and twisted her arms behind her to undo her buttons. In no time at all they were ready, Nynaeve in green wool, Elayne in blue, with the bundles on their backs. Nynaeve carried the scrip with her herbs and the money, Elayne the blanket-wrapped boxes. The deep curving brims of the bonnets hid their faces so well that Nynaeve thought they could have walked right by Galad without him knowing them, especially with her hair down; he would remember the braid. Mistress Jharen, however, might well stop two strange women coming with fat bundles from upstairs.

The back stairs ran down the outside of the inn, narrow stone flights clinging to the wall. Nynaeve felt a moment of sympathy for Thom and Juilin, hauling the heavy chests up these, but mainly her attention was on the stableyard and the slate-roofed stone stable. A yellow dog lay in the shade beneath the coach, sheltering from the already increasing heat, but all of the grooms were inside. Now and again she could see movement beyond the open stable doors, but no one came out; it was shady in there, too.

They trotted quickly across the stableyard to the alley between the stable and a tall stone fence. A full dung cart, swarming with flies and scarcely narrower than the alleyway, was just rumbling by. Nynaeve suspected that the glow of *saidar* surrounded Elayne, though she could not see it. She herself was hoping that the dog did not decide to bark, that no one came out of the kitchens or the stable. Using the Power was no way to sneak off quietly, and talking their way clear would leave traces for Galad to follow.

The rough wooden gate at the end of the alley had only a lift-latch, and the narrow street beyond, lined with simple stone houses with more thatched roofs than otherwise, was empty except for a handful of boys playing some game that seemed to involve hitting each other with a beanbag. The only adult in sight was a man feeding a cote of pigeons on a roof opposite, his head and shoulders up through a trapdoor. Neither he nor the boys more than glanced at them as they shut the gate and started along the winding street as if they had every right to be there.

They had walked a good five miles west of Sienda along the dusty road before Thom and Juilin caught up, Thom driving what looked like a Tinker's wagon, save that it was all one color, a drab green, with the paint flaked off in large patches. Nynaeve was grateful to stuff her bundles under the driver's seat and climb up beside him, but not so pleased to see Juilin riding Skulker. "I told you not to go back to the inn," she told him, vowing to hit him with something if he looked at Thom.

"I did not go back," he said, unaware that he had saved himself a sore head. "I told the head stableman that my Lady wanted berries fresh from the country, and Thom and I had to go fetch them. It's the sort of nonsense that some no—" He cut off, clearing his throat, as Elayne gave him a cool, expressionless look from the other side of Thom. Sometimes he forgot that she really was of royalty.

"We had to have some reason to leave the inn and the stables," Thom said, whipping up the horses. "I suppose you two said you were taking to your room with fainting spells, or the Lady Morelin was, but the grooms would have been wondering why we wanted to wander about in the heat instead of staying in a nice cool hayloft with no work to do, and maybe a pitcher of ale. Perhaps we'll not be worth talking about, now."

Elayne gave Thom a level look—no doubt for the "fainting spells"—that he pretended not to see. Or perhaps did not. Men could be blind when it suited them. Nynaeve sniffed loudly; he could not miss that. He certainly cracked his whip over the lead horses sharply enough right after. It was all just an excuse so they could take turns riding. That was another thing men did; made excuses to do exactly what they wanted. At least Elayne was frowning at him slightly instead of simpering.

"There is something else I learned last night," Thom went on after a time. "Pedron Niall is trying to unite the nations against Rand."

"Not that I don't believe it, Thom," Nynaeve said, "but how could you learn that? I cannot think some Whitecloak simply told you."

"Too many people were saying the same thing, Nynaeve. There's a false Dragon in Tear. A false Dragon, and never mind prophecies about the Stone of Tear falling, or *Callandor*. This fellow is dangerous, and the nations ought to unite, the way they did in the Aiel War.

And who better to lead them against this false Dragon than Pedron Niall? When so many tongues say the same thing, the same thought exists higher up, and in Amadicia, not even Ailron expresses a thought without asking Niall first."

The old gleeman always seemed to put together rumors and whispers and come up with right answers far more often than not. No, not a gleeman; she had to remember that. Whatever he might claim, he had been a court-bard, and had probably seen court intrigue like that in his stories at close hand. Perhaps even dabbled in it himself, if he had been Morgase's lover. She eyed him sideways, that leathery face with bushy white eyebrows, those long mustaches as snowy as the hair on his head. There was no accounting for some women's taste.

"It isn't as if we should not have expected something like this." She never had. But she should have.

"Mother will support Rand," Elayne said. "I know she will. She knows the Prophecies. And she has as much influence as Pedron Niall."

The slight shake of Thom's head denied the last, at least. Morgase ruled a wealthy nation, but there were Whitecloaks in every land and from every land. Nynaeve realized she was going to have to start paying more attention to Thom. Perhaps he really did know as much as he pretended. "So now you think we should have let Galad escort us to Caemlyn?"

Elayne leaned forward to give her a firm look past Thom. "Certainly not. For one thing, there is no way to be sure that that would be his decision. And for another . . ." She straightened, obscuring herself behind the man; she seemed to be talking to herself, reminding herself. "For another, if Mother really has turned against the Tower, I want to do all my speaking to her by letter for the time being. She is quite capable of holding us both in the palace for our own good. She may not be able to channel, but I do not want to try going against her until I am full Aes Sedai. If then."

"A strong woman," Thom said pleasantly. "Morgase would teach you manners quickly enough, Nynaeve." She gave him another loud sniff—all that loose hair

hanging over her shoulders was no good for gripping—
but the old fool only grinned at her.

The sun stood high by the time they reached the
menagerie, still camped exactly where they had left it, in
the clearing by the road. In the still heat, even the oaks
looked a bit wilted. Except for the horses and the great
gray boar-horses, the animals were all back in their cages
and the humans were out of sight, too, no doubt inside
the wagons that looked not much different from theirs.
Nynaeve and the others had all climbed down before
Valan Luca appeared, still in that ridiculous red silk
cape.

There were no flowery speeches this time, no cape-
swirling bows. His eyes widened when he recognized
Thom and Juilin, narrowed at the boxlike wagon behind
them. He bent to peer into the deep bonnets, and his
smile was not pleasant. "So, come down in the world,
have we, my *Lady* Morelin? Or maybe we were never up
at all. Stole a coach and some clothes, did you? Well, I
would hate to see such a pretty forehead branded. That is
what they do here, in case you don't know, if they do not
do worse. So since it seems you've been found out—else
why are you running?—I would suggest you hurry on as
fast as you can. If you want your bloody penny back, it's
somewhere up the road. I threw it after you, and it can lie
there till Tarmon Gai'don for all I care."

"You wanted a patron," Nynaeve said as he was
turning away. "We can be your patrons."

"You?" he sneered. But he stopped. "Even if a few
coins stolen from some lord's purse would help, I will
not accept stolen—"

"We will pay your expenses, Master Luca," Elayne
broke in with that coolly arrogant tone of hers, "and one
hundred gold marks besides, if we can travel with you to
Ghealdan, and if you agree not to stop until you reach
the border." Luca stared at her, running his tongue over
his teeth.

Nynaeve groaned softly. A hundred marks, and gold!
A hundred silver would cover his expenses easily, to
Ghealdan and further, whatever those so-called boar-
horses ate.

"You stole that much?" Luca said cautiously. "Who is after you? I won't risk Whitecloaks, or the army. They'll throw us all into prison, and probably kill the animals."

"My brother," Elayne replied before Nynaeve could angrily deny that they had stolen anything. "It seems that a marriage has been arranged while I was away, and my brother was sent to find me. I have no intention of returning to Cairhien to marry a man a head shorter, three times my weight and thrice my age." Her cheeks colored in only a fair imitation of anger; her throat clearing did it better. "My father has dreams of claiming the Sun Throne if he can gain enough support. My dreams concern a red-haired Andorman whom I *shall* wed, whatever my father says. And that, Master Luca, is as much as you need know of me and more."

"Maybe you are who you say you are," Luca said slowly, "and maybe you are not. Show me some of this money you claim you'll give me. Promises buy small cups of wine."

Angrily Nynaeve fumbled in her scrip for the fattest purse and shook it at him, then stuffed it out of sight when he reached for it. "You'll get what you need as you need it. And the hundred marks after we reach Ghealdan." A hundred marks gold! They would have to find a banker and use those letters-of-rights if Elayne kept on like this.

Luca gave a sour grunt. "Whether you stole that or not, you are still running from somebody. I won't risk my show for you, whether it's the army or some Cairhienin lord who might come looking. The lord might be worse, if he thinks I have stolen his sister. You will have to blend in." That unpleasant smile came on his face again; he was not going to forget that silver penny. "Everybody who travels with me works at something, and you must as well, if you mean not to stand out. If the others know you are paying your way, they will talk, and you would not want that. Cleaning the cages will do; the horse handlers are always complaining about having to do that. I'll even find that penny and give it back to you for pay. Never let it be said Valan Luca is not generous."

Nynaeve was about to say in no uncertain terms that they would not pay his way to Ghealdan and work, too, when Thom laid a hand on her arm. Wordlessly, he bent to scuffle up pebbles from the ground and began juggling them, six in a circle.

"I have jugglers," Luca said. The six became eight, then ten, a dozen. "You are not bad." The circle became two, intertwining. Luca rubbed at his chin. "Maybe I could find a use for you."

"I can also eat fire," Thom said, letting the stones fall, "perform with knives," he fanned his empty hands, then seemingly pulled a pebble from Luca's ear, "and do a few other things."

Luca suppressed his quick grin. "That does for you, but what about the rest?" He seemed angry with himself for showing any enthusiasm or approval.

"What is that?" Elayne asked, pointing.

The two tall poles Nynaeve had seen being erected now each had ropes to stay it and a flat platform at its top, with a rope stretched taut over the thirty paces between. A rope ladder hung from each platform.

"That is Sedrin's apparatus," Luca replied, then shook his head. "Sedrin the highwalker, dazzling with feats ten paces up on a thin rope. The fool."

"I can walk on it," Elayne told him. Thom reached for her arm as she took off her bonnet and started forward, but he subsided at a small shake of her head and a smile.

Luca barred her way, though. "Listen, Morelin, or whatever your name is, your forehead may be too pretty to brand, but your neck is far too pretty to snap. Sedrin knew what he was doing, and we finished burying him not more than an hour ago. That's why everyone is in their wagons. Of course, he drank too much last night, after we were chased out of Sienda, but I've seen him highwalk with a bellyful of brandy. I will tell you what. You do not have to clean cages. You move into my wagon, and we will tell everyone you're my ladylove. Just as a tale, of course." His sly smile said he hoped for more than a tale.

Elayne's smile in return should have raised frost on

him. "I do thank you for the offer, Master Luca, but if you will kindly step aside. . . ." He had to, or else have her walk over him.

Juilin crumpled that cylindrical hat in his hands, then crammed it back onto his head as she began climbing one of the rope ladders, having a little difficulty with her skirts. Nynaeve knew what the girl was doing. The men should have, and perhaps Thom did, at least, but he still looked ready to rush over to catch her if she fell. Luca moved nearer, as though the same thought was in his head.

For a moment Elayne stood on the platform, smoothing her dress. The platform looked much smaller, and higher, with her on it. Then, delicately holding her skirts up as if to keep them out of mud, she stepped out onto the narrow rope. She might as well have been walking across a street. In a way, Nynaeve knew, she was. She could not see the glow of *saidar,* but she knew that Elayne had woven a path between the two platforms, of Air, no doubt, turned hard as stone.

Abruptly Elayne put her hands down and turned two cartwheels, raven-black hair flailing, silk-stockinged legs flashing in the sun. For the merest instant as she righted herself, her skirts seemed to brush a flat surface before she snatched them up again. Two more steps took her to the far platform. "Did Master Sedrin do that, Master Luca?"

"He did somersaults," he shouted back. In a mutter, he added, "But he did not have legs like that. A lady! Hah!"

"I am not the only one with this skill," Elayne called. "Juilin and—" Nynaeve gave a fierce shake of her head; channeling or no channeling, her stomach would enjoy that high rope as much as it did a storm at sea. "—and I have done this many times. Come on, Juilin. Show him."

The thief-catcher looked as if he would rather clean the cages with his bare hands. The lions' cages, with the lions inside. He closed his eyes, mouth moving in a silent prayer, and went up the rope ladder in the manner of a man mounting the scaffold. At the top, he stared from Elayne to the rope with a fearful concentration. Abruptly, he stepped out, walking rapidly, arms stretched out to either side, eyes fixed on Elayne and mouth moving in prayer. She climbed partway down the ladder to make room for him on the platform, then had to help him find the rungs with his feet and guide him down.

Thom grinned at her proudly as she came back and took her bonnet from Nynaeve. Juilin looked as if he had been soaked in hot water and wrung out.

"That was good," Luca said, rubbing his chin judiciously. "Not as good as Sedrin, mind, but good. I especially like the way you make it seem so easy, while—Juilin?—Juilin pretends to be frightened to death. That will go over very well." Juilin gave the man a bleak grin that had something of reaching for knives in it. Luca actually swirled that red cape as he turned to Nynaeve; he looked very satisfied indeed. "And you, my dear Nana? What surprising talent do you have? Tumbling, perhaps? Swallowing swords?"

"I dole out the money," she told him, slapping the scrip. "Unless you want to offer *me* your wagon?" She gave him a smile that wiped his clean away and backed him up two steps besides.

The shouting had roused people from the wagons, and everyone gathered around while Luca introduced the troupe's new performers. He was rather vague about Nynaeve, merely calling what she did startling; she needed to have a talk with him.

The horse handlers, as Luca called the men who had no performing talent, were a scruffy, surly lot in general, perhaps because they were paid less. There were not very many of them, compared to the number of wagons. In fact, it turned out that everyone helped with the work, including driving the wagons; there was not much money in a traveling menagerie, even one like this. The others were a mixed lot.

Petra, the strongman, was the biggest man Nynaeve had ever seen. Not tall, but wide; his leather vest showed arms the size of tree trunks. He was married to Clarine, the plump, brown-cheeked woman who trained dogs; she looked undersized beside him. Latelle, who performed with the bears, was a stern-faced, dark-eyed woman with short black hair and the beginnings of a sneer permanently on her lips. Aludra, the slender woman who was supposed to be an Illuminator, might even have been one. She did not wear her dark hair in Taraboner braids, not surprising given the feelings in Amadicia, but she had the proper accents, and who could say what had happened to the Guild of Illuminators? Their chapter house in Tanchico had certainly closed its doors. The acrobats, on the other hand, claimed to be brothers named Chavana, but though they were all short, compact men, they ranged in coloring from green-eyed Taeric—his high cheekbones and hooked nose proclaiming Saldaean blood—to Barit, who was darker than Juilin and had Sea Folk tattoos on his hands, though he wore no earrings or noserings.

All but Latelle greeted the newcomers warmly; more performers meant more people attracted to the show, and more money. The two jugglers, Bari and Kin—they really were brothers, it turned out—engaged Thom in talk of their trade, once they found out that he did not work the same way they did. Drawing more people was one thing, competition another. Yet it was the pale-haired woman who cared for the boar-horses who attracted Nynaeve's immediate interest. Cerandin stood stiffly on the fringes and barely spoke—Luca claimed she had come from Shara with the animals—but her soft, slurred manner of speech made Nynaeve's ears go to points.

It took a little time to get their wagon in place. Thom and Juilin seemed more than pleased to have the horse handlers' help with the team, sullenly as it was given, and invitations were given to Nynaeve and Elayne. Petra and Clarine asked them to have tea once they were settled. The Chavanas wanted the two women to have supper with them, and Kin and Bari did, too, all of which made Latelle's sneer become a scowl. Those invitations they declined gracefully, Elayne perhaps a bit more so than Nynaeve; the memory of herself goggling at Galad like a frog-eyed girl was too fresh for her to be more than minimally polite to any man. Luca had his own invitation, for Elayne alone, spoken where Nynaeve could not hear. It earned him a slapped face, and Thom ostentatiously flashed knives that seemed to roll across his hands until the man went away growling to himself and rubbing his cheek.

Leaving Elayne putting her things away in the wagon —throwing them, really, and muttering to herself furiously—Nynaeve went off to where the boar-horses were hobbled. The huge gray animals seemed placid enough, but remembering that hole in the stone wall of The King's Lancer, she was not too sure about the leather cords connecting their massive front legs. Cerandin was scratching the big male with her bronze-hooked goad.

"What are they really called?" Diffidently, Nynaeve patted the male's long nose, or snout, or whatever it was. Those tusks were as big around as her leg and a good three paces long, and only a little larger than the female's at that. The snout snuffled at her skirt and she stepped back hastily.

"*S'redit,*" the pale-haired woman said. "They are *s'redit,* but Master Luca thought a name more easily said was better." That drawling accent was unmistakable.

"Are there many *s'redit* in Seanchan?"

The goad stopped moving for an instant, then resumed scratching. "Seanchan? Where is that? The *s'redit* are from Shara, as I am. I have never heard of—"

"Perhaps you've seen Shara, Cerandin, but I doubt it. You are Seanchan. Unless I miss my guess, you were part of the invasion on Toman Head, left behind after Falme."

"There is no doubt," Elayne said, stepping up beside her. "We heard Seanchan accents in Falme, Cerandin. We will not hurt you."

That was more than Nynaeve was willing to promise; her memories of the Seanchan were not fond ones. And yet . . . *A Seanchan helped you when you needed it. They are not all evil. Only most of them.*

Cerandin let out a long sigh, and sagged a little. It was as if a tension so old that she was no longer aware of it had gone. "Very few people I have met know anything approaching the truth of The Return, or Falme. I have heard a hundred tales, each more fanciful than the last, but never the truth. As well for me. I *was* left behind, and many of the *s'redit,* also. These three were all I could gather. I do not know what happened to the rest. The bull is Mer, the cow Sanit, and the calf Nerin. She is not Sanit's."

"Is that what you did?" Elayne asked. "Train *s'redit*?"

"Or were you a *sul'dam*?" Nynaeve added before the other woman could speak.

Cerandin shook her head. "I was tested, as all girls are, but I could do nothing with the *a'dam.* I was glad to be chosen to work with *s'redit.* They are magnificent animals. You know a great deal, to know of *sul'dam* and *damane.* I have encountered no one before who knows of them." She showed no fear. Or perhaps it had been used up since finding herself abandoned in a strange land. Then again, maybe she was lying.

The Seanchan were as bad as Amadicians when it came to women who could channel, perhaps worse. They did not exile or kill; they imprisoned and used. By means of a device called an *a'dam*—Nynaeve was sure it must be a sort of *ter'angreal*—a woman who had the ability to wield the One Power could be controlled by another woman, a *sul'dam,* who forced the *damane* to use her talents for whatever the Seanchan wanted, even as a weapon. A *damane* was no better than an animal, if a well-tended one. And they made *damane* of every last woman found with the ability to channel or the spark born in her; the Seanchan had scoured Toman Head more thoroughly than the Tower had ever dreamed of. The mere thought of *a'dam* and *sul'dam* and *damane* made Nynaeve's stomach churn.

"We know a little," she told Cerandin, "but we want to know more." The Seanchan were gone, driven away by Rand, but that was not to say they would not return one day. It was a distant danger beside everything else they had to face, yet just because you had a thorn in your foot did not mean that a briar scratch on your arm would not fester eventually. "You would do well to answer our questions truthfully." There would be time on the journey north.

"I promise that nothing will happen to you," Elayne added. "I will protect you, if need be."

The pale-haired woman's eyes shifted from one of them to the other, and suddenly, to Nynaeve's amazement, she prostrated herself on the ground in front of Elayne. "You are a High Lady of this land, just as you told Luca. I did not realize. Forgive me, High Lady. I submit myself to you." And she kissed the ground in front of Elayne's feet. Elayne's eyes looked ready to leap out of her face.

Nynaeve was sure she was no better. "Get up," she hissed, looking around frantically to see if anyone was watching. Luca was—curse him!—and Latrelle, still wearing that scowl, but there was nothing to be done. "Get up!" The woman did not stir.

"Stand on your feet, Cerandin," Elayne said. "No one requires people to behave that way in this land. Not even a ruler." As Cerandin scrambled erect, she added, "I will teach you the proper way to behave in return for your answers to our questions."

The woman bowed, hands on her knees and head down. "Yes, High Lady. It will be as you say. I am yours."

Nynaeve sighed heavily. They were going to have a fine time traveling to Ghealdan.

CHAPTER
18

A Hound of Darkness

Liandrin guided her horse through the crowded streets of Amador, the sneer on her rosebud lips hidden by her deep, curving bonnet. She had hated to give up her multitude of braids, and hated even more the ludicrous fashions of this ludicrous land; the reddish yellow of hat and riding dress she rather liked, but not the large velvet bows on both. Still, the bonnet hid her eyes—combined with honey-yellow hair, brown eyes would have named her Taraboner in an instant, not a good thing in Amadicia just now—and it hid what would have been even worse to show here, an Aes Sedai's face. Safely hidden, she could smirk at the Whitecloaks, who seemed to be every fifth man in the streets. Not that the soldiers who made another fifth would have been any better. None of them ever thought to look inside the bonnet, of course. Aes Sedai were outlawed here, and that meant there were none.

Even so, she felt a little better when she turned in at the elaborate iron gates in front of Jorin Arene's house. Another fruitless trip looking for word from the White Tower; there had been nothing since she had learned that Elaida thought she was in control of the Tower, and that the Sanche woman had been disposed of. Siuan had escaped, true, but she was a useless rag now.

The gardens behind the gray stone fence were full of plants going rather brown from lack of rain, but trimmed and trained into cubes and balls, though one was shaped like a leaping horse. Only one, of course. Merchants like Arene mimicked their betters, but they dared not go too far lest someone think their conceit too high. Elaborate balconies decorated the large wooden house with its red-tiled roofs, and even a colonnade of carved columns, but unlike the lord's dwelling it was meant to copy, it stood on a stone foundation no more than ten feet tall. A childish pretense at a noble's manor.

The stringy, gray-haired man who scurried out deferentially to hold her stirrup while she dismounted, and take her reins, was clad all in black. Whatever colors a merchant chose for livery, they were sure to be some real lord's colors, and even a minor lord could cause trouble for the richest seller of goods. People in the streets called black "merchant's livery," and snickered when they said it. Liandrin despised the groom's black coat as much as she did Arene's house and Arene himself. She would have true manors, one day. Palaces. They had been promised to her, and the power that went with them.

Stripping off her riding gloves, she stalked up the ridiculous ramp that slanted along the foundations to the vine-carved front doors. The lords' fortress manors had ramps, so of course a merchant who thought well of himself could not have steps. A black-clad young serving girl took gloves and hat in the round entrance hall, with its many doors and carved and brightly painted columns and its encircling balcony. The ceiling was lacquered in imitation of a mosaic, stars within stars in gold and black. "I will have my bath in one hour," she told the woman. "It will be the proper temperature this time, yes?" The maid went pale as she curtsied, stammering agreement before scurrying away.

Amellia Arene, Jorin's wife, came through one of the doors deep in conversation with a fat balding man in a spotless white apron. Liandrin breathed contemptuously. The woman had pretensions, yet she not only spoke to the cook herself, she brought the man out of his kitchens to discuss meals. She treated the servant like—like a friend!

Fat Evon saw her first and gulped, his piggy eyes darting away immediately. She did not like men looking at her, and she had spoken sharply to him on her first day here about the way his gaze sometimes lingered. He had tried to deny it, but she knew men's vile habits. Without waiting to be dismissed by his mistress, Evon all but ran back the way he had come.

The graying merchant's wife had been a stern-faced woman when Liandrin and the others came. Now she licked her lips and smoothed her bow-draped green silk needlessly. "There is someone upstairs with the others, my Lady," she said diffidently. She had thought that she could use Liandrin's name that first day. "In the front withdrawing room. From Tar Valon, I believe."

Wondering who it could be, Liandrin started for the nearest of the curving staircases. She knew few others of the Black Ajah, of course, for safety's sake; what others did not know, they could not betray. In the Tower she had known only one of the twelve who went with her when she left. Two of the twelve were dead, and she knew at whose feet to lay the blame. Egwene al'Vere, Nynaeve al'Meara, and Elayne Trakand. Everything had gone so badly in Tanchico that she would have thought those three upstart Accepted had been there, except that they were fools who had twice walked tamely into traps she had set. That they had escaped each was of no consequence. Had they been in Tanchico, they would have fallen into her hands, whatever Jeaine claimed to have seen. The next time she found them, they would never escape anything again. She would be done with them whatever her orders.

"My Lady," Amellia stammered. "My husband, my Lady. Jorin. Please, will one of you help him? He did not mean it, my Lady. He has learned his lesson."

Liandrin paused with one hand on the carved banister, looking back over her shoulder. "He should not have thought that his oaths to the Great Lord could be conveniently forgotten, no?"

"He *has* learned, my Lady. Please. He lies beneath

blankets all day—in this heat—shivering. He weeps when anyone touches him, or speaks above a whisper."

Liandrin paused as if considering, then nodded graciously. "I will ask Chesmal to see what she can do. Yet you understand that I make no promises." The woman's unsteady thanks followed her up, but she paid them no mind. Temaile had let herself be carried away. She had been Gray Ajah before becoming Black, and she always made a point of spreading the pain evenly when she mediated; she had been very successful as a mediator, for she liked spreading pain. Chesmal said he might be able to do small tasks in a few months, so long as they were not too hard and no one raised a voice. She had been one of the best Healers in generations among the Yellow, so she should know.

The front withdrawing room startled her when she went in. Nine of the ten Black sisters who had come with her stood around the room against the carved and painted paneling, though there were plenty of silk-cushioned chairs on the gold-fringed carpet. The tenth, Temaile Kinderode, was handing a delicate porcelain cup of tea to a dark-haired, sturdily handsome woman in a bronze-colored gown of unfamiliar cut. The seated woman looked vaguely familiar, though she was not Aes Sedai; she was plainly approaching her middle years, and despite smooth cheeks there was nothing of agelessness about her.

Yet the mood made Liandrin cautious. Temaile was deceptively fragile in appearance, with big, childlike blue eyes that made people trust her; those eyes appeared worried now, or uneasy, and the teacup rattled on the saucer before the other woman took it. Every face looked uneasy, except that of the oddly familiar woman. Coppery-skinned Jeaine Caide, in one of those disgusting Domani garments that she wore inside the house, had tears still glistening on her cheeks; she had been a Green, and liked flaunting herself in front of men even more than most Greens. Rianna Andomeran, once White and always a coldly arrogant killer, nervously kept touching the pale streak in her black hair above her left ear. Her arrogance had been flattened.

"What has happened here?" Liandrin demanded. "Who are you, and what—?" Suddenly the memory flashed into her head. A Darkfriend, a servant in Tanchico who had continually gotten above herself. "Gyldin!" she snapped. This servant had followed them in some fashion and obviously was trying to pass herself off as a Black courier with some dire news. "You have overstepped yourself too far this time." She reached to embrace *saidar,* yet even as she did the glow surrounded the other woman, and Liandrin's reach ran into a thick invisible wall shutting her away from the Source. It hung there like the sun, tantalizingly out of reach.

"Stop gaping, Liandrin," the woman said calmly. "You look like a fish. It is not Gyldin, but Moghedien. This tea needs more honey, Temaile." The slender, fox-faced woman darted to take the cup, breathing heavily.

It had to be so. Who else could have so cowed the others? Liandrin looked at them standing around the walls. Round-faced Eldrith Jhondar, for once not looking vague at all despite an ink smudge on her nose, nodded vigorously. The others seemed afraid to twitch. Why one of the Forsaken—they were not supposed to use that name, but usually did, among themselves—why Moghedien would have masqueraded as a servant, she could not understand. The woman had or could have everything that she herself wanted. Not just knowledge of the One Power beyond her dreams, but power. Power over others, power over the world. And immortality. Power for a lifetime that would never end. She and her sisters had speculated on dissension among the Forsaken; there had been orders at odds with each other, and orders given to other Darkfriends at odds with theirs. Perhaps Moghedien had been hiding from the rest of the Forsaken.

Liandrin spread her divided riding skirts as best she could in a deep curtsy. "We welcome you, Great Mistress. With the Chosen to lead us, we shall surely triumph before the Day of the Great Lord's Return."

"Nicely said," Moghedien said dryly, taking the cup back from Temaile. "Yes, this is much better." Temaile looked absurdly grateful, and relieved. What had Moghedien done?

Suddenly a thought came to Liandrin, an unwelcome one. She had treated one of the Chosen as a servant. "Great Mistress, in Tanchico I did not know that you—"

"Of course you did not," Moghedien said irritably. "What good to bide my time in the shadows if you and these others knew me?" Abruptly a small smile appeared on her lips; it touched nothing else. "Are you worried about those times you sent Gyldin to the cook to be beaten?" Sweat beaded suddenly on Liandrin's face. "Do you truly believe I would allow such a thing? The man no doubt reported to you, but he remembered what I wanted him to remember. He actually felt sorry for Gyldin, so cruelly treated by her mistress." That seemed to amuse her greatly. "He gave me some of the desserts that he made for you. It would not displease me if he still lives."

Liandrin drew a relieved breath. She would not die. "Great Mistress, there is no need to shield me. I also serve the Great Lord. I swore my oaths as a Darkfriend before ever I went to the White Tower. I sought the Black Ajah from the day that I knew that I could channel."

"So you will be the only one in this ill-ordered pack who does not need to learn who her mistress is?" Moghedien quirked an eyebrow. "I would not have thought it of you." The glow around her vanished. "I have tasks for you. For all of you. Whatever you have been doing, you will forget. You are an inept lot, as you proved in Tanchico. With my hand on the dog whip, perhaps you will hunt more successfully."

"We await orders from the Tower, Great Mistress," Liandrin said. Inept! They had almost found what they were hunting for in Tanchico, when the city exploded in riots; they had barely escaped destruction at the hands of Aes Sedai who had somehow wandered into the middle of their plan. Had Moghedien revealed herself, or even taken part on their behalf, they would have triumphed. If their failure was anyone's fault, it was Moghedien's herself. Liandrin reached toward the True Source, not to embrace it, but to be certain that the shield had not merely been tied off. It was gone. "We have been given great responsibilities, great works to perform, and surely we will be commanded to continue—"

Moghedien cut her off sharply. "You serve whichever of the Chosen chooses to snap you up. Whoever sends you orders from the White Tower, she takes her own from one of us now, and very likely grovels on her belly when she does. You will serve me, Liandrin. Be sure of it."

Moghedien did not know who headed the Black Ajah. It was a revelation. Moghedien did not know everything. Liandrin had always imagined the Forsaken as close to omnipotent, something far beyond ordinary mortals. Perhaps the woman truly was in flight from the other Forsaken. To hand her over to them would surely earn her a high place. She might even become one of them. She had a trick, learned in childhood. And she could touch the Source. "Great Mistress, we serve the Great Lord, as you do. We also were promised eternal life, and power, when the Great Lord re—"

"Do you think that you are my equal, little sister?" Moghedien grimaced in disgust. "Did you stand in the Pit of Doom to dedicate your soul to the Great Lord? Did you taste the sweetness of victory at Paaran Disen, or the bitter ashes at the Asar Don? You are a barely trained puppy, not the packmistress, and you will go where I point until I see fit to give you a better place. These others thought themselves more than they are, too. Do you wish to try your strength against me?"

"Of course not, Great Mistress." Not when she was forewarned and ready. "I—"

"You will do so sooner or later, and I prefer to put it out of the way now, in the beginning. Why do you think your companions look so cheerful? I have taught each of them the same lesson already today. I will not wonder when you must be taught, too. I will be done with it now. Try."

Licking her lips fearfully, Liandrin looked around at the women standing rigidly against the walls. Only Asne Zeramene so much as blinked; she shook her head ever so slightly. Asne's tilted eyes, high cheekbones and strong nose marked her Saldaean, and she had all the vaunted Saldaean boldness. If she counseled against, if her dark eyes held a tinge of fear, then it was surely best to grovel however much was needed to make Moghedien relent. And yet, there was her trick.

She went to her knees, head low, looking up at the Forsaken with a fear that was only partly feigned. Moghedien lounged in her chair, sipping the tea. "Great Mistress, I beg you to forgive me if I have presumed. I know that I am but a worm beneath your foot. I beg, as one who would be your faithful hound, for your mercy on this wretched dog." Moghedien's eyes dropped to her cup, and in a flash, while the words still tumbled from her mouth, Liandrin embraced the Source and channeled, seeking the crack that must be in the Forsaken's confidence, the crack that was in everyone's façade of strength.

Even as she lashed out, the light of *saidar* surrounded the other woman, and pain enveloped Liandrin. She crumpled to the carpet, trying to howl, but agony beyond anything she had ever known silenced her gaping mouth. Her eyes were going to burst from her head; her skin was going to peel away in strips. For an eternity she thrashed, and when it vanished as suddenly as it had begun, all she could do was lie there, shuddering and weeping open-mouthed.

"Do you begin to see?" Moghedien said calmly, handing the empty cup to Temaile with, "That was very good. But next time a little stronger." Temaile looked as though she might faint. "You are not quick enough, Liandrin, you are not strong enough, and you do not know enough. That pitiful little thing you tried against me. Would you like to see what it is really like?" She channeled.

Liandrin gazed up at her adoringly. Crawling across the floor, she pushed words through the sobs she still could not stop. "Forgive me, Great Mistress." This magnificent woman, like a star in the heavens, a comet, above all kings and queens in wonder. "Forgive, please," she begged, pressing kisses against the hem of

Moghedien's skirt as she babbled. "Forgive. I am a dog, a worm." It shamed her to her core that she had not meant those things before. They were true. Before this woman, they were all true. "Let me serve you, Great Mistress. Allow me to serve. Please. Please."

"I am not Graendal," Moghedien said, pushing her away roughly with one velvet-slippered foot.

Suddenly the sense of worship was gone. Lying there in a heap, weeping, Liandrin could remember it clearly, though. She stared at the Forsaken in horror.

"Are you convinced yet, Liandrin?"

"Yes, Great Mistress," she managed. She was. Convinced that she dared not even think of trying again until she was certain of success. Her trick was only the palest shadow of what Moghedien had done. Could she but learn that . . .

"We shall see. I think you may be one of those who needs a second lesson. Pray it is not so, Liandrin; I make second lessons exceedingly sharp. Now take your place with the others. You will find that I have taken some of the objects of power that you had in your room, but you may keep the trinkets that remain. Am I not kind?"

"The Great Mistress is kind," Liandrin agreed around hiccoughs and occasional sobs that she could not stifle.

Limply she staggered to her feet and went to stand beside Asne; the wall panel against her back helped to hold her upright. She saw the flows of Air being woven; only Air, but she still flinched as they bound her mouth shut and stopped sound from her ears. She certainly did not try to resist. She did not even let herself think of *saidar*. Who knew what one of the Forsaken could do? Perhaps read her thoughts. That almost made her run. No. If Moghedien knew her thoughts, she would be dead by now. Or still screaming on the floor. Or kissing Moghedien's feet and begging to serve. Liandrin shivered uncontrollably; if that weave had not bound her mouth, her teeth would have been chattering.

Moghedien wove the same around all of them save Rianna, whom the Forsaken beckoned with an imperious finger to kneel before her. Then Rianna left, and Marillin Gemalphin was unbound and summoned.

From where she stood, Liandrin could see their faces even if their mouths moved soundlessly for her. Plainly each woman was receiving orders the others knew nothing of. The faces told little, though. Rianna merely listened, a touch of relief in her eyes, bowed her head in assent and went. Marillin looked surprised, and then eager, but she had been a Brown, and Browns could be enthusiastic over anything that allowed them a chance to unearth some moldy bit of lost knowledge. Jeaine Caide donned a slow mask of horror, shaking her head at first and trying to cover herself and that disgustingly sheer gown, but Moghedien's face hardened, and Jeaine nodded hurriedly and fled, if not as eagerly as Marillin, just as quickly. Berylla Naron, lean almost to scrawniness and as fine a manipulator and plotter as there was, and Falion Bhoda, long-faced and cold despite her obvious fear, showed as little expression as Rianna had. Ispan Shefar, like Liandrin from Tarabon, though dark-haired, actually kissed Moghedien's hem before she rose.

Then the flows were unwoven around Liandrin. She thought that it was her turn to be sent away on the Shadow knew what errand, until she saw the bonds dispelled around the others remaining as well. Moghedien's finger beckoned peremptorily, and Liandrin knelt between Asne and Chesmal Emry, a tall, handsome woman, dark-haired and dark-eyed. Chesmal, once Yellow, could Heal or kill with equal ease, but the intensity of her gaze on Moghedien, the way her hands trembled as they clutched her skirts, said she intended only to obey.

She would have to go by such signs, Liandrin realized. Approaching one of the others with her belief that rewards could be had for handing Moghedien to the rest of the Forsaken might well be disastrous if the one she spoke to had decided that it was in her best interests to be Moghedien's lapdog. She almost whimpered at the thought of a "second lesson."

"You, I keep with me," the Forsaken said, "for the most important task. What the others do may bear sweet fruit, but to me yours will be the most important harvest. A personal harvest. There is a woman named Nynaeve al'Meara." Liandrin's head came up, and Moghedien's dark eyes sharpened. "You know of her?"

"I despise her," Liandrin replied truthfully. "She is a filthy wilder who ought never to have been allowed in the Tower." She loathed all wilders. Dreaming of being Black Ajah, she herself had begun learning to channel a full year before going to the Tower, but she was in no way a wilder.

"Very good. You five are going to find her for me. I want her alive. Oh, yes, I do want her alive." Moghedien's smile made Liandrin shiver; giving Nynaeve and the other two to her might be entirely suitable. "The day before yesterday she was in a village called Sienda, perhaps sixty miles east of here, with another young woman in whom I may be interested, but they have vanished. You will . . ."

Liandrin listened eagerly. For this, she could be a faithful hound. For the other, she would wait patiently.

CHAPTER
19

Memories

My Queen?"

Morgase looked up from the book on her lap. Sunlight slanted through the window of the sitting room next to her bedchamber. The day was already hot, with no breeze, and sweat dampened her face. It would be noon before much longer, and she had not stirred from the room. That was unlike her; she could not remember why she had decided to laze the morning away with a book. She seemed unable to concentrate on reading of late. By the golden clock on the mantel above the marble fireplace, an hour had passed since she last turned a page, and she could not recall its words. It must be the heat.

The red-coated young officer of her Guards, kneeling with one fist pressed to the red-and-gold carpet, looked vaguely familiar. Once she had known the name of every Guard assigned to the Palace. Perhaps it was all the new faces. "Tallanvor," she said, surprising herself. He was a tall, well-made young man, but she could not tell why she remembered him in particular. Had he brought someone to her once? Long ago? "Guardsman Lieutenant Martyn Tallanvor."

He glanced at her, startlingly rough-eyed, before putting his gaze back on the carpet. "My Queen, forgive me, but I am surprised that you remain here, given the morning's news."

"What news?" It would be good to learn something besides Alteima's gossip of the Tairen court. At times she felt that there was something else she wanted to ask the woman, but all they ever did was gossip, which she could never remember doing before. Gaebril seemed to enjoy listening to them, sitting in that tall chair in front of the fireplace with his ankles crossed, smiling contentedly. Alteima had taken to wearing rather daring dresses; Morgase would have to say something to her. Dimly she seemed to remember thinking that before. *Nonsense. If I had, I would have spoken to her already.* She shook her head, realizing that she had drifted away from the young officer entirely, that he had begun speaking and stopped when he saw she was not listening. "Tell me again. I was distracted. And stand."

He rose, face angry, eyes burning on her before they dropped again. She looked where he had been staring and blushed; her dress was cut extremely low. But Gaebril liked her to wear them so. With that thought she ceased fretting about being nearly naked in front of one of her officers.

"Be brief," she said curtly. *How dare he look at me in that manner? I should have him flogged.* "What news is so important that you think you can walk into my sitting room as if it were a tavern?" His face darkened, but whether from proper embarrassment or increased anger she could not say. *How dare he be angry with his queen! Does the man think all I have to do is listen to him?*

"Rebellion, my Queen," he said in a flat tone, and all thought of anger and stares vanished.

"Where?"

"The Two Rivers, my Queen. Someone has raised the old banner of Manetheren, the Red Eagle. A messenger came from Whitebridge this morning."

Morgase drummed her fingers on the book, her thoughts coming more clearly than it seemed they had in a very long time. Something about the Two Rivers, some spark she could not quite fan to life, tugged at her. The region was hardly part of Andor at all, and had not been for generations. She and the last three queens before her had been hard pressed to maintain a modicum of control over the miners and smelters in the Mountains of Mist, and even that modicum would have been lost had there been any way to get the metals out save through the rest of Andor. A choice between holding the mines' gold and iron and other metals and keeping the Two Rivers' wool and tabac had not been difficult. But rebellion unchecked, even rebellion in a part of her realm that she ruled only on a map, could spread like wildfire, to places that were hers in fact. And Manetheren, destroyed in the Trolloc Wars, Manetheren of legend and story, still had a hold on some men's minds. Besides, the Two Rivers *was* hers. If they had been left to go their own way for far too long, they were still a part of her realm.

"Has Lord Gaebril been informed?" Of course he had not. He would have come to her with the news, and suggestions on how to deal with it. His suggestions were always clearly right. *Suggestions?* Somehow, it seemed that she could remember him telling her what to do. That was impossible, of course.

"He has, my Queen." Tallanvor's voice was still bland, unlike his face, where slow anger yet smoldered. "He laughed. He said the Two Rivers seemed to throw up trouble, and he would have to do something about it one day. He said this minor annoyance would have to wait its turn behind more important matters."

The book fell as she sprang to her feet, and she thought Tallanvor smiled in grim satisfaction as she swept by him. A serving woman told her where Gaebril was to be found, and she marched straight to the colonnaded court, with its marble fountain, the basin full of lily pads and fish. It was cooler there, and shaded a little.

Gaebril sat on the broad white coping of the fountain, lords and ladies gathered around him. She recognized fewer than half. Dark square-faced Jarid of House Sarand, and his shrewish honey-haired wife, Elenia. That simpering Arymilla of House Marne, melting brown eyes always so wide in feigned interest, and bony, goat-faced Nasin of House Caeren, who would tumble any woman he could corner despite his thin white hair. Naean of House Arawn, as usual with a sneer marring her pale beauty, and Lir of House Baryn, a whip of a man, wearing a sword of all things, and Karind of House Anshar, with the same flat-eyed stare that some said had put three husbands under the ground. The others she did not know at all, which was strange enough, but these she never allowed into the Palace except on state occasions. Every one had opposed her during the Succession. Elenia and Naean had wanted the Lion Throne for themselves. What could Gaebril be thinking to actually bring them here?

". . . the size of our estates in Cairhien, my Lord," Arymilla was saying, leaning over Gaebril, as Morgase approached. None of them more than glanced at her. As if she were a servant with the wine!

"I want to speak with you concerning the Two Rivers, Gaebril. In private."

"It has been dealt with, my dear," he said idly, dabbling his fingers in the water. "Other matters concern me now. I thought you were going to read during the heat of the day. You should return to your room until the evening's coolness, such as it is."

My dear. He had called her my dear in front of these interlopers! As much as she thrilled to hear that on his lips when they were alone . . . Elenia was hiding her mouth. "I think not, Lord Gaebril," Morgase said coldly. "You will come with me now. And these others will be out of the Palace before I return, or I will exile them from Caemlyn completely."

Suddenly he was on his feet, a big man, towering over her. She seemed unable to look at anything but his dark eyes; her skin tingled as if an icy wind were blowing through the courtyard. "You will go and wait for me, Morgase." His voice was a distant roar filling her ears. "I have dealt with all that needs dealing with. I will come to you this evening. You will go now. You will go."

She had one hand lifted to open the door of her sitting room before she realized where she was. And what had happened. He had told her to go, and she had gone. Staring at the door in horror, she could see the smirks on the men's faces, open laughter on some of the women's. *What has happened to me? How could I become so besotted with any man?* She still felt the urge to enter, and wait for him.

Dazed, she forced herself to turn and walk away. It was an effort. Inside, she cringed at the idea of Gaebril's disappointment in her when he did not find her where he expected, and cringed further at recognizing the fawning thought.

At first she had no notion of where she was going or why, only that she would not wait obediently, not for Gaebril, not for any man or woman in the world. The fountained courtyard kept repeating in her head, him telling her to go, and those hateful, amused faces watching. Her mind still seemed fogged. She could not comprehend how or why she could have let it happen. She had to think of something that she could understand, something she could deal with. Jarid Sarand and the others.

When she assumed the throne she had pardoned them for everything they had done during the Succession, as she had pardoned everyone who opposed her. It had seemed best to bury all animosities before they could fester into the sort of plotting and scheming that infected so many lands. The Game of Houses it was called—*Daes Dae'mar*—or the Great Game, and it led to endless, tangled feuds between Houses, to the toppling of rulers; the Game was at the heart of the civil war in Cairhien, and no doubt had done its part in the turmoil enveloping Arad Doman and Tarabon. The pardons had had to go to all to stop *Daes Dae'mar* being born in Andor, but could she have left any unsigned, they would have been the parchments with those seven's names.

Gaebril knew that. Publicly she had shown no disfavor, but in private she had been willing to speak of her distrust. They had had to pry their jaws open to swear fealty, and she could hear the lie on their tongues. Any one would leap at a chance to pull her down, and all seven together . . .

There was only one conclusion she could reach. Gaebril must be plotting against her. It could not be to put Elenia or Naean on the throne. *Not when he has me already,* she thought bitterly, *behaving like his lapdog.* He must mean to supplant her himself. To become the first king that Andor had ever had. And she still felt the desire to return to her book and wait for him. She still ached for his touch.

It was not until she saw the aged faces in the hallway around her, the creased cheeks and often bent backs, that she became aware of where she was. The Pensioners' Quarters. Some servants returned to their families when they grew old, but others had been so long in the Palace that they could think of no other life. Here they had their own small apartments, their own shaded garden and a spacious courtyard. Like every queen before her, she supplemented their pensions by letting them buy food through the Palace kitchens for less than its cost, and the infirmary treated their ills. Creaky bows and unsteady curtsies followed her, and murmurs of "The Light shine upon you, my Queen," and "The Light bless you, my Queen," and "The Light protect you, my Queen." She acknowledged them absently. She knew where she was going now.

Lini's door was like all the others along the green-tiled corridor, unadorned save for a carving of the rearing Lion of Andor. She never thought of knocking before entering; she was the Queen, and this was her Palace. Her old nurse was not there, though a teakettle steaming over a small fire in the brick fireplace said she would not be long.

The two snug rooms were neatly furnished, the bed made to perfection, the two chairs precisely aligned at the table, where a blue vase in the exact center held a small fan of greenery. Lini had always been a great one for neatness. Morgase was willing to wager that within the wardrobe in the bedchamber every dress was arranged just so with every other, and the same for pots in the cupboard beside the fireplace in the other room.

Six painted ivory miniatures in small wooden stands made a line on the mantelpiece. How Lini could have afforded them on a nurse's stipend was more than Morgase had ever been able to imagine; she could not ask such a question, of course. In pairs, they showed three young women and the same three as babes. Elayne was there, and herself. Taking down the portrait of herself at fourteen, a slender filly of a girl, she could not believe that she had ever looked so innocent. She had worn that ivory silk dress the day she had gone to the White Tower, never dreaming at the time that she would be Queen, only harboring the vain hope that she might become Aes Sedai.

Absentmindedly she thumbed the Great Serpent ring on her left hand. She had not earned that, precisely; women who could not channel were not awarded the ring. But short of her sixteenth nameday she had returned to contest the Rose Crown in the name of House Trakand, and when she won the throne nearly two years later, the ring had been presented to her. By tradition, the Daughter-Heir of Andor always trained in the Tower, and in recognition of Andor's long support of the Tower was given the ring whether or not she could channel. She had only been the heir to House Trakand in the Tower, but they gave it to her anyway once the Rose Crown was on her head.

Replacing her own portrait, she took down her mother's, taken at perhaps two years older. Lini had been nurse to three generations of Trakand women. Maighdin Trakand had been beautiful. Morgase could remember that smile, when it had become a mother's loving beam. It was Maighdin who should have had the Lion Throne. But a fever had carried her away, and a young girl had found herself High Seat of House Trakand, in the middle of a struggle for the throne with no more support in the beginning than her House retainers and the House bard. *I won the Lion Throne. I will not give it up, and I will not see a man take it. For a thousand years a queen has ruled Andor, and I will not let that end now!*

"Meddling in my things again, are you, child?"

That voice triggered long-forgotten reflexes. Morgase had the miniature hidden behind her back before she knew it. With a rueful shake of her head she put the portrait back on its stand. "I am not a girl in the nursery any longer, Lini. You must remember that, or one day you will say something where I must do something about it."

"My neck is scrawny and old," Lini said, setting a net bag of carrots and turnips on the table. She looked frail in her neat gray dress, her white hair drawn back in a bun from a narrow face with skin like thin parchment, but her back was straight, her voice clear and steady, and her dark eyes as sharp as ever. "If you want to give it to hangman or headsman, I am almost done with it anyway. 'A gnarled old branch dulls the blade that severs a sapling.'"

Morgase sighed. Lini would never change. She would not curtsy if the entire court were watching. "You do grow tougher as you grow older. I am not certain a headsman could find an axe sharp enough for your neck."

"You've not been to see me in some time, so I suppose there's something you need to work out in your mind. When you were in the nursery—and later—you always used to come to me when you couldn't work matters out. Shall I make a pot of tea?"

"Some time, Lini? I visit you every week, and a wonder I do, given how you speak to me. I would exile the highest lady in Andor if she said half what you do."

Lini gave her a level look. "You have not darkened my doorway since the spring. And I talk as I always have; I'm too old to change now. Do you want tea?"

"No." Morgase put a hand to her head in confusion. She did visit Lini every week. She could remember. . . . She could not remember. Gaebril had filled her hours so completely that sometimes it was hard to remember anything other than him. "No, I do not want tea. I do not know why I came. You cannot help me with the problem I have."

Her old nurse snorted, though somehow she made it a delicate sound. "Your trouble is with Gaebril, isn't it? Only now you're ashamed to tell me. Girl, I changed you in your cradle, tended you when you were sick and heaving your stomach up, and told you what you needed to know about men. You have never been too shamed to discuss anything with me, and now is no time to begin."

"Gaebril?" Morgase's eyes widened. "You know? But how?"

"Oh, child," Lini said sadly, "everyone knows, though no one's had the courage to tell you. I might have, if you hadn't stayed away, but it is hardly something I could go running to you with, now is it? It is the kind of thing a woman won't believe until she finds out for herself."

"What are you talking about?" Morgase demanded. "It was your duty to come to me if you knew, Lini. It was everyone's duty! Light, I am the last to know, and now it may be too late to stop it!"

"Too late?" Lini said incredulously. "Why should it be too late? You bundle Gaebril out of the Palace, out of Andor, and Alteima and the others with him, and it is done with. Too late, indeed."

For a moment Morgase could not speak. "Alteima," she said finally, "and . . . the others?"

Lini stared at her, then shook her head in disgust. "I am an old fool; my wits are dryrooted. Well, you know now. 'When the honey's out of the comb, there's no putting it back.'" Her voice became gentler and at the same time brisk, the voice she had used for telling Morgase that her pony had broken a leg and had to be put down. "Gaebril spends most of his nights with you, but Alteima has nearly as much of his time. He spreads himself thin with the other six. Five have rooms in the Palace. One, a big-eyed young thing, he sneaks in and out for some reason all swathed in a cloak, even in this heat. Perhaps she has a husband. I'm sorry, girl, but truth is truth. 'Better to face the bear than run from it.'"

Morgase's knees sagged, and if Lini had not hurriedly pulled a chair from the table to shove under her, she would have sat down on the floor. Alteima. Him watching the two of them as they gossiped took on a new image, now. A man fondly watching two of his pet cats at play. And *six* others! Rage boiled up in her, a rage that had been lacking when she only thought he was after her throne. That she had considered coldly, clearly; as clearly as she could consider anything recently. That was a danger that had to be looked at with cold reason. But this! The man had ensconced his jades in her palace. He had made her just another of his trulls. She wanted his head. She wanted him flayed alive. The Light help her, she wanted his touch. *I must be going mad!*

"That will be solved along with everything else," she said coldly. Much depended on who was in Caemlyn, and who on their country estates. "Where is Lord Pelivar? Lord Abelle? Lady Arathelle?" They led strong Houses, and many retainers.

"Exiled," Lini said slowly, giving her an odd look. "You exiled them from the city last spring."

Morgase stared back. She remembered none of that. Except that now, dim and distant, she did. "Lady Ellorien?" she said slowly. "Lady Aemlyn, and Lord Luan?" More strong Houses. More Houses that had been behind her before she gained the throne.

"Exiled," Lini replied just as slowly. "You had Ellorien flogged for demanding to know why." She bent to brush Morgase's hair back, gnarled fingers lingering on her cheek as they had when she checked for fever. "Are you well, girl?"

Morgase nodded dully, but it was because she was remembering, in a shadowy way. Ellorien, screaming in outrage as her gown was ripped down the back. House Traemane had been the very first to throw its support to Trakand, brought by a plumply pretty woman only a few years older than Morgase. Brought by Ellorien, now one of her closest friends. At least, she had been. Elayne had been named after Ellorien's grandmother. Vaguely she could recall others leaving the city; distancing themselves from her, it seemed obvious now. And those who remained? Houses too weak to be of any use, or else sycophants. She seemed to recall signing numerous documents Gaebril had laid in front of her, creating new titles. Gaebril's toadeaters and her enemies; they were all she could count on being strong in Caemlyn.

"I do not care what you say," Lini said firmly. "You have no fever, but there's something wrong. You need an Aes Sedai Healer is what you need."

"No Aes Sedai." Morgase's voice was even harder. She

fingered her ring again, briefly. She knew that her animosity toward the Tower had grown recently beyond what some might say was reasonable, yet she could no longer make herself trust a White Tower that seemed to be trying to hide her daughter from her. Her letter to the new Amyrlin demanding Elayne's return—no one *demanded* anything of an Amyrlin Seat, but she had—that letter was yet unanswered. It had barely had time to reach Tar Valon. In any case, she knew for cold fact that she would not have an Aes Sedai near her. And yet, right alongside that, she could not think of Elayne without a swell of pride. Raised Accepted after so short a time. Elayne might well be the first woman to sit on the throne of Andor as full Aes Sedai, not just Tower trained. It made no sense that she could feel both things at once, but very little made any sense just now. And her daughter would never have the Lion Throne if Morgase did not secure it for her.

"I said no Aes Sedai, Lini, so you might as well stop looking at me like that. This is one time you will not make me take bad-tasting medicine. Besides which, I doubt there is an Aes Sedai of any stripe to be found in Caemlyn." Her old supporters gone, exiled by her own signature, and maybe her enemies for good over what she had done to Ellorien. New lords and ladies in their places in the Palace. New faces in the Guards. What loyalty remained there? "Would you recognize a Guardsman Lieutenant named Tallanvor, Lini?" At the other woman's quick nod, she went on. "Find him for me, and bring him here. But do not let him know you are bringing him to me. In fact, tell everyone in the Pensioners' Quarters that, should anyone ask, I am not here."

"There is more to this than Gaebril and his women, isn't there?"

"Just go, Lini. And hurry. There is not much time." By the shadows she could see in the tree-filled garden through the window, the sun had passed its height. Evening would be there all too soon. Evening, when Gaebril would be looking for her.

When Lini left, Morgase remained in the chair, sitting rigidly. She dared not stand; her knees were stronger now, but she feared that if she began moving she would not stop until she was back in her sitting room, waiting for Gaebril. The urge was that strong, especially now that she was alone. And once he looked at her, once he touched her, she had no doubt that she would forgive him everything. Forget everything, maybe, based on how fuzzy and incomplete her memories were. Had she not known better, she could have thought that he had used the One Power on her in some way, but no man who could channel survived to his age.

Lini had often told her that there was always one man in the world for whom a woman would find herself behaving a brainless fool, but she had never believed that she could succumb. Still, her choices in men had never been good, however right they seemed at the time.

Taringail Damodred she had wed for political reasons. He had been married to Tigraine, the Daughter-Heir whose disappearance had set off the Succession when Mordrellen died. Marrying him had made a link with the old queen, smoothing the doubts of most of her opponents, and more importantly, had maintained the alliance that had ended the ceaseless wars with Cairhien. In such ways did queens choose their husbands. Taringail had been a cold, distant man, and there was never love, despite two wonderful children; it had been almost a relief when he died in a hunting accident.

Thomdril Merrilin, House bard and then Court-bard, had been a joy at first, intelligent and witty, a laughing man who used the tricks of the Game of Houses to aid her to the throne and help strengthen Andor once she had it. He had been twice her age then, yet she might have married him—marriages with commoners were not unheard of in Andor—but he vanished without a word, and her temper got the better of her. She never had learned why he had gone, but it did not matter. When he finally returned she would surely have rescinded the arrest order, but for once instead of softly turning her anger aside he had met her harsh word for harsh word, saying things she could never forgive. Her ears still burned to remember being called a spoiled child and a puppet of Tar Valon. He had actually shaken her, his queen!

Then there had been Gareth Bryne, strong and capable, as bluff as his face and as stubborn as she; he had turned out to be a treasonous fool. He was well out of her life. It seemed years since she had seen him instead of little more than half of one.

And finally Gaebril. The crown to her list of bad choices. At least the others had not tried to supplant her.

Not so many men for one woman's life, but in another way, too many. Another thing that Lini sometimes said was that men were only good for three things, though very good for those. She had been on the throne before Lini had thought her old enough to tell what the three things were. *Perhaps if I'd kept just to the dancing,* she thought wryly, *I'd not have so much trouble with them.*

The shadows in the garden beyond the window had shifted an hour's worth before Lini returned with young Tallanvor, who went to one knee while she was still shutting the door. "He didn't want to come with me at first," she said. "Fifty years ago I suppose I could have shown what you are displaying to the world, and he'd have followed quick enough, but now I must needs use sweet reason."

Tallanvor turned his head to look up at her sourly. "You threatened to harry me here with a stick if I did not come. You are lucky I wondered what was so important to you, instead of having somebody drag you to the infirmary." Her stern sniff did not faze him. His acrid gaze turned angry as it shifted to Morgase. "I see your meeting with Gaebril did not go well, my Queen. I had hoped for . . . more."

He was looking straight at her eyes, but Lini's comment had made her aware of her dress again. She felt as though glowing arrows were pointing to her exposed bosom. It was an effort to keep her hands calmly in her lap. "You are a sharp lad, Tallanvor. And loyal, I believe, else you would not have come to me with the news of the Two Rivers."

"I am not a boy," he snapped, jerking upright where

he knelt. "I am a man who has sworn his life in service to his queen."

She let her temper flare right back at him. "If you are a man, behave as one. Stand, and answer your queen's questions truthfully. And remember that I *am* your queen, *young* Tallanvor. Whatever you think may have happened, I am Queen of Andor."

"Forgive me, my Queen. I hear and obey." The words were properly said, if not exactly contrite, but he stood, head high, staring at her as defiantly as ever. Light, the man was as stubborn as Gareth Bryne had ever been.

"How many loyal men are there among the Guards in the Palace? How many will obey their oaths and follow me?"

"I will," he said quietly, and suddenly all of his anger was gone, though he still stared intently at her face. "For the rest . . . If you wish to find loyal men, you must look to the outlying garrisons, perhaps as far as Whitebridge. Some who were in Caemlyn were sent to Cairhien with the levies, but the rest in the city are Gaebril's to a man. Their new . . . Their new oath is to throne and law, not the Queen."

It was worse than she had hoped for, but no more than she had expected, really. Whatever he was, Gaebril was no fool. "Then I must go elsewhere to begin reestablishing my rule." The Houses would be difficult to rally after the exiles, after Ellorien, but it had to be done. "Gaebril may try to stop me leaving the Palace"—she found a faint memory of trying to leave, twice, and being halted by Gaebril—"so you will procure two horses and wait in the street behind the south stables. I will meet you there, dressed for riding."

"Too public," he said. "And too close. Gaebril's men might recognize you, however you disguised yourself. I know a man. . . . Could you find an inn called The Queen's Blessing, in the western part of the New City?" The New City was new only in comparison with the Inner City it surrounded.

"I can." She did not like being opposed, even when it made sense. Bryne had done that, too. It would be a pleasure to show this young man just how well she could disguise herself. It was her habit once a year, though she realized that she had not done it so far this year, to dress as a commoner and walk the streets to feel the pulse of the people. No one had ever recognized her. "But can this man be trusted, young Tallanvor?"

"Basel Gill is as loyal to you as I am myself." He hesitated, anguish crossing his face then being replaced by anger once more. "Why have you waited so long? You must have known, you must have seen, yet you have waited while Gaebril tightened his hands around Andor's neck. Why have you waited?"

So. His anger was honestly come by, and it deserved an honest answer. Only she had no answer, certainly not one she could tell him. "It is not your place to question your Queen, young man," she said with a gentle firmness. "A loyal man, as I know that you are loyal, serves without question."

He let out a long breath. "I will await you in the stable of The Queen's Blessing, my Queen." And with a bow suitable for a state audience, he was gone.

"Why do you keep calling him young?" Lini demanded once the door closed. "It puts his back up. 'A fool puts a burr under the saddle before she rides.'"

"He *is* young, Lini. Young enough to be my son."

Lini snorted, and this time there was nothing delicate about it. "He has a few years on Galad, and Galad is too old to be yours. You were playing with dolls when Tallanvor was born, and thinking babes came the same way as dolls."

Sighing, Morgase wondered if the woman had treated her mother like this. Probably. And if Lini lived long enough to see Elayne on the throne—which somehow she did not doubt, Lini would last forever—she would probably treat Elayne no differently. That was assuming that a throne remained for Elayne to inherit. "The question is, is he as loyal as he seems, Lini? One faithful Guardsman, when every other loyal man in the Palace has been sent away. Suddenly it seems too good to be true."

"He swore the new oath." Morgase opened her mouth, but Lini forestalled her. "I saw him afterwards, alone

behind the stables. That's how I knew who you meant; I
found out his name. He did not see me. He was on his
knees, tears streaming down his face. He alternated
apologizing to you and repeating the old oath. Not just to
'the Queen of Andor,' but to 'Queen Morgase of Andor.'
He swore in the old way, on his sword, slicing his arm to
show he would shed his last drop before breaking it. I
know a thing or two of men, girl. That one will follow
you against an army with nothing but his bare hands."

That was good to know. If she could not trust him, she
would have to doubt Lini next. No, never Lini. He had
sworn in the old way? That was something for stories,
now. And she was letting her thoughts drift again. Surely
Gaebril's clouding of her mind was finished now, with all
she knew. Then why did a part of her still want to go
back to her sitting room and wait? She had to concentrate. "I will need a simple dress, Lini. One that does not
fit too well. A little soot from the fireplace, and . . ."

Lini insisted on coming, too. Morgase would have had
to tie her to a chair to leave her behind, and she was not
certain that the old woman would have let herself be
tied; she had always seemed frail, and had always been
far stronger than she seemed.

When they slipped out through a small side gate,
Morgase did not look very much like herself. A bit of
soot had darkened her red-gold hair, taken its sheen away
and made it lank. Sweat rolling down her face helped, as
well. No one believed that queens sweated. A shapeless
dress of rough—very rough—gray wool, with divided
skirts, completed her disguise. Even her shift and stockings were coarse wool. She looked a farm woman who
had ridden the cart horse to market and now wanted to
see a little of the city. Lini looked herself, straight-backed
and no-nonsense, in a green woolen riding dress, well cut
but ten years out of fashion.

Wishing she could scratch, Morgase also wished that
the other woman had not taken her so to heart about the
dress not fitting very well. Stuffing the low-necked gown
away under the bed, her old nurse had muttered some
saying about displaying wares you did not mean to sell,
and when Morgase claimed she had just made it up, her

reply was *At my age, if I make it up, it's still an old saying.*
Morgase more than half-suspected that her itchy, ill-draped dress was punishment for that gown.

The Inner City was built on hills, streets following the natural curve of the land and planned to give sudden views of parks full of trees and monuments, or tile-covered towers glittering a hundred colors in the sun. Sudden rises hurled the eye across Caemlyn entire, to the rolling plains and forests beyond. Morgase saw none of it as she hurried through the crowds thronging the streets. Usually she would have tried to listen to the people, to gauge their mood. This time she heard only the hum and babble of a great city. She had no thought of trying to rouse them. Thousands of men armed mainly with stones and rage could overwhelm the Guards in the Royal Palace, but if she had not known it before, the riots in the spring that had brought Gaebril to her attention, and the near riots the year before, had shown what mobs could do. She meant to rule again in Caemlyn, not see it burned.

Beyond the white walls of the Inner City, the New City had its own beauties. Tall slender towers, and domes gleaming white and gold, huge expanses of red-tiled roofs, and the great, towered outer walls, pale gray streaked with silver and white. Broad boulevards, split down the middle by wide expanses of trees and grass, were jammed with people and carriages and wagons. Except to notice in passing that the grass was dying for lack of rain, Morgase kept her mind on what she was hunting.

From the experience of her annual forays, she chose the people she questioned carefully. Men, mostly. She knew how she looked, even with soot in her hair, and some women would give wrong directions from jealousy. Men, on the other hand, racked their brains to be right, to impress her. None with too smug a face, or too rough. The first were often offended at being approached, as though they were not afoot themselves, and the others were likely to think a woman asking directions had something else on her mind.

One fellow with a chin too big for his face, hawking a

tray of pins and needles, grinned at her and said, "Did anyone ever tell you you look a mite like the Queen? Whatever mess she's made of us, she's a pretty one."

She gave him a raucous laugh that earned a stern look from Lini. "You save your flattery for your wife. The second turn to the left, you say? I thank you. And for the compliment, too."

As she pushed on through the crowd, a frown settled on her face. She had heard too much of that. Not that she looked like the Queen, but that Morgase had made a mess of things. Gaebril had raised taxes heavily to pay for his levies, it seemed, but she took the blame, and rightly so. The responsibility was the Queen's. Other laws had come out of the Palace, as well, laws that made little sense, but did make people's lives more difficult. She heard whispers about herself, that maybe Andor had had queens long enough. Only murmurs, but what one man dared speak in a low voice, ten thought. Perhaps it would not have been as easy as she had thought to rouse mobs against Gaebril.

Eventually she found her goal, a broad stone inn, the sign over the door bearing a man kneeling before a golden-haired woman in the Rose Crown, one of her hands on his head. The Queen's Blessing. If it was meant to be her, it was not a good likeness. The cheeks were too fat.

Not until she stopped in front of the inn did she realize that Lini was puffing. She had set a quick pace, and the woman was far from young. "Lini, I am sorry. I should not have walked so—"

"If I can't keep up with you, girl, how will I be able to tend Elayne's babes? Do you mean to stand there? 'Dragging feet never finish a journey.' He said he would be in the stable."

The white-haired woman stalked off, muttering to herself, and Morgase followed her around the inn. Before stepping into the stone stable, she shaded her eyes to look at the sun. No more than two hours until dusk; Gaebril would be looking by then, if he was not already.

Tallanvor was not alone in the stall-lined stable. When he went to one knee on the straw-covered floor, in a green wool coat with his sword belted over it, two men and a woman knelt with him, if a bit hesitantly, unsure of her as she was. The stout man, pink-faced and balding, must be Basel Gill, the innkeeper. An old leather jerkin, studded with steel discs, strained around his girth, and he wore a sword at his hip, too.

"My Queen," Gill said, "I've not carried a sword in years—not since the Aiel War—but I'd count it an honor if you allowed me to follow you." He should have looked ridiculous, but he did not.

Morgase studied the other two, a hulking fellow in a rough gray coat, with heavy-lidded eyes, an oft-broken nose, and scars on his face, and a short, pretty woman approaching her middle years. She seemed to be with the street tough, but her high-necked blue wool dress appeared too finely woven for one like him to have bought.

The fellow sensed her doubts, for all his lazy-eyed appearance. "I am Lamgwin, my Queen, and a good Queen's man. 'Tisn't right, what's been done, and it has to be put straight. I want to follow you, too. Me and Breane, both."

"Rise," she told them. "It may be some days yet before it is safe for you to acknowledge me as your queen. I will be glad of your company, Master Gill. And yours, Master Lamgwin, but it will be safer for your woman if she remains in Caemlyn. There are hard days ahead."

Brushing straw from her skirts, Breane gave her a sharp look, and Lini a sharper. "I have known hard days," she said in a Cairhienin accent. Nobly born, unless Morgase missed her guess; one of the refugees. "And I never knew a good man until I found Lamgwin. Or until he found me. The loyalty and love he bears for you, I bear for him tenfold. He follows you, but I follow him. I will not stay behind."

Morgase drew breath, then nodded her acceptance. The woman seemed to take it for granted in any case. A fine seed for the army to retake her throne: One young soldier who scowled at her as often as not, a balding innkeeper who looked as if he had not been on a horse in twenty years, a street tough who appeared more than half-asleep, and a refugee Cairhienin noblewoman who had made it clear that her loyalties went only as far as the tough. And Lini, of course. Lini, who treated her as though she were still in the nursery. Oh, yes, a very fine seed.

"Where do we go, my Queen?" Gill asked as he began leading already saddled horses out of their stalls. Lamgwin moved with surprising speed to throw another high-cantled saddle on a horse for Lini.

Morgase realized that she had not considered that. *Light, Gaebril can't still be fogging my mind.* She still felt that urge to return to her sitting room, though. It was not he. She had had to concentrate on getting out of the Palace and reaching here. Once she would have gone to Ellorien first, but Pelivar or Arathelle would do. Once she had reasoned out how to explain away their exiles.

Before she could open her mouth, Tallanvor said, "It must be to Gareth Bryne. There is hard feeling against you among the great Houses, my Queen, but with Bryne following you, they will reswear allegiance, if only because they know he will win every battle."

She clamped her teeth shut to hold back instant refusal. Bryne was a traitor. But he was also one of the finest generals alive. His presence would be a convincing argument when she had to make Pelivar and the rest forget that she had exiled them. Very well. No doubt he would leap at the chance to be Captain-General of the Queen's Guards once more. And if not, she would manage well enough without him.

When the sun touched the horizon, they were five miles out of Caemlyn and riding hard for Kore Springs.

Night was when Padan Fain felt most comfortable. As he padded through the tapestry-bedecked corridors of the White Tower, it seemed as though the darkness outside made a cloak to hide him from his enemies, despite the stand-lamps, gilded and mirrored, burning along his way. A false feeling, he knew; his enemies were many and everywhere. Right that moment, as in every waking hour, he could feel Rand al'Thor. Not where he was, but that he was still alive, somewhere. Still alive. It was a gift received at Shayol Ghul, in the Pit of Doom, that awareness of al'Thor.

His mind skittered away from memories of what had been done to him in the Pit. He had been distilled there, remade. But later, in Aridhol, he had been reborn. Reborn to smite old enemies and new.

He could feel something else as he stalked the empty night hallways of the Tower, a thing that was his, stolen from him. A sharper desire drew him at this moment than his longing for al'Thor's death, or the Tower's destruction, or even revenge against his ancient foe. A hunger to be whole.

The heavy paneled door had thick hinges and iron straps, and a black iron lock set in it as big as his head. Few doors in the Tower were ever locked—who would dare steal in the midst of Aes Sedai?—yet some things the Tower accounted too dangerous to be easily accessible. The most dangerous of all they kept behind this door, guarded by a stout lock.

Giggling softly, he took two thin, curved metal rods from his coat pocket, inserted them into the keyhole, probing and pressing, twisting. With a slow snap, the bolt came back. For a moment he sagged against the door, laughing hoarsely. Guarded by a stout lock. Surrounded by Aes Sedai power, and guarded by simple metal. Even the servants and novices should be done with their chores at this hour, but someone still might be awake, might just wander by. Occasional ripples of mirth still shook him as he replaced the lockpicks in his pocket and took out a fat beeswax candle, lighting the wick at a nearby stand-lamp.

He held the candle high as he closed the door behind him, peering around. Shelves lined the walls, holding plain boxes and inlaid chests of various sizes and shapes, small figures in bone or ivory or darker material, things of metal and glass and crystal that sparkled in the candlelight. Nothing that appeared dangerous. Dust covered everything; even the Aes Sedai came here seldom, and they allowed no one else in. What he was seeking pulled him to it.

On a waist-high shelf stood a dark metal box. He opened it, revealing lead walls two inches thick, with just enough space inside for a curved dagger in a golden sheath, a large ruby set in its hilt. Neither the gold nor the ruby, glittering dark as blood, interested him. Hastily he spilled a little wax to hold the candle beside the box and snatched up the dagger.

He sighed as soon as he touched it, stretched languorously. He was whole again, one with what had bound him so long ago, one with what in a very real way had given him life.

Iron hinges creaked faintly, and he darted for the door, baring the curved blade. The pale young woman opening the door had only time to gape, to try to leap back, before he slashed her cheek; in the same motion he dropped the sheath and seized her arm, jerked her past him into the storeroom. Putting his head out, he peered up and down the hallway. Still empty.

He took his time about pulling his head back and shutting the door again. He knew what he would find.

The young woman lay thrashing on the stone floor, trying and failing to scream. Her hands clawed at a face already black and bloated beyond recognition, the dark swelling oozing down onto her shoulders like thick oil. Her snowy skirts, banded in colors at the hem, flailed as her feet scrabbled uselessly. He licked at a splash of blood on his hand and giggled as he picked up the sheath.

"You are a fool."

He spun, dagger reaching, but the air around him seemed to turn solid, encasing him from his neck to the sole of his boots. He hung there, on the balls of his feet, dagger extended to stab, staring at Alviarin as she shut the door behind her and leaned against it to study him. There had been no creak this time. The soft scraping of the dying girl's slippers on the floorstones could never have masked it. He blinked away sweat that was suddenly stinging his eyes.

"Did you really think," the Aes Sedai went on, "that there would be no guard on this room, no watch kept? A ward was set on that lock. That young fool's task tonight was to monitor it. Had she done as she was supposed to, you would find a dozen Warders and as many Aes Sedai outside this door now. She is paying the price of her stupidity."

The thrashing behind him stilled, and his eyes narrowed. Alviarin was not Yellow Ajah, but even so she could have made an attempt to Heal the young woman. And she had not raised the alarm the Accepted should have, either, or she would not now be here alone. "You are Black Ajah," he whispered.

"A dangerous accusation," she said calmly. It was not clear to which of them it was dangerous. "Siuan Sanche tried to claim the Black Ajah was real when she was under the question. She begged to tell us of them. Elaida would not hear it, and will not. Tales of the Black Ajah are a vile slander against the Tower."

"You are Black Ajah," he said in a louder voice.

"You want to steal that?" She sounded as though he had not spoken. "The ruby is not worth it, Fain. Or whatever your name is. That blade is tainted so none but a fool would touch it except with tongs, or be near it for a moment longer than necessary. You can see what it did to Verine. So why did you come here and go straight to what you should not have known was here? You cannot have had time for any search."

"I could dispose of Elaida for you. One touch of this, and even Healing will not save her." He tried to gesture with the dagger, but could not budge it a hair; if he could have moved it, Alviarin would be dead by now. "You could be first in the Tower, not second."

She laughed at him, cool contemptuous chimes. "Do you think I would not be first if I had wished it? Second suits me. Let Elaida claim credit for what she calls successes, and sweat for her failures, too. I know where the power lies. Now, answer my questions, or two corpses will be found here in the morning instead of one."

There would be two in any case, whether he answered her with suitable lies or not; she did not mean to let him live. "I have seen Thakan'dar." Saying that hurt; the memories it brought were agony. He refused to whimper, forced the words out. "The great sea of fog, rolling and crashing in silence against the black cliffs, the fires of the forges glowing red beneath, and lightning stabbing up into a sky fit to drive men mad." He did not want to go on, but he made himself. "I have taken the path down to the belly of Shayol Ghul, down the long way with stones like fangs brushing my head, to the shore of a lake of fire and molten rock—" *No, not again!* "—that holds the Great Lord of the Dark in its endless depths. The heavens above Shayol Ghul are black at noon with his breath."

Alviarin was standing upright now, eyes wide. Not fearful, but impressed. "I have heard of . . ." she began softly, then shook herself and stared at him piercingly. "Who are you? Why are you here? Did one of the For—the Chosen send you? Why was I not informed?"

He threw back his head and laughed. "Are the tasks given to the likes of me for the likes of you to be knowing?" The accents of his native Lugard were strong again; in a way it was his native city. "Do the Chosen confide everything in you, then?" Something inside seemed to shout that this was not the way, but he hated Aes Sedai, and that something inside him did, too. "Be careful, pretty little Aes Sedai, or they'll be giving you to a Myrddraal for its sport."

Her glare was icicles stabbing his eyes. "We shall see, Master Fain. I will clear away this mess you have made, and then we shall see which of us stands higher with the Chosen." Eyeing the dagger, she backed from the room. The air around him did not soften until she had been gone a full minute.

Silently he snarled at himself. Fool. Playing the Aes Sedai's game, groveling for them, then one moment of anger to ruin all. Sheathing the dagger, he nicked himself, and licked the wound before sticking the weapon under his coat. He was not at all what she thought. He had been a Darkfriend once, but he was beyond that, now. Beyond it, above it. Something different. Something more. If she managed to communicate with one of the Forsaken before he could dispose of her . . . Better not to try. No time to find the Horn of Valere now. There were followers awaiting him outside the city. They should still be waiting. He had put fear into them. He hoped some of the humans were still alive.

Before the sun rose he was out of the Tower, off the island of Tar Valon. Al'Thor was out there, somewhere. And he was whole again.

CHAPTER
20

Jangai Pass

Under the looming Spine of the World, Rand guided Jeade'en up the stony slope from the foothills that began the foot of Jangai Pass. The Dragonwall pierced the sky, dwarfing all other mountains, its snowcapped peaks defying the baking afternoon sun. The tallest thrust well above clouds that mocked the Waste with promises of rain that had never come. Rand could not imagine why a man would want to climb a mountain, but it was said that men who had tried to scale these heights turned back, overcome with fear and unable to breathe. He could well believe that a man might grow too afraid to breathe, attempting to climb so high.

". . . yet though the Cairhienin are consumed with the Game of Houses," Moiraine was saying at his shoulder, "they will follow you so long as they know that you are strong. Be firm with them, but I would ask you to be fair also. A ruler who gives true justice . . ."

He tried to ignore her, as he did the other riders, and the creak and rumble of Kadere's wagons, making heavy going further back. The broken gorges and gullies of the

Waste were behind them, but these rugged rising hills, nearly as barren, were little better for wagons. No one had traveled this path in over twenty years.

Moiraine talked at him that way from daybreak to sunset whenever he let her. Her lectures could be on small things—details of court behavior, say, in Cairhien or Saldaea or somewhere else—or on large: the political influence of the Whitecloaks, or perhaps the effects of trade on rulers' decisions to go to war. It was as if she meant to see him educated, as a noble would be, or should be, before he reached the other side of the mountains. It was surprising how often what she said reflected what anyone back in Emond's Field would have called simple common sense. And also how often it did not.

Occasionally she came out with something startling; for instance, that he should trust no woman of the Tower except herself, Egwene, Elayne and Nynaeve, or the news that Elaida was now the Amyrlin Seat. Oath to obey or no, she would not tell him how she knew that. She said it was someone else's place to tell if she chose, someone else's secret, and she could not usurp it. He suspected the Wise One dreamwalkers, though they had stared him right in the eye and refused to say aye or nay. He wished he could make them swear Moiraine's oath; they interfered between him and the chiefs continually, as if they wanted him to go through them to reach the chiefs.

Right that minute he did not want to think about Elaida or the Wise Ones, or listen to Moiraine. Now he wanted to study the pass ahead, a deep gap in the mountains that twisted as though a blunt axe had tried to chop through again and again, never quite succeeding. A few minutes' hard ride, and he could be in it.

On one side of the pass mouth a sheer cliff had been smoothed over a hundred-pace width and carved, a wind-weathered snake entwining a staff a good three hundred spans high; monument or marker or ruler's sigil, it surely dated from some lost nation before Artur Hawkwing, perhaps even before the Trolloc Wars. He had seen remnants before from nations long vanished; often even Moiraine did not know their source.

High on the other side, so far up that he was not sure he was seeing what he thought, just below the snow line, stood something even stranger. Something that made the first monument of a few thousand years a commonplace. He could have sworn it was the remnants of shattered buildings, shining gray against the darker mountain, and stranger still, what appeared to be a dock of the same material, as for ships, slanting drunkenly down the mountain. If he was not imagining it, that had to date from before the Breaking. The face of the world had been changed utterly in those years. This could well have been an ocean's floor, before. He would have to ask Asmodean. Even if he had had the time, he did not think he would want to try reaching that altitude to find out for himself.

At the foot of the huge snake lay Taien, a high-walled town of moderate size, a remnant itself, of the time when Cairhien had been allowed to send caravans across the Three-fold Land, and wealth had flowed from Shara along the Silk Path. There appeared to be birds above the town, and dark blotches at regular intervals along the gray stone walls. Mat stood in Pips' stirrups, shading his eyes with that broad-brimmed hat to peer up the pass, frowning. Lan's hard face wore no expression at all, yet he appeared just as intent; a gust of wind, a little cooler here, whipped his color-shifting cloak around him, and for a moment all of him from shoulders to boots seemed to blend into the rocky hills and sparse thornbushes.

"Are you listening to me?" Moiraine said suddenly, reining her white mare closer. "You must—!" She took a deep breath. "Please, Rand. There is so much that I must tell you, so much that you need to know."

The hint of pleading in her tone made him glance at her. He could remember when he had been overawed by her presence. Now she seemed quite small, for all her regal manner. A fool thing, that he should feel protective of her. "There is plenty of time ahead of us, Moiraine," he said gently. "I don't pretend to think I know as much of the world as you. I mean to keep you close from now on." He barely realized how great a change that was from when *she* was keeping *him* close. "But I have something else on my mind right now."

"Of course." She sighed. "As you wish. We have plenty of time yet."

Rand heeled the dappled gray stallion to a trot, and the others followed. The wagons quickened, too, though they could not keep up on the slope. Asmodean's—Jasin Natael's—patch-covered gleeman's cloak rippled behind him like the banner he carried at his stirrup, brilliant red with the white-and-black symbol of the ancient Aes Sedai at its center. His face wore a sullen glower; he had not been best pleased at having to be the bannerman. Under that sign he would conquer, the Prophecy of Rhuidean said, and perhaps it would not frighten the world so much as the Dragon Banner, Lews Therin's banner, that he had left flying over the Stone of Tear. Few would know this sign.

The blotches on the walls of Taien were bodies, contorted in their final agonies, bloated in the sun and hanging by their necks in a row that seemed to encircle the town. The birds were glossy black ravens, and vultures with their heads and necks befouled. Some ravens perched on corpses, gorging, unconcerned for the new arrivals. The sickly sweet stench of corruption hung in the dry air, and the acrid smell of char. Iron-strapped gates stood gaping open on an expanse of ruin, soot-streaked stone houses and collapsed roofs. Nothing moved except the birds.

Like Mar Ruois. He tried to shake the thought away, but in his head he could see that great city after it was retaken, immense towers blackened and collapsing, the remains of great bonfires at every street crossing, where those who had refused to swear to the Shadow had been bound and thrown alive to the flames. He knew whose memory it had to be, though he had not discussed it with Moiraine. *I am Rand al'Thor. Lews Therin Telamon is dead three thousand years. I am myself!* That was one battle he meant to win. If he did have to die at Shayol Ghul, he would die as himself. He made himself think of something else.

Half a month since he had left Rhuidean. Half a month, though the Aiel had set a pace afoot from sunup to sundown that wearied the horses. But Couladin had been moving this way a week before he learned of it. If they had not managed to close any ground, he would have that long to ravage Cairhien before Rand could reach it. Longer, before the Shaido could be brought to bay. Not a much happier thought.

"There's someone watching us from those rocks to the left," Lan said quietly. He seemed to be completely engrossed in studying what remained of Taien. "Not Aiel, or I doubt I would have seen a glimmer."

Rand was glad that he had made Egwene and Aviendha stay with the Wise Ones. The town gave him a new reason, but the watcher fit in with his original plan, when he had hoped that Taien had escaped. Egwene still wore the same Aiel clothes as Aviendha, and Aiel would not have been very welcome in Taien. They were even less likely to be welcome among the survivors.

He looked back at the wagons drawing to a halt a short distance downslope. Mutters drifted up from the drivers now that they could see the town clearly, and the wall's decorations. Kadere, his bulk all in white again today, mopped at his hawk-nosed face with a large kerchief; he appeared unperturbed, merely pursing his lips thoughtfully.

Rand expected that Moiraine would have to find new drivers once they were through the pass. Kadere and his crew would likely flee as soon as they had the chance. And he would have to let them go. It was not right—it was not justice—but it was necessary to protect Asmodean. How long now had he been doing what was necessary instead of what was right? In a fair world, they would be one and the same. That made him laugh, a hoarse wheeze. He was far from the village boy he had been, but sometimes that boy sneaked up on him. The others looked at him, and he fought the urge to tell them that he was not mad yet.

Long minutes passed before two coatless men and a woman emerged from the rocks, all three ragged and dirty and barefoot. They approached hesitantly, heads tilted uneasily, eyes darting from rider to rider, to the wagons and back, as though they might take flight at a shout. Gaunt cheeks and wavering steps spoke of hunger.

"Thank the Light," one of the men said finally. He was gray-haired—none of the three was young—his face deeply creased. His eyes lingered a moment on Asmodean, with falls of lace at collar and cuffs, but the leader of this train would not be riding a mule and carrying a banner. It was Rand's stirrup that he clutched anxiously. "The Light be praised that you came out of those terrible lands alive, my Lord." That might have been Rand's blue silk coat, embroidered in gold on the shoulders, or the banner, or simple flattery. The man certainly had no reason to think them other than merchants, if well dressed for it. "Those murdering savages have risen again. It is another Aiel War. They were over the wall in the night before anybody knew, killing everyone who raised a hand, stealing everything not mortared in place."

"In the night?" Mat said sharply. Hat pulled low, he was still studying the ruined town. "Were your sentries asleep? You did have sentries this close to your enemies? Even Aiel would have a hard time coming at you if you kept a good watch." Lan gave him an appraising look.

"No, my Lord." The gray-haired man blinked at Mat, then gave his answer to Rand. Mat's green coat was fine enough for a lord, but it hung open and looked slept in. "We . . . We had only a watchman at each gate. It has been long since any have even seen one of the savages. But this time . . . Whatever they did not steal, they burned, and drove us out to starve. Filthy animals! Thank the Light you have come to save us, my Lord, or we would all have died here. I am Tal Nethin. I am—I was—a saddlemaker. A good one, my Lord. This is my sister Aril, and her husband, Ander Corl. He makes fine boots."

"They stole people too, my Lord," the woman said, her voice raw. Somewhat younger than her brother, she might have been handsome once, but haggard worry had etched lines in her face that Rand suspected would never entirely go away. Her husband had a lost look in his eyes, as if not exactly sure where he was. "My daughter, my Lord, and my son. They took all the young ones, everyone above sixteen, and some twice that or more. Said they were guy-something, and stripped them naked right in the street and herded them off. My Lord, can you . . . ?" She trailed off, eyes squeezing shut as the impossibility overwhelmed her, swaying. Small odds that she would ever see her children again.

Moiraine was out of her saddle in an instant and by Aril's side. The haggard woman gave a loud gasp as soon as the Aes Sedai's hands touched her, shivering to her toetips. Her wondering look turned to Moiraine questioningly, but Moiraine only held her as if supporting her.

The woman's husband suddenly gaped, staring at Rand's gilded belt buckle, the gift from Aviendha. "His arms were marked like that. Like that. All twined around, like the cliff snake."

Tal looked up at Rand uncertainly. "The savages' leader, my Lord. He—had markings like that on his arms. He wore those strange clothes they all do, but he had his coatsleeves cut off, and he made sure everybody saw."

"A gift I received in the Waste," Rand said. He made sure to keep his hands still on his pommel; his coatsleeves hid his own Dragons, except for the heads; they would be visible on the backs of his hands to anyone who looked closely. Aril had forgotten about wondering what Moiraine had actually done, and all three looked on the point of running. "How long since they left?"

"Six days, my Lord," Tal said uneasily. "They did what they did in a night and a day and were gone the next. We would have gone, too, but what if we met them coming back? Surely they were turned back at Selean?" That was the town at the other end of the pass. Rand doubted that Selean was in any better condition than Taien by this time.

"How many survivors are there besides you three?"

"Maybe a hundred, my Lord. Maybe more. Nobody has counted."

Abruptly anger flared in him, though he tried to hold it

down. "A hundred of you?" His voice was icy iron. "And six days? Then why are your dead left for the ravens? Why do corpses still decorate your town walls? Those are your people filling your nostrils with their stink!" Huddling together, the three backed away from his horse.

"We were afraid, my Lord," Tal said hoarsely. "They went, but they could come back. And he told us . . . The one with the markings on his arms told us not to touch anything."

"A message," Ander said in a dull voice. "He chose them out to hang, just pulling them out until he had enough to line the wall. Men, women, he did not care." His eyes were fixed on Rand's buckle. "He said they were a message for some man who would be following him. He said he wanted this man to know . . . know what they were going to do on the other side of the Spine. He said . . . He said he would do worse to this man."

Aril's eyes widened suddenly, and the three stared beyond Rand for a moment, gaping. Then, screaming, they turned and ran. Black-veiled Aiel rose from the rocks they had come from, and they darted off in another direction. Veiled Aiel appeared there, too, and they collapsed to the ground, sobbing and holding each other as they were surrounded. Moiraine's face was cool and composed, but her eyes were not serene.

Rand twisted in his saddle. Rhuarc and Dhearic were coming up the slope, unveiling themselves and unwrapping the *shoufa* from around their heads. Dhearic was thicker than Rhuarc, with a prominent nose and paler streaks through his golden hair. He had brought the Reyn Aiel as Rhuarc had said he would.

Timolan and his Miagoma had been paralleling them to the north for three days, exchanging occasional messengers but giving no clue to his intentions. The Codarra and the Shiande and the Daryne were still somewhere to the east; following, so Amys and the others said from dreamtalking to their Wise Ones, but slowly. Those Wise Ones had no more idea of their clan chiefs' aims than Rand did of Timolan's.

"Was that necessary?" he said as the two chiefs came up to him. He had frightened the people first, but for cause, and had not made them think that they were going to die,

Rhuarc simply shrugged, and Dhearic said, "We put spears in place around this hold unseen, as you wished, and there seemed no reason to wait since no one remained here to dance spears. Besides, they are only treekillers."

Rand drew a deep breath. He had known this might be as large a problem as Couladin, in its own way. Nearly five hundred years ago the Aiel had presented Cairhien with a sapling, a cutting from *Avendesora,* and with it a right granted to no other nation, to trade across the Three-fold Land to Shara. They had given no reason— they did not like wetlanders very much at the best—but to the Aiel it had been required by *ji'e'toh.* During the long years of journey that had brought them to the Waste, only one people had not attacked them, only one had allowed them water uncontested when the world grew parched. And finally they had found the descendants of those people. The Cairhienin.

For five hundred years riches had flowed into Cairhien with the silk and the ivory. Five hundred years, and *Avendoraldera* grew in Cairhein. And then King Laman had the tree cut down to make a throne. The nations knew why the Aiel had crossed the Spine of the World twenty years ago—Laman's Sin, they called it, and Laman's Pride—but few knew that to the Aiel it had not been a war. Four clans had come to find an oathbreaker, and when they had killed him, they returned to the Three-fold Land. But their contempt for the treekillers, the oathbreakers, had never died. Moiraine being Aes Sedai offset her being Cairhienin, but Rand was never sure how much.

"These folk broke no oaths," he told them. "Find the others; the saddlemaker says there are about a hundred. And be gentle with them. If any of them were watching, they're probably running away into the mountains by now." The two Aiel started to turn away, and he added, "Did you hear what they told me? What do you think of what Couladin did here?"

"They killed more than they had to," Dhearic said

with a disgusted shake of his head. "Like black ferrets falling on rockhens' nests in a gully." Killing was as easy as dying, so the Aiel said; any fool could do either.

"And the other thing? Taking prisoners. *Gai'shain.*"

Rhuarc and Dhearic exchanged looks, and Dhearic's mouth tightened. Clearly they had heard, and it made them uncomfortable. It took a great deal to make an Aiel uncomfortable.

"It cannot be so," Rhuarc said at last. "If it is . . . *Gai'shain* is a thing of *ji'e'toh.* No one can be made *gai'shain* who does not follow *ji'e'toh,* else they are only human animals, such as the Sharans keep."

"Couladin has abandoned *ji'e'toh.*" Dhearic sounded as though he were saying stones had grown wings.

Mat guided Pips closer, using his knees. He had never been more than an indifferent rider, but sometimes, when he was thinking of something else, he rode as though born on a horse's back. "That surprises you?" he said. "After everything he has done already? The man would cheat at dice with his mother."

They gave him flat-eyed stares, like blue stones. In many ways, Aiel *were ji'e'toh.* And whatever else Couladin was, he was still Aiel in their eyes. Sept before clan, clan before outsiders, but Aiel before wetlanders.

Some of the Maidens joined them, Enaila and Jolien and Adelin, and wiry, white-haired Sulin, who had been chosen roofmistress of the Roof of the Maidens in Rhuidean. She had told the Maidens who stayed to choose another, and now she led the Maidens here. They sensed the mood, and said nothing, only grounded their spearpoints patiently. An Aiel who wanted to could make the rocks look hasty.

Lan broke the silence. "If Couladin expects you to be following him, he may have left a surprise somewhere in the pass. A hundred men could hold some of those narrows against an army. A thousand . . ."

"We will camp here, then," Rand said, "and send scouts ahead to make sure the way is clear. *Duadhe Mahdi'in?*"

"Water Seekers," Dhearic agreed, sounding pleased. That had been his society before he became clan chief.

Sulin and the other Maidens gave Rand flat stares as the Reyn chief walked away downslope. He had chosen scouts from other societies for the last three days, when he had begun to fear what he might find here, and he had the feeling they knew he was not just giving the others their turns. He tried to ignore their looks. Sulin's was especially difficult; the woman could have driven nails with those pale blue eyes.

"Rhuarc, once the survivors are found, see that they're fed. And well treated. We will take them with us." His gaze was drawn to the town wall. Some Aiel were already using their curved horn bows to kill ravens. Sometimes Shadowspawn used ravens and other animals that fed on death as spies; Shadoweyes, the Aiel called them. These barely paused in the frenzied feeding until they fell transfixed with an arrow, but a wise man did not take chances with ravens or rats. "And see that the dead are buried." At least in that, right and necessity were the same.

CHAPTER
21

The Gift of a Blade

The camp began to go up quickly, in the mouth of Jangai Pass, if away from Taien, and spreading over the hills around the approaches, among the scattered thornbushes, and even onto the slopes of the mountains. Not that anything was very visible except what was inside the pass; Aiel tents blended into the stony soil so well that you could miss them even when you knew what you were looking for and where. In the hills the Aiel camped by clan, but those in the pass itself grouped themselves by society. They were mostly Maidens, but the men's societies sent their representatives, too, some fifty each, spreading tents well above the ruins of Taien in slightly separated camps. Everyone understood, or thought they did, about the Maidens carrying Rand's honor, but all societies wanted to guard the *Car'a'carn*.

Moiraine—and Lan, of course—went to get Kadere's wagons settled, just below the town; the Aes Sedai fussed over what was in those wagons nearly as much as she did over Rand. The drivers muttered and cursed about the town's smell, and avoided watching the Aiel cut bodies down from the wall, but after their months in the Waste, they seemed to like being close even to the wreckage of what they saw as civilization.

Gai'shain were erecting the Wise Ones' tents—those of Amys and Bair and Melaine—below the town, astride the faded track that led up out of the hills. Rand was sure they would say they had chosen the spot to be available to him as well as to the countless dozens of Wise Ones below, but he thought it no coincidence that anyone coming up from the hills to him would have to go through or around their camp to reach him. He was a little surprised to see Melaine directing the white-robed figures. Only three nights before, she had married Bael, in a ceremony that made her his wife and first-sister to his other wife, Dorindha. That part had been just as important as the marriage, apparently; Aviendha had been shocked at his surprise, or maybe angry.

When Egwene arrived with Aviendha up behind her on the gray mare, those full skirts pushed above their knees, they looked a matched pair despite their different coloring and Aviendha being tall enough to look over Egwene's shoulder without stretching, each with just one ivory bracelet and one necklace. The work of removing the hanged corpses had barely begun. Most of the ravens lay dead, bundles of black feathers littering the ground, and the rest had flown, but vultures too gorged to flap aloft still waddled through the ashes inside the walls.

Rand wished that there was some way he could keep the two women from having to see, but to his surprise, neither went running to empty her stomach. Well, he had not really expected anything of the sort from Aviendha; she had seen death often enough, and dealt it out, too, and her face remained expressionless. But he had not expected the pure pity in Egwene's eyes as she gazed at the bloated dead coming down.

She drew Mist over to Jeade'en and leaned to put a hand on his arm. "I am so sorry, Rand. There was no way you could have stopped this."

"I know," he told her. He had not even known there *was* a town here until Rhuarc mentioned it casually five days ago—his councils with the chiefs had all been on whether they could cover more ground in a day, and what Couladin would do when he cleared the Jangai— and by that time the Shaido had finished here and gone. He had done with cursing himself for a fool then.

"Well, just you remember it. It was not your fault." She heeled Mist on, and began talking to Aviendha before she was out of earshot. "I am glad he is taking it so well. He has the habit of feeling guilty over things he cannot control."

"Men always believe they are in control of everything around them," Aviendha replied. "When they find out they are not, they think they have failed, instead of learning a simple truth women already know."

Egwene giggled. *"That* is the simple truth. Once I saw those poor people, I thought we would find him heaving somewhere."

"Is his stomach so tender? I . . ."

Their voices faded away as the mare ambled on. Rand pulled himself back upright in the saddle, flushing. Trying to eavesdrop on them; he was behaving like an idiot. That did not stop him frowning at their departing backs. He only took responsibility for what he was accountable for, if only to himself. Just for things he could do something about. And what he should have done something about. He did not like them talking about him. Behind his back, or under his nose. The Light only knew what they were saying.

Dismounting, he led Jeade'en in search of Asmodean, who seemed to have wandered off. After so many days in the saddle, it was good to walk. Various clusters of tents were springing up along the pass; the mountain slopes and cliffs made formidable barriers, but the Aiel still arranged themselves as if they could expect attack from them. He had tried walking with the Aiel, but half a day was enough to put him back on the horse. It was hard enough to keep up with them mounted; they could wear out horses when they pressed.

Mat was down, too, squatting with his reins in one hand and that black-hafted spear across his knees, peering at the gaping gates, studying the town and muttering to himself while Pips tried to nibble at a thornbush. Mat was studying, not just staring. Where had that remark about sentries come from? Mat said odd things at times now, since their first visit to Rhuidean. Rand wished that he were willing to talk about what had happened, but he still denied that anything had, despite the foxhead medallion, the spear, and that scar around his neck. Melindhra, the Shaido Maiden that Mat had taken up with, was off to one side, watching Mat, until Sulin came and chased her away on some errand. Rand wondered if Mat knew the Maidens were laying bets on whether Melindhra would give up the spear for him. And on whether she would teach him to sing, too, though they only laughed when Rand asked what that meant.

The sound of music drew him to Asmodean, seated by himself on a granite outcrop with his harp on his knee. The crimson banner's staff had been twisted into the rocky soil, and the mule tethered to it. "You see, my Lord Dragon," he said cheerfully, "your bannerman keeps loyally to his duties." His voice and expression changed, and he said, "If you must have this thing, why not let Mat carry it, or Lan? Or Moiraine, for that matter? She would be glad to carry your banner, and clean your boots. Be careful of her. She is a devious woman. When a woman says she will obey you, of her own will, it is time to sleep lightly and watch your back."

"You carry it because you were chosen, Master Jasin Natael." Asmodean gave a start and looked around, though everyone else was too far away, and too busy, to be listening. None but they two would have understood, anyway. "What do you know about those ruins up near the snow line? They must come from the Age of Legends."

Asmodean did not even glance up the mountain. "This world is very changed from the world I . . . went to sleep in." He sounded weary, and he shivered slightly. "What I know of what lies where, I have learned since waking." The mournful sounds of "The March of Death" rose from his harp. "That could be what is left of the city where I was born, for all I know. Shorelle was a port."

The sun had maybe an hour before the Spine of the World hid it; this close to high mountains, night came

early. "I am too tired for one of our discussions tonight."
That was what they called Asmodean's lessons in public,
even when no one was around. Added to practice
sessions with Lan or Rhuarc, those lessons had left him
little time for sleep since leaving Rhuidean. "You take to
your tent when you're ready, and I will see you in the
morning. With the banner." There *was* no one else to
carry the bloody thing. Maybe he could find somebody in
Cairhien.

As he was turning away, Asmodean plucked something
discordant and said, "No burning nets woven around my
tent tonight? Do you finally begin to trust me?"

Rand looked back over his shoulder. "I trust you like a
brother. Until the day you betray me. You have a parole
for what you've done, in return for your teaching, and a
better bargain than you deserve, but the day you turn
against me, I will tear it up and bury it with you."
Asmodean opened his mouth, but Rand forestalled him.
"That is me talking, Natael. Rand al'Thor. Two Rivers
folk don't like people who try to stab them in the back."

Irritably, he pulled at the dapple's reins and went on
before the other man could say anything. He was not sure
whether Asmodean had any inkling that a dead man was
trying to take him over, but he should not let himself give
the man hints. Asmodean was sure enough already that
his was a helpless cause; if he began to think that Rand
was not in full control of his own mind, perhaps that he
was going mad, the Forsaken would abandon him in a
heartbeat, and there was too much Rand had to learn
yet.

White-robed *gai'shain* were erecting his tent under
Aviendha's direction, well into the pass mouth, with that
huge carved snake rearing above. The *gai'shain* had their
own tents, but those would be the last erected, of course.
Adelin and a dozen or so Maidens squatted nearby,
watching, waiting to guard his sleep. Even with over a
thousand Maidens encamped around him every night,
they still put a guard on his tent.

Before approaching, he reached out through the
angreal in his coat pocket to seize *saidin*. There was no
need to actually touch the carving of the fat little man

with a sword, of course. Mingled filth and sweetness filled him, that raging river of fire, that crushing avalanche of ice. Channeling as he had done every night since leaving Rhuidean, he set wards around the entire encampment, not only what was in the pass but every tent in the hills below as well, and on the slopes of the mountains. He needed the *angreal* to set wardings so large, but only just. He had thought that he was strong before, but Asmodean's teachings were making him stronger. No human or animal crossing the line of that ward would notice anything, but Shadowspawn that touched it would sound a warning that everyone in the tents would hear. Had he done this in Rhuidean, the Darkhounds could never have entered without him knowing.

The Aiel themselves would have to keep watch for human enemies. Wardings were complex weaves, if tenuous, and trying to make them do more than one thing could render them useless, in practicality. He could have made this one to kill Shadowspawn instead of merely giving warning, but that would have been like a beacon to any male Forsaken who might be searching, and to Myrddraal, too. No need to bring his enemies down on him when they might not know where he was. This, even one of the Forsaken would not know until he was close, and a Myrddraal not until it was too late.

Letting go of *saidin* was an exercise in self-control, despite the foulness of the taint, despite the way the Power tried to scour him away like sand on a riverbed, to burn him, obliterate him. He floated in the vast emptiness of the Void, yet he could feel the air stirring against each hair on his head, see the weave of the *gai'shain*'s robes, smell Aviendha's warm scent. He wanted more. But he could smell the ashes of Taien, too, smell the dead who had been burned, the corruption of those who had not, even the ones already buried, mingled with the dry soil of their graves. That helped. For a while after *saidin* was gone, all he did was take deep breaths of hot, arid air; compared to before, the whiff of death seemed absent, and the air itself pure and wonderful.

"Look what was here before us," Aviendha said as he

let a meek-faced white-robed woman take Jeade'en. She
held up a brown snake, dead, but as thick as his forearm
and nearly three paces long. The bloodsnake took its
name from the effect of its bite, turning the blood to jelly
in minutes. Unless he missed his guess, the neat wound
behind its head had come from her belt knife. Adelin
and the other Maidens looked approving.

"Did you ever for one minute think that it could have
bitten you?" he said. "Did you ever think of using the
Power instead of a bloody belt knife? Why didn't you
kiss it first? You had to be close enough."

She drew herself up, and her big green eyes should
have brought on the night's chill early. "The Wise Ones
say it is not good to use the Power too often." The
clipped words were as cold as her eyes. "They say it is
possible to draw too much and harm yourself." Frowning slightly, she added, more to herself than him,
"Though I have not come near what I can hold yet. I am
sure of it."

Shaking his head, he ducked into the tent. The woman
would not listen to reason.

No sooner had he settled himself against a silk cushion
near the still unlit fire than she followed him. Without
the bloodsnake, thankfully, but gingerly carrying something long wrapped in thick layers of gray-striped blanket. "You were worried for me," she said in a flat voice.
There was no expression at all on her face.

"Of course not," he lied. *Fool woman. She'll get herself
killed yet because she doesn't have the sense to be careful
when it's needed.* "I'd have been as worried for anyone. I
would not want anyone bitten by a bloodsnake."

For a moment she eyed him doubtfully, then gave a
quick nod. "Good. So long as you do not presume
toward me." Tossing the bundled blanket at his feet, she
sat on her heels across the firepit from him. "You would
not accept the buckle as canceling debt between us . . ."

"Aviendha, there is no debt." He thought that she had
forgotten about that. She went on as if he had not
spoken.

". . . but perhaps that will cancel it."

Sighing, he unwrapped the striped blanket—warily,

since she had held it far more uneasily than she had the snake; she had held the bloody snake as if it were a piece of cloth—unwrapped it, and gasped. What lay inside was a sword, the scabbard so encrusted with rubies and moonstones that it was hard to see the gold except where a rising sun of many rays had been inset. The ivory hilt, long enough for two hands, had another inlaid rising sun in gold; the pommel was thick with rubies and moonstones, and still more made a solid mass along the quillons. This had never been made to use, only to be seen. To be stared at.

"This must have cost . . . Aviendha, how could you pay for it?"

"It cost little," she said, so defensively that she might as well have added that she lied.

"A sword. How did you ever come by a sword? How did *any* Aiel come by a sword? Don't tell me Kadere had *this* hidden in his wagons."

"I carried it in a blanket." She sounded even more touchy now than she had about the price. "Even Bair said that would make it all right, so long as I did not actually touch it." She shrugged uncomfortably, shifting and reshifting her shawl. "It was the treekiller's sword. Laman's. It was taken from his body as proof that he was dead, because his head could not be brought back so far. Since then it has passed from hand to hand, young men or fool Maidens who wanted to own the proof of his death. Only, each began to think of what it was, and soon sold it to another fool. The price has come down very far since it first was sold. No Aiel would lay hand to it even to remove the stones."

"Well, it is very beautiful," he said, as tactfully as he could manage. Only a buffoon would carry something this gaudy. And that ivory hilt would twist in a hand slippery with sweat or blood. "But I cannot let you . . ." He trailed off as he bared a few inches of the blade, out of habit, to examine the edge. Etched into the shining steel stood a heron, symbol of a blademaster. He had carried a sword marked like that once. Suddenly he was ready to bet that this blade was like it, like the raven-marked blade on Mat's spear, metal made with Power that would never break and never need sharpening. Most blademasters' swords were only copies of those. Lan could tell him for certain, but he was sure already in his own mind.

Pulling the scabbard off, he leaned across the firepit to place it in front of her. "I will take the blade to cancel the debt, Aviendha." It was long and slightly curved, with a single edge. "Just the blade. You can have the hilt back, too." He could have a new hilt and scabbard made in Cairhien. Maybe one of Taien's survivors was a decent bladesmith.

She stared wide-eyed from the scabbard to him and back, mouth open, stunned for the first time that he had ever seen. "But those gems are worth much, much more than I— You are trying to put me in your debt again, Rand al'Thor."

"Not so." If this blade had lain untouched, and untarnished, in its scabbard for over twenty years, it had to be what he thought. "I did not accept the scabbard, so it has been yours all along." Tossing one of the silk cushions into the air, he executed the seated version of the form called Low Wind Rising; feathers rained down as the blade sliced neatly through. "And I don't accept the hilt, either, so that's yours, too. If you have made a profit, it's your own doing."

Instead of looking happy at her good fortune—he suspected she had given everything that she had for the sword, and likely gotten back a hundred times as much or more in the scabbard alone—instead of seeming glad, or thanking him, she glared through the feathers as indignantly as any goodwife in the Two Rivers seeing her floor littered. Stiffly, she clapped, and one of the *gai'shain* appeared, immediately going to her knees to begin cleaning up the mess.

"It is my tent," he said pointedly. Aviendha sniffed at him in perfect imitation of Egwene. Those two women were definitely spending too much time together.

Supper, when it came at full dark, consisted of the usual flat pale bread, and a spicy stew of dried peppers and beans with chunks of nearly white meat. He only grinned at her when he learned that it was the bloodsnake; he had eaten snake and worse since coming to the Waste. *Gara*—the poisonous lizard—was the worst in his estimation; not for the taste, which was rather like chicken, but because it was lizard. It sometimes seemed that there must be more poisonous things —snakes, lizards, spiders, plants—in the Waste than in the rest of the world combined.

Aviendha appeared disappointed that he did not spit the stew out in disgust, though sometimes it was difficult to tell what she was feeling. At times she seemed to take great pleasure in discomfiting him. Had he been trying to pretend that he was Aiel, he would have thought she was trying to prove he was not.

Tired and eager for sleep, he only took off his coat and boots before crawling into his blankets and turning his back to Aviendha. Aiel men and women might take sweatbaths together, but a short time in Shienar, where they did something much the same, had convinced him that he was not made for that sort of thing, not without going so red in the face that he died of it. He tried not to listen to the rustle of her undressing beneath her own blankets. At least she had that much modesty, but he kept his back turned anyway, just in case.

She claimed she was supposed to sleep there to continue his lessons on Aiel ways and customs, since he spent so much of his days with the chiefs. They both knew that was a lie, though what the Wise Ones thought she could find out this way, he could not imagine. She gave little grunts every now and then as she tugged at something, and muttered to herself.

To cover the sounds, and stop himself thinking of what they must mean, he said, "Melaine's wedding was impressive. Did Bael really know nothing about it until Melaine and Dorindha told him?"

"Of course not," she replied scornfully, pausing for what he thought was a stocking coming off. "Why should he know before Melaine laid the bridal wreath at his feet and asked him?" Abruptly she laughed. "Melaine nearly drove herself and Dorindha to distraction finding *segade* blossoms for the wreath. Few grow so close to the Dragonwall."

"Does that mean something special? *Segade* blossoms?" That was what he had sent her, the flowers she had never acknowledged.

"That she has a prickly nature and means to keep it." Another pause, broken by mutters. "Had she used leaves or flowers from sweetroot, it would have meant she claimed a sweet nature. Morning drop would mean she would be submissive, and . . . There are too many to list. It would take me days to teach all the combinations to you, and you do not need to know them. You will not have an Aiel wife. You belong to Elayne."

He nearly looked at her when she said "submissive." A word less likely to describe any Aiel woman he could not conceive. *Probably means she gives warning before she stabs you.*

There had been more of a muffled sound to her voice at the end. Pulling her blouse over her head, he realized. He wished the lamps were out. No, that would have made it worse. But then, he had been through this every single night since Rhuidean, and every single night it was worse. He had to put an end to it. The woman was going to sleep with the Wise Ones, where she belonged, from now on; he would learn what he could from her as he could. He had thought exactly the same thing for fifteen nights now.

Trying to chase the pictures out of his head, he said, "That bit at the end. After the vows were said." No sooner had half a dozen Wise Ones pronounced their blessings than a hundred of Melaine's blood kin had rushed in to surround her, all carrying their spears. A hundred of Bael's kin had rallied to him, and he had fought his way to her. No one had been veiled, of course—it was all part of custom—but blood had still been shed on both sides. "A few minutes before, Melaine was vowing that she loved him, but when he reached her, she fought like a cornered ridgecat." If Dorindha had not punched her in the shortribs, he did not think Bael would ever have gotten her over his shoulder to carry off. "He still has the limp and the black eye she gave him."

"Should she have been a weakling?" Aviendha said sleepily. "He had to know the worth of her. She was not a trinket for him to put in his pouch." She yawned, and he heard her nestling deeper into her blankets.

"What does 'teaching a man to sing' mean?" Aiel men did not sing, not once they were old enough to take up a spear, except for battle chants and laments for the dead.

"You are thinking of Mat Cauthon?" She actually giggled. "Sometimes, a man gives up the spear for a Maiden."

"You're making that up. I never heard of anything like that."

"Well, it is not really giving up the spear." Her voice held a thick muzziness. "Sometimes a man desires a Maiden who will not give up the spear for him, and he arranges to be taken *gai'shain* by her. He is a fool, of course. No Maiden would look at *gai'shain* as he hopes. He is worked hard and kept strictly to his place, and the first thing that is done is to make him learn to sing, to entertain the spear-sisters while they eat. 'She is going to teach him to sing.' That is what Maidens say when a man makes a fool of himself over one of the spear-sisters." A very peculiar people.

"Aviendha?" He had said he was not going to ask her this again. Lan said it was Kandori work, a pattern called snowflakes. Probably loot from some raid up north. "Who gave you that necklace?"

"A friend, Rand al'Thor. We came far today, and you will start us early tomorrow. Sleep well and wake, Rand al'Thor." Only an Aiel would wish you a good night by hoping you did not die in your sleep.

Setting the much smaller if much more intricate ward on his dreams, he channeled the lamps out and tried to sleep. A friend. The Reyn came from the north. But she had had the necklace in Rhuidean. Why did he care? Aviendha's slow breathing seemed loud in his ears until he fell asleep, and then he dreamed a confused dream of Min and Elayne helping him throw Aviendha, wearing nothing but that necklace, over his shoulder, while she beat him over the head with a wreath of *segade* blossoms.

CHAPTER
22

Birdcalls by Night

Lying facedown on his blankets with his eyes closed, Mat luxuriated in the feel of Melindhra's thumbs kneading their way down his spine. There was nothing quite as good as a massage after a long day in the saddle. Well, some things were, but right then, he was willing to settle for her thumbs.

"You are well muscled for such a short man, Matrim Cauthon."

He opened one eye and glanced back at her, kneeling astride his hips. She had built the fire up twice as high as needed, and sweat trickled down her body. Her fine golden hair, close-cut except for that Aiel tail at the nape of her neck, clung to her scalp. "If I'm too short, you can always find somebody else."

"You are not too short for my taste," she laughed, ruffling his hair. It was longer than hers. "And you are cute. Relax. This does no good if you tense."

Grunting, he closed his eyes again. Cute? *Light!* And short. Only Aiel could call him short. In every other land he had been in, he was taller than most men, if not always by much. He could remember being tall. Taller than Rand, when he rode against Artur Hawkwing. And a hand shorter than he was now when he fought beside Maecine against the Aelgari. He had spoken to Lan, claiming he had overheard some names; the Warder said Maecine had been a king of Eharon, one of the Ten Nations—that much Mat already knew—some four or five hundred years before the Trolloc Wars. Lan doubted that even the Brown Ajah knew more; much had been lost in the Trolloc Wars, and more in the War of the Hundred Years. Those were the earliest and latest of the memories that had been planted in his skull. Nothing after Artur Paendrag Tanreall, and nothing before Maecine of Eharon.

"Are you cold?" Melindhra said incredulously. "You shivered." She scrambled off him, and he heard her add wood to the fire; there was enough scrub here for burning. She slapped his bottom hard as she climbed back on, murmuring, "Good muscle."

"If you keep on like that," he muttered, "I'll think you mean to spit me for supper, like a Trolloc." It was not that he did not enjoy Melindhra—as long as she refrained from pointing out that she was taller, anyway— but the situation made him uncomfortable.

"No spits for you, Matrim Cauthon." Her thumbs dug hard into his shoulder. "That is it. Relax."

He supposed that he would marry someday, settle down. That was what you did. A woman, a house, a family. Shackled to one spot for the rest of his life. *I never heard of a wife yet that liked her husband having a drink or a gamble.* And there was what those folk on the other side of the doorframe *ter'angreal* had said. That he was fated "to marry the Daughter of the Nine Moons." *A man has to marry sooner or later, I suppose.* But he certainly did not mean to take an Aiel wife. He wanted to dance with as many women as he could, while he could.

"You are not made for spits, but for great honor, I think," Melindhra said softly.

"Sounds fine to me." Only now he could not get another woman to look at him, not the Maidens or the others. It was as if Melindhra had hung a sign on him saying OWNED BY MELINDHRA OF THE JUMAI SHAIDO. Well, she would not have put that last bit on, not here. Then again, who knew what an Aiel would do, especially a Maiden of the Spear? Women did not think the same as men, and Aiel women did not think like anybody else in the world.

"It is strange that you efface yourself so."

"Efface myself?" he mumbled. Her hands did feel good; knots were coming out that he had not known were there. "How?" He wondered if it had something to do with that necklace. Melindhra seemed to set great store by it, or by receiving it, anyway. She never wore the thing, of course. Maidens did not. But she carried it in her pouch, and showed it to every woman who asked. A lot of them seemed to.

"You put yourself in the shadow of Rand al'Thor."

"I'm not in anybody's shadow," he said absently. It could not be the necklace. He had given jewelry to other women, Maidens and others; he liked giving things to pretty women, even if all he got in return was a smile. He never expected more. If a woman did not enjoy a kiss and a cuddle as much as he did, what was the point?

"Of course, there is honor of a sort in being in the shadow of the *Car'a'carn.* To be near the mighty, you must stand in their shade."

"Shade," Mat agreed, not really hearing. Sometimes the women accepted and sometimes not, but none had decided they owned him. That was what rankled, really. He was not about to be owned by any woman, however pretty she was. And no matter how good her hands were at loosening knotted muscles.

"Your scars should be scars of honor, earned in your own name, as a chief, not this." One finger traced along the hanging scar on his neck. "Did you earn this serving the *Car'a'carn*?"

Shrugging her hand away, he pushed up on his elbows and twisted to look at her. "Are you sure 'Daughter of the Nine Moons' doesn't mean anything to you?"

"I have told you it does not. Lie down."

"If you are lying to me, I swear I'll welt your rump."

Hands on hips, she looked down at him dangerously. "Do you think that you can . . . welt my rump, Mat Cauthon?"

"I'll give it my best try." She would probably put a

spear through his ribs. "Do you swear you've never heard of the Daughter of the Nine Moons?"

"I never have," she said slowly. "Who is she? Or what? Lie down, and let me—"

A blackbird called, seemingly everywhere in the tent and outside as well, and a moment later, a redwing. Good Two Rivers birds. Rand had chosen his warnings from what he knew, birds not found in the Waste.

Melindhra was off him in an instant, wrapping her *shoufa* around her head, veiling herself as she snatched up spears and bucklers. She darted from the tent like that.

"Blood and bloody ashes!" Mat muttered as he struggled into his breeches. A redwing meant the south. He and Melindhra had put up their tent to the south, with the Chareen, as far from Rand as they could get and stay in the encampment. But he was not going outside in those thornbushes naked, the way Melindhra had. The blackbird meant north, where the Shaarad were camped; they were coming from two sides at once.

Stamping his feet in his boots as best he could in the low tent, he looked at the silver foxhead lying beside his blankets. Shouts were rising outside, the clash of metal on metal. He had finally figured out that that medallion had somehow kept Moiraine from Healing him on her first try. So long as he had been touching it, her channeling had not affected him. He had never heard of Shadowspawn able to channel, but there was always the Black Ajah—so Rand said, and he believed it—and always the chance that one of the Forsaken had finally come after Rand. Pulling the leather thong over his head so the medallion hung on his chest, he snatched up his raven-marked spear and ducked out into cold moonlight.

He had no time to feel the icy chill. Before he was completely out of the tent, he almost lost his head to a scythe-curved Trolloc sword. The blade brushed his hair as he threw himself into a low dive, rolling to his feet with the spear ready.

At first glance in the darkness, the Trolloc might have been a bulky man, though half again as tall as any Aielman, garbed all in black mail with spikes at elbows and shoulders, and a helmet with goat's horns attached. But these horns grew out of that too human head, and below the eyes a goat's muzzle thrust out.

Snarling, the Trolloc lunged at him, and howled in a harsh language never meant for a human tongue. Mat spun his spear like a quarterstaff, knocking the heavy, curved blade to one side, and thrust his long spearpoint into the creature's middle, mail parting for that Power-made steel as easily as the flesh beneath. The goat-snouted Trolloc folded over with a harsh cry, and Mat pulled his weapon free, dodging aside as it fell.

All around him Aiel, some unclothed or only half but all black-veiled, fought Trollocs with tusked boars' snouts or wolves' muzzles or eagles' beaks, some with heads horned or crested with feathers, wielding those oddly curved swords and spiked axes, hooked tridents and spears. Here and there one used a huge bow to shoot barbed arrows the size of small spears. Men fought alongside the Trollocs, too, in rough coats, with swords, shouting desperately as they died among the thornbushes.

"Sammael!"

"Sammael and the Golden Bees!"

The Darkfriends *were* dying, most as soon as they engaged an Aiel, but the Trollocs died harder.

"I am no bloody hero!" Mat shouted to no one in particular as he battled a Trolloc with a bear's muzzle and hairy ears, his third. The creature carried a long-handled axe, with half a dozen sharp spikes and a flaring blade big enough to split a tree, throwing it about like a toy in those great hairy hands. It was being near Rand that got Mat into these things. All he wanted from life was some good wine, a game of dice, and a pretty girl or three. "I don't want to be mixed up in this!" Especially not if Sammael was around. "Do you hear me?"

The Trolloc went down with a ruined throat, and he found himself facing a Myrddraal, just as it finished killing two Aiel who had come at it together. The Halfman looked like a man, pasty pale, armored in black overlapping scales like a snake's. It moved like a snake, too, boneless and fluid and quick, night-black cloak hanging still however it darted. And it had no eyes. Just a dead-white sweep of skin where eyes should be.

That eyeless gaze turned on him, and he shivered, fear oozing along his bones. "The look of the Eyeless is fear," they said in the Borderlands, where they should know, and even Aiel admitted that a Myrddraal's stare sent chills through the marrow. That was the creature's first weapon. The Halfman came at him in a flowing run.

With a roar, Mat rushed to meet it, spear spinning like a quarterstaff, thrusting, ever moving. The thing carried a blade as dark as its cloak, a sword hammered at the forges of Thakan'dar, and if that cut him, he was as good as dead unless Moiraine appeared quickly with her Healing. But there was only one sure way to take down a Fade. All-out attack; you had to overwhelm it before it overwhelmed you, and a thought for defense could be a good way to die. He could not even spare a glance for the battle raging around him in the night.

The Myrddraal's blade flickered like a serpent's tongue, darted like black lightning, but to counter Mat's attack. When raven-marked Power-wrought steel met Thakan'dar-made metal, blue light flashed around them, a crackle of sheet lightning.

Suddenly Mat's slashing attack struck flesh. Black sword and pale hand flew away, and the reverse stroke sliced open the Myrddraal's throat, but Mat did not stop. Thrust through the heart, cut to one hamstring, then the other, all in rapid succession. Only then did he step away from the thing still thrashing on the ground, flailing about with its good hand and severed stump, wounds spilling inky blood. Halfmen took a long time to admit that they were dead; they did not die completely except with a setting sun.

Looking around, Mat realized that the attack was over. Whatever Darkfriends or Trollocs were not dead, had fled; at least, he saw none standing except Aiel. Some of them were down, too. He plucked a kerchief from the neck of a Darkfriend corpse to wipe the Myrddraal's black blood from his spearpoint. It would etch the metal if left too long.

This night assault made no sense. By the bodies he

could see in the moonlight, Trolloc and human, none had made it much past the first line of tents. And without far greater numbers, they could not have hoped for more.

"What was that you called out? *Carai* something. The Old Tongue?"

He turned to look at Melindhra. She had unveiled, but she still wore not a stitch more than her *shoufa*. There were other Maidens about, and men, wearing as little, and showing as little concern, though most did seem to be heading back to their tents without lingering. They had no modesty, that was it. No modesty at all. She did not even seem to feel the cold, though her breath made wisps of mist. He was as sweaty as she, and freezing now that he had no fight for his life to occupy his mind.

"Something I heard once," he told her. "I liked the sound of it," *Carai an Caldazar!* For the honor of the Red Eagle. The battle cry of Manetheren. Most of his memories were from Manetheren. Some of those he had had before the twisted doorway. Moiraine said it was the Old Blood coming out. Just as long as it did not come out of his veins.

She put an arm around his shoulders as he started back toward their tent. "I saw you with the Nightrunner, Mat Cauthon." That was one of the Aiel names for Myrddraal. "You are as tall as a man needs to be."

Grinning, he slipped his arm around her waist, but he could not get the attack out of his head. He wanted to—his thoughts were too snarled in his borrowed memories—but he could not. Why had anyone launched such a hopeless assault? No one but a fool attacked overwhelming force without a reason. That was the thought he could not pry out of his head. No one attacked without a reason.

The birdcalls pulled Rand awake immediately, and he seized *saidin* as he tossed the blankets aside and ran out, coatless, in his stocking feet. The night was cold and moonlit, faint sounds of battle drifting up from the hills below the pass. Around him, Aiel stirred like scurrying ants, rushing into the night to where an attack might come here in the pass. The wards would signal again—

Shadowspawn in the pass would cause a winterfinch to call—until he unraveled them in the morning, but there was no point in taking foolish chances.

Soon the pass was still again, the *gai'shain* in their tents, forbidden weapons even now, the other Aiel off at the places that might need defending. Even Adelin and the other Maidens had gone, as if they knew he would have held them back if they waited. He could hear a few mutters from the wagons near the town walls, but neither the drivers nor Kadere showed themselves; he did not expect them to. The faint sounds of battle—men shouting, screaming, dying—came from two directions. Both below, well away from him. People were out around the Wise Ones' tents, too; staring toward the fighting, it seemed.

An attack down there made no sense. It was not the Miagoma, not unless Timolan had taken Shadowspawn into his clan, and that was as likely as Whitecloaks recruiting Trollocs. He turned back toward his tent, and even enclosed in the Void he gave a start.

Aviendha had come out into the moonlight, a blanket wrapped around her. Just beyond her stood a tall man shrouded in a dark cloak; moonshadows drifted over a gaunt face that was too pale, with eyes too large. A crooning rose, and the cloak opened into wide, leathery wings like those of a bat. Moving as in a dream, Aviendha drifted toward the waiting embrace.

Rand channeled, and finger-thin balefire burned past her, an arrow of solid light, to take the Draghkar in the head. The effect of that narrower stream was slower, but no less sure than with the Darkhounds. The creature's colors reversed, black to white, white to black, and it became sparkling motes that melted in air.

Aviendha shook herself as the crooning ended, stared at the last particles as they vanished, and turned to Rand, gathering the blanket closer. Her hand came up, and a stream of fire as thick as his head roared toward him.

Startled even inside the emptiness, never thinking of the Power, he threw himself to the ground beneath the billowing flames. They died in an instant.

"What are you doing?" he barked, so angry, so shocked, that the Void cracked and *saidin* vanished from him. He scrambled to his feet, stalking toward her. "This tops any ingratitude I ever heard of!" He was going to shake her until her teeth rattled. "I just saved your life, in case you failed to notice, and if I offended some bloody Aiel custom, I don't give a—!"

"The next time," she snapped back, "I will leave the great *Car'a'carn* to deal with matters by himself!" Awkwardly clutching the blanket close, she ducked stiff-backed into the tent.

For the first time, he looked behind him. At another Draghkar, crumpled on the ground in flames. He had been so angry that he had not heard the crackling and popping as it burned, had not smelled the odor of burning grease. He had not even sensed the evil of it. A Draghkar killed by first sucking the soul away, and then life. It had to be close, touching, but this one lay no more than two paces from where he had been standing. He was not certain how effective a Draghkar's crooning embrace was against someone filled with *saidin,* but he was glad he had not found out.

Drawing a deep breath, he knelt beside the tent flap. "Aviendha?" He could not go in. A lamp was lit in there, and she could be sitting there naked for all he knew, mentally ripping him up and down the way he deserved. "Aviendha, I am sorry. I apologize. I was a fool to speak as I did without asking why. I should know that you wouldn't harm me, and I . . . I . . . I'm a fool," he finished weakly.

"A great deal you know, Rand al'Thor," came a muffled reply. "You *are* a fool!"

How *did* Aiel apologize? He had never asked her that. Considering *ji'e'toh,* teaching men to sing, and wedding customs, he did not think he would. "Yes, I am. And I apologize." There was no answer this time. "Are you in your blankets?" Silence.

Muttering to himself, he stood, working his stockinged toes on the icy ground. He was going to have to remain out here until he was sure she was decently covered. Without boots or coat. He seized hold of *saidin,* taint and all, just to be distanced from the bone-grinding cold, inside the Void.

The three Wise One dreamwalkers came running, of course, and Egwene, all staring at the burning Draghkar as they skirted it, drawing their shawls around them with almost the same motion.

"Only one," Amys said. "I thank the Light, but I am surprised."

"There were two," Rand told her. "I . . . destroyed the other." Why should he be hesitant just because Moiraine had warned him against balefire? It was a weapon like any other. "If Aviendha had not killed this one, it might have gotten me."

"The feel of her channeling drew us," Egwene said, looking him up and down. At first he thought she was checking for injuries, but she paid special attention to his stocking feet, then glanced at the tent, where a crack in the tent flap showed lamplight. "You've upset her again, haven't you? She saved your life, and you . . . Men!" With a disgusted shake of her head, she brushed past him and into the tent. He heard faint voices, but could not make out what was being said.

Melaine gave a hitch to her shawl. "If you do not need us, then we must see what is happening below." She hurried off without waiting for the other two.

Bair cackled as she and Amys followed. "A wager on who she will check on first? My amethyst necklace that you like so much against that sapphire bracelet of yours?"

"Done. I choose Dorindha."

The older Wise One cackled again. "Her eyes are still full of Bael. A first-sister is a first-sister, but a new husband . . ."

They moved on out of earshot, and he bent toward the tent flap. He still could not hear what they were saying, not unless he stuck his ear to the crack, and he was not about to do that. Surely Aviendha had covered herself with Egwene in there. Then again, the way Egwene had taken to Aiel ways, it was just as likely she had peeled out of her clothes instead.

The soft sound of slippers announced Moiraine and

Lan, and Rand straightened. Though he could hear both of them breathing, the Warder's steps still made barely an audible noise. Moiraine's hair hung about her face, and she held a dark robe around her, the silk shining with the moon. Lan was fully dressed, booted and armed, wrapped in that cloak that made him part of the night. Of course. The clamor of fighting was dying down in the hills below.

"I am surprised you were not here sooner, Moiraine." His voice sounded cold, but better his voice than him. He held onto *saidin,* fought it, and the night's icy chill remained something far off. He was aware of it, aware of each hair on his arms stirring with cold beneath his shirtsleeves, but it did not touch him. "You usually come looking for me as soon as you sense trouble."

"I have never explained all that I do or do not do." Her voice was as coolly mysterious as it had ever been, yet even in the moonlight Rand was certain that she was blushing. Lan looked troubled, though with him it was difficult to tell. "I cannot hold your hand forever. Eventually, you must walk alone."

"I did that tonight, didn't I?" Embarrassment slid across the Void—that sounded as though he had done everything himself—and he added, "Aviendha all but took that one off my back." The flames on the Draghkar were burning low.

"As well she was here, then," Moiraine said calmly. "You did not need me."

She had not been afraid, of that he was sure. He had seen her rush into the midst of Shadowspawn, wielding the Power as skillfully as Lan did his sword, seen it too often to believe fear in her. So why had she not come when she sensed the Draghkar? She could have, and Lan as well; that was one of the gifts a Warder received from the bond between him and an Aes Sedai. He could make her tell, catch her between her oath to him and her inability to lie straight out. No, he could not. Or would not. He would not do that to someone who was trying to help him.

"At least now we know what the attack below was about," he said. "To make me think something important was happening there while the Draghkar slipped in on me. They tried that at Cold Rocks Hold, and it did not work there either." Only, maybe it almost had, this time. If that *had* been the intent. "You would think they would try something different." Couladin ahead of him; the Forsaken everywhere, it seemed. Why could he not face one enemy at a time?

"Do not make the mistake of thinking the Forsaken simple," Moiraine said. "That could easily be fatal." She shifted her robe as though wishing it were thicker. "The hour is late. If you have no further need of me . . . ?"

Aiel began to drift back as she and the Warder left. Some exclaimed over the Draghkar, and roused some of the *gai'shain* to drag it away, but most simply looked at it before going to their tents. They seemed to expect such things of him now.

When Adelin and the Maidens appeared, their soft-booted feet dragged. They stared at the Draghkar being hauled away by white-robed men, and exchanged long looks before approaching Rand.

"There was nothing here," Adelin said slowly. "The attack was all below, Darkfriends and Trollocs."

"Shouting 'Sammael and the Golden Bees,' I heard," another added. With her head wrapped in a *shoufa*, Rand could not make out who she was. She sounded young; some of the Maidens were no more than sixteen.

Taking a deep breath, Adelin held out one of her spears, horizontally in front of him, rock-steady. The others did the same, one spear each. "We—I—failed," Adelin said. "We should have been here when the Draghkar came. Instead we ran like children to dance the spears."

"What am I supposed to do with those?" Rand asked, and Adelin replied without hesitation.

"Whatever you wish, *Car'a'carn*. We stand ready, and will not resist."

Rand shook his head. *Bloody Aiel and their bloody* ji'e'toh. "You take those and go back to guarding my tent. Well? Go." Looks passed between them before they began to obey, as reluctantly as they had approached him in the first place. "And one of you tell Aviendha that I will be coming in when I return," he added. He was not going to spend the entire night outside wondering whether it was safe. He stalked away, the stony ground hard under his feet.

Asmodean's tent was not very far from his. There had not been a sound out of it. He whipped open the flap and ducked in. Asmodean was sitting in the dark, chewing his lip. He flinched when Rand appeared, and gave him no chance to speak.

"You did not expect me to take a hand, did you? I felt the Draghkar, but you could deal with those; you did. I have never liked Draghkar; we should never have made them. They have fewer brains than a Trolloc. Give them an order, and they still sometimes kill whatever is closest. If I had come out, if I had done something. . . . What if someone noticed? What if they realized it could not be you channeling? I—"

"Well for you that you didn't," Rand cut him off, sitting cross-legged in the dark. "If I had felt you full of *saidin* out there tonight, I might have killed you."

The other man's laugh was shaky. "I thought of that, too."

"It was Sammael who sent the attack tonight. The Trollocs and Darkfriends, anyway."

"It is not like Sammael to throw men away," Asmodean said slowly. "But he'll see ten thousand dead, or ten times that, if it gains him what he thinks is worth the cost. Maybe one of the others wants you to think it was him. Even if the Aiel took prisoners . . . Trollocs do not think of much besides killing, and Darkfriends believe what they are told."

"It was him. He tried to bait me into attacking him once in the same way, at Serendahar." *Oh, Light!* The thought drifted across the surface of the Void. *I said "me."* He did not know where Serendahar had been, or anything but what he had said. The words had just come out.

After a long silence, Asmodean said quietly, "I never knew that."

"What I want to know is, why?" Rand chose his words carefully, hoping that they were all his. He remembered

Sammael's face, a man—*Not mine. Not my memory*—a compact man with a short yellow beard. Asmodean had described all the Forsaken, but he knew this image was not made from that description. Sammael had always wanted to be taller, and resented it that the Power could not make him so. Asmodean had never told him that. "From what you've told me, he is not likely to want to face me unless he is sure of victory, and maybe not then. You said he'd likely leave me to the Dark One, if he could. So why is he sure he'll win now, if I decide to go after him?"

They discussed it in the dark for hours without coming to any conclusion. Asmodean held to the opinion that it had been one of the others, hoping to send Rand against Sammael and thus get rid of one or both; at least, Asmodean said that he did. Rand could feel the man's dark eyes on him, wondering. That slip had been too big to cover.

When he finally returned to his own tent, Adelin and the dozen Maidens all sprang to their feet, all of them at once telling him that Egwene was gone and Aviendha long asleep, that she was angry with him, they both were. They gave so many different pieces of advice on handling the two women's anger, all at the same time, that he could understand none of it. Finally they fell silent, looks passing between them, and Adelin spoke alone.

"We must speak of tonight. Of what we did, and what we failed to do. We—"

"It was nothing," he told her, "and if it was something, it's forgiven and forgotten. I would like to have a few hours' sleep for once. If you want to discuss it go talk to Amys or Bair. I am sure they'll understand what you're after more than I do." That shut them up, surprisingly, and let him get inside.

Aviendha was in her blankets, with one slim, bare leg sticking out. He tried not to look at it, or her. She had left a lamp lit. He climbed into his own blankets gratefully and channeled the lamp out before releasing *saidin*. This time he dreamed of Aviendha hurling fire, only she was not hurling it at a Draghkar, and Sammael was sitting at her side, laughing.

CHAPTER
23

"The Fifth, I Give You"

Reining Mist around on a grassy hilltop, Egwene watched the streams of Aiel coming down from the Jangai Pass. The saddle had pushed her skirts above her knees again, but she hardly noticed that now. She could not spend every minute fussing with them. And she had on stockings; it was not as though she were bare-legged.

In trotting columns the Aiel flowed by below her, arranged by clan and sept and society. Thousands upon thousands, with their packhorses and mules, the *gai'shain* who would tend the camps while the rest fought, spreading a mile wide, and more still in the pass or already out of sight ahead. Even without families, it seemed a nation on the march. The Silk Path had been a road here, a full fifty paces wide and paved with broad white stones, slicing straight through hills carved to make a level. Only occasionally was it visible through the mass of Aiel, although they seemed to prefer running on the grass, but many of the paving stones had lifted up at a corner or sunk down at one end. More than twenty years had gone by since this road had carried more than local farmers' carts and a handful of wagons.

It was startling to see trees again, real trees, towering oaks and leatherleaf in actual thickets rather than an occasional wind-twisted, stunted shape, and tall grass waving in the breeze across the hills. There was real forest to the north, and clouds in the sky, thin and high, yet clouds. The air seemed blessedly cool after the Waste, and moist, though brown leaves and large brown swaths through the grass told her that in reality it might be hotter and drier than usual for the time of year. Still, the countryside of Cairhien was a lush paradise compared to the other side of the Dragonwall.

A small stream meandered north beneath a nearly flat bridge, bordered by the dried clay of a broader bed; the River Gaelin lay not too many miles away in that direction. She wondered what the Aiel would make of that river; she had seen Aiel near a river once before. The shrunken band of water marked a definite break in the steady flow of people, as men and Maidens paused to stare in amazement before leaping across.

Kadere's wagons rumbled by on the road, the long mule teams working hard, but still losing ground to the Aiel. It had taken four days to traverse the twists and turns of the pass, and Rand apparently intended to go as far into Cairhien as he could in the few hours of daylight remaining. Moiraine and Lan rode with the wagons; not ahead of them, or even with Kadere's boxlike little white house on wheels, but alongside the second wagon, where the canvas-covered shape of the doorframe *ter'angreal* made a hump above the rest of the load. Some of the load was wrapped carefully or packed in boxes or barrels that Kadere had brought into the Waste full of his goods, and some was simply stuck in wherever it would fit, odd shapes of metal and glass, a red crystal chair, two child-sized statues of a nude man and woman, rods of bone and ivory and strange black materials in varying lengths and thicknesses. All sorts of things, including some Egwene could hardly begin to describe. Moiraine had used every inch of space in all of the wagons.

Egwene wished that she knew why the Aes Sedai was

so concerned with that particular wagon; perhaps no one else had noticed that Moiraine paid it more attention than all the others combined, but she had. Not that she was likely to find out any time soon. Her newfound equality with Moiraine was a tender thing, as she had learned when she asked that question, in the heart of the pass, and was told that her imagination was too vivid and if she had time to spy on the Aes Sedai, perhaps Moiraine should speak to the Wise Ones about intensifying her training. She had apologized profusely, of course, and the soft words seemed to have worked. Amys and the others were not taking any more of her nights than they had before.

A hundred or so Taardad *Far Dareis Mai* went trotting by on her side of the road, moving easily, veils hanging but ready to be donned, full quivers at hips. Some carried their curved horn bows, arrows nocked, while others had their bows cased on their backs, spears and bucklers swinging rhythmically as they ran. At their rear a dozen *gai'shain* in their white robes leading pack mules struggled to keep up. One wore black, not white; Isendre labored hardest of all. Egwene could pick Adelin out, and two or three others who had been guarding Rand's tent the night of the attack. Each clutched a doll in addition to her weapons, a rough-made doll clothed in full skirts and white blouse; they looked even more stone-faced than usual, trying to pretend that they held no such thing.

She was not sure what that was about. The Maidens who stood that guard had come in a group to see Bair and Amys when their stint was done, and had spent a long time with them. The next morning, while camp was still breaking in the grayness before dawn, they had begun making those dolls. She had not been able to ask, of course, but she had commented on it to one, a red-haired Tomanelle of the Serai sept named Maira, and the woman said it was to remind her that she was not a child. Her tone made it clear that she did not want to talk. One of the Maidens carrying a doll was no more than sixteen, yet Maira was at least as old as Adelin. It made little sense, and that was frustrating. Every time

Egwene thought she understood Aiel ways, something demonstrated that she did not.

Despite herself, her eyes were drawn back to the mouth of the pass. The row of stakes was still there, just visible, stretching from steep mountain slope to steep mountain slope except where Aiel had kicked some of them down. Couladin had left another message, men and women impaled across their path, standing there seven days dead. The tall gray walls of Selean clung to the hills at the right of the pass, nothing showing above them. Moiraine said it had held only a shadow of its one-time glory, yet it had still been a considerable town, much larger than Taien; no more remained of it, however. No survivors, either—except whoever the Shaido had carried off—although here some had probably run for places they thought safe. There had been farms on these hills; most of eastern Cairhien had been abandoned after the Aiel War, but a town needed farms for food. Now soot-streaked chimneys thrust up from blackened stone farmhouse walls; here a few charred rafters remained above a stone barn, there barn and farmhouse had collapsed from the heat. The hill where she sat Mist's saddle had been sheep pasture; near the fence at the foot of the hill, flies still buzzed over the refuse of butchering. Not an animal remained in any pasture, not a chicken scratching in a barnyard. The crop fields were burned stubble.

Couladin and the Shaido were Aiel. But so were Aviendha, and Bair and Amys and Melaine, and Rhuarc, who said she reminded him of one of his daughters. They had been disgusted at the impalements, yet even they seemed to think it little more than the treekillers deserved. Perhaps the only way to truly know the Aiel was to be born Aiel.

Casting a last glance at the destroyed town, she rode slowly down to the rough stone fence and let herself out at the gate, leaning down to refasten the rawhide thong out of habit. The irony was that Moiraine had said that Selean might actually go over to Couladin. In the shifting currents of *Daes Dae'mar*, in balancing an Aiel invader against a man who had sent Tairens into Cairhien, for whatever reason, the decision could have tipped either way, had Couladin given them a chance to choose.

She rode along the broad road until she caught up with Rand, in his red coat today, and joined Aviendha and Amys and thirty or more Wise Ones she barely knew besides the other two dreamwalkers, all following at a short distance. Mat, with his hat and his black-hafted spear, and Jasin Natael, leather-cased harp slung on his back and crimson banner rippling in the breeze, were riding, but hurrying Aiel passed the party by on both sides, because Rand led his dapple stallion, talking with the clan chiefs. Skirts or no skirts, the Wise Ones would have made a good job of keeping up with the passing columns if they were not sticking to Rand like pine sap. They barely glanced at Egwene, their eyes and ears focused on him and the six chiefs.

". . . and whoever comes through after Timolan," Rand was saying in a firm voice, "has to be told the same thing." Stone Dogs left to watch at Taien had returned to report the Miagoma entering the pass a day behind. "I've come to stop Couladin despoiling this land, not to loot it."

"A hard message," Bael said, "for us as well, if you mean we cannot take the fifth." Han and the rest, even Rhuarc, nodded.

"The fifth, I give you." Rand did not raise his voice, yet suddenly his words were driven nails. "But no part of that is to be food. We will live on what can be found wild or hunted or bought—if there is anyone with food to sell—until I can have the Tairens increase what they're bringing up from Tear. If any man takes a penny more than the fifth, or a loaf of bread without payment, if he burns so much as a hut because it belongs to a treekiller, or kills a man who is not trying to kill him, that man will I hang, whoever he is."

"Dark to tell the clans this," Dhearic said, almost as stony. "I came to follow He Who Comes With the Dawn, not to coddle oathbreakers." Bael and Jheran opened their mouths as if to agree, but each saw the other and snapped his teeth shut again.

"Mark what I said, Dhearic," Rand said. "I came to

save this land, not ruin it further. What I say stands for every clan, including the Miagoma and any more who follow. Every clan. You mark me well." This time no one spoke, and he swung back into Jeade'en's saddle, letting the stallion walk on among the chiefs. Those Aiel faces showed no expression.

Egwene drew breath. Those men were all old enough to be his father and more, leaders of their people as surely as kings for all they disclaimed it, hardened leaders in battle. It seemed only yesterday that he had been a boy in more than age, a youth who asked and hoped rather than commanded and expected to be obeyed. He was changing faster than she could keep up with now. A good thing, if he kept these men from doing to other cities what Couladin had done to Taien and Selean. She told herself that. She only wished he could do it without showing more arrogance every day. How soon before he expected her to obey him as Moiraine did? Or all Aes Sedai? She hoped it was only arrogance.

Wanting to talk, she kicked a foot free of its stirrup and held a hand down for Aviendha, but the Aiel woman shook her head. She really did not like to ride. And maybe all those Wise Ones striding in a pack made her reluctant, too. Some of them would not have ridden had both their legs been broken. With a sigh, Egwene climbed down, leading Mist by the reins, settling her skirts a little grumpily. The soft, knee-high Aiel boots she wore looked comfortable and were, but not for walking very far on that hard, uneven pavement.

"He truly is in command," she said.

Aviendha barely shifted her eyes from Rand's back. "I do not know him. I cannot know him. Look at the thing he carries."

She meant the sword, of course. Rand did not precisely carry it; it hung at the pommel of his saddle, in a plain scabbard of brown boarhide, the long hilt covered in the same leather, rising as high as his waist. He had had hilt and scabbard made by a man from Taien, on the journey through the pass. Egwene wondered why, when he could channel a sword of fire, and do other things that made swords seem toys. "You did give it to him, Aviendha."

Her friend scowled. "He tries to make me accept the hilt, too. He used it; it is his. Used it in front of me, as if to mock me with a sword in his hand."

"You are not angry about the sword." She did not think Aviendha was; she had not said a word about it, that night in Rand's tent. "You are still upset over how he spoke to you, and I do understand. I know he is sorry. He sometimes speaks without thinking, but if you would only let him apologize—"

"I do not want his apologies," Aviendha muttered. "I do not want . . . I can bear this no more. I cannot sleep in his tent any longer." Suddenly she took Egwene's arm, and if Egwene had not known better, she would have thought her on the brink of tears. "You must speak to them for me. To Amys and Bair and Melaine. They will listen to you. You are Aes Sedai. They must let me return to their tents. They must!"

"Who must do what?" Sorilea said, dropping back from the others to walk alongside them. The Wise One of Shende Hold had thin white hair and a face like leather drawn tight over her skull. And clear green eyes that could knock a horse down at ten paces. That was the way she normally looked at anyone. When Sorilea was angry, other Wise Ones sat quietly and clan chiefs made excuses to leave.

Melaine and another Wise One, a graying Black Water Nakai, started to join them too, until Sorilea turned those eyes on them. "If you were not so busy thinking of that new husband, Melaine, you would know Amys wants to talk with you. You, also, Aeron." Melaine flushed bright red, and *scurried* back to the others, but the older woman got there first. Sorilea watched them go, then put her full attention on Aviendha. "Now we can have a quiet talk. So you do not want to do something. Something you were told to do, of course. And you think this child Aes Sedai can get you out of doing it."

"Sorilea, I—" Aviendha got no further.

"In my day, girls jumped when a Wise One said jump, and continued jumping until they were told to stop. As I am still alive, it is still my day. Need I make myself clearer?"

Aviendha took a deep breath. "No, Sorilea," she said meekly.

The old woman's eyes came to rest on Egwene. "And you? Do you think you are going to beg her off?"

"No, Sorilea." Egwene felt as though she should curtsy.

"Good," Sorilea said, not sounding satisfied, just as if it was what she had expected. It almost certainly was. "Now I can speak to you of what I really want to know. I hear the *Car'a'carn* has given you an interest gift like no other ever heard of, rubies and moonstones."

Aviendha jumped as if a mouse had run up her leg. Well, she probably would not, but it was the way Egwene would have jumped in that circumstance. The Aiel explained about Laman's sword and the scabbard so hastily that her words tripped over one another.

Sorilea shifted her shawl, muttering about girls touching swords, even wrapped in blankets, and about having a sharp word with "young Bair." "So he has not captured your eye. A pity. It would bind him to us; he sees too many people as his, now." For a moment she eyed Aviendha up and down. "I will have Feran look at you. His greatfather is my sister-son. You have other duties to the people than learning to be a Wise One. Those hips were made for babes."

Aviendha stumbled over an upraised paving stone and just caught herself short of falling. "I . . . I will think on him, when there is time," she said breathlessly. "I have much to learn yet, of being a Wise One, and Feran is *Seia Doon*, and the Black Eyes have vowed not to sleep beneath roof or tent until Couladin is dead." Couladin was *Seia Doon*.

The leathery-faced Wise One nodded as though everything had been settled. "You, young Aes Sedai. You know the *Car'a'carn* well, it is said. Will he do as he has threatened? Hang even a clan chief?"

"I think . . . maybe . . . that he will." More quickly, Egwene added, "But I am sure he can be brought to see reason." She was not sure of any such thing, or even that it was reason—what he had said sounded only just—but justice would do him no good if he found the others turning against him as well as the Shaido.

Sorilea glanced at her in surprise, then turned a gaze on the chiefs around Rand's horse that should have knocked the lot of them flat. "You mistake me. He must show that mangy pack of wolves that he is the chief wolf. A chief must be harder than other men, young Aes Sedai, and the *Car'a'carn* harder than other chiefs. Every day a few more men, and even Maidens, are taken by the bleakness, but they are the soft outer bark of the ironwood. What remains is the hard inner core, and he must be hard to lead them." Egwene noticed that she did not include herself or the other Wise Ones among those who would be led. Muttering to herself about "mangy wolves," Sorilea strode ahead, and soon had all the Wise Ones listening as they walked. Whatever she was saying, it did not carry.

"Who is this Feran?" Egwene asked. "I've never heard you speak of him. What does he look like?"

Frowning at Sorilea's back, more than half hidden by the women clustered around her, Aviendha spoke absently. "He looks much like Rhuarc, only younger, taller and more handsome, with much redder hair. For over a year he has been trying to attract Enaila's interest, but I think she will teach him to sing before she gives up the spear."

"I don't understand. Do you mean to share him with Enaila?" It still felt odd, speaking so casually of that.

Aviendha stumbled again, and stared at her. "Share him? I want no part of him. His face is beautiful, but he laughs like a braying mule and picks at his ears."

"But from the way you talked to Sorilea, I thought you . . . liked him. Why didn't you tell her what you just told me?"

The other woman's low laugh sounded pained. "Egwene, if she thought I was trying to balk in this, she would make the bridal wreath herself and drag both Feran and me by the neck to be wed. Have you ever seen anyone say 'no' to Sorilea? Could you?"

Egwene opened her mouth to say that of course she

could, and promptly closed it again. Making Nynaeve step back was one thing, and trying the same with Sorilea quite another. It would be like standing in the path of a landslide and telling it to stop.

To change the subject, she said, "I will speak to Amys and the others for you." Not that she really thought it would do much good now. The right time had been before it began. At least Aviendha saw the impropriety of the situation finally. Perhaps . . . "If we go to them together, I am sure they will listen."

"No, Egwene. I must obey the Wise Ones. *Ji'e'toh* requires it." Just as if she had not been asking for intercession a moment earlier. Just as if she had not all but begged the Wise Ones not to make her sleep in Rand's tent. "But why is my duty to the people never what I wish? Why must it be what I would rather die before doing?"

"Aviendha, no one is going to make you marry, or have babies. Not even Sorilea." Egwene wished she had sounded a bit less limp on that last.

"You do not understand," the other woman said softly, "and I cannot explain it to you." She gathered her shawl around her and would not speak of it further. She was willing to discuss their lessons, or whether Couladin would turn and give battle, or how marriage had affected Melaine—who seemed to have to work at being prickly now—or anything at all except what it was that she could not, or would not, explain.

CHAPTER
24

A Message Sent

The land changed as the sun began to sink. The hills grew lower, the thickets larger. Often the toppled stone fences of what had been fields had become mounds sprouting wild hedges, or ran through long stands of oak and leatherleaf and hickory, pine and paperbark and trees Egwene did not know. The few farmhouses had no roofs, and trees ten or fifteen paces high grew in them here, little woods enclosed inside the stone walls, complete with twittering birds and black-tailed squirrels. The occasional rivulet caused as much talk among the Aiel as the small forests did, and the grass. They had heard tales of the wetlands, read of them in books bought from merchants and peddlers like Hadnan Kadere, but few had actually seen them since the hunt for Laman. They adapted quickly, though; the gray-brown of the tents blended well with dead leaves under the trees and with the dying grass and weeds. The camp spread over miles, marked by thousands of small cookfires in the golden dusk.

Egwene was more than happy to crawl into her tent once the *gai'shain* had it up. Inside the lamps were lit and a small fire burned in the firepit. Unlacing her soft boots, she tugged them off and her woolen stockings as well, and sprawled on the bright layered rugs, wriggling her toes. She wished she had a basin of water to soak her feet. She could not pretend to be as hardy as the Aiel, but she was growing soft if a few hours of walking made her feet feel twice their size. Of course, water would be no problem here. Or it should not be—she remembered that shrunken stream—but surely she could even have a proper bath again.

Cowinde, meek and silent in her white robes, brought her supper, some of that pale flat bread made from *zemai* flour and in a red-striped bowl, a thick stew that she ate mechanically, though she felt more tired than hungry. She recognized the dried peppers and beans, but did not ask what the dark meat was. *Rabbit,* she told herself firmly, and hoped that it was. The Aiel ate things that would put more curl in her hair than Elayne had. She was willing to bet that Rand could not even look at what he was eating. Men were always picky eaters.

Once done with the stew, she stretched out near an ornately worked silver lamp that had a polished silver disc to reflect and increase its light. She had felt a little guilty once she realized that most of the Aiel had no light at night but their fires; few had brought lamps or oil except the Wise Ones and the chiefs of clans and septs. But there was no point to sitting in the dim illumination of the firepit when she could have proper light. That reminded her: the nights here would not be so drastic a contrast with the days as in the Waste; the tent was already beginning to feel uncomfortably warm.

She channeled briefly, flows of Air to smother the fire, and dug into her saddlebags for the worn leather-bound book that she had borrowed from Aviendha. It was a small fat volume with crowded lines of small print, hard to read except in good light, but easily portable. *The Flame, the Blade and the Heart,* it was called, a collection of tales about Birgitte and Gaidal Cain, Anselan and Barashelle, Rogosh Eagle-eye and Dunsinin, and a dozen more. Aviendha claimed that she liked it for the adventures and battles, and maybe she did, but every last story told of the love of a man and a woman, too. Egwene was willing to admit that that was what she liked, the sometimes stormy, sometimes tender threads of undying love. To herself she would admit it, anyway. It was hardly the sort of enjoyment a woman with any pretensions to sense at all could confess publicly.

In truth she did not feel like reading any more than she had felt like eating—all she really wanted to do was bathe and sleep, and she might be willing to forgo bathing—but tonight she and Amys were to meet Nynaeve in *Tel'aran'rhiod*. It would not be night yet wherever Nynaeve was, on her way to Ghealdan, and that meant remaining awake.

Elayne had made the menagerie sound quite exciting, at their last meeting, though Egwene hardly thought that Galad's presence was reason enough to go haring off like that. Nynaeve and Elayne had simply grown to like adventure, in her opinion. It was too bad about Siuan; they needed a firm hand to settle them down. Odd that she should think of Nynaeve so; Nynaeve had always been the one with the firm hand. But since that episode in the Tower of *Tel'aran'rhiod*, Nynaeve had become less and less someone she had to struggle against.

Guiltily, she realized as she turned a page that she was looking forward to seeing Nynaeve tonight. Not because Nynaeve was a friend, but because she wanted to see if the effects had lingered. If Nynaeve tugged at her braid, she would arch a cool eyebrow at her, and . . . *Light, I hope it's held. If she lets out about that jaunt, Amys and Bair and Melaine will take turns skinning me, if they don't just tell me to go.*

Her eyes kept trying to drift shut as she read, fuzzily half-dreaming the stories in the book. She could be as strong as any of these women, as strong and brave as Dunsinin or Nerein or Melisinde or even Birgitte, as strong as Aviendha. *Would* Nynaeve have sense enough to hold her tongue in front of Amys tonight? She had a vague thought of taking Nynaeve by the scruff of the neck and shaking her. Silly. Nynaeve was years the older. Arch an eyebrow at her. Dunsinin. Birgitte. As hardy and strong as a Maiden of the Spear.

Her head slipped down to the pages, and she tried to cradle the small book under her cheek as her breathing slowed and deepened.

She gave a start at finding herself among the great redstone columns of the Heart of the Stone, in the strange light of *Tel'aran'rhiod,* and another at realizing that she wore the *cadin'sor.* Amys would not be pleased to see her in that; not amused at all. Hastily she changed it, and was surprised when her clothes flickered back and forth between the *algode* blouse and bulky wool skirt and a fine gown of brocaded blue silk before finally settling on the Aiel garb, complete with her ivory bracelet of flames and her gold-and-ivory necklace. That indecision had not happened to her in some time.

For a moment she thought of stepping out of the World of Dreams, but she suspected she was soundly asleep, back in her tent. Very likely she would only step into a dream of her own, and she did not yet always have awareness in her dreams; without that, she could not return to *Tel'aran'rhiod.* She was not about to leave Amys and Nynaeve alone together. Who knew what Nynaeve would say, if Amys got her temper up? When the Wise One arrived, she would simply say that she had just arrived herself. The Wise Ones had always been a bit ahead of her, or arrived at the same time, before this, but surely if Amys believed she had only been there a second it would not matter.

She had almost grown accustomed to the feel of unseen eyes in this vast chamber. *Only the columns, and the shadows, and all this empty space.* Still, she hoped that Amys was not too long in coming, nor Nynaeve. But they would be. Time could be as strange in *Tel'aran'rhiod* as in any dream, but it had to be a good hour yet before the arranged meeting. Perhaps she had time to . . .

Suddenly she realized that she could hear voices, like faint whispers among the columns. Embracing *saidar,* she moved cautiously toward the sound, toward the place where Rand had left *Callandor* beneath the great dome. The Wise Ones claimed that control of *Tel'aran'rhiod* was as strong as the One Power here, but she knew her abilities with the Power far better, and trusted them more. Still hidden well back among the thick redstone columns, she stopped and stared.

It was not a pair of Black sisters, as she had feared, and not Nynaeve, either. Instead, Elayne stood near the glittering shaft of *Callandor* rising out of the floorstone, deep in quiet conversation with as oddly dressed a woman as Egwene had ever seen. She wore a short white coat of peculiar cut and wide yellow trousers gathered in folds at her ankles, above short boots with raised heels. An intricate braid of golden hair hung down her back, and she held a bow that gleamed like polished silver. The arrows in the quiver shone, too.

Egwene squeezed her eyes shut. First the difficulty with her dress, and now this. Just because she had been reading about Birgitte—a silver bow told the name for certain—was no reason to imagine that she saw her. Birgitte waited—somewhere—for the Horn of Valere to call her and the other heroes to the Last Battle. But when Egwene opened her eyes again, Elayne and the oddly dressed woman were still there. She could not quite make out what they were saying, but she believed her eyes this time. She was on the point of going out to announce herself when a voice spoke, behind her.

"Did you decide to come early? Alone?"

Egwene whirled to face Amys, her sun-darkened face too youthful for her white hair, and leathery-cheeked Bair. Both stood with their arms folded beneath their breasts; even the way their shawls were pulled tight spoke of displeasure.

"I fell asleep," Egwene said. It was too much before time for her story to work. Even as she explained hastily about dozing off and why she had not gone back—minus the part about not wanting Nynaeve and Amys to talk alone—she was surprised to feel a tinge of shame that she had intended to lie and relief that she had not. Not that the truth would necessarily save her. Amys was not as strict as Bair—not quite—but she was perfectly capable of setting her to piling up rocks the rest of the night. Many of the Wise Ones were great believers in useless labor for punishment; you could not tell yourself you were doing anything other than being punished while you were burying ashes with a spoon. That was provided they did not simply refuse to teach her any more, of course. The ashes would be much preferable.

She could not hold back a sigh of relief when Amys nodded and said, "It can happen. But next time, return and dream your own dreams; I could have heard what Nynaeve has to say, and tell her what we know. If Melaine was not with Bael and Dorindha tonight, she would be here, as well. You frightened Bair. She is proud of your progress, and if anything happened to you . . ."

Bair did not look proud. If anything, she scowled even more deeply as Amys paused. "You are lucky Cowinde found you when she returned to clear away your supper, and was worried when she could not rouse you to move to your blankets. If I thought you had been here more than a few minutes alone . . ." The glare sharpened in dire promise for a moment, and then her voice turned grumpy. "Now I suppose we have to wait for Nynaeve to arrive, just to stop you begging if we send you back. If we must, we must, but we will use the time to advantage. Concentrate your mind on—"

"It isn't Nynaeve," Egwene said hastily. She did not want to know what a lesson would be like with Bair in this mood. "It is Elayne, and . . ." She trailed off, as she turned. Elayne, in elegant green silk suitable for a ball, was pacing up and down not far from *Callandor*. Birgitte was nowhere to be seen. *I did not imagine her.*

"She is here already?" Amys said, moving to where she could see, too.

"Another young fool," Bair muttered. "Girls today have no more brains or discipline than goats." She stalked out ahead of Egwene and Amys and planted herself across *Callandor's* glittering shape from Elayne, fists on hips. "You are not my pupil, Elayne of Andor—though you've wheedled enough out of us to keep you from killing yourself here, if you are careful—but if you were, I would welt you from your toes up and send you back to your mother until you were grown enough to be let out of her sight. Which I think might take as many more years as you have lived already. I know you have been coming into the World of Dreams alone, you and Nynaeve. You are both fools to do it."

Elayne gave a start when they first appeared, but as Bair's tirade washed over her, she drew herself up, that chilly tilt to her chin. Her gown became red and took on a finer sheen, and grew embroidery down the sleeves and across the high bodice, including rearing lions in white and golden lilies, her own sigil. A thin golden diadem rested in her red-gold curls, a single rearing lion set in moonstones above her brows. She did not yet have the best control over such things. Then again, maybe she wore exactly what she intended this time. "I do thank you for your concern," she said regally. "Yet it is true that I am not your pupil, Bair of the Haido Shaarad. I am grateful for your instruction, but I must go my own way, on the tasks given me by the Amyrlin Seat."

"A dead woman," Bair said coldly. "You claim obedience to a dead woman." Egwene could all but feel Bair's hackles standing erect in anger; if she did not do something, Bair might decide to teach Elayne a painful lesson. The last thing they needed was that sort of squabble.

"What . . . why are you here instead of Nynaeve?" She had been going to ask what Elayne was doing there, but that would have given Bair an opening, and maybe sounded as if she were on the Wise One's side. What she wanted to ask was what Elayne had been doing talking to Birgitte. *I did not imagine it.* Maybe it had been someone dreaming she was Birgitte. But only those who entered *Tel'aran'rhiod* knowingly remained for more than minutes, and Elayne surely would not have been speaking with one of them. Where *did* Birgitte and the others wait?

"Nynaeve is nursing a sore head." The diadem vanished, and Elayne's gown became simpler, with only a few golden scrolls around the bodice.

"Is she ill?" Egwene asked anxiously.

"Only with a headache, and a bruise or two." Elayne giggled and winced at the same time. "Oh, Egwene, you would not have believed it. All four of the Chavanas had come to have supper with us. To flirt with Nynaeve, really. They tried flirting with me the first few days, but Thom had a talk with them, and they stopped. He did not have any right to do that. Not that I *wanted* them to flirt, you understand. Anyway, there they were, flirting with Nynaeve—or trying to, because she paid them no more mind than buzzing flies—when Latelle stalked up and began hitting Nynaeve with a stick, calling her all sorts of terrible names."

"Was she hurt?" Egwene was not sure which of them she meant. If Nynaeve's temper was roused . . .

"Not her. The Chavanas tried to pull her off Latelle, and Taeric will likely limp for days, not to mention Brugh's swollen lip. Petra had to carry Latelle to her wagon, and I doubt she'll put her nose out for some time." Elayne shook her head. "Luca did not know who to blame—one of his acrobats lamed and his bear trainer weeping on her bed—so he blamed everybody, and I thought Nynaeve was going to box his ears as well. At least she did not channel; I thought she was going to once or twice, until she had Latelle down on the ground."

Amys and Bair exchanged unreadable glances; this certainly was not how they expected Aes Sedai to behave.

Egwene felt a little confused herself, but it was mainly over keeping up with all these people she had only heard of briefly before. Odd people, traveling with lions, dogs and bears. And an Illuminator. She did not believe this Petra could possibly be as strong as Elayne claimed. But then, Thom was eating fire as well as juggling, and what Elayne and Juilin were doing sounded as strange, even if she was using the Power.

If Nynaeve had come close to channeling . . . Elayne must have seen the glow of her embracing *saidar*. Whether they had a real reason to be hiding or not, they would not remain hidden long if one of them channeled and let people see it. The Tower's eyes-and-ears would certainly hear; that sort of news traveled quickly, especially if they were not out of Amadicia yet.

"You tell Nynaeve from me that she had best hold her temper, or I'll have some words to say to her that she will not like." Elayne looked startled—Nynaeve had certainly not told her what had passed between them—and Egwene added, "If she channels, you can be sure Elaida will hear of it as soon as a pigeon can fly to Tar Valon." She could not say more; as it was, it brought another exchange of glances between Amys and Bair. What they really thought of a Tower divided, and an Amyrlin who as far as they knew had given orders for Aes Sedai to be drugged, they had never let on. They could make Moiraine look like the village gossip when they wished. "In fact, I wish I had both of you alone. If we were in the Tower, in our old rooms, I'd say a few words to the pair of you."

Elayne stiffened, as queenly and cool as she had been with Bair. "You may say them to me whenever you wish."

Had she understood? Alone; away from the Wise Ones. In the Tower. Egwene could only hope. Best to change the subject and hope the Wise Ones were not picking over her words as carefully as she hoped that Elayne was. "Will this fight with Latelle cause problems?" What had Nynaeve been thinking of? Back home, she would have had any woman her age who did the same up before the Women's Circle so fast that her eyes would pop. "You must be almost to Ghealdan by now."

"Three more days, Luca says, if we are lucky. The menagerie does not move very fast."

"Perhaps you should leave them now."

"Perhaps," Elayne said slowly. "I really would like to highwalk just once in front of . . ." With a shake of her head, she glanced at *Callandor*; the neckline of her gown dipped precipitously, then rose again. "I do not know, Egwene. We could not travel much faster alone than we are traveling, and we don't know where to go exactly, yet." That meant Nynaeve had not remembered where the Blues were gathering. If Elaida's report had been right. "Not to mention that Nynaeve might burst if we had to abandon the wagon and buy saddle horses, or another coach. Besides, we are both learning a great deal about the Seanchan. Cerandin served as a *s'redit* handler at the Court of the Nine Moons, where the Seanchan Empress sits. Yesterday she showed us things that she took when she fled Falme. Egwene, she had an *a'dam*."

Egwene stepped forward, her skirts brushing *Callandor*. Rand's traps were not physical, whatever Nynaeve seemed to think. "Can you be sure she was not a *sul'dam*?" Her voice trembled with anger.

"I am certain," Elayne said soothingly. "I put the *a'dam* on her myself, and it had no effect."

That was a little secret that the Seanchan themselves did not know, or hid well if they did. Their *damane* were women born with the spark, women who would channel eventually even if untaught. But the *sul'dam*, who controlled the *damane*—they were the women who needed to be taught. The Seanchan thought that women who could channel were dangerous animals who had to be controlled, and yet unknowingly gave many of them honored positions.

"I do not understand this interest in the Seanchan." Amys said the name awkwardly; she had never heard it until Elayne spoke it at their last meeting. "What they do is terrible, but they are gone. Rand al'Thor defeated them, and they fled."

Egwene turned her back and stared at the huge polished columns running off into shadow. "Gone is not to say they will never come back." She did not want them to see her face, not even Elayne. "We must know whatever we can learn, in case they ever return." They had put an *a'dam* on her in Falme. They had meant to send her over the Aryth Ocean to Seanchan, to spend the rest of her life as a dog on a leash. Fury welled up in her every time she thought of them. And fear, too. The fear that if they did return, they would succeed in taking and holding her this time. That was what she could not allow them to see. The stark terror that she knew was in her eyes.

Elayne put a hand on her arm. "We will be ready for them if they do come back," she said gently. "They will not find us in surprise and ignorance again." Egwene patted her hand, though she wanted to clutch it; Elayne understood more than Egwene wished, yet it was comforting that she did.

"Let us finish what we are here for," Bair said briskly. "You need to be asleep in truth, Egwene."

"We had the *gai'shain* undress you, and put you in your blankets." Surprisingly, Amys sounded as gentle as Elayne. "When you return to your body, you can sleep until morning."

Egwene's cheeks colored. Given Aiel ways, it was as likely as not that some of those *gai'shain* had been men. She would have to speak to them about that—delicately, of course; they would not understand, and it was not a thing she could be comfortable explaining.

The fear was gone, she realized. *Apparently I'm more afraid of being embarrassed than I am of the Seanchan.* It was not true, but she held to the thought.

There was really little to tell Elayne. That they were in Cairhien finally, that Couladin had devastated Selean and ravaged the surrounding land, that the Shaido were still days ahead and moving west. The Wise Ones knew more than she; they had not taken to their tents straight-away. There had been skirmishes in the evening, small ones and only a few, with mounted men who quickly fled, and other men on horses who had been sighted ran without fighting. There had been no prisoners taken. Moiraine and Lan seemed to think that the riders could have been bandits, or supporters of one or another of the Houses trying to claim the Sun Throne. All had been equally ragged. Whoever they were, word would soon spread that there were more Aiel in Cairhien.

"They had to learn sooner or later" was Elayne's only comment.

Egwene watched Elayne as she and the Wise Ones faded away—to her it seemed as though Elayne and the Heart of the Stone became more and more attenuated—but her golden-haired friend gave no sign as to whether she had understood the message.

CHAPTER

25

Dreams of Galad

Instead of returning to her own body, Egwene floated in darkness. She seemed to be darkness herself, without substance. Whether her body lay up or down or sideways from her, she did not know—there was no direction here—but she knew that it was near, that she could step into it easily. All around her in the blackness, fireflies seemingly twinkled, a vast horde fading away into unimaginable distance. Those were dreams, dreams of the Aiel in the camp, dreams of men and women across Cairhien, across the world, all glittering there.

She could pick out some among the nearer and name the dreamer, now. In one way those sparkles were just as alike as fireflies—that was what had given her so much trouble in the beginning—but in another, somehow, they now seemed as individual as faces. Rand's dreams, and Moiraine's, appeared muted, dimmed by the wards they had woven. Amys' and Bair's were bright and regular in their pulsing; they had taken their own advice, apparently. Had she not seen those, she would have been into her body in an instant. Those two could rove this darkness much more ably than she; she would not have known they were there until they pounced on her. If she ever learned to recognize Elayne and Nynaeve in the same way, she would be able to find them in that great constellation wherever they were in the world. But tonight she did not mean to observe anyone's dream.

Carefully she formed a well-remembered image in her mind, and she was back in *Tel'aran'rhiod*, inside the small, windowless room in the Tower where she had lived as a novice. A narrow bed was built against one white-painted wall. A washstand and a three-legged stool stood opposite the door, and the current occupant's dresses and shifts of white wool hung with a white cloak on pegs. There could as easily have been none; the Tower had not been able to fill the novices' quarters in many years. The floor was almost as pale as walls and clothes. Every day the novice who lived there would scrub that floor on hands and knees; Egwene had done so herself, and Elayne, in the next room. If a queen came to train in the Tower, she would start in a room like this, scrubbing the floor.

The garments were arranged differently when she glanced at them again, but she ignored that. Ready to embrace *saidar* in a heartbeat, she opened the door just enough to stick her head out. And drew a relieved breath when she found Elayne's head coming just as slowly out of the next doorway. Egwene hoped she did not appear as wide-eyed and uncertain. She motioned hurriedly, and Elayne scurried across in novice white that became a pale gray silk riding dress as she darted inside. Egwene hated gray dresses; that was what *damane* wore.

For an instant more she stayed there, scanning the railed galleries of the novices' quarters. Layer on layer they rose, and fell as many levels to the Novices' Court below. Not that she really expected Liandrin or worse to be out there, but it never hurt to be careful.

"I thought this was what you meant," Elayne said as she shut the door. "Do you have any idea how difficult it is to remember what I can say in front of whom? Sometimes I wish we could just tell the Wise Ones everything. Let them know we are only Accepted, and be done with it."

"You would be done with it," Egwene said firmly. "I happen to be sleeping not twenty paces from them."

Elayne shivered. "That Bair. She reminds me of Lini when I'd broken something I was not supposed to touch."

"You wait until I introduce you to Sorilea." Elayne gave her a doubtful look, but then, Egwene was not sure that she would have believed Sorilea herself until she met her. There was no way to do this easily. She shifted her shawl. "Tell me about meeting Birgitte. It was Birgitte, wasn't it?"

Elayne staggered as if hit in the stomach. Her blue eyes closed for a moment, and she took a breath that must have filled her to the toes. "I cannot talk to you about that."

"What do you mean you can't talk? You have a tongue. Was it Birgitte?"

"I *cannot*, Egwene. You must believe me. I would if I could, but I cannot. Perhaps . . . I can ask . . ." If Elayne had been the kind of woman to wring her hands, she would have been doing it then. Her mouth opened and closed without any words coming out; her eyes darted around the room as if seeking inspiration or aid. Taking a deep breath, she fixed an urgent blue gaze on Egwene. "Anything I say violates confidences I promised to hold. Even that. Please, Egwene. You must trust me. And you must not tell *anyone* what you . . . think you saw."

Egwene forced the stern frown from her face. "I will trust you." At least she knew now for a fact that she had not been seeing things. *Birgitte? Light!* "I hope that one day you will trust me enough to tell me."

"I *do* trust you, but . . ." Shaking her head, Elayne sat down on the edge of the neatly made bed. "We keep secrets too often, Egwene, but sometimes there is a reason."

After a moment Egwene nodded and sat next to her. "When you can," was all she said, but her friend gave her a relieved hug.

"I told myself I was not going to ask this, Egwene. Just once I was not going to have my head full of him." The gray riding dress became a shimmering green gown;

Elayne could not possibly have been aware of how deeply the neckline swooped. "But . . . is Rand well?"

"He is alive and unharmed, if that is what you mean. I thought he was hard in Tear, but today I heard him threaten to hang men if they go against his commands. Not that they are bad orders—he won't let anyone take food without paying, or murder people—but still. They were the first to hail him as He Who Comes With the Dawn; they followed him out of the Waste without hesitation. And he threatened them, as hard as cold steel."

"Not a threat, Egwene. He is a king, whatever you or he or anyone else says, and a king or queen must dispense justice without fear of enemies or favor for friends. Anyone who does that has to be hard. Mother can make the city walls seem soft, sometimes."

"He doesn't have to be so arrogant about it," Egwene said levelly. "Nynaeve said I should remind him he's only a man, but I've not figured out how yet."

"He *does* have to remember he is only a man. But he has a right to expect to be obeyed." There was something of a haughty tone to Elayne's voice, until she glanced down at herself. Then her face went crimson, and the green gown suddenly had a lace neck under her chin. "Are you sure you are not mistaking that for arrogance?" she finished in a strangled voice.

"He's as overweening as a pig in a pea field." Egwene shifted herself on the bed; she remembered it as hard, but the thin mattress felt softer than what she slept on in the tent. She did not want to talk about Rand. "Are you certain this fight will not cause more trouble?" A feud with this Latelle could not make their traveling easier.

"I do not think so. Latelle's grievance against Nynaeve was that all the unattached men were no longer hers to pick and choose from. Some women do think that way, I suppose. Aludra keeps to herself, and Cerandin wouldn't have said boo to a goose until I started teaching her to stand up for herself, and Clarine is married to Petra. But Nynaeve has made it clear that she'll box the ears of any man who even *thinks* he can flirt with her, *and* she apologized to Latelle, so I hope that may settle it."

"She *apologized*?"

The other woman nodded, her face as bemused as Egwene knew her own must be. "I thought she *would* thump Luca when he told her she must—he doesn't seem to think her injunction holds to him, by the way—but she did it, after grumping about for an hour. Muttering about you, actually." She hesitated, giving Egwene a sidelong look. "Did you say something to her at your last meeting? She has been . . . different . . . since then, and sometimes she talks to herself. Argues, really. About you, from the little I've heard."

"I said nothing that did not have to be said." So it was holding, whatever it was that had happened between them. Either that, or Nynaeve was storing up her anger for the next time they met. She was not going to put up with the woman's temper anymore, not now that she knew she did not have to. "You tell her from me that she is too old to be rolling about on the ground fighting. If she gets into another, I'll have worse to say to her. You tell her that exactly. It will be worse." Let Nynaeve chew on that until next time. Either she would be mild as a lamb . . . Or else Egwene would just have to carry through on her threat. Nynaeve might be stronger in the Power, when she could channel, but here, Egwene was. One way or another, she was finished with Nynaeve's tantrums.

"I will tell her," Elayne said. "You have changed, too. There seems to be something of Rand's attitude about you."

It took Egwene a moment to realize what she meant, helped by that amused little smile. "Don't be silly."

Elayne laughed aloud and gave her another hug. "Oh, Egwene, you will be Amyrlin Seat one day, when I am Queen of Andor."

"If there is a Tower then," Egwene said soberly, and Elayne's laughter faded.

"Elaida cannot destroy the White Tower, Egwene. Whatever she does, the Tower will remain. Perhaps she will not stay Amyrlin. Once Nynaeve remembers the name of that town, I will wager that we find a Tower in exile, with every Ajah but the Red."

"I hope so." Egwene knew she sounded sad. She wanted Aes Sedai to support Rand and oppose Elaida, but that meant the White Tower broken for sure, maybe never to be made whole again.

"I must get back," Elayne said. "Nynaeve insists that whichever of us does not enter *Tel'aran'rhiod* remain awake, and with her headache, she needs to drink one of her herb teas and sleep. I do not know why she is so insistent. Whoever is watching can do nothing to help, and we both know enough to be perfectly safe here, now." Her green dress flickered to Birgitte's white coat and voluminous yellow trousers for an instant, then snapped back. "She said I wasn't to tell you this, but she thinks that Moghedien is trying to find us. Her and me."

Egwene did not ask the obvious question. Clearly it was something that Birgitte had told them. Why did Elayne persist in trying to keep that secret? *Because she promised to. Elayne never broke a promise in her life.* "You tell her to be careful." Small chance that Nynaeve was sitting and waiting, if she thought one of the Forsaken was after her. She would be remembering that she had defeated the woman once, and she had always had more courage than sense. "The Forsaken are nothing to take lightly. And neither are Seanchan, even if they are supposedly just animal trainers. You tell her that."

"I do not suppose you would listen if I told you to be careful, too."

She gave Elayne a startled look. "I am always careful. You know that."

"Of course." The last thing Egwene saw as the other woman faded away was a very amused smile.

Egwene herself did not go. If Nynaeve could not remember where that gathering of Blues was, perhaps she could discover it here. It was hardly a new idea: this was not her first trip to the Tower since her last meeting with Nynaeve. She put on a copy of Enaila's face, with flame-colored hair to her shoulders, and an Accepted's dress with its banded hem, then formed the image of Elaida's ornately furnished study.

It was as it had been before, though on every visit fewer of the vine-carved stools stood in that arc in front of the wide writing table. The paintings still hung above the fireplace. Egwene strode straight to the table, pushing aside that thronelike chair with its inlaid ivory Flame of Tar Valon, so she could reach the lacquered letterbox. Lifting the lid, all fighting hawks and clouds, she began scanning parchments as fast as she could. Even so, some melted away half-read, or changed. There was no way to tell what was important and what insignificant beforehand.

Most seemed reports of failure. Still no word of where the Lord of Bashere had taken his army, and a note of frustration and worry tinging the words. That name tickled the back of her mind, but with no time to waste she pushed it firmly away and snatched up another sheet. No word on Rand's whereabouts, either, said a cringing report filled with near panic. That was good to know, and worth the trip by itself. More than a month had passed since the last news from Tanchico by any Ajah's eyes-and-ears, and others in Tarabon had also gone silent; the writer blamed the anarchy there; rumors that someone had taken Tanchico could not be confirmed, but the writer suggested that Rand himself was involved. Even better, if Elaida was looking in the wrong place by a thousand leagues. A confused report said that a Red sister in Caemlyn claimed to have seen Morgase at a public audience, but various Ajahs' agents in Caemlyn said the Queen had been in seclusion for days. Fighting in the Borderlands, possibly minor rebellions in Shienar and Arafel; the parchment was gone before she reached the reason. Pedron Niall calling in Whitecloaks to Amadicia, possibly to move against Altara. A good thing that Elayne and Nynaeve had only another three days there.

The next parchment was about Elayne and Nynaeve. First the writer advised against punishing the agent who had allowed them to escape—Elaida had scratched that out in bold strokes and written "Make an example!" in the margin—and then, just when the woman began to detail the search for the pair in Amadicia, the single sheet became a fistful, a sheaf of what seemed to be builders' and masons' estimates for constructing a private residence for the Amyrlin Seat on the Tower grounds. More like a palace, by the number of pages.

She let the pages fall, and they vanished before they finished scattering across the tabletop. The lacquered box was closed again. She could spend the rest of her life here, she knew; there would always be more documents in the box, and they would always be changing. The more ephemeral something was in the waking world—a letter, a piece of clothing, a bowl that might be frequently moved—the less firm its reflection in *Tel'aran'rhiod*. She could not remain here too long; sleep while in the World of Dreams was not as restful as sleep undisturbed.

Hurrying out to the antechamber, she was about to reach for the neat piles of scrolls and parchments, some with seals, on the Keeper's writing table, when the room seemed to flicker. Before she had time to even consider what that meant, the door opened, and Galad stepped in, smiling, his brocaded blue coat fitting his shoulders perfectly, snug breeches showing the shape of his calves.

She took a deep breath, her stomach fluttering. It just was not fair for a man to have a face so beautiful.

He stepped closer, dark eyes twinkling, and brushed her cheek with his fingers. "Will you walk with me in the Water Garden?" he said softly.

"If you two wish to canoodle," a brisk woman's voice said, "you will not do so here."

Egwene spun, wide-eyed, staring at Leane seated behind the table with the Keeper's stole on her shoulders and a fond smile on her copper-cheeked face. The door to the Amyrlin's study was open, and inside Siuan stood beside her simple, well-polished writing table, reading a long parchment, the striped stole of office on her shoulders. This was madness.

She fled without thinking of what image she was forming, and found herself gulping for breath on the Green in Emond's Field, with the thatch-roofed houses all around, and the Winespring gushing from the stone outcrop on the broad expanse of grass. Near the swift, rapidly widening stream stood her father's small inn, its lower floor stone, the overhanging upper whitewashed. "The only roof like it in the Two Rivers," Bran al'Vere had often said of his red tiles. The large stone foundation near the Winespring Inn, a huge, spreading oak rising from its center, was far older than the inn, but some said an inn of some sort had stood there beside the Winespring Water for more than two thousand years.

Fool. After warning Nynaeve so firmly about dreams in *Tel'aran'rhiod,* she had nearly let herself be caught in one of her own. Though it was odd that it had been Galad. She did dream of him, sometimes. Her face heated; she certainly did not love him, or even like him very much, but he was beautiful, and in those dreams he had been much more what she could have wished him. It was his brother Gawyn that she dreamed of more often, but that was just as silly. Whatever Elayne said, he had never made any feelings known to her.

It was that fool book, with all those tales of lovers. As soon as she woke in the morning she was going to give the thing back to Aviendha. And tell her that she did not think that she read it for the adventures at all.

She was reluctant to leave, though. Home. Emond's Field. The last place that she had really felt safe. More than a year and a half had passed since she last saw it, yet everything seemed as she remembered. Not quite everything. On the Green stood two tall poles with large banners, one a red eagle, the other an equally red wolf's head.

Had Perrin anything to do with those? She could not imagine how. Yet he had come home, so Rand said, and she had dreamed of him with wolves more than once.

Enough idle standing about. It was time to—

Flicker.

Her mother stepped out of the inn, graying braid pulled over one shoulder. Marin al'Vere was a slim woman, still handsome, and the best cook in the Two Rivers. Egwene could hear her father laughing inside the common room, where he was meeting with the rest of the Village Council.

"Are you still out here, child?" her mother said, gently chiding and amused. "You've certainly been married long enough to know you shouldn't let your husband know you mope about waiting on him." With a shake of her head, she laughed. "Too late. Here he comes."

Egwene turned eagerly, eyes darting past the children playing on the Green. The timbers of the low Wagon Bridge thrummed as Gawyn galloped across and swung down from his saddle in front of her. Tall and straight in his gold-embroidered red coat, he had his sister's red-gold curls, and marvelous deep blue eyes. He was not so handsome as his half-brother, of course, but her heart beat faster for him than it had for Galad—*For Galad? What?*—and she had to press her hands to her stomach in a vain attempt to still gigantic butterflies.

"Did you miss me?" he said, smiling.

"A little." *Why did I think of Galad? As if I'd just seen him a moment ago.* "Now and then, when there was nothing interesting to occupy my time. Did you miss me?"

For answer, he pulled her off her feet and kissed her. She was not aware of very much else until he set her back down on unsteady legs. The banners were gone. *What banners?*

"Here he is," her mother said, approaching with a babe wrapped in swaddling. "Here's your son. He is a fine boy. He never cries at all."

Gawyn laughed as he took the child, held him aloft. "He does have your eyes, Egwene. He will be a fine one with the girls one day."

Egwene backed away from them, shaking her head. There *had* been banners, red eagle and red wolf's head. She *had* seen Galad. In the Tower. "NOOOOOOO!"

She fled, leaping from *Tel'aran'rhiod* to her own body. Awareness remained only long enough for her to wonder how she could possibly have been fool enough to let her own fancies nearly trap her, and then she was deep in her own safe dream. Gawyn galloped across the Wagon Bridge, swinging down. . . .

Stepping out from behind a thatch-roofed house, Moghedien wondered idly where this little village was. Not the sort of place she would expect to see banners flying. The girl had been stronger than she had thought, to escape her weaving of *Tel'aran'rhiod*. Even Lanfear could not improve on her abilities here, whatever she claimed. Still, the girl had just been of interest because she was speaking to Elayne Trakand, who might lead her to Nynaeve al'Meara. The only reason to trap her had simply been to rid *Tel'aran'rhiod* of one who could walk it freely. It was bad enough that she must share it with Lanfear.

But Nynaeve al'Meara. That woman she meant to make beg to be bound in her service. She would take her in the flesh, perhaps ask the Great Lord to grant her immortality, so Nynaeve could have forever to regret opposing Moghedien. She and Elayne were scheming with Birgitte, were they? That was another she had reason to punish. Birgitte had not even known who Moghedien was, so long ago, in the Age of Legends, when she foiled Moghedien's finely wrought plan to lay Lews Therin by his heels. But Moghedien had known her. Only, Birgitte—Teadra, she had been then—had died before she could deal with her. Death was no punishment, no end, not when it meant living on here.

Nynaeve al'Meara, Elayne Trakand, and Birgitte. Those three she would find, and deal with. From the shadows, so that they would not know until too late. All three, without exception.

She vanished, and the banners waved on in the breeze of *Tel'aran'rhiod*.

CHAPTER
26

Sallie Daera

The halo of greatness, blue and gold, flickered fitfully around Logain's head, though he rode slumped in his saddle. Min did not understand why it had appeared more often of late. He no longer even bothered to lift his eyes from the weeds in front of his black stallion to the low, wooded hills rolling by all around them.

The other two women rode together a little ahead, Siuan as awkward on shaggy Bela as she had ever been, Leane guiding her gray mare deftly, with knees more than reins. Only an unnaturally straight ribbon of ferns, poking through the leaf-covered forest floor, hinted that there had ever been a road here. The lacy ferns were withering, and the leaf mold rustled and crackled dryly under the horses' hooves. Thickly woven branches gave a little shelter from the noonday sun, but it was hardly cool. Sweat rolled down Min's face, despite an occasional breeze that stirred from behind them.

Fifteen days now they had ridden west and south from Lugard, guided only by Siuan's insistence that she knew exactly where they were heading. Not that she shared her destination, of course; Siuan and Leane were as close-mouthed as sprung bear traps. Min was not even sure that Leane actually knew. Fifteen days, while towns and villages grew fewer and farther between, until finally there were none. Day by day Logain's shoulders had sagged a little more, and day by day the halo appeared more often. At first he had only begun muttering that they were chasing Jak o' the Mists, but Siuan had regained her leadership without opposition as he turned more and more inward. For the past six days he had not seemed to have the energy to care where they were going or whether they would ever get there.

Siuan and Leane talked quietly up ahead, now. All Min could hear was a barely audible murmur that might as well have been the wind in the leaves. And if she tried to ride closer, they would tell her to keep an eye on Logain, or simply stare at her until only a stone-blind fool could keep her nose where it did not belong. They had done both often enough. From time to time, though, Leane twisted in her saddle to look at Logain.

Finally Leane let Moonflower fall back beside his black stallion. The heat did not seem to be bothering her; not so much as a sheen of perspiration marred her coppery face. Min reined Wildrose aside to give her room.

"It won't be long now," Leane told him in a sultry voice. He did not look up from the weeds in front of his horse. She leaned closer, holding his arm for balance. Pressing against it, really. "A little while longer, Dalyn. You will have your revenge." His eyes stayed dully on the road.

"A dead man would pay more notice," Min said, and meant it. She had been taking notes in her head of everything Leane did, and talking with her of an evening, though trying not to let on why. She would never be able to behave the way that Leane did—*not unless I had enough wine in me that I couldn't think at all*—yet a few pointers might come in handy. "Maybe if you kissed him?"

Leane shot her a glare that could have frozen a rushing stream, but Min merely looked back. She had never had the problems with Leane that she did with Siuan—well, not as many, anyway—and the few difficulties had grown less since the other woman had left the Tower. Much fewer since they had begun discussing men. How could you be intimidated by a woman who had told you in dead seriousness that there were one hundred and seven different kisses, and ninety-three ways to touch a man's face with your hand? Leane actually seemed to believe these things.

Min had not meant it as a jibe, really, the suggestion of a kiss. Leane had been cooing at him, giving him smiles that should have made steam rise from his ears, since the day he had had to be hauled out of his blankets instead of rising first to chivvy the rest of them. Min did not know whether Leane actually felt something for the man, though she did find it hard to credit even the possibility; or was just trying to keep him from giving up and dying, to keep him alive for whatever Siuan had planned.

Leane certainly had not given up flirting with others besides him. She and Siuan had apparently worked out that Siuan would deal with women, Leane with men, and so it had been ever since Lugard. Her smiles and glances had twice gotten them rooms where the innkeeper had said there were none, lowered the bill at those and three more, and on two nights earned barns instead of bushes for sleeping. They had also gotten the four of them chased off by one farmwife with a pitchfork, and a breakfast of cold porridge *thrown* at them by another, but Leane had thought the incidents funny, if no one else did. The last few days, however, Logain had stopped reacting like every other man who saw her for more than two minutes. He had stopped reacting to her or anything else.

Siuan pulled Bela back stiffly, elbows out and managing to look on the point of falling off any moment. The heat was not touching her, either. "Have you viewed him today?" She hardly glanced at Logain.

"It is still the same," Min said patiently. Siuan refused to understand or believe, however many times she told her, and so did Leane. It would not have mattered if she had not seen the aura since her first viewing of it in Tar

Valon. Had Logain been lying in the road, rasping his death rattle, she would have wagered all she had and more on a miraculous recovery, somehow. The appearance of an Aes Sedai to Heal him. Something. What she saw was always true. It always happened. She knew the same way that she had known the first time she saw Rand al'Thor that she would fall desperately, helplessly in love with him, the same way she had known she would have to share him with two other women. Logain was destined for glory such as few men had dreamed of.

"Don't you take that tone with me," Siuan said, that blue-eyed gaze sharpening. "It is bad enough we have to spoon-feed this great hairy carp to make him eat, without you going sulky as a fisher-bird in winter. I may have to put up with him, girl, but if you start giving me trouble too, you will regret it in short order. Do I make myself clear?"

"Yes, Mara." *At least you could have put a touch of sarcasm in it,* she thought scornfully. *You don't have to be meek as a goose. You've told Leane off to her face.* The Domani woman had suggested that she practice what they had been discussing on a farrier in the last village. A tall, handsome man, with strong-looking hands and a slow smile, but still . . . "I will try not to be sulky." The worst part was that she realized she had tried to sound sincere. Siuan had that effect. Min could not even begin to imagine Siuan discussing how to smile at a man. Siuan would look a man in the eye, tell him what to do, and expect to see it done promptly. Just the way she did with everyone else. If she did anything else, as she had with Logain, it would only be because the point did not matter enough to press.

"It is not much farther, is it?" Leane said briskly. She saved the other voice for men. "I do not like the look of him, and if we have to stop for another night . . . Well, if he helps any less than he did this morning, I don't know that we will be able to get him into his saddle again."

"Not much, if those last directions I had are right." Siuan sounded irritated. She had asked questions at that last village, two days ago—not letting Min hear, of course; Logain had showed no interest—and she did not like to be reminded of them. Min could not understand why. Siuan could hardly expect Elaida to be behind them.

She herself hoped it was not much farther. It was hard to be sure how far south they had drifted since leaving the highway to Jehannah. Most villagers had only vague notions of where their village actually was in relation to anything except the nearest towns, but when they crossed the Manetherendrelle into Altara, just before Siuan took them away from the well-traveled road, the grizzled old ferryman had been studying a tattered map for some reason, a map that stretched as far as the Mountains of Mist. Unless her estimate was off, they were going to reach another wide river in not many miles. Either the Boern, which meant they were already into Ghealdan, where the Prophet and his mobs were, or else the Eldar, with Amadicia and Whitecloaks on the far side.

She was betting on Ghealdan, Prophet or no Prophet, and even that was a surprise if they really were close. Only a fool would think to find a gathering of Aes Sedai any nearer to Amadicia than they had to be, and Siuan was anything but that. Whether they were in Ghealdan or Altara, Amadicia had to be not many miles distant.

"Gentling would have to catch up to him now," Siuan muttered. "If he can only hang on a few more days . . ." Min kept her mouth shut; if the woman would not listen, there was no use in speaking.

Shaking her head, Siuan heeled Bela back into the lead, gripping her reins as though expecting the stout mare to bolt, and Leane returned to silken-voiced cajoling of Logain. Maybe she did have feelings for him; it would be no odder a choice than Min's own.

Forested hills slid on by with never a sign of change, all trees and tangles of weeds and brambles. The ferns that marked the old road ran on, arrow-straight; Leane had said the soil was different where the road had been, as if Min should have known that. Squirrels with tufted ears sometimes chattered at them from a branch, and occasionally birds called. Which birds, Min could not begin to guess. Baerlon might not be a city when compared to

Caemlyn or Ilian or Tear, but she thought of herself as a city woman; a bird was a bird. And she did not care what kind of dirt a fern grew in.

Her doubts began to surface again. They had oozed up more than once after Kore Springs, but back then it had been easier to push them down. Since Lugard they had bubbled to the top more often, and she found herself considering Siuan in ways she would never have dared, once. Not that she had the nerve to actually confront Siuan with any of them, of course; it galled her to admit that, even to herself. But maybe Siuan did *not* know where she was going. She could lie, since stilling broke her away from the Three Oaths. Maybe she was still just hoping that if she continued searching she would find some trace of what she needed desperately to find. In a small way, a peculiar way surely, Leane had begun making a life for herself apart from concerns of power and the Power and Rand. Not that she had abandoned them entirely, but Min did not think there *was* anything else for Siuan. The White Tower and the Dragon Reborn were the whole of her life, and she would hold to them even if she had to lie to herself.

Woodland gave way to a large village so quickly that Min stared. Sweetgum and oak and scrubby pine—those were trees she could recognize—running to within fifty paces of thatch-roofed houses made of rounded river stones and clinging to low hills. She was willing to wager that not so long ago the forest had grown right through. A good many trees actually stood in narrow little thickets among some of the houses, crowding against the walls, and here and there unweathered stumps stood close by the front of a house. The streets still had a look of new-turned earth, not the hard-packed surface that came from generations of feet. Men in their shirtsleeves were up laying new thatch atop three large stone cubes that had to have been inns—one actually had the remains of a faded, weathered sign dangling above the door—yet no old thatch lay anywhere that she could see. There were far too many women out and about for the number of men in sight, and far too few children playing for the number of women. The smells of midday cooking in the air were the only normal things about the place.

If the first glimpse startled Min, when she really saw what lay in front of her she nearly fell out of her saddle. The younger women, shaking blankets from a window or hurrying on some errand, wore plain woolen dresses, but no village of any size had ever contained so many women in riding dresses of silk or fine wool, in every color and cut. Around those women, and around most of the men, auras and images floated before her eyes, changing and flickering; most people rarely had anything for her viewing, but Aes Sedai and Warders seldom lacked an aura for as much as an hour. The children must have belonged to Tower servants. Aes Sedai who married were few and far between, but knowing them, they would have made every effort to bring their servants, with their families, out of any place they felt that they must flee themselves. Siuan had found her gathering.

There was an eerie stillness as they rode into the village. No one spoke. Aes Sedai stood without moving, watching them, and so did younger women and girls who must be Accepted or even novices. Men who a moment before had been moving with wolfish grace were frozen, one hand hidden in thatch, or reaching into a doorway, doubtless where weapons were hidden. The children vanished, hurriedly herded away by the adults who had to be servants. Under all those unwinking stares, the hair on the back of Min's neck tried to stand up.

Leane appeared uneasy, casting sidelong glances at the people they rode past, but Siuan stayed smooth-faced and calm as she led the way straight to the largest inn, the one with the unreadable sign, and scrambled down to tie Bela to the iron ring of one of the stone hitching posts that appeared to have been only recently set upright. Helping Leane help Logain to the ground—Siuan never offered a hand in getting him up or down—Min found her eyes darting around. Everyone staring, no one moving. "I never expected to be greeted like a long-lost daughter," she murmured to the other woman, "but why isn't anyone at least saying hello?"

Before Leane could answer—if she meant to—Siuan said, "Well, don't stop pulling oar with the shore in reach. Bring him on in." She disappeared inside while Min and Leane were still guiding Logain to the door. He

went easily, but when they ceased to urge him he took
only one step before stopping.

The common room looked like none Min had ever
seen before. The wide fireplaces were cold, of course, and
had gaps where stones had fallen out; the plaster ceiling
looked rotten, with holes in it as big as her head where
the lathing showed. Mismatched tables of every size and
shape stood about on an age-roughened floor that several
girls were sweeping. Women with ageless faces sat examining parchments, giving orders to Warders, a few of
whom wore their color-shifting cloaks, or to other wom-
en, some of whom had to be Accepted or novices. Others
were too old for that, perhaps half of them graying and
clearly showing their years, and there were men who
were not Warders, too, most either darting off as though
carrying messages or else fetching parchments or cups of
wine to the Aes Sedai. The bustle had a satisfying air of
something being done. Auras and images danced around
the room, wreathing heads, so many that she had to try
to ignore them before they overwhelmed her. It was not
easy, but it was a trick she had had to learn when around
more than a handful of Aes Sedai at once.

Four Aes Sedai glided forward to meet the newcomers,
all grace and cool serenity in their divided skirts. For
Min, seeing their familiar features was like reaching
home after being lost.

Sheriam's tilted green eyes fixed immediately on Min's
face. Rays of silver and blue flashed about her fiery hair,
and a soft golden light; Min could not say what it meant.
Slightly plump in her dark blue silk, at the moment she
was sternness itself. "I would be happier to see you,
child, if I knew how you discovered our presence here,
and if I had some inkling of why you conceived the
crackbrained idea of bringing him." Half a dozen Warders had drifted near, hands resting on swords, eyes sharp
on Logain; he did not seem to see them at all.

Min gaped. Why were they asking *her*? "*My*
crackbr—?" She had no chance to say more.

"It would be far better," pale-cheeked Carlinya cut in
icily, "if he had died as the rumors say." It was not the
ice of anger, but of cold reason. She was White Ajah. Her

ivory-colored dress looked as if it had had hard wear. For
an instant Min saw an image of a raven floating beside
her dark hair; more a drawing of the bird than the bird
itself. She thought it was a tattoo, but she did not know
its meaning. She concentrated on faces, tried not to see
anything else. "He looks nearly dead in any event,"
Carlinya continued, hardly taking breath. "Whatever
you thought, you have wasted your effort. But I, too,
would like to know how you came to Salidar."

Siuan and Leane stood there exchanging smugly
amused glances, while the onslaught went on. No one
even *looked* at them.

Myrelle, darkly beautiful in green silk embroidered on
the bodice with slanting lines of gold, her face a perfect
oval, usually wore a knowing smile that at times could
rival Leane's new tricks. She was not smiling now as she
jumped in right behind the White sister. "Speak up, Min.
Don't stand there gaping like a dolt." She was noted for
her fiery temper, even among the Greens.

"You must tell us," Anaiya added in a more kindly
voice. Exasperation tinged it, though. A blunt-featured
woman, and motherly despite Aes Sedai smoothness to
her face, at the moment stroking her pale gray skirts, she
looked like a mother who was trying not to reach for a
switch. "We will find a place for you and these other two
girls, but you must tell us how you came here."

Min shook herself, and closed her mouth. Of course.
These other two girls. She had grown so used to them as
they were that she no longer thought of how much they
had changed. She doubted whether any of these women
had seen either since they were hauled off to the dun-
geons beneath the White Tower. Leane looked ready to
laugh, and Siuan all but shook her head in disgust at the
Aes Sedai.

"I am not the one you want to talk to," Min told
Sheriam. *Let "these other two girls" have those stares on
them for a change.* "Ask Siuan, or Leane." They stared at
her as if she were mad, until she nodded to her two
companions.

Four sets of Aes Sedai eyes shifted to the others, but
there was no instant recognition. They studied and

frowned and passed glances between them. None of the Warders took their eyes from Logain or their hands from their swords.

"Stilling might produce this effect," Myrelle murmured finally. "I have read accounts that imply as much."

"The faces are close, in many ways," Sheriam said slowly. "Someone could have found women who look much like them, but why?"

Siuan and Leane did not look smug any longer. "We are who we are," Leane said crisply. "Question us. No impostor could know what we know."

Siuan did not wait for questions. "My face may be changed, yet at least I know what I am doing and why. That is more than I can say for you, I'll wager."

Min groaned at her steely tone, but Myrelle nodded, saying, "That is Siuan Sanche's voice. It is she."

"Voices can be trained," Carlinya said, still coolly calm.

"But how far can memories be taught?" Anaiya frowned sternly. "Siuan—if that is who you are—on your twenty-second nameday we had an argument, you and I. Where did it occur, and what was the outcome?"

Siuan smiled confidently at the motherly woman. "During your lecture to the Accepted on why so many of the nations carved out of Artur Hawkwing's empire after his death failed to survive. I still disagree with you on some points, by the way. The outcome was that I spent two months working three hours a day in the kitchens. 'In the hope that the heat will overpower and diminish your ardor,' I think you said."

If she had thought that one answer would be sufficient, she was wrong. Anaiya had more questions, for both women, and so did Carlinya and Sheriam, who apparently had been novices and Accepted with the pair. They were all about the sort of thing no impostor would be able to learn, scrapes gotten into, pranks successful and not, opinions generally held of various Aes Sedai teachers. Min could not believe that the women who would become the Amyrlin Seat and the Keeper of the Chronicles could have dropped themselves into the soup so often, but she had the impression that this was only the tip of a buried mountain, and it appeared that Sheriam herself might not have been far behind them. Myrelle, the youngest by years, confined herself to amused comments, until Siuan said something about a trout put into Saroiya Sedai's bath and a novice taught to mind her ways for half a year. Not that Siuan had much room to talk of anyone minding her ways. Washing a disliked Accepted's shifts with itchweed when she was a novice? Sneaking out of the Tower to go fishing? Even Accepted needed permission to leave the Tower grounds except during certain hours. Siuan and Leane together had even chilled a bucket of water to near freezing and set it so it would douse an Aes Sedai who had had them switched, unfairly as they saw it. From the glint in Anaiya's eyes, it was a good thing for them that they had not been found out that time. From what Min knew of novice training, and Accepted for that matter, these women were lucky that they had been allowed to remain long enough to become Aes Sedai, much less that they still had whole hides.

"I am satisfied," the motherly woman said at last, glancing at the others.

Myrelle nodded after Sheriam did, but Carlinya said, "There is still the question of what to do with her." She stared right at Siuan, unblinking, and the others suddenly seemed uneasy. Myrelle pursed her lips, and Anaiya studied the floor. Smoothing her dress, Sheriam seemed to avoid looking at the newcomers at all.

"We still know everything we knew before," Leane told them, her sudden frown at least half-worry. "We can be of use."

Siuan was dark-faced—Leane had seemed amused if anything at her recounted girlhood misdeeds and penalties, but Siuan had not liked the telling one bit—yet in contrast to her near-glare, her voice was only a little tight. "You wanted to know how we found you. I made contact with one of my agents who also works for the Blue, and she told me of Sallie Daera."

Min did not understand that about Sallie Daera at all—who was she?—but Sheriam and the others nodded at one another. Siuan had done something other than tell them how, Min realized; she had let them know that she still had access to the eyes-and-ears who had served her as Amyrlin.

"You sit over there, Min," Sheriam told Min, pointing to the one table not in use, in a corner. "Or are you still Elmindreda? And keep Logain with you." She and the other three gathered Siuan and Leane, herding them toward the back of the common room. Two more women in riding dresses joined them before they vanished through a new-made door of uncured boards.

Sighing, Min took Logain's arm and led him to the table, sat him down on a rough bench and took a shaky ladder-back chair herself. Two of the Warders positioned themselves nearby, leaning against the wall. They did not appear to be watching Logain, but Min knew the Gaidin; they saw everything, and they could have their swords out in less than a heartbeat while sleeping.

So there were to be no open arms in welcome, even with Siuan and Leane recognized. Well, what did she expect? Siuan and Leane had been the two most powerful women in the White Tower; now they were not even Aes Sedai. The others very likely did not know how to behave toward them. And appearing with a gentled false Dragon. Siuan had better not be lying or wishing about having a plan for him. Min did not think Sheriam and the others would be as patient as Logain had been.

And Sheriam, at least, had recognized her. She stood again, long enough to peer through a crack-paned window into the street. Their horses were still at the hitching posts, but one of those Warders who were not watching would have her before she had Wildrose's reins untied. This last time in the Tower, Siuan had gone to great lengths to disguise her. To no end, it seemed. She did not think any of them knew about her viewings, though. Siuan and Leane had held that tightly to themselves. Min would be just as glad if it remained that way. If these Aes Sedai learned of it, they would entangle her just as Siuan had, and she would never reach Rand. She was not going to be able to show off what she had learned from Leane if they kept her on a leash here.

Helping Siuan find this gathering, helping bring Aes Sedai to Rand's aid, was all very well and important, but she still had a personal goal. Making a man who had never looked at her twice fall in love with her before he went mad. Maybe she was as mad as he was fated to be. "Then we'll make a matched pair," she muttered to herself.

A freckled, green-eyed girl who had to be a novice stopped at her table. "Would you like something to eat or drink? There is venison stew, and wild pears. There might be some cheese, too." She put so much effort into not looking at Logain that she might as well have stared pop-eyed.

"Pears and cheese sound very good," Min told her. The last two days had been hungry; Siuan had managed to catch some fish in a stream, but Logain had done all the hunting when they had not eaten at an inn or a farm. Dried beans did not make a meal, in her opinion. "And some wine, if you have it. But first, I would like some information. Where are we, if it isn't a secret here too? This village is called Salidar?"

"In Altara. The Eldar is about a mile to the west. Amadicia is on the other side." The girl put on a poor imitation of Aes Sedai mystery. "Where better to hide Aes Sedai than where they would never be looked for?"

"We should not have to hide," a dark, curly-haired young woman snapped, stopping. Min recognized her, an Accepted named Faolain; she would have expected her to be in the Tower still. Faolain had never liked anyone or anything as far as Min knew, and had often spoken of choosing the Red Ajah when she was raised. A perfect follower for Elaida. "Why did you come here? With *him*! Why did *she* come?" There was no doubt in Min's mind who she meant. "It is her fault we have to hide. I did not believe she helped Mazrim Taim escape, but if she appears here with *him,* maybe she did."

"That will be enough, Faolain," a slender woman with black hair spilling down her back to her waist told the round-faced Accepted. Min thought she knew the woman in the dark golden silk riding dress. Edesina. A Yellow, she believed. "Go about your duties," Edesina

said. "And if you mean to bring food, Tabiya, do it."
Edesina did not watch Faolain's sullen curtsy—the
novice gave a better and scurried away—but put a hand
on Logain's head instead. Eyes on the table, he did not
seem to notice.

To Min's eyes, a silvery collar suddenly appeared, snug
around the woman's neck, and as suddenly seemed to
shatter. Min shivered. She did not like viewings connected to the Seanchan. At least Edesina would escape
somehow. Even if Min had been willing to expose
herself, there was no point in warning the woman; it
would not change anything.

"It is the gentling," the Aes Sedai said after a moment.
"He has given up on wanting to live, I suppose. There is
nothing I can do for him. Not that I am sure I should if I
could." The look she gave Min before leaving was far
from friendly.

An elegant, statuesque woman in russet silk paused a
few feet away, coolly examining Min and Logain with
expressionless eyes. Kiruna was a Green, and regal in her
manner; she was a sister of the King of Arafel, so Min
had heard, but she had been friendly to Min in the
Tower. Min smiled, but those large dark eyes swept over
her without recognition, and Kiruna glided out of the
inn, four Warders, disparate men but all with that
deadly-seeming way of moving, suddenly heeling her.

Waiting for her food, Min hoped that Siuan and Leane
were finding a warmer reception.

CHAPTER
27

The Practice of Diffidence

Y ou are rudderless," Siuan told the six women facing her in six different sorts of chair. The room itself was a muddle. Two large kitchen tables against the walls held pens and ink jars and sand bottles in neat arrays. Mismatched lamps, some glazed pottery and some gilded, and candles in every thickness and length stood ready to provide light at nightfall. A scrap of Illianer silk carpet, rich in blues and reds and gold, lay on a floor of rough, weathered planks. She and Leane had been seated across the piece of carpet from the others, in such a way that they were the focus of every eye. Open casement windows with panes cracked or replaced by oiled silk let a breath of air stir in, but not enough to cut the heat. Siuan told herself that she did not envy these women their ability to channel—she was past that, surely—but she did envy the way none of them perspired. Her own face was quite damp. "All that activity out there is play and show. You might be fooling each other, and maybe even the Gaidin—though I'd not count on that, were I you—but you can't fool me."

She wished that Morvrin and Beonin had not been

added to the group. Morvrin was skeptical of everything despite her placid, sometimes vaguely absent look, a stout Brown with gray-streaked hair who demanded six pieces of evidence before she would believe fish had scales. And Beonin, a pretty Gray with dark honey hair and blue-gray eyes so big they constantly made her appear slightly startled—Beonin made Morvrin seem gullible.

"Elaida has the Tower in her fist, and you know she will mishandle Rand al'Thor," Siuan said scornfully. "It will be pure luck if she doesn't panic and have him gentled before Tarmon Gai'don. You know that whatever you feel about a man channeling, Reds feel ten times more. The White Tower is at its weakest when it should be at its strongest, in the hands of a fool when it must have skilled command." She wrinkled her nose, staring them in the eye one by one. "And you sit here, drifting with your sails down. Or can you convince me that you are doing more than twiddling your thumbs and blowing bubbles?"

"Do you agree with Siuan, Leane?" Anaiya asked mildly. Siuan had never been able to understand why Moiraine liked the woman. Trying to get her to do anything she did not want to was like hitting a sack of feathers. She did not stand up to you, or argue; she just silently refused to move. Even the way she sat, with her hands folded, looked more like a woman waiting to knead dough than an Aes Sedai.

"In part I do," Leane replied. Siuan gave her a sharp look that she ignored. "About Elaida, certainly. Elaida will misuse Rand al'Thor, as surely as she is misusing the Tower. For the rest, I know that you have worked hard to gather as many sisters here as you have, and I expect that you are working just as hard to do something about Elaida."

Siuan sniffed loudly. On her way through the common room she had snatched glimpses of some of those parchments being examined so assiduously. Lists of provisions, allotments of timber for rebuilding, assignments for woodcutting and repairing houses and cleaning out wells. Nothing more. Nothing that looked the least like a report on Elaida's activities. They were planning to winter here. All it took was one Blue being captured after she had learned of Sàlidar, one woman being put to the question—she would not hold back much if Alviarin had charge of it—and Elaida would know exactly where to net them. While they worried about planting vegetable gardens and having enough firewood cut before the first freeze.

"Then that is out of the way," Carlinya said coolly. "You do not seem to understand that you are not Amyrlin and Keeper any longer. You are not even Aes Sedai." Some had the grace to look embarrassed. Not Morvrin or Beonin, but the others. No Aes Sedai liked to speak of stilling, or be reminded of it; they would think it especially harsh in front of the two of them. "I do not say this to be cruel. We do not believe the charges against you—despite your traveling companion—or we would not be here, but you cannot assume your old places among us, and that is a simple fact."

Siuan remembered Carlinya well as novice and Accepted. Once a month she had committed some minor offense, a small thing that earned her an extra hour or two of chores. Exactly once each month. She had not wanted the others to think her a prig. Those had been her only offenses—she never broke another rule or put a foot wrong; it would not have been logical—yet she had never understood why the other girls had considered her an Aes Sedai pet anyway. A great deal of logic and not much common sense: that was Carlinya.

"While what was done to you followed the letter of the law narrowly," Sheriam said gently, "we agree that it was malignantly unjust, an extreme distortion of the law's spirit." The chairback behind her fire-red head was incongruously carved with what seemed to be a mass of snakes fighting. "Whatever rumor might say, most of the charges laid against you were so thin that they should have been laughed away."

"Not the charge that she knew of Rand al'Thor and conspired to hide him from the Tower," Carlinya broke in sharply.

Sheriam nodded. "But be that as it may, even that was

not sufficient for the penalty given. Nor should you have been tried in secret, without even a chance to defend yourself. Never fear that we will turn our backs on you. We will see that you both are cared for."

"I thank you," Leane said, her voice soft and almost trembling.

Siuan grimaced at them. "You haven't even asked me about the eyes-and-ears I can use." She had liked Sheriam when they were students together, though years and position had opened water between them. "Cared for" indeed! "Is Aeldene here?" Anaiya started to shake her head before stopping herself. "I suspected not, or you would know more of what is going on. You've left them sending their reports to the Tower." Slow realization dawned on their faces; they had not known Aeldene's office. "I headed the Blue Ajah's net of eyes-and-ears, before I was raised Amyrlin." More surprise. "With a little effort every Blue agent, and those who served me as Amyrlin too, can be sending her reports to you, by routes that keep her ignorant of their final destination." It would take considerably more than a little work, but she had already sketched most of it out in her head, and there was no need for them to know more at the moment. "And they can continue sending reports to the Tower, reports containing what . . . you want Elaida to believe." She had almost said "we"; she had to watch her tongue.

They did not like it, of course. The women who tended the networks might be unknown to all but a few, but they were every one Aes Sedai. They had always been Aes Sedai. But that was her only lever with which to pry her way into the circles where decisions were made. Otherwise, they would likely stuff her and Leane into a cottage with a servant to look after them, and maybe a rare visit from Aes Sedai who wanted to examine women who had been stilled, until they died. They would die soon, in those circumstances.

Light, they might even marry us off! Some thought that a husband and children could occupy a woman enough to replace the One Power in her life. More than one woman, stilled by drawing too much of *saidar* to herself, or in testing *ter'angreal* for their uses, had found herself being matched with potential husbands. Since those who did marry always put as much distance as possible between themselves and the Tower and its memories, the theory remained unproven.

"It should not be difficult," Leane said diffidently, "to put myself in touch with those who were my eyes-and-ears before I was Keeper. More importantly, as Keeper of the Chronicles I had agents in Tar Valon itself." Startlement widened a few eyes, though Carlinya's narrowed. Leane blinked, shifted uneasily, smiled weakly. "I always thought it foolish that we paid more attention to the mood of Ebou Dar or Bandar Eban than to the mood of our own city." They had to see the value of eyes-and-ears in Tar Valon.

"Siuan." Leaning forward in her thick-armed chair, Morvrin said the name firmly, as though to emphasize that she had not said Mother. That round face looked more stubborn than placid now, her stoutness a threatening mass. When Siuan had been a novice, Morvrin rarely seemed to notice the mischief of the girls around her, but when she did, she had taken care of matters herself, in ways that had everyone sitting straight and walking small for days. "Why should we allow you to do as you want? You have been stilled, woman. Whatever you were, you are no longer Aes Sedai. If we want these agents' names, you will both give them to us." There was a flat certainty to that last; they would give them, one way or another. They would, if these women wanted them enough.

Leane shivered visibly, but Siuan's chair creaked as she stiffened her back. "I know that I am not Amyrlin anymore. Do you think I don't know I was stilled? My face is changed, but not what is inside. Everything I ever knew is still in my head. Use it! For the love of the Light, use me!" She took a deep breath to calm herself—*Burn me if I let them shove me aside to rot!*—and Myrelle spoke into the pause.

"A young woman's temper to go with a young woman's face." Smiling, she sat on the edge of a stiff-backed armchair that could have stood in front of a farmer's fireplace, if the farmer had not cared that the varnish was flaking. The smile was not her usual one, though, languid and knowing at the same time, and her dark eyes, nearly as large as Beonin's, were full of sympathy. "I am sure that no one wants you to feel useless, Siuan. And I am sure that we all want to employ your knowledge fully. What you know will be of great use to us."

Siuan did not want her sympathy. "You seem to have forgotten Logain, and why I dragged him all the way here from Tar Valon." She had not meant to bring this up herself, but if they were going to let it lie wallowing . . . "My 'crackbrained' idea?"

"Very well, Siuan," Sheriam said. "Why?"

"Because the first step to pulling Elaida down is for Logain to reveal to the Tower, to the world if need be, that the Red Ajah set him up as a false Dragon so that he could be pulled down." She certainly had their attention now. "He was found by Reds in Ghealdan at least a year before he proclaimed himself, but instead of bringing him to Tar Valon to be gentled, they planted the idea in his head of claiming to be the Dragon Reborn."

"You are certain of this?" Beonin asked quietly, in a heavy Taraboner accent. She sat very still in her tall, cane-bottomed chair, watching carefully.

"He does not know who Leane and I are. He talked with us sometimes on the journey here, late at night when Min was sleeping and he could not rest. He said nothing before because he thinks the entire Tower was behind it, but he knows that it was Red sisters who shielded him and talked to him of the Dragon Reborn."

"Why?" Morvrin demanded, and Sheriam nodded. "Yes, why? Any of us would go out of our way to see a man like that gentled, but the Red Ajah lives for nothing else. Why would they create a false Dragon?"

"Logain did not know," she told them. "Perhaps they think they gain more by capturing a false Dragon than gentling a poor fool who might terrorize one village. Perhaps they have some reason to want more turmoil."

"We do not suggest they've had anything to do with Mazrim Taim or any of the others," Leane added quickly. "Elaida will no doubt be able to tell you what you want to know."

Siuan watched them mull it over in silence. They never considered the possibility that she was lying. *An advantage to having been stilled.* It did not seem to occur to them that being stilled might have broken all ties to the Three Oaths. Some Aes Sedai studied stilled women, true, but gingerly and reluctantly. No one wanted to be reminded of what might happen to herself.

For Logain, Siuan had no worry. Not as long as Min continued to see whatever it was that she saw. He would live long enough to reveal what Siuan wanted him to, once she had talked to him. She had not dared risk his deciding to go his own way, which he might well have done had she told him before. But it was his one chance for revenge now against those who had gentled him, surrounded by Aes Sedai again as he was. Revenge only against the Red Ajah, true, but he would have to settle for that. A fish in the boat was worth a school in the water.

She glanced at Leane, who smiled the faintest possible smile. That was good. Leane had disliked being kept in the dark about her plan for the man until this morning, but Siuan had lived too long wrapped in secrecy to be easy revealing more than she had to, even to a friend. She thought that the idea of Red Ajah involvement with other false Dragons had been neatly planted. Reds had been the leaders in overthrowing her. There might not be a Red Ajah once this was done with.

"This changes a great deal," Sheriam said after a time. "We cannot possibly follow an Amyrlin who would do such a thing."

"Follow her!" Siuan exclaimed, for the first time truly startled. "You were actually considering going back to kiss Elaida's ring? Knowing what she has done, and will do?" Leane quivered in her seat as if she wanted to say a few choice words herself, but they had agreed that Siuan was to be the one to lose her temper.

Sheriam looked a trifle embarrassed, and spots of color floated in Myrelle's olive cheeks, but the others took it as calmly as sunshine.

"The Tower must be strong," Carlinya said in a voice as hard as winter stone. "The Dragon has been Reborn, the Last Battle is coming, and the Tower must be whole."

Anaiya nodded. "We understand your reasons for disliking Elaida, even hating her. We do understand, but we must think of the Tower, and the world. I confess I do not like Elaida myself. But then, I have never liked Siuan, either. It is not necessary to *like* the Amyrlin Seat. There is no need to glare so, Siuan. You have had a file for a tongue since you were a novice, and it has only roughened with the years. And as Amyrlin, you pushed sisters where you wanted and only seldom explained why. The two do not make a likable combination."

"I will try to . . . smooth my tongue," Siuan said dryly. Did the woman expect the Amyrlin Seat to treat every sister like a childhood friend? "But I hope what I've told you changes your desire to kneel at Elaida's feet?"

"If that is your smoother tongue," Myrelle said idly, "I may have to smooth it myself, if we do allow you to run the eyes-and-ears for us."

"We cannot go back to the Tower now, of course," Sheriam said. "Not knowing this. Not until we are in position to see Elaida deposed."

"Whatever she has done, the Reds, they will continue to support her." Beonin stated it as fact, not objection. It was no secret that the Reds resented the fact that there had not been an Amyrlin from their Ajah since Bonwhin.

Morvrin nodded heavily. "Others will, as well. Those who have thrown themselves too much behind Elaida to believe they have any other choice. Those who will support authority, however vile. And some who will believe we are dividing the Tower when it must be whole at any cost."

"All but the Red sisters can be approached," Beonin said judiciously, "negotiated with." Mediation and negotiation were her Ajah's reason for existence.

"It seems we will have a use for your agents, Siuan." Sheriam looked around at the others. "Unless anyone still thinks we should take them away from her?" Morvrin was the last to shake her head, but she did it, finally, after a long study that made Siuan feel she had been stripped, weighed and measured.

She could not stop a sigh of relief. Not a short life drying up in a cottage, but a life of purpose. It might still be a short life—no one knew how long a stilled woman could live given something to replace the One Power in her life—but with purpose it would be long enough. So Myrelle was going to smooth her tongue for her, was she? *I'll show that fox-eyed Green—I will hold my tongue and be glad she isn't doing more than look at me is what I'll do. I knew how this would go. Burn me, but I did.*

"Thank you, Aes Sedai," she said in the meekest tone she could find. To call them that pained her; it was another break, another reminder of what she was not any longer. "I will try to give good service." Myrelle did not have to nod in such a satisfied way. Siuan ignored a small voice that said she would have done as much or more in Myrelle's place.

"If I may suggest," Leane said, "it is not enough to wait until you have enough support in the Hall of the Tower to depose Elaida." Siuan put on an interested look, as though hearing this for the first time. "Elaida sits in Tar Valon, in the White Tower, and to the world she is Amyrlin. At the moment, you are only a flock of dissidents. She can call you rebels and agitators, and coming from the Amyrlin Seat, the world will believe it."

"We can hardly stop her being Amyrlin before she is deposed," Carlinya said, shifting on her chair in icy contempt. Had she been wearing her white-fringed shawl, she would have snapped it around her.

"You can give the world a true Amyrlin." Leane spoke not to the White sister, but to all of them, eyeing each in turn, sure of what she was saying yet at the same time offering a suggestion that she merely hoped they would take. It had been Siuan who pointed out that the techniques she employed on men could be adapted for women. "I saw Aes Sedai from every Ajah save the Red in the common room, and in the streets. Have them elect a Hall of the Tower here, and let that Hall select a new Amyrlin. Then you can present yourselves to the world as the true White Tower, in exile, and Elaida as a usurper. With Logain's revelations added in, can you doubt who the nations will accept as the real Amyrlin Seat?"

The idea took hold. Siuan could see them turning it over in their minds. Whatever the others thought, only Sheriam voiced a word against. "It will mean that the Tower truly is broken," the green-eyed woman said sadly.

"It already is broken," Siuan told her tartly, and instantly wished she had not when they all looked at her. This was supposed to be purely Leane's notion. She herself had a reputation as a deft manipulator, and they could well be suspicious of anything she proposed. That was why she had begun by scathing them; they would not have believed her if she had begun with mild words. She would come at them as if she still thought herself Amyrlin, and let them put her in her place. By comparison, Leane would seem more cooperative, only offering the little she could, and they would be more likely to listen to her. Doing her own part had not been difficult— until it came to pleading; then she had wanted to hang them all in the sun to dry. Sitting here, doing nothing!

You didn't have to worry about them being suspicious. They think you are a broken reed. If everything went properly, they would not learn differently. A useful reed, but a weak one, not to be thought of twice. It was a painful accommodation to make, but Duranda Tharne had shown her the necessity in Lugard. They would accept her only on their terms, and she would have to make the best of it.

"I wish I had thought of this myself," she went on. "Now that I hear it, Leane's idea gives you a way to build the Tower again without having to tear it down completely first."

"I still cannot like it." Sheriam's voice firmed. "But what must be must be. The Wheel weaves as the Wheel wills, and the Light willing, it will weave Elaida out of the stole."

"We will need to negotiate with those sisters who remain in the Tower," Beonin mused, only half to herself. "The Amyrlin we choose, she must be a skilled negotiator, yes?"

"Clear thinking will be needed," Carlinya put in. "The new Amyrlin must be a woman of cool reason and logic."

Morvrin's snort was loud enough to make everyone jump in their chairs. "Sheriam is the highest among us, and she has kept us together when we'd have been running in ten different directions."

Sheriam shook her head vigorously, but Myrelle gave her no chance to speak. "Sheriam is an excellent choice. I can promise every Green sister here behind her, I know." Anaiya opened her mouth, agreement plain on her face.

It was time to put a stop to this before it got out of hand. "If I may suggest?" Siuan thought she managed diffidence much better than she had meekness. It was a strain, but she thought she had better learn to maintain it. *Myrelle isn't the only one who will try to stuff me in the bilges if they think I've overstepped my place. Whatever it is.* Only, they would not try; they would do. Aes Sedai expected—no, required—respect from those who were not. "It seems to me that whoever you choose should be someone who was not in the Tower when I . . . was deposed. Would it not be best if the woman who unites the Tower again was one whom no one could accuse of choosing a side on that day?" If she had to keep this up, she was going to burst a seam in her head.

"Someone very strong in the Power," Leane added. "The stronger she is, the more she can stand for all that the Tower means. Or will again, once Elaida is gone."

Siuan could have kicked her. That thought was supposed to wait a full day, to be tossed in once they actually began considering names. Between them, she and Leane knew enough of every sister to find some weakness, some doubt to be dangled subtly as to her fitness for stole and staff. She would rather wade naked through a school of silverpike than have these women realize that she was trying to manipulate them.

"A sister who was out of the Tower," Sheriam said, nodding. "That makes excellent sense, Siuan. Very good." How easily they slipped into patting her on the head.

Morvrin pursed her lips. "It will not be easy, finding whoever we choose."

"Strength narrows the possibilities." Anaiya looked around at the others. "It will not only make her a better symbol, to the other sisters at least, but strength in the Power often goes with strength of will, and whoever we choose will surely need that."

Carlinya and Beonin were the last to join in agreement.

Siuan kept her face smooth, her smile on the inside. The breaking of the Tower had changed many things, many ways of thinking besides her own. These women had led the sisters gathered here, and now they were discussing who should be presented to their new Hall of the Tower as if that should not be the Hall's choice. It would not be difficult to bring them around, ever so gently, to the belief that the new Amyrlin should be one who could be guided by them. And unknowing, they and the Amyrlin she chose for her replacement would be guided by herself. She and Moiraine had worked too long to find Rand al'Thor and prepare him, given too much of their lives, for her to risk the rest of it being bungled by someone else.

"If I may make another suggestion?" Diffidence was simply not in her nature; she was going to have to find something else. She waited, trying not to grit her teeth, for Sheriam to nod before going on. "Elaida will be attempting to discover where Rand al'Thor is; the farther south I came, the more rumors I heard that he has left Tear. I think that he has, and I think that I have reasoned out where he went."

There was no need for her to say that they had to find him before Tar Valon did. They all understood. Not only would Elaida mishandle him, certainly, but should she put her hands on him, display him shielded and in her control, any hope of toppling her would be gone. Rulers knew the Prophecies, if their people usually did not; they would forgive her a dozen false Dragons out of necessity.

"Where?" Morvrin barked, a hair ahead of Sheriam, Anaiya and Myrelle all together.

"The Aiel Waste."

There was a moment of silence before Carlinya said, "That is ridiculous."

Siuan bit back an angry reply and smiled what she hoped was an apologetic smile. "Perhaps, but I read something of the Aiel when I was Accepted. Gitara Moroso thought that some of the Aiel Wise Ones might be able to channel." Gitara had been Keeper then. "One of the books she had me read, an old thing from the dustiest corner of the library, claimed that the Aiel call themselves the People of the Dragon. I did not remember it until I tried puzzling out where Rand could have vanished to. The Prophecies say 'the Stone of Tear shall never fall till the People of the Dragon come,' and there were Aiel in the taking of the Stone. That, every rumor and tale agrees on."

Morvrin's eyes suddenly seemed to look elsewhere. "I remember speculation about the Wise Ones when I was newly raised to the shawl. It would be fascinating, if true, but Aiel are little more welcoming to Aes Sedai than to anyone else who enters the Waste, and their Wise Ones apparently have some law or custom against speaking to strangers, so I understand, which makes it extremely hard to come close enough to one to feel if she—" Suddenly she gave herself a shake, staring at Siuan and Leane as though her wandering had been their fault. "A thin straw to weave a basket, something you remember from a book likely written by someone who never saw an Aiel."

"A very thin straw," Carlinya said.

"But worth sending someone to the Waste?" It took effort to make that a question instead of a demand. Siuan thought she might sweat down to nothing if she could not find another way. She still had enough control of herself to ignore the heat, usually, but not while trying to drag these women along without letting them notice her fist in their hair. "I do not think the Aiel would try to harm an Aes Sedai." Not if she was quick enough to show that she was Aes Sedai. Siuan did not think they would. It had to be risked. "And if he is in the Waste, the Aiel will know of it. Remember those Aiel at the Stone."

"Perhaps," Beonin said slowly. "The Waste is large. How many would we need to send?"

"If the Dragon Reborn is in the Waste," Anaiya said, "the first Aiel met will know of it. Events follow this Rand al'Thor, by all accounts. He could not slip into the ocean without making a splash heard in every corner of the world."

Myrelle smiled. "She should be Green. None of the rest of you will bond more than one Warder, and two or three Gaidin might be very useful in the Waste until the Aiel know her for Aes Sedai. I have always wanted to see an Aiel." She had been a novice during the Aiel War, and not allowed out of the Tower. Not that any Aes Sedai had taken part beyond Healing, of course. The Three Oaths had bound them unless Tar Valon, or maybe even the Tower itself, were attacked, and that war had never crossed the rivers.

"Not you," Sheriam told her, "or any other member of this council. You agreed to see this through, Myrelle, when you agreed to sit with us, and that does not include gallivanting off because you are bored. I fear there will be more excitement than any of us could wish, before we finish." She would have made an excellent Amyrlin in other circumstances; in these, she was simply too strong and sure of herself. "But Greens . . . Yes, I think so. Two?" Her green eyes swept along the others. "To be certain?"

"Kiruna Nachiman?" Anaiya offered, and Beonin added, "Bera Harkin?" The others nodded, except for Myrelle, who shifted her shoulders irritably. Aes Sedai did not pout, but she came close.

Siuan took her second relieved breath. She was certain her reasoning was correct. He had vanished to somewhere, and if he was anywhere between the Spine of the World and the Aryth Ocean, rumors would have been flying. And wherever he was, Moiraine would be there with a hand on his collar. Kiruna and Bera would surely be willing to carry a letter to Moiraine, and they had seven Warders between them to keep the Aiel from killing them.

"We do not want to tire you and Leane," Sheriam went on. "I will ask one of the Yellow sisters to look at both of you. Perhaps she can do something to help, to ease you in some way. I will have rooms found for you, where you can rest."

"If you are to be our mistress of eyes-and-ears," Myrelle added solicitously, "you must maintain your strength."

"I am not so frail as you seem to think," Siuan protested. "If I were, could I have followed you nearly two thousand miles? Whatever weakness I had after being stilled is gone, believe me." The truth was that she had found a center of power again, and she did not want to leave it, but she could hardly say that. All those concerned eyes on her, and Leane. Well, not Carlinya's particularly, but the rest. *Light! They're going to have a novice tuck us into bed for a nap!*

A knock at the door was followed immediately by Arinvar, Sheriam's Warder. Cairhienin, he was not tall, and slender besides, but in spite of gray at his temples he was hard of face, and he moved like a stalking leopard. "There are twenty-odd riders to the east," he said without preamble.

"Not Whitecloaks," Carlinya said, "or I presume you would have reported as much."

Sheriam gave her a look. Many sisters could be prickly when it came to another stepping between them and their Gaidin. "We cannot allow them to get away, and perhaps carry word of our presence. Can they be captured, Arinvar? I would prefer that to killing them."

"Either may be difficult," he replied. "Machan says they are armed and have the look of veterans. Worth ten times their number of younger men."

Morvrin made a vexed sound. "We must do one or the other. Forgive me, Sheriam. Arinvar, can the Gaidin sneak some of the more agile sisters close enough to weave Air around them?"

He shook his head fractionally. "Machan says they may have seen some of the Warders keeping watch. They would certainly see if we tried to bring more than one or two of you near. They are still coming, though."

Siuan and Leane were not the only ones to exchange startled glances. Few men saw a Warder who did not want to be seen, even without the Gaidin cloak.

"Then you must do as you think best," Sheriam said. "Capture them, if possible. But none must escape to betray us."

Before Arinvar could complete his bow, hand to sword hilt, another man was beside him, a dark bear of a man, tall and wide, with hair to his shoulders and a short beard that left his upper lip bare. That flowing Warder movement seemed odd on him. He winked at Myrelle, his Aes Sedai, even as he said in a thick Illianer accent, "Most of the riders do be stopped, but one does come on by himself. If my aged mother did say different, I would still name him Gareth Bryne from the glimpse I did get."

Siuan stared at him; her hands and feet suddenly felt cold. Strong rumor said that Myrelle had actually married this Nuhel and her other two Warders, in defiance of convention and law in every land Siuan had ever heard of. It was the sort of incongruous thought that drifted through a stunned mind, and right then she felt as if a mast had fallen on her head. Bryne, here? *It's impossible! It is mad!* Surely the man could not have followed them all this way for . . . *Oh yes, he could and would. That one would.* As they journeyed, she had told herself that it was only sensible caution to leave no trace behind, that Elaida knew they were not dead, whatever the rumors said, and she would not stop hunting until they were found or she was pulled down. Siuan had been irritated at having to ask directions finally, yet the thought that had snapped at her like a shark had not been that Elaida might somehow find a blacksmith in one small Altaran village, but that the blacksmith would be like a painted sign for Bryne. *Told yourself it was foolish, didn't you? And now here he is.*

She well remembered her confrontation with him, when she had had to bend him to her will on that matter of Murandy. It had been like bending a thick iron bar, or some huge spring that would leap back if she let up for an instant. She had had to bring all of her force to bear, had had to humiliate him publicly, in order to make certain he would remain bent for as long as she needed. He could hardly go against what he had agreed to on his knees, begging her pardon, with fifty nobles watching. Morgase had been difficult enough herself, and Siuan had not been willing to risk Bryne giving Morgase an excuse to go against her instructions. Strange to think that she and Elaida had worked together then, bringing Morgase to heel.

She had to take hold of herself. She was in a daze, thinking of everything except what she needed to. *Concentrate. This is no time to panic.* "You must send him away. Or kill him."

She knew it for a mistake while the words were still leaving her mouth, all too full of urgency. Even the Warders looked at her, and the Aes Sedai. . . . She had never before known what it felt like for someone who lacked the Power to have those eyes turned on them at full strength. She felt naked, her very mind laid bare. Even knowing that Aes Sedai could not read thoughts, she still wanted to confess before they listed her lies and crimes. She hoped that her face was not like Leane's, red-cheeked and wide-eyed.

"You know why he is here." Sheriam's voice was calmly certain. "Both of you do. And you do not want to confront him. Enough so that you would have us kill him for you."

"There do be few great captains living." Nuhel marked them off on gauntleted fingers. "Agelmar Jagad and Davram Bashere will no leave the Blight, I think, and Pedron Niall will surely no be of use to you. If Rodel Ituralde do be alive, he do be mired somewhere in what do remain of Arad Doman." He raised his thick thumb. "And that do leave Gareth Bryne."

"Do you think that we will need a great captain, then?" Sheriam asked quietly.

Nuhel and Arinvar did not look at one another, but Siuan still had the feeling that they had exchanged glances. "It is your decision, Sheriam," Arinvar replied just as quietly, "yours and the other sisters, but if you mean to return to the Tower, we could use him. If you intend to remain here until Elaida sends for you, then not." Myrelle gazed at Nuhel questioningly, and he nodded.

"It seems that you were right, Siuan," Anaiya said wryly. "We have not fooled the Gaidin."

"The question is whether he will agree to serve us," Carlinya said, and Morvrin nodded, adding, "We must make him see our cause in such a way that he wishes to serve. It will not help us if it becomes known that we killed or imprisoned so notable a man before we have even begun."

"Yes," Beonin said, "and we must offer him the rewards that will bind him to us firmly."

Sheriam turned her eyes on the two men. "When Lord Bryne reaches the village, tell him nothing, but bring him to us." As soon as the door closed behind the Warders, her gaze firmed. Siuan recognized it; the same clear green stare that had novices' knees knocking before a word was said. "Now. You will tell us exactly why Gareth Bryne is here."

There was no choice. If they caught her in even the tiniest lie, they would begin to question everything. Siuan took a deep breath. "We took shelter for the night in a barn near Kore Springs, in Andor. Bryne is the lord there, and . . ."

CHAPTER
28

Trapped

A Warder in a gray-green coat approached Bryne as soon as he rode Traveler past the first stone houses of the village. Bryne would have known the man for a Warder after watching him walk two strides, even without all the Aes Sedai faces staring at him in the street. What in the name of the Light were so many Aes Sedai doing this close to Amadicia? Rumor in villages behind said Ailron meant to claim this bank of the River Eldar, which meant the Whitecloaks did. Aes Sedai could defend themselves well, but if Niall sent a legion across the Eldar, a good many of these women would die. Unless he could no longer tell how long a stump had been exposed to air, this place had been buried in the forest two months ago. What had Mara gotten herself into? He was sure he would find her here; village men remembered three pretty young women traveling together, especially when one of them asked directions to a town abandoned since the Whitecloak War.

The Warder, a big man with a broad face, an Illianer by his beard, planted himself in the street in front of

Bryne's big-nosed bay gelding and bowed. "Lord Bryne? I am Nuhel Dromand. If you will come with me, there are those who do wish to speak with you."

Bryne dismounted slowly, pulling off his gauntlets and tucking them behind his sword belt as he studied the town. The plain buff-colored coat he wore now was much better for a journey of this sort than the gray silk he had started in; that, he had given away. Aes Sedai and Warders, and others, watched him silently, but even those who had to be servants did not look surprised. And Dromand knew his name. His face was not unknown, but he suspected more than that. If Mara was—if *they* were Aes Sedai agents, it did not alter the oath they had taken. "Lead on, Nuhel Gaidin." If Nuhel was surprised at the address, he did not show it.

The inn that Dromand took him to—or what had been an inn once—had the look of headquarters for a campaign, all bustle and scurry. That is, if Aes Sedai had ever commanded a campaign. He spotted Serenla before she did him, seated in the corner with a big man who was very likely Dalyn. When she did see him, her chin dropped almost to the table, and then she squinted at him as if not believing her eyes. Dalyn appeared to be asleep with his eyes open, staring at nothing. None of the Aes Sedai or Warders seemed to notice as Dromand led him through, but Bryne would have wagered his manor and lands that any one of them had seen ten times as much as all the staring servants combined. He should have turned and ridden away as soon as he realized who was in this village.

He took careful note as he made his bows while the Warder introduced him to the six seated Aes Sedai— only a fool was careless around Aes Sedai—but his mind was on the two young women standing against the wall beside the fresh-swept fireplace and looking chastened. The willowy Domani minx was offering him a smile more tremulous than seductive for a change. Mara was frightened, too—terrified out of her skin, he would say—but those blue eyes still met his full of defiance. The girl had courage to suit a lion.

"We are pleased to greet you, Lord Bryne," the flame-haired Aes Sedai said. Just slightly plump, and with those tilted eyes, she was pretty enough to make any man look twice despite the Great Serpent ring on her finger. "Will you tell us what brings you here?"

"Of course, Sheriam Sedai." Nuhel stood at his shoulder, but if any women needed less guarding from one old soldier, Bryne could not imagine who. He was sure that they knew already, and watching their faces while he told the tale confirmed it. Aes Sedai let nothing be seen that they did not want seen, but at least one of them would have blinked when he spoke of the oath if they had not known beforehand.

"A dreadful story to relate, Lord Bryne." That was the one called Anaiya; ageless face or not, she looked more like a happy, prosperous farmwife than an Aes Sedai. "Yet I am surprised that you followed so far, even after oathbreakers." Mara's fair cheeks flushed a furious red. "Still, a strong oath, one that should not be broken."

"Unfortunately," Sheriam said, "we cannot let you take them quite yet."

So they were Aes Sedai agents. "A strong oath that should not be broken, yet you mean to keep them from honoring it?"

"They will honor it," Myrelle said, with a glance at the pair by the fireplace that made them both stand straighter, "and you may rest assured that they already regret running away after giving it." This time it was Amaena who reddened; Mara looked ready to chew rocks. "But we cannot allow it yet." No Ajahs had been mentioned, yet he thought the darkly pretty woman was Green, and the stout, round-faced one called Morvrin was Brown. Perhaps it was the smile that Myrelle had given Dromand when the man brought him in, and Morvrin's air of thinking of something else. "In truth, they did not say when they would serve, and we have a use for them."

This was foolish; he should apologize for disturbing them and leave. And that was foolish, too. He had known before Dromand reached him in the street that he was unlikely to leave Salidar alive. There were probably fifty Warders in the forest around where he had left his men, if not a hundred. Joni and the others would give a good account of themselves, but he had not brought them all this way to die. Yet if he was a fool to have let a pair of eyes lure him into this trap, he might as well go the last mile for it. "Arson, theft and assault, Aes Sedai. Those were the crimes. They were tried, sentenced, and sworn. But I have no objection to remaining here until you are done with them. Mara can act as my dog robber when you do not need her. I will mark the hours she works for me, and count them against her service."

Mara opened her mouth angrily, but almost as if the women had known that she would try to speak, six pairs of Aes Sedai eyes swiveled to her in unison. She shifted her shoulders, snapped her mouth shut, and then glared at him, fists rigidly at her sides. He was glad she did not have a knife in her hand.

Myrelle appeared close to laughter. "Better to choose the other, Lord Bryne. From the way she is looking at you, you would find her far more . . . congenial."

He half-expected Amaena to go crimson, but she did not. And she was eyeing him—appraisingly. She even shared a smile with Myrelle. Well, she was Domani after all, and considerably more so than when he saw her last, it seemed.

Carlinya, cold enough to make the others seem warm, leaned forward. He was wary of her, and of the big-eyed one named Beonin. He was not sure why. Except that if he were in the Game of Houses here, he would say both women reeked of ambition. Maybe he was involved in exactly that.

"You should be aware," Carlinya said coolly, "that the woman you know as Mara is in reality Siuan Sanche, formerly the Amyrlin Seat. Amaena is really Leane Sharif, who was Keeper of the Chronicles."

It was all he could do not to gape like a country lout. Now that he knew, he could see it in Mara's face—in Siuan's—the face that had made him back down, softened into youth. "How?" was all he said. It was almost all he could have managed to say.

"There are some things men are better off not knowing," Sheriam replied coolly, "and most women."

Mara—no, he might as well think of her by her right name—Siuan had been stilled. He knew that. It must be something to do with stilling. If that swan-necked Domani had been Keeper, he was ready to wager she had been stilled, too. But talking about stilling around Aes Sedai was a good way to find out how tough you were. Besides, when they began going mysterious with you, Aes Sedai would not give a straight answer if you asked whether the sky was blue.

They were very good, these Aes Sedai. They had lulled him, then hit hard when his guard was down. He had a sinking feeling that he knew what they were softening him for. It would be interesting to learn whether he was right. "It does not change the oath they took. If they were still Amyrlin and Keeper, they could be held to that oath by any law, including that of Tar Valon."

"Since you have no objection to remaining here," Sheriam said, "you may have Siuan as your bodyservant, when we do not need her. You may have all three of them, if you wish, including Min, whom you apparently know as Serenla, all the time." For some reason, that seemed to irritate Siuan as much as what had been said about her; she muttered to herself, not loud enough to be heard. "And since you have no objections, Lord Bryne, while you remain with us there is a service that you can give us."

"The gratitude of Aes Sedai is not inconsiderable," Morvrin said.

"You will be serving the Light and justice in serving us," Carlinya added.

Beonin nodded, speaking in serious tones. "You served Morgase and Andor faithfully. Serve us as well, and you will not find exile at its end. Nothing we ask of you will go against your honor. Nothing we ask will harm Andor."

Bryne grimaced. He was in the Game, all right. He sometimes thought that Aes Sedai must have invented *Daes Dae'mar*; they seemed to play it in their sleep. Battle was surely more bloody, but it was more honest, too. If they meant to pull his strings, then his strings would be pulled—they would manage it one way or another—but it was time to show them he was not a brainless puppet.

"The White Tower is broken," he said flatly. Those Aes Sedai eyes widened, but he gave them no chance to speak. "The Ajahs have split. That is the only reason you can all be here. You certainly don't need an extra sword or two"—he eyed Dromand and got a nod in return—"so the only service you can want out of me is to lead an army. To build one, first, unless you have other camps with a good many more men than I saw here. And that means you intend to oppose Elaida." Sheriam looked vexed, Anaiya worried, and Carlinya on the point of speaking, but he went on. Let them listen; he expected he would be doing a great deal of listening to them in the months to come. "Very well. I've never liked Elaida, and I cannot believe she makes a good Amyrlin. More importantly, I can make an army to take Tar Valon. So long as you know the taking will be bloody and long.

"But these are my conditions." They stiffened to a woman at that, even Siuan and Leane. Men did not make conditions for Aes Sedai. "First, the command is mine. You tell me what to do, but I decide how. You give commands to me, and I give them to the soldiers under me, not you. Not unless I have agreed to it first." Several mouths opened, Carlinya's and Beonin's first, but he continued. "I assign men, I promote them, and I discipline them. Not you. Second, if I tell you it can't be done, you will consider what I say. I don't ask to usurp your authority"—small chance they would allow that—"yet I do not want to waste men because you do not understand war." It would happen, but no more than once, if he was lucky. "Third, if you begin this, you will stay the course. I will be putting my head in a noose, and every man who follows along with me, and should you decide half a year from now that Elaida as Amyrlin is preferable to war, you will pull that noose tight for every one of us who can be hunted down. The nations may stay out of a civil war in the Tower, but they'll not let us live if you abandon us. Elaida will see to that.

"If you will not agree to these, then I do not know that

I can serve you. Whether you bind me with the Power for Dromand here to slit my throat or I end attainted and hung, death is still the end."

The Aes Sedai did not speak. For a long moment they stared at him, until the itch between his shoulder blades made him wonder if Nuhel was ready to plunge a dagger in. Then Sheriam rose, and the others followed her to the windows. He could see their lips moving, but he heard nothing. If they wanted to hide their deliberations behind the One Power, so be it. He was not certain how much of what he wanted he could wring out of them. All, if they were sensible, but Aes Sedai could decide that strange things were sensible. Whatever they decided, he would have to accede with as good a grace as he could muster. It was a perfect trap that he had made for himself.

Leane gave him a look and a smile that said as plain as words that he would never know what he had missed; he thought it would have been a fine chase, with him being led by the nose. Domani women never promised half what you thought they did, and they gave only as much as they chose and changed their minds either way in a blink.

The bait in his trap stared at him levelly, strode across the floor until she stood so close that she had to crane her neck to stare up at him, and spoke in a low, furious voice. "Why did you do this? Why did you follow us? For a barn?"

"For an oath." For a pair of blue eyes. Siuan Sanche could not be more than ten years younger than he, but it was hard to remember that she was Siuan Sanche while looking at a face nearer thirty years younger. The eyes were the same, though, deep blue and strong. "An oath you gave to me, and broke. I should double your time for that."

Dropping her gaze from his, she folded her arms beneath her breasts, growling, "That has already been taken care of."

"You mean they punished you for oathbreaking? If you've had your bottom switched for it, it doesn't count unless I do it."

Dromand's chuckle sounded more than half scandalized—the man had to be still struggling with who Siuan had been; Bryne was not certain that he was not, too—and her face darkened until he thought she might have apoplexy. "My time has already been doubled, if not more, you pile of rancid fish guts! You and your marking hours! Not an hour will count until you have all three of us back at your manor, not if I must be your . . . your . . . *dog robber,* whatever that is . . . for twenty years!"

So they had planned for this too, Sheriam and the others. He glanced to their conference by the windows. They seemed to have divided into two opposing groups; Sheriam, Anaiya and Myrelle on one side, Morvrin and Carlinya on the other, with Beonin standing between. They had been ready to give him Siuan and Leane and—Min?—as bribe or sop, before he ever walked in. They were desperate, which meant he was on the weaker side, but maybe they were desperate enough to give him what he needed for a chance of victory.

"You are taking pleasure from this, aren't you?" Siuan said fiercely the moment his eyes moved. "You buzzard. Burn you for a carp-brained fool. Now that you know who I am, it pleases you that I'll have to bow and scrape to you." She did not seem to be doing much of that yet. "Why? Is it because I made you back down over Murandy? Are you so small, Gareth Bryne?"

She was trying to make him angry; she realized that she had said too much, and did not want to give him time to think on it. Maybe she was no longer Aes Sedai, but manipulation was in her blood.

"You were the Amyrlin Seat," he said calmly, "and even a king kisses the Amyrlin's ring. I can't say that I liked how you went about it, and we may have a quiet talk sometime on whether it was necessary to do what you did with half the court looking on, but you will remember that I followed Mara Tomanes here, and it was Mara Tomanes I asked for. Not Siuan Sanche. Since you keep asking why, let me ask it. Why was it so important for me to allow the Murandians to raid across the border?"

"Because your interference then could have ruined important plans," she said, driving each word home in a tight voice, "just as your interference with me now can. The Tower had identified a young border lord named Dulain as a man who could one day truly unify Murandy, with our help. I could hardly allow the chance your soldiers might kill him. I have work to do here, *Lord* Bryne. Leave me to do it, and you may see victory. Meddle out of spite, and you ruin everything."

"Whatever your work is, I am sure Sheriam and the others will see you do it. Dulain? I've never heard of him. He cannot be succeeding yet." It was his opinion that Murandy would remain a patchwork of all but independent lords and ladies until the Wheel turned and a new Age came. Murandians called themselves Lugarders or Mindeans or whatever before they named a nation. If they even bothered to name one. A lord who could unite them, and who had Siuan's leash around his throat, could bring a considerable number of men.

"He . . . died." Scarlet spots appeared in her cheeks, and she seemed to struggle with herself. "A month after I left Caemlyn," she muttered, "some Andoran farmer put an arrow through him on a sheep raid."

He could not help laughing. "It was the farmers you should have made kneel, not me. Well, you no longer need concern yourself with such things." That was certainly true. Whatever use the Aes Sedai had for her, they would never let her near power or decisions again now. He felt pity for her. He could not imagine this woman giving up and dying, but she had lost about as much as it was possible to lose short of dying. On the other hand, he had not liked being called a buzzard, or a pile of reeking fish guts. What was the other thing? A carp-brained fool. "From now on, you can concern yourself with keeping my boots clean and my bed made."

Her eyes narrowed to slits. "If that is what you want, *Lord* Gareth Bryne, you should choose Leane. *She* might be fool enough."

Only barely did he stop himself from goggling. The way women's minds worked never ceased to amaze him. "You vowed to serve me however I choose." He managed to chuckle. Why was he doing this? He knew who she was, and what she was. But those eyes still haunted him, staring a challenge even when she thought there was no hope, just as they were now. "You will discover the kind of man I am, Siuan." He meant it to soothe her after his jest, but from the way her shoulders stiffened, she seemed to take it as a threat.

Suddenly he realized that he could hear the Aes Sedai, a soft murmur of voices that went silent immediately. They stood together, staring at him with unreadable expressions. No, at Siuan. Their eyes followed her as she started back to where Leane still stood; as if she could feel the pressure of them, each step came a little quicker than the one before. When she turned again, beside the fireplace, her face told no more than theirs. A remarkable woman. He was not sure he could have done as well, in her place.

The Aes Sedai were waiting for him to approach. When he did, Sheriam said, "We accept your conditions without reservation, Lord Bryne, and pledge ourselves to hold to them. They are most reasonable."

Carlinya, at least, did not look as though she thought they were reasonable at all, but he did not care. He had been prepared to give up all but the last, that they stay the course, if need be.

He knelt where he was, right fist pressed to the scrap of carpet, and they encircled him, each laying a hand on his bowed head. He did not care whether they used the Power to bind him to his oath or search for truth—he was not sure they could do either, but who really knew what Aes Sedai could do?—and if they meant something else, there was nothing he could do about it. Trapped by a pair of eyes, like a bullgoose fool country boy. He *was* carp-brained. "I do pledge and vow that I will serve you faithfully until the White Tower is yours . . ."

Already, he was planning. Thad and maybe a Warder or two across the river to see what the Whitecloaks were up to. Joni, Barim and a few others down to Ebou Dar; it would keep Joni from swallowing his tongue every time he looked at "Mara" and "Amaena," and every man he sent would know how to recruit.

". . . building and directing your army to the best of my ability. . . ."

When the low buzz of talk in the common room died, Min looked up from the patterns she had been idly sketching on the table with a finger dipped in wine. Logain stirred, too, for a wonder, but only to stare at the people in the room, or maybe through them; it was hard to tell.

Gareth Bryne and that big Illianer Warder came out of the back room first. In the watchful silence, she heard Bryne say, "Tell them an Ebou Dari tavern maid sent you, or they'll put your head on a stake."

The Illianer roared with laughter. "A dangerous city, Ebou Dar." Pulling leather gauntlets from behind his sword belt, he stalked out into the street drawing them on.

The talk began to pick up again as Siuan appeared. Min could not hear what Bryne said to her, but she strode after the Warder snarling to herself. Min had a sinking feeling that the Aes Sedai had decided that they were going to honor that fool oath Siuan had been so proud of, honor it right now. If she could convince herself that the pair of Warders lounging against the wall would not notice, she would be out of the door and into Wildrose's saddle in a flash.

Sheriam and the other Aes Sedai came out last, with Leane. Myrelle sat Leane down at one of the tables and began discussing something, while the rest circulated through the room, stopping to speak to each Aes Sedai. Whatever they said, it produced reactions from outright shock to pleased grins, despite that fabled Aes Sedai serenity.

"Stay here," Min told Logain, scraping back her rickety chair. She hoped he was not going to start trouble. He was staring at Aes Sedai faces, one by one, and appearing to see more than he had in days. "Just stay at this table till I get back, Dalyn." She was out of the habit of being around people who knew his real name. "Please."

"She sold me to Aes Sedai." It was a shock to hear him

speak after being so long silent. He shivered, then nodded. "I will wait."

Min hesitated, but if two Warders could not stop him from doing anything stupid, a roomful of Aes Sedai certainly could. When she reached the door, a chunky bay gelding was being led away by a man with the look of a groom. Bryne's horse, she supposed. Their own mounts were nowhere in sight. So much for any dash for freedom. *I'll honor the bloody thing! I will! But they can't keep me from Rand now. I've done what Siuan wanted. They have to let me go to him.* The only problem was that Aes Sedai decided for themselves what they had to do, and usually what other people had to do as well.

Siuan nearly knocked her down, bustling back in with a scowl on her face, a blanket roll under her arm and saddlebags over her shoulder. "Watch Logain," she hissed under her breath without slowing. "Let no one talk to him." She marched to the foot of the stairs, where a gray-haired woman, a servant, was starting to lead Bryne up, and fell in behind. From the stare she fixed on the man's back, he should have been praying she did not reach for her belt knife.

Min smiled at the tall, slender Warder who had followed her to the door. He stood ten feet away, barely glancing at her, but she had no illusions. "We're guests now. Friends." He did not return the smile. *Bloody stone-faced men!* Why could they not at least give you a hint what they were thinking?

Logain was still studying the Aes Sedai when she got back to the table. A fine time for Siuan to want him kept silent, just when he was beginning to show life again. She needed to talk to Siuan. "Logain," she said softly, hoping neither of the Warders lounging against the wall could hear. They had hardly seemed to breathe since taking their positions, except when one had followed her. "I don't think you should say anything until Mara tells you what she has planned. Not to anyone."

"Mara?" He gave her a dark sneer. "You mean Siuan Sanche?" So he remembered what he had heard in his daze. "Does anyone here look as if they want to talk to me?" He returned to his frowning study.

No one did look as if they wanted to talk with a gentled false Dragon. Except for the two Warders, no one seemed to be paying them any mind at all. If she had not known better, she would have said the Aes Sedai in the room were excited. They had hardly appeared lethargic before, but they certainly seemed to have more energy now, talking in small groups, issuing brisk orders to Warders. The papers they had been so intent on largely lay abandoned. Sheriam and the others who had taken Siuan away had returned to the room at the back, but Leane had two clerks at her table now, both women writing as fast as they could. And a steady stream of Aes Sedai were coming into the inn, disappearing through that rough plank door and not coming out. Whatever had happened in there, Siuan had surely stirred them up.

Min wished she had Siuan at the table, or better yet somewhere alone, for five minutes. Doubtless at that moment she was beating Bryne over the head with his saddlebags. No, Siuan would not resort to that, for all of her glares. Bryne was not like Logain, larger than life in every dimension, every emotion; Logain had managed to overpower Siuan for a time with sheer hugeness. Bryne was quiet, reserved, not a small man certainly, but hardly overbearing. She would not want the man she remembered from Kore Springs as an enemy, but she did not think that he would hold out long against Siuan. He might think she was going to meekly serve out her time as his servant, but Min had no doubts who would end doing what who wanted. She just had to talk to the woman about him.

As if Min's thoughts had brought her, Siuan came stumping down the stairs, a bundle of white under her arm. Stalked down was nearer truth; if she had had a tail, she would have been lashing it. She paused for one instant, staring at Min and Logain, then marched toward the door that led to the kitchens.

"Stay here," Min cautioned Logain. "And please, say nothing until . . . Siuan can talk to you." She was going to have to get used to calling people by their right names again. He did not even look at her.

She caught up with Siuan in a hallway short of the

kitchen; the rattle and splash of pots being scrubbed and dishes washed drifted through gaps where boards had dried in the kitchen door.

Siuan's eyes widened in alarm. "Why did you leave him? Is he still alive?"

"He'll live forever, for all I can see. Siuan, no one *wants* to talk to him. But I have to talk with you." Siuan stuffed the white bundle into her arms. Shirts. "What is this?"

"Gareth bloody Bryne's bloody laundry," the other woman snarled. "Since you are one of his *serving girls,* too, you can wash them. I must speak with Logain before anyone else."

Min caught her arm as she tried to brush past. "You can spare one minute to listen. When Bryne came in, I had a viewing. An aura, and a bull ripping roses from around its neck, and . . . None of it matters except the aura. I didn't even really understand that, but more than anything else."

"How much did you understand?"

"If you want to stay alive, you had better stay close to him." Despite the heat, Min shivered. She had only ever had one other viewing with an "if" in it, and both had been potentially deadly. It was bad enough sometimes knowing what *would* happen; if she started knowing what *might* . . . "All I know is this. If he stays close to you, you live. If he gets too far away, for too long, you are going to die. Both of you. I don't know why I should have seen anything about you in his aura, but you seemed like part of it."

Siuan's smile would have done to peel a pear. "I'd as soon sail in a rotting hull full of last month's eels."

"I never thought he'd follow us. Are they really going to make us go with him?"

"Oh, no, Min. He is going to lead our armies to victory. And make my life the Pit of Doom! So he's going to save my life, is he? I don't know that it is worth it." Taking a deep breath, she smoothed her skirts. "When you have those washed and ironed, bring them to me. I will take them up to him. You can clean his boots before you go to sleep tonight. We have a room—a cubbyhole

—near him, so we will be close if he calls to have his bloody pillows plumped!" She was gone before Min could protest.

Staring down at the wadded shirts, Min was sure that she knew who was going to be doing all of Gareth Bryne's laundry, and it was not Siuan Sanche. *Rand bloody al'Thor.* Fall in love with a man, and you ended up doing laundry, even if it did belong to another man. When she marched into the kitchen to demand a washtub and hot water, she was snarling every bit as much as Siuan.

CHAPTER

29

Memories of Saldaea

Lying on his bed in the dark, in his shirtsleeves, Kadere idly twirled one of his large kerchiefs between his hands. The wagon's open windows let in moonlight, but not much breeze. At least Cairhien was cooler than the Waste. Someday he hoped to return to Saldaea, to walk in the garden where his sister Teodora had taught him his first letters and numbers. He missed her as much as he did Saldaea, the deep winters when trees burst from their sap freezing and the only way to travel was by snowshoes or skis. In these southlands, spring felt like summer, and summer like the Pit of Doom. Sweat rolled out of him in streams.

With a heavy sigh, he pushed his fingers into a small gap where the bed was built into the wagon. The folded scrap of parchment rustled. He left it there. He knew the words on it by heart.

You are not alone among strangers. A way has been chosen.

Just that, without signature, of course. He had found it slipped under his door when he retired for the night. There was a town not a quarter of a mile away, Eianrod, but even if a soft bed remained empty there, he doubted whether the Aiel would allow him to spend a night away from the wagons. Or that the Aes Sedai would. For the moment, his plans fit in well enough with Moiraine's. Perhaps he would get to see Tar Valon again. A dangerous place, for his sort, but the work there was always important, and invigorating.

He put his mind back on the note, though he wished he could afford to ignore it. The word "chosen" made him sure it came from another Darkfriend. The first surprise had been receiving it now, after crossing most of Cairhien. Nearly two months ago, right after Jasin Natael attached himself to Rand al'Thor—for reasons the man had never deigned to explain—and his new partner Keille Shaogi had disappeared—he suspected she was buried in the Waste, with a thrust from Natael's knife through her heart, and small riddance—soon after that, he had been visited by one of the Chosen. By Lanfear herself. She had given him his instructions.

Automatically his hand went to his chest, feeling through his shirt the scars branded there. He mopped his face with the kerchief. Part of his mind thought coldly, as it had at least once a day since, that they were an effective way to prove to him that it had not been an ordinary dream. An ordinary nightmare. Another part of him almost gibbered with relief that she had not returned.

The second surprise of the note had been the hand. A woman's hand, unless he missed his guess by a mile, and some of the letters formed in what he now knew for an Aiel way. Natael had told him that there must be Darkfriends among the Aiel—there were Darkfriends in every land, among every people—but he had never wanted to find brothers in the Waste. Aiel would kill you as soon as look at you, and you could put a foot wrong with them by breathing.

Taken all in all, the note spelled disaster. Possibly Natael had told some Aiel Darkfriend who he was. Angrily twirling the kerchief to a long thin cord, he snapped it tight between his hands. If the gleeman and Keille had not had proofs that they stood high in Darkfriend councils, he would have killed them both before going near the Waste. The only other possibility made his stomach leaden. "A way has been chosen." Maybe that had only been to put the word "chosen" down, and maybe it was meant to tell him that one of the Chosen had decided to use him. The note had not come from Lanfear; she would simply have spoken to him in his dreams once more.

In spite of the heat, he shivered, yet he had to wipe his face again, too. He had the feeling that Lanfear was a jealous mistress to serve, but if another of the Chosen wanted him he would have no choice. Despite all the promises made when he had given his oaths as a boy, he was a man of few illusions. Caught between two of the Chosen, he could be flattened like a kitten beneath a wagon wheel, and they would notice as much as the wagon did. He wished he were home in Saldaea. He wished he could see Teodora again.

A scraping at the door brought him to his feet; for all his bulk, he was more agile than he let anyone see. Mopping his face and neck, he made his way past the brick stove that he certainly had no need for here, and the cabinets with their ornately carved and painted uprights. When he pulled the door open, a slender figure swathed in black robes scurried in past him. He took one quick look around the moonlit darkness to make certain no one was watching—the drivers were all snoring beneath the other wagons and the Aiel guards never came among the wagons themselves—and quickly shut the door again.

"You must be hot, Isendre," he chuckled. "Take off that robe and make yourself comfortable."

"Thank you, no," she said bitterly from the shadowed depths of her cowl. She stood stiffly, but every now and then she twitched; the wool must be even itchier than usual tonight.

He chuckled again. "As you wish." Beneath those robes, he suspected, the Maidens of the Spear still allowed her to wear nothing but the stolen jewelry, if that. She had become prudish in ways, since the Maidens had her. Why the woman had been stupid enough to steal, he could not understand. He had certainly made no objections when they dragged her screaming from the wagon by her hair; he was only glad that they had not thought he was involved. Her greediness had certainly made his task more difficult. "Have you anything to report on al'Thor or Natael?" A major part of Lanfear's instruction had been to keep a close eye on those two, and he knew no better way to keep an eye on a man than to put a woman in his bed. Any man told his bedmate things he had vowed to keep secret, boasted of his plans, revealed his weaknesses, even if he was the Dragon Reborn and this Dawn fellow the Aiel called him.

She shuddered visibly. "At least I can come near Natael." Come near him? Once the Maidens had caught her sneaking to the man's tent, they had practically begun stuffing her into it every night. She always put the best face on matters. "Not that he tells me anything. Wait. Be patient. Keep silent. Make accommodation with fate, whatever that means. He says that every time I try to ask a question. For the most part, all he wants to do is play music I've never heard before and make love." She never had anything more to say about the gleeman. For the hundredth time he wondered why Lanfear wanted Natael watched. The man was supposed to be as high as a Darkfriend could reach, only a step below the Chosen themselves.

"I take it that means you still have not managed to wriggle into al'Thor's bed?" he asked, brushing past her to sit down on the bed.

"No." She writhed uncomfortably.

"Then you will have to try harder, won't you? I am growing tired of failure, Isendre, and our masters are not as patient as I. He's only a man, whatever his titles." She had often boasted to him that she could have any man she wanted, and make him do whatever she wanted. She had shown him the truth of her boasts. She had not needed to steal jewelry; he would have bought her anything she wanted. He *had* bought her more than he could afford. "The bloody Maidens can't watch him every second, and once you are in his bed, he'll not let them harm you." One taste of her would be enough for that. "I have full faith and confidence in your abilities."

"No." If anything, the word was shorter this time.

He rolled and unrolled the kerchief irritably. " 'No' is not a word our masters like to hear, Isendre." That meant their lords among the Darkfriends; not all lords or ladies by any means—a groom might give orders to a lady, a beggar to a magistrate—but their commands were at least as strictly enforced as any noble's, and usually more so. "Not a word our mistress will like to hear."

Isendre shuddered. She had not believed his tale until he showed her the burns on his chest, but since then, one mention of Lanfear had been enough to quell any rebellion on her part. This time, she began to weep.

"I cannot, Hadnan. When we stopped tonight, I thought I might have a chance in a town instead of tents, but they caught me before I got within ten paces of him." She pushed back her hood, and he gaped as moonlight played over her bare scalp. Even her eyebrows were gone. "They shaved me, Hadnan. Adelin and Enaila and Jolien, they held me down and shaved every hair. They beat me with with nettles, Hadnan." She shook like a sapling in high wind, sobbing slack-mouthed and mumbling the words. "I itch from shoulders to knees, and I burn too much to scratch. They said they'd make me *wear* nettles, the next time I so much as looked in his direction. They meant it, Hadnan. They did! They said they'd give me to Aviendha, and they told me what she would do. I cannot, Hadnan. Not again. I cannot."

Stunned, he stared at her. She had had such lovely dark hair. Yet she was beautiful enough that even being bald as an egg only made her seem exotic. Her tears and sagging face detracted only a little. If she could put herself into al'Thor's bed for just one night . . . It was not going to happen. The Maidens had broken her. He had broken people himself, and he knew the signs. Eagerness to avoid more punishment became eagerness to obey. The mind never wanted to admit it was running from something, so she would soon convince herself that she really wanted to obey, that she really wanted nothing more than to please the Maidens.

"What does Aviendha have to do with it?" he muttered. How soon before Isendre felt the need to confess her sins, as well?

"Al'Thor has been bedding her since Rhuidean, you fool! She spends every night with him. The Maidens think she will marry him." Even through her sobs he could detect resentful fury. She would not like it that another had succeeded where she failed. Doubtless that was why she had not told him before.

Aviendha was a beautiful woman despite her fierce eyes, full-breasted compared to most of the Maidens, yet he would stack Isendre against her if only . . . Isendre slumped in the moonlight coming through the windows, quivering from head to toe, sobbing openmouthed, tears rolling down her cheeks that she did not even bother to wipe away. She would grovel on the ground if Aviendha frowned at her.

"Very well," he said gently. "If you cannot, then you cannot. You can still pry something out of Natael. I know you can." Rising, he took her shoulders to turn her toward the door.

She flinched away from his touch, but she did turn. "Natael will not want to look at me for days," she said petulantly around hiccoughs and sniffs. Sobs threatened to break out again any moment, but his tone seemed to have soothed her. "I'm red, Hadnan. As red as if I had laid naked in the sun for a day. And my hair. It will take forever to grow ba—"

As she reached for the door, her eyes going to the handle, he had the kerchief spun to a cord in an instant and around her neck. He tried to ignore her rasping gurgles, the frantic scraping of her feet on the floor. Her fingers clawed at his hands, but he stared straight ahead. Even keeping his eyes open, he saw Teodora; he always did, when he killed a woman. He had loved his sister, but she had discovered what he was, and she would not have kept silent. Isendre's heels drummed violently, but after what seemed an eternity they slowed, went still, and she became a dead weight dragging at his hands. He held the cord tight for a count of sixty before unwinding it and letting her fall. She would have been confessing, next. Confessing to being a Darkfriend. Pointing a finger at him.

Rummaging in the cabinets by touch, he pulled out a butchering knife. Disposing of a whole corpse would be difficult, but luckily the dead did not bleed much; the robe would absorb what little there was. Maybe he could find the woman who had left the note under his door. If she was not pretty enough, she must have friends who were also Darkfriends. Natael would not care if it was an Aiel woman who visited him—Kadere would rather have bedded a viper himself; Aiel were dangerous—and maybe an Aiel would have a better chance than Isendre against Aviendha. Kneeling, he hummed quietly to himself as he worked, a lullaby that Teodora had taught him.

CHAPTER
30

A Wager

A soft night breeze stirred across the small town of Eianrod, then faded. Sitting on the stone rail of the wide flat bridge in the heart of the town, Rand supposed the breeze was hot, yet it hardly felt so after the Waste. Warm for nighttime perhaps, but not enough to make him unbutton his red coat. The river below him had never been large, and was half its normal width now, yet he still enjoyed watching the water flow north, moonshadows cast by scudding clouds playing across the darkly glittering surface. That was why he was out here in the night, really; to look at running water for a time. His wards were set, surrounding the Aiel encampment that itself surrounded the town. The Aiel themselves kept a watch a sparrow could not pierce unseen. He could waste an hour being soothed by the flow of a river.

It was surely better than another night where he had to order Moiraine to leave so he could study with Asmodean. She had even taken to bringing his meals to him and talking while he ate, as if she meant to cram everything she knew into his head before they reached the city of Cairhien. He could not face her begging to remain—actually begging!—as she had the previous night. For a woman like Moiraine, that behavior was so unnatural that he had wanted to agree simply to stop it. Which was very likely why she had done it. Much better an hour listening to the quiet liquid ripplings of the river. With luck, she would have given up on him for tonight.

The eight or ten paces of clay between water and weeds on both sides below him was dried and cracked. He peered up at the clouds crossing the moon. He could try to make those clouds give rain. The town's two fountains were both dry, and dust lay in a third of the wells not fouled beyond cleaning. Try was the word, though. He had made it rain once; remembering how was the trick. If he managed that, then he could try not to make it a drowning deluge and a tree-snapping windstorm this time.

Asmodean would be no help; he did not know much about weather, it seemed. For every thing the man taught him, there were two more that made Asmodean either throw up his hands or give a lick and a promise. Once he had thought that the Forsaken knew everything, that they were all but omnipotent. But if the others were like Asmodean, they had ignorances as well as weaknesses. It might actually be that he already knew more of some things than they. Than some of them, at least. The problem would be finding out who. Semirhage was almost as poor at handling weather as Asmodean.

He shivered as if this were night in the Three-fold Land. Asmodean had never told him that. Better to listen to the water and not think, if he meant to sleep at all tonight.

Sulin approached him, the *shoufa* around her shoulders so it uncovered her short white hair, and leaned on the railing. The wiry Maiden was armed for battle, bow and arrows, spears and knife and buckler. She had taken command of his bodyguard tonight. Two dozen more *Far Dareis Mai* squatted easily on the bridge ten paces away. "An odd night," she said. "We were gambling, but suddenly everyone was throwing nothing but sixes."

"I am sorry," he told her without thinking, and she gave him a peculiar look. She did not know, of course; he had not spread it about. The ripples he gave off as *ta'veren* spread out in odd, random ways. Even the Aiel would not want to be within ten miles of him, if they knew.

The ground had given way beneath three Stone Dogs today, dropping them into a viper pit, but none of the dozens of bites had found anything but cloth. He knew that had been him, bending chance. Tal Nethin, the saddlemaker, had survived Taien to trip on a stone this very noon and break his neck falling on flat, grassy ground. Rand was afraid that had been him, too. On the other hand, Bael and Jheran had mended the blood feud between Shaarad and Goshien while he was with them, eating a midday meal of dried meat on the move. They still did not like each other, and hardly seemed to understand what they had done, but it *was* done, with pledges and water oaths given, each man holding the cup for the other to drink. To Aiel, water oaths were stronger than any other; it might be generations before Shaarad and Goshien so much as raided each other for sheep or goats or cattle.

He had wondered if those random effects would ever work in his favor; maybe this was as close as it came. What else had happened today that might be laid at his feet, he did not know; he never asked, and would as soon not hear. The Baels and Jherans could only partly make up for the Tal Nethins.

"I've not seen Enaila or Adelin for days," he said. It was as good a change of subject as any. That pair in particular had seemed to be jealous of their places guarding him. "Are they ill?"

If anything, the look Sulin gave him was even more peculiar. "They will return when they learn to stop playing with dolls, Rand al'Thor."

He opened his mouth, then closed it again. Aiel were strange—Aviendha's lessons often made them more so, not less—but this was ridiculous. "Well, tell them they are grown women and they ought to act it."

Even by moonlight he could tell that her smile was pleased. "It shall be as the *Car'a'carn* wishes." What did that mean? She eyed him a moment, lips pursed thoughtfully. "You have not eaten yet tonight. There is still enough food for everyone, and you will not fill one belly by going hungry yourself. If you do not eat, people will worry that *you* are ill. You will become ill."

He laughed softly, a hoarse wheeze. The *Car'a'carn* one minute, and the next . . . If he did not fetch something to eat, Sulin would probably go get it for him. And try to feed him to boot. "I will eat. Moiraine must be in her blankets by now." This time her odd look was satisfying; for a change he had said something that she did not understand.

As he swung his feet down, he heard the ring of horses' hooves walking down the stone-paved street toward the bridge. Every Maiden was upright in an instant, face veiled; half nocked arrows. His hand went to his waist by instinct, but the sword was not there. The Aiel felt strange enough about him riding a horse and carrying the thing at his saddle; he had not seen any need to offend their customs more by wearing it. Besides, there were not many horses, and they were coming at a walk.

When they appeared, surrounded by an escort of fifty Aiel, the riders numbered fewer than twenty, slumping in their saddles dejectedly. Most wore rimmed helmets and Tairen coats with puffy, striped sleeves beneath their breastplates. The pair in the lead had ornately gilded cuirasses, and large white plumes attached to the front of their helmets, and the stripes on their sleeves had the glisten of satin in the moonlight. Half a dozen men at the rear, though, shorter and slighter than the Tairens, two with small banners called *con* on short staffs harnessed to their backs, wore dark coats and helmets shaped like bells cut away to expose their faces. Cairhienin used the banners to pick out officers in battle, and also to mark a lord's personal retainers.

The Tairens with plumes stared when they saw him, exchanged startled glances, then scrambled down to come kneel before him, helmets under their arms. They were young, little older than he, both with dark beards trimmed to neat points in the fashion of Tairen nobility. Dents marred their breastplates, and the gilding was chipped; they had been crossing swords somewhere.

Neither as much as glanced at the Aiel surrounding them, as if when ignored they would disappear. The Maidens unveiled, though they looked no less ready to put spear or arrow through the kneeling men.

Rhuarc followed the Tairens, with a gray-eyed Aiel younger and slightly taller than he, and stood behind. Mangin was of the Jindo Taardad, and one of those who had gone to the Stone of Tear. Jindo had brought in the riders.

"My Lord Dragon," the plump, pink-cheeked lordling said, "burn my soul, but have they taken *you* prisoner?" His companion, jug ears and potato nose making him look a farmer despite his beard, kept sweeping lanky hair from his forehead nervously. "They said they were taking us to some Dawn fellow. The *Car'a'carn*. Means something about chiefs, if I remember what my tutor said. Forgive me, my Lord Dragon. I am Edorion of House Selorna, and this is Estean of House Andiama."

"I am He Who Comes With the Dawn," Rand told them quietly. "And the *Car'a'carn*." He had them placed now: young lords who had spent their time drinking, gambling and chasing women when he was in the Stone. Estean's eyes nearly popped out of his face; Edorion looked as surprised for a moment, then nodded slowly, as if he suddenly saw how it made sense. "Stand. Who are your Cairhienin companions?" It would be interesting to meet Cairhienin who were not running for their lives from the Shaido, and any other Aiel they saw. For that matter, if they were with Edorion and Estean, they might be the first supporters he had met in this land. If the two Tairens' fathers had followed his orders. "Bring them forward."

Estean blinked in surprise as he rose, but Edorion barely paused in turning to shout, "Meresin! Daricain! Come here!" Much like calling dogs. The Cairhienins' banners bobbed as they dismounted slowly.

"My Lord Dragon." Estean hesitated, licking his lips as though thirsty. "Did you . . . Did you send the Aiel against Cairhien?"

"They've attacked the city, then?"

Rhuarc nodded, and Mangin said, "If these are to be

believed, Cairhien still holds. Or did three days ago." There was little doubt that he did not think it still did, and less that he cared about a city of treekillers.

"I did not send them, Estean," Rand said as they were joined by the two Cairhienin, who knelt, doffing their helmets to reveal men of an age with Edorion and Estean, their hair shaved back in line with their ears and their dark eyes wary. "Those who attack the city are my enemies, the Shaido. I mean to save Cairhien if it can be saved."

He had to go through the business of telling the Cairhienin to rise; his time with the Aiel had almost made him forget the habit this side of the Spine of the World, bowing and kneeling right and left. He had to ask for introductions, too, and the Cairhienin gave them themselves. Lieutenant Lord Meresin of House Daganred—his *con* was all wavy vertical lines of red and white—and Lieutenant Lord Daricain of House Annallin, his *con* covered with small squares of red and black. It was a surprise that they were lords. Though lords commanded and led soldiers in Cairhien, they did not shave their heads and become soldiers. Or had not; much had changed, apparently.

"My Lord Dragon." Meresin stumbled a bit saying that. He and Daricain were both pale, slender men, with narrow faces and long noses, but he was a bit the heavier. Neither looked as if he had had much to eat lately. Meresin rushed on as if afraid of being interrupted. "My Lord Dragon, Cairhien can hold. For days yet, perhaps as many as ten or twelve, but you must come quickly if you are to save it."

"That is why we came out," Estean said, shooting Meresin a dark look. Both Cairhienin returned it, but their defiance was tinged with resignation. Estean raked stringy hair from his forehead. "To find help. Parties have been sent in every direction, my Lord Dragon." He shivered despite the sweat on his brow, and his voice turned distant and hollow. "There were more of us when we started. I saw Baran go down, screaming with a spear through his guts. He'll never turn a card at chop again. I could use a mug of strong brandy."

Edorion turned his helmet in gauntleted hands, frowning. "My Lord Dragon, the city can hold a while longer, but even if these Aiel will fight those, the question is, can you bring them there in time? I think ten or twelve days is a more than generous estimate, myself. In truth, I only came because I thought dying with a spear through me would be better than being taken alive when they made it over the walls. The city is packed with refugees who fled ahead of the Aiel; there isn't a dog or a pigeon left in the city, and I doubt there will be a rat left soon. The one good thing is that no one seems to be worrying very much about who will take the Sun Throne, not with this Couladin outside."

"He called on us to surrender to He Who Comes With the Dawn, on the second day," Daricain put in, earning a sharp look from Edorion for the interruption.

"Couladin has some sport with prisoners," Estean said. "Out of bowshot, but where anyone on the walls can see. You can hear them screaming, too. The Light burn my soul, I don't know whether he is trying to break our will or simply likes it. Sometimes they let peasants make a run for the city, then shoot them full of arrows when they're almost safe. However safe Cairhien is. Only peasants, but . . ." He trailed off and swallowed hard, as if he had just remembered what Rand's opinions were of "only peasants." Rand just looked at him, but he seemed to shrivel, and muttered under his breath about brandy.

Edorion leaped into the momentary silence. "My Lord Dragon, the point is that the city can hold until you come, if you can come quickly. We only beat back the first assault because the Foregate caught fire. . . ."

"Flames nearly took the city," Estean interjected. The Foregate, a city in itself outside the walls of Cairhien, had been mostly wood, as Rand remembered. "Would have been disaster if the river was not right there."

The other Tairen went on right over him. ". . . but Lord Meilan has the defense well planned, and the Cairhienin appear to be keeping their backbones for the time." That earned him frowns from Meresin and Daricain that he either did not see or pretended not to. "Seven days with luck, perhaps eight at most. If you can . . ." A heavy sigh abruptly seemed to deflate Edorion's plumpness. "I did not see one horse," he said as if to himself. "The Aiel do not ride. You will never be able to move men afoot so far in time."

"How long?" Rand asked Rhuarc.

"Seven days" was the reply. Mangin nodded, and Estean laughed.

"Burn my soul, it took us as long to reach here on horses. If you think you can make the return in the same afoot, you must be . . ." Becoming aware of the Aiel eyes on him, Estean scrubbed the hair from his face. "Is there any brandy in this town?" he muttered.

"It isn't how fast we can make it," Rand said quietly, "but how fast you can, if you dismount some of your men and use their horses for spares. I want to let Meilan and Cairhien know that help is on the way. But whoever goes will have to be sure he can keep his mouth shut if the Shaido take him. I do not intend to let Couladin know any more than he can learn on his own." Estean went whiter in the face than the Cairhienin.

Meresin and Daricain were on their knees together, each seizing one of Rand's hands to kiss. He let them, with as much patience as he could find; one bit of Moiraine's advice that had the ring of common sense was not to offend people's customs, however strange or even repulsive, unless you absolutely had to, and even then think twice.

"We will go, my Lord Dragon," Meresin said breathlessly. "Thank you, my Lord Dragon. Thank you. Under the Light, I vow I will die before revealing a word to any but my father or the High Lord Meilan."

"Grace favor you, my Lord Dragon," the other added. "Grace favor you, and the Light illumine you forever. I am your man to the death." Rand let Meresin say that he also was Rand's man before taking his hands back firmly and telling them to stand. He did not like the way they were looking at him. Edorion had called them like hounds, but men should not look at anyone as if they were dogs gazing at a master.

Edorion drew a deep breath, puffing his pink cheeks, and let it out slowly. "I suppose if I made it out in one piece, I can make it back in. My Lord Dragon, forgive me if I offend, but would you care to wager, say, a thousand gold crowns, that you can really come in seven days?"

Rand stared at him. The man was as bad as Mat. "I don't have a hundred crowns silver, much less a thousand in—"

Sulin broke in. "He has it, Tairen," she said firmly. "He will meet your wager, if you make it ten thousand by weight."

Edorion laughed. "Done, Aiel. And worth every copper if I lose. Come to think, I'll not live to collect if I win. Come, Meresin, Daricain." It sounded as if he were summoning dogs to heel. "We ride."

Rand waited until the three had made their bows and were halfway back to the horses before rounding on the white-haired Maiden. "What do you mean, I have a thousand gold crowns? I've never *seen* a thousand crowns, much less ten thousand."

The Maidens exchanged glances as if he were demented; so did Rhuarc and Mangin. "A fifth of the treasure that was in the Stone of Tear belongs to those who took the Stone, and will be claimed when they can carry it away." Sulin spoke as to a child, instructing it in the simple facts of everyday life. "As chief and battle leader there, one tenth of that fifth is yours. Tear submitted to you as chief by right of triumph, so one tenth of Tear is yours as well. And you have said we can take the fifth in these lands—a . . . tax, you called it." She fumbled the word; the Aiel did not have taxes. "The tenth part of that is yours also, as *Car'a'carn*."

Rand shook his head. In all of his talks with Aviendha, he had never thought to ask whether the fifth applied to him; he was not Aiel, *Car'a'carn* or no, and it had not seemed anything to do with him. Well, it might not be a tax, but he could use it as kings did taxes. Unfortunately, he had only the vaguest idea how that was. He would have to ask Moiraine; that was one thing she had missed in her lectures. Perhaps she thought it so obvious that he should know.

Elayne would have known what taxes were used for; it had certainly been more fun taking advice from her than from Moiraine. He wished he knew where she was. Still in Tanchico, probably; Egwene told him little more than a constant string of well-wishings. He wished he could sit Elayne down and make her explain those two letters. Maiden of the Spear or Daughter-Heir of Andor, women were strange. Except maybe Min. She had laughed at him, but she had never made him think she was speaking some strange language. She would not laugh, now. If he ever saw her again, she would run a hundred miles to get away from the Dragon Reborn.

Edorion dismounted all his men, taking one of their horses and stringing the others together by their reins, along with Estean's. No doubt he was saving his own for the final sprint through the Shaido. Merisin and Daricain did the same with their men. Though it meant that the Cairhienin had only two spare mounts apiece, no one seemed to think they should have any of the Tairen horses. They clattered off together westward at a trot, with a Jindo escort.

Carefully not looking at anyone, Estean started to drift toward the soldiers standing uneasily in a circle of Aiel at the foot of the bridge. Mangin caught his red-striped sleeve. "You can tell us conditions inside Cairhien, wetlander." The lumpy-faced man looked ready to faint.

"I am certain he will answer any questions you ask," Rand said sharply, emphasizing the final word.

"They will only be asked," Rhuarc said, taking the Tairen's other arm. He and Mangin seemed to be holding the much shorter man up between them. "Warning the city's defenders is well and good, Rand al'Thor," Rhuarc went on, "but we should send scouts. Running, they can reach Cairhien as soon as those men on horses, and meet us coming back with word of how Couladin has disposed the Shaido."

Rand could feel the Maiden's eyes on him, but he looked straight at Rhuarc. "Thunder Walkers?" he suggested.

"*Sha'mad Conde,*" Rhuarc agreed. He and Mangin turned Estean—they *were* holding him up—and started toward the other soldiers.

"Ask!" Rand called after them. "He is your ally, and

my liege man." He had no idea whether Estean was that last or not—it was another thing to ask Moiraine—or even how much of an ally he really was—his father, the High Lord Torean, had plotted against Rand enough—but he would allow nothing close to Couladin's ways.

Rhuarc turned his head and nodded.

"You tend your people well, Rand al'Thor." Sulin's voice was flat as a planed plank.

"I try," he told her. He was not about to rise to the bait. Whoever went to scout the Shaido, some would not return, and that was that. "I think I will have something to eat now. And get some sleep." It could not be much more than two hours to midnight, and sunrise still came early this time of year. The Maidens followed him, watching the shadows warily as if they expected attack, handtalk flickering among them. But then, Aiel always seemed to expect attack.

CHAPTER

31

The Far Snows

The streets of Eianrod ran straight and met at right angles, where necessary slicing through hills that were otherwise neatly terraced with stone. The slate-roofed stone buildings had an angular look, as if they were all vertical lines. Eianrod had not fallen to Couladin; no people had been there when the Shaido swept through. A good many of the houses were only charred beams and hollow ruined shells, however, including most of the wide three-story marble buildings with balconies that Moiraine said had belonged to merchants. Broken furniture and clothes littered the streets, along with shattered dishes and shards of glass from windows, single boots and tools and toys.

The burning had come at different times—Rand could tell that much himself, from the weathering of blackened timbers and how much smell of char lingered where—but Lan had been able to chart the flow of battles by which the town had been taken and retaken. By different Houses contending for the Sun Throne, most likely, though from the look of the streets, the last to hold Eianrod had been brigands. A good many of the bands roaming Cairhien held allegiance to no one, and to nothing except gold.

It was to one of the merchants' houses that Rand went, on the largest of the town's two squares, three square stories of gray marble with heavy balconies and wide steps with thick angular stone siderails overlooking a silent fountain with a dusty round basin. A chance to sleep in a bed again had been too good to pass up, and he had hopes that Aviendha would choose to remain in a tent; whether his or with the Wise Ones, he did not care, so long as he did not have to try going to sleep while listening to her breathe a few paces away. Recently he had begun imagining he could hear her heart beat even when he had not taken hold of *saidin.* But if she did not stay away, he had taken precautions.

The Maidens stopped at the steps, some trotting around the building to take positions on all sides. He had feared that they would try declaring this a Roof of the Maidens, even for the one night, and so as soon as he had chosen the building, one of the few in town with a sound roof and most of the windows unbroken, he had told Sulin that he was declaring it the Roof of the Winespring Brothers. No one could enter who had not drunk from the Winespring, in Emond's Field. From the look she had given him, she knew very well what he was up to, but none of them followed him beyond the wide doors that seemed to be all narrow vertical panels.

Inside, the large rooms were bare, though white-robed *gai'shain* had spread a few blankets for themselves in the broad entry hall, its high plaster ceiling worked in a pattern of severe squares. Keeping *gai'shain* out was beyond him even had he wanted to, as much so as keeping Moiraine out if she was not asleep elsewhere. Whatever orders he gave about not being disturbed, she always found a way to make the Maidens let her by, and it always took a direct command for her to go before she would leave.

The *gai'shain* rose smoothly, men and women, before he had the door closed. They would not sleep until he did, and some would take turns remaining awake in case he wanted something in the night. He had tried ordering them not to, but telling a *gai'shain* not to serve according to custom was like kicking a bale of wool; whatever impression you made was gone as soon as your toes were. He waved them away and climbed the marble stairs. Some of those *gai'shain* had salvaged a few bits of furniture, including a bed and two feather mattresses, and he was looking forward to washing and—

He froze as soon as he opened the door to his bedchamber. Aviendha had not chosen to remain with the tents. She stood before the washstand, with its mismatched, cracked bowl and pitcher, a cloth in one hand and a bar of yellow soap in the other. She had no clothes on. She seemed as stunned as he, as incapable of moving.

"I . . ." She stopped to swallow, big green eyes locked on his face. "I could not make a sweat tent here in this . . . town, so I thought I would try your way of . . ." She was hard muscle and soft curves; she glistened damply from head to feet. He had never imagined that her legs were so long. "I thought you would remain longer at the bridge. I . . ." Her voice rose in pitch; her eyes widened in panic. "I did not arrange for you to see me! I must get away from you. As far away as I can! I must!"

Suddenly a shimmering vertical line appeared in the air near her. It widened, as if rotating, into a gateway. Icy wind rushed through it into the room, carrying thick curtains of snow.

"I must get away!" she wailed, and darted through into the blizzard.

Immediately the gateway began to narrow again, turning, but without thought Rand channeled, blocking it at half its former width. He did not know what he had done or how, but he was sure this was a gateway for Traveling, such as Asmodean had told him of and been unable to teach him. There was no time for thinking. Wherever Aviendha had gone, she had gone naked into the heart of a winter storm. Rand tied off the flows he had woven as he ripped all the blankets from the bed and tossed them onto her clothes and pallet. Seizing blankets, clothes and rugs all together, he plunged through only moments behind her.

Icy wind screamed through night air filled with swirling white. Even wrapped in the Void, he could feel his body shivering. Dimly he could make out scattered shapes in the darkness; trees, he thought. There was nothing for him to smell but cold. Ahead of him, a form moved, obscured by darkness and the snowstorm; he might have missed it but for the sharpness of his eyes in the Void. Aviendha, running as hard as she could. He lumbered after her through snow to his knees, clutching the thick bundle to his chest.

"Aviendha! Stop!" He was afraid that the howling wind would sweep his shout away, but she heard. And if anything, ran faster. He forced himself to more speed, staggering and tripping as the deepening snow tugged at his boots. The prints left by her bare feet were filling fast. If he lost sight of her in this. . . . "Stop, you fool woman! Are you trying to kill yourself?" The sound of his voice seemed to flog her to run harder.

Grimly, he pushed himself, half-falling and scrambling back up, knocked down by the hurtling wind as often as stumbling in the snow, blundering into trees. He had to keep his eyes on her. He was only thankful this forest, or whatever it was, had trees so far apart.

Plans skittered across the Void and were discarded. He could try quelling the storm—and maybe the result would turn the air to ice. A shelter of Air to keep the falling snow away would do nothing for that underfoot. He could melt a path for himself with Fire—and slog through mud instead. Unless . . .

He channeled, and the snow ahead of him melted in a band a span wide, a band that ran ahead of him as he did. Steam rose, and falling snow vanished a foot above the sandy soil. He could feel the heat of it through his boots. Down almost to his ankles, his body shook with the bone-chilling cold; his feet sweated and flinched away from the heated ground. But he was catching up now. Another five minutes and . . .

Suddenly the vague shape he had been following vanished as if she had fallen into a hole.

Keeping his eyes fixed on the spot where he had last seen her, he ran as hard as he could. Abruptly he was splashing in icy flowing water to his ankles, halfway to his knees. Ahead of him, the melting snow revealed more, and an edge of ice inching slowly back. No steam rose from the black water. Stream or river, it was too big for the amount of his channeling to warm the swift-moving flow even a hair. She must have run out onto the ice and fallen through, but he would not save her by trying to wade into this. Filled with *saidin,* he was barely aware of the cold, but his teeth chattered uncontrollably.

Retreating to the bank, gaze locked on where he thought Aviendha had gone down, he channeled flows of Fire into ground still bare, well back from the stream, until the sand melted and fused and glowed white. Even in this storm, that would stay hot for a time. He set the bundle down in the snow beside it—her life would depend on finding the blankets and rugs again—then waded through the deep white to one side of the melted path and lay flat. Slowly he crawled out onto the snow-covered ice.

The wind shrieked across him. His coat might as well not have existed. His hands were numb now, and his feet going; he had stopped shivering except for an occasional shudder. Coldly calm inside the Void, he knew what was happening; there were blizzards in the Two Rivers, perhaps even as bad as this. His body was being overwhelmed. If he did not find warmth soon, he would be able to calmly watch from the Void as he died. But if he died, Aviendha would too. If she had not already.

He felt rather than heard the ice cracking beneath his weight. His probing hands fell into water. This was the place, but with snow whirling about, he could barely see. He flailed, searching, numb hands splashing. One hit something at the edge of the ice, and he commanded his fingers to close, felt frozen hair crackling.

Got to pull her out. He crawled backward, hauling at her. She was a dead weight, sliding slowly out of the water. *Don't care if the ice scrapes her. Better that than freezing or drowning.* Back. *Keep moving. If you quit, she dies. Keep moving, burn you!* Crawling. Pulling with his legs, pushing with one hand. The other locked in Aviendha's hair; no time to get a better grip; she could not feel it anyway. *You've had it easy for too long. Lords kneeling, and* gai'shain *running to fetch your wine, and Moiraine doing as she's told.* Back. *Time to do something yourself, if you still can. Move, you flaming fatherless son of a spavined goat! Keep moving!*

Suddenly his feet hurt; the pain began creeping up his legs. It took him a moment to look back, and then he rolled off the steaming patch of melted sand. Tendrils of smoke, where his breeches had begun smoldering, were whisked away by the wind.

Fumbling for the bundle he had left, he swathed Aviendha from head to foot in all of it, the blankets, the rugs of her pallet, her clothes. Every bit of protection was vital. Her eyes were closed, and she did not move. He parted the blankets enough to put an ear to her chest. Her heart beat so slowly that he was not sure he was really hearing it. Even four blankets and half a dozen rugs were not enough, and he could not channel heat into her as he had the ground; even fining the flow as much as possible, he was more likely to kill than warm. He could feel the weave he had used to block open her gateway, a mile or perhaps two away through the storm. If he tried to carry her that far, neither of them would survive. They needed shelter, and they needed it here.

He channeled flows of Air, and snow began to move across the ground against the wind, building into thick square walls three paces on a side with one gap for a door, building higher, compacting the snow till it glistened like ice, roofing it over high enough to stand. Scooping Aviendha into his arms, he stumbled into the dark interior, weaving and tying flames dancing in the corners for light, channeling to scoop more snow to close the doorway.

Just with the wind shut away it felt warmer, but that would not be enough. Using the trick Asmodean had shown him, he wove Air and Fire, and the air around them grew warmer. He did not dare tie that weave off; if he feel asleep, it could grow and melt the hut. For that matter, the flames were almost as dangerous to leave, but he was too bone-weary and chilled to maintain more than one weave.

The ground inside had been cleared as he built, bare

sandy soil with only a few brown leaves he did not recognize and some scruffy low dead weeds that were equally strange to him. Releasing the weave that warmed the air, he heated the ground enough to take away the iciness, then took up the other weave again. It was all he could do to lay Aviendha down gently rather than drop her.

He pushed a hand inside the blankets to feel her cheek, her shoulder. Trickles of water ran across her face as her hair melted. He was cold, but she was ice. She needed every scrap of warmth he could find for her, and he did not dare warm the air more. Already the insides of the walls shone with a faint layer of melt. However frozen he felt, he had more heat in him than she did.

Stripping off his clothes, he climbed into the coverings with her, arranging his own damp garments on the outside; they could help hold in the body heat. His sense of touch, enhanced by the Void and *saidin,* soaked in the feel of her. Her skin made silk feel rough. Compared to her skin, satin was . . . *Don't think.* He smoothed damp hair away from her face. He should have dried it, but the water no longer felt so cold, and there was nothing but the blankets or their clothes to use anyway. Her eyes were closed; her chest stirred against him slowly. Her head lay on his arm, snuggled against his chest. If she had not felt like winter itself, she could have been sleeping. So peaceful; not angry at all. So beautiful. *Stop thinking.* It was a sharp command outside the emptiness surrounding him. *Talk.*

He tried talking of the first thing that came to mind, Elayne and the confusion her two letters brought, but that soon had thoughts of golden-haired Elayne drifting across the Void, of kissing her in secluded spots in the Stone. *Don't think of kissing, fool!* He shifted to Min. He had never thought about Min that way. Well, a few dreams could not count. Min would have slapped his face if he had ever tried to kiss her, or else laughed and called him a woolhead. Only it seemed that speaking of any woman reminded him that he had his arms around a woman who had no clothes on. Filled with the Power, he could smell the scent of her, feel every inch of her as clearly as if he were running his hands . . . The Void trembled. *Light, you're only trying to warm her! Keep your mind out of the pigsty, man!*

Trying to drive thought away, he talked of his hopes for Cairhien, to bring peace and an end to the famine, to bring the nations behind him without any more bloodshed. But that had its own life, too, its own inevitable path, to Shayol Ghul, where he must face the Dark One and die, if the Prophecies were true. It seemed cowardly to say that he hoped he might live through that somehow. Aiel did not know cowardice; the worst of them was brave as a lion. "The Breaking of the World killed the weak," he had heard Bael say, "and the Three-fold Land killed the cowards."

He began speaking of where they might be, where she had brought them with her wild senseless flight. Somewhere far and strange, to have snow at this time of year. It had been worse than a senseless flight. Mad. Yet he knew that she had fled from him. *Fled* from him. How she must hate him, if she had to flee as far as she could rather than just tell him to leave her to her bath in privacy.

"I should have knocked." At his own bedroom door? "I know you do not want to be around me. You don't have to be. Whatever the Wise Ones want, whatever they say, you are going back to their tents. You will not have to come near me again. In fact, if you do, I . . . I'll send you away." Why hesitate on that? She gave him anger, coldness, bitterness when she was awake, and asleep. . . . "It *was* a crazy thing to do. You could have killed yourself." He was stroking her hair again; he could not seem to stop. "If you ever do anything half so crazy again, I'll break your neck. Do you have any idea how I will miss hearing you breathe at night?" Miss it? She drove him crazy with it! He was the one who was mad. He had to stop this. "You are going away, and that's that, if I have to send you back to Rhuidean. The Wise Ones can't stop me if I speak as *Car'a'carn*. You won't have to run away from me again."

The hand that he could not stop from stroking her hair froze as she stirred. She was warm, he realized. Very warm. He should be wrapping one of the blankets about himself decently and moving away. Her eyes opened, clear and deep green, staring at him seriously from not a foot away. She did not seem surprised to see him, and she did not pull back.

He took his arms from around her, started to slither away, and she seized a handful of his hair in a painful grip. If he moved, he would have a bald patch. She gave him no chance to explain anything. "I promised my near-sister to watch you." She seemed to be speaking to herself as much as to him, in a low, almost expressionless voice. "I ran from you as hard as I could, to shield my honor. And you followed me even here. The rings do not lie, and I can run no more." Her tone firmed decisively. "I will run no more."

Rand tried to ask her what she meant while attempting to untangle her fingers from his hair, but she clutched another handful on the other side and pulled his mouth to hers. That was the end of rational thought; the Void shattered, and *saidin* fled. He did not think he could have stopped himself had he wanted to, only he could not think of wanting to, and she certainly did not seem to want him to. In fact, the last thought he had of any coherency for a very long time was that he did not think he could have stopped *her*.

Some considerable time later—two hours, maybe three; he could hardly be sure—he lay atop the rugs with the blankets over him and his hands behind his head, watching Aviendha examine the slick white walls. They had held a surprising amount of the warmth; there was no need to latch on to *saidin* again, either to shut out cold or to try warming the air. She had done no more than rake her fingers through her hair on rising, and she moved completely unashamed at her nakedness. Of course, it was a bit late to be ashamed of something as small as having no clothes on. He had been worried about hurting her when dragging her out of the water, but she showed fewer scrapes than he did, and somehow they did not seem to mar her beauty at all.

"What is this?" she asked.

"Snow." He explained what snow was as best he could,

but she only shook her head, partly in wonderment, partly disbelief. For someone who had grown up in the Waste, frozen water falling from the sky must seem as impossible as flying. According to the records, the only time it had ever even rained in the Waste was the time he had made it.

He could not stop a sigh of regret when she began pulling her shift over her head. "The Wise Ones can marry us as soon as we get back." He could still feel his weave holding her gateway open.

Aviendha's dark reddish head popped through the neck of the shift, and she stared at him flatly. Not unfriendly, but not friendly, either. Determined, though. "What makes you think a man has the right to ask me that? Besides, you belong to Elayne."

After a moment he managed to close his mouth. "Aviendha, we just . . . The two of us . . . Light, we *have* to marry now. Not that I'm doing it because I have to," he added hastily. "I want to." He was not sure of that at all, really. He thought he might love her, but he thought he might love Elayne, too. And for some reason, Min kept creeping in. *You're as big a lecher as Mat.* But for once he could do what was right because it was right.

She sniffed at him and felt her stockings to be sure they were dry, then sat down to don them. "Egwene has spoken to me of your Two Rivers marriage customs."

"You want to wait a year?" he asked incredulously.

"The year. Yes, that is what I meant." He had never realized before how much leg a woman showed pulling on a stocking; odd that that could seem so thrilling after he had seen her naked and sweating and . . . He concentrated on listening to her. "Egwene said she thought of asking her mother's permission for you, but before she mentioned it her mother told her she had to wait another year even if she did have her hair in a braid." Aviendha frowned, one knee almost under her chin. "Is that right? She said a girl was not allowed to braid her hair until she was old enough to marry. Do you understand what I am saying? You look like that . . . fish . . . Moiraine caught in the river." There were no fish in the Waste; Aiel knew them only from books.

"Of course I do," he said. He might as well have been deaf and blind for all he understood. Shifting under the blankets, he made himself sound as sure as he could manage. "At least . . . Well, the customs are complicated, and I am not certain which part you are talking about."

She looked at him suspiciously for a moment, but Aiel customs were so intricate that she believed him. In the Two Rivers, you walked out for a year, and if you suited, then you became betrothed and finally married; that was as far as custom went. She went on as she dressed. "I meant about a girl asking her mother's permission during the year, and the Wisdom's. I cannot say I understand that." The white blouse going over her head muffled her words for a moment. "If she wants him, and she is old enough to marry, why should she need permission? But you see? By my customs," her tone of voice said they were the only ones that mattered, "it is my place to choose whether to ask you, and I will not. By your customs," fastening her belt, she shook her head dismissively, "I did not have my mother's permission. And you would need your father's, I suppose. Or your father-brother's, since your father is dead? We did not have them, so we cannot marry." She began folding the scarf to wrap around her forehead.

"I see," he said weakly. Any boy in the Two Rivers who asked his father for that kind of permission was asking to have his ears soundly boxed. When he thought of the lads who had sweated themselves silly worrying that someone, *anyone,* would find out what they were doing with the girl they meant to marry . . . For that matter, he remembered when Nynaeve caught Kimry Lewin and Bar Dowtry in Bar's father's hayloft. Kimry had had her hair braided for five years, but when Nynaeve was through with her, Mistress Lewin had taken over. The Women's Circle had nearly skinned poor Bar alive, and that was nothing to what they had done to Kimry over the month they thought was the shortest decent time to wait for a wedding. The joke told quietly, where it would not get to the Women's Circle, had been that neither Bar nor Kimry had been able to sit down the whole first week they were married. Rand supposed Kimry had failed to ask permission. "But I guess Egwene wouldn't know all the men's customs, after all," he continued. "Women don't know everything. You see, since I started it, we have to marry. It doesn't matter about permissions."

"You started it?" Her sniff was pointed and meaning. Aiel, Andoran or anything else, women used those noises like sticks, to prod or thump. "It does not matter anyway, since we are going by Aiel customs. This will not happen again, Rand al'Thor." He was surprised—and pleased—to hear regret in her voice. "You belong to the near-sister of my near-sister. I have *toh* to Elayne, now, but that is none of your concern. Are you going to lie there forever? I have heard that men turn lazy, after, but it cannot be long until the clans are ready to begin the morning's march. You must be there." Suddenly a stricken look crossed her face, and she sagged to her knees. "If we can return. I am not certain that I remember what I did to make the hole, Rand al'Thor. You must find our way back."

He told her how he had blocked her gateway and could still feel it holding. She looked relieved, and even smiled at him. But it became increasingly clear as she folded her legs and arranged her skirts that she did not mean to turn her back while he dressed.

"Fair's fair," he muttered after a long moment, and scrambled out of the blankets.

He tried to be as nonchalant as she had been, but it was not easy. He could feel her eyes like a touch even when he turned away from her. She had no call to tell him he had a pretty behind; he had not said anything about how pretty hers was. She only said it to make him blush, anyway. Women did not look at men that way. *And they don't ask their mother's permission to . . . ?* He had an idea that life with Aviendha had not become one bit easier.

CHAPTER
32

A Short Spear

There was little discussion. Even if the storm still raged outside, they could make it back to the gateway using the blankets and rugs for cloaks. Aviendha began dividing them while he seized *saidin*, filling himself with life and death, molten fire and liquid ice.

"Split them equally," he told her. He knew his voice was cold and emotionless. Asmodean had said he could go beyond that, but he had not managed to so far.

She gave him a surprised look, but all she said was "There is more of you to cover," and went on as she was.

There was no point in arguing. In his experience, from Emond's Field to the Maidens, if a woman wanted to do something for you, the only way to stop her was to tie her up, especially if it involved sacrifice on her part. The surprise was that she had not sounded acid, had not said anything about him being a soft wetlander. Maybe something good besides a memory had come out of this. *She can't* really *mean never again.* He suspected that she meant exactly that, though.

Weaving a finger-thin flow of Fire, he sliced the outline

of a door in one wall, widening the gap at the top. Startlingly, daylight shone through. Releasing *saidin,* he exchanged surprised looks with Aviendha. He knew he had lost track of time— *You lost track of the year*—but they could not have been inside that long. Wherever they were, it was a great distance from Cairhien.

He pushed against the block, but it did not budge until he put his back to it, dug in his heels and shoved with all of his might. Just as it occurred to him that he very probably could have done this more easily with the Power, the block toppled outward, taking him with it into cold, crisp pale daylight. Not all the way, though. It stopped at an angle, propped against snow that had built up around the hut. Lying on his back, with only a bit of his head sticking out, he could see other mounds, some smooth drifts around sparse, stunted trees that he did not recognize, others maybe burying bushes or boulders.

He opened his mouth—and forgot what he was going to say as *something* swept through the air not fifty feet above him, a leathery gray shape far bigger than a horse, on slow-beating widespread wings, a horny snout thrust out before and clawed feet and thin, lizardlike tail trailing behind. His head twisted on its own to follow the thing's flight over the trees. There were two people on its back; despite what seemed to be some sort of hooded garments, it was plain that they were scanning the ground below. If he had had more than his head showing, if he had not been directly under the creature, they would surely have seen him.

"Leave the blankets," he said as he ducked back inside. He told her what he had seen. "Maybe they'd be friendly and maybe not, but I'd as soon not find out." He was not sure he wanted to meet people who rode something like that in any case. If they were people. "We are going to *sneak* back to the gateway. As quickly as we can, but sneaking."

For a wonder she did not argue. When he commented on it as he was helping her climb over the ice block— that was a wonder, too; she accepted his hand without so much as a glare—she said, "I do not argue when you make sense, Rand al'Thor." That was hardly the way he remembered it.

The land around them lay flat beneath its deep blanket of snow, but to the west sharp, white-tipped mountains rose, peaks wreathed in cloud. He had no difficulty knowing they lay west, for the sun was rising. Less than half its golden ball stuck above the ocean. He stared at that. The land slanted down enough for him to see waves crashing in violent spray on a rocky, boulder-strewn shore maybe half a mile away. An ocean to the east, stretching endlessly to horizon and sun. If the snow had not been enough, that told him they were in no land he knew.

Aviendha stared at the rolling breakers and pounding waves in amazement, then frowned at him as it hit home. She might never have seen an ocean, but she had seen maps.

In her skirts the snow gave her even more trouble than it did him, and he floundered, digging his way through as much as walking, sometimes sinking to his waist. She gasped as he scooped her up in his arms, and her green eyes glared.

"We have to move faster than you can dragging those skirts," he told her. The glare faded, but she did not put an arm around his neck, as he had half-hoped. Instead she folded her hands and put on a patient face. A bit touched with sullenness. Whatever changes what they had done might have wrought in her, she was not completely different. He could not understand why that should be a relief.

He could have melted a path through the snow as he had in the storm, but if another of those flying things came, that cleared path would lead straight to them. A fox trotted by across the snow well to his right, pure white except for a black tip to its bushy tail, occasionally eyeing him and Aviendha warily. Rabbit tracks marred the snow in places, blurred where they had leapt, and once he saw the prints of a cat that had to be as large as a leopard. Maybe there were larger animals still, maybe some flightless relative of that leathery creature. Not something he wanted to encounter, but there was always the chance the . . . *fliers* . . . might take the plowed furrow he was leaving now as the track of some animal.

He still made his way from tree to tree, wishing there were more of them, and closer together. Of course, if there had been, he might not have found Aviendha in the storm—she grunted, frowning up at him, and he loosened his hold on her again—but it would surely have helped now. It was because he was creeping in that way, though, that he saw the others first.

Less than fifty paces away, between him and the gateway—right at the gateway; he could feel his weave holding it—were four people on horseback and more than twenty afoot. The mounted were all women shrouded in long thick, fur-lined cloaks; two of them each wore a silvery bracelet on her left wrist, connected by a long leash of the same shining stuff to a bright collar tight around the neck of a gray-clad, cloakless woman standing in the snow. The others afoot were men in dark leather, and armor painted green and gold, overlapping plates down their chests and the outsides of their arms and fronts of their thighs. Their spears bore green-and-gold tassels, their long shields were painted in the same colors, and their helmets seemed to be the heads of huge insects, faces peering out through the mandibles. One was clearly an officer, lacking spear or shield, but with a curved, two-handed sword on his back. Silver outlined the plates of his lacquered armor, and thin green plumes, like feelers, heightened the illusion of his painted helmet. Rand knew where he and Aviendha were now. He had seen armor like that before. And women collared like that.

Setting her down behind something that looked a little like a wind-twisted pine, except that its trunk was smooth and gray, streaked with black, he pointed, and she nodded silently.

"The two women on leashes can channel," he whispered. "Can you block them?" Hurriedly he added, "Don't embrace the Source yet. They're prisoners, but they still might warn the others, and even if they don't, the women with the bracelets might be able to feel them sense you."

She looked at him oddly, but wasted no time on foolish questions such as how he knew; they would come later, he knew. "The women with the bracelets can channel also," she replied just as softly. "It feels very strange, though. Weak. As if they had never practiced it. I cannot see how that can be."

Rand could. *Damane* were the ones who were supposed to be able to channel. If two women had somehow slipped through the Seanchan net to become *sul'dam* instead—and from the little he knew of them, that would not be easy, for the Seanchan tested every last woman during the years that she might first show signs of channeling—they would surely never dare to betray themselves. "Can you shield all four?"

She gave him a very smug look. "Of course. Egwene taught me to handle several flows at once. I can block them, tie those off, and wrap them up in flows of Air before they know what is happening." That self-satisfied little smile faded. "I am fast enough to handle them, and their horses, but that leaves the rest to you until I can bring help. If any get away . . . They can surely cast those spears this far, and if one of them pins you to the ground . . ." For a moment she muttered under her breath, as if angry that she could not complete a sentence. Finally she looked at him, her gaze as furious as he had ever seen it. "Egwene has told me of Healing, but she knows little, and I less."

What could she be angry about now? *Better to try understanding the sun than a woman,* he thought wryly. Thom Merrilin had told him that, and it was simple truth. "You take care of shielding those women," he told her. "I will do the rest. Not until I touch your arm, though."

He could tell she thought he was boasting, but he would not have to split flows, only weave one intricate flow of Air that would bind arms to sides and hold horses' feet as well as human. Taking a deep breath, he grabbed hold of *saidin,* touched her arm and channeled.

Shocked cries rose from the Seanchan. He should have thought of gags, too, but they could be through the gateway before they attracted anyone else. Holding on to the Source, he seized Aviendha's arm and half-dragged her through the snow, ignoring her snarls that she could walk. At least this way he broke a trail for her, and they had to hurry.

The Seanchan quieted, staring as he and Aviendha made their way around in front of them. The two women who were not *sul'dam* had thrown back their hoods, struggling against his weave. He held it rather than tying; he would have to release it when he went anyway, for the simple reason that he could not leave even Seanchan bound in the snow. If they did not freeze to death, there was always the big cat whose tracks he had seen. Where there was one, there must be more.

The gateway was there all right, but instead of looking into his room in Eianrod, it was a gray blank. It seemed narrower than he remembered, too. Worse, he could see the weave of that grayness. It had been woven from *saidin*. Furious thought slid across the Void. He could not tell what it was meant to do, yet it could easily be a trap for whoever stepped through, woven by one of the male Forsaken. By Asmodean, most likely; if the man could hand him over to the others, he might be able to regain his place among them. Yet there could be no question of staying here. If Aviendha only remembered how she had woven the gateway in the first place, she could open another, but as it was, they were going to have to use this, trap or no.

One of the mounted women, a black raven in front of a stark tower on the gray breast of her cloak, had a severe face and dark eyes that seemed to want to drill into his skull. Another, younger and paler and shorter, yet more regal, wore a silver stag's head on her green cloak. The little fingers of her riding gloves were too long. Rand knew from the shaven sides of her scalp that those long fingers covered nails grown long and no doubt lacquered, both signs of Seanchan nobility. The soldiers were stiff-faced and stiff-backed, but the officer's blue eyes glittered behind the jaws of the insectlike helmet, and his gauntleted fingers writhed as he struggled futilely to reach his sword.

Rand did not care very much about them, but he did not want to leave the *damane* behind. At the least he could give them a chance to escape. They might be staring at him as they would a wild animal with bared fangs, but they had not chosen to be prisoners, treated little better than domestic animals themselves. He put a hand to the collar of the nearest, and felt a jolt that nearly numbed his arm; for an instant the Void shifted, and *saidin* raged through him like the snowstorm a thousandfold. The *damane*'s short yellow hair flailed as she convulsed at his touch, screaming, and the *sul'dam* connected to her gasped, face going white. Both would have fallen if not held by bonds of Air.

"You try it," he told Aviendha, working his hand. "A woman must be able to touch the thing safely. I don't know how it unfastens." It looked of a piece, linked somehow, just like bracelet and leash. "But it went on, so it must be able to come off." A few moments could not make any difference to whatever had happened to the gateway. Was it Asmodean?

Aviendha shook her head, but began fumbling at the other woman's collar. "Hold still," she growled as the *damane,* a pale-faced girl of sixteen or seventeen, tried to flinch back. If the leashed women had looked on Rand as a wild beast, they stared at Aviendha like a nightmare made flesh.

"She is *marath'damane,*" the pale girl wailed. "Save Seri, mistress! Please, mistress! Save Seri!" The other *damane,* older, almost motherly, began weeping uncontrollably. Aviendha glared at Rand as hard as she did the girl for some reason, muttering angrily under her breath as she worked at the collar.

"It is he, Lady Morsa," the other *damane*'s *sul'dam* said suddenly in a soft drawl that Rand could barely understand. "I have borne the bracelet long, and I could tell if the *marath'damane* had done more than block Jini."

Morsa did not look surprised. In fact, there seemed to be a light of horrified recognition in her blue eyes as she gazed at Rand. There was only one way that could be.

"You were at Falme," he said. If he went through first, it meant leaving Aviendha behind, although only for a moment.

"I was." The noblewoman looked faint, but her slow,

slurring voice was coolly imperious. "I saw you, and what you did."

"Take a care I don't do the same here. Give me no trouble, and I will leave you in peace." He could not send Aviendha first, into the Light knew what. If emotion had not been so distant, he would have grimaced the way she was grimacing over that collar. They had to go through together, and be ready to face anything.

"Much has been kept secret about what happened in the lands of the great Hawkwing, Lady Morsa," the severe-faced woman said. Her dark eyes were as hard on Morsa as they had been on him. "Rumors fly that the Ever Victorious Army has tasted defeat."

"Do you now seek truth in rumor, Jalindin?" Morsa asked in a cutting tone. "A Seeker above all should know when to keep silent. The Empress herself has forbidden speech of the *Corenne* until she calls it again. If you—or I—speak so much as the name of the city where that expedition landed, our tongues will be removed. Perhaps you would enjoy being tongueless in the Tower of Ravens? Not even the Listeners would hear you scream for mercy, or pay heed."

Rand understood no more than two words in three, and it was not the odd accents. He wished he had time to listen. *Corenne*. The Return. That was what the Seanchan in Falme had called their attempt to seize the lands beyond the Aryth Ocean—the lands where he lived—that they considered their birthright. The rest—Seeker, Listeners, the Tower of Ravens—were a mystery. But apparently the Return had been called off, for the time being at least. That was worth knowing.

The gateway *was* narrower. Maybe as much as a finger width narrower than moments before. Only his block held it open; it had tried to close as soon as Aviendha released her weave, and it was still trying to.

"Hurry," he told Aviendha, and she gave him a look so patient it could as well have been a stone between his eyes.

"I am trying, Rand al'Thor," she said, still working at the collar. Tears trickled down Seri's cheeks; a continuous low moan came from her throat, as if the Aiel woman intended to slit it. "You nearly killed the other two, and maybe yourself. I could feel the Power rushing into both of them wildly when you touched the other collar. So leave me to it, and if I can do it, I will." Muttering a curse, she tried at the side.

Rand thought about making the *sul'dam* remove the collars—if anyone knew how the things came off, they would—but from the set frowns on their faces, he knew he would have to force them to it. If he could not kill a woman, he could not very well torture one.

With a sigh he glanced at the gray blankness filling the gateway again. The flows appeared to be woven into his; he could not slice one without the other. Passing through might trigger the trap, but cutting away the grayness, even if that act did not trip it, would allow the gateway to snap shut before they had a chance to leap through. It would have to be a blind jump into the Light knew what.

Morsa had listened carefully to every word he and Aviendha said, and now she was gazing thoughtfully at the two *sul'dam,* but Jalindin had never taken her eyes from the noblewoman's face. "Much has been kept secret that should not be held from the Seekers, Lady Morsa," the stern woman said. "The Seekers must know all."

"You forget yourself, Jalindin," Morsa snapped, her gloved hands jerking; had her arms not been bound to her sides, she would have sawed the reins. As it was, she tilted her head to stare down her nose at the other woman. "You were sent to me because Sarek looks above himself and has designs on Serengada Dai and Tuel, not to ask of what the Empress has—"

Jalindin broke in harshly. "It is you who forgets herself, Lady Morsa, if you think that you are proof against the Seekers for Truth. I myself have put both a daughter and a son of the Empress, may the Light bless her, to the question, and in gratitude for the confessions I wrenched from them she allowed me to gaze upon her. Think you that your minor House stands higher than the Empress' own children?"

Morsa remained upright, not that she had much choice, but her face went gray, and she licked her lips.

"The Empress, may the Light illumine her forever, already knows far more than I can tell. I did not mean to imply—"

The Seeker cut her off again, twisting her head to speak to the soldiers as if Morsa did not exist. "The woman Morsa is in the custody of the Seekers for Truth. She will be put to the question as soon as we return to Merinloe. And the *sul'dam* and *damane,* as well. It seems they too have hidden what they should not." Horror painted the faces of the named women, but Morsa could have stood for any of them. Eyes wide and suddenly haggard, she slumped as much as her invisible bonds would allow, voicing not a word of protest. She looked as if she wanted to scream, yet she—accepted. Jalindin's gaze turned to Rand. "She named you Rand al'Thor. You will be well treated if you surrender to me, Rand al'Thor. However you came here, you cannot think to escape even if you kill us. There is a wide search for a *marath'damane* who channeled in the night." Her eyes flickered to Aviendha. "It will find you as well, inevitably, and you might be slain by accident. There is sedition in this district. I do not know how men like you are treated in your lands, but in Seanchan your sufferings can be eased. Here, you can find great honor in the use of your power."

He laughed at her, and she looked offended. "I cannot kill you, but I vow I should stripe your hide at least for that." He certainly would not have to worry about being gentled in Seanchan hands. In Seanchan, men who could channel were killed. Not executed. Hunted and shot down on sight.

The gray-filled gateway was another finger narrower, barely wide enough now for both of them to pass through together. "Leave her, Aviendha. We have to go now."

She released Seri's collar and gave him an exasperated look, but her eyes went past him to the gateway, and she hoisted her skirts to stump through the snow to him, muttering to herself about frozen water.

"Be ready for anything," he told her, putting an arm around her shoulders. He told himself they had to be close together to fit. Not because she felt good. "I don't know what, but be ready." She nodded, and he said, "Jump!"

Together they leaped into the grayness, Rand releasing the weave that had held the Seanchan in order to fill himself to bursting with *saidin* . . .

. . . and landed stumbling in his bedchamber in Eianrod, lamplit, with darkness outside the windows.

Asmodean sat against the wall beside the door with his legs crossed. He was not embracing the Source, but Rand slammed a block between the man and *saidin* anyway. Whirling with his arm still around Aviendha, he found the gateway gone. No, not gone—he could still see his weaving, and what he knew must be Asmodean's—but there seemed to be nothing there at all. Without pause he slashed his weave, and suddenly the gateway appeared, a rapidly narrowing view of Seanchan, the Lady Morsa slumped in her saddle, Jalindin shouting orders. A green-and-white tasseled spear lanced through the opening, just before it snapped shut. Instinctively, Rand channeled Air to snatch the suddenly wobbling two-foot length of spear. The shaft ended as smoothly as any craftsman could have worked it. Shivering, he was glad that he had not tried removing the gray barrier—whatever it had been—*before* jumping through.

"A good thing neither of the *sul'dam* recovered in time," he said, taking the severed spear in his hand, "or we'd have had worse than this coming after us." He watched Asmodean from the corner of his eye, but the man only sat there, looking slightly ill. He could not know whether Rand meant to stuff that spear down his throat.

Aviendha's sniff was her most pointed yet. "Do you think I released them?" she said heatedly. She removed his arm firmly, but he did not think her temper was for him. Or not for his arm, anyway. "I tied their shields as tightly as I could. They are your enemies, Rand al'Thor. Even the ones you called *damane* are faithful dogs who would have killed you rather than be free. You must be hard with your enemies, not soft."

She was right, he thought, hefting the spear. He had left enemies behind that he might well have to face one day. He had to become harder. Or else he would be ground to flour before he ever reached Shayol Ghul.

Abruptly she began smoothing her skirts, and her voice became almost conversational. "I notice that you did not save that whey-faced Morsa from her fate. From the way you looked at her, I thought big eyes and a round bosom had caught your eye."

Rand stared at her in amazement that oozed across the emptiness surrounding him like syrup. She could have been saying the soup was ready. He wondered how he was supposed to have noticed Morsa's bosom, hidden as it was in a fur-lined cloak. "I should have brought her," he said. "To question her about the Seanchan. I will be troubled by them again, I am afraid."

The glint that had appeared in her eye vanished. She opened her mouth, but stopped, glancing at Asmodean, when he raised a hand. He could all but see the questions about Seanchan piled up behind her eyes. If he knew her, once begun she would not stop digging until she had uncovered scraps he did not even remember he knew. Which might not be a bad thing. Another time. After he had wrung a few answers out of Asmodean. She was right. He had to be hard.

"That was a smart thing you did," she said, "hiding the hole I made. If a *gai'shain* had come in here, a thousand of the spear-sisters might have marched through seeking you."

Asmodean cleared his throat. "One of the *gai'shain* did come. Someone named Sulin had told her she must see you eat, my Lord Dragon, and to stop her from bringing the tray in here and finding you gone, I took the liberty of telling her that you and the young woman did not want to be disturbed." A slight tightening of his eyes caught Rand's attention.

"What?"

"Just that she took it strangely. She laughed out loud and went running off. A few minutes later, there must have been twenty *Far Dareis Mai* beneath the window, shouting and beating their spears on their bucklers for a good hour or more. I must say, my Lord Dragon, some of the suggestions they called up startled even me."

Rand felt his cheeks burning—it had happened on the other side of the bloody world, and still the Maidens knew!—but Aviendha only narrowed her eyes.

"Did she have hair and eyes like mine?" She did not wait for Asmodean's nod. "It must have been my first-sister Niella." She saw the startled question on Rand's face and answered it before he could speak. "Niella is a weaver, not a Maiden, and she was taken half a year ago by Chareen Maidens during a raid on Sulara Hold. She tried to talk me out of taking the spear, and she has always wanted me wed. I am going to send her back to the Chareen with a welt on her bottom for every one she told!"

Rand caught her arm as she started to stalk out of the room. "I want to talk with Natael. I don't suppose there is much time left until dawn . . ."

"Two hours, maybe," Asmodean put in.

". . . so there will be little sleeping now. If you want to try, would you mind making your bed elsewhere for what's left of the night? You need new blankets anyway."

She nodded curtly before pulling loose, and slammed the door behind her. Surely she was not angry at being tossed out of his bedchamber—how could she be; she had said nothing more would happen between them— but he was glad he was not Niella.

Bouncing the shortened spear in his hand, he turned to Asmodean.

"A strange scepter, my Lord Dragon."

"It will do for one." To remind him that the Seanchan were still out there. For once he wished his voice was even colder than the Void and *saidin* made it. He had to be hard. "Before I decide whether to skewer you with it like a lamb, why did you never mention this trick of making something invisible? If I hadn't been able to see the flows, I'd never have known the gateway was still there."

Asmodean swallowed, shifting as though he did not know whether Rand meant his threat. Rand was not sure himself. "My Lord Dragon, you never asked. A matter of bending light. You always have so many questions, it is hard to find a moment to speak of anything else. You must realize by now that I've thrown my lot in with yours completely." Licking his lips, he got up. As far as his knees. And began to babble. "I felt your weave—anybody within a mile could have felt it—I never saw anything like it—I didn't know that anyone but Demandred could block a gateway that was closing, and maybe Semirhage—and Lews Therin—I felt it, and came, and a hard time I had getting past those Maidens—I used the same trick—you *must* know I am your man now. My Lord Dragon, I am your man."

It was the repetition of what the Cairhienin had said that got through as much as anything else. Gesturing with the half-spear, he said roughly, "Stand. You aren't a dog." But as Asmodean slowly rose, he laid the long spearpoint alongside the man's throat. He had to be hard. "From now on, you will tell me two things I *don't* ask about every time we talk. Every time, mind. If I think you are trying to hide anything from me, you will be glad to let Semirhage have you."

"As you say, my Lord Dragon," Asmodean stammered. He looked ready to bow and kiss Rand's hand.

To avoid the chance, Rand moved to the blanketless bed and sat on the linen sheet, the feather mattresses yielding under him as he studied the spear. A good idea to keep it for remembrance, if not as a scepter. Even with everything else, he had best not forget the Seanchan. Those *damane.* If Aviendha had not been there to block them from the Source . . .

"You have tried showing me how to shield a woman and failed. Try showing me how to avoid flows I cannot see, how to counter them." Once Lanfear had sliced his weavings as neatly as with a knife.

"Not easy, my Lord Dragon, without a woman to practice against."

"We have two hours," Rand said coldly, letting the man's shield unravel. "Try. Try very hard."

CHAPTER

33

A Question of Crimson

The knife brushed Nynaeve's hair as it thunked into the board she was leaning against, and she flinched behind her blindfold. She wished she had a decent braid instead of locks hanging loose about her shoulders. If that blade had cut even one strand . . . *Fool woman,* she thought bitterly. *Fool, fool woman.* With the scarf folded over her eyes she could just see a narrow line of light at the bottom. It seemed bright, from the darkness behind the thick folds. There had to be enough light yet, even if it was late afternoon. Surely the man would not throw when he could not see properly. The next blade struck on the other side of her head; she could feel it vibrating. She thought it almost touched her ear. She was going to kill Thom Merrilin and Valan Luca. And maybe any other man she could get her hands on, on sheer principle.

"The pears," Luca shouted, as if he were not just thirty paces from her. He must think the blindfold made her deaf as well as blind.

Fumbling in the pouch at her belt, she brought out a pear and carefully balanced it atop her head. She *was* blind. A pure blind fool! Two more pears, and she gingerly extended her arms to either side between the knives that outlined her, holding one in either hand by the stems. There was a pause. She opened her mouth to tell Thom Merrilin that if he so much as nicked her, she would—

Tchunk-tchunk-tchunk! The blades came so fast she would have yelped if her throat had not contracted like a fist. She held only the stem in her left hand, the other pear trembled faintly with the knife through it, and the pear on her head leaked juice into her hair.

Snatching the scarf off, she stalked toward Thom and Luca, both of them grinning like maniacs. Before she could speak one of the words boiling up in her, Luca said admiringly, "You are magnificent, Nana. Your bravery is magnificent, but you are more so." He swirled that ridiculous red silk cloak in a bow, one hand over his heart. "I shall call this 'Rose Among Thorns.' Though truly, you are more beautiful than any mere rose."

"It doesn't take much bravery to stand like a stump." A rose, was she? She would show him thorns. She would show both of them. "You listen to me, Valan Luca—"

"Such courage. You never even flinch. I tell you, I would not have the stomach to do what you are doing."

That was the simple truth, she told herself. "I am no braver than I have to be," she said in a milder tone. It was hard to shout at a man who insisted on telling you how brave you were. Certainly better to hear than all that blather about roses. Thom knuckled his long white mustaches as if he saw something funny.

"The dress," Luca said, showing all of his teeth in a smile. "You will look wonderful in—"

"No!" she snapped. Whatever he had gained, he had just lost by bringing this up again. Clarine had made the dress Luca wanted her to wear, in silk more crimson than his cloak. It was her opinion that the color was to hide blood if Thom's hand slipped.

"But, Nana, beauty in danger is a *great* draw." Luca's voice crooned as if whispering sweetness in her ear. "You will have every eye on you, every heart pounding for your beauty and courage."

"If you like it so much," she said firmly, "you wear it." Aside from the color, she was not about to show that much bosom in public, whether or not Clarine thought it was proper. She had seen Latelle's performing dress, all black spangles, with a high neck to her chin. She could wear something like . . . What was she thinking? She had no intention of actually going through with this. She had only agreed to this practice to stop Luca scratching at the wagon door every night to try convincing her.

The man was nothing if not deft at knowing when to change the subject. "What happened here?" he asked, suddenly all smooth solicitude.

She flinched as he touched her puffy eye. It was his bad luck to choose that. He would have done better to continue trying to stuff her into that red dress. "I did not like the way it looked at me in the mirror this morning, so I bit it."

Her flat tone and bared teeth made Luca snatch his hand back. From the wary gleam in his dark eyes, he suspected she might bite again. Thom was stroking his mustaches furiously, red in the face from the effort of not laughing. He knew what had happened, of course. He would. And as soon as she left, he would no doubt regale Luca with his version of events. Men could not avoid gossiping; it was in them at birth, and nothing women could do ever got it out of them.

The daylight was dimmer than she had thought. The sun sat red on the treetops to the west. "If you ever try this again without better light . . ." she growled, shaking a fist at Thom. "It's almost dusk!"

"I suppose," the man said, bushy eyebrow lifting, "this means you want to leave out the bit where *I* am blindfolded?" He was joking, of course. He had to be joking. "As you wish, Nana. From now on, only in the most perfect light."

It was not until she stalked away, swishing her skirts angrily, that she realized that she had agreed to actually do this fool thing. By implication, at least. They would try to hold her to it, as surely as the sun would set tonight. *Fool, fool,* fool *woman!*

The clearing where they—or Thom, at least, burn him

and Luca both!—had been practicing stood some little distance from the camp over beside the road north. Doubtless Luca had not wanted to upset the animals should Thom put one of his knives through her heart. The man would likely have fed her corpse to the lions. The only reason he wanted her to wear that dress was so he could ogle what she had no intention of showing to anyone but Lan, and burn him, too, for a stubborn fool man. She wished she had him there so she could tell him so. She wished she had him there so she could be sure he was safe. She broke a dead dogfennel and used its feathery brown length like a whip to snap the heads off weeds that poked through the leaves on the ground.

Last night, Elayne had said, Egwene reported fighting in Cairhien, skirmishes with brigands, with Cairhienin who saw any Aiel as an enemy, with Andoran soldiers trying to claim the Sun Throne for Morgase. Lan had been involved in them; whenever Moiraine let him out of her sight, he apparently managed to take himself to the fighting, as if he could sense where it would be. Nynaeve had never thought that she would want the Aes Sedai to keep Lan on a short leash at her side.

This morning Elayne had still been disturbed about her mother's soldiers being in Cairhien, fighting Rand's Aiel, but what worried Nynaeve was the brigands. According to Egwene, if anyone could identify stolen property in a brigand's possession, if anyone could swear to seeing him kill anyone or burn so much as a shed, Rand was hanging him. He did not put his hands on the rope, but it was the same thing, and Egwene said he watched every execution with a face cold and hard as the mountains. That was not like him. He had been a gentle boy. Whatever had happened to him in the Waste had been very much for the worse.

Well, Rand was far away, and her own problems—hers and Elayne's—were no nearer solution. The River Eldar lay less than a mile north, spanned by a single lofty stone bridge built between tall metal pillars that glistened without a speck of rust. Remnants of an earlier time, certainly, perhaps even an earlier Age. She had gone up to it at midday, right after they arrived, but there had not been a boat in the river worthy of the name. Rowboats, small fishing boats working along the reed-lined banks, some strange, narrow little things that skittered over the water propelled by kneeling men with paddles, even a squat barge that looked to be moored in mud—there seemed to be a lot of mud showing on both sides, some of it dried hard and cracked, yet that was no wonder with the heat holding on so unseasonably—but nothing that could carry them swiftly away downriver as she wanted. Not that she knew where it was to take them, yet.

Rack her brains as she would, she could not remember the name of the town where the Blue sisters were supposed to be. She swiped savagely at a scatterhead, and it burst in little white feathers that floated to the ground. They probably were not there anymore in any case, if they ever had been. But it was the only clue they had to a safe place short of Tear. If she could only remember it.

The only good thing on the entire journey north was that Elayne had stopped flirting with Thom. There had not been an incident since joining the show. At least, it would have been good if Elayne had not apparently decided to pretend nothing had ever happened. Yesterday Nynaeve had congratulated the girl on coming to her senses, and Elayne had cooly replied, *Are you trying to find out if I will stand in your way with Thom, Nynaeve? He's rather old for you, and I did think you had planted your affections elsewhere, but you are old enough to make your own decisions. I am fond of Thom, as I think he is of me. I look on him like a second father. If you want to flirt with him, you have my permission. But I really did think you were more constant.*

Luca meant to cross the river in the morning, and Samara, the town on the other side, in Ghealdan, was no fit place to be. Luca had spent most of the day since their arrival over in Samara, securing a place to set up his show, he was only concerned that a number of other menageries had beaten him there, and he was not the only one to have more than animals. That was why he had grown particularly insistent about her letting Thom throw knives at her. She was lucky he did not want it done highwalking with Elayne. The man seemed to think the most important thing in the world was that his show should be bigger and better than any other. For herself, the worrisome thing was that the Prophet was in Samara, his followers crowding the town and spilling out into tents, huts and shanties around it, a city that overwhelmed Samara's own not inconsiderable size. It had a high stone wall, and most of the buildings were stone as well, many as much as three stories, and there were more roofs of slate or tile than thatch.

This side of the Eldar was no better. They had passed three Whitecloak encampments before reaching their stopping place, hundreds of white tents in neat rows, and there had to be more they had not seen. Whitecloaks on this side of the river, the Prophet and maybe a riot waiting to happen on the other, and she had no idea where to go and no way to get there except in a lumbering wagon that moved no faster than she could walk. She wished she had never let Elayne talk her into abandoning the coach. Not seeing a weed close enough to snap without stepping aside, she broke the dogfennel in half, then again, until the pieces were no longer than her hand, and tossed them to the ground. She wished she could do the same with Luca. And Galad Damodred, for sending them running here. And al'Lan Mandragoran, for not being here. Not that she *needed* him, of course. But his presence would have been . . . a comfort.

The camp was quiet, with evening meals cooking over small fires beside the wagons. Petra was feeding the black-maned lion, thrusting huge pieces of meat through the bars on a stick. The female lions were already hunkered down over theirs companionably, letting out an occasional growl if someone came too close to their cage. Nynaeve stopped near Aludra's wagon; the Illuminator was working with wooden mortar and pestle on a table let down from the side of her wagon, muttering to herself over whatever she was compounding. Three of the Chavanas smiled at Nynaeve enticingly, motioning her to join them. Not Brugh, who still glowered over his lip, though she had given him a salve to make the swelling go down. Maybe if she hit the rest of them as hard, they would listen to Luca—and more importantly, to her!—and realize that she did not want their smiles. Too bad Master Valan Luca could not follow his own instructions. Latelle turned from the bear cage and gave her a tight smile; more of a smirk, really. Mainly, though, Nynaeve stared at Cerandin, who was filing the blunt toenails of one of the huge gray *s'redit* with what looked like a tool suitable for metal.

"That one," Aludra said, "she uses the hands and the feet with remarkable ability, no? Do not glare at me so, Nana," she added, dusting her hands. "I am not your enemy. Here. You must try these new firesticks."

Nynaeve took the wooden box from the dark-haired woman gingerly. It was a cube she could have held easily with one hand, but she used both. "I thought you called them strikers."

"Maybe yes, maybe no. Firesticks, it says what they are much better than strikers, yes? I have smoothed the little holes that hold the sticks so they can no longer ignite on the wood. A good idea, no? And the heads, they are a new formulation. You will try them and tell me what you think?"

"Yes, of course. Thank you."

Nynaeve hurried on before the woman could press another box on her. She held the thing as if it might explode, which she was not certain it would not. Aludra had everyone trying out her strikers, or firesticks, or whatever she would decide to call them next. They certainly would light a fire or a lamp. They could also burst into flame if the blue-gray heads rubbed against each other or anything else rough. For herself, she would stick with flint and steel, or a coal kept properly banked in a box of sand. Much safer.

Juilin caught her before she could set foot on the steps of the wagon she shared with Elayne, his gaze going straight to her swollen eye. She glared at him so hard that he stepped back and snatched that ridiculous conical cap from his head. "I've been over the river," he said. "There are a hundred or so Whitecloaks in Samara. Just watching, and being watched as hard themselves by

Ghealdanin soldiers. But I recognized one. The young fellow who was sitting across from The Light of Truth in Sienda."

She smiled at him, and he took another hasty step back, eyeing her warily. Galad in Samara. That was all they needed. "You always bring such wonderful news, Juilin. We should have left you in Tanchico, or better, on the dock in Tear." That was hardly fair. Better he told her of Galad than that she walked around a corner into the man. "Thank you, Juilin. At least we know to keep an eye out for him, now." His nod was hardly a proper response to graciously offered thanks, and he hurried away, clapping his hat on, as if he expected her to hit him. Men had no manners.

The interior of the wagon was far cleaner than it had been when Thom and Juilin purchased it. The flaking paint had all been scraped off—the men had grumbled about doing that—and the cabinets and the tiny table that was fastened to the floor oiled until they shone. The small brick stove with its metal chimney was never used—the nights were warm enough, and if they began cooking in here, Thom and Juilin would never take another turn—but it made a good place to keep their valuables, the purses and the jewelry boxes. The washleather pouch holding the seal—that she had stuffed in as far as it would go and had not touched since.

Elayne, seated on one of the narrow beds, stuffed something under the blankets when Nynaeve climbed inside, but before she could ask what it was, Elayne exclaimed, "Your eye! What happened to you?" They needed to wash her hair in henpepper again; faint hints of gold were showing at the roots of those black tresses. It had to be done every few days.

"Cerandin hit me when I wasn't looking," Nynaeve muttered. The remembered taste of boiled catfern and powdered mavinsleaf made her tongue curl. That was *not* why she had let Elayne go to the last meeting in *Tel'aran'rhiod*, too. She was *not* avoiding Egwene. It was just that she made most of the journeys into the World of Dreams between meetings, and it was only fair to give Elayne her chances to go. That was it.

Carefully she put the box of firesticks into one of the cabinets, next to two more. The one that had actually caught fire was long since discarded.

She did not know why she was hiding the truth. Elayne had obviously not been outside the wagon, or she would know already. She and Juilin were probably the only people in camp who did not know, now that Thom had surely revealed every disgusting detail to Luca.

Taking a deep breath, she sat down on the other bed and made herself meet Elayne's eyes. Something in the quiet of the other woman said she knew that more was coming.

"I . . . asked Cerandin about *damane* and *sul'dam*. I am certain she knows more than she lets on." She paused for Elayne to voice doubts that she had asked rather than demanded, to say that the Seanchan woman had already told them all she knew, that she had not had much contact with *damane* or *sul'dam*. But Elayne kept silent, and Nynaeve realized that she was only hoping to postpone the moment with an argument. "She got quite heated about not knowing any more, so I shook her. You've really gone too far with her. She waggled her finger under my nose!" Still Elayne only watched her, those cool blue eyes barely blinking. It was all Nynaeve could do not to look away as she went on. "She . . . threw me, somehow, over her shoulder. I got up and slapped her, and she knocked me down with her fist. That is how I got the eye." She might as well tell the rest; Elayne would hear soon enough; better it came from her. She would rather have pulled out her tongue. "I wasn't about to put up with that, certainly. We scuffled a little more." Not much of a scuffle on her part, for all that she had refused to quit. The bitterest truth was that Cerandin had only stopped flipping her about and tripping her in sneaky ways because it had been like manhandling a child. Nynaeve had had as much chance as that child. If only no one had been watching, so she could have channeled; she had certainly been angry enough. If only no one had been watching, period. She wished Cerandin had pounded her with her fists until she bled. "Then Latelle gave her a stick. You know how that woman wants to get back at me." There was certainly no need to say that Cerandin had been holding her head down over a wagon tongue at the time. No one had manhandled her like that since she threw a pitcher of water at Neysa Ayellin when she was sixteen. "Anyway, Petra broke it up." Just in time, too. The huge man had taken the pair of them by the scruff of the neck like kittens. "Cerandin apologized, and that was that." Petra had made the Seanchan woman apologize, true, but he had made Nynaeve do so as well, refusing to loose that gentle yet iron-hard grip on her neck until she did. She had hit him as hard as she could, right in the stomach, and he had not even blinked. Her hand felt as if it might swell, too. "Nothing much to it, really. I suppose Latelle will try to spread some story of her own making about it. That is the woman I ought to shake. I didn't hit her half hard enough."

She felt better for telling the truth, but Elayne had doubt on her face that made her want to change the subject. "What is that you're hiding?" She reached over and pulled the blanket back, revealing the silvery length of the *a'dam* they had gotten from Cerandin. "Why under the Light do you want to look at that? And if you do, why hide it? It is a filthy thing, and I cannot understand how you can touch it, but if you want to, that is entirely up to you."

"Don't sound so prim," Elayne told her. A slow smile broke across her face, a flush of excitement. "I think I could make one."

"Make one!" Nynaeve lowered her voice, hoping no one came running to see who was killing whom, but she did not soften it any. "Light, why? Make an open cesspit first. A midden heap. At least there's some decent use for those."

"I do not mean to actually make an *a'dam*." Elayne held herself erect, chin tilted in that cool way of hers. She sounded offended, and icily calm. "But it is a *ter'angreal*, and I have puzzled out how it works. I saw you attend at least one lecture on linking. The *a'dam* links the two women; that is why the *sul'dam* must be a woman who can channel too." She frowned slightly. "It is a strange link, though. Different. Instead of two or more sharing, with one guiding, it is one taking full control, really. I think that is the reason a *damane* cannot do anything the *sul'dam* doesn't want her to. I don't really believe there is any need for the leash. The collar and bracelet would work as well without it, and in just the same ways."

"Work as well," Nynaeve said dryly. "You've studied the matter a great deal for someone who has no intention of making one." The woman did not even have the grace to blush. "What use would you put it to? I cannot say I would take it amiss if you put one around Elaida's neck, but that doesn't make it any less disgus—"

"Don't you understand?" Elayne broke in, haughtiness all gone in excitement and fervor. She leaned forward to put a hand on Nynaeve's knee, and her eyes shone, she was so delighted with herself. "It is a *ter'angreal,* Nynaeve. And I think I can make one." She said each word slowly and deliberately, then laughed and rushed on. "If I can make this one, I can make others. Maybe I can even make *angreal* and *sa'angreal.* No one in the Tower has been able to do that in thousands of years!" Straightening, she shivered, and laid fingers across her mouth. "I never really thought of *making* anything myself before. Not anything *useful.* I remember seeing a craftsman once, a man who had made some chairs for the palace. They were not gilded, or elaborately carved—they were meant for the servants' hall—but I could see the pride in his eyes. Pride in what he had made, a thing well crafted. I would love to feel that, I think. Oh, if we only knew a fraction of what the Forsaken do. The knowledge of the Age of Legends inside their heads, and they use it to serve the Shadow. Think what we could do with it. Think what we could *make.*" She took a deep breath, dropping her hands in her lap, her enthusiasm barely diminished. "Well, be that as it may, I'll wager I could puzzle out how Whitebridge was made, too. Buildings like spun glass, but stronger than steel. And *cuendillar,* and—"

"Slow down," Nynaeve said. "Whitebridge is five or six hundred miles from here at least, and if you think you're going to go channeling at the seal, you can think again. Who knows what could happen? It stays in its pouch, in the stove, until we find somewhere safe for it."

Elayne's eagerness was very odd. Nynaeve would not have minded a little of the Forsaken's knowledge herself —far from it—but if she wanted a chair, she paid a carpenter. She had never wanted to make anything, aside from poultices and salves. When she was twelve, her mother had stopped going through the motions of teaching her to sew, after it became apparent that she did not care whether she sewed a straight seam and could not be made to care. As for cooking . . . She thought she was a good cook, actually, but the point was that she knew what was significant. Healing was important. Any man could build a bridge, and leave him to it was what she said.

"With you and your *a'dam*," she went on, "I nearly forgot to tell you. Juilin saw Galad on the other side of the river."

"Blood and bloody ashes," Elayne muttered, and when Nynaeve raised her eyebrows, she added very firmly, "I will not listen to a lecture on my language, Nynaeve. What are we going to do?"

"As I see it, we can remain on this side of the river and have Whitecloaks looking us over, wondering why we left the menagerie, or we can cross the bridge and hope the Prophet doesn't spark a riot and Galad doesn't denounce us, or we can try to buy a rowboat and flee downriver. Not very good choices. And Luca will want his hundred marks. Gold." She tried not to scowl, but that still rankled. "You promised it to him, and I suppose it would not be honest to sneak away without paying him." She would have done it in a minute if there was anywhere to go.

"It certainly would not be," Elayne said, sounding shocked. "But we do not have to worry about Galad, at least not as long as we stay close to the menagerie. Galad won't go near one. He thinks putting animals in cages is cruel. He doesn't mind hunting them, mind, or eating them, only caging them."

Nynaeve shook her head. The truth was that Elayne would have found some way to delay, if only for one day, had there been any way to leave. The woman really wanted to highwalk in front of people other than the rest of the performers. And she herself was probably going to have to let Thom throw knives at her again. *I am not wearing that bloody dress, though!*

"The first boat that comes large enough to take four people," she said. "We are hiring it. Trade on the river can't have stopped altogether."

"It would help if we knew where we were going." The other woman's tone was much too gentle. "We could simply head for Tear, you know. We do not have to stay fixed to this just because you . . ." She trailed off, but Nynaeve knew what she had been going to say. Just because *she* was stubborn. Just because she was so furious that she could not remember a simple name that she intended to remember it and go there if it killed her. Well, none of that was true. She intended to find these Aes Sedai who might just support Rand and bring them to him, not trail into Tear like a pitiful refugee fleeing for safety.

"I will remember," she said in a level tone. *It ended with "bar." Or was it "dar"? "Lar"?* "Before you are tired of flaunting yourself highwalking, I will." *I will not wear that dress!*

CHAPTER
34

A Silver Arrow

Elayne had the cooking that evening, which meant
that none of the food was simple, despite the fact
that they were eating on stools around a cookfire,
with crickets chirping in the surrounding woods, and
now and again some night-bird's thin, sad cry in the
deepening darkness. The soup was served cold and
jellied, with chopped green ferris sprinkled on top. The
Light knew where she had found ferris, or the tiny
onions she put in with the peas. The beef was sliced
nearly thin enough to see through and wrapped around
something made from carrots, sweetbeans, chives and
goatcheese, and there was even a small honeycake for
dessert.

It was all tasty, though Elayne fretted that nothing was
exactly the way it should be, as if she thought she could
duplicate the cooks' work in the Royal Palace in
Caemlyn. Nynaeve was fairly sure the girl was not fishing
for compliments. Elayne would always brush away compliments and tell you exactly what was not right. Thom
and Juilin grumbled about there being so little beef, but
Nynaeve noticed that they not only ate every scrap but

looked disappointed when the last pea was gone. When she cooked, for some reason they always seemed to eat at one of the other wagons. When one of them made supper, it was always stew or else meat and beans so full of dried peppers that your tongue blistered.

They did not eat alone, of course. Luca saw to that, bringing his own stool and placing it right next to her, his red cloak spread to best effect and his long legs stretched out so that his calves showed well, above his turned-down boots. He was there almost every night. Oddly, the only nights he missed were when she cooked.

It was interesting, really, having his eyes on her when a woman as pretty as Elayne was there, but he did have his motives. He sat altogether too close—tonight she moved her stool three times, but he followed without missing a word or seeming to notice—and he alternated comparing her with various flowers, to the blossoms' detriment, ignoring the black eye he could not miss without being blind, and musing over how beautiful she would be in that red dress, with compliments on her courage thrown in. Twice, he slipped in suggestions that they take a stroll by moonlight, hints so veiled that she was not entirely sure that was what they were until she thought about it.

"That gown will frame your unfolding bravery to perfection," he murmured in her ear, "yet not a quarter so well as you display yourself, for night-blooming dara lilies would weep with envy to see you stroll beside the moonlit water, as I would do, and make myself a bard to sing your praises by this very moon."

She blinked at him, working that out. Luca seemed to believe she was fluttering her lashes; she accidentally hit him in the ribs with her elbow before he could nibble her ear. At least that seemed to be his intention, even if he was coughing now and claiming he had swallowed a cake crumb the wrong way. The man was certainly handsome—*Stop that!*—and he did have a shapely calf—*What are you doing, looking at his legs?*—but he must think her a brainless ninny. It was all in aid of his bloody show.

She moved her stool again while he was trying to get his breath back; she could not move it far without making it clear that she was running from him, though she held her fork ready in case he followed again. Thom studied his plate as though more than a smear remained on the white glaze. Juilin whistled tunelessly and nearly silently, peering into the dying fire with false intensity. Elayne looked at her and shook her head.

"It was so pleasant of you to join us," Nynaeve said, and stood up. Luca stood when she did, a hopeful look in his eye along with the shine of the firelight. She set her plate atop the one in his hand. "Thom and Juilin will be grateful for your help with the dishes, I am sure." Before his mouth finished falling open, she turned to Elayne. "It is late, and I expect we'll be moving across the river early."

"Of course," Elayne murmured, with just the hint of a smile. And she put her plate atop Nynaeve's before following her into the wagon. Nynaeve wanted to hug her. Until she said, "Really, you should not encourage him." Lamps mounted in wall brackets sprang alight.

Nynaeve planted her fists on her hips. "*Encourage* him! The only way I could encourage him less would be to stab him!" Sniffing for emphasis, she frowned at the lamps. "Next time, use one of Aludra's firesticks. Strikers. You are going to forget one day and channel where you shouldn't, and then where will we be? Running for our lives with a hundred Whitecloaks after us."

Stubborn to a fault, the other woman refused to be diverted. "I may be younger than you, but sometimes I think I know more of men than you ever will. For a man like Valan Luca, that coy little flight of yours tonight was only asking him to keep pursuing you. If you would snap his nose off the way you did the first day, he might give up. You don't tell him to stop, you do not even ask! You kept smiling at him, Nynaeve. What is the man supposed to think? You haven't smiled at *any*one in days!"

"I am trying to hold my temper," Nynaeve muttered. Everybody complained about her temper, and now that she was trying to control it, Elayne complained about that! It was not that she was fool enough to be taken in by his compliments. She certainly was not so big a fool as that. Elayne laughed at her, and she scowled.

"Oh, Nynaeve. 'You cannot hold the sun down at dawn.' Lini could have been thinking of you."

With an effort Nynaeve smoothed her face. She could too hold her temper. *Didn't I just prove it out there?* She held out her hand. "Let me have the ring. He *will* want to cross the river early tomorrow, and I want at least some real sleep after I'm done."

"I thought I would go tonight." Concern touched Elayne's voice. "Nynaeve, you've been entering *Tel'aran'rhiod* practically every night except the meetings with Egwene. That Bair intends to pick a bone with you, by the way. I had to tell them why you weren't there yet again, and she says you should not need rest however often you enter, unless you are doing something wrong." Concern became firmness, and the younger woman planted *her* fists on her hips. "I had to listen to a lecture that was meant for you, and it was not pleasant, with Egwene standing there nodding her head to every word. Now, I really think that tonight I should—"

"Please, Elayne." Nynaeve did not lower her outstretched hand. "I have questions for Birgitte, and her answers might make me think of more." She did have, sort of; she could always think of questions for Birgitte. It had nothing to do with avoiding Egwene, and the Wise Ones. If she visited *Tel'aran'rhiod* so often that Elayne always went to the meetings with Egwene, that was simply how it fell out.

Elayne sighed, but fished the twisted stone ring from the neck of her dress. "Ask her again, Nynaeve. It is very difficult facing Egwene. She *saw* Birgitte. She doesn't say anything, but she looks at me. It is worse when we meet again after the Wise Ones have gone. She *could* ask then, and she still doesn't, and that makes it far worse." She frowned as Nynaeve transferred the small *ter'angreal* to the leather cord around her own neck, with Lan's heavy ring and her Great Serpent. "Why do you suppose none of the Wise Ones ever come with her then? We don't learn very much in Elaida's study, but you would think they would at least want to *see* the Tower. Egwene doesn't even want to talk about it in front of them. If I seem to come close, she gives me such a look that you'd think she meant to hit me."

"I think they want to avoid the Tower as much as

possible." And wise they were indeed for that. If not for Healing, she would avoid it, and Aes Sedai, too. She was *not* becoming Aes Sedai; she was just hoping to learn more of Healing. And to help Rand, certainly. "They are free women, Elayne. Even if the Tower was not in the mess it is, would they really want Aes Sedai traipsing through the Waste, scooping them up to carry back to Tar Valon?"

"I suppose that is it." Elayne's tone said she could not understand it, though. *She* thought the Tower wonderful, and could not see why any woman would want to evade Aes Sedai. Sealed to the White Tower forever, they said when they put that ring on your finger. And they meant it. Yet the fool girl did not see it as onerous at all.

Elayne helped her undress, and she stretched out on her narrow bed in her shift, yawning. It had been a long day, and it was surprising how tiring standing still could be when someone unseen was hurling knives at you. Idle thoughts drifted through her head as she closed her eyes. Elayne had claimed she was practicing when she had acted the fool with Thom. Not that the fond-father-and-favorite-daughter they tried on now was much less foolish to watch. Maybe she could practice herself, just a bit, with Valan. Now, that *was* foolish. Men's eyes might wander—Lan's had *better* not!—but she knew how to be constant. She was simply not going to wear that dress. Far too much bosom.

Vaguely, she heard Elayne say, "Remember to ask her again."

Sleep took her.

She stood outside the wagon, in the night. The moon was high, and drifting clouds cast shadows over the camp. Crickets chirruped, and the night-birds called. The lions' eyes shone as they watched her from their cages. The white-faced bears were dark sleeping mounds behind the iron bars. The long picket line stood empty of horses, Clarine's dogs were not on their leashes beneath her and Petra's wagon, and the space where the *s'redit* stood in the waking world was bare. She had come to understand that only wild creatures had reflections here, but whatever the Seanchan woman claimed, it was hard to think that those huge gray animals had been domesticated so long that they were no longer wild.

Abruptly she realized that she was wearing the dress. Blazing red, far too snug around the hips for decency, and a square neck cut so low she thought she might pop out. She could not imagine any woman but Berelain donning it. For Lan, she might. If they were alone. She *had* been thinking of Lan when she drifted off. *I was, wasn't I?*

In any case, she was not about to let Birgitte see her in the thing. The woman claimed to be a soldier, and the more time Nynaeve spent with her, the more she realized that some of her attitudes—and comments—were as bad as any man's. Worse. A combination of Berelain and a tavern brawler. The comments did not come out all the time, but they certainly did whenever Nynaeve allowed idle thoughts to put her in anything like this dress. She changed to good stout Two Rivers wool, dark, with a plain shawl she did not need, her hair decently braided again, and opened her mouth to call Birgitte.

"Why did you change?" the woman said, stepping out from the shadows to lean on her silver bow. Her intricate golden braid hung over her shoulder, and moonlight shone on her bow and arrows. "I remember wearing a gown that could have been twin to that, once. It was only to attract attention so Gaidal could sneak by—the guards' eyes bulged like frogs'—but it was fun. Especially when I wore it dancing with him later. He *always* hates dancing, but he was so intent on keeping any other man from getting close that he danced every dance." Birgitte laughed fondly. "I won fifty gold solids from him that night at spin, because he stared so much he never looked at his tiles. Men are peculiar. It was not as if he had never seen me—"

"That's as may be," Nynaeve cut in primly, wrapping the shawl firmly around her shoulders.

Before she could add her question, Birgitte said, "I have found her," and all thought of the question fled.

"Where? Did she see you? Can you take me to her? Without her seeing?" Fear fluttered in Nynaeve's belly—a fat lot Valan Luca would say about her courage if he could see her now—but she was sure it would turn to anger as soon as she saw Moghedien. "If you can bring me close . . ." She trailed off as Birgitte raised a hand.

"I cannot think she saw me, or I doubt I would be here now." She was all seriousness now; Nynaeve found it much easier to be around her when she showed this side of being a soldier. "I can take you close for a moment, if you want to go, but she is not alone. At least . . . You will see. You must be silent, and you must take no action against Moghedien. There are other Forsaken. Perhaps you could destroy her, but can you destroy five of them?"

The fluttering in Nynaeve's middle spread to her chest. And her knees. Five. She should ask what Birgitte had seen or heard and let it go at that. Then she could return to her bed and . . . But Birgitte was looking at her. Not questioning her courage, only looking. Ready to do this thing if she said. "I will be silent. And I won't even think of channeling." Not with five Forsaken together. Not that she could have channeled a spark at that moment. She stiffened her knees to keep them from knocking. "Whenever you are ready."

Birgitte hefted her bow and put a hand on Nynaeve's arm . . .

. . . and Nynaeve's breath caught in her throat. They were standing on nothing, infinite blackness all around, no way to tell up from down, and in every direction a fall that would last forever. Head spinning, she made herself look where Birgitte pointed.

Below them, Moghedien also stood on darkness, garbed nearly as black as what surrounded her, bent and listening intently. And as far below her, four huge, high-backed chairs, each different, sat on an expanse of glistening white-tiled floor floating in the blackness. Strangely, Nynaeve could hear what those in the chairs said as well as if she had been among them.

". . . never been a coward," a plumply pretty, sun-haired woman was saying, "so why begin?" Seemingly attired in silvery-gray mist and sparkling gems, she lounged in a chair of ivory worked so it appeared made of naked acrobats. Four carved men held it aloft, and her arms rested along the backs of kneeling women; two men and two women held a white silk cushion behind her head, while above more were contorted into shapes Nynaeve did not believe a human body could attain. She blushed when she realized that some were performing more than acrobatic tricks.

A compact man of middling height, with a livid scar across his face and a square golden beard, leaned forward angrily. His chair was heavy wood, carved with columns of armored men and horses, a steel-gauntleted fist clasping lighting at the back's peak. His red coat made up for the lack of gilding on the chair, for golden scrollwork rolled across his shoulders and down his arms. "No one names me coward," he said harshly. "But if we continue as we are, he will come straight for my throat."

"That has been the plan from the beginning," said a woman's melodious voice. Nynaeve could not see the speaker, hidden behind the towering back of a chair that seemed all snow-white stone and silver.

The second man was large and darkly handsome, with white wings streaking his temples. He toyed with an ornate golden goblet, leaning back in a throne. That was the only possible word for the gem-encrusted thing; a mere hint of gold showed here and there, but Nynaeve would not have doubted that it was solid gold beneath all those glittering rubies and emeralds and moonstones; it had an air of weight quite apart from its massive size. "He will concentrate on you," the big man said in a deep voice. "If need be, one close to him will die, plainly at your order. He will come for you. And while he is fixed on you alone, the three of us, linked, will take him. What has changed to alter any of that?"

"Nothing has changed," the scarred man growled. "Least of all, my trust for you. I *will* be part of the link, or it ends now."

The golden-haired woman threw back her head and laughed. "Poor man," she said mockingly, waving a beringed hand at him. "Do you think he would not *notice* that you were linked? He has a teacher, remember. A poor one, but not a complete fool. Next you will ask to include enough of those Black Ajah children to take the circle beyond thirteen, so you or Rahvin must have control."

"If Rahvin trusts us enough to link when he must allow one of us to guide," the melodious voice said, "you can display an equal trust." The big man looked into his goblet, and the mist-clad woman smiled faintly. "If you cannot trust us not to turn on you," the unseen woman continued, "then trust that we will be watching each other too closely to turn. You *agreed* to all of this, Sammael. Why do you begin to quibble now?"

Nynaeve gave a start as Birgitte touched her arm . . .

. . . and they were back among the wagons, with the moon shining through the clouds. It seemed almost normal compared to where they had been.

"Why . . . ?" Nynaeve began, and had to swallow. "Why did you bring us away?" Her heart leaped into her throat. "Did Moghedien see us?" She had been so intent on the other Forsaken—on the mingled strangeness and commonplaceness of them—that she had forgotten to keep an eye on Moghedien. She heaved a fervent sigh when Birgitte shook her head.

"I never took my gaze from her for more than a moment, and she never moved a muscle. But I do not like being so exposed. If she *had* looked up, or one of the others . . ."

Nynaeve wrapped her shawl tightly around her shoulders and still shivered. "Rahvin and Sammael." She wished she did not sound hoarse. "Did you recognize the others?" Of course Birgitte had; it was a foolish way to phrase it, but she was shaken.

"Lanfear was the one hidden by her chair. The other was Graendal. Do not think her a fool because she lolls in a chair that would make a Senje no-room keeper blush. She is devious, and she uses her *pets* in rites to cause the roughest soldier I ever knew to swear celibacy."

"Graendal is devious," Moghedien's voice said, "but not devious enough."

Birgitte whirled, silver bow coming up, silver arrow almost flying to nock—and abruptly hurtled thirty paces through the moonlight to crash against Nynaeve's wagon so hard that she bounced back five and lay in a crumpled heap.

Desperately Nynaeve reached for *saidar*. Fear streaked through her anger, but there was anger enough—and it ran into an invisible wall between her and the warm glow of the True Source. She almost howled. Something seized her feet, jerking them backward and up off the ground; her hands flew up and back until wrists met ankles above her head. Her clothes became powder that slid from her skin, and her braid dragged her head back until the braid rested on her bottom. Frantic, she tried to step out of the dream. Nothing happened. She hung doubled in midair like some netted creature, every muscle strained to its limit. Tremors ran through her; her fingers twitched feebly, brushing her feet. She thought if she tried to move anything else, her back would break.

Strangely, her fear was gone, now that it was too late. She was certain that she could have been quick enough, if not for the terror that had laced through her when she needed to act. All she wanted was a chance to put her hands around Moghedien's throat. *Much good that does now!* Every breath came in strained panting.

Moghedien moved to where Nynaeve could see her, between the quivering triangle of her arms. The glow of *saidar* surrounded the woman mockingly. "A detail from Graendal's chair," the Forsaken said. Her dress was mist like Graendal's, sliding from black fog to nearly transparent and back to gleaming silver. The fabric changed almost constantly. Nynaeve had seen her wear it before, in Tanchico. "Not something I would have thought of on my own, but Graendal can be . . . edifying." Nynaeve glared at her, but Moghedien did not appear to notice. "I can hardly believe that *you* actually came hunting *me*. Did you really believe that because once you were lucky enough to catch me off guard, you might be my equal?" The woman's laugh was cutting. "If you only knew the effort I have put into finding you. And you came to me." She glanced around at the wagons, studying the lions and bears for a moment before turning back to Nynaeve. "A menagerie? That would make you easy enough to find. If I needed to, now."

"Do your worst, burn you," Nynaeve snarled. As best she could. Doubled up as she was, she had to force the words out one by one. She did not dare look straight toward Birgitte—not that she could have shifted her head enough to—but rolling her eyes as if caught between fury and fear, she caught a glimpse. Her stomach went hollow, even stretched tight as a sheepskin for drying. Birgitte lay sprawled on the ground, silver arrows spilling from the quiver at her waist, her silver bow a span from her unmoving hand. "Lucky, you say? If you hadn't managed to sneak up on me, I'd have striped you till you wailed. I'd have wrung your neck like a chicken." She had only one chance, if Birgitte was dead, and a bleak one. To make Moghedien so angry that she killed her quickly in a rage. If only there was some way to warn Elayne. Her dying would have to do it. "Remember how you said you'd use me for a mounting block? And later, when I said I'd do the same for you? That was after I had beaten you. When you were whimpering and pleading for your life. Offering me anything. You are a gutless coward! The leavings from a nightjar! You piece of—!" Something thick crawled into her mouth, flattening her tongue and forcing her jaws wide.

"You are so simple," Moghedien murmured. "Believe me, I am quite angry enough with you already. I do not think I *will* use you for a mounting block." Her smile made Nynaeve's skin crawl. "I think I will turn you into a horse. It is quite possible, here. A horse, a mouse, a frog . . . ." She paused, listening. ". . . a cricket. And every time you come to *Tel'aran'rhiod,* you'll be a horse, until I change it. Or some other with the knowledge does so." She paused again, looking almost sympathetic. "No, I'd not want to give you false hope. There are only nine of us now who know that binding, and you would not want any of the others to have you any more than myself. You will be a horse every time I bring you here. You will have your own saddle and bridle. I will even braid your mane." Nynaeve's braid jerked almost out of her scalp. "You will remember who you are even then, of course. I think I will enjoy our rides, though you may not." Moghedien took a deep breath, and her dress darkened to something that glistened in the pale light; Nynaeve could not be sure, but she thought it might be the color of wet blood. "You make me approach Semirhage. It will be well to be done with you, so I can turn my full attention to matters of importance. Is the little yellow-haired chit with you in this menagerie?"

The thickness vanished from Nynaeve's mouth. "I am alone, you stupid—" Pain. As if she had been beaten from ankles to shoulders, every stroke landing at once. She bellowed shrilly. Again. She tried to clamp her teeth shut, but her own endless shriek filled her ears. Tears rolled shamingly down her cheeks as she sobbed, waiting hopelessly for the next.

"Is she with you?" Moghedien said patiently. "Do not waste time trying to make me kill you. I won't. You will live many years serving me. Your rather pitiful abilities might be of some use once I train them. Once I train you. But I can make you think that what you just felt was a lover's caress. Now, answer my question."

Nynaeve managed to gather breath. "No," she wept. "She ran off with a man after we left Tanchico. A man old enough to be her grandfather, but he had money. We heard what happened in the Tower"—she was sure Moghedien must know of that—"and she was afraid to go back."

The other woman laughed. "A delightful tale. I can almost see what fascinates Semirhage about breaking the spirit. Oh, you are going to provide me with a great deal of entertainment, Nynaeve al'Meara. But first, you are going to bring the girl Elayne to me. You will shield her and bind her and bring her to lie at my feet. Do you know why? Because some things are actually stronger in *Tel'aran'rhiod* than in the waking world. That is why you will be a glossy white mare whenever I bring you here. And it is not only hurts taken here that last into waking. Compulsion is another. I want you to think of it for a moment or two, before you begin believing it your own idea. I suspect that the girl is your friend. But you are going to bring her to me like a pet—" Moghedien screamed as a silver arrow suddenly stuck its head out from below her right breast.

Nynaeve fell to the ground like a dropped sack. The fall knocked every speck of breath from her lungs as surely as a hammer in the belly. Straining to breathe, she struggled to make racked muscles move, to fight through pain to *saidar*.

Staggering on her feet, Birgitte fumbled another arrow from her quiver. "Go, Nynaeve!" It was a mumbling shout. "Get away!" Birgitte's head wavered, and the silver bow wobbled as she raised it.

The glow around Moghedien increased until it seemed as if the blinding sun surrounded her.

The night folded in over Birgitte like an ocean wave, enveloping her in blackness. When it passed, the bow dropped atop empty clothes as they collapsed. The clothes faded like fog burning off, and only the bow and arrows remained, shining in the moonlight.

Moghedien sank to her knees, panting, clutching the protruding arrow shaft with both hands as the glow around her faded and died. Then she vanished, and the silver arrow fell where she had been, stained dark with blood.

After what seemed an eternity, Nynaeve managed to push up to hands and knees. Weeping, she crawled to Birgitte's bow. This time it was not pain that made tears come. Kneeling, naked and not caring, she clutched the bow. "I'm sorry," she sobbed. "Oh, Birgitte, forgive me. Birgitte!"

There was no answer except the mournful cry of a night-bird.

Liandrin leaped to her feet as the door to Moghedien's bedchamber crashed open and the Chosen staggered into the sitting room, blood soaking her silk shift. Chesmal and Temaile rushed to her side, each taking an arm to keep the woman on her feet, but Liandrin remained by her chair. The others were out; perhaps out of Amador, for all Liandrin knew. Moghedien told only what she wanted the hearer to know, and punished questions she did not like.

"What happened?" Temaile gasped.

Moghedien's brief look should have fried her where

she stood. "You have some small ability with Healing," the Chosen told Chesmal thickly. Blood stained her lips, trickled from the corner of her mouth in an increasing stream. "Do it. Now, fool!"

The dark-haired Ghealdanin woman did not hesitate in laying hands to Moghedien's head. Liandrin sneered to herself as the glow surrounded Chesmal; concern painted Chesmal's handsome face, and Temaile's delicate, foxlike features were contorted with pure fright and worry. So faithful, they were. Such obedient lapdogs. Moghedien lifted up onto her toes, head flung back; eyes wide, she shook, breath rushing from her gaping mouth as if she had been plunged into ice.

In moments it was done. The glow around Chesmal disappeared, and Moghedien's heels settled to the blue-and-green patterned carpet. Without Temaile's support, she might have fallen. Only a part of the strength for Healing came from the Power; the rest came from the person being Healed. Whatever wound had caused all that bleeding would be gone, but Moghedien was surely as weak as if she had lain in bed an invalid for weeks. She pulled the fine gold-and-ivory silk scarf from Temaile's belt to wipe her mouth as the woman helped her turn toward the bedchamber door. Weak, and her back turned.

Liandrin struck as hard as she ever had, with everything she had puzzled out of what the woman had done to her.

Even as she did, *saidar* seemed to fill Moghedien like a flood. Liandrin's probe died as the Source was shielded from her. Flows of Air picked her up and slammed her against the paneled wall hard enough to make her teeth rattle. Spread-eagled, helpless, she hung there.

Chesmal and Temaile exchanged confused glances, as if they did not understand what had occurred. They continued to support Moghedien as she came to stand in front of Liandrin, still calmly wiping her mouth on Temaile's scarf. Moghedien channeled, and the blood on her shift turned black and flaked away, falling to the carpet.

"Y-you do not understand, Great M-mistress,"

Liandrin said frantically. "I only wished to help you to have the good sleep." For once in her life, slipping back into the accents of a commoner did not concern her in the least. "I only—" She cut off with a strangled gagging as a flow of Air seized her tongue, stretching it out between her teeth. Her brown eyes bulged. A hair more pressure, and . . .

"Shall I pull it out?" Moghedien studied her face, but spoke as if to herself. "I think not. A pity for you that the al'Meara woman makes me think like Semirhage. Otherwise, I might only kill you." Suddenly she was tying off the shield, the knot growing ever more intricate, until Liandrin lost the twists and turns completely. And still it went on. "There," Moghedien said finally in tones of satisfaction. "You will search a very long time to find anyone who can unravel that. But you will have no opportunity to search."

Liandrin searched Chesmal's face, and Temaile's, for some sign of sympathy, pity, anything. Chesmal's eyes were cold and stern; Temaile's shone, and she touched her lips with the tip of her tongue and smiled. Not a friendly smile.

"You thought you had learned something of compulsion," Moghedien went on. "I will teach you a bit more." For an instant Liandrin shivered, Moghedien's eyes filling her vision as the woman's voice filled her ears, her entire head. "Live." The instant passed, and sweat beaded on Liandrin's face as the Chosen smiled at her. "Compulsion has many limits, but a command to do what someone wants to do in their inmost depths will hold for a lifetime. You will live, however much you think you want to take your life. And you will think of it. You will lie weeping many nights, wishing for it."

The flow holding Liandrin's tongue vanished, and she barely paused to swallow. "Please, Great Mistress, I swear I did not mean—" Her head rang and silvery black spots danced before her eyes from Moghedien's slap.

"There are . . . attractions . . . to doing a thing physically," the woman breathed. "Do you wish to beg more?"

"Please, Great Mistress—" The second slap sent her hair flying.

"More?"

"Please—" A third nearly unhinged her jaw. Her cheek burned.

"If you cannot be more inventive than that, I will not listen. You will listen instead. I think what I have planned for you would delight Semirhage herself." Moghedien's smile was almost as dark as Temaile's. "You will live, not stilled, but knowing that you could channel again, if only you found someone to untie your shield. Yet that is only the beginning. Evon will be glad of a new scullery girl, and I am sure the Arene woman will want to have long talks with you about her husband. Why, they will enjoy your company so much that I doubt you will see the outside of this house during the years to come. Long years in which to wish that you had served me faithfully."

Liandrin shook her head, mouthing "no" and "please"; she was crying too hard to force the words out.

Turning her head to Temaile, Moghedien said, "Prepare her for them. And tell them they are not to kill or maim her. I want her always to believe she *might* escape. Even futile hope will keep her alive to suffer." She turned away on Chesmal's arm, and the flows holding Liandrin to the wall vanished.

Her legs gave way like straw, crumpling her to the carpet. Only the shield remained; she hammered at it futilely as she crawled after Moghedien, trying to catch the hem of her shift, sobbing brokenly. "Please, Great Mistress."

"They are with a menagerie," Moghedien told Chesmal. "All of your searching, and I had to find them myself. A menagerie should not be too difficult to locate."

"I will serve faithfully," Liandrin wept. Fear turned her limbs to water; she could not crawl fast enough to catch up. They did not even look back at her, scrabbling across the carpet after them. "Bind me, Great Mistress. Anything. I will be the faithful dog!"

"There are many menageries traveling north,"

Chesmal said, eagerness to negate her failure filling her voice. "To Ghealdan, Great Mistress."

"Then I must to Ghealdan," Moghedien said. "You will procure fast horses and follow—" The bedchamber door closed on her words.

"I will be the faithful dog," Liandrin sobbed in a heap on the carpet. Lifting her head, she blinked tears away to see Temaile watching her, rubbing her arms and smiling. "We could overwhelm her, Temaile. We three together could—"

"We *three*?" Temaile laughed. "You could not overwhelm fat Evon." Her eyes narrowed as she studied the shield fastened to Liandrin. "You might as well be stilled."

"Listen. Please." Liandrin swallowed hard, trying to clear her voice, but it was still thick, if burning with urgency, when she went on at frantic speed. "We have spoken of the dissension that must rule among the Chosen. If Moghedien hides herself so, she must hide from the other Chosen. If we take her and give her to them, think of the places we could have. We could be exalted above kings and queens. We could be Chosen ourselves!"

For a moment—one blessed, wonderful moment— the child-faced woman hesitated. Then she shook her head. "You have never known how high to lift your eyes. 'Who reaches for the sun will be burned.' No, I think that I will not be burned for reaching too high. I think that I will do as I am told, and soften you for Evon." Suddenly she smiled, showing teeth that made her even more vulpine. "How surprised he will be when you crawl to kiss his feet."

Liandrin started screaming before Temaile even began.

CHAPTER
35

Ripped Away

Yawning, Elayne watched Nynaeve from her bed, her head propped up on one elbow and black hair spilling down her arm. It was really quite ridiculous, this insistence that whoever did not go to *Tel'aran'rhiod* remain awake. She did not know how long an interval Nynaeve had experienced in the World of Dreams, but Elayne had been lying here for a good two hours, with no book to read, no needlework to do, nothing at all to occupy her except staring at the other woman stretched out on her own narrow bed. Studying the *a'dam* was no good; she thought she had wrung everything out of it that she could. She had even tried a slight touch of Healing on the sleeping woman, perhaps all the Healing she knew. Nynaeve would never have consented to it awake—she did not think much of Elayne's abilities in that direction—or maybe she would have, in this case—but her black eye was gone. In truth, that was the most complicated Healing Elayne had ever done, and it really had exhausted her skill. Nothing to do. If she had some silver, she might have tried making an *a'dam;* silver was not the only metal, but she would have to melt coins to get enough. The other woman would be less pleased at that than at finding a second *a'dam*. If Nynaeve had been willing to tell Thom and Juilin about this, at least she could have invited Thom in for conversation.

They really did have the most delightful talks. Like a father passing on his knowledge to his daughter. She had never realized that the Game of Houses was so deeply embedded in Andor, if thankfully not so deeply as it was in some other lands. Only the Borderlands escaped it entirely, according to Thom. With the Blight right to the north, and Trolloc raids a daily fact, they had no time for maneuvering and scheming. She and Thom had wonderful talks, now that he was sure she was not going to try snuggling into his lap. Her face burned at the memory; she had actually thought of that once or twice, and mercifully had not quite brought herself to it.

"'Even a queen stubs her toe, but a wise woman watches the path,'" she quoted softly. Lini was a wise woman. Elayne did not think she would make that particular mistake again. She knew she made many, but seldom the same twice. One day, perhaps, she would make few enough to be worthy to follow her mother on the throne.

Suddenly she sat up. Tears were leaking from Nynaeve's closed eyes, trickling down the sides of her face; what Elayne had taken for a faint snore—Nynaeve *did* snore, whatever she said—was a tiny, whimpering sob deep in her throat. That should not be. If she had been injured, the hurt would have appeared, although she would not feel it here until she woke.

Perhaps I should wake her. But she hesitated, even as her hand stretched toward the other woman. Waking someone out of *Tel'aran'rhiod* was far from easy—shaking, even icy water in the face would not always do—and Nynaeve would not appreciate being pummeled awake after the bruising Cerandin had given her. *I wonder what really happened. I will have to ask Cerandin.* Whatever was going on, Nynaeve should be able to step out of the dream whenever she wished. Unless . . . Egwene said that the Wise Ones could hold someone in

Tel'aran'rhiod against their will, though if they had taught her the trick, she had not passed it on to Elayne or Nynaeve. If someone was holding Nynaeve now, hurting her, it could not be Birgitte, or the Wise Ones. Well, the Wise Ones might, if they caught her wandering where they thought she should not. But if not them, that left only . . .

She took hold of Nynaeve's shoulders to shake her—if that did not work, she would freeze the pitcher of water on the table, or slap her face silly—and Nynaeve's eyes popped open.

Immediately Nynaeve began to weep aloud, the most despairing sound Elayne had ever heard. "I killed her. Oh, Elayne, I killed her with my foolish pride, thinking I could . . ." The words trailed off in openmouthed sobs.

"You killed who?" It could not be Moghedien; that woman's death would surely not bring this grief. She was about to take Nynaeve in her arms to comfort her, when a pounding came at the door.

"Send them away," Nynaeve mumbled, curling herself into a trembling ball in the middle of the bed.

Sighing, Elayne made her way to the door and pulled it open, but before she could say a word, Thom pushed past her out of the night, rumpled shirt bagging out of his breeches, carrying someone shrouded in his cloak in his arms. Only a woman's bare feet showed.

"She was just there," Juilin said behind him, as if he did not believe the words coming out of his own mouth. Both men were barefoot, and Juilin was stripped to the waist, lean and hairless-chested. "I woke for a moment, and suddenly she was standing there, naked as the day she was born, collapsing like a cut net."

"She's alive," Thom said, laying the cloak-wrapped figure on Elayne's bed, "but only barely. I could hardly hear her heart."

Frowning, Elayne pulled aside the cloak's hood—and found herself staring at Birgitte's face, pale and wan.

Nynaeve scrambled stiffly from the other bed to kneel beside the unconscious woman. Her face glistened with tears, but her weeping had stopped. "She is alive," she breathed. "She is alive." Abruptly she seemed to realize that she was in her shift in front of the men, but she barely spared them a glance, and all she said was "Get them out of here, Elayne. I can do nothing with them gawking like sheep."

Thom and Juilin rolled their eyes toward each other when Elayne made a herding motion at them, and shook their heads slightly, but they backed toward the door without complaint. "She is . . . a friend," Elayne told them. She felt as if she were moving in a dream, floating, without feeling. How could this be? "We will take care of her." How could it possibly have happened? "Now, don't say a word to anyone." The looks they gave her as she closed the door nearly made her blush. Of course they knew better than to talk. But men did have to be reminded of the simplest things sometimes, even Thom. "Nynaeve, how under the Light," she began, turning, and cut off as the glow of *saidar* surrounded the kneeling woman.

"Burn her!" Nynaeve growled, channeling fiercely. "Burn her forever for doing this!" Elayne recognized the flows being woven for Healing, but recognition was as far as she could go. "I will find her, Birgitte," Nynaeve muttered. Strands of Spirit predominated, but Water and Air were in there, and even Earth and Fire. It looked as complicated as embroidering one dress with either hand, and two more with your feet. Blindfolded. "I will make her pay." The glow shining about Nynaeve grew and grew, until it overwhelmed the lamps, until it hurt to look at her except through slitted eyes. "I swear it! By the Light and my hope of salvation and rebirth, I will!" The anger in her voice changed, becoming deeper if anything. "It isn't working. There is nothing wrong with her to Heal. She is as perfect as anyone can be. But she is dying. Oh, Light, I can feel her slipping away. Burn Moghedien! Burn her! And burn me along with her!" She was not giving up, though. The weaving continued, complex flows weaving into Birgitte. And the woman lay there, golden braid flung over the side of the bed, the rise and fall of her chest slowing.

"I can do something that might help," Elayne said slowly. You were supposed to have permission, but it had not always been so. Once it had been done almost as often without as with. There was no reason it should not work on a woman. Except that she had never heard of it being done to any but men.

"Linking?" Nynaeve did not look away from the woman on the bed, or stop her efforts with the Power. "Yes. You will have to do it—I don't know how—but let me guide. I do not know half what I am doing right this minute, but I know that I *can* do it. You could not Heal a bruise."

Elayne's mouth tightened, but she let the remark lie. "Not linking." The amount of *saidar* that Nynaeve had drawn into herself was amazing. If she could not Heal Birgitte with that, what Elayne could add would not make a difference. Together, they would be stronger than either apart, but not as strong as if their two strengths were simply added. Besides, she was not certain that she could link. She had only been linked once, and an Aes Sedai had done it, to show her what it was like more than how. "Stop, Nynaeve. You said yourself it is not working. Stop and let me try. If it doesn't work, you can . . ." She could what? If Healing worked, it worked; if it did not . . . There was no point in trying again if it failed.

"Try what?" Nynaeve snapped, yet she moved away awkwardly, letting Elayne come close. The weave of Healing faded, but not the shining nimbus.

Instead of answering, Elayne put one hand on Birgitte's forehead. Physical contact was as necessary for this as for Healing, and the two times she had watched it done in the Tower, the Aes Sedai had touched the man's forehead. The flows of Spirit she wove were complex, if not so intricate as Nynaeve's of a moment before. She barely understood some of what she was doing, and none at all of other parts, yet she had paid close attention, from her hiding place, to how the weave was shaped. Watched closely because she had built up a stock of stories in her head, made silly romances where there so seldom were any. After a moment, she sat down on the other bed and let *saidar* go.

Nynaeve frowned at her, then bent to examine Birgitte. The unconscious woman's color was perhaps a little better, her breathing a little stronger. "What did you do, Elayne?" Nynaeve did not take her eyes from Birgitte, but the glow around her faded away slowly. "It wasn't Healing. I think I could do it myself, now, but it was not Healing."

"Will she live?" Elayne asked faintly. There was no visible link between her and Birgitte, no flows, but she could sense the woman's weakness. A terrible weakness. She would know the moment Birgitte died, even if she was sleeping, or hundreds of miles away.

"I do not know. She isn't fading anymore, but I do not know." Weariness made Nynaeve's voice soft, and pain touched it strongly, as if she shared Birgitte's injury. Wincing, she rose and unfolded a red-striped blanket to spread over the woman lying there. "What did you do?"

Silence held Elayne long enough for Nynaeve to join her, lowering herself awkwardly onto the bed. "Bonding," Elayne said finally. "I . . . bonded her. As a Warder." The incredulous stare on the other woman's face made her rush on. "Healing was doing no good. I had to do something. You know the gifts a Warder gets from being bonded. One is strength, energy. He can keep going when other men would collapse and die, survive wounds that would kill anyone else. It was the only thing I could think of."

Nynaeve drew a deep breath. "Well, it is working better than what I did, at least. A woman Warder. I wonder what Lan will think of that? No reason why she shouldn't be. If any woman can, it would be her." Wincing, she curled her legs up beneath her; her gaze kept returning to Birgitte. "You will have to keep this secret. If anyone learns that an Accepted has bonded a Warder, whatever the circumstances . . ."

Elayne shivered. "I know," she said simply, and quite fervently. It was not quite a stilling offense, but any Aes Sedai would very likely make her wish she had been stilled. "Nynaeve, what happened?"

For a long moment she thought the other woman was going to start crying again as her chin quivered and her lips worked. When she began speaking, her voice was iron, her face a blend of fury and too many tears ever to be shed. She told the tale starkly, almost sketchily, until she came to Moghedien's appearance among the wagons. That she rendered in painful detail.

"I should be welted from the neck down," she said bitterly at last, touching a smooth, unmarked arm. Unmarked or not, she flinched. "I don't understand why I am not. I feel it, but I deserve the welts, for stupid, foolish pride. For being too afraid to do what I should. I deserved being hung up like a ham in a smokehouse. If there was any justice, I would still be dangling there, and Birgitte would not be lying on that bed, with us wondering whether she'll live or not. If only I knew more. If only I could have Moghedien's knowledge for five minutes, I *could* Heal her. I am sure of it."

"If you were still hanging," Elayne said practically, "in a very short while you would be waking up and shielding me. I don't doubt Moghedien would have seen to it that you were angry enough to channel—she knows us all too well, remember—and I do doubt very much that I would have suspected anything until you had done it. I do not fancy being carted off to Moghedien, and I cannot believe you do either." The other woman did not look at her. "It must have been a link, Nynaeve, like an *a'dam*. That is how she made you feel pain without marking you." Nynaeve still sat there in a glowering sulk. "Nynaeve, Birgitte is alive. You did everything you could for her, and the Light willing, she will live. It was Moghedien who did this to her, not you. A soldier who takes blame for comrades who fall in battle is a fool. You and I are soldiers in a battle, but you are not a fool, so stop behaving like one."

Nynaeve did look at her then, a scowl that lasted only a moment before she turned her face completely away. "You don't understand." Her voice sank almost to a whisper. "She . . . *was* . . . one of the heroes bound to the Wheel of Time, destined to be born again and again to make legends. She wasn't born this time, Elayne. She was ripped out of *Tel'aran'rhiod* as she stood. Is she still bound to the Wheel? Or has she been ripped away from that, too? Ripped away from what her own courage earned her, because I was so proud, so man-stubborn stupid, that I made her hunt for Moghedien?"

Elayne had hoped that those questions had not occurred to Nynaeve yet, would not until she had had a little time to recover first. "Do you know how badly Moghedien was hurt? Maybe she is dead."

"I hope not," the other woman almost snarled. "I want to make her pay. . . ." She took a deep breath, but instead of invigorating her, it seemed to make her sag. "I would not count on her dying. Birgitte's shot missed her heart. A wonder she managed to hit the woman at all, staggering as she was. I could not have stood up if I were thrown that far, hard enough to bounce like that. I couldn't even stand up after what Moghedien did to me. No, she is alive, and we had best believe that she can have her wound Healed and be after us by morning."

"She would still need time to rest, Nynaeve. You know that. Can she even know where we are? From what you said, she had no time to do more than see that this is a menagerie."

"What if she did see more?" Nynaeve rubbed her temples as if it were difficult to think. "What if she knows *exactly* where we are? She could send Darkfriends after us. Or send word to Darkfriends in Samara."

"Luca is livid because eleven menageries are already around the city, and three more are waiting to cross the bridge. Nynaeve, it will take her days to regain strength after a wound like that, even if she does find some Black sister to Heal her, or one of the other Forsaken. And more days to search through fifteen menageries. That is if there are not more on the road behind us, or coming from Altara. If she does come after us or send Darkfriends, either one, we are forewarned, and we have days to find a boat that can carry us downriver." She paused a moment, thinking. "Do you have anything to dye your hair in that bag of herbs? I'll wager anything that you had your hair braided in *Tel'aran'rhiod.* Mine is always its real color, there. If yours is loose, as it is now, and another color, it will make us that much harder to find."

"Whitecloaks everywhere," Nynaeve sighed. "Galad. The Prophet. No boats. It is as if everything is conspiring to hold us here for Moghedien. I am so tired, Elayne. Tired of being afraid of who might be around the next corner. Tired of being afraid of Moghedien. I cannot seem to think of what to do next. My hair? Nothing that would make it any color I'd have."

"You need to sleep," Elayne said firmly. "Without the ring. Give it to me." The other woman hesitated, but Elayne merely waited with her hand outstretched until Nynaeve fished the flecked stone ring from the cord around her neck. Stuffing it into her pouch, Elayne went on. "Now you lie down here, and I will watch Birgitte."

Nynaeve stared at the woman stretched out on the other bed for a moment, then shook her head. "I can't sleep. I . . . need to be alone. To walk." Getting to her feet as stiffly as if she really had been beaten, she took her dark cloak from its peg and swung it over her shift. At the door she paused. "If she wants to kill me," she said bleakly, "I do not know that I could make myself stop her." She went into the night barefoot and sad-faced.

Elayne hesitated, unsure which woman needed her more, before settling back where she sat. Nothing she said could make things better for Nynaeve, but she had faith in the woman's resilience. Time alone to work it all over in her mind, and she would see that blame lay at Moghedien's door, not hers. She had to.

CHAPTER
36

A New Name

For a long time Elayne sat there, watching Birgitte sleep. It did seem to be sleep. Once she stirred, muttering in a desperate voice, "Wait for me, Gaidal. Wait. I'm coming, Gaidal. Wait for . . ." Words trailed off into slow breath again. Was it stronger? The woman still looked deathly ill. Better than she had, but pale and drawn.

After perhaps an hour, Nynaeve returned, her feet dirty. Fresh tears shone on her cheeks. "I could not stay away," she said, hanging her cloak back on its peg. "You sleep. I will watch her. I have to watch her."

Elayne rose slowly, smoothing her skirts. Perhaps watching over Birgitte for a time would help Nynaeve work matters out. "I don't feel like sleeping yet, either." She was exhausted, but not sleepy any longer. "I think I will stroll outside myself." Nynaeve only nodded as she took Elayne's place on the bed, her dusty feet dangling over the side, her eyes fastened to Birgitte.

To Elayne's surprise, Thom and Juilin were not asleep either. They had built a small fire beside the wagon and sat on either side of it, cross-legged on the ground, smoking their long-stemmed pipes. Thom had tucked his shirt in, and Juilin had donned his coat, though no shirt, and turned the cuffs back. She took a look around before joining them. No one stirred in the camp, dark except for the light of this one fire and the glow of the lamps from their wagon's windows.

Neither man said anything while she settled her skirts; then Juilin looked at Thom, who nodded, and the thief-catcher took something from the ground and held it out to her. "I found it where she was lying," the dark man said. "As if it had dropped from her hand."

Elayne took the silver arrow slowly. Even the fletching feathers appeared to be silver.

"Distinctive," Thom said conversationally around his pipe. "And added to the braid . . . Every story mentions the braid for some reason. Though I've found some I think might be her under other names, without it. And some under other names with."

"I do not care about stories," Juilin put in. He sounded no more agitated than Thom. But then, it took a great deal to agitate either one of them. "Is it her? Bad enough if it isn't, a woman appearing naked out of nothing like that, but . . . What have you gotten us into, you and N . . . Nana?" He *was* troubled; Juilin did not make mistakes, and his tongue *never* slipped. Thom merely bubbled at his pipe, waiting.

Elayne turned the arrow in her hands, pretending to study it. "She is a friend," she said finally. Until—unless—Birgitte released her, her promise held. "She is not Aes Sedai, but she has been helping us." They looked at her, waiting for her to say more. "Why didn't you give this to Nynaeve?"

One of those glances passed between them—men seemed to carry on entire conversations through glances, around women at least—saying as clearly as spoken words what they thought of her keeping secrets. Especially when they all but knew for certain already. But she had given her word.

"She seemed upset," Juilin said, sucking at his pipe judiciously, and Thom took his from between his teeth and blew out his white mustaches.

"Upset? The woman came out in her shift, looking lost, and when I asked if I could help her, she didn't snap my head off. She cried on my shoulder!" He plucked at his linen shirt, muttering something about dampness. "Elayne, she *apologized* for every cross word she has ever said to me, which is very nearly every other word out of her mouth. Said she ought to be switched, or maybe that she had been; she was incoherent half the time. She said she was a coward, and a stubborn fool. I don't know what is the matter with her, but she isn't herself by a mile."

"I knew a woman who behaved like this, once," Juilin said, peering into the fire. "She woke to find a burglar in her bedchamber and stabbed the man through the heart. Only, when she lit a lamp, it was her husband. His boat had come back to the docks early. She walked around like Nynaeve for half a month." His mouth tightened. "Then she hanged herself."

"I hate to lay this burden on you, child," Thom added gently, "but if she can be helped, you are the only one of us who can do it. I know how to take a man out of his miseries. Give him a swift kick, or else get him drunk and find him a pr—" He harrumphed loudly, trying to make it seem a cough, and knuckled his mustaches. The one bad thing about him seeing her as a daughter was that now sometimes he seemed to think she was perhaps twelve. "Anyway, the point is that I do not know how to do this. And while Juilin might be willing to dandle her on his knee, I doubt she'd thank him for it."

"I would sooner dandle a fangfish," the thief-catcher muttered, but not as roughly as he would have yesterday. He was as concerned as Thom, though less willing to admit it.

"I will do what I can," she assured them, turning the arrow again. They were good men, and she did not like lying to them, or hiding things from them. Not unless it was absolutely necessary, anyway. Nynaeve claimed that you had to manage men for their own good, but there was such a thing as taking it too far. It was not right to lead a man into dangers he knew nothing of.

So she told them. About *Tel'aran'rhiod* and the Forsaken being loose, about Moghedien. Not quite everything, of course. Some events in Tanchico had been too shaming for her to want to think of them. Her promise held her concerning Birgitte's identity, and there was certainly no need to go into detail about what Moghedien had done to Nynaeve. It made explaining this night's happenings a little difficult, yet she managed. She did tell them everything she thought they should know, enough to make them aware for the first time what they were really up against. Not just the Black Ajah—that had certainly made them stare cross-eyed when they learned it—but the Forsaken, and one of them very likely hunting her and Nynaeve. And she made it quite plain that they two would be hunting Moghedien as well, and that anyone close to them was in danger of being caught between hunter and prey either way.

"Now that you know," she finished, "the choice to stay or go is yours." She left it at that, and was careful not to look at Thom. She hoped almost desperately that he would stay, but she would not let him think that she was asking, not by so much as a glance.

"I haven't taught you half what you need to know if you're to be as good a queen as your mother," he said, trying to sound gruff and spoiling it by brushing a strand of black-dyed hair from her cheek with a gnarled finger. "You'll not rid yourself of me this easily, child. I mean to see you mistress of *Daes Dae'mar* if I must drone in your ear until you go deaf. I haven't even taught you to handle a knife. I tried to teach your mother, but she always said she could tell a man to use a knife if one needed using. Fool way to look at it."

She leaned forward and kissed his leathery cheek, and he blinked, bushy eyebrows shooting up, then smiled and stuck his pipe back into his mouth.

"You can kiss me, too," Juilin said dryly. "Rand al'Thor will have my guts for fish bait if I don't hand you back to him in the same health he last saw you."

Elayne lifted her chin. "I will not have you stay for Rand al'Thor, Juilin." Hand her back? Indeed! "You will stay only if you want to. And I do not release you—or you, Thom!"—he had grinned at the thief-catcher's comment—"from your promise to do as you are told." Thom's startled look was quite satisfying. She turned back to Juilin. "You will follow *me,* and Nynaeve of course, knowing full well the enemies we face, or you may pack your belongings and ride Skulker where you wish. I will give him to you."

Juilin sat up straight as a post, his dark face going darker. "I have never abandoned a woman in danger in my life." He pointed his pipestem at her like a weapon. "You send me away, and I will be on your heels like a soarer on a stern-chase."

Not exactly what she wanted, but it would do. "Very well, then." Rising, she held herself erect, the silver arrow at her side, and kept her slightly frosty manner. She thought they had finally realized who was in charge. "Morning is not far off." Had Rand actually had the nerve to tell Juilin to "hand her back"? Thom would just have to suffer along with the other man for a time, and it served him right for that grin. "You will put out this fire and go to sleep. Now. No excuses, Thom. You'll be no good at all tomorrow without sleep."

Obediently they began scuffing dirt over the flames with their boots, but when she reached the plain wooden steps of the wagon, she heard Thom say, "Sounds like her mother sometimes."

"Then I am glad I have never met the woman," Juilin grumbled in reply. "Flip for first guard?" Thom murmured an assent.

She almost went back, but found herself smiling instead. *Men!* It was a fond thought. Her good mood lasted until she was inside.

Nynaeve sat on the very edge of the bed, holding herself up with both hands, eyes trying to drift shut as she watched Birgitte. Her feet were still dirty.

Elayne put Birgitte's arrow into one of the cupboards behind some rough sacks of dried peas. Luckily, the other woman never so much as glanced at her. She did not think the sight of the silver arrow was what Nynaeve needed right at that moment. But what was?

"Nynaeve, it is past time for you to wash your feet and go to sleep."

Nynaeve swayed in her direction, blinking sleepily. "Feet? What? I must watch her."

It would have to be one step at a time. "Your feet, Nynaeve. They are dirty. Wash them."

Frowning, Nynaeve peered down at her dusty feet, then nodded. She spilled water tipping the big white pitcher over the washbasin, and sloshed more out before she was washed and ready to towel dry, but even then she resumed her seat. "I must watch. In case . . . In case . . . She cried out once. For Gaidal."

Elayne pressed her back on the mattress. "You need sleep, Nynaeve. You can't keep your eyes open."

"I can," Nynaeve muttered sullenly, trying to sit up against Elayne's pressure on her shoulders. "I must watch her, Elayne. I must."

Nynaeve made the two men outside look sensible and biddable. Even if Elayne had had a mind to, there was no way to get her drunk and find her a—a pretty young man, she supposed it would have to be. That left a swift kick. Sympathy and common sense had surely made no impression. "I have had enough of this sulking and self-pity, Nynaeve," she said firmly. "You are going to sleep *now,* and in the morning you are not going to say one word about what a miserable wretch you are. If you cannot behave like the clearheaded woman you are, I will ask Cerandin to give you two black eyes for the one I took away. You did not even thank me for that. Now go to sleep!"

Nynaeve's eyes widened indignantly—at least she did not look on the point of tears—but Elayne slid them shut with her fingers. They closed easily, and despite softly murmured protests, the deep slow breath of sleep followed quickly.

Elayne patted Nynaeve's shoulder before straightening. She hoped it was a peaceful sleep, with dreams of Lan, but any sort of sleep was better for her now than none. Fighting a yawn, she bent to check Birgitte. She could not tell whether the woman's color or breathing was any better. There was nothing to do but wait and hope.

The lamps did not seem to be bothering either of the

women, so she left them alight and sat on the floor between the beds. They should help keep her awake. Not that she knew why she should remain awake, really. She had done what she could as much as Nynaeve had. Unthinkingly she leaned back against the front wall, and her chin sank slowly to her chest.

The dream was a pleasant one, if odd. Rand knelt before her, and she put a hand on his head and bonded him as her Warder. One of her Warders; she would *have* to choose Green now, with Birgitte. There were other women there, faces changing between one glance and the next. Nynaeve, Min, Moiraine, Aviendha, Berelain, Amathera, Liandrin, others she did not know. Whoever they were, she knew that she had to share him with them, because in the dream she was certain that that was what Min had viewed. She was not sure how she felt about that—some of those faces she wanted to claw to shreds —but if it was fated by the Pattern, it would have to be. Yet she would have one thing of him the others could never have, the bond between Warder and Aes Sedai.

"Where is this place?" Berelain said, raven-haired and so beautiful that Elayne wanted to bare her teeth. The woman wore the low-cut red dress that Luca wanted Nynaeve to wear; she always dressed revealingly. "Wake up. This is not *Tel'aran'rhiod.*"

Elayne started awake to find Birgitte leaning over the side of the bed, gripping her arm weakly. Her face was too pale, and damp with sweat as if a fever had broken, but her blue eyes were sharp and intent on Elayne's face.

"This is not *Tel'aran'rhiod.*" It was not a question, but Elayne nodded, and Birgitte sank back with a long sigh. "I remember everything," she whispered. "I am here as I am, and I remember. All is changed. Gaidal is out there, somewhere, an infant, or even a young boy. But even if I find him, what will he think of a woman more than old enough to be his mother?" She scrubbed angrily at her eyes, muttering, "I do not cry. I never cry. I remember that, the Light help me. I never cry."

Elayne got up on her knees beside the woman's bed. "You will find him, Birgitte." She kept her voice low. Nynaeve still seemed sound asleep—a small, rasping snore rose from her regularly—but she needed rest, not to confront this all over again now. "Somehow you will. And he will love you. I know he will."

"Do you think that is what matters? I could stand him not loving me." Her glistening eyes gave her the lie. "He will need me, Elayne, and I will not be there. He always has more courage than is good for him; I always must supply him with caution. Worse, he will wander, searching for me, not knowing what he is looking for, not knowing why he feels incomplete. We are always together, Elayne. Two halves of a whole." The tears welled up, flowing across her face. "Moghedien said she would make me cry forever, and she . . ." Suddenly her features contorted; low ragged sobs came as if ripped from her throat.

Elayne gathered the taller woman into her arms, murmuring words of comfort she knew were useless. How would she feel if Rand were taken away from her? The thought was nearly enough to make her put her head down atop Birgitte's and join her weeping.

She was not sure how long it took Birgitte to cry herself out, but eventually she pushed Elayne away and settled back, wiping her cheeks with her fingers. "I have never done that except as a small child. Never." Twisting her neck, she frowned at Nynaeve, still asleep on the other bed. "Did Moghedien hurt her badly? I have not seen anyone trussed like that since the Tourag took Mareesh." Elayne must have looked confused, because she added, "In another Age. Is she hurt?"

"Not badly. Her spirit, mainly. What you did allowed her to escape, but only after . . ." Elayne could not make herself say it. Too many wounds were too fresh. "She blames herself. She thinks that . . . everything . . . is her fault, for asking you to help."

"If she had not asked me, Moghedien would be teaching her to beg right now. She has as little caution as Gaidal." Birgitte's dry tone sounded odd with her wet cheeks. "She did not drag me into this by my hair. If she claims responsibility for the consequences, then she claims responsibility for my actions." If anything, she sounded angry. "I am a free woman, and I made my own choices. She did not decide for me."

"I must say you are taking this better than . . . I would." She could not say "better than Nynaeve." That was true, but the other was as well.

"I always say, if you must mount the gallows, give a jest to the crowd, a coin to the hangman, and make the drop with a smile. on your lips." Birgitte's smile was grim. "Moghedien sprang the trap, but my neck is not yet snapped. Perhaps I will surprise her before it is done." The smile faded into a frown as she studied Elayne. "I can . . . feel you. I think I could close my eyes and point to you a mile away."

Elayne took a very deep breath. "I bonded you as a Warder," she said in a rush. "You were dying, and Healing did no good, and . . ." The woman was looking at her. Not frowning anymore, but her eyes were disconcertingly sharp. "There was no other choice, Birgitte. You would have died, else."

"A Warder," Birgitte said slowly. "I think I remember hearing a tale of a female Warder, but it was in a life so long ago that I cannot remember more than that."

It was time for another deep breath, and this time she had to force the words. "There is something you should know. You will discover it sooner or later, and I've decided not to keep things from people who have a right to know, not unless I absolutely must." A third breath. "I am not Aes Sedai. I am only Accepted."

For a long moment, the golden-braided woman stared up at her, then slowly shook her head. "An Accepted. In the Trolloc Wars, I knew an Accepted who bonded a fellow. Barashelle was due to be tested the next day for raising to full Aes Sedai, and certain to be given the shawl, but she was afraid that a woman testing that same day would take him. In the Trolloc Wars, the Tower tried to raise women as quickly as possible, from necessity."

"What happened?" Elayne could not stop herself from asking. Barashelle? That name sounded familiar.

Lacing her fingers over the blanket atop her bosom, Birgitte shifted her head on the pillow and put on a look of mock sympathy. "Needless to say, she was not allowed to take the tests once it was discovered. Necessity did not outweigh such an offense. They made her pass the poor fellow's bond to another, and to teach her patience, put her into the kitchens among the scullions and spit-girls. I heard that she stayed there three years, and when she did receive her shawl, the Amyrlin Seat herself chose her Warder, a leather-faced, stone-stubborn man named Anselan. I saw them a few years after, and I could not tell which of them gave the commands. I do not think Barashelle was certain either."

"Not pleasant," Elayne muttered. Three years in the . . . Wait. Barashelle and *Anselan*? It could not be the same pair; that story said nothing about Barashelle being Aes Sedai. But she had read two versions and heard Thom tell another, and all had Barashelle doing some long, arduous service to earn Anselan's love. Two thousand years could change a great deal in a story.

"Not pleasant," Birgitte agreed, and suddenly her eyes were much too large and innocent in her pale face. "I suppose, since you wish me to keep your dreadful secret, you will not ride me as hard as some Aes Sedai ride their Warders. It would not do to push me to tell just to escape you."

Elayne's chin came up instinctively. "That sounds very like a threat. I do not take well to threats, from you or anyone else. If you think—"

The reclining woman caught her arm and cut her off apologetically; her grip was noticeably stronger. "Please. I did not intend it that way. Gaidal claims I have a sense of humor like a rock tossed into a shoja-circle." A cloud swept across her face at Gaidal's name, and was gone. "You saved my life, Elayne. I will keep your secret and serve you as Warder. And be your friend, if you will have me."

"I will be proud to have you for friend." Shoja-circle? She would ask another time. Birgitte might be stronger, but she needed rest, not questions. "And for Warder." It seemed that she really was going to choose the Green Ajah; aside from everything else, that was the only way she could bond Rand. The dream was still clear in her mind, and she intended to convince him to accept it one way or another. "Perhaps you could try to . . . moderate . . . your sense of humor?"

"I will try." Birgitte sounded as if she were saying she would try to pick up a mountain. "But if I am to be your Warder, even in secret, then I will be Warder to you. You can barely hold your eyes open. It is time for you to sleep." Elayne's eyebrows and chin shot up together, but the woman gave her no opportunity to speak. "Among many other things, it is a Warder's place to tell his—her —Aes Sedai when she pushes herself too hard. Also to provide a dose of caution when she thinks she can walk into the Pit of Doom. And to keep her alive so she can do what she must. I will do these things for you. Never fear for your back when I am near, Elayne."

She did need sleep, she supposed, but Birgitte needed it more. Elayne dimmed the lamps and got the woman settled and asleep, though not until Birgitte had seen her put a pillow and blankets on the floor between the beds for herself. There was some slight argument over who would sleep on the floor, but Birgitte was still weak enough that Elayne had no trouble making her stay in the bed. Well, not very much anyway. At least Nynaeve's soft snore never broke.

She herself did not go to sleep immediately, whatever she had told Birgitte. The woman could not put her nose outside the wagon until she had something to wear, and she was taller than Elayne or Nynaeve. Sitting down between the beds, Elayne began letting out the hem on her dark gray silk riding dress. There would hardly be time in the morning for more than a quick fitting and stitching the new hem. Sleep overtook her with her ripping no more than half done.

She had the dream of bonding Rand again, more than once. Sometimes he knelt voluntarily, and sometimes she had to do what she had done with Birgitte, even sneaking into his bedchamber while he slept. Birgitte was one of the other women now. Elayne did not mind that *too* much. Not her, or Min, or Egwene, or Aviendha, or Nynaeve, though she could not imagine what Lan would say to that last. Others, though . . . She had just ordered Birgitte, in a Warder's color-shifting cloak, to drag Berelain and Elaida to the kitchens for three years, when suddenly the two women began pummeling her. She awakened to find Nynaeve trampling her to reach Birgitte and check on the woman. The gray light just before dawn showed in the small windows.

Birgitte woke claiming she was as strong as ever, and ravenous besides. Elayne was not certain whether Nynaeve had finished her bout of self-blame. She did not wring her hands or speak of it, but while Elayne washed her face and hands, and explained about the menagerie and why they had to remain with it a while longer, Nynaeve hastily peeled and cored red pears and yellow apples, sliced cheese, and handed it all to Birgitte on a plate with a cup of watered wine with honey and spices. She would have fed the woman had Birgitte let her. Nynaeve washed Birgitte's hair in white henpepper herself, until it was as black as Elayne's—Elayne did her own, of course—donated her best stockings and shift, and looked disappointed when a pair of Elayne's slippers fit better. She insisted on helping Birgitte into the gray silk as soon as her hair had been toweled dry and braided again—the hips and bosom needed letting out, too, but that would have to wait—and even wanted to stitch the hem herself, until Elayne's incredulous stare made her retreat to her own ablutions, muttering as she scrubbed her face that she could sew as well as anyone. When she wanted to.

When they went outside at last, the first sharp golden edge of the sun was peeking above the trees to the east. For this little while, the day felt deceptively comfortable. There was not a cloud to be seen in the sky, and by noon the air would be hot and gritty.

Thom and Juilin were hitching the team to the wagon, and the whole camp bustled in preparation for moving. Skulker was already saddled, and Elayne made a note to herself to speak up about riding today herself before one of the men took possession of the saddle. Even if Thom or Juilin got there first, though, she would not be too disappointed. This very afternoon she would highwalk in front of people for the first time. The costume Luca had shown her made her a little nervous, but at least she was not moaning about it as Nynaeve did.

Luca himself came striding rapidly through the camp, red cloak fluttering behind, chivvying and shouting unneeded instructions. "Latelle, wake those bloody bears! I want them on their feet, snarling, when we drive through Samara. Clarine, you watch those dogs this time. If one of them goes chasing after a cat again . . . Brugh, you and your brothers do your tumbling just ahead of my wagon, mind. *Just* ahead. This is supposed to be a stately procession, not a race to see which of you can backflip the fastest! Cerandin, keep those boar-horses in hand. I want people to gasp in amazement, not run in terror!"

He stopped at their wagon, glowering at Nynaeve and herself equally with a bit left over for Birgitte. "Kind of you to decide to come with the rest of us, Mistress Nana, *my Lady* Morelin. I thought you meant to sleep until midday." He nodded toward Birgitte. "Having a chat with someone from across the river, are you? Well, we've no time for visitors. I mean to be set up and performing by noon."

Nynaeve looked taken aback by the onslaught, but by the end of his second sentence she was meeting him glare for glare. Whatever her awkwardness toward Birgitte, it apparently did not hinder her temper where others were concerned. "We will be ready as soon as anyone, and you know it, Valan Luca. Besides, an hour or two will make no difference anyway. There are enough people gathered on the other side of the river that if one in a hundred comes to your show it will be more than you ever dreamed. If we decide to make a leisurely breakfast, you can just twiddle your thumbs and wait. You'll not get what you want if you leave us behind."

That was her bluntest reminder yet of the promised hundred gold marks, but for once it did not slow him. "Enough people? Enough people! People must be attracted, woman. Chin Akima has been in place three days, and he has a fellow who juggles swords and axes. And nine acrobats. Nine! Some woman I've never heard of has two women acrobats who do things on a hanging rope that would make the Chavanas' eyes pop. You would not believe the crowds. Sillia Cerano has men with their faces painted like court fools, splashing each other with water and hitting each other over the head with bladders, and people are paying an extra silver penny just to watch!" Suddenly his eyes narrowed, focusing on Birgitte. "Would you be willing to paint your face? Sillia doesn't have a woman among her fools. Some of the horse handlers would be willing. It doesn't hurt, getting hit with an inflated bladder, and I will pay you. . . ." He trailed off, musing—he did not like parting with money any more than Nynaeve did—and Birgitte spoke into his momentary silence.

"I am not a fool, and will not be a fool. I am an archer."

"An archer," he muttered, eyeing the intricate glossy black braid pulled over her left shoulder. "And I suppose you call yourself Birgitte. What are you? One of those idiots hunting the Horn of Valere? Even if the thing exists, what chance any one of you will find it more than another? I was in Illian when the Hunters' oaths were given, and there were thousands in the Great Square of Tammaz. But for glory that you *can* attain, nothing can outshine the applause of—"

"I am an archer, pretty man," Birgitte broke in firmly. "Fetch a bow, and I will outshoot you or anyone you name, a hundred crowns gold to your one." Elayne expected Nynaeve to yelp—it was they who would have to cover the wager if Birgitte lost, and whatever she claimed, Elayne did not think Birgitte could be fully recovered already—yet all Nynaeve did was close her eyes briefly and draw a deep, long breath.

"Women!" Luca growled. Thom and Juilin did not have to look as if they agreed. "You are a fine match for the *Lady* Morelin and Nana, or whatever their names are." He swept his silk cloak in a wide gesture at the surrounding hustle of men and horses. "It may have escaped your keen eye, *Birgitte,* but I have a show to get under way, and my rivals are already draining Samara of coin like the cutpurses they are."

Birgitte smiled, a slight curving of her lips. "Are you

afraid, pretty man? We can make your side a silver penny."

Elayne thought Luca might have apoplexy from the color that crept into his face. His neck suddenly looked too big for his collar. "I will fetch my bow," he almost hissed. "You can work off the hundred marks with your face painted, or cleaning cages for all I care!"

"Are you sure that you are well enough?" Elayne asked Birgitte as he stalked off muttering to himself. The only word she caught was a repeat of "women!" Nynaeve was looking at the woman with the braid as if she wanted the ground to open and swallow her; herself, not Birgitte. A number of the horse handlers had gathered around Thom and Juilin for some reason.

"He has nice legs," Birgitte said, "but I have never liked tall men. Add a pretty face, and they are always insufferable."

Petra had joined the group of men, twice as wide as any other. He said something, then shook hands with Thom. The Chavanas were there as well. And Latelle, talking earnestly with Thom while darting dark looks at Nynaeve and the two women with her. By the time Luca returned with an unstrung bow and a quiver of arrows, no one was making preparations any longer. The wagons and horses and cages—even the tethered boar-horses— stood abandoned, the people all clustered around Thom and the thief-catcher. They followed as Luca led the way a short distance out of the camp.

"I am accounted a fair shot," he said, carving a white cross chest-high to himself on the trunk of a tall oak. He had some of his jauntiness back, and he swaggered as he strode off fifty paces. "I will take the first shot, so you can see what you face."

Birgitte plucked the bow from his hand and walked off another fifty as he stared after her. She shook her head over the bow, but braced it on her slippered foot and strung it in one smooth motion before Luca joined her and Elayne and Nynaeve. Birgitte pulled an arrow from the quiver he held, examined it a moment, then tossed it aside like rubbish. Luca frowned and opened his mouth, but she was already discarding a second shaft. The next three went to the leaf-covered ground as well before she stuck one point-down in the soil beside her. Of twenty-one, she kept only four.

"She can do it," Elayne whispered, trying to sound certain. Nynaeve nodded bleakly; if they had to pay out a hundred gold crowns, they would soon be selling the jewelry Amathera had given them. The letters-of-rights were all but useless, as she had explained to Nynaeve; their use would eventually point a finger to where they had been been for Elaida, if not where they were. *If I had just spoken up in time, I could have stopped this. As my Warder, she has to do as I say. Doesn't she?* From the evidence so far, obedience was no part of the bond. Had those Aes Sedai she had spied on made the men give oaths as well? Now that she thought of it, she believed one of them had.

Birgitte nocked an arrow, raised the bow, and loosed seemingly without pausing to aim. Elayne winced, but the steel point struck dead center in the middle of the carved white cross. Before it stopped quivering, the second brushed in beside it. Birgitte did wait a moment then, but only for the two arrows to still. A gasp rose from the onlookers as the third shaft *split* the first, but that was nothing to the absolute silence as the last split the other just as neatly. Once could have been chance. Twice . . .

Luca looked as if his eyes were coming out of his head. Mouth hanging open, he stared at the tree, then at Birgitte, at the tree then Birgitte. She proffered the bow, and he shook his head weakly.

Suddenly he flung the quiver away, spreading his arms wide with a glad cry. "Not knives! Arrows! From a hundred paces!"

Nynaeve sagged against Elayne as the man explained what he wanted, but she made not one sound of protest. Thom and Juilin were collecting money; most handed over coins with a sigh or a laugh, but Juilin had to snag Latelle's arm as she tried to slip away, and speak some angry words before she dug coins from her pouch. So that was what they had been up to. She would have to speak to them firmly. But later. "Nana, you don't have to go through with this." The woman only stared at Birgitte, eyes haggard.

"Our wager?" Birgitte said when Luca ran out of wind. He grimaced, then fished slowly into his pouch and tossed her a coin. Elayne caught the glint of gold in the sun as Birgitte examined it, then tossed it right back. "The bet was a silver penny on your part."

Luca's eyes widened in startlement, but the next moment he was laughing and pressing the gold crown into her hand. "You are worth every copper of it. What do you say? Why, the Queen of Ghealdan herself might come to see a performance such as yours. Birgitte and her arrows. We will paint them silver, and the bow!"

Desperately Elayne wanted Birgitte to look at her. They might as well put up a sign for Moghedien as do what the man suggested.

But Birgitte only bounced the coin on her hand, grinning. "Paint will ruin an already shabby bow," she said finally. "And call me Maerion; I was called that, once." Leaning on the bow, she let her smile widen. "Can I have a red dress, too?"

Elayne heaved a sigh of fervent relief. Nynaeve looked as if she were going to sick up.

CHAPTER
37

Performances in Samara

For what seemed the hundredth time, Nynaeve held a lock of her hair up to look at it and sighed. Thick murmurs of talk and laughter from hundreds if not thousands of throats, distant music that was nearly drowned out, drifted in through the wagon walls. She had not minded spending the parade through the streets of Samara in the wagon with Elayne—occasional peeks through the windows had convinced her that she would just as soon not be out in those packed crowds, yelling and barely making way for the wagons—but every time she looked at the brassy red of her hair, she wished she had been doing somersaults with the Chavanas rather than dyeing it.

Carefully not looking at herself, she wrapped up completely in her plain dark gray shawl, turned, and gave a start to find Birgitte standing in the doorway. The woman had ridden in Clarine and Petra's wagon during the parade, with Clarine altering a spare red dress she had been making for Nynaeve at Luca's direction; he had given Clarine her instructions before Nynaeve ever agreed. Birgitte wore it now, her black-dyed braid pulled over her shoulder so it nestled between her breasts, totally unconscious of the low square neck. Just looking at her made Nynaeve fold her shawl tighter; Birgitte could not show a fingernail more of pale bosom and retain the slightest claim to decency. As it was, such a claim would be feeble, really quite laughable. Looking at her made Nynaeve's stomach knot up, but not for reasons of clothes or skin.

"If you are going to wear the dress, why cover up?" Birgitte came inside and closed the door behind her. "You are a woman. Why not be proud of it?"

"If you think I shouldn't," Nynaeve replied hesitantly, and slowly let the shawl slide down to her elbows, revealing the twin of the other woman's garment. She felt all but naked. "I only thought . . . I thought . . ." Gripping her silk skirts hard to keep her hands at her sides, she held her gaze on the other woman. Even knowing she wore exactly the same herself, it was easier that way.

Birgitte grimaced. "And if I wanted you to lower the neck another inch?"

Nynaeve opened her mouth, face going as scarlet as the gown, but for a moment nothing came out. When it did, she sounded as if she were being strangled. "There isn't an inch to lower it. Look at your own. There isn't a *tenth*!"

Three quick, frowning strides, and Birgitte bent slightly to put her face right in Nynaeve's. "And if I said I wanted you to rid yourself of that inch?" she snarled, showing teeth. "What if I wanted to paint your face, so Luca could have his fool? What if I stripped you out of it altogether and painted you from head to toe? A fine target you would make then. Every man inside fifty miles would come to see."

Nynaeve's mouth worked, but this time no sound emerged at all. She wanted very much to close her eyes; maybe when she opened them, none of this would be happening.

With a disgusted shake of her head, Birgitte took a seat on one of the beds, one elbow on her knee and her blue eyes sharp. "This must stop. When I look at you, you flinch. You run about waiting on me hand and foot. If I glance for a stool, you fetch one. If I lick my lips, you have a cup of wine in my hands before I know I am thirsty. You would wash my back and put the slippers on my feet if I let you. I am neither monster nor invalid nor child, Nynaeve."

"I am only trying to make up for—" she began timidly, and jumped when the other woman roared.

"Make up? You are trying to make me less!"

"No. No, it is not that, truly. I am to blame—"

"You take responsibility for my actions," Birgitte broke in fiercely. "*I* chose to speak to you in *Tel'aran'rhiod. I* chose to help you. *I* chose to track Moghedien. And *I* chose to take you to see her. *Me!* Not you, Nynaeve, me! I was not your puppet, your pack hound, then, and I will not be now."

Nynaeve swallowed hard and gripped her skirts more tightly. She had no right to be angry with this woman. No right at all. But Birgitte had every right. "You did what I asked. It is my fault that you . . . that you are here. It is all my fault!"

"Have I mentioned fault? I see none. Only men and dim-witted girls take blame where there is none, and you are neither."

"It was my foolish pride that made me think I could best her again, and my cowardice that let her . . . that let her . . . If I had not been so afraid I could not spit, I might have done something in time."

"A coward?" Birgitte's eyes widened, openly incredulous, and scorn touched her voice. "You? I thought you had more sense than to confuse fear with cowardice. You could have fled *Tel'aran'rhiod* when Moghedien released you, but you stayed to fight. No fault or blame to you that you could not." Drawing a deep breath, she rubbed her forehead for a moment, then leaned forward intently again. "Listen to me close, Nynaeve. I take no blame for what was done to you. I saw, but I could not twitch. Had Moghedien tied you into a knot or cored you like an apple, still I would take no blame. I did what I could, when I could. And you did the same."

"It was not the same." Nynaeve tried to take the heat

out of her voice. "It *was* my fault that you were there. My fault that you are here. If you . . ." She stopped to swallow again. "If you . . . miss . . . when you shoot at me today, I want you to know that I will understand."

"I do not miss where I aim," Birgitte said dryly, "and where I aim will not be at you." She began taking things from one of the cabinets and laying them on the small table. Half-finished arrows, scraped shafts, steel arrow points, stone glue pot, fine cord, gray goose feathers for fletchings. She had said she would make her own bow, too, as soon as she could. Luca's she called "a knot-riddled branch broken from a cross-grained tree by a blind idiot in the middle of the night." "I liked you, Nynaeve," she said as she laid everything out. "Thorns, warts and all. I no longer do, as you are now . . ."

"You have no reason to like me, now," Nynaeve said miserably, but the other woman spoke right over her without looking up.

". . . and I will not allow you to make me less, to make my decisions less, by claiming responsibility for them. I have had few women friends, but most have had tempers like snowghosts."

"I wish you could be my friend once more." What under the Light was a snowghost? Something from another Age, no doubt. "I would never try to make you less, Birgitte. I only—"

Birgitte paid her no mind, except to raise her voice. Her attention seemed all on her arrow shafts. "I would like to like you again, whether you return the liking or not, but I cannot until you are yourself again. I could live with you a milk-tongued sniveling wretch if that was what you were. I take people as they are, not as I would like them to be, or else I leave them. But that is not what you are, and I will not accept your reasons for playing at it. So. Clarine told me of your encounter with Cerandin. Now I know what to do the next time you claim my decisions as your own." She swished a length of ashwood vigorously. "I am sure Latelle will be happy to provide the switch."

Nynaeve forced her jaws to unclench, forced her tone as smooth as she could make it. "You have a perfect right to do whatever you wish to me." Her fists in her skirts quivered more than her voice.

"A touch of temper showing? Just at the edges?" Birgitte grinned at her, at once amused and startlingly feral. "How long before it bursts into flame? I am willing to wear out any number of switches, if need be." The grin faded into seriousness. "I will make you see the right of this, or I will drive you away. There is no other course. I cannot—will not—leave Elayne. That bond honors me, and I will honor it, and her. And I will not allow you to think that you make my decisions, or made them. I am myself, not an appendage to you. Now go away. I must finish these arrows if I am to have even a few shafts that will fly true. I do not mean to kill you, and I would not have it happen by accident." Unstopping the glue pot, she bent over the table. "Do not forget to curtsy like a good girl on your way out."

Nynaeve made it as far as the foot of the steps before pounding her fist on her thigh in a fury. How dare the woman? Did she think that she could just . . . ? Did she think that Nynaeve would put up with . . . ? *I thought she could do anything she wanted to you,* a small voice whispered in her head. *I said she could kill me,* she snarled at it, *not humiliate me!* Before much longer *everybody* would be threatening her with that bloody Seanchan woman!

The wagons stood abandoned, except for a few rough-coated horse handlers for guards, near the tall sprawling canvas fence erected to contain Luca's show. From this large brown-grass meadow half a mile from Samara the gray stone walls of the city were clearly visible, with squat towers at the gates, and a few of the taller buildings showing roofs of thatch or tile. Outside the walls, villages of huts and rude shanties sprouted like mushrooms in every direction, full of the Prophet's followers, and they had stripped every tree for miles either for building or for firewood.

The show's entrance for patrons was on the other side, but two of the horse handlers, with stout cudgels, stood on this side to discourage any who did not want to pay from entering as the performers did. Nynaeve was almost upon them, striding as hard as she could and muttering angrily to herself, when their idiotic grins made her realize that the shawl was still looped over her elbows. Her stare wiped their faces blank. Only then did she cover herself properly, and slowly; she was not about to have these louts think they could make her yelp and leap. The skinny one, with a nose that took up half of his face, held the canvas flap aside, and she ducked through into pandemonium.

Everywhere people thronged, in noisy milling clusters of men and women and children, in chattering streams flowing from one attraction to the next. All but the *s'redit* performed on raised wooden stages Luca had had built. Cerandin's boar-horses had the largest crowd, the huge gray animals actually balancing on their forelegs, even the baby, long snouts curved up sinuously, while Clarine's dogs had the smallest, for all they did backsprings and flips over each others' backs. A good many people paused to stare at the lions and the hairy boarlike *capars* in their cages, the strangely horned deer from Arafel and Saldaea and Arad Doman and the bright birds from the Light knew where, and some waddling, brown-furred creatures with big eyes and round ears that sat placidly eating leaves from branches gripped in their forepaws. Luca's tale on where they came from varied— she supposed he did not know—and he had not been able to make up a name for them that pleased him. A huge snake from the marshes of Illian, four times as long as a man, earned nearly as many gasps as the *s'redit,* although simply lying there, apparently asleep, but she was pleased to see that Latelle's bears, at the moment standing atop huge red wooden balls that they rolled in circles with their feet, attracted few more than the dogs. Bears these people could see in their own forests, even if these did have white faces.

Latelle sparkled in the afternoon sunlight in her black spangles. Cerandin glittered almost as much in blue, and Clarine in green, though neither had quite as many sequins sewn on as Latelle, but every last one of the dresses had a collar right up under the chin. Of course, Petra and the Chavanas were performing attired only in bright blue breeches, but that was to show off their muscles. Only understandable. The acrobats were standing one atop the other's shoulders, four high. Not far from them, the strongman took a long bar with a large iron ball at each end—two men were needed to hand the thing up to him—and immediately began twirling it in his thick hands, even spinning the bar around his neck and across his back.

Thom was juggling fire, and eating it as well. Eight flaming batons made a perfect circle: then suddenly he had four in each hand, one sticking up from each cluster. Deftly popping each upraised flaming end into his mouth in turn, he appeared to swallow, and took them out extinguished, looking as if he had just had something tasty. Nynaeve could not fathom how he did not scorch his mustaches off, much less burn his throat. A twist of his wrists, and the unlit batons folded into the lit like fans. A moment later they were making two interlinked circles above his head. He wore the same brown coat he always did, though Luca had given him a red one sewn with sequins. From the way Thom's bushy eyebrows rose as she stalked past, he did not understand why she glared at him. His own coat, indeed!

She hurried on toward the thick, impatiently buzzing crowd circled around the two tall poles with the rope stretched tightly between. She had to use her elbows to reach the front row, though two women did glare and snatch their men out of her way when the shawl slipped. She would have glared back had she not been so busy blushing and covering herself. Luca was there, frowning as anxiously as a husband outside a birthing room, next to a thick fellow with his head shaved except for a grizzled topknot. She slipped in on the other side of Luca. The shaven-headed man had a villainous look; a long scar sliced down his left cheek, and a patch over that eye was painted with a scowling red replacement. Few of the men she had seen here were armed with more than a belt knife, but he wore a sword strapped to his back, the long hilt rising above his right shoulder. He looked vaguely familiar for some reason, but her mind was all on the highrope. Luca frowned at the shawl, smiled at her, and tried to put an arm around her waist.

While he was still trying to catch his breath from her elbow and she was still getting her shawl decently back in place, Juilin came staggering out of the crowd on the other side, conical red hat tilted jauntily, coat half off one shoulder and a wooden mug in his fist slopping over the rim. With the overcareful steps of a man whose head contains more wine than brains, he approached the rope ladder leading up to one of the high platforms and stared at it.

"Go on!" someone shouted. "Break your fool neck!"

"Wait, friend," Luca called, starting forward with smiles and flourishes of his cloak. "That is no place for a man with a belly full of—"

Setting the mug on the ground, Juilin scampered up the ladder and stood swaying on the platform. Nynaeve held her breath. The man had a head for heights, and well he should after a life of chasing thieves across the rooftops of Tear, but still . . .

Juilin turned as if lost; he appeared too drunk to see or remember the ladder. His eyes fixed on the rope. Tentatively, he put one foot onto the narrow span, then drew it back. Pushing the hat back to scratch his head, he studied the taut rope, and abruptly brightened visibly. Slowly he got down on hands and knees and crawled wobbling out onto the rope. Luca shouted for him to come down, and the crowd roared with laughter.

Halfway across, Juilin stopped, swaying awkwardly, and peered back, his eyes latching onto the mug he had left on the ground. Plainly he was considering how to get back to it. Slowly, with exceeding care, he stood, facing the way he had come and wavering from side to side. A gasp rose from the crowd as his foot slipped and he fell, somehow catching himself with one hand and a knee hooked around the rope. Luca caught the Taraboner hat as it fell, shouting to everyone that the man was mad, and whatever happened was no responsibility of his. Nynaeve pressed both hands tight against her middle; she could imagine being up there, and even that was enough to make her feel ill. The man was a fool. A pure bull-goose fool!

With an obvious effort, Juilin managed to catch the rope with his other hand, and pulled himself along it hand-over-hand. To the far platform. Swaying from side to side, he brushed his coat, tried to pull it straight and succeeded only in changing which shoulder hung down —and spotted his mug at the floor of the other pole. Pointing to it gleefully, he stepped out onto the rope again.

This time at least half the onlookers shouted for him to go back, shouted that there was a ladder behind him; the others only laughed uproariously, no doubt waiting for him to break his neck. He walked across smoothly, slid down the rope ladder with his hands and feet on the outside, and snatched up the wooden mug to take a deep drink. Not until Luca clapped the red hat on Juilin's head and they both bowed—Luca flourishing his cloak in such a way that Juilin was behind it half the time— did the watchers realize that it had all been part of the show. A moment of silence, and then they exploded with applause and cheers and laughter. Nynaeve had half-thought they might turn ugly after being duped. The fellow with the topknot looked villainous even while laughing.

Leaving Juilin standing beside the ladder, Luca came back to stand between Nynaeve and the man with the topknot. "I thought that would go well." He sounded incredibly self-satisfied, and he made little bows to the crowd as if he had been the one up on the rope.

Giving him a sour frown, she had no time to speak the acid comment on her tongue, because Elayne came bounding through the crowd to stand beside Juilin with her arms upraised and one knee bent.

Nynaeve's mouth tightened, and she shifted her shawl irritably. Whatever she thought of the red dress that she had found herself wearing without really knowing how, she was not sure that Elayne's costume was not worse. The Daughter-Heir of Andor was all in snow white, with a scattering of white sequins sparkling on her short coat and snug breeches. Nynaeve had not really believed that

Elayne would actually appear in the clothes in public, but she had been too concerned over her own attire to give her opinion. The coat and breeches made her think of Min. She had never approved of Min wearing boy's clothes, but the color and spangles made these even more—flagrant.

Juilin held the rope ladder for Elayne to climb, though there was no need. She went up as adeptly as he could have. He vanished into the crowd as soon as she reached the top, where she posed again, beaming at the thunderous applause as if at the adulation of her subjects. As she stepped out onto the rope—somehow it seemed even thinner than when Juilin had been on it—Nynaeve all but ceased breathing, and she stopped thinking of Elayne's clothes, or her own, at all.

Elayne made her way out onto the rope, arms outstretched to either side, and she was not channeling a platform of Air. Slowly she stepped her way across, one foot in front of the other, never wavering, supported only by the rope. Channeling would be far too dangerous if Moghedien had even a clue to where they were; the Forsaken or Black sisters could be in Samara, and they would be able to feel the weave. And if they were not in Samara now, they might be soon. On the far platform, Elayne paused to considerably more applause than Juilin had received—Nynaeve could not understand that—and started back. Almost to the end, she pivoted smoothly, walked back halfway, pivoted again. And wobbled, just catching herself. Nynaeve felt as though a hand had her by the throat. At a slow steady pace, Elayne highwalked to the platform, once more posing to thunderous shouts and clapping.

Nynaeve swallowed her heart and breathed again, raggedly, but she knew it was not over.

Raising her hands above her head, Elayne suddenly cartwheeled herself along the rope, black tresses whipping, white-sheathed legs flashing in the sun. Nynaeve yelped and clutched Luca's arm as the girl reached the far platform, stumbled in landing and caught herself just short of going over the edge.

"What's the matter?" he murmured beneath the gasp

rising from the crowd. "You've seen her do this every evening since Sienda. And a good many other places, too, I would think."

"Of course," she said weakly. Eyes fixed on Elayne, she barely noticed the arm he slipped around her shoulders, certainly not enough to do anything about it. She had tried to talk the girl into feigning a sprained ankle, but Elayne insisted that after all of that practice with the Power, she did not need it now. Maybe Juilin did not—apparently he did not—but Elayne had never gone scrambling over rooftops in the night.

The return cartwheels went perfectly, and the landing, but Nynaeve did not look away, or loose her hold on Luca's sleeve. After what now seemed the inevitable pause for applause, Elayne returned to the rope for more pivots, one leg raised and whipping down and up so quickly that it seemed she kept it outstretched the whole while, and for a slow handstand that lifted her straight as a dagger, white-slippered toes pointed to the sky. And a backflip that had the crowd gasping and her swaying from side to side, only just catching her balance. Thom Merrilin had taught her that, and the handstand.

From the corner of her eye Nynaeve caught Thom, two places down from her, eyes riveted to Elayne, poised on the balls of his feet. He looked as proud as a peacock. He looked ready to rush forward and catch her if she fell. If she did fall, it would be at least partly his fault. He should never have taught her those things!

One last passage of cartwheels, white legs flashing and glittering in the sun, faster than before. A passage that had never been mentioned to Nynaeve! She would have eviscerated Luca with her tongue had he not muttered angrily that Elayne adding to the act just for applause was a good way to break her neck. One last pause to pose for more of that applause, and Elayne at last climbed down.

Shouting, the crowd rushed in on her. Luca and four horse handlers with cudgels appeared around her as if by the Power, but even so Thom beat them to her, limp and all.

Nynaeve jumped as high as she could, just managing

to see over enough heads to make out Elayne. The girl did not seem frightened, or even taken aback, by all the waving hands trying to touch her, stretching between her encircling guards. Head high, face flushed from effort, she still managed a cool and regal grace as she was escorted away. How she could do that, garbed as she was, Nynaeve simply could not imagine.

"Face like a bloody queen," the one-eyed man muttered to himself. He had not gone running with the others, but merely let them stream past. Roughly dressed in a plain coat of dark gray wool, he certainly looked solid enough to have no fears of being knocked down and trampled. He appeared as if he could use that sword. "Burn me for a sheep-gutted farmer, but she's flaming well brave enough for a bloody queen."

Nynaeve gaped at him as he strode away through the crowd, and it was not his language. Or rather, it was, partly. Now she remembered where she had seen him, a one-eyed man with a topknot who could not say two sentences without the vilest curses.

Forgetting about Elayne—she was certainly safe enough—Nynaeve began pushing her way through the throng after him.

CHAPTER
38

An Old Acquaintance

With the crowds, it took Nynaeve some little time to catch up, muttering every time she was jostled by a man gaping at everything in sight or a woman dragging a child with either hand, children usually trying to drag *her* to two different attractions at once. The one-eyed man barely paused to look at anything except the big snake and the lions, until he reached the boar-horses. He had to have seen them earlier, situated as they were near the patrons' entrance. Every time the *s'redit* stood on their hind legs, as they were doing now, the great tusked heads of the adults could be seen by those outside the canvas fence, and the press to enter intensified a little more.

Beneath a wide red sign that said VALAN LUCA in ornate gold script on both sides, two of the horse handlers collected admission from people funneled between two thick ropes, taking the money in clear blown-glass pitchers—both thick and flawed; Luca would never lay out coin for better—so they could see that the coins were right without touching them. They dumped the money straight from the pitchers through a hole in the top of an iron-strapped box so wrapped about with chain that Petra had to have put it in place before the first silver penny went in. Another pair of horse handlers—thick-shouldered, broken-nosed men with the sunken knuckles of brawlers—stood nearby with cudgels to make sure that the crowd remained orderly. And to keep an eye on the men taking the money, Nynaeve suspected. Luca was not a trusting man, especially when it came to coin. In fact, he was as tight as the skin on an apple. She had never met anyone so stingy.

Slowly she elbowed close to the man with the gray-streaked topknot. *He* had had no trouble reaching the front rank before the *s'redit,* of course; his scar and painted eyepatch would have seen to that, even without the sword on his back. At the moment he was watching the big gray animals with a grin and what she supposed was wonder on that stony face.

"Uno?" She thought that was the right name.

His head turned to stare at her. Once she had the shawl back in place, he raised the stare to her face, but no recognition lit in his dark eye. The other, the painted red glaring one, made her a little queasy.

Cerandin waved her goad, shouting something slurred beyond intelligibility, and the *s'redit* turned, Sanit, the cow, placing her feet on Mer's broad, rounded back while he remained upright. Nerin, the calf, put her feet low on Sanit's back.

"I saw you in Fal Dara," Nynaeve said. "And again on Toman Head, briefly. After Falme. You were with . . ." She did not know how much she could say with people cheek-by-jowl around her; rumors of the Dragon Reborn had circulated all through Amadicia, and some even had his name right. "With Rand."

Uno's real eye narrowed—she tried not to see the other—and after a moment he nodded. "I remember the face. I never forget a flaming pretty face. But the hair was bloody well different. Nyna?"

"Nynaeve," she told him sharply.

He shook his head, eyeing her up and down, and before she could say another word, he had seized her arm and was all but dragging her out through the entrance.

The horse handlers there recognized her, of course, and the broken-nosed fellows started forward hefting their cudgels. She waved them away furiously even as she was yanking her arm free; it took three tries, and still it was more a matter of his letting go. The man had a grip like iron. The men with the clubs hesitated, then drifted back to their places when they saw Uno drop his grip. Apparently they knew what Valan Luca would prefer them to be guarding.

"What do you think you are doing?" she demanded, but Uno only motioned her to follow, watching to see that she did so without more than slowing his stride through the crowd waiting to get in. He had slightly bowed legs, and moved like a man more used to the back of a horse than his own feet. Growling to herself, she picked up her skirts and stalked after him toward the town.

Two other menageries were set up behind brown canvas walls not far off, and beyond them more lay scattered among the crowded shanty villages. None too close to the city walls, though. Apparently the governor, as they called the woman Nynaeve could have named mayor—though she had never heard of a woman mayor—had decreed half a mile as the distance, to protect the town in case any of the animals got loose.

The sign over the entrance to the nearest show said MAIRIN GOME in florid green and gold. Two women were clearly visible above the sign, clinging to a rope hanging from a tall framework of poles that had not been there when Luca's walls went up. Apparently the boar-horses' rearing high enough to be seen was having an effect. The women contorted themselves into positions that made Nynaeve think uncomfortably of what Moghedien had done, and somehow even managed to hold themselves out in horizontal handstands to either side of the rope. The crowd waiting impatiently in front of Mistress Gome's sign was almost as large as the one in front of Luca's. None of the other shows had anything visible that she could see, and their crowds were much smaller.

Uno refused to answer her questions or say a word or

do more than give her dire frowns until they were out of the jam of people and onto a cart path of hard-packed dirt. "What I am flaming trying to do," he growled then, "is to take you where we can flaming well talk without you being torn to flaming bits by flaming folk trying to kiss your flaming hem when they find out you flaming know the Lord Dragon." There was no one within thirty paces of them, but he still stared around for anyone who might hear. "Blood and bloody ashes, woman! Don't you know what these flaming goat-heads are like? Half of them think the Creator talks to him over bloody supper every night, and the other half think he *is* the bloody Creator!"

"I will thank you to moderate your language, Master Uno. And I will thank you to slow down, too. We are not running a footrace. Where are you going, and why should I stir another step with you?"

He rolled his eye toward her, chuckling wryly. "Oh, I do remember you. The one with the fla—the mouth. Ragan thought you could skin and butcher a blo—a bull at ten paces with your tongue. Chaena and Nangu thought fifty." At least he did shorten his stride.

Nynaeve stopped dead. "Where and why?"

"Into the town." He did not stop. He strode right on, flipping a hand for her to follow. "I don't know what you're flam—what you're doing here, but I remember you were mixed up with that *blue* woman."

Snarling under her breath, she gathered her skirts and hurried after him again; it was the only way to hear. He continued as if she had been beside him the whole time. "This is no blood—no place for you to be. I can scrape together enough blo—aagh!—enough coin to get you to Tear, I think. Rumor says that's where the Lord Dragon is." Again he looked around warily. "Unless you want to go to the island instead." He must have meant Tar Valon. "There's blo—there's odd rumors floating around about that, too. Peace, if there aren't!" He came from a land that had not known peace in three thousand years; Shienarans used the word as talisman and oath both. "They say the old Amyrlin's been deposed. Executed maybe. Some say they fought and burned the whole—" He paused, taking a deep breath and grimacing horribly. "—the whole city."

Walking along, she studied him in amazement. She had not seen him in nearly a year, had never spoken more than two words together to him, and yet he . . . Why did men always think a woman needed a man to look after her? Men could not lace up their own shirts without a woman to help! "We are doing quite well as we are, thank you. Unless you know when a river trader will dock on his way downriver."

"We? Is the blue woman with you, or the brown?" That had to be Moiraine and Verin. He was certainly being cautious.

"No. Do you remember Elayne?" He gave a blunt nod, and a mischievous impulse seized her; nothing seemed to faze the man, and he obviously expected to just take charge of her welfare. "You saw her again just now. You said she had a"—she made her voice gruff in imitation of his—"face like a bloody queen."

He stumbled in a quite satisfactory way, and glared around him so fiercely that even two Whitecloaks riding by skirted wide around him, though they tried to pretend he had nothing to do with it, of course. "Her?" he growled incredulously. "But her bloody hair was black as a raven's. . . ." He glanced at hers, and the next minute he was pacing up the cart path again, muttering half to himself, "The flaming woman is daughter to a queen. A bloody queen! Showing her bloody legs that way." Nynaeve nodded in agreement. Until he added, "You bloody southlanders are bloody strange! No flaming decency at all!" He had fine room to talk. Shienarans might dress properly, but she still blushed to remember that in Shienar men and women bathed together as often as not, and thought no more of it than of eating together.

"Did your mother never teach you to talk decently, man?" His real eye frowned at her almost as darkly as the painted one, and he rolled his shoulders. In Fal Dara he and everyone else had treated her as nobly born, or the next thing to. Of course, it was hard to pass herself off as a lady in that dress, and with her hair a shade that nature never made. She arranged her shawl more snugly and folded her arms to hold it in place. The gray wool was terribly uncomfortable in that dry heat, and she herself was not feeling very dry at all; she had never heard of anyone who died of sweating, but she thought she might well be the first. "What are you doing here, Uno?"

He looked around before answering. Not that he had need; there was little traffic on the path—an occasional ox-drawn cart, a few folk in farm clothes or rougher, here and there a man on a horse—and no one seemed willing to come any closer to him than they had to. He appeared a man who might cut somebody's throat on a whim. "The blue woman gave us a name in Jehannah, and said we were to wait there until she sent instructions, but the woman in Jehannah was dead and buried when we arrived. An old woman. Died in her sleep, and none of her relatives had ever heard the blue woman's name. Then Masema started talking to people, and . . . Well, there was no point staying there for orders we'd never hear if they did come. We stay close to Masema because he slips us enough to live on, though none except Bartu and Nengar listen to his trash." The grizzled topknot swung as he shook his head in irritation.

Suddenly Nynaeve realized that there had not been a single obscene word in that. He looked about to swallow his tongue. "Perhaps if you cursed only occasionally?" She sighed. "Maybe once every other sentence?" The man smiled at her so gratefully that she wanted to throw up her hands in exasperation. "How is it that Masema has money when the rest of you do not?" She remembered Masema: a dark sour man who liked no one and nothing.

"Why, he's the bloody Prophet they've all come to hear. Would you like to meet him?" He gave the impression of counting his sentences. Nynaeve breathed deeply; the man was going to take her literally. "He might find you a flaming boat, if you want one. In Ghealdan, what the Prophet wants, the Prophet usually gets. No, he always flaming gets it in the end, one way or another. The man was a good soldier, but who'd have ever thought he would turn out like this?" His frown took in all the rude villages and the people, even the shows and the city ahead.

Nynaeve hesitated. The dreaded Prophet, rousing mobs and riots, was Masema? But he *did* preach the coming of the Dragon Reborn. They were almost to the town gate, and there was time yet before she must stand up and let Birgitte shoot arrows at her. Luca had been more than disappointed that the woman insisted on being called Maerion. If Masema *could* find a boat heading downriver . . . Today, maybe. On the other hand, there *were* the riots. If rumor inflated them tenfold, then only hundreds had died in towns and cities farther north. Only hundreds.

"Just don't remind him that you have anything to do with that bloody island," Uno went on, eyeing her thoughtfully. Now that she thought of it, she realized that he very likely did not know what her connection to Tar Valon actually was. Women did go there without becoming Aes Sedai, after all, to seek help or answers. He was aware that she was involved in some way, but no more than that. "He isn't much friendlier to women from there than the Whitecloaks are. If you just keep your mouth bloody well shut about it, he'll likely pass it over. For somebody who comes from the same village as the Lord Dragon, Masema will probably have a flaming boat *built*."

The crowds were thicker at the city gates, flanked by squat gray towers, men and women streaming in and out, afoot and mounted, in every sort of garb from rags to embroidered silk coats and dresses. The gates themselves, thick and iron-bound, stood open under the guard of a dozen spearmen in scaled tunics and round steel caps with flat rims. Actually, the guards paid more attention to half their number of Whitecloaks lounging nearby than to anything else. It was the men in snowy cloaks and burnished mail who watched the flow of people.

"Do the Whitecloaks cause much trouble?" she asked quietly.

Uno pursed his lips as if to spit, glanced at her, and did

not. "Where do they bloody not? There was a woman with one of these traveling shows who did tricks, sleight of hand. Four days ago a flaming mob of pigeon-gutted sheep-heads tore the show apart." Valan Luca had certainly never mentioned that! "Peace! What they wanted was the woman. Claimed she was"—he glowered at the folk hurrying by, and lowered his voice—"Aes Sedai. And a Darkfriend. Broke her bloody neck getting her to a rope, so I hear, but they hung her corpse anyway. Masema had the ringleaders beheaded, but it was Whitecloaks whipped up the bloody mob." His scowl matched the red eye painted on his patch. "There's been too many flaming hangings and beheadings, if you bloody well ask me. Bloody Masema's as bad as the bloody Whitecloaks when it comes to finding a Darkfriend under every flaming rock."

"Once every other sentence," she murmured, and the man actually blushed.

"Don't know what I'm thinking," he grumped, coming to a stop. "Can't take you in there. It's half festival and half riot, with a cutpurse every third step and a woman not safe out-of-doors after dark." He sounded more scandalized about the last than the rest; in Shienar, a woman was safe anywhere, any time—except from Trollocs and Myrddraal, of course—and any man would die to see it so. "Not safe. I'll take you back. When I find a way, I'll come for you."

That settled it for her. Pulling her arm loose before he could get a grip on it, she quickened her pace toward the gates. "Come along, Uno, and do not dawdle. If you dawdle, I will leave you behind." He caught up to her, grumbling under his breath about the stubbornness of women. Once she understood that that was his subject, and that apparently he did not think her injunction against cursing held when talking to himself, she stopped listening.

CHAPTER
39

Encounters in Samara

The Whitecloaks at the gates gave Uno and Nynaeve no more mind than they gave anyone else in the steady throng, which was to say a cold suspicious stare, searching yet quick. Too many people made anything else impossible, and maybe the scale-armored guards did, too. Not that there was any reason for more except in her mind. Her Great Serpent ring and Lan's heavy gold ring both nestled in her pouch—the dress's low neckline meant she could not wear them on the thong—but somehow she almost expected Children of the Light to pick out a Tower-trained woman by instinct. Her relief was palpable when those icy, unfeeling eyes swept past her.

The soldiers paid the two of them as little attention—once she rearranged her shawl yet again. Uno's scowl might have helped send their eyes back to the Whitecloaks, but the man had no right to scowl in the first place. It was her business.

Rewrapping the folded length of gray wool one more time, she tied the ends around her waist. The shawl defined her bosom more than she wished, and still exposed a bit of cleavage, yet it was a considerable improvement on the dress alone. At least she would not have to worry about the shawl slipping again. If only the thing were not so hot. The weather really should be turning soon. They were not *that* far south of the Two Rivers.

Uno patiently waited on her for a change. She was of two minds as to whether this was simple courtesy—his scarred face looked a deal *too* patient—but finally they walked together into Samara. Into chaos.

A babble of noise hung over everything, no one sound distinguishable. People jammed the rough stone-paved streets all but shoulder to shoulder from slate-roofed taverns to thatch-roofed stables, from raucous inns with simple painted signs like The Blue Bull or The Dancing Goose to shops where the signs had no words, only a knife-and-scissors here, a bolt of cloth there, a gold-smith's scales or a barber's razor, a pot or a lamp or a boot. Nynaeve saw faces as pale as that of any Andorman and as dark as that of any of the Sea Folk, some clean, some dirty, and coats with high collars, low collars, no collars, drably colored and bright, plain and embroi-dered, shabby and near new-made, in styles strange as often as familiar. One fellow with a dark forked beard wore silver chains across the chest of his plain blue coat, and two with their hair in braids—*men,* with a black braid over each ear below their shoulders!—had tiny brass bells sewn to their red coatsleeves and the turned-down tops of thigh-high boots. Whatever land they hailed from, those two were not fools; their dark eyes were hard and searching as Uno's, and they carried curved swords on their backs. A bare-chested man in a bright yellow sash, skin a deeper brown than aged wood and hands intricately tattooed, had to be one of the Sea Folk, though he wore neither earrings nor nose ring.

The women were equally as diverse, hair ranging from raven black to yellow so pale it was nearly white, braided or gathered or hanging loose, cut short, to the shoulders, to the waist, dresses in worn wool or neat linen or shimmering silk, collars brushing chins with lace or embroidery and necklines every bit as low as the one she hid. She even saw a copper-complexioned Domani wom-an in a barely opaque red gown that covered her to the neck and hid next to nothing! She wondered how safe that woman would be after dark. Or in this broad daylight, for that matter.

The occasional Whitecloaks and soldiers in that milling mass seemed overwhelmed, struggling to make ground as hard as anyone else. Oxcarts and horse-drawn wagons inched along the haphazardly crisscrossing streets, bearers jostled sedan chairs through the crowds, and now and then a lacquered coach with a plumed team of four or six made its laborious way, liveried footman and steel-capped guards vainly trying to clear a path. Musicians with flute or zither or bittern played at every corner where there was not a juggler or an acrobat— their skill certainly nothing to make Thom or the Chavanas worry—always with another man or woman holding out a cap for coins. Ragged beggars wove through it all, plucking at sleeves and proffering grimy hands, and hawkers bustled with trays of everything from pins to ribbons to pears, their cries lost in the din.

Her head spun by the time Uno drew her into a narrower street where the throng seemed thinner, if only by comparison. She paused to straighten her clothes, disarrayed from plunging through the crowd, before following him. It was a trifle quieter here, too. No street entertainers, and fewer hawkers and beggars. Beggars kept clear of Uno, even after he tossed a few coppers to a wary pack of urchins, for which she did not blame them. The man just did not look . . . charitable.

The town's buildings loomed over these narrow ways, despite being only two or three stories, putting the streets themselves in shadow. But there was good light in the sky, hours yet till dusk. Still plenty of time to get back to the show. If she had to. With luck, they could all be boarding a riverboat by sunset.

She gave a start when another Shienaran suddenly joined them, sword on his back and head shaven but for that topknot, a dark-haired man only a few years older than she. Uno gave curt introductions and explanation without slowing.

"Peace favor you, Nynaeve," Ragan said, the skin of his dark cheek dimpling around a triangular white scar. Even smiling, his face was hard; she had never met a soft

Shienaran. Soft men did not survive along the Blight, nor soft women either. "I remember you. Your hair was different, was it not? No matter. Never fear. We will see you safely to Masema and to wherever you would go after. Just be sure not to mention Tar Valon to him." No one was sparing them a second glance, but he lowered his voice anyway. "Masema thinks the Tower will try to control the Lord Dragon."

Nynaeve shook her head. Another fool man who was going to take care of her. At least he did not try to engage her in conversation; the mood she was in, she would have given him the rough side of her tongue if he so much as commented on the heat. Her own face felt a trifle damp, and no wonder, having to wear a shawl in this weather. Abruptly she remembered what the one-eyed man had said concerning Ragan's opinion of her tongue. She did not think she more than glanced at him, but Ragan moved to the other side of Uno as if for shelter and eyed her warily. Men!

The streets grew still narrower, and though the stone buildings lining them did not grow smaller, it was more often than not the backs of the buildings they saw, and rough gray walls that could hide only small yards. Eventually they turned down an alley barely wide enough for all three of them abreast. At the far end, a lacquered and gilded coach stood surrounded by scale-armored men. More immediately, halfway between her and the coach, fellows lounged thickly along both sides of the alley. In a motley of coats, most clutched clubs or spears or swords as different as their garb. They could have been a pack of street toughs, but neither of the Shienarans slowed, so she did not either.

"The street out front will be full of bloody fools hoping to catch a glimpse of Masema at a bloody window." Uno's voice was pitched for her ears alone. "The only way to get in is by the back." He fell silent as they came close enough for the waiting men to hear.

Two of those were soldiers with rimmed steel helmets and scaled tunics, swords at hip and spears in hand, but it was the others who studied the three newcomers and fingered their weapons. They had disturbing eyes, too intent, almost feverish. For once, she would have been pleased to see an honest leer. These men did not care whether she was a woman or a horse.

Without a word Uno and Ragan unfastened the scab-barded blades from their backs and handed them and their daggers to a plump-faced man who might have been a shopkeeper once, from the look of his blue woolen coat and breeches. The clothing had been good; it was clean, but heavily worn, and wrinkled as if it had been slept in for a month. Plainly he recognized the Shienarans, and though he frowned at her for a moment, especially at her belt knife, he silently nodded to a narrow wooden gate in the stone wall. That was perhaps the most off-putting fact of all; none of them made a sound.

On the other side of wall was a small yard where weeds stuck up between cobblestones. The tall stone house—three broad, pale-gray stories, with wide windows and scroll-worked eaves and gables, roofed in dark red tiles—must have been one of the finest in Samara. Once the gate was closed behind them, Ragan spoke softly. "There have been attempts to kill the Prophet."

It took Nynaeve a moment to realize that he was explaining why their weapons had been taken. "But you are his friends," she protested. "You all followed Rand to Falme together." She was not about to start calling him the Lord Dragon.

"That's why we're bloody let in at all," Uno said dryly. "I told you we don't see everything the way . . . the Prophet does." The slight pause, and the quick half-glance back at the gate to see if anyone was listening, spoke volumes. It had been Masema, before. And Uno was clearly a man who did not temper his tongue easily.

"Just watch what you say for once," Ragan told her, "and likely you will get the help you want." She nodded, as agreeably as anyone could wish—she knew sense when she heard it, even if he had no right to offer it—and he and Uno exchanged doubtful glances. She was going to stuff these two into a sack with Thom and Juilin and switch anything that stuck up.

Fine house as it might be, the kitchen was dusty, and empty except for one bony, gray-haired woman, her drab gray dress and white apron the only clean things in sight as they walked through. Sucking her teeth, the old woman hardly glanced up from stirring a small kettle of soup over a tiny blaze in one of the wide stone fireplaces. Two battered pots hung on hooks where twenty could have, and a cracked pottery bowl on a blue-lacquered tray stood on the broad table.

Beyond the kitchen, moderately fine hangings decorated the walls. Nynaeve had developed something of an eye in the last year, and these scenes of feasts and hunts for deer and bear and boar were only good, not excellent. Chairs and tables and chests lined the halls, dark lacquer streaked with red, inlaid with mother-of-pearl. Hangings and furniture alike were also dusty, and the red-and-white tiled floor had had only a halfhearted lick with a broom. Cobwebs decorated the corners and cornices of the high plaster ceiling.

There were no other servants—or anyone else—in sight until they came to a weedy fellow sitting on the floor beside an open door, his grimy red silk coat much too large for him and at odds with a filthy shirt and worn woolen breeches. One of his cracked boots had a large hole in the sole; a toe poked through another in the other one. He held up a hand, whispering, "The Light shine on you, and praise the name of the Lord Dragon?" He made it sound a question, querulously twisting a narrow face as unwashed as his shirt, but then he did the same with everything. "The Prophet can't be disturbed now? He's busy? You'll have to wait a bit?" Uno nodded patiently, and Ragan leaned against the wall; they had been through this before.

Nynaeve did not know what she had expected of the Prophet, not even now that she was aware who he was, but certainly not filth. That soup had smelled like cabbage and potatoes, hardly the fare for a man who had an entire city dancing for him. And only two servants, both of whom could well have come from the rudest huts outside the city.

The skinny guard, if such he was—he had no weapon; perhaps he was not trusted either—seemed to have no objection when she moved to where she could see through the doorway. The man and woman inside could not have been more different. Masema had shaved even his topknot, and his coat was plain brown wool, heavily wrinkled but clean, although his knee-high boots were scuffed. Deep-set eyes turned his permanently sour look to a scowl, and a scar made a pale triangle on his dark cheek, a near mirror image of Ragan's, only more faded with age and a hair nearer the eye. The woman, in elegantly gold-embroidered blue silk, was short of her middle years and quite lovely despite a nose perhaps too long for beauty. A simple blue net cap gathered dark hair spilling almost to her waist, but she wore a broad necklace of gold and firedrops with a matching bracelet, and gemmed rings decorated nearly every finger. Where Masema seemed poised to rush at something, teeth bared, she bore herself with stately reserve and grace.

". . . so many follow wherever you go," she was saying, "that order flies over the wall when you arrive. People are not safe in themselves or their property—"

"The Lord Dragon has broken all bonds of law, all bonds made by mortal men and women." Masema's voice was heated, but intense, not angry. "The Prophecies say that the Lord Dragon will break all chains that bind, and it is so. The Lord Dragon's radiance will protect us against the Shadow."

"It is not the Shadow that threatens here, but cutpurses and slipfingers and headcrackers. Some who follow you—many—believe that they can take what they wish from whoever has it without payment or leave."

"There is justice in the hereafter, when we are born again. Concern with things of this world is useless. But very well. If you wish earthly justice"—his lip curled contemptuously—"let it be this. Henceforth, a man who steals will have his right hand cut off. A man who interferes with a woman, or insults her honor, or commits murder will be hung. A woman who steals or commits murder will be flogged. If any accuses and finds twelve who will agree, it will be done. Let it be so."

"As you say, of course," the woman murmured. Aloof elegance remained on her face, but she sounded shaken. Nynaeve did not know how Ghealdanin law ran, but she did not think it could be so casual as that. The woman took a deep breath. "There is still the matter of food. It becomes difficult to feed so many."

"Every man, woman and child who has come to the Lord Dragon must have a full belly. It must be so! Where gold can be found, food can be found, and there is too much gold in the world. Too much concern with gold." Masema's head swung angrily. Not angry with her, but in general. He looked to be searching for those who concerned themselves with gold so he could unleash fury on their heads. "The Lord Dragon has been Reborn. The Shadow hangs over the world, and only the Lord Dragon can save us. Only belief in the Lord Dragon, submission and obedience to the word of the Lord Dragon. All else is useless, even where it is not blasphemy."

"Blessed be the name of the Lord Dragon in the Light." It had the sound of a rote reply. "It is no longer simply a matter of gold, my Lord Prophet. Finding and transporting food in sufficient—"

"I am not a lord," he broke in again, and now he was angry. He leaned toward the woman, spittle on his lips, and though her face did not change, her hands twitched as if they wanted to clutch her dress. "There is no lord but the Lord Dragon, in whom the Light dwells, and I am but one humble voice of the Lord Dragon. Remember that! High or low, blasphemers earn the scourge!"

"Forgive me," the begemmed woman murmured, spreading her skirts in a curtsy fit for a queen's court. "It is as you say, of course. There is no lord save the Lord Dragon, and I am but a humble follower of the Lord Dragon—blessed be the name of the Lord Dragon— who comes to hear the wisdom and guidance of the Prophet."

Wiping his mouth with the back of his hand, Masema was suddenly cold. "You wear too much gold. Do not let earthly possession seduce you. Gold is dross. The Lord Dragon is all."

Immediately she began plucking rings from her fingers, and before the second was off, the weedy fellow scurried to her side, pulling a pouch from his coat pocket and holding it for her to drop them in. The bracelet and necklace followed as well.

Nynaeve looked at Uno and raised an eyebrow.

"Every penny goes to the poor," he told her in a low voice that barely reached her ear, "or somebody who needs it. If some merchant hadn't bloody given him her house, he'd be in a bloody stable, or one of those huts outside the city."

"Even his food comes as a gift," Ragan said just as quietly. "They used to bring him dishes fit for a king, until they learned he just gave away everything but a little bread, and soup or stew. He hardly drinks wine, now."

Nynaeve shook her head. She supposed it was one way to find money for the poor. Simply rob anyone who was *not* poor. Of course, that would just make everyone poor in the end, but it might work for a time. She wondered if Uno and Ragan knew the whole of it. People who claimed they were collecting money to help others often had a way of letting a good bit stick in their own pockets, or else they liked the power that spreading it about gave them, liked it far too much. She had better feeling for the man who freely gave one copper from his own purse than for the fellow who wrested a gold crown from someone else's. And less for fools who abandoned their farms and shops to follow this . . . this *Prophet,* with no idea where their next meal would come from.

Inside the room, the woman curtsied to Masema even more deeply than before, spreading her skirts wide and bowing her head. "Until I once again have the honor of the Prophet's words and counsel. The name of the Lord Dragon be blessed in the Light."

Masema waved her away absently, already half forgotten. He had seen them in the hall, and was looking at them with as close to pleasure as his dour face could come. It was not very close. The woman swept out, not even appearing to see Nynaeve or the two men. Nynaeve sniffed as the weedy fellow in the red coat waved anxiously for them to come in. For someone who had just given up her jewelry on demand, that woman managed a fine queenly air.

The skinny man scampered back to his place by the door as the other three men shook hands in the Borderlands fashion, gripping forearms.

"Peace favor your sword," Uno said, echoed by Ragan.

"Peace favor the Lord Dragon" was the reply, "and his

Light illumine us all." Nynaeve's breath caught. There was no doubt to his meaning; the *Lord Dragon* was the source of the Light. And he had the nerve to speak of blasphemy from others! "Have you come to the Light at last?"

"We walk in the Light," Ragan said carefully. "As always." Uno kept silent, his face blank.

Weary patience made an odd play on Masema's sour features. "There is no way to the Light save through the Lord Dragon. You will see the way and the truth in the end, for you have seen the Lord Dragon, and only those whose souls are swallowed in the Shadow can see and not believe. You are not such. You will believe."

In spite of the heat and the wool shawl, goose bumps crawled along Nynaeve's arms. Total conviction filled the man's voice, and this close she could see a glint in his nearly black eyes that bordered on madness. He swept those eyes over her, and she stiffened her knees. He made the most rabid Whitecloak she had ever seen appear mild. Those fellows in the alley were only a pale imitation of their master.

"You, woman. Are you ready to come to the Light of the Lord Dragon, abandoning sin and flesh?"

"I walk in the Light as best I can." She was irritated to find herself speaking as carefully as Ragan. Sin? Who did he think he was?

"You are too concerned with the flesh." Masema's gaze was withering as it swept over her red dress and the shawl wrapped tightly around her.

"And what do you mean by that?" Uno's eye widened in startlement, and Ragan made small shushing motions, yet she could as soon have flown as stopped. "Do you think you have a right to tell me how to dress?" Before she quite realized what she was doing, she had untied the shawl and looped it over her elbows; it really was much too hot, anyway. "*No* man has that right, for me or any other woman! If I chose to go *naked*, it would be none of your concern!"

Masema contemplated her bosom for a moment—not so much as a hint of admiration lit his deep eyes, only acid contempt—then raised that stare to her face. Uno's real eye and painted made a perfect match, scowling at nothing, and Ragan winced, surely muttering to himself inside his head.

Nynaeve swallowed hard. So much for guarding her tongue. For perhaps the first time in her life, she truly regretted speaking her mind without thinking first. If this man could order men's hands cut off, order men hung, with only a jack-fool excuse of a trial, what was he not capable of? She thought she was angry enough to channel.

But if she did . . . If Moghedien or any Black sisters *were* in Samara . . . *But if I don't . . . !* She wanted very much to wrap the shawl back around her, up to her chin. But not with him staring at her. Something in the back of her mind shouted at her not to be a complete woolhead —only men let pride overcome sense—but she met Masema's gaze defiantly, even if she did have to stop herself from swallowing again.

His lip curled. "Such garments are worn to entice men, and for no other reason." She could not understand how his voice could be so fervent and so icy at the same time. "Thoughts of the flesh distract the mind from the Lord Dragon and the Light. I have considered banning dresses that distract men's eyes, and minds. Let women who would waste time in attracting men, and men who would attract women, be scourged until they know that only in perfect contemplation of the Lord Dragon and the Light can joy be found." He was not really looking at her any longer. That dark burning stare looked through her, to something distant. "Let taverns, and places that sell strong drink, and all places that would take the minds of people from that perfect contemplation, be closed and burned to the ground. I frequented such places in my days of sin, but now I heartily regret, as all should regret their transgressions. There is only the Lord Dragon and the Light! All else is illusion, a snare set by the Shadow!"

"This is Nynaeve al'Meara," Uno said quickly into the first pause for breath. "From Emond's Field, in the Two Rivers, whence the Lord Dragon comes." Masema's head turned slowly to the one-eyed man, and she hastily took the opportunity to re-do the shawl as she had had it. "She was at Fal Dara with the Lord Dragon, and at

Falme. The Lord Dragon rescued her at Falme. The Lord Dragon cares for her as for a mother."

Another time, she would have given him a few choice words, and maybe a well-boxed ear. Rand had *not* rescued her—or not exactly, anyway—and she was only a handful of years older than he. A mother, indeed!

Masema turned back to her. The zealous light that had burned in his eyes before was nothing to what was there now. They almost glowed.

"Nynaeve. Yes." His voice quickened. "Yes! I remember your name, and your face. Blessed are you among women, Nynaeve al'Meara, none more so save the blessed mother of the Lord Dragon herself, for you watched the Lord Dragon grow. You attended the Lord Dragon as a child." He seized her arms, hard fingers biting in painfully, but he seemed unaware of it. "You will speak to the crowds of the Lord Dragon's boyhood, of his first words of wisdom, of the miracles that accompanied him. The Light has sent you here to serve the Lord Dragon."

She was not exactly sure what to say. There had never been any miracles around Rand that *she* had seen. She had *heard* of things, in Tear, but you could hardly call what a *ta'veren* caused miracles. Not really. Even what had occurred at Falme had a rational explanation. Sort of. And as for words of wisdom, the first she had heard out of him had been a fervent promise never to throw a rock at anyone again, offered after she had paddled his young backside for it. She did not believe she had heard another word since that she could call wise. In any case, if Rand had given sage advice from his cradle, if there had been comets by night and apparitions in the sky by day, she still would not have stayed with this madman.

"I must travel downriver," she said guardedly. "To join him. The Lord Dragon." That name curdled on her tongue, so soon after her promise to herself, but Rand was apparently never anything as simple as "he" around the Prophet. *I am just being sensible. That's all it is.* "A man is an oak, a woman a willow," the saying ran. The oak fought the wind and was broken, while the willow bent when it must and survived. That did not mean she had to like bending. "He . . . the Lord Dragon . . . is in Tear. The Lord Dragon has summoned me there."

"Tear." Masema took his hands away, and she surreptitiously rubbed her arms. She did not have to try hiding it, though; he was staring at something beyond sight again. "Yes, I have heard." Speaking to something beyond sight, too, or to himself. "When Amadicia has come to the Lord Dragon as Ghealdan has, I will lead the people to Tear, to bask in the radiance of the Lord Dragon. I will send disciples to spread the word of the Lord Dragon throughout Tarabon and Arad Doman, to Saldaea and Kandor and the Borderlands, to Andor, and I will lead the people to kneel at the Lord Dragon's feet."

"A wise plan . . . uh . . . O Prophet of the Lord Dragon." A fool plan if she had ever heard one. That was not to say it would not work. Fool plans often did, for some reason, when men made them. Rand might even enjoy having all those people kneel to him, if he was half as arrogant as Egwene claimed. "But we . . . I cannot wait. I have been summoned, and when the Lord Dragon summons, mere mortals must obey." Some day she was going to get a chance to box Rand's head for her need to do this! "I have to find a boat going downriver."

Masema stared at her for so long that she began to grow nervous. Sweat trickled down her back, and between her breasts, and it was only partly the heat. That stare would have made Moghedien sweat.

Finally he nodded, fiery zealotry fading to leave only his usual dour scowl. "Yes," he sighed. "If you have been summoned, you must go. Go with the Light, and in the Light. Dress more appropriately—those who have been close to the Lord Dragon must be virtuous above all others—and meditate on the Lord Dragon and his Light."

"A riverboat?" Nynaeve insisted. "You must know whenever a boat reaches Samara, or any village along the river. If you could just tell me where I might find one, it would make my journey much . . . swifter." She had been going to say "easier," but she did not think ease mattered much to Masema.

"I do not concern myself with such things," he said testily. "But you are right. When the Lord Dragon commands, you must come on the hour. I will ask. If a vessel can be found, someone will tell me of it eventually." His eyes shifted to the other two men. "You must see that she is safe until then. If she persists in clothing herself in this manner, she will attract men with vile thoughts. She must be protected, like a wayward child, until she is reunited with the Lord Dragon."

Nynaeve bit her tongue. A willow, not an oak, when a willow was needed. She managed to mask her irritation behind a smile that had to carry all the gratitude the idiot man could wish. A dangerous idiot, however. She had to remember that.

Uno and Ragan made their goodbyes quickly, with more forearm clasping, and hustled her out, one on either arm, as if they thought it necessary to hurry her away from Masema for some reason. Masema appeared to have forgotten them before they reached the door; he was already frowning at the weedy man, waiting next to a bluff fellow in a farmer's coat who was crumpling his cap in thick hands, awe painted across his broad face.

She did not say a word as they retraced their steps through the kitchen, where the gray-haired woman was sucking her teeth and stirring the soup as if she had not moved in the interval. Nynaeve held her tongue while they retrieved their weapons, held it until they were out of the alleyway, into something approaching the width of a street. Then she rounded on them, shaking her finger under each nose alternately. "How dare you *drag* me out like that!" People passing by grinned—men ruefully, women appreciatively—though none could have had an idea what she was berating them over. "Another five minutes, and I would have had him finding a boat today! If you ever lay hands on me again—!" Uno snorted so loudly that she cut off with a start.

"Another five bloody minutes, and Masema would have bloody well laid hands on *you*. Or rather, he'd have said that someone should, and then someone flaming well would have! When he says something should be done, there are always fifty flaming hands, or a hundred, or a flaming thousand if need be, to do it!" He stalked off down the street, Ragan at his side, and she had to go with them or be left. Uno paced on as if he knew she would trail after. She almost went the other way just to prove him wrong. Following had nothing to do with fear of getting lost in that rabbit warren of streets. She could have found her way out. Eventually. "He had a flaming Lord of the Crown High Council flogged—flogged!—for half the heat in his voice that you had," the one-eyed man growled. "Contempt for the word of the Lord Dragon, he called it. Peace! Demanding what bloody right he had to comment on your flaming clothes! For a few minutes you did well enough, but I saw your face there at the end. You were ready to flaming lace into him again. The only thing worse you could have done would be to bloody name the Lord Dragon. He calls that blasphemy. As well name the flaming Dark One."

Ragan's topknot bobbed as he nodded. "Remember the Lady Baelome, Uno? Right after the first rumors came from Tear naming the Lord Dragon, Nynaeve, she said something about 'this Rand al'Thor' in Masema's hearing, and he called for an axe and a chopping block without pause for breath."

"He had someone beheaded for *that*?" she said incredulously.

"No," Uno muttered in disgust. "But only because she bloody well groveled when she realized he flaming meant it. She was dragged out and hung up by her flaming wrists from the back of her own coach, then strapped the bloody length of whatever village it was we were in then. Her own flaming retainers stood like a bunch of sheep-gutted farmers and watched it."

"When it was done," Ragan added, "she thanked Masema for his mercy, the same as Lord Aleshin did." His tone had too much pointedness to suit her; he was delivering a moral, and intended her to take it in. "They had reason, Nynaeve. Theirs would not have been the first heads he has put on a stake. Yours could have been the latest. And ours with it, if we tried to give aid. Masema plays no favorites."

She drew breath. How could Masema have all this power? And not only among his own followers, apparently. But then, there was no reason lords or ladies could be not as great fools as any farmer; a good many were greater, in her estimation. That idiot woman with her rings had surely been a lady; no merchant ever wore firedrops. Yet surely Ghealdan had laws and courts and judges. Where was the queen, or the king? She could not remember which Ghealdan had. No one in the Two Rivers had ever had much truck with kings or queens, yet that was what they were for, them and lords and ladies, seeing justice fairly done. But whatever Masema did here was no concern of hers. She had more important problems than worrying over a flock of imbeciles who let a madman trample them.

Still, curiosity made her say, "Does he mean that about trying to stop men and women looking at one another? What does he think will happen if there are no marriages, no children? Will he stop people farming next, or weaving or making shoes, so they can think about Rand al'Thor?" She enunciated the name deliberately. These two went around calling him "the Lord Dragon" at the drop of a pin almost as much as Masema did. "I will tell you this. If he tries telling women how to dress, he *will* start a riot. Against him." Samara must have something like a Women's Circle—most places did, even if they called it something else, even when it was not a formal arrangement at all; there were some things men just did not have the sense to see to—and they surely could and did call women down for wearing inappropriate clothes, but that was not the same as a man putting his finger into it. Women did not meddle in men's affairs—well, no more than was necessary—and men should not meddle in women's. "And I expect the men will react no better if he tries closing taverns and the like. I never knew a man yet who wouldn't cry himself to sleep if he could not put his nose in a mug now and then."

"Maybe he will," Ragan said, "and maybe he won't. Sometimes he orders things, and sometimes he forgets, or puts it off anyway, because something more important comes along. You would be surprised," he added dryly, "at what his followers will accept from him without a whimper." He and Uno were flanking her, she realized, and watching the other folk in the street warily. Even to her, the pair of them appeared ready to draw swords in a heartbeat. If they actually thought to carry out Masema's instructions, they had another think coming.

"He isn't against bloody marriage," Uno growled, staring so hard at a peddler with meat pies on a tray that the man turned and ran without taking the coins from two women holding pies in their hands. "You're lucky he did not remember you have no husband, or he might have sent you to the Lord Dragon with one. Sometimes he picks out three or four hundred unmarried men and as many women, and flaming well marries them. Most have never seen each other before that day. If the pigeon-gutted dirt-grubbers don't bloody complain about that, do you think they'll open their flaming mouths about ale?"

Ragan muttered something under his breath, but she caught enough to narrow her eyes. "Some man doesn't know how bloody lucky *he* is." That was what he had said. He did not even notice her glare. He was too busy scanning the street, watching against someone who might try to abscond with her like a pig in a sack. She was half tempted to take off the shawl and throw it away. He did not seem to hear her sniff, either. Men could be insufferably blind and deaf when they wished to.

"At least he didn't try to steal my jewelry," she said. "Who was that fool woman who gave him hers?" She could not have much sense if she had become one of Masema's followers.

"That," Uno said, "was Alliandre, Blessed of the Light, Queen of bloody Ghealdan. And a dozen more titles, the way you southlanders like to pile them up."

Nynaeve stubbed her toe on a cobblestone and almost fell. "So that is how he does it," she exclaimed, shaking off their helping hands. "If the *queen* is fool enough to listen to him, no wonder he can do whatever he wants."

"Not a fool," Uno said sharply, flashing a frown at her before returning to watching the street. "A wise woman. When you bloody find yourself straddling a wild horse, you bloody well ride it the way it's bloody going, if you're smart enough to pour water out of a bloody boot. You think she's a fool because Masema took her rings? She's flaming smart enough to know he might demand more if she stopped wearing jewelry when she comes to him. The first time, he went to her—been the other way round, since—and he *did* take the rings right off her flaming fingers. She had strands of pearls in her hair, and he broke the strings pulling them out. All of her ladies-in-waiting were down on their knees gathering the bloody things off the floor. Alliandre even picked up a few herself."

"That doesn't sound so wise to me," she said stoutly. "It sounds like cowardice." *Whose knees were shaking because he looked at her?* a voice in her head asked. *Who was sweating herself silly?* At least she had managed to face up to him. *I did. Bending like a willow isn't the same as cowering like a mouse.* "Is she the queen, or isn't she?"

The two men exchanged those irritating looks, and Ragan said quietly, "You don't understand, Nynaeve. Alliandre is the fourth to sit on the Light Blessed Throne since we came to Ghealdan, and that's barely half a year. Johanin wore the crown when Masema began attracting a few crowds, but he thought Masema a harmless madman and did nothing even when the crowds grew and his nobles told him he had to put an end to it. Johanin died in a hunting accident—"

"Hunting accident!" Uno interjected, sneering. A hawker who happened to be looking at him dropped his tray of pins and needles. "Not unless he didn't know one bloody end of a flaming boar spear from the other. Flaming southlanders and their flaming Game of Houses!"

"And Ellizelle succeeded," Ragan took up. "She had the army dispersing the crowds, until finally there was a pitched battle and it was the army that was chased off."

"Bloody poor excuse for soldiers," Uno muttered. She was going to have to speak to him about his language again.

Ragan nodded agreement, but went on with what he had been saying. "They say Ellizelle took poison after that, but however she died, she was replaced by Teresia, who lasted a full ten days after her coronation, just until she had a chance to send two thousand soldiers against ten thousand folk who had gathered to hear Masema outside Jehannah. After her soldiers were routed, she abdicated to marry a rich merchant." Nynaeve stared at him incredulously, and Uno snorted. "That is what they say," the younger man maintained. "Of course, in this land, marrying a commoner means giving up any claim to the throne forever, and whatever Beron Goraed feels about having a pretty young wife with royal blood, I hear he was dragged from his bed by a score of Alliandre's retainers and hauled to Jheda Palace for a wedding in the small hours of the morning. Teresia went off to live on her husband's new country estate while Alliandre was being crowned, all before sunrise, and the new queen summoned Masema to the palace to tell him he would not be troubled again. Inside two weeks *she* was calling on *him*. I do not know whether she really believes what he preaches, but I know she took the throne of a land on the edge of civil war, with Whitecloaks ready to move in, and she stopped it the only way she could. That is a wise queen, and a man could be proud to serve her, even if she is a southlander."

Nynaeve opened her mouth, and forgot what she was going to say when Uno said, in a casual tone, "There's a flaming Whitecloak following us. Don't look around, woman. You have more bloody sense than that."

Her neck stiffened with the effort of keeping her eyes forward; prickles crawled up her back. "Take the next turn, Uno."

"That carries us away from the main streets, and the flaming gates. We can flaming lose him in the crowds."

"Take it!" She inhaled slowly, made her voice less shrill. "I need a sight of him."

Uno glowered so fiercely that people stepped out of their way for ten paces ahead, but they turned down the next narrow street. She shifted her head a trifle as they made the turn, just enough to peek from the edge of her eye before the corner of a small stone tavern cut off her view. The snowy cloak with the flaring sun stood out among the thin crowd. There was no mistaking that beautiful face, the face she had been sure she would see. No other Whitecloak than Galad could have a reason to follow her, and none to follow Uno or Ragan.

CHAPTER
40

The Wheel Weaves

As soon as the building hid Galad, Nynaeve's eyes darted down the street ahead. Fury bubbled up, at herself as much as Galadedrid Damodred. *You witless woolhead!* It was a narrow way like all the rest, paved with rounded stones, lined with gray shops and houses and taverns, populated with a scattered afternoon crowd. *If you hadn't come into town, he'd never have found you!* Too scattered to hide anyone. *You had to go see the Prophet! You had to go believing the Prophet would whisk you away before Moghedien gets here! When are you going to learn you can't depend on anyone but yourself?* In an instant she made her choice. When Galad turned that corner and did not see them, he would begin looking into shops, and maybe taverns as well.

"This way." Gathering her skirts, she darted into the nearest alley and pressed her back against the wall. No one glanced at her twice, furtive as she was, and what that had to say about the way things were in Samara she did not want to consider. Uno and Ragan were beside her before she finished setting her feet, crowding her farther down the dusty dirt alleyway, past an old splintered bucket and a rain barrel dried to the point of collapse inside its hoops. At least they were doing what she wanted. In a manner of speaking. Tense hands on long sword hilts rising above their shoulders, they were ready to protect her whether she desired it or not. *Let them, you fool! Do you think you can protect yourself?*

She was certainly angry enough. Galad, of all people! She should never have left the menagerie! A fool whim, and one that might ruin everything. She could no more channel here than against Masema. Just the possibility that Moghedien or Black sisters were in Samara made her dependent on two men for her safety. It was enough to screw her anger tight; she could have chewed a hole in the stone wall behind her. She knew why Aes Sedai had Warders—all but Reds, anyway. In her head, she did. In her heart, it just made her want to snarl.

Galad appeared, threading his way slowly through the folk out in the street, eyes searching. By all reason, he should have gone on by—he should have—yet almost immediately his gaze settled on the alleyway. On them. He did not even have the grace to appear pleased or surprised.

Uno and Ragan moved together as Galad turned toward the alley. The one-eyed man had his sword out in the blink of an eye, and Ragan was scarcely slower for all he paused to push her deeper into the narrow passage. They positioned themselves one behind the other; should Galad make it past Uno, he would still have Ragan to face.

Nynaeve ground her teeth. She could make all these swords unnecessary, useless; she could sense the True Source, like a light unseen over her shoulder, waiting for her embrace. She could do it. If she dared.

Galad stopped at the alley mouth, cloak thrown back, one hand resting nonchalantly on his sword hilt, a picture of spring-steel grace. Except for his burnished mail, he could have been at a ball.

"I do not want to kill either of you, Shienaran," he said calmly to Uno. Nynaeve had heard Elayne and Gawyn speak of Galad's sword skill, but for the first time she realized that he might really be as good as they said. At least, *he* thought he was. Two seasoned soldiers with blades bare, and he eyed them as a wolfhound would eye a pair of lesser dogs, not seeking a fight yet utterly confident he could take both. Never quite looking away from the two men, he addressed her. "Someone else might have run into a shop or an inn, but you never do what is expected. Will you let me speak with you? There is no need to make me kill these men."

None of the passersby were stopping, but even with three men blocking her view she could see heads swiveling for a glimpse of what had drawn the Whitecloak. And plainly taking in the swords. Rumors would be hatching in all those minds and taking flight on wings that made duskswallows seem slow.

"Let him by," she commanded. When Uno and Ragan did not budge, she repeated herself, even more firmly. They did move aside then, slowly, as much as the narrow alley would allow, yet though neither said a word, there was an air of muttering about them. Galad came by smoothly, seeming to forget the Shienarans. She suspected that believing so would be a mistake; the top-knotted men plainly did not.

Aside from one of the Forsaken, she could not imagine a man she would less like to see right then, but with that face in front of her, she was all too conscious of her own breathing, her own heartbeat. It was ludicrous. Why could the man not be ugly? Or at least plain.

"You knew I knew that you were following." Accusation rang strongly in her voice, though she was not sure what she was accusing him of. Not doing what she had expected and wanted, she imagined ruefully.

"I assumed as much as soon as I recognized you, Nynaeve. I remember that you generally see more than you let on."

She would not let him divert her with compliments. Look where that had gotten her with Valan Luca. "What are you doing in Ghealdan? I thought you were on your way to Altara."

For a moment he stared down at her with those dark, beautiful eyes, then abruptly laughed. "In all the world, Nynaeve, only you would ask me the question I should be asking you. Very well. I'll answer you, for all it should be the other way round. I did have orders for Salidar, in

Altara, but all changed when this Prophet fellow—What is the matter? Are you unwell?"

Nynaeve forced her face to smoothness. "Of course not," she said irritably. "My health is quite good, thank you very kindly." Salidar! Of course! The name was like one of Aludra's firesticks going off in her head. All of that racking of her brain, and Galad casually handed her what she had been unable to dig up on her own. Now if only Masema found a ship quickly. If only she could make sure Galad would not betray them. Without letting Uno and Ragan kill him, of course. Whatever Elayne said, Nynaeve could not believe she would appreciate having her brother cut down. Small chance he would believe Elayne was not with her. "I just cannot get over my shock at seeing you."

"A small patch on mine, when I learned you had slipped out of Sienda." Sternness became that handsome face to an unfortunate degree, but his tone offset it. Somewhat. He could have been lecturing a small girl who had sneaked out of the house after her bedtime to climb trees. "I was sick near to death with worry. What under the Light possessed you? Have you any idea of the risks you ran? And to come here, of all places. Elayne always chooses to saddle a horse at the gallop if she can, but I thought that you, at least, had more sense. This so-called Prophet—" He cut off, eyeing the other two men. Uno had grounded his swordpoint, scarred hands folded atop the pommel. Ragan appeared to be inspecting his blade's edge to the exclusion of everything else.

"I have heard rumors," Galad went on slowly, "that he is Shienaran. You *cannot* have been witless enough to get yourself mixed up with him." There was too much question in that for her taste by far.

"Neither of them is the Prophet, Galad," she said wryly. "I've known them both for some little time, and I can assure you of that. Uno, Ragan, unless you intend to prune your toenails, put those things up. Well?" They hesitated before doing as they were told, Uno grumping under his breath and glaring, but they did it finally. Men usually responded to a firm voice. Most did. Sometimes, anyway.

"I hardly thought they were, Nynaeve." Galad's tone,

even more arid than hers, made her bristle, but when he went on, he sounded annoyed rather than superior. And worried. Which made her bristle even more, of course. *He* all but gave her palpitations, and *he* had the nerve to be worried. "I do not know what you and Elayne have fallen into here, and I do not care, so long as I can extract you from it before you are hurt. Trade is slow on the river, but a suitable boat of some sort should call in the next few days. Let me know where I can find you, and I will secure you passage to somewhere in Altara. From there, you can make your way to Caemlyn."

She gaped in spite of herself. "You mean to find us a ship?"

"It is all I can do, now." He sounded apologetic, and shook his head as if arguing with himself. "I cannot escort you to safety; my duty is here."

"We wouldn't want to take you from your duty," she said, a touch breathless. If he wanted to misunderstand, let him. The most she had hoped for was that he would leave them be.

He seemed to feel the need to defend himself. "It is hardly safe to send you off alone, but a boat will take you away before the entire border explodes. Which it will, soon or late; all it needs is one spark, and the Prophet is sure to strike it if no one else does. You must see to getting yourselves to Caemlyn, you and Elayne. All I ask is your promise that you will go there. The Tower is no place for either of you. Or for—" He clamped his teeth shut, but he might as well have gone ahead and named Egwene.

It could not hurt, having Galad looking for a boat too. If Masema could forget whether he intended to close the taverns, he could forget to have anyone find a riverboat. Especially if he thought a convenient bout of forgetfulness might keep her there to further his own plans. It could not hurt—if she could trust Galad. If she could not, then she would have to hope he was not as good with that sword as he thought he was. A stark thought, but not so stark as what might happen—*would* happen—if he proved untrustworthy.

"I am what I am, Galad, and Elayne is the same." Dodging around Masema had put a bad taste on her tongue. A little White Tower sidestepping was as close as she could come. "And you are what you are, now." She raised her eyebrows significantly at his white cloak. "That lot hates the Tower, and they hate women who can channel. Now that you are one of them, why shouldn't I think there will be fifty of you after me inside the hour, trying to put an arrow in my back if they can't haul me off to a cell? Me, and Elayne as well."

Galad's head jerked in irritation. Or maybe he was offended. "How often must I tell you? I would never let harm come to my sister. Or to you."

It truly was annoying, realizing that she was annoyed at the pause that made it clear she was an afterthought. She was not some silly girl, to lose her wits because a man had eyes that somehow managed to be melting and incredibly penetrating at the same time. "If you say it so," she told him, and his head tossed again.

"Tell me where you are put up, and I will bring word, or send it, as soon as I locate a suitable vessel."

If Elayne was right, he could no more lie than could an Aes Sedai who had sworn the Three Oaths, but still she hesitated. A mistake here could be her last. She had a right to take risks for herself, but this risk involved Elayne too. And Thom and Juilin, for that matter; they were her responsibility, whatever they wanted to think. But she was here, and the decision had to be hers. Not that it might be any other way, frankly.

"Light, woman, what more do you want of me?" Galad growled, half-raising his hands as though to grab her shoulders. Uno's blade was between them in a flash of bright steel, but Elayne's brother actually brushed it aside like a twig, and paid it no more mind than one. "I mean no harm to you, now or ever; I swear it by my mother's name. You say that you are what you are? I know what you are. And what you are not. Perhaps half the reason I wear this," he touched an edge of his snowy cloak, "is because the Tower sent you out—you and Elayne and Egwene—for the Light knows what reason, when you are what you are. It was like sending a boy who has just learned to hold a sword into battle, and I will never forgive them. There is still time for both of you to turn aside; you do not have to carry that sword. The

Tower is too dangerous for you or my sister, especially now. Half the world is become too dangerous for you! Let me help you to safety." The tightness slid from his voice, though it took on a raw edge. "I beg you, Nynaeve. If anything happened to Elayne . . . I half-wish that Egwene were with you, so I could . . ." Scrubbing a hand through his hair, he looked left and right, searching for how to convince her. Uno and Ragan held their blades ready to drive through his body, but he did not appear to see them. "In the name of the Light, Nynaeve, please allow me to do what I can."

It was a simple thing that finally tipped the balance in her mind. They were in Ghealdan. Amadicia was the only land that actually made a crime out of a woman being able to channel, and they were on the opposite bank of the river. That left only Galad's oaths as a Child of the Light to battle against his duty to Elayne. She gave blood the edge in that struggle. Besides, he really was too gorgeous for her to let Uno and Ragan kill him. Not that that had anything to do with her decision, of course.

"We are with Valan Luca's show," she said at last.

He blinked at her, frowned. "Valan Luca's . . . ? You mean one of the menageries?" Incredulity and disgust fought in his voice. "What under the Light are you doing in company like that? Those who keep such shows are no better than . . . No matter. If you need coin, I can supply some. Enough to see you in a decent inn."

His tone bespoke his certainty that she would do as he wanted. Not a "can I help you with a few crowns?" or a "would you like me to find a room for you?" He thought they should be in an inn, so into an inn they would go. The man might have observed enough to know she would duck into an alley, but he did not know her at all, it seemed. Besides, there were reasons to stay with Luca.

"Do you think there is a room, or a hayloft, not taken in all of Samara?" she asked, a touch more tartly than intended.

"I am certain I can find—"

She cut him off. "The last place anyone would look for us is among the shows." The last place anyone but Moghedien would look, at least. "You'll agree we should keep from sight as much as possible? If you *did* find a room, more than likely you'd have to have someone put out of it. A Child of the Light securing a room so for two women? That would set tongues wagging and draw eyes like flies to a midden."

He did not like it, grimacing, and glaring at Uno and Ragan as if it were their fault, but he had enough sense to see sense. "It is no fit place for either of you, but it is probably safer than anywhere inside the city at that. Since you have at least agreed to go to Caemlyn, I will say no more on it."

She kept her face smooth and let him think as he wished. If he thought she had promised what she had not, that was his affair. She had to keep him away from the show as much as possible, though. One glimpse of his sister in those spangled white breeches, and the uproar would overshadow any riot Masema could raise. "You will have to stay clear of the menagerie, mind. Until you find a ship, anyway. Then come to the performers' wagons at nightfall and ask for Nana." He liked that even less, if possible, but she forestalled him firmly. "I've not seen a single Child of the Light near any of the shows. If you visit one, don't you think people will notice and ask why?"

His smile was still gorgeous, but it showed too many teeth. "You have an answer for everything, it seems. Do you have any objection to my escorting you back there, at least?"

"I most certainly do. There will be rumors as it is—a hundred people must have noticed us talking here"— she could no longer see the street past the three men, yet she had no doubt passersby were still glancing into the alley, and Uno and Ragan had not resheathed their swords—"but if you accompany me, we'll be seen by ten times as many."

His wince was half rueful, half mirthful. "An answer for everything," he muttered. "But you have the right of it." Clearly he wished she did not. "Hear me, Shienarans," he said, turning his head, and suddenly his voice was steel. "I am Galadedrid Damodred, and this woman is under my protection. As for her companion, I would count it small loss to die in order to save her the smallest harm. If you allow either to come to that

smallest harm, I will find you both and kill you."
Ignoring the sudden, dangerous blankness of their faces
as completely as he did their swords, he swung his eyes
back to her. "I suppose you still will not tell me where
Egwene is?"

"All you need know is that she is far from here."
Folding her arms beneath her breasts, she could feel her
heart beating through her ribs. Was she making a dangerous mistake because of a pretty face? "And safer than
any action of yours can make her."

He looked as if he did not believe her, but he made no
more of it. "With luck, I will find a vessel in a day or two.
Until then, stay close to this Valan Luca's . . . show. Stay
low and avoid notice. As much as you can with your hair
that color. And tell Elayne not to run away from me
again. The Light shone on you to let me find you still in
one piece, and it will have to shine twice as brightly to
keep you from harm if you try haring off across
Ghealdan. This Prophet's blasphemous ruffians are
everywhere, without respect for law or persons, and that
does not count brigands taking advantage of disorder.
Samara itself is a wasp nest, but if you will sit quietly—
and convince my headstrong sister to do the same—I
will find a way to get you out of it before you are stung."

It was an effort to keep her mouth shut. Taking what
she told him and making it an injunction to her! Next
thing the man would want to pack her and Elayne in
wool and sit them on a shelf! *Wouldn't it be best if*
someone *did?* a tiny voice asked. *Haven't you caused*
enough trouble going your own way? She told the voice to
be quiet. It did not listen, but began listing disasters and
near disasters sprung from her own stubbornness.

Apparently taking her silence for acquiescence, he
turned away from her—and stopped. Ragan and Uno
had moved to block his way to the street, glancing at her
with that strange, deceptive calm men so often adopted
when they were a hairsbreadth from sudden violence.
The air seemed to crackle, until she motioned hurriedly.
The Shienarans lowered their blades and stood aside,
and Galad took his hands from his sword, brushed
past them and melded into the crowd without a backward glance.

Nynaeve gave Uno and Ragan each a good glare before stalking off in the opposite direction. There she had had everything arranged properly, and they had to nearly ruin it all. Men always seemed to think violence could solve anything. If she had had a stout stick, she would have thumped all three of them about the shoulders until they saw reason.

The Shienarans seemed to see a little of it, now; they caught up to her, swords scabbarded on their backs once more, and followed without a word, even when she twice took a wrong turn and had to double back. It was especially well for them that they kept silent then. She had had enough of holding her tongue. First Masema, and then Galad. All she wanted was a wafer-thin excuse to tell someone exactly what she thought. Especially that little voice in her head, pushed back to an insect buzz now but refusing to be quiet.

By the time they were out of Samara and on that dirt cart track, with its sparse traffic, the voice refused to be denied. She worried over Rand's arrogance, but hers had brought herself and others as near calamity as made no never mind. For Birgitte, perhaps it was well over the line, even if she was alive. The best thing was for Nynaeve not to confront them again, not the Black Ajah and not Moghedien, not until someone who knew what they were doing could decide what should be done. Protest welled up, but she stamped on it as firmly as she ever had on Thom or Juilin. She would go to Salidar and hand the matter over to the Blues. That was how it would be. She was set on it.

"Have you eaten something that disagrees with you?" Ragan said. "Your mouth is twisted as if you had chewed a ripe duckberry."

She gave him a look that snapped his teeth shut and stalked on. The two Shienarans kept pace to either side.

What was she going to do with them? That she should put them to some use was never in doubt; their appearance was too providential to throw away. For one thing, two additional pairs of eyes—well, three eyes anyway; she was going to learn to look at that patch without swallowing if it killed her—more eyes hunting for a ship might mean finding one sooner. All very well if Masema or Galad found a vessel first, but she did not want either to know more of her doings than she had to allow. There was no telling what either might do.

"Are you following me because Masema told you to look after me," she demanded, "or because Galad did?"

"What flaming difference does it make?" Uno muttered. "If the Lord Dragon has summoned you, you bloody well—" He cut off, frowning, as she raised one finger. Ragan eyed it as if it were a weapon.

"Do you mean to help Elayne and me reach Rand?"

"We've nothing better to do," Ragan said dryly. "As it is, we'll not see Shienar again till we are gray and toothless. We might as well ride with you to Tear or wherever he is."

She had not considered that, but it made sense. Two more to help Thom and Juilin with chores and standing guard. No need to let them know how long that might take, or how many stops and detours could lie along the way. The Blues in Salidar might not let any of them go further. Once they reached Aes Sedai, they would be only Accepted again. *Stop thinking about it! You are going to do it!*

The crowd waiting in front of Luca's garish sign appeared no smaller than it had before. A stream of people trickled into the meadow to join the throng as another stream meandered out, exclaiming over what they had seen. Now and again the "boar-horses" were visible, rearing above the canvas wall, to *oohs* and *aahs* from those waiting to get in. Cerandin was putting them through their paces again. The Seanchan woman always saw that the *s'redit* got plenty of rest. She was very firm about that, whatever Luca wanted. Men *did* do as they were told when you left no doubt that anything else was inconceivable. Usually they did.

Short of the well-trampled brown grass, Nynaeve stopped and turned to face the two Shienarans. She kept her face calm, but they looked suitably wary, though in Uno's case, regrettably, that involved fiddling with his eyepatch in a queasy-making way. The folk heading to or from the show paid no heed to them.

"Then it will not be because of Masema *or* Galad," she said firmly. "If you are going to travel with me, you will do as *I* say, else you can go your own way, for I'll have none of you."

Of course they had to exchange glances before nodding acceptance. "If that's how it flaming has to be," Uno growled, "then well enough. If you don't have somebody to bloody well look after you, you'll never flaming live to reach the Lord Dragon. Some sheep-gutted farmer will have you for breakfast because of your tongue." Ragan gave him a guarded look that said he agreed with every word but strongly doubted Uno's wisdom in voicing them. Ragan, it seemed, had the makings of a wise man in him.

If they accepted her terms, it did not really matter why. For now. There would be plenty of time later to set them straight.

"I don't doubt the others will agree, too," Ragan said.

"Others?" she said, blinking. "You mean there are more than the two of you? How many?"

"There are only fifteen of us altogether now. I don't think Bartu or Nengar will come."

"Sniffing after the bloody *Prophet*." Uno turned his head and spat copiously. "Only fifteen. Sar went over that bloody cliff in the mountains, and Mendao had to get himself into a flaming duel with three Hunters for the Horn, and . . ."

Nynaeve was too busy stopping herself from gaping to listen. Fifteen! She could not help toting up in her head what it would cost to feed fifteen men. Even when they were not particularly hungry, Thom or Juilin either one ate more than Elayne and her combined. Light!

On the other hand, with fifteen Shienaran soldiers, there was no need to wait for a ship. A riverboat was certainly the fastest way to travel—she remembered what she had heard of Salidar, now; a river town, or close by; a boat could take them right to it—yet a Shienaran escort would make their wagon just as safe, from Whitecloaks or bandits or followers of the Prophet. But much slower. And a lone wagon heading away from Samara with such an escort would certainly stand out. A signpost for Moghedien, or the Black Ajah. *I will let the Blues deal with them, and that is that!*

"What is wrong?" Ragan asked, and Uno added

apologetically, "I shouldn't have mentioned how Sakaru died." Sakaru? That must have been after she stopped listening. "I don't spend much time around fla—, around ladies. I forget you have weak bell—, I mean, uh, delicate stomachs." If he did not stop tugging at that eyepatch he was going to find out how delicate her stomach was.

The number changed nothing. If two Shienarans were good, fifteen were wonderful. Her own private army. No need to worry about Whitecloaks or brigands or riots, or whether she had made a mistake about Galad. How many hams could fifteen men eat every day? A firm voice. "Right, then. Every night just after dark, one of you—one, mind!—will come here and ask for Nana. That's the name I am known by." She had no reason for the order, except to put them in the habit of doing what she told them. "Elayne goes by Morelin, but you ask for Nana. If you need coin, come to me, not Masema." She had to suppress a wince as the words left her mouth. There was still gold in the wagon's stove, but Luca had not demanded his hundred gold crowns yet, and he would. There was always the jewelry, if need be, though. She had to be sure they were weaned away from Masema. "Aside from that, none of you are to come near me, or the show." Without that, they would likely set a guard, or some such idiocy. "Not unless a riverboat arrives. In that case, you come running on the instant. Do you understand me?"

"No," Uno muttered. "Why do we flaming have to keep away—?" His head jerked back as her admonitory finger almost touched his nose.

"Do you remember what I said about your language?" She had to make herself give him a level look; that glaring red eyepatch made her stomach do flips. "Unless you do remember, you will learn why men in the Two Rivers have decent tongues in their mouths."

She watched him turn that over in his mind. He did not know what her connection with the White Tower was, only that it existed. She might be an agent of the Tower, or Tower-trained. Or even Aes Sedai, though one not long to the shawl. And the threat was vague enough for him to put his own worst interpretation to it. She had

known that technique long before hearing Juilin mention
it to Elayne.

When it appeared the idea had taken hold—and
before he could ask any questions—she lowered her
hand. "You will stay away for the same reason Galad
does. So as not to draw attention. For the rest, you will
do it because I say so. If I must explain my every decision
to you, I'll have time for nothing else, so you must make
the best of it."

That was a suitably Aes Sedai comment. Besides, they
had no choice if they intended to help her reach Rand, as
they thought, which meant they had no choice. All in all,
she was feeling quite satisfied with herself as she shooed
them off back toward Samara and strode past the waiting
crowd and under the sign bearing Valan Luca's name.

To her surprise, there was an addition to the show. On
a new platform not far from the entry, a woman in gauzy
yellow trousers was standing on her head, arms outstretched to either side with a pair of white doves on
each hand. No, not on her head. The woman was
gripping some sort of wooden frame in her *teeth* and
balancing on that. As Nynaeve watched, aghast, the
peculiar acrobat lowered her hands to the platform for a
moment while bending herself double, until she seemed
to be sitting on her own head. Even that was not enough.
Her legs curved down in front of her, then impossibly
back up under her arms, whereupon she transferred the
doves to the upturned soles of her feet, now the highest
part of the contorted ball she had knotted herself into.
The onlookers gasped and applauded, but the sight made
Nynaeve shiver. It was all too good a reminder of what
Moghedien had done to her.

That isn't why I mean to hand her over to the Blues, she
told herself. *I just do not want to cause calamity again.*
That was true, but she was also afraid that the next time,
she would not escape so easily or so lightly. She would
not have admitted that to another soul. She did not like
admitting it to herself.

Giving the contortionist one last puzzled glance—she
could not begin to puzzle out what the woman had
twisted herself into now—she turned away. And started
as Elayne and Birgitte suddenly appeared at her side out

of the milling crowd. Elayne had a cloak decently covering her white coat and breeches; Birgitte was all but flaunting her low-necked red gown. No, there was no "all but" to it. She stood even straighter than usual and had tossed back her braid to remove even its minimal covering. Nynaeve fingered the knot of her shawl at her waist, wishing every glance at Birgitte did not remind her how much she herself would be showing once the gray wool came off. The other woman's quiver hung at her belt, and she carried the bow Luca had found for her. Surely the day was too late for her to go through with the shooting.

A glance at the sky told Nynaeve she was wrong. Despite everything that had happened, the sun still stood well above the horizon. Shadows stretched long, but not long enough to dissuade Birgitte, she suspected.

In an attempt to cover checking the sun, she nodded toward the woman in the gauzy trousers, who had now begun to twist herself into something that Nynaeve *knew* was impossible. While still balancing on her teeth. "Where did she come from?"

"Luca hired her," Birgitte answered calmly. "He bought some leopards, as well. Her name is Muelin."

If Birgitte was all self-possessed coolness, Elayne very nearly quivered with emotion. "'Where did she *come* from?'" she spluttered. "She came from a show that a mob nearly destroyed!"

"I heard about that," Nynaeve said, "but that isn't what is important. I—"

"Not important!" Elayne rolled her eyes to the heavens as if for guidance. "Did you also hear *why*? I don't know whether it was Whitecloaks or this Prophet, but somebody whipped up that mob because they thought . . ." She glanced around without slowing and lowered her voice; none of the crowd had stopped, but every passerby stared at two obvious performers standing. ". . . that a woman in the show might wear a shawl." She emphasized the last word significantly. "Fools to think she'd be with a traveling menagerie, but then, you and I are. And you go dashing into the city without a word to anyone. We've heard everything from a bald-headed man carrying you off over his shoulder to you kissing a Shienaran and traipsing away with him arm in arm."

Nynaeve was still gaping when Birgitte added, "Luca was upset, whatever the tale. He said . . ." She cleared her throat and made her voice deep. "'So she likes rough men, does she? Well, I can be as rough as a winter cob!' And off he set, leading two lads with shoulders like s'Gandin quarrymen, to fetch you back. Thom Merrilin and Juilin Sandar went as well, in not much better temper. That did not improve Luca's, but they were all so upset over you it left no room for anger at each other."

For a moment Nynaeve stared in confusion. She liked rough men? What could he possibly mean by . . . ? Slowly it sank in, and she groaned. "Oh, that is just what I need." And Thom and Juilin running around Samara. The Light knew what trouble they could get into.

"I still want to know what you thought you were doing," Elayne said, "but we are wasting time here."

Nynaeve let them start her off through the crowd, one to either side, but even with the news of Luca and the others, she felt satisfied with her day's work. "We should be out of here in a day or two, with luck. If Galad doesn't find us a boat, Masema will. It turns out he is the Prophet. You remember Masema, Elayne. That sour-faced Shienaran we saw—" Realizing that Elayne had stopped, Nynaeve paused for her to catch up again.

"Galad?" the younger woman said disbelievingly, forgetting to hold her cloak closed. "You saw—you *spoke* to Galad? *And* the Prophet? You must have, or how would they be trying to find a vessel? Did you have tea with them, or did you just meet them in a common room? Where the bald-headed man carried you, no doubt. Maybe the King of Ghealdan was there, too? Would you please convince me I am dreaming so I can wake up?"

"Get a grip on yourself," Nynaeve said firmly. "It is a queen, now, not a king, and yes, she was. And he wasn't bald; he had a topknot. The Shienaran, I mean. Not the Prophet. *He's* as bald as—" She glared at Birgitte until the woman stopped snickering. The glower slipped a little when Nynaeve remembered who she was glowering at and what she had done to her, but if the woman had not smoothed her features, they might have found out whether she could bring herself to slap Birgitte cross-eyed. They began walking again, and she said as levelly as she could manage, "This is what happened. I saw Uno, one of the Shienarans who was at Falme, watching you highwalk, Elayne. He doesn't think any better of the Daughter-Heir of Andor showing her legs than I do, by the way. In any case, Moiraine sent them here after Falme, but . . ."

She related everything quickly as they made their way through the crowd, riding roughshod over Elayne's increasingly incredulous exclamations, answering their questions in as few words as possible. Despite a quick interest in the shifts of the Ghealdanin throne, Elayne concentrated on *exactly* what Galad had said and why Nynaeve had been fool enough to approach the Prophet, *whoever* he was. That word—*fool*—popped up often enough to make Nynaeve keep a tight leash on her temper. She might doubt whether she could slap Birgitte, but Elayne had no such protection, Daughter-Heir or not. A few more repetitions, and the girl would discover it. Birgitte was more interested in Masema's intentions on the one hand and the Shienarans on the other. It seemed she had encountered Borderlanders in previous lives, though their nations had had different names, and thought well of them by and large. She said little, really, but she appeared to approve of holding on to the Shienarans.

Nynaeve expected the news about Salidar to startle them, or excite them, or anything but what it did. Birgitte took it as matter-of-factly as if she had said they would eat supper with Thom and Juilin that night. Plainly she meant to go where Elayne did, and all else mattered little. Elayne looked doubtful. Doubtful!

"Are you certain? You have tried so hard to remember, and . . . Well, it seems awfully fortuitous that Galad should just happen to mention it to you."

Nynaeve glowered. "Of course I am certain. Coincidences *do* happen. The Wheel weaves as the Wheel wills, as you may have heard. I remember now that he mentioned it in Sienda, too, but I was so concerned over *you* being concerned about him that I didn't—" She cut off short.

They had arrived at a long narrow area near the north wall, marked off by ropes. At one end stood something like a segment of wooden fence, two paces wide and two tall. People lined the ropes four deep, with children crouching down in front or holding a father's leg or a mother's skirts. A buzz rose as the three women appeared. Nynaeve would have stopped dead, but Birgitte had her by the arm, and it was walk or be dragged.

"I thought we were going to the wagon," she said faintly. Busy with talking, she had paid too little attention to where they were going.

"Not unless you want to see me shoot in the dark," Birgitte replied. She sounded all too willing to give it a try.

Nynaeve wished she could have made some other comment than a squeak. The bit of fence filled her vision as they progressed down the open space, to the exclusion of the onlookers. Even their increasing murmurs sounded distant. The fence looked a mile from where Birgitte would stand.

"Are you sure that he said he swore by . . . our mother?" Elayne demanded sourly. Acknowledging Galad as her brother even that far was unpleasant for her.

"What? Yes. I said so, didn't I? Listen. If Luca is in the city, he would not know whether we did this or not until it was too late to . . ." Nynaeve knew she was babbling, but she could not seem to stop her tongue. Somehow she had never realized how *far* a hundred paces really was. In the Two Rivers, grown men always shot targets at twice that. But then, none of those targets had ever been *her*. "I mean, it already is very late. The shadows . . . The glare . . . We really should do this in the morning. When the light is—"

"If he swore by her," Elayne broke in as if she had not been listening, "then he will hold to it no matter what. He would sooner break an oath on his hope of salvation and rebirth than that. I think . . . no, I *know* we can trust him." She did not sound as if she particularly liked it, though.

"The light is just fine," Birgitte said, a hint of amusement in her calm voice. "I might try it blindfolded. This lot will want it to look difficult, I think."

Nynaeve opened her mouth, but nothing came out. This time she would have settled for a squeak. Birgitte was only making a bad joke. She had to be joking.

They positioned her with her back against the rough wooden fence, and Elayne began tugging at the knot in the shawl as Birgitte turned back the way they had come, drawing an arrow from her quiver.

"You really did something foolish this time," Elayne muttered. "We can trust Galad's oath, I'm sure, but you could not know what he might do beforehand. And to approach the Prophet!" She jerked the shawl from Nynaeve's shoulders roughly. "You could have had *no* idea whatsoever what *he* might do. You worried everybody and risked everything!"

"I know," Nynaeve managed to get out. The sun was in her eyes; she could no longer see Birgitte at all. But Birgitte could see her. Of course she could. That was the important thing.

Elayne looked at her suspiciously. "You know?"

"I know I risked everything. I should have talked with you, asked you. I know I've been a fool. I should not be allowed outside without a keeper." It all came in a breathless rush. Birgitte *must* be able to see her.

Suspicion became concern. "Are you all right? If you really do not want to do this . . ."

The woman thought she was afraid. Nynaeve could not, would not, allow that. She forced a smile, hoped her eyes were not too wide. Her face felt tight. "Of course I want to. I'm looking forward to it, actually."

Elayne gave her a dubious frown, but nodded at last. "You are *sure* about Salidar?"

She did not wait for an answer, but hurried off to one side, folding the shawl. For some reason, Nynaeve could not work up a proper indignation over the question, or Elayne not waiting. Her breath was coming so fast that she was dimly aware that she might come right out of the dress's low neck, yet even that thought could not catch her. The sun filled her view; had she squinted, she might have been able to make out Birgitte after a fashion, but her eyes had a will of their own, increasingly widening.

There was nothing she could do now. It was a punishment for taking foolish risks. She could manage only the tiniest pique over being punished after working everything out so well. And Elayne did not even believe her about Salidar! She would have to take it stoically. She would—

Seemingly out of nowhere an arrow *tchunked* into the wood, vibrating against her right wrist, and stoic resolve broke with a low wail. It was all she could do to keep her knees straight. A second arrow brushed the other wrist, producing a slightly higher pitch to her yelp. She could as soon stop Birgitte's shafts as silence herself. Arrow by arrow the yelps rose higher, and it seemed to her almost as if the crowd was cheering her cries. The louder she shrieked, the louder they cheered and applauded. By the time she was outlined from knees to head, the applause was thunderous. In truth, she felt some irritation at the finish, when the crowd all rushed to throng around Birgitte, leaving her standing there staring at the fletchings around her. Some still quivered. *She* still quivered.

Pushing away, she scurried off toward the wagons as quickly as she could before anyone noticed how much her legs were wobbling. Not that anyone was paying any attention to *her*. All she had done was stand there and pray Birgitte did not sneeze, or get an itch. And tomorrow she would have to go through it again. That or let Elayne—and worse, Birgitte—know she could not face it.

When Uno came that night asking after Nana, she told him in no uncertain terms to prod Masema as much as he dared and to find Galad and tell him he *must* find a boat quickly, whatever it required. Then she took to her bed without eating and tried to make herself believe that she could convince Elayne and Birgitte that she was too ill to stand against that wall. Only, she was all too certain they would know exactly what her illness was. That even Birgitte would likely be all sympathy just made it worse. One of those fool men *had* to find a riverboat!

CHAPTER
41

The Craft of Kin Tovere

One hand on his sword hilt, the other holding the green-and-white tasseled length of Seanchan spear, Rand ignored the others on the sparsely treed hilltop for the moment while he studied the three camps spread out below in the midmorning sun. Three distinct camps, and that was the rub. They were all the Cairhienin and Tairen forces at his disposal. Every man else who could use sword or spear was penned in the city, or the Light alone knew where.

The Aiel had rounded up refugees in hordes between the Jangai Pass and here, and a few had even straggled in on their own, lured by rumors that *these* Aiel at least were not killing everyone in sight, or else too dispirited to care so long as they had a meal before dying. Too many thought they would die, at the hands of the Aiel or the Dragon Reborn, or in the Last Battle, which they seemed to think was shaping up for any day now. A goodly number all together, but farmers and craftsmen and shopkeepers for the most part. Some knew how to use bow or sling to fetch a rabbit, but there was not a soldier in the lot and no time to teach them. The city of

Cairhien itself lay little more than five miles to the west, some of the fabled "topless towers of Cairhien" visible above the intervening forest. The city sprawled across hills hard by the River Alguenya, encircled by Couladin's Shaido and those who had joined him.

One haphazard set of tents and cookfires in the long shallow valley below Rand held some eight hundred Tairens, armored men. Nearly half were Defenders of the Stone in burnished breastplates and rimmed helmets, their plump coatsleeves striped black and gold. The rest were levies from a double handful of lords whose banners and pennants made a circle in the camp's center around the silver Crescent-and-Stars of the High Lord Weiramon. Guards stood thickly along their picket lines as if they expected a raid against the horses any minute.

Three hundred paces away, the second camp guarded their horses as tightly. The animals were a mixed lot, few approaching the fine arch-necked stock of Tear, and some former plow and cart horses were tied along those ropes or Rand missed his guess. The Cairhienin numbered perhaps a hundred more than the Tairens, but their tents were fewer and most often patched, and their banners and *con* represented some seventy-odd lords. Few Cairhienin nobles still had many retainers, and the army had broken apart early in the civil war.

The last gathering lay another five hundred paces along, full of Cairhienin for the most part, yet well and truly separated from the others by more than distance. Larger than the other pair combined, this camp held few tents or horses. It displayed no banners, and only the officers wore *con,* the small pennants on their backs in solid colors meant to pick them out for their men rather than signify a House. Infantry might be necessary, but rare was the lord of Tear or Cairhien, either one, who would admit it. Certainly none would agree to actually lead such. It was the most orderly of the camps, though, the cookfires in neat rows, the long pikes stacked upright where they could be seized in a moment and clusters of archers or crossbowmen dotted along the lines. According to Lan, discipline kept men alive in battle, but infantry were more likely to know it and believe than cavalry.

The three groups were supposedly together, under the same command—the High Lord Weiramon had brought them in from the south late the day before—but the two camps of horsemen watched each other nearly as warily as they did the Aiel on the surrounding hills, the Tairens with a dose of contempt that the Cairhienin echoed in ignoring the third, which in turn eyed the others sullenly. Rand's followers, his allies, and as ready to fight each other as anyone else.

Still pretending to study the camps, Rand examined Weiramon, helmetless and iron-spined straight nearby. Two younger men, minor Tairen lords, hung at the High Lord's heels, dark beards trimmed and oiled in perfect imitation of Weiramon's except that his was streaked with gray, and their breastplates, worn over brightly striped coats, bore goldwork only a touch less ornate than his. Aloof, apart from everyone else on the hilltop yet close to Rand, they could have been waiting for some martial ceremony at a royal court, except for the sweat rolling down their faces. They ignored that as well, though.

The High Lord's sigil lacked only a few stars to duplicate Lanfear's, but the long-nosed fellow was not her in disguise, with his mainly gray hair oiled like his beard and combed in a vain attempt to hide its thinness. He had been coming north with reinforcements from Tear when he heard that Aiel were attacking the city of Cairhien itself. Instead of turning back or sitting still, he continued north as hard as his horses could stand, gathering what forces he found along the way.

That was the good news of Weiramon. The bad was that he had fully expected to dispel the Shaido around Cairhien with what he had brought. He still did. And he was none too happy that Rand would not let him be about it or that he was surrounded by Aiel. One Aiel was no different from another to Weiramon. To the others, too, for that matter. One of the young lords pointedly sniffed a scented silk handkerchief whenever he looked at an Aiel. Rand wondered how long the fellow would survive. And what Rand would have to do about it when he died.

Weiramon noticed Rand watching, and cleared his throat. "My Lord Dragon," he began in a gravelly bark, "one good charge will scatter them like quail." He slapped his gauntlets against his palm loudly. "Foot never stands up to horse. I will send in the Cairhienin to flush them, then follow with my—"

Rand cut him off. Could the man count at all? Did the number of Aiel he could see here give him no clue to how many might be around the city? It did not matter. Rand had heard as much of this as he could stomach. "You are certain of the news you bring from Tear?"

Weiramon blinked. "News, my Lord Dragon? What—? Oh, that. Burn my soul, there's nothing to that. Illianer pirates often try to raid along the coast." They were more than trying, by what the man had said when he arrived.

"And the attacks on the Plains of Maredo? Do they often do that, as well?"

"Why, burn my soul, those are just brigands." It was more statement of fact than protest. "Perhaps not Illianers at all, but certainly not soldiers. The jumble those Illianers make of things, who can say whether king or Assemblage or Council of Nine has the whiphand on any given day, yet if they do decide to move, it will be armies striking at Tear under the Golden Bees, not raiders burning merchants' wagons and border farms. You can mark me on that."

"If you wish it," Rand replied, as politely as he could. Whatever power the Assemblage, or the Council of Nine, or Mattin Stepaneos den Balgar had, it was what Sammael chose to leave them. But relatively few knew that the Forsaken were loose already. Some who should know refused to believe, or ignored it—as if that would make the Forsaken go away—or seemed to think that if it had to happen, it would be in some vague and preferably distant future. There was no point in trying to convince Weiramon, whichever group he belonged in. The man's belief or disbelief changed nothing.

The High Lord scowled at the hollow between the hills. More specifically, at the two Cairhienin camps. "With no proper rule here as yet, who can say what riffraff have drifted south?" Grimacing, he slapped his gauntlets even harder before turning back to Rand. "Well, we will bring them to heel soon enough for you, my Lord Dragon. If you will only give the order, I can drive. . . ."

Rand brushed past him, not listening, though Weiramon followed, still asking authority to attack, the other two trailing him like heelhounds. The man was a stone-blind fool.

They were not alone, of course. The hilltop was crowded, really. Sulin had a hundred *Far Dareis Mai* arrayed around the peak, for one thing, every last one looking even more ready to don her veil than Aiel usually did. It was not only the nearness of the Shaido that had Sulin on edge. In mockery of Rand's contempt for the suspicions in the camps below, Enaila and two Maidens were never far from Weiramon and his lordlings, and the closer they stood to Rand, the more the three Maidens looked about to don veils.

Not far off, Aviendha stood talking with a dozen or more Wise Ones, shawls looped over their elbows, all but she decked in bracelets and necklaces. Surprisingly, it was a bony white-haired woman, even older than Bair, who seemed to be taking the lead. Rand would have expected Amys or Bair, but even they shut up as soon as Sorilea spoke. Melaine was with Bael, halfway between the other Wise Ones and the other clan chiefs. She kept adjusting the coat of Bael's *cadin'sor* as if he did not know how to dress himself, and he had the patient look of a man reminding himself of all the reasons he had married. It might be personal, but Rand suspected the Wise Ones were trying to influence the chiefs again. If that was the case, he would learn the particulars soon enough.

It was Aviendha who held Rand's eye, though. She smiled at him briefly before returning to listening to Sorilea. A friendly smile, but no more. That was something, he supposed. She had not lashed out at him once since what had happened between them, and if she sometimes made an acid comment it was no sharper than what he might have expected from Egwene. Except the one time he had brought up marriage again; then she had scorched his ears so thoroughly that he had left it alone thereafter. But friendly was as far as it went, though she was sometimes careless now about undressing in front of him at night. She still insisted on sleeping no more than three paces from him.

The Maidens, at any rate, seemed sure that there was a lot less than three paces between their blankets, and he kept expecting that certainty to spread, but so far it had not. Egwene would come down on him like a falling tree if she even *suspected* something like that. It was easy enough for her to talk of Elayne, but he could not even puzzle out Aviendha, and she was right there in front of him. All in all, he was tenser than ever when he as much as looked at Aviendha, but she seemed more relaxed than he had ever seen her. Somehow or other, that seemed the opposite of how it should be. It all seemed topsy-turvy with her. But then, Min was the only woman who had *not* made him feel as if he were standing on his head half the time.

Sighing, he walked on, still not listening to Weiramon. One day he was going to understand women. When he had the time to apply to it. He suspected a lifetime would not be enough, though.

The clan chiefs had their own gathering, of sept chiefs and representatives from the societies. Rand recognized some of them. Dark Heirn, chief of the Jindo Taardad, and Mangin, who gave him a companionable nod and the Tairens a contemptuous grimace. Spear-slender Juranai, leader of *Aethan Dor,* the Red Shields, on this expedition despite a few streaks of white in his pale brown hair, and Roidan, thick-shouldered and gray, who led *Sha'mad Conde,* the Thunder Walkers. Those four had sometimes joined him in practicing the Aiel way of fighting without weapons since leaving the Jangai Pass.

"Do you want to go hunting today?" Mangin asked as Rand passed, and Rand looked at him in surprise.

"Hunting?"

"There is not much to give sport, but we could try catching sheep in a sack." The wry glance Mangin darted at the Tairens left little doubt what "sheep" he meant, though Weiramon and the others did not see. Or affected not to. The lordling with the perfumed handkerchief sniffed it again.

"Another time, maybe," Rand replied, shaking his head. He thought he could have been friends with any of the four, but especially Mangin, who had a sense of humor much like Mat's. If he had no time to study women, he certainly had no time for making new friends. Little time for old friends, for that matter. Mat worried him.

On the highest part of the hill, a heavy framework tower of logs thrust above the treetops, the wide platform at the top twenty spans or more above the ground. The Aiel knew nothing about working with wood on that scale, but there had been plenty among the Cairhienin refugees who did.

Moiraine was waiting at the base of the first slanting ladder with Lan, and Egwene. Egwene had been getting a good bit of sun; she really could have passed for Aiel except for her dark eyes. A short Aiel. He scanned her face quickly, but detected nothing except tiredness. Amys and the others must be working her too hard with her training. She would not thank him for interceding, though.

"Have you decided?" Rand asked, stopping. Weiramon fell silent at last.

Egwene hesitated, but Rand noted that she did not look at Moiraine before nodding. "I will do what I can."

Her reluctance bothered him. He had not asked Moiraine—she could not use the One Power as a weapon against the Shaido, not unless they threatened her or he managed to convince her they were all Darkfriends— but Egwene had not taken the Three Oaths, and he had been sure she would see the necessity. Instead, she had gone white-faced when he suggested it and had avoided for him for three days until now. At least she had agreed. Whatever made the fight shorter against the Shaido must be for the good.

Moiraine's face never changed, though he had no doubt what she thought. Those smooth Aes Sedai features, those Aes Sedai eyes, could register icy disapproval without altering a jot.

Thrusting the piece of spear through his belt, he put foot to the first rung—and Moiraine spoke.

"Why are you wearing a sword again?"

The last question he would have expected. "Why shouldn't I?" he muttered, and scrambled upward. Not a good answer, but she had caught him off balance.

The half-healed wound in his side tugged as he climbed, not quite hurting but seeming about to break open just the same. He paid it no mind; it often felt that way when he exerted himself.

Rhuarc and the other clan chiefs came after him, Bael leaving Melaine last of all, but thankfully Weiramon and his two toadies remained on the ground. The High Lord *knew* what was to be done; he needed and wanted no more information. Feeling Moiraine's eyes following him, Rand glanced down. Not Moiraine. It was Egwene watching him climb, her face so close to Aes Sedai that he could not have slid a hair through the difference. Moiraine had her head together with Lan's. He hoped Egwene was not going to change her mind.

On the broad platform at the top, two short, sweating young men in shirtsleeves were setting a brass-bound wooden tube, three paces long and bigger around than either's arm, on a pivoting frame fastened to the railing. An identical tube already sat a few paces away, where it had been almost since the tower was completed the day before. A third coatless man wiped his bald head with a striped kerchief while he growled at them.

"Easy with it. *Easy,* I said! You motherless weasels knock a lens out of alignment, and I will knock your brainless heads backward to front. Fasten it tight, Jol. Tight! If it falls while the Lord Dragon is looking through it, you both had better jump after it. Not just for him. You break my work and you will wish you had broken your fool skulls."

Jol and the other fellow, Cail, worked on, quickly but not very visibly perturbed. They had had years to grow used to Kin Tovere's way of talking. It had been finding a craftsman who made lenses and looking glasses—and his two apprentices—among the refugees that had first given Rand the idea for this tower.

At first none of the three noticed they were not alone. The clan chiefs climbed on silent feet, and Tovere's harangue was enough to cover the sound of Rand's boots. Rand himself was startled when Lan's head popped through the open trap after Bael; boots or no, the Warder made no more noise than the Aiel. Even Han stood a head taller than the Cairhienin.

When they finally did see the new arrivals, the two apprentices gave wide-eyed starts as if they had never seen an Aiel before, then bent themselves in half bowing to Rand and stayed that way. The lensmaker jerked almost as much at the sight of the Aiel, but made a more restrained bow, wiping his head again in the middle of it.

"Told you I would have the second finished today, my Lord Dragon." Tovere managed to get respect into his tone without making his voice one bit less gruff. "A wonderful thought, this tower. I would never have conceived it, but once you started asking how far you could see with a looking glass . . . Give me time, and I will make you one to see Caemlyn from here. If the tower is built high enough," he added judiciously. "There are limits."

"What you've done already is more than enough, Master Tovere." More than Rand had hoped for, certainly. He had already had a look through the first looking glass.

Jol and Cail were still bent at right angles, heads down. "Perhaps you had best take your apprentices below," Rand said. "So we don't get crowded."

There was room for four times as many, but Tovere immediately poked Cail's shoulder with a thick finger. "Come along, you ham-fisted stableboys. We are in the Lord Dragon's way."

The apprentices barely straightened enough to follow him, gazing round-eyed at Rand even more than at the Aiel as they vanished down the ladder. Cail was a year older than he, Jol two. Both had been born in bigger

towns than he had imagined before leaving the Two
Rivers, had visited Cairhien and seen the king and the
Amyrlin Seat, if at a distance, while he was still tending
sheep. Very likely, they still knew more of the world than
he in some ways. Shaking his head, he bent to the new
looking glass.

Cairhien leaped into view. The forests, never particularly thick to one used to Two Rivers' woods, stopped
completely well short of the city, of course. High gray,
square-towered walls in a perfect square against the river
mocked the hills' flowing curves. Within, more towers
rose in precise pattern, marking the points of a grid,
some twenty times as high as the walls or more, yet all
surrounded by scaffolding. The legendary topless towers
were still being rebuilt after their burning in the Aiel
War.

When last he had seen the city, another city had
surrounded it from riverbank to riverbank—Foregate, a
rabbit warren as raucous as Cairhien was solemn, all in
wood. Now only a wide stretch of ash and charred
timbers bordered the walls. How that fire had been kept
from spreading into Cairhien itself, he could not understand.

Banners decked every tower in the city, too distant to
make out clearly, but scouts had described them to him.
Half bore the Crescents of Tear; the other half, perhaps
not surprisingly, duplicated the Dragon banner he had
left flying over the Stone of Tear. Not one bore the Rising
Sun of Cairhien.

Moving the looking glass only a little swept the city
from his sight. On the far side of the river still stood the
blackened stone shells of the granaries. Some of the
Cairhienin Rand had talked to claimed the torching of
the granaries had led to riots and then King Galldrian's
death, and thus to the civil war. Others said Galldrian's
assassination had caused the riots and the burning. Rand
doubted that he would ever know which was the truth, or
whether either was.

A number of burned-out hulks dotted both banks of
the wide river, but none lay close to the city. Aiel had an
uneasiness—fear might be too strong a word—about

bodies of water they could not step across or wade, but Couladin had managed to put barriers of floating logs across the Alguenya both above and below Cairhien, along with enough men to see they were not cut. Fire-arrows had done the rest. Nothing except rats and birds could get into or out of Cairhien without Couladin's leave.

The hills around the city showed little sign of a besieging army. Here and there vultures flapped heavily, no doubt feasting on the remains of some attempt to break out, but no Shaido were visible. Aiel seldom were unless they wanted to be.

Wait. Rand swung the looking glass back to a treeless hilltop perhaps a mile from the city walls. Back to a cluster of men. He could not discern faces, or much else aside from the fact that they all wore the *cadin'sor*. One thing more. One of those men had bare arms. Couladin. Rand was sure it must be imagination, but he thought that when Couladin moved he could see sunlight glittering off the metallic scales encircling the man's forearms in imitation of his own. Asmodean had put those there. Just an attempt to divert Rand's attention, to occupy him while Asmodean worked his own plans, but without that, how much would have turned out differently? Certainly, he would not be standing on this tower, watching a besieged city and awaiting a battle.

Suddenly, something streaked through the air on that distant hilltop, a long blur, and two of the men there went down thrashing. Staring at the fallen men, both apparently transfixed with the same spear, Couladin and the others seemed as stunned as Rand. Twisting the looking glass, Rand scanned for the man who had thrown with such force. He had to be brave—and a fool—to get close enough. Rand's search widened quickly, beyond any possible range of a human arm. He was beginning to think of Ogier—not likely; it took a great deal to rouse an Ogier into violence—when another streaking blur caught his eye.

Startled, he half-straightened before jerking the glass back to Cairhien's walls. That spear—or whatever it was—had come from there. He was certain of it. How was another matter entirely. At this distance it was all he could do to make out an occasional someone moving on the walls or atop a tower.

Raising his head, Rand found Rhuarc just stepping away from the other looking glass, giving up his place to Han. That was the whole reason for the tower and the glasses. Scouts brought back what word they could of how the Shaido were deployed, but this way the chiefs could see for themselves the terrain on which the battle would be fought. They had worked out a plan between them already, but one more look at the land could never go amiss. Rand did not know much about battles, but Lan thought their plan a good one. At least, Rand did not know much in his own mind; sometimes those other memories crept in, and then he seemed to know more than he wanted.

"Did you see that? Those . . . spears?"

Rhuarc looked as puzzled as Rand knew he himself must, but the Aiel nodded. "The last took another Shaido, but he crawled away. Not Couladin, worse luck." He gestured to the looking glass, and Rand let him take his place.

Was it such bad luck? Couladin's death would not end the threat to Cairhien, or to anywhere else. Now they were this side of the Dragonwall, the Shaido would not tamely return just because the man they thought was the true *Car'a'carn* died. It might well shake them, but not enough for that. And after all Rand had seen, he did not think Couladin deserved so easy a way out. *I can be as hard as I must,* he thought, stroking his sword hilt. *For him, I can.*

CHAPTER

42

Before the Arrow

The inside of a tent roof had to be the most boring sight in the world, but lying back in his shirtsleeves on scarlet-tasseled cushions that Melindhra had acquired, Mat studied the gray-brown cloth intently. Or rather, he stared beyond it. One arm curled behind his head, he swirled a hammered-silver goblet full of good wine from the south of Cairhien. A small cask had cost him as much as two good horses would—as much as two horses would have if the world and everything in it had not been stood on its head—but he counted it a small price for something decent. Sometimes a drop or two splashed over onto his hand, but he never noticed and he never took a drink.

By his book, matters had long since gone beyond merely serious. Serious was being stuck in the Waste with no idea of the way out. Serious was Darkfriends popping up when you least expected, Trolloc attacks in the night, the odd Myrddraal freezing your blood with an eyeless stare. That sort of thing came quickly, and usually was done before you had much chance to think. It was certainly not what you would seek out, yet if you had to, you could live with it if you could live through it. But for days he had known where they were heading, and why. Nothing quick about it. Days to think.

I am no bloody hero, he thought grimly, *and I'm no bloody soldier.* Fiercely he pushed down a memory of walking fortress walls, ordering his last reserves to where another crop of Trolloc scaling ladders had sprung up. *That was* not *me, the Light burn whoever it was! I'm . . .* He did not know what he was—a sour thought—but whatever he was, it involved gambling and taverns, women and dancing. That he was sure of. It involved a good horse and every road in the world to choose from, not sitting and waiting for somebody to shoot arrows at him or try to stick a sword or a spear through his ribs. Any different would make him a fool, and he would not be that, not for Rand or Moiraine or anybody else.

As he sat up, the silver foxhead medallion, hanging on its leather thong, slipped from the unlaced neck of his shirt. He tucked it back before taking a long swallow of wine. The medallion made him safe from Moiraine, or any other Aes Sedai, as long as they did not get it away from him—surely one or another would try sooner or later—but nothing except his own wits kept him safe from some fool killing him along with a few thousand other fools. Or from Rand, or from being *ta'veren.*

A man ought to be able to find a profit in something like that, having events twist themselves around him. Rand certainly had, in a way. He himself had never noticed anything twisting around him except the fall of dice. He would not turn away from some of the things that happened to *ta'veren* in stories. Wealth and fame dropped into their pockets as if from the sky; men who wanted to kill them decided to follow instead, and women with ice in their eyes decided to melt.

Not that he was complaining at what he had, really. And certainly not that he wanted anything like Rand's bargain; the price to get into the game was too high. It was just that he seemed to be stuck with all the burdens of being *ta'veren* and none of the pleasure.

"It is time to go," he told the empty tent, then paused thoughtfully and sipped at the goblet. "It is time to get on Pips and ride. Ride to Caemlyn, maybe." Not a bad city, so long as he avoided the Royal Palace. "Or Lugard." He had heard rumors about Lugard. A fine place, that, for the likes of him. "Time to leave Rand in my dust. He's got a bloody Aiel army and more Maidens than he can count taking care of him. He doesn't need me."

That last was not strictly true. In some strange way he was tied to Rand's success or failure in Tarmon Gai'don, him and Perrin both, three *ta'veren* all tangled together. The histories would probably only mention Rand. Small chance he or Perrin would find any place in the stories. And then there was the Horn of Valere. Which he did not want to think about, and would not. Not until he had to. There might be some way out of that particular mess yet. Any way he looked at it, the Horn was a problem for another day. A distant day. With luck, all those bills would come due on a very distant day. Only, that might take more luck than he had.

The point now was that he had said all of that about going and felt scarcely a twinge. Not long ago, he had been unable even to speak of leaving; when he got too far from Rand, he had been drawn back like a hooked fish on some invisible line. Then he had become able to say it, even to lay plans, but the slightest thing would distract him, make him put off his schemes for stealing away. Even in Rhuidean, when he had told Rand he was going, he had been sure something would get in the way. It had, in a manner of speaking; Mat had made it out of the Waste, but he was no further from Rand than before. This time, he did not think he would be diverted.

"Not like I was abandoning him," he muttered. "If he can't bloody take care of himself by now, he'll never be able to. I'm not his bloody nursemaid."

Draining the goblet, he scrambled into his green coat, settled his knives in their hiding places, arranged a dark yellow silk scarf to hide the hanging scar on his throat, then snatched up his hat and ducked out.

Heat hit him in the face after the relatively cool shade inside. He was not sure how the seasons changed here, but summer was hanging on too long to suit him. One thing he had looked forward to on leaving the Waste was the arrival of autumn. A little coolness. No luck here. At least the hat's wide brim kept the sun off.

This hilly Cairhienin forest was a pitiful thing, more clearings than trees and half of them going brown in the drought. Not a patch on the Westwood, back home. Low Aiel tents were everywhere, though at any distance they took on the look of a pile of dead leaves or a bare hummock of ground unless the side flaps were up, and even then they were not easy to see. The Aiel going about their business did not look at him twice.

From one crest as he crossed the encampment, he caught sight of Kadere's wagons, all in a circle, the drivers lying in the shade underneath and the peddler nowhere in view. Kadere kept to his wagon more and more, seldom poking his nose out except when Moiraine came to inspect the ladings. The Aiel ringing the wagons, small knots with spears and bucklers, bows and quivers, made little pretense of being anything but guards. Moiraine must think Kadere or some of his men would try to make off with what she had brought out of Rhuidean. Mat wondered whether Rand realized that he was giving her anything and everything she asked. For a while Mat had thought Rand had gotten the upper hand there, but he was not so sure any longer, even if Moiraine did do everything but curtsy and fetch Rand's pipe.

Rand's tent was on a hilltop by itself, naturally, that red banner on a staff at its front. It rippled in a light breeze, sometimes standing out enough to show the black-and-white disc. The thing made Mat's skin crawl as much as the Dragon banner had. If a man wanted to avoid Aes Sedai entanglements, as any but an idiot would, the last thing to do was wave that symbol about.

The slopes of the hill were bare, but Maidens' tents encircled the foot of the hill and spread through the trees up surrounding slopes and down the other side. That was as usual, too, and so was the Wise Ones' camp within the *Far Dareis Mai,* dozens of low tents in shouting distance of Rand's hill, with white-robed *gai'shain* bustling about.

There were only a few of the Wise Ones to be seen, yet they made up for lack of numbers with the stares that followed him. He had no idea how many could channel in that bunch, but they were a fair equal of Aes Sedai weighing and measuring when it came to stares. He picked up his pace, making an effort not to shrug uncomfortably; he could feel those eyes on his back as surely as he could have a poke from a stick. And he would have to run the same gauntlet coming out. Well, a few words with Rand, and it would be the last time he had to run it.

Only, when he pulled off his hat and ducked into Rand's tent, no one was there except Natael, lounging on the cushions with his gilded, dragon-carved harp propped against his knee and a gold goblet in his hand.

Mat grimaced, and swore under his breath. He should have known as much. If Rand had been here, he would have had to pass through a circle of Maidens right around the tent. Most likely he was up at that new-built tower. A good idea, that. Know the terrain. That was the second rule, close behind "Know your enemy," and not much to choose between them.

The thought put a sour twist to his mouth. Those rules came from other men's memories; the only rules he wanted to remember were "Never kiss a girl whose brothers have knife scars" and "Never gamble without knowing a back way out." He almost wished those memories of other men were still separate lumps in his brain instead of oozing into his thoughts when he least expected.

"Trouble with a bilious stomach?" Natael asked lazily. "One of the Wise Ones might have a root to cure it. Or you could try Moiraine."

Mat could not like the man; he always seemed to be thinking of a joke he did not mean to share. And he always looked as if he had three servants taking care of his clothes. All that snowy lace at collar and cuffs, always seeming freshly laundered. The fellow never appeared to sweat, either. Why Rand wanted him around was a mystery. He almost never played anything merry on that harp. "Will he be back soon?"

Natael shrugged. "When he decides to. Perhaps soon, perhaps late. No man clocks the Lord Dragon. And few women." There it was again, that secretive smile. A touch bleak, this time.

"I'll wait." He meant to go through with this. Too many times he had found himself putting off going.

Natael sipped at his wine, studying him across the goblet's rim.

It was bad enough that Moiraine and the Wise Ones watched him in that silent, searching way—sometimes Egwene did too; she had certainly changed, half Wise One and half Aes Sedai—but from Rand's gleeman, it was enough to set his teeth on edge. The best thing about leaving would be not having anyone look at him as if they would know in a minute what he was thinking, and already knew whether his smallclothes were clean.

Two maps lay spread out near the firepit. One, copied in detail from a tattered map found in a half-burned town, covered northern Cairhien from west of the Alguenya halfway to the Spine of the World, while the other, newly drawn and sketchy, showed the land around the city. Slips of parchment held down with pebbles dotted both. If he was going to stay, and ignore Natael's searching look at the same time, there was nothing for it but to study the maps.

With the toe of his boot he shifted a few pebbles on the map of the city so he could read what was written on the parchments. In spite of himself, he winced. If the Aiel scouts could count, Couladin had nearly one hundred and sixty thousand spears—Shaido and those who had supposedly gone to join their societies among the Shaido. A hard nut to crack, and prickly. This side of the Spine of the World had not seen an army like that since Artur Hawkwing's time.

The second map showed the other clans that had crossed the Dragonwall. All had now, in one force or another, strung out according to when they had left the Jangai and spread apart, but too close to here for comfort. The Shiande, the Codarra, the Daryne, and the Miagoma. Between them, they apparently had at least as many spears as Couladin; they had not left many behind, if that was true. The seven clans with Rand almost doubled that, easily enough to face Couladin or the four clans. Either or. Not both, not at once. But both at once might be what Rand had to fight.

What the Aiel called the bleakness had to be affecting those clans too—every day still men tossed down their weapons and vanished—but only a fool would think it lessened their numbers any more than it did Rand's. And there was always the possibility that some of those were going to Couladin. The Aiel did not speak of it very much or very freely, and masked the idea behind talk of joining societies, but even now, men and Maidens decided they could not accept Rand or what he had told them of themselves. Every morning some were missing, and not all left their spears behind.

"A pretty situation, wouldn't you say?"

Mat's head jerked up at Lan's voice, but the Warder had entered the tent alone. "Just something to look at while I waited. Is Rand coming back?"

"He will be with us soon." Thumbs tucked behind his sword belt, Lan stood beside Mat, looking down at the map. His face gave away as much as a statue's would. "Tomorrow should bring the largest battle since Artur Hawkwing."

"You don't say?" Where was Rand? Still up on that tower, probably. Maybe he should go there. No, he could end up haring all over the camp, always one step behind. Rand would come here eventually. He wanted to talk about something besides Couladin. *This fight is none of mine. I'm not running away from anything that concerns me in the least.* "What about them?" He gestured to the slips representing the Miagoma and the others. "Any word on whether they mean to join Rand, or do they just intend to sit there watching?"

"Who can say? Rhuarc doesn't seem to know any more than I do, and if the Wise Ones do, they are not telling. The only thing certain is that Couladin is not going anywhere."

Couladin again. Mat shifted uncomfortably and took a half-step toward the entrance. No, he *would* wait. Fastening his gaze on the maps, he pretended to study them further. Perhaps Lan would leave him in silence. He just wanted to say his piece to Rand and go.

The Warder appeared to want to talk, though. "What do you think, Master Gleeman? Should we rush down on Couladin with everything and crush him tomorrow?"

"That sounds as good to me as any other plan," Natael replied dourly. Emptying the goblet down his throat, he dropped it on the carpets and picked up the harp to begin softly strumming something dark and funereal. "I lead no armies, Warder. I command nothing save myself, and not always that."

Mat grunted, and Lan glanced at him before returning to his study of the maps. "You do not think it a good plan? Why not?"

He said it so casually that Mat answered without thinking. "Two reasons. If you surround Couladin, trap him between you and the city, you might crush him against it." How long was Rand going to be? "But you might push him right over the walls, too. From what I hear, he's nearly gotten over twice already, even without miners or siege engines, and the city is hanging on by its teeth." Say his piece and go, that was it. "Press him enough, and you'll find yourself fighting inside Cairhien. Nasty thing, fighting in a city. And the idea is to save the place, not finish ruining it." Those slips laid out on the maps, the maps themselves, made it all so clear.

Frowning, he squatted with his elbows on his knees. Lan got down with him, but he hardly noticed. A dicey problem. And fascinating. "Best if you try to shove him away. Hit him from the south, mainly." He pointed to the River Gaelin; it joined the Alguenya some miles north of the city. "There are bridges up here. Leave the Shaido a clear path to them. Always leave a way out, unless you really want to find out how hard a man can fight when he's nothing to lose." His finger slid east. Wooded hills for the most part, it seemed. Probably not much different from right around here. "A blocking force here on this side of the river will make sure they go for the bridges, if it's big enough and positioned right. Once they are moving, Couladin won't want to try fighting someone ahead of him while you're coming behind." Yes. Almost exactly the same as at Jenje. "Not unless he's a complete fool, anyway. They might make it to the river in good order, but those bridges will choke them. I don't see Aiel swimming, or hunting out fords for that matter. Keep the pressure on, shove them across. With luck you'll be able to harry them all the way to the mountains." It was like Cuaindaigh Fords, too, late in the Trolloc Wars, and on much the same scale. Not much different from the Tora Shan, either. Or Sulmein Gap, before Hawkwing found his stride. The names flickered through his head, the images of bloody fields forgotten even by historians. Absorbed in the map as he was, they did not register as anything but his own remembrances. "Too bad you don't have more cavalry. Light cavalry is best for the harrying. Bite at the flanks, keep them running, and never let them settle to fight. But Aiel should do almost as well."

"And the other reason?" Lan asked quietly.

Mat was caught up in it, now. He more than merely liked gambling, and battle was a gamble to make dicing in taverns a thing for children and toothless invalids. Lives were the stake here, your own and other men's, men who were not even there. Make the wrong wager, a foolish bet, and cities died, or whole nations. Natael's somber music was fit accompaniment. At the same time, this was a game that set the blood racing.

Without lifting his eyes from the map, he snorted. "You know as well as I. If even one of those four clans decides to side with Couladin, they'll take you from behind while your hands are still full of Shaido. Couladin will be the anvil and they the hammer, with you the nut between. Only take half of what you have against Couladin. That makes it an even fight, but you have to settle for it." There was no such thing as fairness in war. You took your enemy from behind, when he least expected it, when and where he was weakest. "You still have an edge. He has to worry about a sortie from the city. The other half, you split in three parts. One to funnel Couladin to the river, the other two a few miles apart, between the city and the four clans."

"Very neat," Lan said, nodding. That slab-carved face never changed, but approval touched his voice, if lightly. "It would gain a clan nothing to attack either force, especially not when the other could take it in the rear. And none will try to interfere in what happens around the city for the same reason. Of course, all four could join. Not likely, if they haven't already, but if they do, everything changes."

Mat laughed aloud. "Everything always changes. The best plan lasts until the first arrow leaves the bow. This would be easy enough for a child to handle, except for Indirian and the rest not knowing their own minds. If they all decide to go over to Couladin, you toss the dice and hope, because the Dark One's in the game for sure. At least you'll have enough strength clear of the city nearly to match them. Enough to hold them for the time you need. Abandon the idea of pursuing Couladin and turn everything on them as soon as he's well and truly begun crossing the Gaelin. But it's my bet they'll wait and watch, and come to you once Couladin is done for. Victory settles a lot of arguments in most men's heads."

The music had stopped. Mat glanced at Natael, and found the man holding his harp rigidly, staring at him over it harder than ever. Staring as if he had never seen him before, did not know what he was. The gleeman's eyes were dark polished glass, his knuckles white on the harp's gilding.

With that it all crashed home, what he had been saying, the memories he had been embracing. *Burn you for a fool, for not guarding your tongue!* Why had Lan had to take the conversation that way? Why could he not have talked about horses, or the weather, or just kept his mouth shut? The Warder had never seemed all that eager to talk before. Usually the man made a tree seem talkative. Of course, he could have kept his own mind focused and his own mouth shut, too. At least he had not been babbling in the Old Tongue. *Blood and ashes, but I hope I wasn't!*

Springing to his feet, Mat turned to go, and found Rand standing just inside the tent, absently twisting that odd bit of tasseled spear as if he did not realize he was holding it. How long had he been there? It did not matter. Mat spilled it all out in a rush. "I'm leaving, Rand. Come first light in the morning, I am in the saddle and gone. I'd go this minute if I could get far enough in half a day to suit me for stopping. I mean to put as many miles between me and the Aiel—*any* Aiel—as Pips can cover before I make camp." No point in bedding down close enough to be snapped up and hung out to dry by somebody's scouts; Couladin must have them out too, and even the others might not recognize him before he had a spear in his liver.

"I will be sorry to see you go," Rand said quietly.

"Don't try to talk me out of—" Mat blinked. "That's it? You'll be sorry to see me go?"

"I've never tried to make you stay, Mat. Perrin went when he had to, and so can you."

Mat opened his mouth, then closed it again. Rand had never tried to make him stay, true. He had just done it without trying. But there was not the slightest bit of *ta'veren* tugging, now, no vague feelings that he was doing the wrong thing. He was firm and clear in his purpose.

"Where will you go?"

"South." Not that there was much choice of direction. The others led to the Gaelin, with nothing north of the river that he was interested in, or else to Aiel, one lot that would certainly kill him and one that might or might not, depending on how close by Rand was and what they had had for supper the night before. Not good odds, by his reckoning. "To begin, anyway. Then somewhere there's a tavern, and some women who don't carry spears." Melindhra. She might present a problem. He had the feeling she might be the sort of woman who did not let go until *she* wanted. Well, one way or another, he would deal with her. Maybe he could just ride out before she knew it. "This isn't for me, Rand. I don't know anything about battles, and I don't want to know." He avoided looking at Lan and Natael. If either man cracked his teeth, he would punch him right in the mouth. Even the Warder. "You understand, don't you?"

Rand's nod could have been understanding. Maybe it was. "I'd forget saying goodbye to Egwene, were I you. I am no longer certain how much of what I tell her I might as well be telling Moiraine, or the Wise Ones, or both."

"I reached that conclusion a long time ago. She's left Emond's Field further behind than either of us. And regrets it less."

"Maybe," Rand said sadly. "The Light shine on you, Mat," he added, sticking out his hand, "and send you smooth roads, fair weather and pleasant company until we meet again."

That would not be soon, if Mat had his way. He felt a little sad about that, and a little foolish for feeling sad, yet a man had to look after himself. When all was said and done, that was the long and short of it.

Rand's grip was as hard as it had ever been—all that swordwork had only added new calluses atop older bowman's—but the ridged heron brand in his palm was distinct against Mat's hand. Just a little reminder, in case he should forget the markings under his friend's coatsleeves, or those even stranger things inside his head that let him channel. If he could forget that Rand could channel—and he had not thought of it once in days; days!—then it was *far* past time to be gone.

A few more awkward words standing there—Lan seemed to ignore them, arms folded, silently studying the maps, while Natael had begun idly plucking his harp; Mat had an ear for music, and to him the unfamiliar tune had an ironic sound; he wondered why the fellow had chosen it—a few more moments and Rand half-stepping around actually putting an end to it, and then Mat was outside. There was a crowd out there, a good hundred Maidens spread about the hilltop and walking on tiptoe they were so ready to spear somebody, all seven clan chiefs waiting patient and still as stone, three Tairen lords trying to pretend that they were not sweating and the Aiel did not exist.

He had heard about the lords' arrival, and had even gone to take a look at their camp—or camps—but there had been no one there he knew, and no one wanting to take a turn at dice or cards. These three eyed him up and down, frowning disdainfully, and apparently decided he was no better than the Aiel, which was to say not worth seeing.

Clapping his hat on his head and pulling the brim low over his eyes, Mat studied the Tairens coldly in return for a moment. He had the pleasure of seeing the younger pair, at least, become uncomfortably aware of him again before he started down the hill. The gray-beard still looked all barely concealed impatience to enter Rand's tent, but it did not matter anyway. He would never see any of them again.

He had no idea why he had not simply ignored them. Except that his step was lighter and he felt full of vinegar. No wonder, really, leaving tomorrow at last. The dice seemed to be spinning in his head, and there was no knowing what pips would show when they landed. Odd, that. It must be Melindhra worrying him. Yes. He would definitely leave early, and as quietly as a mouse tiptoeing on feathers.

Whistling, he set off for his tent. What was the tune? Oh, yes. "Dance with Jak o' the Shadows." He had no intention of dancing with death, but it had a merry sound, so he whistled it anyway as he tried to plan the best route away from Cairhien.

Rand stood staring after Mat long after the tent flaps had fallen to hide him. "I only heard the last bit," he said finally. "Was it all like that?"

"Very nearly," Lan replied. "With only a few minutes to study the maps, he laid out close to the battle plan that Rhuarc and the others made. He saw the difficulties and the dangers, and how to meet them. He knows about miners and siege engines, and using light cavalry to harry a defeated foe."

Rand looked at him. The Warder showed no surprise, not the twitch of an eyelash. Of course, he was the one who had said Mat seemed surprisingly knowledgeable about military matters. And Lan was not going to ask the obvious question, either, which was good. Rand had no right to give the little answer he had.

He could have asked a few questions himself. Such as, What did miners have to do with battles? Or maybe it was only sieges. Whatever the answer, there was not a mine closer than the Kinslayer's Dagger, and no certainty anyone was still digging ore. Well, this battle would be fought without. The important thing was that he knew Mat had gained more on the other side of that doorway *ter'angreal* than a tendency to spout the Old Tongue when not thinking. And knowing that, Rand would surely make use of it.

You don't have to get any harder, he thought bitterly. He had seen Mat climbing toward this tent, and never hesitated in sending Lan in to discover what might come to the surface in idle conversation, alone. That had been deliberate. The rest might or might not be, but it would happen. He hoped Mat had a fine time while he was free. He hoped that Perrin was enjoying himself in the Two Rivers, showing off Faile to his mother and sisters, maybe marrying her. He hoped it because he knew he would draw them back, *ta'veren* pulling at *ta'veren,* and he the strongest. Moiraine had named it no coincidence, three such growing up in the same village, all nearly the same age; the Wheel wove happenstance and coincidence into the Pattern, but it did not lay down the likes of the three of them for no reason. Eventually he would pull his friends back to him, however far they went, and when they came, he would use them, however he could. However he had to. Because he did have to. Because whatever the Prophecy of the Dragon said, he was sure the only chance he had of winning Tarmon Gai'don lay in having all three of them, three *ta'veren* who had been tied together since infancy, tied together once more. No, he did not need to become hard. *You're rank enough already to make a Seanchan spew his supper!*

"Play 'March of Death,' " he commanded in a harsher voice than he wanted, and Natael looked at him blankly for a moment. The man had been listening to everything. He would have questions, but he would find no answers. If Rand could not tell Lan Mat's secrets, he would not spread them before one of the Forsaken, however tame he appeared. This time he deliberately made his tone rough, and pointed the length of spear at the man. "Play it, unless you know a sadder. Play something to make *your* soul weep. If you have one still."

Natael gave him an ingratiating smile and a seated bow, but he went white around the eyes. It was indeed "The March of Death" that he began, yet it had a sharper edge on his harp than ever before, a dirgelike keen that surely would make any soul weep. He stared fixedly at Rand as if hoping to see some effect.

Turning away, Rand stretched out on the carpets with his head to the maps and a red-and-gold cushion under his elbow. "Lan, would you ask the others to come in now?"

The Warder made a formal bow before stepping outside. It was the first time that he had ever done that, but Rand noticed only absently.

The battle would begin tomorrow. It was a polite fiction that he helped Rhuarc and the others plan. He was smart enough to know what he did not know, and despite all of his talks with Lan and Rhuarc, he knew he was not ready. *I've planned a hundred battles this size or more and given orders that led to ten times as many.* Not his thought. Lews Therin knew war—had known war—but not Rand al'Thor, and that was him. He listened, asked questions—and nodded as if he understood when the chiefs said a thing should be done a certain way. Sometimes he did understand and wished he did not, because he knew where that understanding came from. His only real contribution had been to say that Couladin had to be defeated without destroying the city. In any case, this meeting would only add a few touches at most to what had already been decided. Mat would have been useful, with his new-found knowledge.

No. He would not think of his friends, of what he would do to them before it was all done. Even leaving the battle aside, there was plenty to occupy him, things he could do something about. The absence of Cairhienin flags above Cairhien marked a major problem, and the continued skirmishes with Andorans another. What Sammael was up to warranted thought, and . . .

The chiefs filed in in no particular order. This time Dhearic came first, Rhuarc and Erim together at the rear with Lan. Bruan and Jheran took the places next to Rand. They did not concern themselves with precedence among themselves, and *Aan'allein* they seemed to take as all but one of them.

Weiramon entered last, his lordlings at his heels and a tight-mouthed scowl on his face. Precedence certainly mattered to him. Muttering into his oiled beard, he stalked his way around the firepit, taking up a place behind Rand. Until the chiefs' flat stares finally broke through his shell, at least. Among Aiel, a close kinsman or society brother might position himself so, if there was the possibility of a knife in the back. He still frowned at Jheran and Dhearic as though expecting one of them to make room.

Finally Bael gestured to the place beside him, across the maps from Rand, and after a pause, Weiramon strode back to sit cross-legged and rigid, staring straight ahead and looking like a man who had swallowed an unripe plum whole. The younger Tairens stood almost as stiffly at his back, one with the grace to look embarrassed.

Rand took note of him but said not a word, only thumbed his pipe full of tabac and seized *saidin* long enough to light it. He had to do something about Weiramon; the man exacerbated old problems and made new ones. Not a flicker crossed Rhuarc's features, but the other chiefs' expressions ranged from Han's sour disgust to Erim's clear, cold-eyed readiness to dance spears there and then. Perhaps there was a way for Rand to rid himself of Weiramon and make a beginning on another of his worries at the same time.

With Rand's example, Lan and the chiefs began filling pipes.

"I see only small changes necessary," Bael said, puffing his pipe alight, and sparking a glower from Han, as usual.

"Do these small changes concern the Goshien, or perhaps some other clan?"

Putting Weiramon from his mind, Rand bent himself to listening as they worked out what had to be altered from their new view of the terrain. Now and again one of the Aiel would glance at Natael, a brief tightness to eyes or mouth suggesting that the mournful music plucked at something in him. Even the Tairens grimaced sadly. The sounds washed over Rand, though, touching nothing. Tears were a luxury he could no longer afford, not even inside.

CHAPTER
43

This Place, This Day

The next morning Rand was up and dressed well before first light. In truth, he had not slept, and it had not been Aviendha who kept him awake, not even after she began undressing before he could put out the lamps and channeled one alight again as soon as he did, chiding him that she was unable to see in the dark even if he could. He made no reply, and hours later, had hardly noticed when she rose, a good hour before he did, dressed and left. He did not even think to wonder where she was going.

The thoughts that had had him staring up into the blackness still ran through his head. Men would die today. A great many men, even if everything went perfectly. Nothing he did now would change it; today would run out according to the Pattern. But over and over he mulled the decisions he had made since he first entered the Waste. Could he have done something different, something that would have avoided this day, this place? Next time, perhaps. The tasseled length of spear lay atop his sword belt and scabbarded blade beside his blankets. There would be a next time, and one beyond that, and beyond again.

While darkness still held, the chiefs came in a bunch for a few final words, to report that their men were in position and ready. Not that anything else was expected. Stone-faced as they were, some emotion showed. An odd mix, though, a skim of ebullience over somberness.

Erim actually wore a slight smile. "A good day, to see the end of the Shaido," he said finally. He seemed to be walking on his toes.

"The Light willing," Bael said, his head brushing the roof of the tent, "we will wash the spears in Couladin's blood before sunfall."

"Bad luck to talk of what will be," Han muttered. The skim was very thin on him, of course. "Fate will decide."

Rand nodded. "The Light send it does not decide on too many of our number dead." He wished his concern were only that few men should die because men should not have their lives cut short, but there were many more days to come. He would need every spear to bring order to this side of the Dragonwall. That was a bone between him and Couladin every bit as much as the rest.

"Life is a dream," Rhuarc told him, and Han and the others nodded agreement. Life was only a dream, and all dreams had to end. Aiel did not run toward death, yet they did not run from it either.

As they were departing, Bael paused. "Are you certain of what you want the Maidens to do? Sulin has been speaking to the Wise Ones."

So that was what Melaine had been at Bael about. The way Rhuarc stopped to listen, he had been hearing from Amys on the subject, too.

"Everyone else is doing what they are supposed to without complaining, Bael." That was unfair, but this was no game. "If the Maidens want special consideration, Sulin can come to me, not go running to the Wise Ones."

Had they been anything but Aiel, Rhuarc and Bael would have been shaking their heads as they left. Rand supposed each would get an earful from his wife, but they would have to live with it. If *Far Dareis Mai* carried his honor, this time they would carry it where he wanted.

To Rand's surprise Lan appeared just as he was ready to go out himself. The Warder's cloak hung down his back, disturbing the vision as it rippled with his movements.

"Is Moiraine with you?" Rand had expected Lan to be glued to her side.

"She is fretting in her tent. She cannot possibly Heal even all of the worst hurt today." That was her choice of how to help; she could not use the Power as a weapon today, but she could Heal. "Waste always angers her."

"It angers us all," Rand snapped. His taking Egwene away probably upset her, too. As far as he could tell, Egwene was not very good at Healing on her own, but she could have aided Moiraine. Well, he needed her to keep her promise. "Tell Moiraine if she needs help, ask some of the Wise Ones who can channel." But few Wise Ones had any knowledge of Healing. "She can link with them and use their strength." He hesitated. Had Moiraine ever spoken of linking to him? "You didn't come here to tell me Moiraine is brooding," he said irritably. It was difficult sometimes, keeping straight what came from her, what from Asmodean, and what bubbled up from Lews Therin.

"I came to ask why you've taken to wearing a sword again."

"Moiraine asked already. Did she send—?"

Lan's face did not change, but he cut in roughly. "I want to know. You can make a sword from the Power, or kill without, but suddenly you are wearing steel on your hip again. Why?"

Unconsciously, Rand ran one hand up the long hilt at his side. "It's hardly fair to use the Power that way. Especially against someone who can't channel. I might as well fight a child."

The Warder stood silent for a time, studying him. "You mean to kill Couladin yourself," he said at last in flat tones. "That sword against his spears."

"I don't mean to seek him out, but who can say what will happen?" Rand shrugged uncomfortably. Not to hunt for him. But if ever his twisting of chance was to favor him, let it be to bring him face-to-face with

Couladin. "Besides, I'd not put it past him to seek me. The threats I've heard from him have been personal, Lan." Raising one fist, he thrust his arm out of a crimson coatsleeve enough to make the golden-maned Dragon's fore end plainly visible. "Couladin won't rest while I live, not so long as we both wear these."

And truth to tell, he would not rest himself until only one living man bore the Dragons. By rights he should lump Asmodean in with Couladin. Asmodean had marked the Shaido. But Couladin's unrestrained ambition had made it possible; his ambition and refusal to abide by Aiel law and custom had led inevitably to this place, this day. Beyond the bleakness and war between Aiel, there was Taien to be laid at Couladin's feet, and Selean, and dozens of ruined towns and villages since, countless hundreds of burned farms. Unburied men and women and children had fed the vultures. If he was the Dragon Reborn, if he had any right to demand that any nation follow him, much less Cairhien, then he owed them justice.

"Then have him beheaded when he's taken," Lan said harshly. "Set a hundred men, or a thousand, with no purpose but to find and take him. But do not be fool enough to fight him! You are good with a blade now— very good—but Aielmen are all but born with spear and buckler in hand. A spear through your heart, and all has been for naught."

"So I should avoid the fighting? Would you, if Moiraine had no claims on you? Will Rhuarc, or Bael, or any of them?"

"I am not the Dragon Reborn. The fate of the world does not rest on me." But the momentary heat had gone from his voice. Without Moiraine, he would have been wherever the fighting was hottest. If anything, he looked to be regretting those claims at the moment.

"I'll not take needless risks, Lan, but I can't run from them all." The Seanchan spear would remain in the tent today; it would only get in his way if he did find Couladin. "Come. The Aiel will finish it without us if we stand here much longer."

When he ducked outside, only a few stars remained, and a thin brightness outlined the eastern horizon sharply. That was not why he stopped, though, and Lan with him. Maidens made a ring around the tent, shoulder to shoulder, facing inward. A thick ring that spread down the dark shrouded slopes, *cadin'sor*-clad women jammed so a mouse could not have slipped through. Jeade'en was nowhere in sight, though a *gai'shain* had been ordered to have him saddled and waiting.

Not Maidens alone. Two women in the front rank wore bulky skirts and pale blouses, their hair bound back with folded scarves. It was too black yet to discern faces with any certainty, but there was something in the shape of those two, in their folded-arm stance, that named Egwene and Aviendha.

Sulin stepped forward before he could open his mouth to ask what they were up to. "We have come to escort the *Car'a'carn* to the tower with Egwene Sedai and Aviendha."

"Who put you up to this?" Rand demanded. One glance at Lan showed it had not been him. Even in the darkness the Warder looked startled. For a moment anyway, his head jerking up; nothing surprised Lan for long. "Egwene is supposed to be on her way to the tower now, and the Maidens are supposed to be there to guard her. What she will do today is very important. She must be protected while she does it."

"We will protect her." Sulin's voice was as flat as a planed board. "And the *Car'a'carn*, who gave his honor to *Far Dareis Mai* to carry." A murmur of approval rippled through the Maidens.

"It only makes sense, Rand," Egwene said from where she stood. "If one using the Power as a weapon will make the battle shorter, three will shorten it even more. And you are stronger than Aviendha and me together." She did not sound as if she liked saying that last. Aviendha said nothing, but the way she stood was eloquent.

"This is ridiculous," Rand scowled. "Let me through, and go to your assigned place."

Sulin did not budge. *"Far Dareis Mai* carries the honor of the *Car'a'carn*," she said calmly, and others took it up. No louder, but from so many women's voices it made a high rumble. *"Far Dareis Mai* carries the honor of the

Car'a'carn. Far Dareis Mai carries the honor of the *Car'a'carn.*"

"I said let me through," he demanded the instant the sound died.

As if he had told them to begin again, they did. "*Far Dareis Mai* carries the honor of the *Car'a'carn. Far Dareis Mai* carries the honor of the *Car'a'carn.*" Sulin just stood there looking at him.

After a moment Lan leaned close to murmur dryly, "A woman is no less a woman because she carries a spear. Did you ever meet one who could be diverted from anything she really wanted? Give over, or we will stand here all day while you argue and they chant at you." The Warder hesitated, then added, "Besides which, it does make sense."

Egwene opened her mouth as the litany fell off once more, but Aviendha put a hand on her arm and whispered a few words, and Egwene said nothing. He knew what she had intended to say, though. She had been about to tell him he was a stubborn foolish woolhead or some such.

The trouble was that he was beginning to feel like one. It *did* make sense for him to go to the tower. He had nothing to do elsewhere—the battle was in the hands of the chiefs and fate, now—and he would be of more use channeling than riding around hoping to meet with Couladin. If being *ta'veren* could pull Couladin to him, it could draw him to the tower as easily as anywhere else. Not that he would have much chance of seeing the man, not after ordering every last Maiden to defend the tower.

But how to back down and retain a scrap of dignity after blustering left, right and center? "I've decided I can do the most good from the tower," he said, his face going hot.

"As the *Car'a'carn* commands," Sulin replied without a hint of mockery, just as if it had been his idea from the first. Lan nodded, then slipped away, the Maidens making narrow room for him.

The gap closed up right behind Lan, though, and when they began to move, Rand had no choice except to go

with them. He could have channeled, of course, flung
Fire about or knocked them down with Air, but that was
hardly the way to behave with people on his side, let
alone women. Besides, he was not sure he could have
made them leave him short of killing, and maybe not
then. And anyway, he had decided he was of most use at
the tower, after all.

Egwene and Aviendha were as silent as Sulin as they
walked, for which he was grateful. Of course, at least part
of their silence had to do with picking their way uphill
and down in the dark without breaking their necks.
Aviendha did raise a mutter now and then that he barely
caught, something angry about skirts. But neither made
fun of him for backing down so visibly. Though that
might well come later. Women seemed to enjoy jabbing
the needle in just when you thought the danger was past.

The sky began to lighten into gray, and as the log tower
came into sight above the trees, he broke the quiet
himself. "I didn't expect you to be part of this, Aviendha.
I thought you said Wise Ones take no part in battles." He
was sure she had. A Wise One could walk through the
middle of a battle untouched, or into any hold or stand
of a clan that had blood feud with hers, but she took no
part in fighting, certainly not with channeling. Until he
came to the Waste, even most Aiel had not really known
that some Wise Ones could channel, though there were
rumors of strange abilities, and sometimes something
the Aiel thought might be close to channeling.

"I am not a Wise One yet," she replied pleasantly,
shifting her shawl. "If an Aes Sedai like Egwene can do
this, so can I. I arranged it this morning, while you still
slept, but I have thought of it since you first asked
Egwene."

There was enough light now for him to see Egwene
flush. When she saw him glancing at her, she tripped over
nothing, and he had to catch her arm to keep her from
falling. Avoiding his eyes, she jerked free. Maybe he
would not have to worry about any needles from her.
They started uphill through the sparse woods toward the
tower.

"They didn't try to stop you? Amys, I mean, or Bair, or Melaine?" He knew they had not. If they had, she would not be there.

Aviendha shook her head, then frowned thoughtfully. "They talked for a long time with Sorilea, then told me to do as I thought I must. Usually they tell me to do as *they* think I must." Glancing at him sideways, she added, "I heard Melaine say that you bring change to everything."

"I do that," he said, setting his foot on the bottom rung of the first ladder. "The Light help me, that I do."

The view from the platform was magnificent even to the naked eye, the land spreading out in wooded hills. The trees were thick enough to hide the Aiel moving toward Cairhien—most would already be in position—but dawn cast the city itself in golden light. A quick scan through one of the looking glasses showed the barren hills along the river placid and seemingly empty of life. That would change soon enough. The Shaido were there, if concealed for now. They would not remain concealed when he began to direct. . . . What? Not balefire. Whatever he did, it had to unnerve the Shaido as much as possible before his Aiel attacked.

Egwene and Aviendha had been taking turns looking through the other long tube, with pauses for quiet discussion, but now they were simply talking softly. Exchanging nods finally, they moved closer to the railing and stood with their hands on the rough-hewn timber, staring toward Cairhien. Goose bumps suddenly dotted his skin. One of them was channeling, maybe both.

It was the wind that he noticed first, blowing toward the city. Not a breeze; the first real wind he had felt in this country. And clouds were beginning to form above Cairhien, heaviest to the south, growing thicker and blacker as he watched, roiling. Only there, over Cairhien and the Shaido. Everywhere else as far as he could see, the sky was a clear blue, with only a few high thin white wisps. Yet thunder rolled, long and solid. Suddenly lightning stabbed down, a jagged silver streak that rent a hilltop below the city. Before the crack of the first bolt reached the tower, two more crackled earthward. Wild forks danced across the sky, but those single lances of brilliant white struck with the regularity of a heartbeat. Abruptly, ground exploded where no lightning had fallen, fountaining fifty feet, then again somewhere else, and again.

Rand had no idea which woman was doing what, but they certainly looked set to harrow the Shaido out. Time to do his bit, or stand watching. Reaching out, he seized *saidin*. Icy fire scoured the outside of the Void that surrounded what was Rand al'Thor. Coldly, he ignored the oily filth seeping into him from the taint, juggled wild torrents of the Power that threatened to engulf him.

At this distance, there were limits to what he could do. In fact, it was about as far as he could do anything, really, without *angreal* or *sa'angreal*. Very likely that was why the women were channeling one lightning bolt at a time, one explosion; if he was at his boundary, they must be stretching theirs.

A memory slid across the emptiness. Not his; Lews Therin's. For once he did not care. In an instant he channeled, and a ball of fire enveloped the top of a hill nearly five miles away, a churning mass of pale yellow flame. When it faded, he could see without the looking glass that the hill was lower now, and black at the crest, seemingly melted. Between the three of them, there might be no need for the clans to fight Couladin at all.

Ilyena, my love, forgive me!

The Void trembled; for an instant Rand teetered on the brink of destruction. Waves of the One Power crashed through him in a froth of fear; the taint seemed to solidify around his heart, a reeking stone.

Clutching the rail until his knuckles ached, he forced himself back to calmness, forced the emptiness to hold. Thereafter he refused to listen to the thoughts in his head. Instead he concentrated everything on channeling, on methodically searing one hill after another.

Standing well back into what treeline there was on the crest, Mat held Pips' nose under his arm so the gelding would not whicker as he watched a thousand or so Aiel slanting toward him across the hills from the south. The sun was just peeking over the horizon, stretching long rippling shadows to one side of the trotting mass. The night's warmth was already beginning to give way to the heat of day. The air would swelter once the sun reached any height. He was already beginning to sweat.

The Aiel had not seen him yet, but he had few doubts that they would if he waited there much longer. It hardly mattered that they very nearly had to be Rand's men—if Couladin had men to the south, the day was going to get very interesting for those stupid enough to be in the middle of the fighting—hardly mattered because he was not going to run the risk of letting them see him. He had already come too close to an arrow this morning for that kind of carelessness. Absently he fingered the neat slice across the shoulder of his coat. Good shooting, at a moving target only half-seen through trees. He could have admired it more had he not been the target.

Without taking his eyes from the approaching Aiel, he carefully backed Pips deeper into the sparse thicket; if they saw him and picked up their pace, he wanted to know. People said Aiel could run down a man on horseback, and he meant to have a good lead if they tried.

Not until the trees hid them from him did he quicken his own step, leading Pips onto the reverse slope before mounting and turning west. A man could not be too careful if he wanted to stay alive on this day and this ground. He muttered to himself as he rode, hat pulled low to shade his face and black-hafted spear across his pommel. West. Again.

The day had begun so well, a good two hours before first light, when Melindhra had gone off to some meeting of the Maidens. Thinking him asleep, she had not glanced at him as she stalked out muttering half under her breath about Rand al'Thor and honor and "*Far Dareis Mai* above all." She sounded as if she were arguing with herself, but frankly, he did not care whether she wanted to pickle Rand or stew him. Before she was a minute out of the tent, he was stuffing his saddlebags. No one had so much as looked at him twice while he saddled Pips and ghosted away to the south. A good beginning.

Only he had not counted on columns of Taardad and Tomanelle and every other bloody clan sweeping around to the south. No consolation that it was very close to what he had babbled to Lan. He wanted to go south, and those Aiel had forced him toward the Alguenya. Toward where the fighting would be.

A mile or two on, he cautiously turned Pips upslope, pausing deep in the scattered trees on the crest. It was a higher hill than most, and he had a good view. This time there were no Aiel in sight, but the column winding along the bottom of the twisting hill valley was almost as bad. Mounted Tairens had the lead behind a knot of colorful lords' banners, with a gap back to a thick, bristling snake of pikemen in the Tairens' dust, and then another to the Cairhienin horse, with their multitude of banners and pennants and *con*. The Cairhienin maintained no order at all, milling about as lords shifted back and forth for conversation, but at least they had flankers out to either side. In any case, as soon as they were past, he had a clear route south. *And I'll not stop until I'm halfway to the bloody Erinin!*

A flicker of movement caught his eye, well ahead of the column below. He would not have seen it except for being so high. None of the riders could have, certainly. Digging his small looking glass from his saddlebags— Kin Tovere liked the dice—he peered toward what he had seen, and whistled softly through his teeth. Aiel, at least as many as the men in the valley, and if they were not Couladin's, they meant to give a nameday surprise, for they were lying low among the dying bushes and dead leaves.

For a moment he drummed fingers on his thigh. Shortly there were going to be some corpses down there. And not many of them Aiel. *None of my affair. I am out of this, out of here, and heading south.* He would wait a bit, then head off while they were all too busy to notice.

This fellow Weiramon—he had heard the gray-beard's name yesterday—was a stone fool. *No foreguard out, and no scouts, or he'd know what was bloody in store for him.* For that matter, the way the hills lay, the way the valley twisted, the Aiel could not see the column, either, only its thin dust rising skyward. They certainly had had scouts to get themselves in place; they could not just be waiting there on the off chance.

Idly whistling "Dance with Jak o' the Shadows," he put the looking glass back to his eye and studied the hilltops. Yes. The Aiel commander had left a few men where they could signal a warning just before the column entered the killing ground. But even they could not possibly see anything yet. In a few minutes the first Tairens would come in sight, but until then . . .

It came as a shock when he heeled Pips to a gallop downslope. *What under the Light am I doing?* Well, he could not just stand by and let them all go their deaths like geese to the knife. He would warn them. That was all. Tell what lay in wait ahead, then he was gone.

The Cairhienin outriders saw him coming before he reached the bottom of the slope, of course, heard Pips' dead-flat charge. Two or three lowered their lances. Mat did not precisely enjoy having a foot and a half of steel pointed at him, and still less three times over, but obviously one man was no threat, even riding like a madman. They let him pass, and he swung in near the lead Cairhienin lords long enough to shout, "Halt here! Now! By order of the Lord Dragon! Else he'll channel your head into your belly and feed you your own feet for breakfast!"

His heels dug in, and Pips sprang ahead. He only glanced back to be sure they were doing what he said— they were, if showing some confusion over it; the hills hid them from the Aiel still, and once their dust settled, the Aiel would have no way of knowing they were there—and then he was lying low on the gelding's neck, whipping Pips with his hat and galloping up alongside the infantry.

If I wait to let Weiramon pass the orders, it'll be too late. That's all. He would give his warning and go.

The foot marched in blocks of two hundred or so pikemen, with one mounted officer in the front of each and maybe fifty archers or crossbowmen at the rear. Most looked at him curiously as he dashed by, Pips' heels kicking up spurts of dust, but none broke stride.

Some of the officers' mounts frisked as if the riders wanted to come see what had him in such a hurry, but none of them left their places either. Good discipline. They would need it.

Defenders of the Stone brought up the tail end of the Tairens, in their breastplates and puffy black-and-gold striped coatsleeves, plumes of various colors on the rimmed helmets marking officers and underofficers. The rest were armored the same, but bore the colors of various lords on their sleeves. The silk-coated lords themselves rode at the very front in ornate breastplates and large white plumes, their banners rippling behind them in a rising breeze toward the city.

Reining around in front of them so quickly that Pips danced, Mat shouted, "Halt, in the name of the Lord Dragon!"

It seemed the fastest way to stop them, but for a moment he thought they meant to ride right over him. Almost at the last moment, a young lord he remembered from outside Rand's tent flung up a hand, and then they were all drawing rein in a flurry of shouted orders that ran back along the column. Weiramon was not there; not a lord was as much as ten years older than Mat.

"What is the meaning of this?" demanded the fellow who had signaled. Dark eyes glared arrogantly down a sharp nose, chin lifted so his pointed beard looked ready to stab. Sweat trickling down his face spoiled it only a little. "The Lord Dragon himself gave me this command. Who are you to—?"

He cut off as another man Mat knew caught his sleeve, whispering urgently. Potato-faced Estean looked haggard beneath his helmet as well as hot—the Aiel had wrung him out concerning conditions in the city, so Mat had heard—but he had gambled at cards with Mat in Tear. He knew exactly who Mat was. Estean's breastplate alone had chips in the ornate gilding; none of the others had done more than ride around looking pretty. Yet.

Sharp-nose's chin came down as he listened, and when Estean left off, he spoke in a more moderate tone. "No offense intended . . . ah . . . Lord Mat. I am Melanril, of House Asegora. How may I serve the Lord Dragon?"

Moderation slipped into actual hesitation at that last, and Estean broke in anxiously.

"Why should we 'halt'? I know the Lord Dragon told us to hold back, Mat, but burn my soul, there's no honor in sitting and letting the Aiel do all the fighting. Why should we be saddled with chasing them after they're broken? Besides, my father is in the city, and . . ." He trailed off under Mat's stare.

Mat shook his head, fanning himself with his hat. The fools were not even where they should be. There was no chance of turning them back, either. If Melanril would go—and looking at him, Mat was not sure he would, even on supposed orders from the Lord Dragon—there was still no chance. He sat his saddle in plain sight of the Aiel lookouts. If the column started turning around, they would know themselves discovered, and very likely they would attack while the Tairens and the Cairhienin pike were tangled up. It would be a slaughter as surely as if they had gone ahead in ignorance.

"Where is Weiramon?"

"The Lord Dragon sent him back to Tear," Melanril replied slowly. "To deal with the Illianer pirates, and the bandits on the Plains of Maredo. He was reluctant to go, of course, even for so great a responsibility, but . . . Pardon, Lord Mat, but if the Lord Dragon sent you, how is it that you don't know—"

Mat cut him off. "I am no lord. And if you want to question what Rand lets people know, ask him." That set the fellow back; he was not about to question the Lord bloody Dragon about anything. Weiramon was a fool, but at least he was old enough to have been in a battle. Except for Estean, looking like a sack of turnips tied on his horse, all this lot had seen was a tavern fight or two. And maybe a few duels. Fat lot of good that would do them. "Now, you all listen to me. When you pass through that gap ahead between the next two hills, Aiel are going to come down on you like an avalanche."

He might as well have told them there was going to be a ball, with the women all sighing to meet a Tairen lordling. Eager grins broke out, and they started dancing

their horses about, slapping each other on the shoulder
and boasting how many they would kill. Estean was odd
man out, just sighing and easing his sword in its scabbard.

"Don't stare up there!" Mat snapped. The fools. In a
minute they would be calling the charge! "Keep your
eyes on me. On me!"

It was who he was friends with that settled them down.
Melanril and the others in their fine, unmarked armor
frowned impatiently, not understanding why he did not
want to let them begin the business of killing Aiel
savages. If he had not been Rand's friend they probably
would have trampled him and Pips both.

He could let them go charging off. They would do it
piecemeal, leaving the pikes and the Cairhienin horse
behind, though the Cairhienin might join in once they
realized what was happening. And they would all die.
The smart thing would be to let them get on with it while
he headed in the opposite direction. The only trouble
was that once these idiots let the Aiel know they were
discovered, those Aiel might decide to do something
fancy, like swinging around to take the strung-out fools
in the flank. If that happened, there was no certainty that
he would get clear.

"What the Lord Dragon wants you to do," he told
them, "is to ride ahead slowly, just as if there wasn't an
Aiel inside a hundred miles. As soon as the pikes are
through the gap, they'll form a hollow square, and you
get yourselves inside it double quick."

"Inside!" Melanril protested. Angry mutters rose from
the other young lords—except Estean, who looked
thoughtful. "There is no honor in hiding behind stink-
ing—"

"You bloody do it," Mat roared, reining Pips close to
Melanril's horse, "or if the bloody Aiel don't kill you,
Rand will, and whatever he leaves, I'll chop into sausage
myself!" This was taking too long; the Aiel had to be
wondering what they were talking about by now. "With
any luck, you will be set before the Aiel can hit you. If
you have horsebows, use them. Otherwise, hold tight.

You'll get your bloody charge, and you'll know when, but if you move too early . . . !" He could almost feel time running down.

Setting the butt of his spear in his stirrup like a lance, he heeled Pips back down the column. When he glanced over his shoulder, Melanril and the others were talking and peering after him. At least they were not haring up the valley.

The commander of the pikemen proved to be a pale, slender Cairhienin, half a head shorter than Mat and mounted on a gray gelding that looked past ready for the pasture. Daerid had hard eyes, though, an oft-broken nose, and three white scars crisscrossing his face, one of them not very old. He took off his bell-shaped helmet while he talked with Mat; the front of his head was shaved. No lord, he. Maybe he had been part of the army, before the civil war started. Yes, his men knew how to form a hedgehog. He had not faced Aiel, but he had faced brigands, and Andoran cavalry. There was an implication that he had fought other Cairhienin as well, for one of the Houses contesting for the throne. Daerid sounded neither eager nor reluctant; he sounded like a man with a job of work to do.

The column stepped off as Mat turned Pips' head the other way. They marched with a measured pace, and a quick look behind showed the Tairens' horses moving no faster.

He let Pips go a little quicker than a walk, but not much. It seemed he could feel Aiel eyes on his back, feel them wondering what he had said, and where he was going now and why. *Just a messenger who's delivered his message and is going away. Nothing to worry about.* He certainly hoped that was what the Aiel thought, but his shoulders did not untense until he was sure they could no longer see him.

The Cairhienin were still waiting where he had left them. They still had their flankers out, too. Banners and *con* made a thicket where the lords had gathered, one in ten or better of the Cairhienin's number. Most of them wore plain breastplates, and where there was gilt or silverwork, it was battered as though a drunken blacksmith had been at it. Some of their mounts made Daerid's look like Lan's warhorse. Could they even do what was needed? But the faces that turned to him were hard, the gazes harder.

He was in the clear, now, hidden from the Aiel. He could ride on. After telling this lot what was expected of them, anyway. He had sent the others on into the Aiel trap; he could not simply abandon them.

Talmanes of House Delovinde, his *con* three yellow stars on blue and his banner a black fox, was even shorter than Daerid and had three years on Mat at most, but he led these Cairhienin although there were older men and even gray hair present. His eyes held as little expression as Daerid's, and he looked like a coiled whip. His armor and sword were utterly plain. Once he had told Mat his name the man listened quietly while Mat laid out his plan, leaning a little out of the saddle to cut lines in the ground with the sword-bladed spear.

The other Cairhienin lords gathered round on their horses, watching, but none so sharply as Talmanes. Talmanes studied the map he drew, and studied him from boots to hat, even his spear. When he was done, the fellow still did not speak, until Mat barked, "Well? I don't care whether you take it or leave it, but your friends will be hip-deep in Aiel in not much longer."

"The Tairens are no friends of mine. And Daerid is . . . useful. Certainly not a friend." Dry chuckles ran through the onlooking lords at the suggestion. "But I will lead one half, if you lead the other."

Talmanes pulled off one steel-backed gauntlet and put out his hand, but for a moment Mat only stared at it. Lead? Him? *I'm a gambler, not a soldier. A lover.* Memories of battles long gone spun through his head, but he forced them down. All he had to do was ride on. But then maybe Talmanes would leave Estean and Daerid and the rest to roast. On the spit Mat had hung them from. Even so, it was a surprise to him when he grasped the other's hand and said, "You just be there when you're supposed to be."

For reply Talmanes began calling off names in a quick voice. Lords and lordlings reined toward Mat, each followed by a bannerman and perhaps a dozen retainers, until he had four hundred odd of the Cairhienin. Talmanes did not have much to say after, either; he just led the remainder west at a trot, trailing a faint cloud of dust.

"Keep together," Mat told his half. "Charge when I say charge, run when I say run, and don't make any noise you don't have to." There was the creak of saddles and the thud of hooves as they followed him, of course, but at least they did not talk, or ask questions.

A last glimpse of the other bristle of bright banners and *con,* and then a twist in the shallow valley hid them. How had he gotten into this? It had all started so simply. Just give warning and go. Each step after had seemed so small, so necessary. And now he had waded waist deep into the mud, and no choice but to keep on. He hoped Talmanes meant to show up. The man had not even asked who he was.

The hill valley twisted and forked as he angled north, but he had a good sense of direction. For instance, he knew exactly which way lay south and safety, and it was not the way he was heading. Dark clouds were forming up there toward the city, the first he had seen so thick in a long time. Rain would break the drought—good for the farmers, if any remained—and settle the dust—good for horsemen, so they did not announce themselves too early. Maybe if it rained, the Aiel would give up and go home. The wind was beginning to pick up, too, bringing a little cool, for a wonder.

The sound of fighting drifted over the crests, men shouting, men screaming. It had begun.

Mat turned Pips, raised his spear and swung it right and left. He was almost surprised when the Cairhienin formed into one long line to either side of him, facing upslope. The gesture had been instinctive, from another time and place, but then, these men had seen fighting. He started Pips up through the scattered trees at a slow walk, and they kept pace to the quiet jangle of bridles.

His first thought on reaching the height was relief at seeing Talmanes and his men coming into sight on the crest across from him. His second was to curse. Daerid had formed the hedgehog, spiny thickets of pikes four deep interspersed with bowmen to make a large hollow square. Long pikes made it difficult for the Shaido to get close, however they rushed in, and the archers and crossbowmen were exchanging shots hot and fast with the Aiel. Men were falling on both sides, but the pikes simply closed in when one of their number went down, making the square tighter. Of course, the Shaido did not appear to slacken their assault either.

The Defenders were dismounted in the center, and maybe half the Tairen lords with their retainers. Half. That was what made him want to curse. The rest dashed about among the Aiel, slashing and stabbing with sword and lance in knots of five or ten, or alone. Dozens of riderless horses told how well they were doing. Melanril was off with only his bannerman, laying about with his blade. Two Aiel darted in to neatly hamstring the lordling's horse; it fell, head flailing—Mat was sure it screamed, but the din swallowed it—and then Melanril vanished behind *cadin'sor*-clad figures, spears stabbing. The bannerman lasted a moment longer.

Good riddance, Mat thought grimly. Standing in his stirrups, he raised the sword-bladed spear high, then swept it forward, shouting, *"Los! Los caba'drin!"*

He would have had the words back if he could, and not because they were Old Tongue; it was a boiling cauldron down in the valley. But whether or not any of the Cairhienin understood a command of "horsemen forward" in the Old Tongue, they understood the gesture, especially when he dropped back into his saddle and dug in his heels. Not that he really wanted to, but he could not see any choice now. He had put those men down there—some might have gotten away if he had told them to turn and run—and he just did not have a choice.

Banners and *con* waving, the Cairhienin charged downhill with him, shouting battle cries. In imitation of him, no doubt, though what he was shouting was "Blood and bloody ashes!" Across the valley, Talmanes raced down just as hard.

Sure that they had all the wetlanders penned, the Shaido never saw the others until crashed into from behind on both sides. It was then that the lightning began to fall. And after that things really got hairy.

CHAPTER
44

The Lesser Sadness

Rand's shirt clung to him with the sweat of effort,
but he kept his coat on for protection from the
wind gusting toward Cairhien. The sun had at
least another hour to reach its noonday peak, yet already
he felt as if he had run all morning and been beaten with
a club at the finish. Wrapped in the Void, he was only
distantly aware of the weariness, dimly perceiving the
ache in arms and shoulders, in the small of his back, a
throb around the tender scar in his side. That he was
aware of them at all told the story. With the Power in
him, he could make out individual leaves on the trees at a
hundred paces, but whatever happened to him physically
should have been as if it were happening to someone else.

He had long since taken to drawing on *saidin* through
the *angreal* in his pocket, the stone carving of the fat
little man. Even so, working the Power was a strain now,
weaving it at this distance of miles, but only the rancid
threads streaking what he drew kept him from pulling
more, from trying to pull it all to him. The Power was
that sweet, taint or no. After hours of channeling without
rest, he was that tired. At the same time, he had to fight
saidin itself harder, to put more of his strength into

keeping it from burning him to ash where he stood, from burning his mind to ash. It was ever more difficult to hold off *saidin*'s destruction, more difficult to resist the desire to draw more, more difficult to handle what he did draw. A nasty downward spiral, and hours to go before the battle was decided.

Wiping sweat from his eyes, he gripped the platform's rough railing. He was near the brink, yet he was stronger than Egwene or Aviendha. The Aiel woman was standing, peering off toward Cairhien and the storm clouds, occasionally bending to stare through the long looking glass; Egwene sat cross-legged, leaning back against an upright still covered in gray bark, her eyes closed. They both looked as worked out as he felt.

Before he could do anything—not that he knew what; he had no skill at Healing—Egwene's eyes opened, and she stood, exchanging a few quiet words with Aviendha that the wind snatched away from even his *saidin*-enhanced hearing. Then Aviendha sat down in Egwene's place and let her head fall back against the upright. The black clouds around the city continued to stab lightning, but they were wild forks far more often than single lances now.

So they were taking turns, giving each other a rest. It would have been nice to have someone do that with him, but he did not regret telling Asmodean to stay in his tent. He would not have trusted him to channel. Especially not now. Who could say what he would have done when he saw Rand weakened as he was?

Staggering slightly, Rand pulled his looking glass around to study the hills outside the city. Life was certainly visible there now. And death. Wherever he looked there was fighting, Aiel against Aiel, a thousand here, five thousand there, swarming over the treeless hills and too closely meshed for him to do anything. He could not find the column of horse and pike.

Three times he had seen them, once fighting twice their number of Aiel. He was certain they were still out there. Small hope that Melanril had decided to obey his orders at this late juncture. Choosing the man just because he had the grace to be embarrassed by Weiramon's behavior had been a mistake, but there had been little time to make a choice, and he had had to get rid of Weiramon. Nothing to be done about it now. Maybe one of the Cairhienin could be put in command. If even his direct order would make the Tairens follow a Cairhienin.

A milling mass right at the city's high gray wall caught his eye. Tall iron-bound gates stood open, Aiel battling horsemen and spearmen almost in the open while folk tried to close the gates, tried and failed because of the press of bodies. Horses with empty saddles and armored men unmoving on the ground half a mile from the gate marked where the sortie had been driven back. Arrows rained down from the walls, and head-sized chunks of rubble—even occasional spears slashing down with enough force to spit two men, or three, though he still could not see from where exactly—but the Aiel were going over their dead, ever closer to forcing their way in. A quick scan showed him two more columns of Aiel trotting toward the gates, perhaps three thousand all told. He did not doubt that they were Couladin's as well.

He was aware of grinding his teeth. If the Shaido got inside Cairhien, he would never drive them north. He would have to dig them out street by street; the cost in lives would dwarf the number of those already dead, and the city itself would end a ruin like Eianrod, if not Taien. Cairhienin and Shaido were mingled like ants in a bowl, but he had to do something.

Taking a deep breath, he channeled. The two women had set the conditions, bringing the storm clouds; he did not need to be able to see their weavings to take advantage of them. Stark silver-blue lightning struck into the Aiel, once, twice, again, as fast as a man could clap.

Rand jerked his head up, blinking away the burning lines that still seemed to cross his sight, and when he looked through the long tube again, Shaido lay like cut barley all around where the bolts had fallen. Men and horses thrashed on the ground closer to the gates, too, and some did not move at all, but the uninjured were dragging the injured and the gates were beginning to close.

How many won't make it back inside? How many of my

own did I kill? The cold truth was that it did not matter. It had had to be done, and it was done.

And well it was. Distantly he felt his knees wobbling. He would have to pace himself if he was to last the rest of the day. No more laying about him everywhere; he had to spot where he was particularly needed, where he could make a—

The storm clouds were massed only over the city and the hills to the south, but that did not stop lightning from slashing out of the clear, cloudless sky above the tower, flashing down into the gathered Maidens below with a deafening crack.

Hair lifting with the tingle in the air, Rand stared. He could feel that bolt in another way, feel the weaving of *saidin* that had made it. *So Asmodean was tempted even back in the tents.*

There was no time for thought, though. Like rapid beats on a giant drum, bolt followed bolt, marching through the Maidens until the last struck the base of the tower in an explosion of splinters the size of arms and legs.

As the tower slowly began to slant over, Rand threw himself at Egwene and Aviendha. Somehow he managed to scoop them both into one arm, then wrap the other around an upright on what was now the upslope side of the platform. They stared at him wide-eyed, mouths coming open, but there was no more time for speaking than for thinking. The shattered log tower toppled, crashing through the branches of the trees. For an instant he believed they might cushion the fall.

With a snap, the upright he clung to broke off. The ground came up and knocked all the breath out of him a heartbeat before the women came down on top of him. Darkness rolled in.

He regained consciousness slowly. Hearing returned first.

". . . have dug us up like a boulder and sent us rolling downhill in the night." It was Aviendha's voice, low, as if she spoke for her own ears. There was something moving on his face. "You have taken away what we are, what we were. You must give us something in return, something to be. We need you." The moving thing slowed, touched more softly. "I need you. Not for myself, you will understand. For Elayne. What is between her and me now is between her and me, but I will hand you to her. I will. If you die, I will carry your corpse to her! If you die—!"

His eyes popped open, and for a moment they stared at each other almost nose to nose. Her hair was all in disarray, her head scarf gone, and a purple lump marred her cheek. She straightened jerkily, folding a damp cloth stained with blood, and began dabbing at his forehead with considerably more force than before.

"I've no intention of dying," he told her, though in truth he was not sure of that at all. The Void and *saidin* were gone, of course. Just thinking of losing them as he had made him shiver; it was pure luck that *saidin* had not scoured his mind blank in that last instant. Just thinking of seizing the Source again made him groan. Without the Void for buffer, he felt every ache, every bruise and scrape, to the fullest. He was so tired he could have dropped off to sleep at once if he had not hurt so much. As well he did hurt, then, because he surely could not sleep. Not for a long time, yet.

Sliding a hand beneath his coat, he touched his side, then surreptitiously wiped the blood off his fingers onto his shirt before bringing the hand out again. No wonder that a fall like that had broken open the half-healed, never-healed wound. He did not seem to be bleeding too badly, but if the Maidens saw it, or Egwene, or even Aviendha, he might have a fight to keep from being hauled off to Moiraine for Healing. He had too much to do yet for that—being Healed on top of everything else would act on him like a cudgel to the temple—and besides, there must be far worse hurt than what he suffered for her to deal with.

Grimacing, suppressing another groan, he got to his feet with only a little help from Aviendha. And promptly forgot about his injuries.

Sulin sat on the ground nearby, with Egwene bandaging a bloody split in her scalp and muttering fiercely at herself because she did not know how to Heal, but the white-haired Maiden was not the only casualty, and not the worst by far. Everywhere *cadin'sor*-clad women were covering the dead with blankets, and tending those who had merely been burned, if "merely" could be used for lightning burns. Except for Egwene's grumbling, the hilltop lay in near silence, even the injured women quiet save for hoarse breathing.

The log tower, all but unrecognizable now, had not spared the Maidens in its fall, breaking arms and legs, tearing open gashes. He watched as a blanket was laid over the face of a Maiden with red-gold hair almost the shade of Elayne's, head twisted at an unnatural angle and glazed eyes staring. Jolien. One of those who first crossed the Dragonwall to search for He Who Comes With The Dawn. She had gone to the Stone of Tear for him. And now she was dead. For him. *Oh, you've done well at keeping the Maidens from harm,* he thought bitterly. *Very well indeed.*

He could still feel the lightning, or rather the residue of its making. Almost like the after-image burned into his eyes earlier, he could trace the weave, though it was fading. To his surprise, it led west, not back toward the tents. Not Asmodean, then.

"Sammael." He was sure of it. Sammael had sent that attack in the Jangai, Sammael was behind the pirates and the raids in Tear, and Sammael had done this. His lips peeled back in a snarl, and his voice was a harsh whisper. "Sammael!" He did not realize he had taken a step until Aviendha seized his arm.

A moment later, Egwene had the other, the pair of them clinging to him as if they meant to root him to the spot. "Do not be a complete woolhead," Egwene said, giving a start at his glare but not letting go. She had redone the brown scarf around her head, but combing with her fingers had not put her hair back in order, and dust still covered her blouse and skirt. "Whoever did this, why do you think he waited so long, until you must be tired? Because if he missed killing you, and you went after him, you would be easy meat. You can barely stand on your own!"

Aviendha was no readier to let go, meeting his stare

with a flat one of her own. "You are needed here, Rand al'Thor. Here, *Car'a'carn.* Does your honor lie with killing this man, or here with those you have brought to this land?"

A young Aielman came running up through the Maidens, *shoufa* around his shoulders, spears and buckler swinging easily. If he thought it odd to find two women holding Rand between them, he gave no hint of it. He eyed the shattered remnants of the tower and the dead and wounded with a slight curiosity, as though wondering how it might have happened and where the enemy dead might be. Grounding his spearpoints in front of Rand, he said, "I am Seirin, of the Shorara sept of the Tomanelle."

"I see you, Seirin," Rand replied just as formally. Not easy with a pair of women holding him as if they thought he might run.

"Han of the Tomanelle sends word to the *Car'a'carn.* The clans to the east are moving toward each other. All four. Han means to join with Dhearic, and he has sent to Erim to join them."

Rand drew a measured breath, and hoped the women thought his grimace was for the news; his side burned, and he could feel blood spreading slowly down his shirt. So there would be nothing to force Couladin north when the Shaido broke. If they broke; they had given no evidence of it yet that he had seen. Why were the Miagoma and the others joining together? If they meant to come against him, they were only giving warning. But if they meant to come against him, Han and Dhearic and Erim would be outnumbered, and if the Shaido held long enough and the four clans broke through . . . Across the wooded hills he could see that it had begun to rain over the city now that Egwene and Aviendha were not holding the clouds. That would hamper both sides. Unless the women were in better shape than they looked, they might be unable to regain control from this distance.

"Tell Han to do what he must to keep them off our backs."

Young as he was—he was about Rand's age, come to that—Seirin raised an eyebrow in surprise. Of course.

Han would not do differently, and Seirin knew it. He waited only long enough to make certain that Rand had no further message: then he was off and running downhill, just as fast as he had come. No doubt he hoped to get back without missing any more of the fighting than he had to. For that matter, it might already have begun, there to the east.

"I need someone to fetch Jeade'en," Rand said as soon as Seirin had dashed off. If he tried to walk that far, he really would need the women to hold him up. The two of them looked nothing alike, yet they managed practically identical suspicion. Those frowns must have been one of the things every girl was taught by her mother. "I am not going after Sammael." Not yet. "I have to get closer to the city, though." He nodded to the fallen tower; that was the only gesture available with them hanging on. Master Tovere might be able to salvage the lenses from the looking glasses, but there were not three logs of the tower unbroken. No more observing everything from on high today.

Egwene was plainly uncertain, but Aviendha barely paused before asking a young Maiden to go to the *gai'shain*. To fetch Mist, too, which he had not counted on. Egwene began brushing herself off, muttering under her breath at the dust, and Aviendha had found an ivory comb and another scarf somewhere. Despite the fall, somehow they already looked considerably less disheveled than he. Weariness still marked their faces, but as long as they could channel at all, they would be useful.

That gave him pause. Did he ever think of anyone now except as to how useful they were? He should be able to keep them as safe as they had been atop the tower. Not that the tower had been very safe, as it turned out, but this time he would manage things better.

Sulin stood as he approached, a pale cap of *algode* bandage covering the top of her head, her hair a white fringe below.

"I am moving nearer the city," he told her, "where I can see what is happening, and maybe do something about it. Everyone who is injured is to remain here, along with enough others to protect them if need be.

Make it a strong guard, Sulin; I only need a handful with me, and it's poor repayment for the honor the Maidens have shown me if I let their wounded be slaughtered." That should hold the greater part of them away from the fighting. He himself would have to stay clear to keep the rest out, but the way he felt, that would be no burden. "I want you to stay here, and—"

"I am not one of the injured," she said stiffly, and he hesitated, then nodded slowly.

"Very well." He had no doubt that her injury was serious, but neither did he doubt that she was tough. And if she stayed, he might be stuck with someone like Enaila leading his guard. Being treated like a brother was nowhere near as annoying as being treated like a son, and he was in no mood to put up with the latter. "But I trust you to see that no one follows who *is* injured, Sulin. I will have to keep moving. I can't afford anyone who will slow me down or must be left behind."

She nodded so quickly that he was convinced she would make any Maiden with as much as a scratch remain behind. Except herself, of course. This was one time he felt no guilt over using someone. The Maidens had chosen to carry the spear, but they had chosen to follow him, too. Maybe "follow" was not precisely the word, considering some of the things they did, but that did not change anything, to his mind. He would not, he could not, order a woman to her death, and that was that. In truth, he had expected some sort of protest before this. He was only grateful that it had not come. *I must be more subtle than I think.*

Two pale-robed *gai'shain* arrived leading Jeade'en and Mist, and behind them followed a crowd of others, arms full of bandages and ointments and over their shoulders bulging water bags in layers, under the direction of Sorilea and a dozen other Wise Ones whom he had met. At most he thought he might know the names of half.

Sorilea was very definitely in charge, and she quickly had *gai'shain* and other Wise Ones alike circulating among the Maidens tending wounds. She eyed Rand and Egwene and Aviendha, frowning thoughtfully and pursing her thin lips, obviously thinking that all three looked tossed about enough to need their injuries bathed. That look was enough to send Egwene scrambling into the gray's saddle with a smile and a nod for the aged Wise One, though if Aiel had been more familiar with riding, Sorilea would have realized that Egwene's awkward stiffness was not usual. And it was a measure of Aviendha's condition that she let Egwene pull her up behind the saddle without the slightest protest. She smiled at Sorilea, too.

Gritting his teeth, Rand pulled himself into his own saddle in one smooth motion. Aching muscles' protests were buried under an avalanche of pain in his side, as though he had been stabbed anew, and it took a full minute before he could breathe again, but he let none of it show.

Egwene reined Mist close to Jeade'en, near enough to whisper. "If you cannot mount a horse any better than that, Rand al'Thor, maybe you should forget about riding at all for a while." Aviendha wore one of those blank Aiel expressions, but her eyes were intent on his face.

"I noticed you mounting, too," he said quietly. "Maybe you ought to stay here and help Sorilea until you feel better." That shut her up, even if it did tighten her mouth sourly. Aviendha gave Sorilea another smile; the old Wise One was still watching.

Rand booted the dapple to a trot downhill. Every step sent a jolt up his side that had him breathing through his teeth, but he had ground to cover, and he could not do it at a walk. Besides, Sorilea's stare had been starting to get on his nerves.

Mist joined Jeade'en before he was fifty paces down the overgrown slope, and another fifty brought Sulin and a stream of Maidens, some running to position themselves ahead. More than he had hoped for, but it should not matter. What he had to do would not involve getting very close to the fighting. They could stay back in safety with him.

Seizing *saidin* was an effort in and of itself, even through the *angreal,* and the sheer weight of it seemed to press down on him greater than ever, the taint stronger.

At least the Void shielded him from his own pain. Somewhat, anyway. And if Sammael tried to play games with him again . . .

He quickened Jeade'en's pace. Whatever Sammael did, he still had his own job to do.

Rain dripped from the brim of Mat's hat, and periodically he had to lower his looking glass and wipe off the end of the tube. The downpour had slackened in the last hour, but the sparse branches overhead gave no shelter at all. His coat was long since soaked, and Pips' ears were down; the horse stood as if not intending to move however Mat thumped his heels.

He did not know for sure what time of day it was. Somewhere in the middle of the afternoon, he thought, but the dark clouds had not thinned along with the rain, and they hid the sun where he was. On the other hand, it felt very much like three or four days since he had ridden down to warn the Tairens. He was still not sure why he had done that.

It was southward that he peered, and a way out that he looked for. A way out for three thousand men; easily that many survived yet, though they had no idea what he was up to. They believed he was hunting another fight for them, but three so far were three too many by his book. He thought he could have escaped on his own, now, so long as he kept his eyes open and his wits about him. Three thousand men, however, drew eyes whenever they moved, and they did not move quickly, what with more than half their number afoot. That was why he was on this Light-forsaken hilltop, and why the Tairens and Cairhienin were all jammed into the long, narrow hollow between this hill and the next. If he simply made a break for it . . .

Jamming the looking glass back to his eye, he glared south at sparsely wooded hills. Here and there were thickets, some fairly large, but most of the land was scrub or grass even here. He had worked back to the east, using every fold in the ground that would hide a mouse, bringing the column with him out of the treeless terrain and into some proper cover. Out of those bloody light-

ning strikes and fireballs; he was not sure whether it was
worse when they came, or when the earth simply erupted
in a roar for no apparent reason. All that effort to find
that the battle was shifting with him. He could not seem
to get out of the center of the thing.

Where's my bloody luck now that I really need it? He
was a pea-brained fool for staying. Just because he had
managed to keep the others alive this long did not mean
he could keep it up. Soon or late, the dice would come up
the Dark One's Eyes. *They're the flaming soldiers. I
should leave them to it and ride.*

But he kept searching, scanning the wooded peaks and
ridges. They gave cover for Couladin's Aiel as well as for
him, but here and there he could make them out. Not all
were involved in pitched battles, but every last group was
larger than his, every one was between him and safety to
the south, and he had no way to tell who was who until it
might be too late. The Aiel themselves seemed to know
at a glance, but that did him no good.

Some mile or more off, a few hundred *cadin'sor*-clad
shapes running eight abreast and heading east topped a
rise where half-a-dozen leatherleaf made a poor excuse
for a copse. Before the lead runners could start down the
other side, a lightning bolt flashed down into their midst,
splashing men and earth like a stone thrown into a pond.
Pips did not even quiver as the clap reached Mat; the
gelding had grown accustomed to closer strikes than
that.

Some of the fallen men picked themselves up, limping,
and immediately joined those who had kept their feet in
a hasty check of the unmoving. No more than a dozen
were hauled across shoulders before they all dashed
down from the height, back the way they had come.
None paused to look at the crater. Mat had watched
them learn that lesson; waiting only invited a second
silvery lance from the clouds. In moments they were out
of sight. Except for the dead.

He swung the looking glass east. There was a look of
sunlight a few miles that way. The log tower should have
been visible, poking above the trees, but he had not been
able to find it in some time. Maybe he was looking in the

wrong places. It did not matter. The lightning had to be Rand's work, and all the rest of it as well. *If I can get far enough that way . . .*

He would be right back where he started. Even if it was not the pull of *ta'veren* drawing him back, he would have a hard time leaving again once Moiraine found out. And there was Melindhra to consider. He had never heard of a woman who would not take it askance when a man tried to walk out of her life without letting her know.

As he panned the looking glass slowly, hunting the tower, a slope covered in spaced leatherleaf and paperbark abruptly went up in flames, every tree become a torch at the same instant.

Slowly he lowered the brass-bound tube; he hardly required it to see the fire, and the thick gray smoke already making a thick plume into the sky. He did not need signs to recognize channeling when he saw it, not like that. Had Rand finally tipped over the edge of madness? Or maybe Aviendha had finally had enough of being forced to stay around him. Never upset a woman who could channel; that was a rule Mat seldom managed to follow, but he did try.

Save the smart mouth for somebody besides yourself, he thought sourly. He was just trying not to think about the third alternative. If Rand had not finally gone mad, and Aviendha or Egwene or one of the Wise Ones had not decided to be rid of him, then someone else was taking a hand in the day's business. He could add two twos without getting five. *Sammael.* So much for trying that way out; it was no way out of anything. *Blood and bloody ashes! What* has *happened to my—?*

A fallen branch cracked under someone's foot behind him, and he reacted without thinking, knees more than reins pulling Pips in a tight circle, sword-bladed spear whipping across from the pommel of his saddle.

Estean almost dropped his helmet, his eyes going wide, as the short blade stopped a breath short of splitting his head for him. The rain had slicked his hair down into his face. Also afoot, Nalesean grinned, partly startled and partly amused at the other young Tairen's discomfort. Square-faced and blocky, Nalesean was the second since

Melanril to lead the Tairen cavalry. Talmanes and Daerid were there as well, a pace behind as usual, and blank-faced beneath their bell-shaped helmets, also as usual. The four had left their horses farther back in the trees.

"There are Aiel coming straight for us, Mat," Nalesean said as Mat raised the raven-marked spear upright. "The Light burn my soul if there's a one less than five thousand." He grinned at that, too. "I don't think they know we're here waiting for them."

Estean nodded once. "They are keeping to the valleys and hollows. Hiding from . . ." He glanced at the clouds and shivered. He was not the only one to be uneasy about what might come out of the sky; the other three looked up, too. "Anyway, it's plain they mean to go through where Daerid's men are." There was actually a touch of respect in his voice when he mentioned the pikes. Grudging, true, and not very strong, but it was difficult to look down on someone after they had saved your neck a few times. "They will be on top of us before they see us."

"Wonderful." Mat breathed. "That is just bloody wonderful."

He meant it for sarcasm, yet Nalesean and Estean missed the flavor, of course. They looked eager. But Daerid wore as much expression on his scarred face as a rock, and Talmanes lifted an eyebrow at Mat just a fraction, shook his head a hair. That pair knew fighting.

The first encounter with the Shaido had been an even wager at best, one Mat would never have taken if not forced. That all the lightning had shaken the Aiel enough to turn it into a rout changed nothing. Twice more today they had seen action, when Mat discovered himself in a choice of whether to catch or be caught, and neither had come out nearly as well as the Tairens believed. One had been a draw, but only because he had been able to lose the Shaido after they pulled back to regroup. At least they had not come again while he was getting everyone away through the twisting hill valleys. He suspected they had found something else to occupy them; maybe more of that lightning, or fireballs, or the Light knew what. He knew very well what had allowed them to escape their last fight with skins mostly whole. Another bunch of Aiel plowing into the rear of those fighting him, just in time to keep the pikes from being overrun. The Shaido had decided to withdraw to the north, and the others—he still did not know who—had swung off to the west, leaving him in possession of the field. Nalesean and Estean considered it a clear victory. Daerid and Talmanes knew better.

"How long?" Mat asked.

It was Talmanes who answered. "Half an hour. Perhaps a little more, if grace favors us." The Tairens looked doubtful; they still did not seem to realize how quickly Aiel could move.

Mat had no such illusions. He had already studied the surrounding terrain, but he looked at it again and sighed. There was a very good view from this hill, and the only halfway decent stand of trees within half a mile was right where he sat his saddle. The rest was scrub brush, little as much as waist-high, dotted with leatherleaf and paperbark and the occasional oak. Those Aiel would surely send scouts up here for a look, and there was no chance at all that even the horsemen could get out of sight before they did. The pikes would be right out in the open. He knew what had to be done—it was catch or be caught again—but he did not have to like it.

He only took a glance, but before he could open his mouth, Daerid said, "My scouts tell me Couladin himself is with this lot. At least, their leader has his arms bare, and shows marks such as the Lord Dragon is said to carry."

Mat grunted. Couladin, and heading east. If there was any way to step aside, the fellow would run headlong into Rand. That might even be what he was after. Mat realized that he was smoldering, and it had nothing to do with Couladin wanting to kill Rand. The Shaido chief, or whatever the man was, might remember Mat vaguely as somebody hanging about Rand, but Couladin was the reason he was stuck out here in the middle of a battle, trying to stay alive, wondering whether any minute it was going to turn into a personal fight between Rand and

Sammael, the kind of fight that might kill everything within two or three miles. *That's if I don't get a spear through the brisket first.* And no more choice about it than had a goose hanging outside the kitchen door. None of it would be so without Couladin.

A pity no one had killed the man years ago. He certainly gave excuses enough. Aiel seldom let anger show, and when they did, it was cold and tight. Couladin, on the other hand, seemed to flare up two or three times a day, losing his head in a fiery rage as quick as snap a straw. A miracle he was still alive, and the Dark One's own luck.

"Nalesean," Mat said angrily, "swing your Tairens wide to the north and come in on these fellows from behind. We will be holding their attention, so you ride hard and come down like a barn collapsing." *So he has the Dark One's luck, does he? Blood and ashes, but I hope mine is back in.* "Talmanes, you do the same to the south. Move, both of you. We've little time, and it's wasting."

The two Tairens bowed hastily and dashed for their horses, clapping on their helmets. Talmanes' bow was more formal. "Grace favor your sword, Mat. Or perhaps I should say your spear." Then he was gone, too.

Looking up at Mat as the three vanished down the hill, Daerid slashed rain from his eyes with a finger. "So you will stay with the pikes this time. You must not let your anger at this Couladin overcome you. A battle is no place to try fighting a duel."

Mat barely stopped from gaping. A duel? Him? With Couladin? Was that why Daerid thought he was staying with the foot? He had chosen it because it was safer to be behind the pikes. That was his reason. The whole reason. "Not to worry. I can hold myself in rein." And he had thought Daerid the most sensible of the whole lot.

The Cairhienin merely nodded. "I thought that you could. You have seen pikes pushed before, and faced a charge or two, I vow. Talmanes gives praises when there are two moons, yet I heard him say aloud that he would follow wherever you led. Some day I would like to hear your story, Andorman. But you are young—under the

Light, I mean no disrespect—and young men have hot blood."

"This rain will keep it cool if nothing else does." *Blood and ashes!* Were they all mad? Talmanes was praising him? He wondered what they would say if they found out he was only a gambler following bits of memory from men dead a thousand years and more. They would be drawing lots for first chance to spit him like a pig. The lords especially; no one liked being made to look a fool, but nobles seemed to like it least of all, perhaps because they so often managed it on their own. Well, one way or another, he meant to be miles away when that discovery came. *Bloody Couladin. I'd like to shove this spear down his throat!* Heeling Pips, he started for the opposite slope, where the foot waited below.

Daerid climbed into his own saddle and swung in beside him, nodding as Mat spun out his plan. The bowmen on the slopes, where they could cover the flanks, but lying down, hidden in the brush until the last minute. One man on the crest to signal the Aiel in sight. And the pikes to step off as soon as he did, marching straight out toward the approaching enemy. "As soon as *we* can see the Shaido, we'll retreat just as fast as we can, almost back to the gap between these two hills, then turn to face them."

"They will think we wanted to run, realized we could not, and turned at bay like a bear to the hounds. Seeing us less than half their number and fighting only because we must, they should think to roll over us. Can we but hold their attention until the horse comes down on them from behind . . ." The Cairhienin actually grinned. "It is using the Aiel's own tactics against them."

"We had better hold their bloody attention." Mat's tone was as dry as he was wet. "To make sure we do—to make sure *they* don't start putting loops around *our* flanks—I want a cry raised as soon as you stop the retreat. 'Protect the Lord Dragon.'" This time Daerid laughed aloud.

That should bring the Shaido in right enough, especially if Couladin was leading. If Couladin really was leading, if he thought Rand was with the pikes, if the

pikes could hold until the horse arrived . . . A lot of ifs.
Mat could hear those dice rolling in his head again. This
was the biggest gamble he had ever taken in his life. He
wondered how long it was until nightfall; a man should
be able to make his way out in the night. He wished those
dice would get out of his head, or else fall so he knew
what they showed. Scowling into the rain, he booted Pips
on down the hillside.

Jeade'en stopped on a crest where a dozen trees made a
thin topknot, and Rand hunched slightly against the
pain in his side. The crescent moon, riding high, cast a
pale light, yet even to his *saidin*-amplified vision anything more than a hundred paces distant was featureless
shadow. Night swallowed the surrounding hills whole,
and he was only intermittently aware of Sulin hovering
nearby, and Maidens all around him. But then, he could
not seem to keep his eyes more than half open; they felt
grainy, and he thought the gnawing pain in his side might
be all that held him awake. He did not think of it often.
Thought was not only distant now, it was slow.

Was it twice Sammael had attempted his life today, or
three times? More? It seemed that he should be able to
remember how often someone had tried to kill him. No,
not to kill. To bait. *Are you still so jealous of me, Tel
Janin? When did I ever slight you, or give you one finger
less than your due?*

Swaying, Rand scrubbed a hand through his hair.
There had been something odd about that thought, but
he could not recall what. Sammael. . . . No. He could
deal with him when . . . if . . . No matter. Later. Today
Sammael was only a distraction from what was important. He might even be gone.

Vaguely it seemed that there had been no attack
after . . . After what? He recalled countering Sammael's
last move with something particularly nasty, but he
could not pull the memory to the surface. Not balefire.
*Mustn't use that. Threatens the fabric of the Pattern. Not
even for Ilyena? I would burn the world and use my soul
for tinder to hear her laugh again.*

He was drifting again, away from what was important.

However long ago the sun had gone down, it had sunk on fighting, lengthening shadows gradually overwhelming the golden-red light, the men killing and dying. Now, vagrant winds still brought distant shouts and screams. Because of Couladin, true, but at the heart of it, because of himself.

For a moment he could not remember his name.

"Rand al'Thor," he said aloud, and shivered, though his coat was damp with sweat. For an instant, that name had sounded strange to him. "I am Rand al'Thor, and I need to . . . I need to see."

He had not eaten since morning, but then, the taint on *saidin* drove hunger away. The Void quivered constantly, and he hung on to the True Source by his fingernails. It was like riding a bull driven mad by redwort, or swimming naked in a river of fire churned to rapids by jagged boulders of ice. Yet when he was not on the brink of being gored or battered or drowned, it seemed that *saidin* was the only strength left in him. *Saidin* was there, filing at the edges of him, trying to erode or corrode his mind, but ready to be used.

With a jerky nod, he channeled, and something burned high in the sky. Something. A ball of bubbling blue flame that banished shadows in harsh light.

Hills mounded up all around, trees black in the stark illumination. Nothing moved. A faint sound came to him on a gust of wind. Cheering perhaps, or singing. Or maybe he was imagining things; it was so tiny, he could well have been, and it died with the wind.

Suddenly he became aware of the Maidens around him, hundreds of them. Some, including Sulin, were staring at him, but many had their eyes squeezed shut. It took him a moment to realize they were trying to preserve night vision. He frowned, searching. Egwene and Aviendha were no longer there. Another long moment passed before he remembered to loose the weave of his channeling and let blackness reclaim the night. A deep blackness to his eyes, now.

"Where are they?" He was vaguely irritated when he had to say who he meant, and just as vaguely aware that he had no reason for it.

"They went to Moiraine Sedai and the Wise Ones at dusk, *Car'a'carn*," Sulin replied, moving closer to Jeade'en. Her short white hair shone in the moonlight. No, her head was bandaged. How could he have forgotten? "A good two hours gone. They know that flesh is not stone. Even the strongest legs can run only so far."

Rand frowned. Legs? They had been riding Mist. The woman was making no sense. "I have to find them."

"They are with Moiraine Sedai and the Wise Ones, *Car'a'carn*," she said slowly. He thought she was frowning too, but it was hard to be sure.

"Not them," he muttered. "Have to find my people. They're still out there, Sulin." Why was the stallion not moving? "Can you hear them? Out there, in the night. Still fighting. I need to help them." Of course; he had to dig his heels into the dapple's ribs. But when he did, Jaede'en only shifted sideways, with Sulin holding on to his bridle. He did not remember that she had been holding the bridle.

"The Wise Ones must speak to you now, Rand al'Thor." Her voice had changed, but he was too weary to say how.

"Can't it wait?" He must have missed the runner with the message. "I must find them, Sulin."

Enaila seemed to spring up on the other side of the stallion's head. "You have found your people, Rand al'Thor."

"The Wise Ones are waiting for you," Sulin added. She and Enaila turned Jeade'en without waiting on his agreement. Maidens crowded in for some reason as they started along a winding way down the side of the hill, faces reflecting moonlight as they stared up at him, so close their shoulders brushed the horse's flanks.

"Whatever they want," he grumbled, "they had best be quick." There was no need for them to be leading the dapple, but it was too much effort to make a fuss over it. He twisted to look back, grunting at the pain in his side; the crest was already swallowed in the night. "I have a lot to do yet. I need to find . . ." Couladin. Sammael. The men who were fighting and dying for him. "I need to find them." He was so tired, but he could not sleep yet.

Lamps on poles lit the Wise Ones' encampment, and small fires where kettles of water were hauled away and replaced by white-robed men and women as soon as they began boiling. *Gai'shain* scurried everywhere, and Wise Ones as well, tending the wounded whose numbers swelled the camp. Moiraine was moving slowly down the long lines of those who could not stand, only rarely pausing to lay hands on an Aiel who then thrashed in the throes of being Healed. She swayed whenever she straightened, and Lan hovered behind her as if wanting to hold her up, or expecting to have to. Sulin exchanged words with Adelin and Enaila, too low for Rand to make out, and the younger women ran to speak to the Aes Sedai.

Despite the numbers of wounded, not all of the Wise Ones were looking after them. Inside a pavilion off to one side, perhaps twenty sat in a circle listening to one standing in the center. When she sat, another took her place. *Gai'shain* knelt around the outside of the pavilion, but none of the Wise Ones appeared to have any interest in wine, or anything except what they were hearing. Rand thought the speaker was Amys.

To his surprise, Asmodean was also helping out with the wounded, the water bag hanging from each shoulder looking decidedly odd with his dark velvet coat and white lace. Straightening from giving a drink to a man stripped to the waist except for bandages, he saw Rand and hesitated.

After a moment he handed the water bags to one of the *gai'shain* and wove his way through the Maidens toward Rand. They ignored him—they all seemed to be watching Adelin and Enaila speaking to Moiraine or else eyeing Rand—and his face was tight by the time he had to pause for the solid circle of *Far Dareis Mai* around Jeade'en. They were slow in parting, and did so just enough to let him through to Rand's stirrup.

"I was sure you must be safe. I was sure." From his tone of voice, he had been no such thing. When Rand did not speak, Asmodean shrugged uncomfortably. "Moiraine insisted I carry water. A forceful woman, to not allow the Lord Dragon's bard to . . ." Trailing off, he licked his lips quickly. "What happened?"

"Sammael," Rand said, but not in answer. He was just speaking the thoughts that drifted through the Void. "I remember when he was first named Destroyer of Hope. After he betrayed the Gates of Hevan, and carried the Shadow down into the Rorn M'doi and the heart of Satelle. Hope did seem to die that day. Culan Cuhan wept. What is wrong?" Asmodean's face had gone as white as Sulin's hair; he only shook his head mutely. Rand peered at the pavilion. Whoever was speaking now, he did not know her. "Is that where they are waiting for me? Then I should join them."

"They will not welcome you yet," Lan said, appearing beside Asmodean, who jumped, "or any man." Rand had not heard or seen the Warder approach either, but he only turned his head. Even that seemed an effort. It seemed to be someone else's head. "They meet with Wise Ones from the Miagoma, the Codarra, the Shiande and the Daryne."

"The clans are coming to me," Rand said flatly. But they had waited long enough to make today bloodier. It never happened like that in the stories.

"So it seems. But the four chiefs will not meet you until the Wise Ones have made their arrangements," Lan added dryly. "Come. Moiraine can tell you more than I of it."

Rand shook his head. "Done is done. I can hear details later. If Han doesn't need to keep them from our backs any longer, then I need him. Sulin, send a runner. Han—"

"It *is* done, Rand," the Warder said insistently. "All of it. Only a few Shaido remain south of the city. Thousands have been taken prisoner, and most of the rest are crossing the Gaelin. Word would have been sent to you an hour ago, had anyone known where you were. You've kept moving. Come and let Moiraine tell you."

"Done? We've won?"

"You have won. Completely."

Rand peered at the men being bandaged, the patient

lines awaiting bandages and those leaving with them. The rows that lay almost unmoving. Moiraine was still making her way along those, pausing wearily here and there to Heal. Only a few of the wounded would be here, of course. They would have been coming as they could throughout the day, leaving as and when they could. If they could. None of the dead would be here. *Only a battle lost is sadder than a battle won.* He seemed to remember saying that before, long ago. Perhaps he had read it.

No. There were too many living in his responsibility for him to worry over the dead. *But how many faces will I know, like Jolien's? I will never forget Ilyena, not if all the world burns!*

Frowning, he raised a hand to his head. Those thoughts had seemed to come on top of one another, from different places. He was so tired he could hardly think. But he needed to, needed thoughts that did not slide by almost beyond his reach. He released the Source and the Void, and convulsed as *saidin* almost drove him under in that moment of retreat. He barely had time to realize his mistake. With the Power gone, exhaustion and pain crashed down on him.

He was aware of faces turned up to him as he toppled from his saddle, mouths moving, hands reaching to grab him, cushion his fall.

"Moiraine!" Lan shouted, voice hollow in Rand's ears. "He is bleeding badly!"

Sulin had his head cradled in her arms. "Hold on, Rand al'Thor," she said urgently. "Hold on."

Asmodean said nothing, but his face was bleak, and Rand felt a trickle of *saidin* flowing into him from the man. Darkness came.

CHAPTER
45

After the Storm

Sitting on a small boulder jutting from the foot of the slope, Mat winced as he pulled his broad-brimmed hat lower against the midmorning sun. Partly to shield his eyes from the sun. There was another thing he did not want to see, though cuts and bruises reminded him, especially the arrow slash along his temple that the hat pressed against. An ointment from Daerid's saddle-bags had stopped the bleeding, there and elsewhere, yet everything still hurt, and most of it stung. That part would grow worse. The heat of the day was just beginning to take hold, but sweat was beading up on his face and already dampening his smallclothes and shirt. Idly he wondered whether autumn would ever come to Cairhien. At least discomfort kept him from thinking how tired he was; even after a night with no sleep he would have lain awake in a feather bed, much less blankets on the ground. Not that he wanted to be anywhere near his tent in any case.

A fine bloody to-do. Nearly killed, I'm sweating like a pig, I can't find a comfortable place to stretch out, and I don't dare get drunk. Blood and bloody ashes! He stopped fingering a slice across the chest of his coat—an inch difference, and that spear would have gone through his heart; Light, but the man had been good!—and put that part of it out of his mind. Not that it was easy, with what was going on all around him.

For once the Tairens and Cairhienin did not seem to mind seeing Aiel tents in every direction. There were even Aiel right in the camp, and almost as miraculously, Tairens mingling with Cairhienin among the smoky cookfires. Not that anyone was eating; the kettles had not been set on the fires, although he could smell meat burning somewhere. Instead, most were as drunk as they could manage on wine, brandy, or Aiel *oosquai*, laughing and celebrating. Not far from where he sat, a dozen Defenders of the Stone, stripped to sweaty shirtsleeves, were dancing to the claps of ten times as many watchers. In a line, with arms around each others' shoulders, they stepped so quickly that it was a wonder none of them tripped or kicked the man next to them. For another circle of onlookers, near a ten-foot pole stuck in the ground—Mat hastily averted his eyes—as many Aielmen were doing some kicking of their own. Mat assumed it was a dance; another Aiel was playing the pipes for them. They leaped as high as they could, flung one foot even higher, then landed on that foot and immediately leaped upward again, faster and faster, sometimes spinning like horizontal tops at the height of their leaps, or turning somersaults or backflips. Seven or eight Tairens and Cairhienin sat nursing broken bones from trying it, all the while cheering and laughing like madmen, passing a stone crock of something back and forth. In other places other men were dancing, and maybe singing. It was hard to say, in the din. Without stirring, he could count ten flutes, not to mention twice as many tin whistles, and a skinny Cairhienin in a ragged coat was blowing something that looked part flute and part horn with some odd bits tossed in. And there were countless drums, most of them pots being banged with spoons.

In short, the camp was bedlam and a ball rolled into one. He recognized it, mainly from those memories he could still assign to other men if he concentrated hard enough. A celebration of still being alive. One more time they had walked under the Dark One's nose and survived to tell the tale. One more dance along the razor's edge finished. Almost dead yesterday, maybe dead tomorrow, but alive, gloriously alive, today. He did not feel like celebrating. What good was being alive if it meant living in a cage?

He shook his head as Daerid, Estean and a heavyset red-haired Aielman he did not know staggered by, holding each other up. Barely audible through the clamor, Daerid and Estean were trying to teach the taller man between them the words to "Dance with Jak o' the Shadows."

> *"We'll sing all night, and drink all day,*
> *and on the girls we'll spend our pay,*
> *and when it's gone, then we'll away,*
> *to dance with Jak o' the Shadows."*

The sun-dark fellow showed no interest in learning, of course—he would not unless they convinced him it was a proper battle hymn—but he listened, and he was not the only one. By the time the three passed out of sight in the milling crowd, they had acquired a tail of twenty more, waving dented pewter cups and tarred-leather mugs, all bellowing the tune at the top of their lungs.

> *"There're some delight in ale and wine,*
> *and some in girls with ankles fine,*
> *but my delight, yes, always mine,*
> *is to dance with Jak o' the Shadows."*

Mat wished he had never taught any of them the song. The teaching had just kept his mind occupied while Daerid stopped him from bleeding to death; that ointment stung as bad as the gashes themselves had, and Daerid would never make a seamstress jealous with his delicate handling of needle and thread. Only, the song had spread from that first dozen like fire in dry grass. Tairens and Cairhienin, horse and foot, had all been singing it when they returned at dawn.

Returned. Right back to the hill valley where they had started, below the ruin of the log tower, and no chance for him to get away. He had offered to ride ahead, and Talmanes and Nalesean nearly came to blows over who was to provide his escort. Not everyone had become the best of friends. All he needed now was for Moiraine to come asking questions about where he had been and why, nattering at him about *ta'veren* and duty, about the Pattern and Tarmon Gai'don, until his head spun. Doubtless she was with Rand now, but she would get around to him eventually.

He glanced up at the hilltop and the tangle of shattered logs among broken trees. That Cairhienin fellow who had made the looking glasses for Rand was up there with his apprentices, poking about. The Aiel had been full of what happened there. It was definitely past time for him to be gone. The foxhead medallion protected him from women channeling, but he had heard enough from Rand to know a man's channeling was different. He had no interest in finding out whether the thing would shield him from Sammael and his ilk.

Grimacing at darts of pain, he used the black-hafted spear to lever himself to his feet. Around him the celebration went on. If he drifted down to the picket lines now . . . He was not looking forward to saddling Pips.

"The hero should not sit without drinking."

Startled, he jerked around, grunting at the stab of his wounds, to stare at Melindhra. She had a large clay pitcher in one hand, not spears, and her face was not veiled, but her eyes seemed to be weighing him. "Now listen, Melindhra, I can explain everything."

"What must be explained?" she asked, flinging her free arm around his shoulders. Even with the sudden jolt, he tried to stand straighter; he still was not used to having to look up at a woman. "I knew you would seek your own honor. The *Car'a'carn* casts a great shadow, but no man wishes to spend his life in the shade."

Closing his mouth hurriedly, he managed a faint, "Of course." She was not going to try to kill him. "That's it exactly." In his relief, he took the pitcher from her, but his gulp turned into a splutter. It was the rawest double-distilled brandy he had ever tasted.

She retrieved the pitcher long enough to take a draw, then sighed gratefully and pushed it back at him. "He was a man of much honor, Mat Cauthon. Better that you had captured him, but even by killing him, you have gained much *ji*. It was well that you sought him out."

Despite himself, Mat looked at what he had been avoiding, and shivered. A leather cord tied in short flame-red hair held Couladin's head atop the ten-foot pole near where the Aielmen were dancing. The thing seemed to be grinning. At him.

Sought Couladin out? He had done his best to keep the pikes between him and *any* of the Shaido. But that arrow had clipped the side of his head, and he was on the ground before he knew it, struggling to get to his feet with the fight raging all around him, laying about him with the raven-marked spear, trying to make it back to Pips. Couladin had appeared as if springing out of air, veiled for killing, but there had been no mistaking those bare arms, entwined with Dragons glittering gold-and-red. The man had been cutting a swath into the pikemen with his spears, shouting for Rand to show himself, shouting that *he* was the true *Car'a'carn*. Maybe he really believed it by then. Mat still did not know whether Couladin had recognized him, but it had made no difference, not when the fellow decided to carve a hole through him to find Rand. He did not know who had cut off Couladin's head afterward, either.

I was too busy trying to stay alive to watch, he thought sourly. And hoping he would not bleed to death. Back in the Two Rivers he had been as fine a hand with a quarterstaff as anyone, and a quarterstaff was not so different from a spear, but Couladin must have been born with the things in his hands. Of course, that skill had not availed the man much in the end. *Maybe I still have a little bit of luck. Please, Light, let it show itself now!*

He was thinking of how to get rid of Melindhra so he could saddle Pips when Talmanes presented himself with a formal bow, hand to heart in the Cairhienin fashion. "Grace favor you, Mat."

"And you," Mat said absently. She was not going to go because he asked. Asking would certainly put a fox in the henyard. Maybe if he told her he wanted to take a ride. They said Aiel could run down horses.

"A delegation came from the city during the night. There will be a triumphal procession for the Lord Dragon, in gratitude from Cairhien."

"Will there?" She had to have duties of some sort. The Maidens were always flocking around Rand; maybe she would be called off for that. Glancing at her though, he did not think he had better count on it. Her wide smile was . . . proprietary.

"The delegation was from the High Lord Meilan," Nalesean said, joining them. His bow was just as correct, both hands sweeping wide, but hasty. "It is he who offers the procession to the Lord Dragon."

"Lord Dobraine, Lord Maringil and Lady Colavaere, among others, also came to the Lord Dragon."

Mat pulled his mind back to the moment. Each of the pair was trying to pretend the other of them did not exist—both looking right at him, with never the flicker of an eye toward each other—but their faces were as tight as their voices from the strain, their hands white-knuckled on sword hilts. It would be a cap to everything if they came to blows, and him likely still trying to hobble out of reach when one of them ran him through by accident. "What does it matter who sent a delegation, as long as Rand gets his procession?"

"It matters that you should ask him for our rightful place at the head," Talmanes said quickly. "You slew Couladin, and earned us that place." Nalesean closed his mouth and scowled; plainly he had been about to say the same thing.

"You two ask him," Mat said. "It's none of my affair." Melindhra's hand tightened on the back of his neck, but he did not care. Moiraine would surely not be far from Rand. He was not about to put his neck in a second noose while still trying to think his way out of the first.

Talmanes and Nalesean gaped at him as if he were demented. "You are our battle leader," Nalesean protested. "Our general."

"My bodyservant will polish your boots," Talmanes put in with a small smile that he carefully did not direct at the square-faced Tairen, "and brush and mend your clothes. So you will appear at your best."

Nalesean gave his oiled beard a jerk; his eyes darted halfway to the other man before he could stop them. "If I may offer, I have a good coat I think will fit you well. Gold satin and crimson." It was the Cairhienin's turn to glower.

"General!" Mat exclaimed, holding himself up with the spear haft. "I'm no flaming—! I mean, I wouldn't want to usurp your place." Let them figure out which one of them he meant.

"Burn my soul," Nalesean said, "it was your battle skill that won for us, and kept us alive. Not to mention your luck. I've heard how you always turn the right card, but it is more than that. I'd follow you if you had never met the Lord Dragon."

"You are our leader," Talmanes said right on top of him, in a voice more sober if no less certain. "Until yesterday I have followed men of other lands because I must. You I will follow because I want to. Perhaps you are not a lord in Andor, but here, I say that you are, and I pledge myself your man."

Cairhienin and Tairen stared at one another as though startled at voicing the same sentiment, then slowly, relucantly, exchanged brief nods. If they did not like each other—and only a fool would bet against that—they could meet on this point. After a fashion.

"I will send my groom to prepare your horse for the procession," Talmanes said, and barely frowned when Nalesean added, "Mine can share the work. Your mount must do us proud. And burn my soul, we need a banner. Your banner." At that the Cairhienin nodded emphatically.

Mat was not sure whether to laugh hysterically or sit down and cry. Those bloody memories. If not for them, he would have ridden on. If not for Rand, he would not have the things. He could trace the steps that led to them, each necessary as it seemed at the time and seeming an end in itself, yet each leading inevitably to the next. At the beginning of it all lay Rand. And bloody *ta'veren*. He could not understand why doing something that seemed absolutely necessary and as close to harmless as he could make it always seemed to lead him deeper into the mire. Melindhra had begun stroking the back of his neck instead of squeezing it. All he needed now . . .

He glanced up the hill, and there she was. Moiraine, on her delicate-stepping white mare, with Lan on his black stallion towering at her side. The Warder bent toward her as if to listen, and there seemed to be a brief argument, a violent protest on his part, but after a moment the Aes Sedai reined Aldieb around and rode out of sight toward the opposite slope. Lan remained where he was on Mandarb, watching the camp below. Watching Mat.

He shivered. Couladin's head really did appear to be grinning at him. He could almost hear the man speak. *You may have killed me, but you've put your foot squarely in the trap. I'm dead, but you'll never be free.*

"Just bloody wonderful," he muttered, and took a long, choking swallow of the rough brandy. Talmanes and Nalesean seemed to think he meant it as said, and Melindhra laughed agreement.

Some fifty or so Tairens and Cairhienin had gathered to watch the two lords speak to him, and they took his drinking as a signal to serenade him, beginning with a verse of their own.

> *"We'll toss the dice however they fall,*
> *and snuggle the girls be they short or tall,*
> *then follow young Mat whenever he calls,*
> *to dance with Jak o' the Shadows."*

With a wheezing laugh he could not stop, Mat sank back down onto the boulder and set about emptying the pitcher. There had to be some way out of this. There just had to be.

Rand's eyes opened slowly, staring up at the roof of his tent. He was naked beneath a single blanket. The absence of pain seemed almost startling, yet he felt even weaker than he remembered. And he did remember. He had said things, thought things. . . . His skin went cold. *I cannot let him take control. I am me! Me!* Fumbling beneath the blanket, he found the smooth round scar on his side, tender yet whole.

"Moiraine Sedai Healed you," Aviendha said, and he gave a start.

He had not seen her, sitting cross-legged on the layered rugs near the firepit, sipping from a silver cup worked with leopards. Asmodean lay sprawled across tasseled cushions, chin on his arms. Neither appeared to have slept; dark circles underlined their eyes.

"She should not have had to," Aviendha went on in a cool voice. Tired or not, she had every hair in place, and her neat clothes were a sharp contrast to Asmodean's rumpled dark velvets. Now and then she twisted the ivory bracelet of roses-and-thorns that he had given her as if not realizing what she was doing. She wore the silver snowflake necklace, too. She still had not told him who had given it to her, though she had seemed amused when she realized he really wanted to know. She certainly did not look amused now. "Moiraine Sedai herself was near collapse from Healing wounded. *Aan'allein* had to carry her to her tent. Because of you, Rand al'Thor. Because Healing you took the last of her strength."

"The Aes Sedai is on her feet already," Asmodean put in, stifling a yawn. He ignored Aviendha's pointed stare. "She has been here twice since sunrise, though she said you would recover. I think she was not so certain last night. Nor was I." Pulling his gilded harp around in front of him, he fussed with it, speaking in an idle tone. "I did what I could for you, of course—my life and fortune are tied to yours—but my talents lie elsewhere than Healing, you understand." He strummed a few notes to demonstrate. "I understand that a man can kill or gentle himself doing what you did. Strength in the Power is useless if the body is exhausted. *Saidin* can easily kill, if the body is exhausted. Or so I have heard."

"Are you finished sharing your wisdom, Jasin Natael?" Aviendha's tone was chillier, if anything, and she did not wait for a reply before turning a gaze like blue-green ice back to Rand. The interruption, it seemed, was his fault. "A man may behave like a fool sometimes, and little is the worse for it, but a chief must be more than a man, and the chief of chiefs more still. You had no right to push yourself near to death. Egwene and I tried to make you come with us when we grew too tired to continue, but you would not listen. You may be as much stronger than we as Egwene claims, yet you are still flesh. You are the *Car'a'carn,* not a new *Seia Doon* seeking honor. You have *toh,* obligation, to the Aiel, Rand al'Thor, and you cannot fulfill it dead. You cannot do everything yourself."

For a moment he could only gape at her. He had barely managed to do anything at all, had left the battle to others for all practical purposes while he stumbled about trying to be useful. He had not even been able to stop Sammael from striking where and as he chose. And she upbraided him for doing too much.

"I will try to remember," he said finally. Even so, she looked ready to lecture more. "What news of the Miagoma and the other three clans?" he asked, as much to divert her as because he wanted to know. Women seldom seemed willing to stop until they had hammered you into the ground, unless you managed to distract them.

It worked. She was full of what she knew, of course, and as eager to instruct as to scold. Asmodean's soft strumming—for once, something pleasant, even pastoral—made an odd background for her words.

The Miagoma, the Shiande, the Daryne and the Codarra were camped within sight of one another, a few miles to the east. A steady stream of men and Maidens moved between the camps, including Rand's, but only among societies, and Indirian and the other chiefs were not stirring. There was no doubt now that they would come to Rand eventually, but not until the Wise Ones finished their talks.

"They are still talking?" Rand said. "What under the Light do they have to discuss that takes so long? The chiefs are coming to follow me, not them."

She gave him a flat look that would have done credit to

Moiraine. "The Wise Ones' words are for Wise Ones, Rand al'Thor." Hesitating, she added, as if making a concession, "Egwene may tell you something of it. When it is done." Her tone implied that Egwene might not, too.

She resisted his attempts to learn more, and finally he let it lie. Perhaps he would find out before it bit him, and perhaps not, but either way, he was not going to pry one word out of her that she did not want to speak. Aes Sedai had nothing on Aiel Wise Ones when it came to guarding their secrets and surrounding themselves with mystery. Aviendha was absorbing that particular lesson very well.

Egwene's presence at the meeting of Wise Ones came as a surprise, and so did Moiraine's absence—he would have expected her to be in the middle, twitching strings to her plans—but it turned out that one grew from the other. The new-come Wise Ones had wanted to meet with one of the Aes Sedai who followed the *Car'a'carn*, and although she was back on her feet after Healing him, Moiraine claimed to have no time. Egwene had been routed from her blankets as a replacement.

That made Aviendha laugh. She had been outside when Sorilea and Bair practically dragged Egwene from her tent, trying to pull on her clothes while they hustled her along. "I called to her that she would have to dig holes in the ground with her teeth this time if she had been caught in a misdeed, and she was so sleepy she believed me. She began protesting that she would not, so hard that Sorilea began demanding what she had done to think she deserved to. You should have seen Egwene's face." She laughed so hard that she nearly toppled over.

Asmodean actually looked at her askance—though why he should, being what and who he was, was beyond Rand—but Rand only waited patiently until she caught her breath. For Aiel humor, this was mild. More the sort of thing he would have expected from Mat than from any woman, but mild even so.

When she straightened, wiping her eyes, he said, "What of the Shaido, then? Or are their Wise Ones also at this conclave?"

She answered still giggling into her wine; she considered the Shaido finished, hardly worth considering now.

Thousands of prisoners had been taken, with a trickle still being brought in, and the fighting had died down except for a few small skirmishes here and there. Yet the more he got out of her, the less he could see them as done for. With the four clans keeping Han occupied, the bulk of Couladin's people had crossed the Gaelin in good order, even carrying away most of the Cairhienin prisoners they had captured. Worse, they had destroyed the stone bridges behind them.

That did not concern her, but it did him. Tens of thousands of Shaido north of the river, no way to get at them until the bridges were replaced, and even wooden spans would take time. It was time that he did not have.

At the very end, when it seemed there was no more to say on the Shaido, she told him what made him forget worrying about the Shaido and what trouble they would cause. She just tossed it in, as if she had almost forgotten.

"Mat killed Couladin?" he said incredulously when she was done. "Mat?"

"Did I not say so?" The words were sharp, but halfhearted. Peering at him over her winecup, she seemed more interested in how he would take the news than in whether he doubted her word.

Asmodean plucked a few chords of something martial; the harp seemed to echo to drums and trumpets. "In some ways, a young man of as many surprises as you. I truly look forward to meeting the third of you, this Perrin, one day."

Rand shook his head. So Mat had not escaped the pull of *ta'veren* to *ta'veren* after all. Or maybe it was the Pattern that had caught him, and being *ta'veren* himself. Either way, he suspected Mat was not too happy right that moment. Mat had not learned the lesson that he had. Try to run away, and the Pattern pulled you back, often roughly; run in the direction the Wheel wove you, and sometimes you could manage a little control over your life. Sometimes. With luck, maybe more than any expected, at least in the long haul. But he had more urgent concerns than Mat, or the Shaido.

A glance at the entrance told him the sun was well up, though all he saw otherwise was two Maidens squatting just outside, spears across their knees. A night and most of a morning with him unconscious, and Sammael had either not tried to find him or had failed.

He was careful to use that name, even to himself, though another floated in the back of his mind now. Tel Janin Aellinsar. No history recorded the name, no fragment in the library at Tar Valon; Moiraine had told him everything the Aes Sedai knew of the Forsaken, and it was little more than was told in village tales. Even Asmodean had always called him Sammael, if for a different reason. Long before the War of the Shadow ended, the Forsaken had embraced the names men had given them, as if symbols of rebirth in the Shadow. Asmodean's own true name—Joar Addam Nessosin— made the man flinch, and he claimed to have forgotten the others in the course of three thousand years.

Perhaps there was no real reason to hide what was going on inside his head—maybe it was only an attempt to deny reality to himself—but Sammael the man would remain. And as Sammael, he would pay in full for every Maiden he had killed. The Maidens Rand had not been able to keep safe.

Even as he made the resolution, he grimaced. He had made a beginning by sending Weiramon back to Tear— the Light willing, only he and Weiramon knew how much of one, so far—but he could not go chasing off after Sammael, whatever he wanted or vowed. Not yet. There were matters to be seen to here in Cairhien, first. Aviendha might think he did not understand *ji'e'toh,* and perhaps he did not, but he understood duty, and he had one to Cairhien. Besides, there were ways to tail it in with Weiramon.

Sitting up—and trying not to show the effort of it—he covered himself as decently as he could in the blanket and wondered where his clothes were; he did not see anything but his boots, standing over behind Aviendha. She probably knew. It might have been *gai'shain* who undressed him, but it could just as easily have been she. "I need to go into the city. Natael, have Jeade'en saddled and brought up."

"Tomorrow, perhaps," Aviendha told him firmly,

catching Asmodean's coatsleeve as he started to rise. "Moiraine Sedai said you would need to rest for—"

"Today, Aviendha. Now. I don't know why Meilan isn't here, if he's alive, but I mean to find out. Natael, my horse?"

She put on a stubborn face, but Asmodean jerked his arm free, smoothing the wrinkled velvet, and said, "Meilan was here, and others."

"He was not to be told—" Aviendha began angrily, then tightened her mouth before finishing, "He needs to rest."

So the Wise Ones thought they could keep things from him. Well, he was not as weak as they believed. He tried to stand, holding the blanket close, and turned the motion into shifting his position when his legs refused to cooperate. Maybe he was as weak as they thought. But he did not intend to let that stop him.

"I can rest when I'm dead," he said, and wished he had not when she flinched as if he had hit her. No, she would not have flinched at a blow. His staying alive was important to her for the Aiel's sake, and a threat there could hurt her more than a fist. "Tell me about Meilan, Natael."

Aviendha kept a sullen silence, though if looks had had anything to do with it, Asmodean would have been struck dumb as well.

A rider had come from Meilan in the night, bearing flowery praises and assurances of undying loyalty. At dawn Meilan himself appeared, with the six other High Lords of Tear who were in the city and a small host of Tairen soldiers who fingered sword hilts and gripped lances as though more than half expecting to fight the Aiel who had stood silently watching them ride in.

"It came close," Asmodean said. "This Meilan is not used to being thwarted, I think, and the others scarcely more so. Especially the lumpy-faced one—Torean?— and Simaan. That one has eyes as sharp as his nose. You know I am used to dangerous company, but these men are as dangerous in their way as any I have known."

Aviendha sniffed loudly. "Whatever they are used to, they had no choice with Sorilea and Amys and Bair and

Melaine on one side, and Sulin with a thousand *Far Dareis Mai* on the other. And there were some Stone Dogs," she conceded, "and a few Water Seekers and some Red Shields. If you truly serve the *Car'a'carn* as you claim, Jasin Natael, you should guard his rest as they do."

"It is the Dragon Reborn I follow, young woman. The *Car'a'carn,* I leave to you."

"Go on, Natael," Rand said impatiently, earning a sniff for himself.

She was right concerning the Tairens' choices, though perhaps the Maidens and others fingering their veils had concerned them more than the Wise Ones. In any case, even Aracome, a graying, slender man with a long-smoldering temper, had been near bursting aflame by the time they reined their horses around, and Gueyam, bald as a stone and wide as a blacksmith, was white-faced in rage. Asmodean was not sure whether it had been the certainty of being overwhelmed that stopped them drawing swords, or the realization that if they somehow managed to cut a path to Rand, he was unlikely to welcome them with his allies' blood on their blades.

"Meilan's eyes were bulging out of his head," the man finished. "But before leaving, he shouted out his allegiance and fealty to you. Perhaps he thought you might hear. The others echoed him quickly, yet Meilan added something that made them stare. 'I make a gift of Cairhien to the Lord Dragon,' he said. Then he announced that he would prepare a grand triumph for you when you're ready to enter the city."

"There's an old saying in the Two Rivers," Rand said dryly. "'The louder a man tells you he's honest, the harder you must hold on to your purse.'" Another said, "The fox often offers to give the duck its pond." Cairhien was his without gifts from Meilan.

He had no doubts about the man's loyalty. It would last just as long as Meilan believed he would be destroyed if caught betraying Rand. If caught; that was the hook. Those seven High Lords in Cairhien had been the most assiduous in trying to see him dead in Tear. That was why he had sent them here. Had he executed every

Tairen noble who plotted against him, there might have been none left. At the time, handing them anarchy, famine and civil war to deal with a thousand miles from Tear had seemed a good way to put a crimp in their schemes while doing some good where it needed doing. Of course, he had not even known Couladin existed then, much less that the man would lead him to Cairhien.

It would be easier if this was a story, he thought. In stories, there were only so many surprises before the hero knew everything he needed; he himself never seemed to know a quarter of everything.

Asmodean hesitated—that old saying about shouting men might be applied to him, too, as he was no doubt aware—but when Rand said no more, he added, "I think he wants to be King of Cairhien. Subject to you, of course."

"And preferably with me far away." Meilan probably expected Rand to return to Tear, and to *Callandor.* Meilan certainly would never be afraid of too much power.

"Of course." Asmodean sounded even drier than Rand had. "There was another visit between those two." A dozen Cairhienin lords and ladies, without retainers, came cloaked and with faces hidden in their hoods despite the heat. Plainly they knew that the Aiel despised Cairhienin, and just as plainly returned the sentiment, yet they were as nervous that Meilan might discover they had come as that the Aiel might decide to kill them. "When they saw me," Asmodean said wryly, "half seemed ready to kill me for fear I was Tairen. You have *Far Dareis Mai* to thank that you still have a bard."

Few as they were, the Cairhienin had still been harder to turn back than Meilan, growing sweatier and more white-faced by the minute, but stubbornly demanding to see the Lord Dragon. It was a measure of their desire that when demands failed, they finally descended to open begging. Asmodean might have thought Aiel humor odd or harsh, but he chuckled over nobles in silk coats and riding dresses trying to pretend he was not there as they knelt to catch at the Wise Ones' woolen skirts.

"Sorilea threatened to have them stripped and flogged back to the city." His muted laughter turned disbelieving. "They actually discussed it among themselves. Had the requirement allowed them to reach you, I do believe some would have accepted."

"Sorilea should have done it," Aviendha put in, surprisingly agreeable. "The oathbreakers have no honor. At last Melaine had the Maidens throw them across their horses like bundles and run the animals from camp, with the oathbreakers hanging on as they might."

Asmodean nodded. "But before that, two of them did speak to me, once they were certain I was not a Tairen spy. Lord Dobraine, and Lady Colavaere. They clouded everything in so many hints and innuendos that I cannot be certain, but I would not be surprised if they mean to offer you the Sun Throne. They could bandy words with . . . some people I used to be acquainted with."

Rand barked a laugh. "Maybe they will. If they can manage the same terms as Meilan." He had not needed Moiraine to tell him that Cairhienin played the Game of Houses in their sleep, nor Asmodean to tell him they would try it with the Forsaken. The High Lords to the left and the Cairhienin to the right. One battle done, and another, of a different sort if no less dangerous, beginning. "In any case, I mean the Sun Throne for someone who has a right to it." He ignored the speculation on Asmodean's face; perhaps the man had tried to help him the night before and perhaps he had not, but he did not trust the fellow enough to let him know half of his plans. However much Asmodean's future might be tied to his, his loyalty was all necessity, and he was still the same man who had chosen to give his soul to the Shadow. "Meilan wants to give me a grand entry when I am ready, does he? So much the better that I see what's what before he expects me." It came to him why Aviendha had become so agreeable, even helping the talk along. As long as he sat here talking, he was doing exactly what she wanted. "Are you going to get my horse, Natael, or must I?"

Asmodean's bow was deep, formal, and on the surface, at least, sincere. "I serve the Lord Dragon."

Other Battles, Other Weapons

Frowning after Asmodean and wondering how far he trusted the man, Rand was startled when Aviendha threw down her cup, splashing wine onto the rugs. Aiel did not waste anything that could be drunk, not only water.

Staring at the wet spot, she appeared just as surprised, but only for a moment. The next instant she had planted fists on hips where she sat and was glaring at him. "So the *Car'a'carn* will enter the city when he can barely sit up. I said the *Car'a'carn* must be more than other men, but I did not know he was more than mortal."

"Where are my clothes, Aviendha?"

"You are only flesh!"

"My clothes?"

"Remember your *toh*, Rand al'Thor. If I can remember *ji'e'toh*, so can you." That seemed a strange thing to say; the sun would rise at midnight before she forgot the smallest scrap of *ji'e'toh*.

"If you keep on like this," he said with a smile, "I will begin thinking you care for me."

He meant it for a jest—there were only two ways to

deal with her, joke or simply override her; arguing was fatal—and a mild one considering they had spent a night in each other's arms, but her eyes went wide in outrage, and she jerked at the ivory bracelet as if to pull it off and throw it at him. "The *Car'a'carn* is so far above other men that he does not need clothes," she spat. "If he wishes to go, let him go in his skin! Must I bring Sorilea and Bair? Or perhaps Enaila, and Somara, and Lamelle?"

He stiffened. Of all the Maidens who treated him as a long-lost son of ten, she had chosen the three worst. Lamelle even brought him soup—the woman could not cook a lick, but she insisted on making him soup! "You bring whoever you wish," he told her in a tight, flat voice, "but I *am* the *Car'a'carn,* and I *am* going into the city." With luck, he could find his clothes before she returned. Somara was nearly as tall as he, and, at the moment, probably stronger. The One Power certainly would do him no good; he could not have embraced *saidin* if Sammael appeared in front of him, much less held onto it.

For a long moment she met his stare, then abruptly picked up the leopard-worked cup and refilled it from a hammered-silver pitcher. "If you can find your clothes and dress yourself without falling down," she said calmly, "you may go. But I will accompany you, and if I think you are too weak to continue, you will return here if Somara must carry you in her arms."

He stared as she stretched out on one elbow, carefully arranged her skirts, and began sipping at her wine. If he mentioned marriage again, no doubt she would snap his head off again, but in some ways she behaved as if they were married. The worst parts of it, at least. The parts that did not seem a pennyworth different from Enaila or Lamelle at *their* worst.

Muttering to himself, he gathered the blanket around him and shuffled past her and the firepit to his boots. Clean woolen stockings were folded up inside, but nothing else. He could summon *gai'shain.* And have the entire matter spread through the camp. Not to mention the possibility that the Maidens would get into it after all; then the question would be whether he was the

Car'a'carn, who must be obeyed, or just Rand al'Thor, another man entirely in their eyes. A rolled rug at the back of the tent caught his eye; rugs were always spread out. His sword was inside, the belt with the Dragon buckle wrapped around the scabbard.

Humming to herself, eyes lidded, Aviendha looked half asleep as she watched him search. "You no longer need . . . *that*." She invested the word with so much disgust that no one would have believed she had given him the sword.

"What do you mean?" There were only a few small chests in the tent, inlaid with mother-of-pearl or worked in brass, or in one case, gold leaf. The Aiel preferred putting things in bundles. None held his clothes. The gold-covered chest, all unfamiliar birds and animals, held tightly tied leather sacks and gave off a smell of spices when he raised the lid.

"Couladin is dead, Rand al'Thor."

Startled, he stopped and stared at her. "What are you talking about?" Would Lan have told her? No one else knew. But why?

"No one told me, if that is what you are thinking. I know you now, Rand al'Thor. I learn you more every day."

"I wasn't thinking any such thing," he growled. "There isn't anything anybody could tell." Irritably, he snatched up the scabbarded sword and carried it awkwardly under his arm as he went on searching. Aviendha continued sipping wine; he thought she might be hiding a smile.

A fine thing. The High Lords of Tear sweated when Rand al'Thor looked at them, and the Cairhienin might offer him their throne. The greatest Aiel army the world had ever seen had crossed the Dragonwall on the orders of the *Car'a'carn*, the chief of chiefs. Nations trembled at mention of the Dragon Reborn. Nations! And if he did not find his clothes, he would sit waiting on permission to go outside from a lot of women who thought they knew better about everything than he did.

He finally found them when he noticed the gold-embroidered cuff of a red coatsleeve sticking out from under Aviendha. She had been sitting on them all along.

She grunted sourly when he asked her to move, but she did it. Finally.

As usual, she watched him shave and dress, channeling the water hot for him without comment—and without being asked—after the third time he nicked himself and muttered about cold water. In truth, this time he was bothered as much because she might see his unsteadiness as for any other cause. *You can become used to anything if it goes on long enough,* he thought wryly.

She misunderstood his head shaking. "Elayne will not mind if I look, Rand al'Thor."

Pausing with the laces of his shirt half done, he stared at her. "Do you really believe that?"

"Of course. You belong to her, but she cannot own the sight of you."

Laughing silently, he went back to the laces. It was good to be reminded that her newfound mystery hid ignorance, aside from anything else. He could not help smiling smugly as he finished dressing, buckled on his sword and took up the tasseled Seanchan spearhead. That last turned the smile a touch toward grimness. He had meant it as a reminder that the Seanchan were still in the world, but it served to recall all the things that he must juggle. Cairhienin and Tairens, Sammael and the other Forsaken, the Shaido and nations that did not know him yet, nations that would have to before Tarmon Gai'don. Dealing with Aviendha was really quite simple compared with that.

Maidens leaped to their feet when he ducked out of the tent quickly to hide the unsteadiness of his legs. He was not sure how far he succeeded. Aviendha kept to his side as though she not only intended to catch him if he fell over but fully expected him to. It did nothing for his mood when Sulin, in her cap of bandages, looked questioningly at her—not him; her!—and waited for her nod before ordering the Maidens to be ready to move.

Asmodean came riding his mule up the hill, leading Jeade'en by the reins. Somehow he had found time to don fresh clothes, all dark green silk. With spills of white lace, of course. The gilded harp hung on his back, but he had given up wearing the gleeman's cloak, and he no longer carried the crimson banner with its ancient symbol of the Aes Sedai. That office fell to a Cairhienin refugee named Pevin, an expressionless fellow in a patched farmer's coat of rough dark gray wool, on a brown mule that should have been put out to grass from pulling a cart some years back. A long scar, still red, ran up the side of his narrow face from jaw to thinning hair.

Pevin had lost his wife and sister to the famine, his brother and a son to the civil war. He had no idea which Houses' men had killed them, or who they had supported for the Sun Throne. Fleeing toward Andor had cost him a second son at the hands of Andoran soldiers and a second brother to bandits, and returning had cost the last son, dead on a Shaido spear, and his daughter as well, carried off while Pevin was left for dead. The man rarely spoke, but as near as Rand could make out, his beliefs had been winnowed down to a bare three. The Dragon had been Reborn. The Last Battle was coming. And if he stayed close to Rand al'Thor, he would see his family avenged before the world was destroyed. The world would end, surely, but it did not matter, nothing did, so long as he saw that vengeance. He bowed silently to Rand from his saddle as the mare reached the crest. His face was absolutely blank, but he held the banner straight and steady.

Climbing onto Jeade'en, Rand pulled Aviendha up behind him without letting her use a stirrup, just to show her that he could, and kicked the dapple into motion before she was settled. She flung both arms around his waist, grumbling only partly under her breath; he caught a few more snippets of her current opinion of Rand al'Thor, and of the *Car'a'carn,* too. She made no move to let go, though, for which he was grateful. Not only was it pleasant having her pressed against his back, the support was welcome. With her halfway to the saddle, he had suddenly not been sure whether she was coming up or he down. He hoped she had not noticed. He hoped that was not why she was holding on to him so tightly.

The crimson banner with its large black-and-white disc rippled behind Pevin as they zigzagged down the hill and along the shallow valleys. As usual, the Aiel gave little attention to the party as it passed, though the banner marked his presence as surely as the encircling escort of several hundred *Far Dareis Mai* easily keeping pace with Jeade'en and the mules. They went on about their business among the tents covering the slopes, at most glancing up at the sound of hooves.

It had been startling to hear of nearly twenty thousand prisoners taken from Couladin's followers—until leaving the Two Rivers, he had never really believed so many people could be in one place—but seeing them was twice the shock. In clusters of forty or fifty, they dotted the hillsides like cabbages, men and women alike sitting naked in the sun, each cluster under the eyes of one *gai'shain* if that. Certainly no one else paid them much mind, though now and again a *cadin'sor*-clad figure approached one of the groups and ordered a man or woman off on an errand. Whoever was called out went at a run, unguarded, and Rand saw several returning to slip back into their places. For the rest, they sat quietly, almost looking bored, as if they had no reason to be elsewhere, or desire to be, either.

Perhaps they would put on white robes just as calmly. Yet he could not help remembering how easily these same people had violated their own laws and customs already. Couladin might have begun the violation or ordered it, but they had followed and obeyed.

Frowning at the prisoners—twenty thousand, and more to come; he would certainly never trust one to hold to *gai'shain*—it took some time before he noticed an oddity among the other Aiel. Maidens and Aielmen who carried the spear never wore anything on their heads except the *shoufa,* and never any color that would not fade into rocks and shadows, but now he saw men with a narrow scarlet headband. Perhaps one in four or five had a strip of cloth knotted around his temples, with a disc embroidered or painted above the brows, two joined teardrops, black and white. Perhaps most strangely of all, *gai'shain* wore it, too; most had their cowls up, but every last bareheaded one wore it. And *algai'd'siswai* in their *cadin'sor* saw and did nothing, whether wearing the headband or not. *Gai'shain* were never to wear anything that those who could touch weapons did. Never.

"I do not know," Aviendha said curtly into his back when he asked what it meant. He tried to sit up straighter; she really did seem to be holding to him more tightly than necessary. After a moment, she went on, so softly that he had to listen sharp to catch it all. "Bair threatened to strike me if I mentioned it again, and Sorilea hit me across the shoulders with a stick, but I think they are those who claim we are *siswai'aman.*"

Rand opened his mouth to ask the meaning—he knew a scant few words of the Old Tongue, no more—when interpretation floated to the surface in his mind. *Siswai'aman.* Literally, the spear of the Dragon.

"Sometimes," Asmodean chuckled, "it is difficult to see the difference between oneself and one's enemies. They want to own the world, but it seems you already own a people."

Turning his head, Rand stared at him until amusement faded and, shrugging uncomfortably, he let his mule fall back beside Pevin and the banner. The trouble was that the name did imply—more than implied—ownership; that was out of Lews Therin's memories, too. It did not seem possible to own people, but if it was, he did not want to. *All I want is to use them,* he thought wryly.

"I see you don't believe it," he said over his shoulder. None of the Maidens had donned the thing.

Aviendha hesitated before saying, "I do not know what to believe." She spoke as quietly as before, yet she sounded angry, and unsure. "There are many beliefs, and the Wise Ones are often silent, as if they do not know the truth. Some say that in following you, we expiate the sin of our ancestors in . . . in failing the Aes Sedai."

The catch in her voice startled him; he had never considered that she might be as worried as any other Aiel about what he had revealed of their past. Ashamed might be a better word than worried; shame was an important part of *ji'e'toh.* They were ashamed of what they had been—followers of the Way of the Leaf—and at the same time ashamed that they had abandoned their pledge to it.

"Too many have heard some version of part of the Prophecy of Rhuidean now," she went on in a more controlled tone, for all the world as if she had heard a word of that prophecy herself before she began training to become a Wise One, "but it has been twisted. They know that you will destroy us . . ." Her control faltered for the space of one deep breath. "But many believe that you will kill us all in endless dances of the spear, a sacrifice to atone for the sin. Others believe that the bleakness itself is a testing, to wear away all but the hard core before the Last Battle. I have even heard some say that the Aiel are now your dream, and that when you wake from this life, we will be no more."

A grim set of beliefs, that. Bad enough that he had revealed a past they saw as shaming. It was a wonder they had not all left him. Or gone mad. "What do the Wise Ones believe?" he asked, as quietly as she.

"That what must be, will be. We will save what can be saved, Rand al'Thor. We do not hope to do more."

We. She included herself among the Wise Ones, just as Egwene and Elayne included themselves among Aes Sedai. "Well," he said lightly, "I expect Sorilea at least believes I should have my ears boxed. Probably Bair does, too. And certainly Melaine."

"Among other things," she mumbled. To his disappointment, she pushed away from him, although keeping a hold on his coat. "They believe many things I could wish they did not."

He grinned in spite of himself. So she did not believe he needed his ears boxed. That was a pleasant change since waking.

Hadnan Kadere's wagons lay a mile or so from his tent, circled in a broad depression between two hills where Stone Dogs kept watch. A cream-colored coat straining over his bulk, the hatchet-nosed Darkfriend looked up, mopping his face with the inevitable large handkerchief, as Rand rode past with his banner and loping escort. Moiraine was there as well, examining the wagon where the doorframe *ter'angreal* was lashed under canvas behind the driver's seat. She did not even glance around until Kadere spoke to her. By his gestures, he was plainly suggesting that she might want to accompany Rand. In fact, he appeared eager for her to go, and small wonder. He had to be congratulating himself on keeping his being a Darkfriend hidden so long, but the more he was in company with an Aes Sedai, the more he was in danger of discovery.

Indeed, it was a surprise to Rand that the man was still there. At least half of the drivers who had entered the Waste with him had slipped away since crossing the Dragonwall, replaced by Cairhienin refugees chosen by Rand himself, to make sure they were not of Kadere's sort. He expected every morning to find the fellow himself gone, too, especially since Isendre's escape. The Maidens had nearly torn the wagons apart looking for the woman, while Kadere sweated his way through three handkerchiefs. Rand would not regret it if Kadere managed to sneak off in the night. The Aiel guards had orders to let him go, so long as he did not try to take Moiraine's precious wagons. More obviously every day, their loads were a treasure to her, and Rand would not see her lose them.

He glanced over his shoulder, but Asmodean was staring straight ahead, ignoring the wagons altogether. He claimed to have had no contact with Kadere since Rand captured him, and Rand thought it might be true. Certainly, the merchant never left his wagons, and was never out of sight of Aiel guards except when inside his own wagon.

Opposite the wagons, Rand half drew rein without thinking. Surely Moiraine would want to accompany him into Cairhien; she might have crammed his head full, but it always seemed there was another piece she wanted to fit in, and this once in particular he could do with her presence and advice. But she merely looked at him for a long moment, then turned back to the wagon.

Frowning, he heeled the dapple on. As well to remember she had other sheep to shear than he knew about. He had become too trusting. Best to be as wary of her as of Asmodean.

Trust no one, he thought bleakly. For an instant he did not know whether it was his thought or Lews Therin's, but in the end he decided it did not matter. Everybody had their own goals, their own desires. Much the best to trust no one completely except himself. Yet he wondered, with another man oozing through the back of his mind, how far could he trust himself?

Vultures filled the sky around Cairhien in spiraling layers of black wings. On the ground they flapped about among clouds of buzzing flies, squawking hoarsely at glossy ravens that tried to usurp their rights to the dead. Where Aiel went across the treeless hills, recovering the bodies of their slain, the birds lumbered aloft fatly, screeching protests, then settled again as soon as the living humans were a few paces gone. Vultures and ravens and flies together could not really have made the sunlight dimmer, yet it seemed so.

Stomach twisting, trying not to see, Rand heeled Jeade'en faster, until Aviendha clung to his back once more and the Maidens were running. No one protested, and he did not believe it was only because Aiel could maintain that speed for hours. Even Asmodean looked pale around the eyes. Pevin's face never changed, though the bright banner whipping above him appeared a mockery in that place.

What lay ahead was little better. Rand remembered the Foregate as a raucous beehive, a tangled warren of streets full of noise and color. Now it was a still, thick band of ashes surrounding the square gray walls of Cairhien on three sides. Charred timbers lay crazily atop stone foundations, and here and there a soot-black chimney yet stood, sometimes tilting precariously. In places, a chair lying somehow untouched in the dirt street, a hasty bundle dropped by someone fleeing, a rag doll, emphasized the desolation.

Breezes stirred some of the banners on the city's towers and along the walls, a Dragon standing out red-and-gold on white at one place, the Crescents of Tear white on red-and-gold at another. The middle set of the Jangai Gates stood open, three tall square arches in the gray stone guarded by Tairen soldiers in rimmed helmets. Some were mounted but most afoot, and the variously colored stripes on their wide sleeves showed they were retainers of several lords.

Whatever was known in the city about the battle being won, and Aiel allies coming to the rescue, the approach of half a thousand *Far Dareis Mai* created some little stir. Hands went uncertainly to sword hilts, or spears and long shields, or lances. Some of the soldiers half moved as if to close the gates even while looking to their officer, with three white plumes on his helmet, who hesitated, standing in his stirrups and shading his eyes against the sun to study the crimson banner. And more particularly, Rand.

Abruptly the officer sat down, saying something that sent two of the mounted Tairens galloping back through the gates. Almost immediately, he was waving the other men aside, calling, "Make way for the Lord Dragon Rand al'Thor! The Light illumine the Lord Dragon! All glory to the Dragon Reborn!"

The soldiers still appeared uneasy about the Maidens, but they formed into lines to either side of the gates, bowing deeply as Rand rode through. Aviendha sniffed loudly at his back, and again when he laughed. She did not understand, and he had no intention of explaining. What amused him was that however hard Tairens or Cairhienin or anyone else tried to puff up his head, he could rely on her and the Maidens, at least, to take the swelling down. And Egwene. And Moiraine. And Elayne and Nynaeve, for that matter, if he ever saw either again. Come to think of it, the lot of them seemed to make that a large part of their life's work.

The city beyond the gates stilled his laughter.

Here the streets were paved, some broad enough for a dozen or more large wagons abreast, all straight as knife cuts and crossing at right angles. The hills that rolled outside the walls were here carved and terraced, faced with stone; they looked as much made by men as the stone buildings with their severe straight lines and sharp angles, or the great towers with their unfinished tops, surrounded by scaffolding. People crowded the streets and the alleys, dull-eyed and hollow-cheeked, huddling beneath makeshift lean-tos or ragged blankets rigged as tents, or simply jammed together in the open, in the dark clothes favored by Cairhienin city dwellers and the bright colors of Foregaters and the rough garb of farmers and villagers. Even the scaffolds were filled, on every level to the very top, where folk looked tiny for the height. Only the middle of the streets remained clear as Rand and the Maidens made their way along, and that only for as long as it took the people to surge out around them.

It was the people who stilled his mirth. Worn and ragged as they were, jammed together like sheep in a too-small pen, they cheered. He had no idea how they knew who he was, unless perhaps the officer's shouts at the gates had been heard, but a roar sprang ahead of him as he circled through the streets, the Maidens forcing a way through the throng. The thunder of it overwhelmed any words except for the occasional "Lord Dragon" when enough shouted it together, but the meaning was clear in men and women holding up children to see him pass, in scarves and scraps of cloth waved from every window, in people who tried to push past the Maidens with outstretched hands.

They certainly seemed to have no fear of Aiel, not at the chance to lay a finger on Rand's boots, and their numbers were such, the pressure of hundreds shoving them forward, that some managed to wriggle through. Actually, a good many touched Asmodean's instead—he certainly looked a lord, in all his dripping lace, and perhaps they thought the Lord Dragon must be an older man than the youth in a red coat—but it made no difference. Whoever managed to put hand to anyone's boot or stirrup, even Pevin's, wore joy on their faces and mouthed "Lord Dragon" into the din even as Maidens forced them back with their bucklers.

Between the clamor of acclaim and the riders sent by the officer at the gate it was no surprise when Meilan appeared, a dozen lesser Tairen lords for retinue and fifty Defenders of the Stone to clear his way, laying about them with the butts of their lances. Gray-haired, hard and lean in his fine silk coat with stripes and cuffs of green satin, the High Lord sat his saddle with the stiff-backed ease of one who had been put on a horse and taught to command it almost as soon as he could walk. He ignored the sweat on his face, and equally the possibility that his escort might trample someone. Both were minor annoyances and the sweat likely the greater.

Edorion, the pink-cheeked lordling who had come to

Eianrod, was among the others, not quite so plump as he had been, so his red-striped coat hung on him. The only other Rand recognized was a broad-shouldered fellow in shades of green; Reimon had liked to play at cards with Mat back in the Stone, as he recalled. The others were older men for the most part. None displayed any more consideration of the crowd they plowed through than Meilan. There was not one Cairhienin in the lot.

The Maidens let Meilan ride through when Rand nodded, but closed behind him to exclude the rest, a fact the High Lord did not notice at first. When he did, his dark eyes smoldered angrily. He was often angry, Meilan was, since Rand had first come to the Stone of Tear.

The noise began to abate with the Tairen arrival, fading to a dull murmur by the time Meilan made a rigid bow to Rand from his saddle. His gaze flickered to Aviendha before he decided to ignore her, just as he was trying to ignore the Maidens. "The Light illumine you, my Lord Dragon. Be you well come to Cairhien. I must apologize for the peasants, but I was unaware you meant to enter the city now. Had I known, they would have been cleared. I meant to give you a grand entry, befitting the Dragon Reborn."

"I have had one," Rand said, and the other man blinked.

"As you say, my Lord Dragon." He went on after a moment, his tone making it clear that he did not understand. "If you will accompany me to the Royal Palace, I have arranged a small greeting. Small indeed, I fear, since I had no warning of you, yet by this even I will make sure—"

"Whatever you have arranged now will do," Rand cut in, and received another bow and a thin, oily smile for reply. The fellow was all subservience now, and in an hour he would be talking as to someone too feeble-witted to understand facts held under his nose, but beneath it all lay a contempt and hatred that he believed Rand did not see although they shone in his eyes. Contempt because Rand was not a lord—not truly, as Meilan saw it, by birth—and hatred because Meilan had had the power of life and death before Rand came, with few his equal and none his superior. To believe that the Prophecies of the Dragon would be fulfilled someday was one thing; to have them fulfilled, and his own power diminished by them, was quite another.

There was a moment of confusion before Rand made Sulin allow the other Tairen lords to bring their horses in behind Asmodean and Pevin's banner. Meilan would have had the Defenders clear the way again, but Rand curtly ordered that they follow behind the Maidens. The soldiers obeyed, faces unchanging beneath the rims of their helmets, though their white-plumed officer shook his head, and the High Lord put on a condescending smile. That smile faded when it became clear that the crowds opened up easily ahead of the Maidens. That they did not have to club a path through, he attributed to the Aiel reputation for savagery, and frowned when Rand made no reply. One thing Rand made note of: Now that he had Tairens with him, the cheers did not rise again.

The Royal Palace of Cairhien occupied the highest hill of the city, exactly in the center, square and dark and massive. In fact, between the palace in all its levels and the stone-faced terracing, it was hard to say there was a hill there at all. Lofty colonnaded walks and tall narrow windows, high above the ground, did no more to relieve the ridigity than did gray, stepped towers precisely placed in concentric squares of increasing height. The street became a long, broad ramp leading up to tall bronze gates, and a huge square courtyard beyond lined with Tairen soldiers standing like statues, spears slanted. More stood on the overlooking stone balconies.

A ripple of murmurs ran through the ranks at the appearance of the Maidens, but it was quickly stilled in chanted shouts of "All glory to the Dragon Reborn! All glory to the Lord Dragon and Tear! All glory to the Lord Dragon and the High Lord Meilan!" From Meilan's expression, you would have thought it all spontaneous.

Dark-garbed servants, the first Cairhienin Rand had seen in the palace, rushed out with worked golden bowls and white linen cloths as he swung a leg over the high pommel and slid from his saddle. Others came to take reins. He took the excuse of bathing his face and hands in cool water to leave Aviendha to climb down by herself.

Trying to help her down might have ended with them both flat on the paving stones.

Unprompted, Sulin chose out twenty Maidens besides herself to accompany him within. On the one hand, he was glad she did not want to keep every last spear around him. On the other hand, he wished Enaila, Lamelle and Somara were not among the twenty. The considering looks they gave him—especially Lamelle, a lean, strong-jawed woman with dark red hair, nearly twenty years older than he—made him grind his teeth while trying to smile reassuringly. Somehow Aviendha must have managed to speak to them, and to Sulin, behind his back. *I may not be able to do anything about the Maidens,* he thought grimly as he tossed a linen towel back to one of the serving men, *but burn me if there isn't* one *Aiel woman who'll learn I'm the* Car'a'carn!

The other High Lords greeted him at the foot of the broad gray stairs that led up from the courtyard, all in colorful silk coats and satin stripes and silver-worked boots. It was plain that none were aware Meilan had gone to meet him until after the fact. Potato-faced Torean, oddly languid for such a lumpy man, sniffed anxiously at a scented handkerchief. Gueyam, oiled beard making his head seem even balder, clenched fists the size of small hams and glared at Meilan even as he bowed to Rand. Simaan's sharp nose seemed to quiver in outrage; Maraconn, with blue eyes rare in Tear, compressed his thin lips until they almost disappeared; and while Hearne's narrow face was all smiles, he tugged unconsciously at one earlobe as he did when furious. Only blade-slender Aracome showed no outward emotion, but then he almost always kept his anger well banked until ready to let it burst into flame.

It was too good an opportunity to miss. Silently thanking Moiraine for her lessons—it was easier to trip a fool than to knock him down, she said—Rand clasped Torean's pudgy hand warmly and clapped Gueyam on the point of a thick shoulder, returned Hearne's smile with one warm enough for a close companion and nodded silently to Aracome with a seemingly significant glance. Simaan and Maraconn he all but ignored after one look as flat and cool as a deep winter pond for each.

That was all it needed for the moment, beyond watching their eyes shift and faces tighten in thought. They had played *Daes Dae'mar,* the Game of Houses, their entire lives, and being among Cairhienin, who could read volumes in a raised eyebrow or a cough, had only heightened their sensitivity. Each man knew Rand had no reason to be friendly toward him, but each had to wonder if his own greeting was only to cover something real with someone else. Simaan and Maraconn appeared the most worried, yet the others eyed those two perhaps the most suspiciously of all. Perhaps his coolness had been the true cover. Or maybe that was what they were meant to think.

For himself, Rand thought that Moiraine would be proud of him, and so would Thom Merrilin. Even if none of these seven was actively plotting against him at the moment—something he did not think even Mat would bet on—men in their positions could do much to disrupt his plans without being seen to, and they would do so from habit if for no other reason. Or they would have. He had them off balance now. If he could keep them that way, they would be too busy watching each other, and too afraid of being watched in turn, to trouble him. They might even obey for once without finding a hundred reasons why things should be done differently from what he wanted. Well, that might be asking too much.

His satisfaction slipped when he saw Asmodean's sardonic grin. Worse was Aviendha's wondering stare. She had been in the Stone of Tear; she knew who these men were, and why he had sent them here. *I do what I must,* he thought sourly, and wished it did not sound as if he were trying to excuse himself.

"Inside," he said, more sharply than he intended, and the seven High Lords jumped as if suddenly recalling who and what he was.

They wanted to crowd around him as he climbed the stairs, but except for Meilan to show the way, the Maidens simply made a solid circle around him, and the High Lords brought up the rear with Asmodean and the lesser lords. Avienda stuck close by . . . of course, and Sulin was on his other side, Somara and Lamelle and

Enaila right behind him. They could have reached out and touched his back without stretching. He gave Aviendha an accusing look, and she arched her eyebrows at him so questioningly that he almost believed she had nothing to do with it. Almost.

The corridors of the palace were empty except for dark-liveried servants who bowed almost chest to knees or curtsied just as deeply as he passed, but when he entered the Grand Hall of the Sun he discovered that the Cairhienin nobility had not been excluded from the palace entirely.

"The Dragon Reborn comes," intoned a white-haired man just inside the huge gilded doors worked with the Rising Sun. His red coat embroidered with six-pointed stars in blue, a little large on him after his time in Cairhien, marked him for an upper servant of Meilan's House. "All hail the Lord Dragon Rand al'Thor. All glory to the Lord Dragon."

A quick roar filled the chamber to its angle-vaulted ceiling, fifty paces up. "Hail the Lord Dragon Rand al'Thor! All glory to the Lord Dragon! The Light illumine the Lord Dragon!" The silence that followed seemed twice as still by comparison.

Between massive square columns of marble thick-streaked with blue so deep it was almost black stood more Tairens than Rand expected, ranks of Lords and Ladies of the Land dressed in their finest, in peaked velvet hats and coats with puffy, striped sleeves, in colorful gowns and lace ruffs and close-fitting caps intricately embroidered or sewn with pearls or small gems.

To their rear were the Cairhienin, darkly garbed except for slashes of color across the breast of gown or knee-length coat. The more stripes in House colors, the higher the rank of the wearer, but men and women with color from neck to waist or lower stood behind Tairens clearly of minor Houses, with yellow embroidery instead of thread-of-gold and wool instead of silk. No few of the Cairhienin men had shaved and powdered the front of their heads; all of the younger men had.

The Tairens looked expectant, if uneasy; the Cairhienin faces could have been chiseled from ice.

There was no way to say who had cheered and who not, but Rand suspected most of those cries had come from the front rows.

"A good many wished to serve you here," Meilan murmured as they made their way up the blue-tiled floor with its great golden mosaic of the Rising Sun. A ripple of silent curtsies and bows followed.

Rand only grunted. They wished to serve him? He did not need Moiraine to know that these lesser nobles hoped to become greater on estates carved out of Cairhien. No doubt Meilan and the other six had already intimated if not promised which lands would be whose.

At the far end of the Grand Hall, the Sun Throne itself stood centered atop a wide dais of deep blue marble. Even here Cairhienin restraint held, for a throne at any rate. The great heavy-armed chair glittered with gilt and golden silk, but somehow it seemed to be all plain vertical lines, except for the wavy-rayed Rising Sun that would stand above the head of whoever sat on it.

That was meant to be him, Rand realized long before reaching the nine steps to the dais. Aviendha climbed up with him, and Asmodean, as his bard, was allowed up as well, but Sulin quickly arrayed the other Maidens around the dais, their casually held spears blocking Meilan as well as the rest of the High Lords. Frustration painted those Tairen faces. The Hall was so quiet that Rand could hear himself breathe.

"This belongs to someone else," he said finally. "Besides, I've spent too long in the saddle to welcome such a hard seat. Bring me a comfortable chair."

There was a moment of shocked silence before a murmur ran through the Hall. Meilan suddenly wore such a look of speculation, quickly suppressed, that Rand nearly laughed. Very likely Asmodean was right about the man. Asmodean himself was eyeing Rand with barely hidden surmise.

It was some minutes before the fellow in the star-embroidered coat ran up panting, followed by two dark-liveried Cairhienin carrying a high-backed chair piled with silk-covered cushions, and pointed out where to place it with a great many worried glances at Rand. Vertical lines of gilt ran up the chair's heavy legs and back, but it seemed insignificant in front of the Sun Throne.

While the three servants were still bowing themselves away, bending double on every step, Rand tossed most of the cushions to one side and sat down gratefully, the Seanchan spearhead on his knee. He was careful not to sigh, though. Aviendha was watching him too carefully for that, and the way Somara kept glancing from her to him and back confirmed his suspicions.

But whatever his problems with Aviendha and *Far Dareis Mai,* most present awaited his words with equal parts eagerness and trepidation. *At least* they'll *jump when I say "toad,"* he thought. They might not like it, but they would do it.

With Moiraine's help he had worked out what he must do here. Some he had known was right even without her suggestions. It would have been good to have her there to whisper in his ear if needed, instead of Aviendha waiting to signal Somara, but there was no point in waiting. Surely every Tairen and Cairhienin noble in the city was in this chamber.

"Why do the Cairhienin hang back?" he said loudly, and the crowd of nobles shifted, exchanging confused glances. "Tairens came to help, but that is no reason for Cairhienin to hold themselves in the rear here. Let everyone sort themselves by rank. Everyone."

It was difficult to say whether Tairens or Cairhienin were the most stunned, though Meilan looked ready to swallow his tongue, and the other six not far behind. Even slow-burning Aracome went white in the face. With much shuffling of boots and twitching aside of skirts, with many icy stares on both sides, it was done, until the front rows were all men and women with stripes across their chests and the second held only a few Tairens. Meilan and his fellows had been joined at the foot of the dais by twice their number of Cairhienin lords and ladies, most graying and everyone stripes from neck nearly to knees, though perhaps "joined" was not the right word. They stood in two groups, with a full three paces between, and looked away from one another so hard that they might as well have shaken fists and shouted. Every eye was on Rand, and if the Tairens were in a fury, the Cairhienin were still ice, with only hints of a thaw in the considering way they studied him.

"I have noticed the banners flying above Cairhien," he went on once the movement stilled. "It is well that so many of the Crescents of Tear fly. Without Tairen grain, Cairhien would have no living to hoist a banner, and without Tairen swords, the people of this city who survived today, noble as well as common, would be learning to obey the Shaido. Tear has earned her honor." That puffed up the Tairens, of course, bringing fierce nods and fiercer smiles, though it certainly seemed to confuse the High Lords, coming on the heels of the other. For that matter, the Cairhienin below the dais were eyeing one another doubtfully. "But I do not need so many banners for myself. Let one Dragon banner remain, on the highest tower of the city so all who approach can see, but let the rest be taken down and replaced with the banners of Cairhien. This is Cairhien, and the Rising Sun must and will fly proudly. Cairhien has her own honor, which she shall keep."

The chamber erupted in a roar so suddenly that Maidens hefted their spears, a roar that reverberated from wall to wall. In an instant Sulin was flashing Maiden handtalk, but already half-raised veils were being let fall. The Cairhienin nobles were cheering every bit as loudly as the people in the streets had, capering and waving their arms like Foregaters at festival. In the pandemonium it was the Tairens' turn to exchange silent stares. They did not look angry. Even Meilan appeared unsure more than anything else, though like Torean and the others, he watched in amazement the lords and ladies of high rank around him, so coldly dignified a moment before, now dancing and shouting for the Lord Dragon.

Rand did not know what any of them read into his words. Certainly he had expected them to hear more than he said, especially the Cairhienin, and perhaps even that some would hear what he really meant, but nothing had prepared him for this display. Cairhienin reserve was an odd thing, he well knew, mixed at times with unexpected boldness. Moiraine had been reticent on the matter, for all her insistence on trying to teach him everything; the most she had said was that if that reserve broke, it could do so to a surprising degree. Surprising, indeed.

When the cheering finally died down, the giving of oaths of fealty began. Meilan was the first to kneel, tight-faced as he pledged under the Light and by his hope of salvation and rebirth to serve faithfully and obey; it was an old form, and Rand hoped it might actually constrain some to keep the oath. Once Meilan had kissed the tip of the Seanchan spearhead, trying to hide a sour grimace by stroking his beard, he was replaced by the Lady Colavaere. A more than handsome woman in her middle years, with dark ivory lace spilling over the hands she placed between Rand's, and horizontal slashes of color from high lace collar to her knees, she gave the oath in a clear, firm voice and the musical accent he was used to hearing from Moiraine. Her dark gaze had something of the weighing-and-measuring look of Moiraine as well, most especially when she eyed Aviendha as she curtsied her way back down the steps. Torean replaced her, sweating as he swore, and Lord Dobraine replaced Torean, deep-set eyes probing, one of the few older men to have shaved the front of his long, mostly gray hair, then Aracome, and . . .

Rand felt impatience as the procession continued, one by one up to kneel before him, Cairhienin succeeding Tairen succeeding Cairhienin, as he had decreed. This was all necessary, so Moiraine said—and so agreed a voice in his head that he knew for Lews Therin's—but to him it was part of the delay. He must have their loyalty, if only on the surface, in order to begin making Cairhien secure, and that beginning, at least, had to be made before he could move on Sammael. *And that I will do! I have too much to do yet to let him go on stabbing at my ankles from the bushes! He will find out what it means to rouse the Dragon!*

He did not understand why those coming before him began to sweat and lick their lips as they knelt and stammered the words of fealty. But then, he could not see the cold light burning in his own eyes.

CHAPTER
47

The Price of a Ship

Finishing her morning wash, Nynaeve toweled herself dry and pulled on a fresh silk shift reluctantly. Silk was not as cool as linen, and even with the sun only just up, the heat in the wagon foretold another scorching day. Besides which, the thing was cut so she was half afraid it would fall in a puddle around her ankles if she breathed wrong. At least it was not damp with nightsweat, as her discarded one was.

Disturbing dreams had racked her sleep, dreams of Moghedien that woke her bolt upright—and those better than the ones she did not wake out of—dreams of Birgitte shooting arrows at her and *not* missing, dreams of the Prophet's followers rioting through the menagerie, of being stranded forever in Samara because no vessel ever came, of reaching Salidar and finding Elaida in charge. Or Moghedien again, there too. She had wakened weeping from that one.

All just worry, of course, and natural enough. Three nights camped here without a ship appearing, three sweltering days of standing blindfolded against that cursed piece of wall. That was enough to put anyone on edge, even without worrying whether Moghedien was closing in. But then, just because the woman knew they were with a menagerie did not mean she had to find them in Samara. There were other traveling menageries in the world besides those gathered here. Thinking up reasons not to worry was easier than not worrying, though.

But why should I be anxious about Egwene? Dipping a split twig into a small dish of salt-and-soda on the washstand, she began scrubbing her teeth vigorously. Egwene had popped up in nearly every dream, yammering at her, but she could not see how Egwene came into them.

In truth, anxiety and lack of sleep were only part of what made her mood vile this morning. The others were such minor things, but they were realities. A pebble in your shoe was small compared to having your head cut off, but if the pebble was there and the chopping block might never be . . .

It was not possible to avoid her own reflection, and her hair hanging loose about her shoulders instead of decently braided. Brush it how she would, the brassy red color never became less loathsome. And she knew all too well that a blue dress was laid out on the bed behind her. A blue to make even a Tinker woman blink, and cut as low as the original red gown hanging on a peg. That was why she had on this precariously clinging shift. One dress like that was not enough, not according to Valan Luca. Clarine was at work on another pair in a virulent yellow, and there was talk of stripes. Nynaeve did not want to know about stripes.

At least the man could let me choose the colors, she thought, working the split twig furiously. Or Clarine. But no, he had his own ideas, and he never asked. Not Valan Luca. His color choices sometimes made her forget the necklines. *I ought to throw it in his face!* Yet she knew she would not. Birgitte flaunted herself in those dresses without the hint of a blush. The woman was certainly *nothing* like any of the stories about her! Not that she was going to wear the fool dress without protest because Birgitte did. She was not competing with the woman in any way. It was just that . . . "If you have to do a thing," she growled around the twig, "best you get used it."

"What did you say?" Elayne asked. "If you're going to talk, please take that out of your mouth. The noise is disgusting otherwise."

Wiping her chin, Nynaeve glared over her shoulder. Elayne was seated on her own narrow bed with her legs drawn up beside her, braiding her black-dyed hair. She already had on her white breeches, all sewn with spangles, and a snowy silk blouse with ruffles at the neck that was much too sheer. Her sequin-splattered white coat lay beside her. White. She also had two suits of clothes for performing, with a third in the making, all in white, if not exactly plain. "If you are going to dress in that fashion, Elayne, you should not sit so. It's indecent."

The other woman glowered sullenly, but she did put her slippered feet on the floor. And raised her chin in that haughty way she had. "I think I may take a walk into the town this morning," she said coolly, still working at the braid. "This wagon is . . . confining."

Rinsing her mouth, Nynaeve spat into the washbowl. Loudly. The wagon certainly did seem smaller by the day. Maybe they did need to keep out of sight as much as possible—it had been her idea, one she was coming to regret—but this was becoming ridiculous. Three days shut up with Elayne except when they went to perform was beginning to feel like three weeks. Or three months. She had never before realized what an acid tongue Elayne had. A ship had to come. Any kind of ship. She would give every last coin hidden in the brick stove, every last jewel, anything, for a ship today. "Well, that wouldn't attract any attention, would it? But perhaps you could use the exercise. Or maybe it's just the way those breeches fit your hips."

Blue eyes flared, but Elayne's chin remained high and her tone cold. "I dreamed about Egwene last night, and between going on about Rand and Cairhien—*I* worry about what is happening there, even if *you* do not—in between, she said you were turning into a screaming harridan. Not that *I* think so, necessarily. *I* would have said a fishmonger."

"Now you listen to me, you ill-tempered little chit! If you don't—"

Still glaring, Nynaeve snapped her mouth shut, then drew breath slowly. With an effort she forced her voice to be level. "You dreamed about Egwene?" Elayne nodded curtly. "And she talked of Rand and Cairhien?" The younger woman rolled her eyes in exaggerated exasperation and went on with her braid. Nynaeve made her hand loose its fistful of brassy red hair, made herself stop thinking of teaching the Daughter-Heir of bloody Andor some simple common courtesy. If they did not find a ship soon . . . "If you can think of anything except how to show more of your legs than you already are, it might interest you to know that she was in my dreams, too. She said Rand won a great victory at Cairhien yesterday."

"I may be exposing my legs," Elayne barked, spots of color rising in her cheeks, "but at least I am not flashing my— You dreamed of her, too?"

It did not take long to compare notes, though Elayne continued to show a viperish tongue; Nynaeve had had a perfectly good reason for screaming at Egwene, and Elayne probably *had* been dreaming of parading in front of Rand in her sequined costume, if not less. Saying so was simple honesty. Even so, it quickly became clear that Egwene had said the same things in both their dreams, and that left little room for doubt.

"She kept saying she was really there," Nynaeve muttered, "but I thought it was just part of the dream." Egwene had told them often enough that it was possible, talking to someone in her dreams, but she had never said that she could. "Why should I have believed? I mean, she said she'd finally recognized some spear he's taken to carrying as Seanchan work. That's preposterous."

"Of course." Elayne arched one eyebrow in an irritating manner. "Just as preposterous as finding Cerandin and her *s'redit*. There *must* be other Seanchan refugees, Nynaeve, and spears are likely the *least* of what they left behind."

Why could the woman not say anything without a barb? "I notice how well *you* believed."

Elayne threw the finished braid over her shoulder, then tossed her head again, superciliously, for good measure. "I do hope Rand is all right." Nynaeve sniffed; Egwene had said he would need days of rest before he was on his feet again but he *had* been Healed. The other woman continued, "No one has ever taught him he mustn't overextend himself. Doesn't he know the Power can kill him if he draws too much, or weaves when tired? That much is the same for him as for us."

So she meant to change the subject, did she? "Perhaps he doesn't know," Nynaeve told her sweetly, "since there isn't a White Tower for men." That made her think of something else. "Do you think it really was Sammael?"

Caught with a retort on the tip of her tongue, Elayne glowered at her sideways, then heaved a peevish sigh. "It hardly matters to us, does it? What we should be thinking about is using the ring again. For more than meeting Egwene. There is so much to learn. The more I do learn, the more I know how much I don't know yet."

"No." Nynaeve did not really expect the other woman to take out the ring *ter'angreal* then and there, but she took a reflexive step toward the brick stove. "No more trips to *Tel'aran'rhiod,* for either of us, except to meet her."

Elayne went right on without appearing to notice. Nynaeve could have been talking to herself. "It isn't as though we need to channel. We won't give ourselves away that way." She did not look at Nynaeve, but there was a hint of bite in her voice. She maintained that they could use the Power, if they were careful. For all Nynaeve knew, Elayne did just that behind her back. "I'll wager if one of us visited the Heart of the Stone tonight, Egwene would be there. Think, if *we* could talk to her in *her* dreams, we'd not need to worry about encountering Moghedien in *Tel'aran'rhiod* any longer."

"You think it's easy to learn, then?" Nynaeve asked dryly. "If that's so, why hasn't she taught us already? Why hasn't she done it before this?" Her heart was not in it, though. She was the one worried about Moghedien. Elayne knew the woman was dangerous, but it was like knowing a viper was dangerous; Elayne knew, but

Nynaeve had been bitten. And being able to communicate without entering the World of Dreams would be valuable quite aside from avoiding Moghedien.

In any case, Elayne still was paying no attention to her. "I wonder why she was so insistent we not tell anyone. That makes no sense." For a moment she worried her underlip with her teeth. "There is another reason to talk to her as soon as we can. It didn't mean anything to me then, but the last time she spoke to me, she vanished in midsentence. What I remember now is that before she did, she suddenly looked surprised, and frightened."

Nynaeve took a deep breath and pressed both hands hard against her stomach in a vain effort to quiet sudden flutters. She managed to keep her voice flat, though. "Moghedien?"

"Light, you do have cheerful thoughts! No. If Moghedien could come into our dreams, I think we would know it by now." Elayne gave a small shiver; she did have some idea of how dangerous Moghedien was. "Anyway, it wasn't that sort of look. She was frightened, but not enough for that."

"Then maybe she isn't in any danger. Maybe . . ." Forcing her hands to her sides, Nynaeve compressed her lips angrily. Only, she was not certain who she was angry with.

Putting the ring away, out of sight, except for meetings with Egwene, had been a good idea. It had. Any venture into the World of Dreams could have found Moghedien, and keeping clear of her was better than a good idea. She already knew she was overmatched. That thought rankled, worse every time she had it, but it was the simple truth.

Yet now there was the chance that Egwene needed help. A small chance. Just because she was properly wary of Moghedien did not mean she was underrating the possibility. And it might be that Rand had one of the Forsaken after him in the same personal way that Moghedien was after her and Elayne. What Egwene reported, both of Cairhien and of the mountains, smacked of one man daring another to knock a chip off his shoulder. Not that she could see anything to do about that. But Egwene . . .

Sometimes it seemed to Nynaeve that she had forgotten why she had left the Two Rivers in the first place. To protect young people from her village who had been caught in Aes Sedai webs. Not that much younger than herself—only a few years—yet the gap seemed wider when you were the village Wisdom. Of course, the Women's Circle in Emond's Field had certainly chosen a new Wisdom by now, but that did not make it less her village, or them less her people. In her heart of hearts, it made her no less the Wisdom. Somehow, though, protecting Rand and Egwene and Mat and Perrin from Aes Sedai had become helping them survive, and finally, without her quite realizing when or how, even that goal had been submerged in other needs. Entering the White Tower to learn how better to pull down Moiraine had become a burning desire to learn how to Heal. Even her hatred for Aes Sedai meddling in people's lives now coexisted with her desire to become one. Not that she really wanted to, but it was the only way to learn what she wanted to learn. Everything had become as tangled as one of those Aes Sedai webs, herself included, and she did not know how to escape.

I am still who I always have been. I will *help them, as much as I can.* "Tonight," she said aloud, "I will use the ring." Sitting down on the bed, she began to pull on her stockings. Stout wool was hardly comfortable in this heat, but at least part of her would be decently clothed. Stout stockings, and stout shoes. Birgitte wore brocaded slippers, and gossamer silk stockings that surely looked cool. She put the thought firmly out of her head. "Just to see if Egwene *is* in the Stone. If she isn't, I will come back, and we won't use the ring again until the next scheduled meeting."

Elayne watched her, with an unblinking stare that made her tug at her stockings in increasing discomfort. The woman did not say a word, but her expressionless gaze implied that Nynaeve might be lying. To Nynaeve it did. It did not help that the thought had flittered on the edge of consciousness, that she could easily make sure the ring was not touching her skin when she went to sleep; there was no real reason to believe that Egwene would be waiting in the Heart of the Stone tonight. She had never really considered it—the thought had drifted up unbidden—but it had been there, and made it hard to meet Elayne's eyes. What if she was afraid of Moghedien? It was only good sense, however it galled to admit it.

I will do what I must. She clamped down firmly on butterflies in the pit of her belly. By the time she tossed the shift down over her stockings, she was eager to don the blue dress and go out into the heat just to escape Elayne's eyes.

Elayne was just finishing helping her with the rows of small buttons up the back—and muttering that no one had helped *her,* as if anyone needed help with breeches —when the wagon door banged open, letting in a wave of hot air. Startled, Nynaeve jumped and covered her bosom with both hands before she could stop herself. When Birgitte climbed in instead of Valan Luca, she tried to pretend she was adjusting the neckline.

Smoothing identical brilliant blue silk over her hip, the taller woman pulled her thick black braid over one bare shoulder with a self-pleased grin. "If you want to draw attention, don't bother fiddling. It is too obvious. Just breathe deeply." She demonstrated, then laughed at Nynaeve's scowl.

Nynaeve made an effort to keep her temper. Though why she should, she did not know. She could hardly imagine that she had felt guilt over what had happened. Gaidal Cain was probably glad to get away from the woman. And Birgitte got to wear her hair the way she wanted. Not that that had anything to do with anything. "I knew someone like you in the Two Rivers, *Maerion.* Calle knew every merchant's guard by his first name, and she certainly had no secrets from any of them."

Birgitte's smile tightened. "And I knew a woman like you, once. Mathena looked down her nose at men, too, and even had a poor fellow executed for coming on her by accident while she swam naked. She had never even been kissed, until Zheres stole one from her. You'd have thought she had discovered men for the first time. She became so besotted, Zheres had to go live on a mountain to escape her. Watch out for the first man to kiss you. One has to come along sooner or later."

Fists clenching, Nynaeve took a step toward her. Or tried to. Somehow Elayne was in between them, hands upraised.

"Both of you stop it this minute," she said, eyeing them in turn with equal haughtiness. "Lini always said 'Waiting turns men into bears in a barn, and women into cats in a sack,' but you will stop clawing at one another right now! I will not put up with it any longer!"

To Nynaeve's surprise, Birgitte actually blushed and mumbled a sullen apology. To Elayne, of course, but the apology itself was the surprise. Birgitte had chosen to stay close to Elayne—there was no need for her to hide—but after three days the heat was apparently affecting her as badly as it did Elayne. For herself, Nynaeve gave the Daughter-Heir her frostiest stare. She had managed to maintain an even disposition while they waited, cooped up together—she had—but Elayne certainly had no room to talk.

"Now," Elayne said, still in that icy tone, "did you have some reason for barging in like a bull, or have you simply forgotten how to knock?"

Nynaeve opened her mouth to say something about cats—just a gentle reminder—but Birgitte forestalled her, if in a tighter voice.

"Thom and Juilin are back from the town."

"Back!" Nynaeve exclaimed, and Birgitte glanced at her before returning to Elayne.

"You did not send them?"

"I did not," Elayne said grimly.

She was out of the door, Birgitte at her heels, before Nynaeve could say a word. There was nothing for it but to follow, grumbling to herself. Elayne had better not suddenly think she was the one giving orders. Nynaeve had still not forgiven her for revealing so much to the men.

The dry heat seemed even worse outside, for all the

sun still sat on the canvas wall around the menagerie. Sweat popped out on her brow before she reached the foot of the ladder, but for once she did not grimace.

The two men sat on three-legged stools beside the cookfire, hair wild and coats looking as if they had rolled in the dirt. A trickle of red ran from beneath a wadded cloth Thom was pressing to his scalp, down across a fan of dried blood that covered his cheek and stained one long white mustache. A purple lump the size of a hen's egg stood out beside Juilin's eye, and he held his thumb-thick staff of pale ridged wood in a hand roughly wrapped with a bloody bandage. That ridiculous conical red cap, sitting on the back of his head, appeared to have been trampled.

From the noises inside the canvas walls, the horse handlers were already at work cleaning cages, and no doubt Cerandin was with her *s'redit*—none of the men would go near them—but there was relatively little stir around the wagons as yet. Petra was smoking his long-stemmed pipe while he helped Clarine prepare their breakfast. Two of the Chavanas were studying some piece of apparatus with Muelin, the contortionist, while the other pair were chatting with two of the six female acrobats Luca had hired away from Sillia Cerano's show. They claimed to be sisters named Murasaka, despite being even more disparate in looks and coloring than the Chavanas. One of the pair lounging in colorful silk robes with Brugh and Taeric had blue eyes and almost white hair, the other skin nearly as dark as her eyes. Everyone else was already garbed for the day's first performance, the men bare-chested in colorful breeches, Muelin in gauzy red and a tight matching vest, Clarine in high-necked green sequins.

Thom and Juilin attracted a few looks, but fortunately no one thought it necessary to come inquire after their health. Perhaps it was the hangdog way they sat, shoulders slumped, eyes on the ground under their boots. Doubtless they knew they were in for a tongue-lashing that would sear their hides. Nynaeve certainly intended to give them one.

Elayne, though, gasped at the sight of them and went running to kneel beside Thom, all the anger of a moment before taking wing. "What happened? Oh, Thom, your poor head. That must hurt so. This is beyond my abilities. Nynaeve will take you inside and see to it. Thom, you are too old to get yourself into scrapes like this."

Indignantly, he fended her off as best he could while holding his compress in place. "Leave over, child. I've had worse than this falling out of bed. Will you leave over?"

Nynaeve was not about to do any Healing, despite being angry enough. She planted herself in front of Juilin, fists on her hips and a brook-no-nonsense, answer-me-right-now look on her face. "What do you mean, sneaking off without telling me?" As well to start letting Elayne know that *she* was not in charge. "If you had gotten your throat cut instead of a mouse on your eye, how would we know what had happened to you? There was no reason for you to go. None! Finding a ship has been seen to."

Juilin glared up at her, shoving his cap forward over his forehead. "Seen to, is it? Is that why the three of you have taken to stalking about like—?" He cut off as Thom groaned loudly and swayed.

Once the old gleeman had quieted Elayne's concerned flutters with protestations that it had just been a momentary pang, that he was fit to attend a ball—and given Juilin a significant glance he obviously hoped the women would not see—Nynaeve turned a dangerous eye back to the dark Tairen, to learn just what it was he thought they had been stalking about like.

"A good thing we did go," he told her instead in a tight voice. "Samara's a school of silverpike around a chunk of bloody meat. There are mobs on every street hunting Darkfriends and anybody else who isn't ready to hail the Prophet as the one true voice of the Dragon Reborn."

"It started three hours or so ago, near the river," Thom put in, giving in with a sigh to Elayne's bathing his face with a damp cloth. He appeared to be ignoring her mutters, which must have taken some doing, since Nynaeve could clearly hear "foolish old man" and "need someone to take care of you before you get yourself killed" among other things in a tone easily as exasperated as it was fond. "How it began, I don't know. I heard Aes Sedai blamed, Whitecloaks, Trollocs, everybody but the Seanchan, and if they knew the name, they'd blame them, too." He winced at Elayne's pressure. "The last hour we were a little too personally involved in getting clear to learn much."

"There are fires," Birgitte said. Petra and his wife noticed her pointing and stood to stare worriedly. Two dark plumes of smoke rose above the canvas wall in the direction of the town.

Juilin rose and looked Nynaeve in the eyes with a hard gaze. "It is time to go. Maybe we'll stand out enough for Moghedien to find us, but I doubt it; there are people running every direction they can run. In another two hours, it won't be a pair of fires, it will be fifty, and avoiding her won't do much good if we're torn to pieces by a mob. They'll turn to the shows once they have smashed what can be smashed in the town."

"Don't use that name," Nynaeve said sharply, with a frown for Elayne that the younger woman did not see. Letting men know too much was always a mistake. The trouble was, he was right, but letting a man know that too quickly was a mistake, too. "I will consider your suggestion, Juilin. I would hate to run away for no reason, and then learn that a ship had come right after we left." He stared at her as if she were mad, and Thom shook his head despite Elayne's holding it still for her washing, but a figure making his way through the wagons brightened Nynaeve. "Perhaps it's come already."

Uno's painted eyepatch and scarred face, his topknot and the sword on his back, attracted casual nods from Petra and the various Chavanas and one shiver from Muelin. He had made each of the evening visits himself, though with nothing to report. His presence now had to mean there was something.

As usual he grinned at Birgitte as soon as he saw her, and rolled his lone eye in an ostentatious stare at her exposed bosom, and as usual she grinned back and eyed him up and down lazily. For once, though, Nynaeve did not care how reprehensibly they behaved. "Is there a ship?"

Uno's grin faded. "There's a bloo—a ship," he said grimly, "if I can get you to it whole."

"We know all about the rioting. Surely fifteen Shienarans can get us safely through."

"You know about the rioting," he muttered, eyeing Thom and Juilin. "Do you fla—do you know Masema's people are fighting Whitecloaks in the streets? Do you know he's bloo—he's ordered his people to take Amadicia with fire and sword? There are thousands across the blo—aagh!—the river already."

"That's as may be," Nynaeve said firmly, "but I expect you to do as you said you would. You promised to obey *me,* if you recall." She put just a slight emphasis on the word, and gave Elayne a meaning look.

Pretending not to see, the woman stood, bloodied washcloth in her hand, and directed her attention to Uno. "I have always been told that Shienarans are among the bravest soldiers in the world." That razor edge to her voice had suddenly become regal silk and honey. "I heard many stories of Shienaran bravery when I was a child." She rested a hand on Thom's shoulder, but her eyes remained on Uno. "I remember them still. I hope I shall always remember them."

Birgitte stepped closer and began massaging the back of Uno's neck while she looked him straight in the eye. That glaring red eye on his eyepatch did not seem to upset her at all. "Three thousand years guarding the Blight," she said gently. Gently. It had been two days since she had spoken to Nynaeve like that! "Three thousand years, and never a step back not paid for ten times over in blood. This may not be Enkara, or the Soralle Step, but I know what you will do."

"What did you do," he growled, "read all the flaming histories of the flaming Borderlands?" Immediately he flinched and glanced at Nynaeve. It had been necessary to tell him she expected absolutely clean language out of him. He was not taking it well, but there was no other way to prevent backsliding, and Birgitte should not frown at her. "Can you talk to them?" he directed at Thom and Juilin. "They're fla—fools to try this."

Juilin flung up his hands, and Thom laughed out loud.

"Did you ever know a woman who listened to sense when she didn't want to?" the gleeman replied. He grunted as Elayne pulled his compress away and began dabbing at his split scalp with perhaps a bit more force than was strictly necessary.

Uno shook his head. "Well, if I'm to be cozened, I suppose I'll be cozened. But mark this. Masema's people found the ship—*Riversnake,* or something like—not an hour after it docked, but Whitecloaks seized it. That's what started this little row. The bad news is the Whitecloaks still hold the docks. The worse is, Masema may have forgotten the ship—I went to see him, and he wouldn't hear of ships; all he can talk about is hanging Whitecloaks, and making Amadicia bend knee to the Lord Dragon if he has to put the whole land to the torch—but he hasn't bothered to tell all of his people. There's been fighting near the river, and may still be. Getting you through the riots will be bad enough, but if there's a battle at the docks, I make no promises. And how I'm to put you on a ship in Whitecloak hands, I don't begin to know." Letting out a long breath, he scrubbed sweat from his forehead with the back of a scarred hand. The strain of so long a speech without cursing was plain on his face.

Nynaeve might have relented on his language at that moment—if she had not been too stunned to speak. It had to be coincidence. *Light, I said anything for a ship, but I didn't mean this. Not this!* She did not know why Elayne and Birgitte were staring at her with such blank expressions. They had known everything she had, and neither had brought up this possibility. The three men exchanged frowns, obviously aware that something was going on and just as obviously unaware what it was, for which thank the Light. Much better when they did not know everything. It just had to be coincidence.

In one way, she was more than happy to focus on another man making his way through the wagons; it gave an excuse to pull her eyes away from Elayne and Birgitte. In another way, the sight of Galad made her stomach settle right to her shoes.

He wore plain brown and a flat velvet cap instead of

his white cloak and burnished mail, but his sword still rested on his hip. He had not been to the wagons before, and the effect of his face was dramatic. Muelin took an unconscious step toward him, and the two slender acrobats leaned forward, mouths open. The Chavanas were plainly forgotten, and scowling for it. Even Clarine smoothed her dress as she watched him, until Petra took his pipe from his mouth and said something. Then she went over to where he sat, laughing, and snuggled his face to her plump bosom. But her eyes still followed Galad over her husband's head.

Nynaeve was in no mood to be affected by a handsome face; her breath hardly quickened at all. "It was you, wasn't it?" she demanded before he even reached her. "You seized the *Riversnake,* didn't you? Why?"

"Riverserpent," he corrected, eyeing her incredulously. "You did ask me to secure you passage."

"I didn't ask you to start a riot!"

"A riot?" Elayne put in. "A war. An invasion. All begun over this vessel."

Galad answered calmly. "I gave Nynaeve my word, sister. My first duty is to see you safely on your way to Caemlyn. And Nynaeve, of course. The Children would have had to fight this Prophet soon or late."

"Couldn't you simply have let us know the ship was here?" Nynaeve asked wearily. Men and their word. It was all very admirable, sometimes, but she should have listened when Elayne said he did what he saw as right no matter who was hurt.

"I don't know what the Prophet wanted the ship for, but I doubt it was so you could take passage downriver." Nynaeve flinched. "Besides which, I paid the captain your passage while he was still unloading his cargo. An hour later, one of the two men I left to make sure he did not sail without you came to tell me the other man was dead and the Prophet had taken the ship. I don't understand what you are so upset about. You wanted a ship, needed a ship, and I got you one." Frowning, Galad addressed Thom and Juilin. "What is the matter with them? Why do they keep staring at one another?"

"Women," Juilin said simply, and got slapped on the

back of the head by Birgitte for his trouble. He glared at her.

"Horseflies have a nasty bite," she grinned, and his glower faded into uncertainty as he readjusted his cap.

"We can sit here all day discussing right and wrong," Thom said dryly, "or we can take this vessel. Passage has been paid, and there's no getting the price back now."

Nynaeve flinched again. However he meant it, she knew how she heard it.

"There may be trouble reaching the river," Galad said. "I donned this clothing because the Children are not popular in Samara at the moment, but the mobs can set on anyone." He eyed Thom doubtfully, with his white hair and long white mustaches, and Juilin a little less so—even disheveled, the Tairen looked hard enough to pound posts—then turned to Uno. "Where is your friend? Another sword might be useful until we reach my men."

Uno's smile was villainous. Clearly, there was no more love between them than at their first meeting. "He's about. And maybe one or two more. I'll see them to the ship, if your Whitecloaks can hold on to it. Or if they can't."

Elayne opened her mouth, but Nynaeve spoke up quickly. "That's enough, both of you!" Elayne would just have tried honeyed words again. They might have worked, but she wanted to lash out. At something, anything. "We need to move quickly." She should have considered, when she flung two madmen at the same target, what might happen if they both hit at once. "Uno, gather the rest of your men, as fast as you can." He tried to tell her they were already waiting on the other side of the menagerie, but she plowed on. They *were* madmen, *both* of them. *All* men were! "Galad, you—"

"Rouse and rise!" Luca's shout cut into her words as he trotted between the wagons, limping, and with a bruise discoloring the side of his face. His scarlet cape was soiled and torn. It seemed Thom and Juilin were not the only ones to have entered the town. "Brugh, go tell the horse handlers to hitch the teams! We'll have to abandon the canvas," he grimaced at the words, "but I mean to be on the road in under an hour! Andaya, Kuan, pull your sisters out! Wake anybody still asleep, and if they're washing, tell them to dress dirty or come naked! Hurry, unless you're ready to proclaim the Prophet and march to Amadicia! Chin Akima's lost his head already, along with half his performers, and Sillia Cerano and a dozen of hers were flogged for being too slow! Move!" By that time, everybody except those around Nynaeve's wagon were at the run.

Luca's limp slowed as he approached, eyeing Galad warily. And Uno, for that matter, though he had seen the one-eyed man twice before. "Nana, I want to talk to you," he said quietly. "Alone."

"We will not be going with you, Master Luca," she told him.

"Alone," he said, and seized her arm, hauling her away.

She looked back to tell the others not to interfere and found there was no need. Elayne and Birgitte were hurrying off toward the canvas wall that encompassed the menagerie, and except for a few glances at her and Luca, the four men were engrossed in conversation. She sniffed loudly. Fine men they were, to watch a woman manhandled and do nothing.

Jerking her arm free, she strode along beside Luca, silk skirts swishing her displeasure. "I suppose you want your money, now that we are going. Well, you shall have it. One hundred gold marks. Though I think you should allow something for the wagon and horses we're leaving behind. And for what we've brought in. We have certainly increased the number of your patrons. Morelin and Juilin with their highwalking, me with the arrows, Thom—"

"Do you think I want the gold, woman?" he demanded rounding on her. "If I did, I'd have asked for it the day we crossed the river! Have I asked? Did you ever think why not?"

In spite of herself, she took a step back, crossing her arms beneath her breasts sternly. And immediately wished she had not; that stance more than emphasized what she was exposing. Stubbornness kept her arms where they were—she was not about to let him think she was flustered, especially since she was—but surprisingly, his eyes remained on hers. Maybe he was ill. He had never avoided looking at her bosom before, and if Valan Luca was not interested in bosoms *or* gold . . . "If not about the gold, then why do you want to talk to me?"

"All the way back here from the town," he said slowly, following her, "I kept thinking that now you would finally go." She refused to back away again, even when he was standing over her and staring down intently. At least he was still looking at her face. "I don't know what you are running from, Nana. Sometimes, I almost believe your story. Morelin certainly has a noblewoman's manner about her, at least. But you were never a lady's maid. The last few days, I've half expected to find the pair of you rolling on the ground tearing one another's hair. And maybe Maerion in the pile." He must have seen something on her face, because he cleared his throat and hurried on. "The point is, I can find someone else for Maerion to shoot at. You do scream so beautifully, anyone would think you were truly terrified, but—" He cleared his throat again, even more hastily, and drew back. "What I am trying to say is that I want you to stay. There's a wide world out there, a thousand towns waiting for a show like mine, and whatever is chasing you will never find you with me. A few of Akima's people, and some of Sillia's who haven't been marched off across the river—they're joining me. Valan Luca's show will be the greatest the world has ever seen."

"Stay? Why should I stay? I told you from the first we only wanted to reach Ghealdan, and nothing has changed."

"Why? Why, to have my children, of course." He took one of her hands in both of his. "Nana, your eyes drink my soul, your lips inflame my heart, your shoulders make my pulse race, your—"

She cut in hurriedly. "You want to marry me?" she said incredulously.

"Marry?" He blinked. "Well . . . uh . . . yes. Yes, of course." His voice picked up strength again, and he pressed her fingers to his lips. "We will be wed at the first town where I can arrange it. I've never asked another woman to marry me."

"I can quite believe it," she said faintly. It took some effort to pull her hand free. "I am sensible of the honor, Master Luca, but—"

"Valan, Nana. Valan."

"But I must decline. I am betrothed to another." Well, she was, in a way. Lan Mandragoran might think his signet ring just a gift, but she saw it differently. "And I am going."

"I should bundle you up and carry you with me." Dirt and rips somewhat spoiled the grandiloquent flourish of his cape as he drew himself up. "With time, you would forget the fellow."

"You try it, and I'll have Uno make you wish you had been sliced for sausage." That barely deflated the fool man at all. She drove a finger hard against his chest. "You do not know me, Valan Luca. You don't know anything about me. My enemies, the ones you dismiss so easily, would make you take off your skin and dance in your bones, and you would be grateful if that was all they did. Now, I am going, and I don't have time to listen to your drivel. No, don't say any more! My mind is set, and you will not change it, so you might as well stop blathering."

Luca sighed heavily. "You are the only woman for me, Nana. Let other men choose boring flutterers with their shy sighs. A man would know he had to walk through fire and tame a lioness with his bare hands every time he approached you. Every day an adventure, and every night . . ." His smile almost earned him boxed ears. "I will find you again, Nana, and you will choose me. I know it in here." Thumping his chest dramatically, he gave his cape an even more pretentious swirl. "And you know it, too, my dearest Nana. In your fair heart, you do."

Nynaeve did not know whether to shake her head or gape. Men *were* mad. *All* of them.

He insisted on escorting her back to her wagon, holding her arm as if they were at a ball.

* * *

Stalking though the turmoil of horse handlers rushing to hitch teams, the din of men shouting, horses whickering, bears growling, leopards coughing, Elayne found herself muttering under her breath to match any of the animals. Nynaeve had no room to talk about her showing her legs. She had seen the way the woman stood up straighter when Valan Luca appeared. And breathed deeper, too. For Galad as well, for that matter. It was not as if she *enjoyed* wearing breeches. They *were* comfortable, true, and cooler than skirts. She could see why Min chose to wear men's clothes. Almost. There was the problem of getting past the feeling that the coat was really a dress that barely covered your hips. She had just managed that, so far. Not that she intended to let Nynaeve know, her and her viperish tongue. The woman should have realized Galad would ignore the cost of keeping his promise. It was not as if Elayne had not told her about him often enough. And involving the Prophet! Nynaeve just acted without thinking about what she was doing.

"Did you say something?" Birgitte asked. She had gathered her skirts over one arm to keep up, unashamedly baring her legs from blue brocaded slippers to *well* above her knees, and those sheer silk stockings did not hide as much as breeches.

Elayne stopped dead. "What do you think of how I am dressed?"

"It allows freedom of movement," the other woman said judiciously. Elayne nodded. "Of course, it's good that your bottom isn't too big, as tight as those—"

Striding on furiously, Elayne tugged the coat down with sharp yanks. Nynaeve's tongue had nothing on Birgitte's. She really should have required some oath of obedience, or at least some show of proper respect. She would have to remember that once it came time to bond Rand. When Birgitte caught up to her, wearing a sour expression as if *she* were driven almost beyond endurance, neither of them spoke.

Dressed in green sequins, the pale-haired Seanchan woman was using her goad to guide the huge bull *s'redit* as his head pushed the heavy wagon holding the black-maned lion's cage. A horse handler in a shabby leather vest held the wagon tongue, steering the wagon around to where its horses could be hitched more easily. The lion stalked back and forth, lashing his tail and now and then giving a hoarse cough that sounded like the beginning of a roar.

"Cerandin," Elayne said, "I must speak to you."

"In a moment, Morelin." Fixed on the tusked gray animal as she was, her quick, slurred way of speaking made her nearly unintelligible.

"Now, Cerandin. We have little time."

But the woman did not halt the *s'redit* and turn until the horse handler called out that the wagon was in position. Then she said impatiently, "What do you need, Morelin? I have much to do, yet. And I would like to change; this dress is not for traveling." The animal stood waiting patiently behind her.

Elayne's mouth tightened slightly. "We are leaving, Cerandin."

"Yes, I know. The riots. Such things should not be allowed. If this Prophet thinks to harm us, he will learn what Mer and Sanit can do." She twisted to scratch Mer's wrinkled shoulder with her goad, and he touched her shoulder with his long nose. A "trunk," Cerandin called it. "Some prefer *lopar* or *grolm* for battle, but *s'redit* properly used—"

"Be quiet and listen," Elayne said firmly. It was an effort to maintain her dignity, with the Seanchan woman being obtuse and Birgitte standing aside with her arms folded. She was certain Birgitte was just waiting to say something else cutting. "I do not mean the show. I mean myself, and Nana, and you. We are taking ship this morning. In a few hours, we will be beyond the Prophet's reach forever."

Cerandin shook her head slowly. "Few river craft can carry *s'redit,* Morelin. Even if you've found one that can, what would they do? What would I do? I do not think I can earn as much by myself as I can with Master Luca, not even with you highwalking and Maerion shooting her bow. And I suppose Thom would juggle. No. No, it is better if we all remain with the show."

"The *s'redit* will have to be left behind," Elayne

admitted, "but I am sure that Master Luca will take care of them. We will not be performing, Cerandin. There's no more need for that. Where I am going, there are those who would like to learn about . . ." She was conscious of the horse handler, a lanky fellow with an incongruously bulbous nose, standing close enough to listen. "About where you came from. Much more than you've told us already." No, not listening. Leering. By turns at Birgitte's bosom and at *her* legs. She looked at him until his insolent grin turned sickly and he scuttled back to his duties.

Cerandin was shaking her head again. "I am to leave Mer and Sanit and Nerin to be cared for by men who are afraid to come near them? No, Morelin. We will stay with Master Luca. You, too. It is much better. Remember how bedraggled you were the day you came? You do not want to return to that."

Drawing a deep breath, Elayne stepped closer. No one but Birgitte was close enough to overhear, but she did not want to take foolish chances. "Cerandin, my true name is Elayne of House Trakand, Daughter-Heir of Andor. One day, I will be Queen of Andor."

Based on the woman's behavior the first day, and even more on what she had told them of Seanchan, that should have been enough to quell any resistance. Instead, Cerandin looked her straight in the eye. "You claimed to be a lady the day you came, but . . ." Pursing her lips, she eyed Elayne's breeches. "You are a very good highwalker, Morelin. With practice, you may be good enough to perform before the Empress one day. Everyone has a place, and everyone belongs in their place."

For a moment, Elayne's mouth worked soundlessly. Cerandin did not believe her! "I have wasted quite enough time, Cerandin."

She reached for the woman's arm, to haul her along bodily if necessary, but Cerandin caught her hand, twisted, and with a wide-eyed yelp Elayne found herself on tiptoe, wondering whether her wrist would break before her arm came out of her shoulder. Birgitte just stood there, arms folded under her breasts, and had the nerve to raise an eyebrow questioningly!

Elayne gritted her teeth. She *would* not ask for help. "Release me, Cerandin," she demanded, wishing she did not sound quite so breathy. "I said, release me!"

Cerandin did, after a moment, and stepped back warily. "You are a friend, Morelin, and always will be. You could be a lady, one day. You have the manner, and if you attract a lord, he may take you for one of his *asa*. *Asa* sometimes become wives. Go with the Light, Morelin. I must finish my work." She held out the goad for Mer to curl his trunk around, and the big animal let her lead him ponderously away.

"Cerandin," Elayne said sharply. "Cerandin!" The pale-haired woman did not look back. Elayne glared at Birgitte. "A great lot of help you were," she growled, and stalked off before the other woman could reply.

Birgitte caught her up and fell in at her side. "From what I hear, and what I've seen, you have spent considerable time teaching the woman she has a backbone. Did you expect me to help you take it away from her again?"

"I was not trying to do any such thing," Elayne muttered. "I was trying to take care of her. She is a long way from home, a stranger wherever she goes, and there are some who would not treat her kindly if they learned where she came from."

"She seems well able to take care of herself," Birgitte said dryly. "But then, perhaps you taught her that, too? Perhaps she was helpless before you found her." Elayne's stare seemed to slide off her like ice sliding down warm steel.

"You just stood and watched her. You are supposed to be my . . ." She glanced around; it was only a glance, but several of the horse handlers ducked their heads away. "My Warder. You are supposed to help me defend myself when I cannot channel."

Birgitte looked around, too, but unfortunately there was no one close enough to make her hold her tongue. "I will defend you when you are in danger, but if the danger is only of being turned over someone's knee because you've behaved like a spoiled child, I will have to decide whether it's better to let you learn a lesson that might save you the same or worse another time. Telling her you

were heir to a throne! Really! If you are going to be Aes
Sedai, you had better start practicing how to bend the
truth, not break it into shards."

Elayne gaped. It was not until she stumbled over her
own feet that she managed to say, "But I am!"

"If you say so," Birgitte said, rolling her eyes at the
spangled breeches.

Elayne could not help herself. Nynaeve wielding her
tongue like a needle, Cerandin stubborn as two mules,
and now this. She threw back her head and screamed
with frustration.

When the sound died, it seemed as if the animals had
quieted. Horse handlers stood about, staring at her.
Coolly, she ignored them. Nothing could worm its way
under her skin now. She was as calm as ice, perfectly in
control of herself.

"Was that a cry for help," Birgitte said, tilting her
head, "or are you hungry? I suppose I could find a wet
nurse in—"

Elayne strode away with a snarl that would have done
any of the leopards proud.

CHAPTER
48

Leavetakings

Once she was back in the wagon, Nynaeve changed into a decent dress, with a few exasperated mutters for having to undo one set of buttons and do up another by herself. The plain gray wool, fine and well cut yet hardly elaborate, would pass without comment almost anywhere, but it was decidedly warmer. Still, it felt good to be decently garbed again. And somehow *odd,* as if she were wearing too many clothes. It must be the heat.

Quickly she knelt in front of the small brick stove with its tin chimney and opened the iron door on their valuables.

The twisted stone ring was fast nestled into her belt pouch beside Lan's heavy signet ring and her gold Great Serpent. The small gilded coffer containing the gems Amathera had given her went into the leather scrip with the pouches of herbs taken from Ronde Macura in Mardecin and the small mortar and pestle for preparing them; she fingered through the latter just to remind herself what each contained, from healall to that dreadful forkroot. The letters-of-rights went in as well, and three of the six purses, none quite as fat as it had been after paying the menagerie's way to Ghealdan. Luca might not be interested in his hundred marks, but he had had no qualms about collecting his expenses. One of the letters authorizing the bearer to do whatever she wished in the name of the Amyrlin Seat joined the rings. No more than vague rumors of some sort of trouble in Tar Valon had reached Samara; she might find a use for it, even with Siuan Sanche's signature. The dark wooden box she left where it sat, next to three of the purses, as well as the rough jute bag containing the *a'dam*—that, she certainly had no wish to touch—and the silver arrow Elayne had found the night of the calamitous encounter with Moghedien.

For a moment she frowned at the arrow, contemplating Moghedien. It *was* best to do whatever was necessary to avoid her. *It was. I bested her once!* And had been hung up like a sausage in the kitchen the second time. If not for Birgitte . . . *She made her own choice.* The woman had said so, and it was true. *I could defeat her again. I could. But if I failed* . . . If she failed . . .

She was only trying to avoid the washleather purse stuffed right to the back, and she knew it, yet there was not a hair's difference for ugliness between the purse and the thought of losing to Moghedien again. Drawing a deep breath, she gingerly reached in and took it up by the drawstrings, and knew she had been wrong. Evil seemed to bathe her hand, stronger than ever, as if the Dark One really was trying to break through the *cuendillar* seal inside. Better to dwell all day on defeat by Moghedien; there was a *world* of difference between thought and reality. It had to be imagination—there had been no such feeling in Tanchico—but she wished she could let Elayne carry that, too. Or leave it there.

Stop being foolish, she told herself firmly. *It holds the Dark One's prison shut. You are just letting your fancies run wild.* But she still dropped it like a week-dead rat onto the red dress Luca had had made, then wrapped and tied the thing securely with more than a little haste. The silken parcel went into the middle of a bundle of clothes she was taking with her, inside her good gray traveling cloak. A few inches' distance was enough to take away the sensation of dark bleakness, but she still wanted to wash her hand. If only she did not know it was there. She *was* being foolish. Elayne would laugh at her, and Birgitte, as well. And rightly.

Actually, the clothes she wanted to keep made two packages, and she regretted every stitch she had to leave behind. Even the low-cut blue silk. Not that she ever wanted to wear anything like it again—she did not intend to *touch* the red dress, certainly, until she handed the intact packet to an Aes Sedai in Salidar—but she could not help totting up the cost of clothes, horses and wagons abandoned since leaving Tanchico. And the coach, and the barrels of dye. Even Elayne would have winced if she had ever thought of it. That young woman believed there would always be coin when she reached into her purse.

She was still making the second bundle when Elayne returned and silently changed into a blue silk dress. Silently, except for mutters when she had to double her arms behind her to fasten the buttons. Nynaeve would have helped, had she been asked, but since she was not, she examined the other woman for bruises while she changed. She thought she had heard a scream only minutes before Elayne arrived, and if she and Birgitte had actually come to blows . . . She was not certain she was glad to find none. A riverboat would be just as confining as this wagon in its own way, and less than pleasant if the two women were at one another's throats. But then again, it might have helped had they worked off some of their beastly tempers.

Elayne said not a word while she gathered her own belongings, not even when Nynaeve asked, quite amiably, where she had gone haring off to as if she had sat on a cockleburr. That got only a raised chin and a chilly stare, as though the girl thought she was already on her mother's throne.

Sometimes Elayne was even more silent, in a way that said far more than words could. Finding three purses remaining, she paused before taking them, and the temperature in the wagon lowered considerably, though the purses were only her share. Nynaeve was tired of the carping over how she doled out coins; let the woman watch them dribble away and realize there might be no more for some time. When Elayne realized the ring was gone, though, and the dark box still sitting there . . .

Elayne hefted the box and opened the lid, pursing her lips as she studied the contents, the other two *ter'angreal* they had carried all the way from Tear. A small iron disc worked on both sides with a tight spiral, and a narrow plaque five inches long, seemingly amber yet harder than steel, and with a sleeping woman somehow carved inside it. Either could be used to enter *Tel'aran'rhiod,* though not so easily or so well as could the ring; to use either it was necessary to channel Spirit, the sole one of the Five Powers that could be channeled in sleep. It had seemed only right to Nynaeve, leaving them for Elayne, since she was taking charge of the ring. Closing the box with a sharp click, Elayne stared at her, absolutely expressionless, then stuffed it into one of her bundles alongside the silver arrow. Her silence was thunderous.

Elayne also made two bundles, but hers were larger; she left nothing out except the spangled coats and breeches. Nynaeve refrained from suggesting that she had overlooked them; she should have, with the sulking that was going on, but *she* knew how to promote harmony. She limited herself to one sniff when Elayne ostentatiously added the *a'dam* to her things, though from the look she got in return, you would have thought she had made her objections known at length. By the time they left the wagon, the quiet could have been chipped and used to chill wine.

Outside, the men were ready. And muttering to themselves, and throwing impatient looks at her and Elayne. It was hardly fair. Galad and Uno had nothing to prepare. Thom's flute and harp hung on his back in leather cases, along with a small bundle, and Juilin, notched sword-breaker at his belt and leaning on his head-high staff, wore an even smaller bundle, neatly tied. Men were willing to wear the same clothes until they rotted off.

Of course, Birgitte was ready, too, bow in hand, quiver

at her hip, and a cloak-wrapped bundle at her feet not much smaller than one of Elayne's. Nynaeve would not have put it past Birgitte to have Luca's dresses in there, but it was what she wore that gave a moment's pause. Her divided skirts could have been the voluminous trousers she had worn in *Tel'aran'rhiod*, except for being more gold than yellow and not being gathered at the ankles. The short blue coat was identical in cut.

The mystery of where the garments had come from was solved when Clarine scurried up, chattering that she had taken too long, with two more of the skirts and another coat to fold into Birgitte's bundle. She stayed to say how sorry she was that they were leaving the show, and she was not the only one to take a few moments from the bustle of hitching horses and packing up. Aludra came with wishes for a safe journey, wherever they were going, in her Taraboner accents. And with two more boxes of her firesticks. Nynaeve tucked them into her scrip with a sigh. She had made a point of leaving the others behind, and Elayne had pushed them to the back of the shelf, behind a sack of beans, when she thought Nynaeve was not looking. Petra offered to help escort them to the river, pretending not to see his wife's eyes tighten with concern, and so did the Chavanas, and Kin and Bari, the jugglers, though when Nynaeve told them there was no need, and Petra frowned, they could barely hide their relief. She had to speak quickly, for Galad and the other men looked on the point of accepting. Surprisingly, even Latelle appeared briefly, with words of regret, smiles, and eyes that said she would carry their bundles if it saw them gone any sooner. Nynaeve was surprised Cerandin did not come, though in a way she was just as glad. Elayne might get on famously with the woman, but since the incident where she had been assaulted, Nynaeve had felt a tension whenever she was around her, perhaps the more because Cerandin gave no outward sign of the same.

Luca himself was the last, thrusting a handful of pitiful, drought-dwarfed wildflowers at Nynaeve—the Light alone knew where he had found them—with protestations of undying love, extravagant praises for her beauty, and dramatic vows to find her again if he had to travel to the corners of the world. She was not sure which made her cheeks grow hotter, but her frosty stare wiped the grin from Juilin's face and astonishment from Uno's. Whatever Thom and Galad thought, they had enough sense to keep their features smooth. She could not make herself look at Birgitte or Elayne.

The worst was that she had to stand there and listen, wilted flowers drooping over her hand, her face growing redder. Trying to send him away with a flea in his ear would likely only have sparked him to greater efforts, and given the others more fodder than they already had. She very nearly heaved a sigh of relief when the idiot man finally bowed himself away in elaborate flourishes of his cape.

She held on to the flowers, striding ahead of the others so she did not have to see their faces and angrily shoving bundles back into place when they shifted, until she was out of sight of the wagons around the canvas wall. Then she threw the bedraggled blossoms down so violently that Ragan and the rest of the rough-clad Shienarans, squatting halfway across the meadow to the road, exchanged glances. Each had a blanket-wrapped bundle on his back—small, of course!—alongside his sword, but they were hung about with enough water bottles to last for days, and every third man had a pot or kettle dangling somewhere. Fine. If there was cooking to be done, let them do it! Not waiting for them to decide whether she was safe to approach, she stalked out to the dirt road alone.

Valan Luca was the source of her fury—Humiliating her that way! She should have thumped his head and the Dark One take what anyone thought!—but its target was Lan Mandragoran. Lan had never given her flowers. Not that that was of any account. He had expressed his feelings in words deeper and more heartfelt than Valan Luca could ever manage. She had meant every word to Luca, but if Lan said he was going to carry you off, threats would never stop him; channeling would not stop him unless you managed it before he turned your brain and your knees to jelly with kisses. Still, flowers would have been nice. Nicer than another explanation of why their love could never be, certainly. Men and their word! Men and their *honor!* Wedded to death, was he? Him and his personal war with the Shadow! He was going to live, he was going to wed her, and if he thought differently on either point, she intended to set him straight. There was only the small matter of his bond to Moiraine to deal with. She could have screamed in frustration.

She was a hundred paces down the road before the others caught up, glancing at her sideways. Elayne only sniffed loudly while struggling to readjust the two large bundles on her back—she *would* have to take everything —but Birgitte strode along pretending to speak under her breath yet quite audibly muttering about women who rushed off like Carpan girls leaping from a river cliff. Nynaeve ignored them equally.

The men spread out, Galad in the lead flanked by Thom and Juilin, the Shienarans in a long file to either side, wary eyes searching every withered bush and fold in the ground. Walking in the middle of them, Nynaeve felt foolish—you would have thought they expected an army to rise up out of the ground; you would have thought she and the other two women were helpless—especially when the Shienarans silently followed Uno's lead and unlimbered their swords. Why, there was not a human being in sight; even the shanty villages appeared abandoned. Galad's blade remained in its scabbard, but Juilin began hefting his thumb-thick staff instead of using it for a walking stick, and knives appeared in Thom's hands and vanished as if he was unconscious of what he was doing. Even Birgitte fitted an arrow to her bow. Nynaeve shook her head. It would take a brave mob to come in eyeshot of this lot.

Then they reached Samara, and she began to wish she had accepted Petra's offer, and the Chavanas', and anyone else's she could have found.

The gates stood open and unguarded, and six black columns of smoke rose above the gray town walls. The streets beyond were still. Shattered glass from broken windows crunched underfoot; that was the only sound except for a distant buzz, like monstrous swarms of wasps scattered through the city. Furniture and bits of clothing littered the paving stones, pots and pottery, things dragged from shops and homes, whether by looters or by people fleeing there was no way to tell.

Not only property had been destroyed. In one place a corpse in a fine green silk coat hung half out of a window, limp and unmoving; in another a fellow garbed in rags dangled by his neck from the eaves of a tinsmith's shop. Sometimes, down a side street or alley, she caught a glimpse of what might have been discarded bundles of old clothes; she knew they were not.

In one doorway, where the splintered door hung crazily by a single hinge, small flames licked up around a wooden staircase, smoke just beginning to trickle out. The street might be empty now, but whoever had done that was not long gone. Head swiveling, trying to watch every way at once, Nynaeve took a firm hold on her belt knife.

Sometimes the angry buzz grew louder, a wordless guttural roar of rage that seemed no more than one street over, and sometimes it faded to a dull murmur; yet when trouble came, it came suddenly and silently. The mass of men stalked around the next corner but one, like a pack of hunting wolves, jamming the street from side to side, soundless but for the thud of boots. The sight of Nynaeve and the others was a torch tossed into a haystack. There was no hesitation; as one they surged forward, howling and rabid, waving pitchforks and swords, axes and clubs, anything that could be taken to hand for a weapon.

Enough anger still clung in Nynaeve for her to embrace *saidar,* and she did it without thinking, even before she saw the glow spring up around Elayne. There were a dozen ways she could halt this mob by herself, a dozen more she could destroy it if she chose. If not for the possibility of Moghedien. She was not sure whether the same thought held Elayne. She only knew that she hung on to her anger and the True Source with equal fervor, and it was Moghedien more than the onrushing rabble that made it hard. She hung on to them, and knew she dared do nothing. Not if there was any other chance.

Almost, she wished she could cut the flows being woven by Elayne. There had to be some other chance.

One man, a tall fellow in a ragged red coat that had belonged to someone else once by its green-and-gold embroidery, ran out in front of the others on long legs, shaking a wood-axe overhead. Birgitte's arrow took him through one eye. He went down in a sprawling heap and was trampled by the others, all contorted faces and wordless screams. Nothing was going to stop them. With a wail, half outrage, half pure fear, Nynaeve jerked her belt knife free and at the same time prepared to channel.

Like a wave striking boulders, the charge splintered on Shienaran steel. The top-knotted men, not much less ragged than those they fought, worked their two-handed swords methodically, craftsmen at their craft, and the onslaught went no farther than their thin line. Men fell screaming for the Prophet, but more scrambled over them. Juilin, the fool, was in that row, flat-topped conical cap perched on his dark head, thin staff a blur that deflected stabs, broke arms and cracked skulls. Thom worked behind the line, his limp strong as he darted from place to place to confront the few who managed to wriggle through; only a dagger in either hand, yet even swordsmen died on those blades. The gleeman's leathery face was grim, but when one bulky fellow in a blacksmith's leather vest nearly reached Elayne with his pitchfork, Thom snarled as viciously as any in the mob and very nearly cut the man's head off while slitting his throat. Through it all Birgitte calmly shifted from spot to spot, every arrow finding an eye.

Yet if they held the mob, it was Galad who broke them. He faced their charge as though awaiting the next dance at a ball, arms folded and unconcerned, not even bothering to bare his blade until they were almost on top of him. Then he did dance, all his grace turned in an instant to fluid death. He did not stand against them; he carved a path into their heart, a clear swath as wide as his sword's reach. Sometimes five or six men closed in around him with swords and axes and table legs for clubs, but only for the brief time it took them to die. In the end, all their

rage, all their thirst for blood, could not face him. It was
from him that the first ran, flinging away weapons, and
when the rest fled, they divided around him. As they
vanished back the way they had come, he stood twenty
paces from anyone else, alone among the dead and the
groans of the dying.

Nynaeve shivered as he bent to clean his blade on a
corpse's coat. He was graceful, even doing that. He was
beautiful, even doing that. She thought she might sick
up.

She had no idea how long it had taken. Some of the
Shienarans were leaning on their swords, panting. And
eyeing Galad with a good deal of respect. Thom was bent
over with one hand on his knee, trying to fend Elayne off
with the other while telling her he just had to catch his
breath. Minutes, an hour; it could have been either.

For once, looking at the injured men lying on the
pavement here and there, the one crawling away, she felt
no desire to Heal, no pity at all. Not far off was a
pitchfork, where someone had flung it; a man's severed
head was impaled on one tine, a woman's on another. All
she felt was queasy, and grateful that it was not her head.
That, and cold.

"Thank you," she said aloud, to no one in particular
and to everyone. "Thank you very much." The words
grated a little—she did not like confessing something
she had not been able to do for herself—but they were
fervent. Then Birgitte nodded in acknowledgment, and
Nynaeve had to struggle with herself. But the woman
had done as much as anyone. Considerably more than
she herself. She thrust her belt knife back into its sheath.
"You . . . shot very well."

With a wry grin, as if she knew exactly how difficult
those words had been, Birgitte set about recovering her
arrows. Nynaeve shuddered and tried not to watch.

Most of the Shienarans had wounds, and Thom and
Juilin both wore their own blood in places—
miraculously, Galad was untouched; or perhaps not so
miraculously, remembering how he had handled his
sword—but, manlike to the bitter end, every one of
them insisted that his hurts were not serious. Even Uno

said they had to keep moving, him with one arm hanging and a gash down the side of his face whose scar would nearly mirror the first if it was not Healed soon.

In truth, she was not reluctant to go, despite telling herself that she should be seeing to injuries. Elayne put a supporting arm around Thom; he responded by refusing to lean on her and beginning to recite a tale in High Chant, so flowery it was difficult to recognize the story of Kirukan, the beautiful soldier queen of the Trolloc Wars.

"She had a temper like a boar caught in briars at the best," Birgitte said softly to no one in particular. "Not at all like anyone close by."

Nynaeve ground her teeth. Catch her complimenting the woman again, no matter what she did. Come to think of it, any man in the Two Rivers could have shot as well at that range. Any boy.

Rumbles followed them, distant roars from other streets, and often she had the feeling of eyes watching from one of the vacant, glassless windows. But word must have spread, or else the watchers had seen what happened, because they saw no one else living until suddenly two dozen Whitecloaks stepped into the street in front of them, half with drawn bows, the rest with bared blades. The Shienarans' blades were up in a heartbeat.

Quick words between Galad and a fellow with a grizzled face beneath his conical helmet passed them through, though the man did eye the Shienarans doubtfully, and Thom and Juilin, and for that matter Birgitte. It was enough to rankle Nynaeve. All very well for Elayne to march along with her chin raised, ignoring the Whitecloaks as though they were servants, but Nynaeve did not like being taken for granted.

The river was not far. Beyond a few small stone warehouses under slate roofs, the town's three stone docks barely reached water over the dried mud. A fat vessel with two masts sat low at the end of one. Nynaeve hoped there would be no problem obtaining separate cabins. She hoped it would not heave too badly.

A small crowd huddled twenty paces from the dock, under the watchful eyes of four white-cloaked guards;

nearly a dozen men, mainly old and all ragged and bruised, and twice as many women, most with two or three children clinging to them, some with a babe in arms beside. Two more Whitecloaks stood right at the dock. The children hid their faces in their mothers' skirts, but the adults gazed yearningly at the ship. The sight wrenched at Nynaeve's heart; she remembered the same gazes, many more of them, in Tanchico. People desperately hoping for a way to safety. She had not been able to do anything for those.

Before she could do anything for these, Galad had seized her and Elayne by the arm and hustled them along the dock and down an unsteady gangplank. Six more stern-faced men in white cloaks and burnished mail stood on the deck, watching a cluster of barefoot and mostly bare-chested men squatting in the bluff bows. It was close whether the captain at the foot of the plank gazed at the Whitecloaks more sourly or at the motley party that trooped onto his ship.

Agni Neres was a tall, bony man in a dark coat, with ears that stood out and a dour cast to his narrow face. He paid no mind to the sweat rolling down his cheeks. "You paid me passage for two women. I suppose you want me to take the other wench and the men for free?" Birgitte eyed him dangerously, but he seemed not to see.

"You shall have your fare money, my good captain," Elayne told him coolly.

"As long as it's reasonable," Nynaeve said, and ignored Elayne's sharp glance.

Neres' mouth thinned, though it hardly seemed possible, and he addressed Galad again. "Then if you'll get your men off my craft, I'll sail. I like being here in daylight now less than ever."

"As soon as you take your *other* passengers on," Nynaeve said, nodding to the people huddled ashore.

Neres looked for Galad only to find that he had moved away to speak with the other Whitecloaks, then eyed the folk ashore and spoke to the air above Nynaeve's head. "Any who can pay. Not many in that lot look like they can. And I could not take the lot if they could."

She raised herself on tiptoe, so he could not possibly

miss her smile. It snapped his chin down into his collar. "Every last one of them, *Captain*. Else I'll shave your ears off for you."

The man's mouth opened angrily; then abruptly his eyes widened, staring past her. "All right," he said quickly. "But I expect some sort of payment, mind. I give alms on Firstday, and that's long past."

Heels settling back to the deck, she looked over her shoulder suspiciously. Thom, Juilin and Uno stood there, blandly watching her and Neres. As blandly as they could manage with Uno's features, and blood all over their faces. Far too blandly.

With a sharp sniff, she said, "I will see them all aboard before anybody touches a rope," and went in search of Galad. She supposed he deserved some thanks. He had thought what he was doing was the right thing. That was the trouble with the best of men. They always thought they were doing the right thing. Still, whatever the three had done, they *had* saved argument.

She found him with Elayne, that handsome face painted with frustration. He brightened at the sight of her. "Nynaeve, I've paid your way as far as Boannda. That's only halfway to Altara, where the Boern runs into the Eldar, but I could not afford to pay further. Captain Neres took every copper in my purse, and I had to borrow besides. The fellow charges ten prices. I'm afraid you will have to make your own way to Caemlyn from there. I truly am sorry."

"You have done quite enough already," Elayne put in, her eyes drifting toward the plumes of smoke rising above Samara.

"I gave my promise," he said with a weary resignation. Plainly they had had the same exchange before Nynaeve came.

Nynaeve managed to offer her thanks, which he dismissed graciously, but with a look as if she, too, did not understand. And she was more than ready to admit as much. He started a war to keep a promise—Elayne was right about that; it would be a war, if it was not already—yet, with his men holding Neres' ship, he would not demand a better price. It was Neres' ship, and

Neres could charge as he chose. As long as he took Elayne and Nynaeve. It was true: Galad never counted the cost of doing right, not to himself or anyone else.

At the gangplank, he paused, staring at the town as if seeing the future. "Stay clear of Rand al'Thor," he said bleakly. "He brings destruction. He *will* break the world again before he is done. Stay clear of him." And he was trotting up to the dock, already calling for his armor.

Nynaeve found herself sharing a wondering gaze with Elayne, though it quickly broke up in embarrassment. It was hard to share a moment like that with someone you knew might rake you with her tongue. At least, that was why she felt discomfited; why Elayne should look flustered, she could not imagine, unless the woman was starting to come to her senses. Surely Galad did not suspect they had no intention of going to Caemlyn. Surely not. Men were never that perceptive. She and Elayne did not look at one another again for some time.

CHAPTER
49

To Boannda

There was little trouble getting the huddled crowd of men, women and children aboard. Not once Nynaeve made it clear to Captain Neres that he *was* going to find room for everyone and whatever *he* thought he was going to charge, *she* knew *exactly* how much she would give for their fares to Boannda. Of course, it might have helped a little that she'd taken the precaution of quietly telling Uno to have the Shienarans do something with their swords. Fifteen hard-faced, rough-dressed men, all with shaved heads and topknots not to mention bloodstains, oiling and sharpening blades, laughing as one recounted how another had almost been spitted like a lamb—well, they had a most salutary effect. She counted the money into his hand, and if it pained her, she only had to summon the memory of those docks at Tanchico to keep counting. Neres was right in one thing: these folk did not look to have much coin; they would need whatever coppers they had. Elayne had no call to ask in that sickly sweet tone if she was having a tooth pulled.

The crew ran at Neres' shouted commands to cast off

while the last of the people were still scrambling aboard carrying their wretched possessions in their arms, those who had anything at all beyond the rags on their backs. In truth, they crowded even the fat vessel so that Nynaeve began to wonder whether Neres had been right about that, too. Yet such hope dawned on their faces once their feet were firmly on the deck that she was embarrassed to have considered it. And when they learned she had paid their passage, they clustered around her, struggling to kiss her hands, the hem of her skirt, crying out thanks and blessings, some with tears streaming down dirty cheeks, men as well as women. She wished she could sink through the planks under her feet.

The decks bustled as sweeps went out and sails rose, and Samara began to dwindle behind before she could put an end to the demonstration completely. If Elayne or Birgitte had said one word, she would have thumped them both twice around the ship for good measure.

Five days they were on *Riverserpent,* five days running down the slowly winding Eldar through baking days and nights not much cooler. Some things changed for the better in that time, but the voyage did not begin well.

The first real problem of the trip was Neres' cabin in the stern, the only accommodation on the ship except the deck. Not that Neres was reluctant about moving out. His haste—breeches and coats and shirts flung over his shoulders and dangling from a great wad in his arms, shaving mug clutched in one hand and razor in the other—made Nynaeve look hard at Thom and Juilin and Uno. It was one thing for her to make use of them when she chose to, quite another for them to go *looking after* her behind her back. Their faces could not have been more open, or their eyes more innocent. Elayne brought up another of Lini's sayings. "An open sack hides nothing, and an open door hides little, but an open man is surely hiding something."

But whatever problem the men might prove to be, the problem now was the cabin itself. It smelled of must and mold even with the tiny windows swung out, and they let little light into its dank confines. "Confines" was the word. The cabin was small, smaller than the wagon, and most of the space was taken by a heavy table and high-backed chair fastened to the floor, and the ladder leading up to the deck. A washstand built into the wall, with a grimy pitcher and bowl and a narrow dusty mirror, crowded the room still more, and completed the furnishings except for a few empty shelves and pegs for hanging clothes. The ceiling beams crouched right overhead, even for them. And there was only one bed, wider than what they had been sleeping on, yet hardly wide enough for two. Tall as he was, Neres might as well have lived in a box. The man surely had not given up one inch that might be stuffed with cargo.

"He came to Samara in the night," Elayne muttered, unburdening herself of her bundles and putting hands on hips as she looked around disparagingly, "and he wanted to leave in the night. I heard him tell one of his men that he meant to sail on through the night whatever the . . . the *wenches* . . . wanted. Apparently, he's not much pleased to be moving in daylight."

Thinking of the other woman's elbows and cold feet, Nynaeve wondered whether she would not have done better to sleep up above with the refugees. "What are you going on about?"

"The man is a smuggler, Nynaeve."

"In *this* vessel?" Dropping her own bundles, Nynaeve laid the scrip on the table and sat down on the edge of the bed. No, she would not sleep on deck. The cabin might smell, but it could be aired out, and if the bed was cramped, it had a thick feather mattress. The ship *did* roll disturbingly; she might as well have what comfort she could. Elayne could not *chase* her out of there. "It is a *barrel*. We will be lucky to reach Boannda in *two* weeks. The Light alone knows how long to Salidar." Neither of them really knew how far Salidar was, and it was not yet time to broach the matter with Captain Neres.

"Everything fits. Even the name. *Riverserpent*. What honest trader would name his craft so?"

"Well, what if he is? It wouldn't be the first time we've made use of a smuggler."

Elayne threw up her hands in exasperation; she always did think obeying the law was important, however fool the law was. She shared more with Galad than she would be willing to admit. So Neres had called them wenches, had he?

The second difficulty was room for the others. *Riverserpent* was not a very large vessel, if wide, and counting everyone there were well over a hundred people aboard. A certain amount of space had to go to the crew working the sweeps and tending ropes and sails, and that did not leave much for the passengers. It did not help that the refugees kept as far from the Shienarans as possible; it seemed they had had their fill of armed men. There was scarcely room for everyone to sit, and none for lying down.

Nynaeve approached Neres straight away. "These folk need more room. Especially the women and children. Since you have no more cabins, your hold will have to do."

Neres' face darkened. Staring straight ahead, somewhere a pace to her left, he growled, "My hold is full of valuable cargo. Very valuable cargo."

"I wonder if customs men are active along the Eldar here?" Elayne said idly, eyeing the tree-lined banks to either side. The river was only a few hundred paces wide here, bordered with dried black mud and bare yellow clay. "Ghealdan to one side and Amadicia to the other. It might seem odd, your hold full of goods from the south and you heading south. Of course, you probably have all the documents showing where you've paid duties. And you could explain that you didn't unload because of the troubles in Samara. I have heard that excise men are quite understanding, really."

The corners of his mouth turning down, he still did not look at either of them.

Which was why he had a very good view when Thom fanned empty hands, made a flourish, and was suddenly twirling a pair of knives through his fingers before making one of them disappear.

"Just keeping in practice," Thom said, scratching one long mustache with the other blade. "I like to maintain certain . . . skills." The gash in his white-haired scalp and the fresh blood on his face, added to a bloodstained rent in one shoulder of his coat and tears elsewhere besides, made him look villainous in any company but Uno's. The Shienaran's toothy smile held no mirth at all, and did unfortunate things to his long scar and the new slash down his face, red and raw. The glaring crimson eye on his patch almost paled in comparison.

Neres shut his eyes and drew a long, long breath.

The hatches came open, and crates and casks went splashing over the side, some heavy, most light and smelling of spices. Neres winced every time the river closed over something else. He brightened—if such a thing could be said of him—when Nynaeve directed that bolts of silk and carpets and bales of fine woolens be left below. Until he realized that she meant them for bedding. If his face had been sour before, now it could have curdled milk in the next room. Through the whole thing he never said a word. When women began drawing up buckets of water on ropes to wash their children right there on the deck, he strode to the stern, hands clenched behind his back, and stared at the few floating casks as they fell behind.

In a way, it was Neres' peculiar attitude toward women that began smoothing the edges from Elayne's acid tongue, and Birgitte's. That was the way Nynaeve saw it; she herself had maintained her usual even disposition, of course. Neres disliked women. The crew spoke quickly when they had to speak to one of the women, all the while darting glances at the captain until they could hurry back to their duties. A fellow who seemed to have nothing to do for a moment was more likely than not to be sent running to some task by a roar from Neres if he exchanged two words with anyone in skirts. Their hasty comments and muttered warnings made Neres' opinions perfectly clear.

Women cost a man money, they fought like alley cats, and they caused trouble. Any and all trouble a man had could be laid to women, one way or another. Neres expected half of them to be rolling on the deck clawing one another before the first sunset. They would all flirt with his crew, and bring on dissension where they did not cause fights. Could he have sent all women off his ship, forever, he might have been happy. Could he have had them out of his life, he would have been ecstatic.

Nynaeve had never encountered the like. Oh, she had heard men mutter about women and money, as if men did not fling coin about like water—they just had no head for money, less than Elayne—and she had even heard them lay various troubles to women, usually when it was they themselves who had caused all the bother. But she could not recall *ever* meeting a man who truly *disliked* women. It was a surprise to learn that Neres had a wife and a horde of children in Ebou Dar, but no surprise that he stayed at home only long enough to load a new cargo. He did not even want to *talk* to a woman. It was simply amazing. Sometimes Nynaeve found herself looking at him sideways, the way she would have at some incredible animal. Far stranger than *s'redit,* or anything else in Luca's menagerie.

Naturally, there was no way that Elayne or Birgitte could vent their bile where he might hear. Rolling eyes and meaningful looks among Thom and the others were bad enough; they at least made some effort to hide them. Neres' open satisfaction at having his ridiculous expectations met—he surely would have seen it so—that would have been unbearable. He left them no choice but to swallow their acid and smile.

For herself, Nynaeve could have done with a little time with Thom and Uno and Juilin away from Neres' eye. They were forgetting themselves again, forgetting they were supposed to do as they were told. The results did not matter; they should wait. And for some reason they had taken to tormenting Neres with darkly smiling comments about cracking heads and slitting throats. But the only place she could be sure of avoiding Neres was in the cabin. They were not particularly large men, though Thom *was* tall and Uno fairly wide, yet crowded in there, they would have filled the tiny space to where they were looming over her. Hardly conducive to the tongue-lashing she wanted to hand out; give a man the chance to loom, and he had the battle half won. So she put on a pleasant mask, ignored startled frowns from Thom and Juilin, incredulous stares from Uno and Ragan, and enjoyed the outward good temper the other women had been forced to adopt.

She managed to keep smiling when she learned why the sails were so full, the undulating riverbanks rushing by under the afternoon as fast as a trotting horse. Neres had had the sweeps pulled in and stored along the railings; he almost looked happy. Almost. A low clay bluff ran along the Amadicia bank: on the Ghealdan side lay a broad ribbon of reeds between river and trees, mainly brown where water had receded. Samara lay only a few hours upriver.

"You channeled," she said to Elayne through her teeth. Wiping sweat from her brow with the back of her hand, she resisted the urge to dash it to the slowly heaving deck. The other passengers left a clear space for the two of them and Birgitte a few paces across, but she still kept her voice low, and as affable as she could manage. Her stomach seemed to move a heartbeat behind the ship's roll; that hardly improved her temper. "This wind is your doing." She hoped there was enough red fennel in her scrip.

From Elayne's damply glowing countenance and wide eyes, milk and honey should have fountained from her mouth. "You are turning into a frightened rabbit. Pull yourself together. Samara is *miles* behind us. No one could sense anything useful from that far. She would have to be on the ship with us to know. I was very quick."

Nynaeve thought her own face might crack if she held her smile any longer, but out of the corner of her eye she could see Neres, studying his passengers and shaking his head. Angry as she was at that moment, she could also see the almost faded residue of the other woman's weaving. Working weather was like rolling a stone downhill; it tended to keep going the way you started it. When it bounced away from the path, as it would sooner or later, you just had to twitch it back. Moghedien might have felt a weave of that size from Samara—maybe— but certainly not well enough to say where it had been done. She herself was a match for Moghedien in raw strength, and if she was not strong enough to do something, it seemed safe to say the Forsaken was not either. And she did want to travel as quickly as possible; right then, one day more than necessary in close quarters with the other two held as much attraction for her as sharing the cabin with Neres. For that matter, an extra day on water was nothing to look forward to. How could a ship move in such a fashion when the river looked so flat?

Smiling was beginning to make her lips ache. "You should have asked, Elayne. You always go and do things without asking, without thinking. It's time you realized if you fall into a hole running blindly, your old nurse isn't going to come pick you up and wash your face." By the last word, Elayne's eyes were as round as teacups, and her bared teeth looked ready to bite.

Birgitte put a hand on each of them, leaning close and beaming as though joy had her by the throat. "If you two don't stop this, I'm going to tip you both into the river to cool off. You are both acting like Shago barmaids with winteritch!"

Sweating faces frozen in amiability, the three women stalked in different directions, just as far apart as the ship would allow. Near sunset Nynaeve heard Ragan say that she and the others must really be relieved to be away from Samara, the way they were all but laughing on one another's shoulder, and the other men seemed to be thinking much the same, but the rest of the women aboard watched them with faces much too smooth. *They* knew trouble when they saw it.

Yet bit by bit, that trouble oozed away. Nynaeve was not exactly sure how. Perhaps the pleasant exteriors Elayne and Birgitte put on just seeped inside in spite of them. Perhaps the ridiculousness of it all, trying to keep a friendly smile on your face while putting a proper bite into your words, struck them more and more. Whatever did it, she could not complain at the outcome. Slowly, day by day, words and tones began to match faces, and now and then one of them even looked embarrassed, plainly remembering how she had been behaving. Neither spoke one word of apology, of course, which Nynaeve quite understood. Had she been as foolish and vicious as they, she certainly would not want to remind anyone.

The children played a part in restoring Elayne and Birgitte to equilibrium, too, though it actually started with Nynaeve looking after the men's wounds that first morning on the river. She brought out her scrip full of herbs, making poultices and ointments, bandaging cuts. Those gashes made her angry enough to Heal—sickness and injury always made her angry—and she did so, for some of the worst, though she had to be careful. Wounds vanishing would have set people talking, and the Light knew what Neres would do if he thought he had an Aes Sedai aboard; very likely sneak a man ashore in Amadicia by night and try to have them arrested. For that matter, the news might have sent some of the refugees over the side.

With Uno, for example, she rubbed a touch of stinging mardroot-oil liniment into his heavily bruised shoulder, dabbed a bit of healall ointment on the fresh slash down his face—no point wasting either—and wrapped his head in bandages until he could hardly move his jaw before Healing him. When he gasped and flailed, she said briskly, "Don't be such a baby. I wouldn't have thought a little pain would bother a big strong man. Now, you leave those alone; if you even touch them in the next three days, I'll dose you with something you won't soon forget."

He nodded slowly, staring at her so uncertainly that it was plain he did not know what she had done. If he realized when he finally took the bandages off, with luck no one else would remember exactly how bad the gash had been, and he should have sense enough to keep his mouth shut.

Once she began, it was only natural to go on to the rest of the passengers. Few of the refugees lacked bruises and scrapes, and some of the children were showing signs of fevers or worms. Those she could Heal without worry; children always made a fuss when they were dosed with anything that did not taste of honey. If they told their mothers it had felt odd, children always had fancies.

She had never really been comfortable around children. True, she wanted to have Lan's babies. Part of her did. Children could make a mess from nothing. They seemed to have the habit of doing the opposite of what you told them as soon as your back was turned, just to see how you would react. Yet she found herself smoothing back the dark hair of a boy no higher than her waist who stared up at her owlishly with bright blue eyes. They looked very like Lan's eyes.

Elayne and Birgitte joined her, just to help keep order at first, but one way or another they gravitated to the children too. Strangely, Birgitte did not look at all silly with a boy of three or four cradled on either hip and a ring of children about her, singing them a nonsense song about dancing animals. And Elayne handed round a sack of sweet red candies. The Light knew where she had gotten them, or why. She did not look guilty at all when Nynaeve caught her sneaking one into her own mouth; she only grinned, gently pulled a little girl's thumb from *her* mouth and replaced it with another candy. The children laughed as if just remembering how, and snuggled themselves into Nynaeve's skirts, or Elayne's or Birgitte's, as easily as into their mothers'. It was very difficult to maintain any sort of temper in those circumstances. She could not even bring herself to do more than sniff, and that faintly, when Elayne resumed her study of the *a'dam* in the privacy of the cabin on the second day. The woman seemed more convinced than ever that the bracelet, necklace and leash created a strange form of linking. Nynaeve even sat with her once or twice; the sight of the vile thing itself was enough to enable her to embrace *saidar* and follow along.

The refugees' stories came out, of course. Families separated, lost or dead. Farms and shops and crafts ruined as ripples of the world's troubles spread out, disrupting trade. People could not buy when they could not sell. The Prophet had only been the last brick on the cart that broke the axle. Nynaeve said nothing when she saw Elayne slipping a gold mark to a fellow with thin gray hair who knuckled a wrinkled forehead and tried to kiss her hand. She would learn how fast gold vanished. Besides, Nynaeve had handed out a few coins herself. Well, perhaps more than a few.

All but two of the men were grizzled or balding, with leathery faces and work-callused hands. Younger men had been snatched into the army if they were not caught up by the Prophet; those who refused one or the other had been hanged. The young pair—little more than boys, really; Nynaeve doubted if either had to shave regularly—wore hunted stares, and flinched if one of the Shienarans looked at them. Sometimes the older men talked of starting over, finding a bit of land to farm or taking up their trade again, but the tone of their voices said it was more bluff and bravado than real hope. Mostly they talked quietly of their families; a wife lost, sons and daughters lost, grandchildren lost. They sounded lost. The second night, a jug-eared fellow who had seemed the most enthusiastic in a sad lot had just vanished; he was simply gone when the sun came up. He might have swum ashore. Nynaeve hoped he had.

Still, it was the women who caught her heart. They had no more prospects than the men, no more certainties, but most had more burdens. None had a husband with her, or even knew if she had a husband alive, yet the responsibilities that weighed them down also kept them moving. No woman with grit could give up when she had children. Even the others meant to find some future, though. They all had at least a scrap of the hope the men only pretended to. Three especially tugged at her.

Nicola was about her age and height, a slender dark-haired weaver with big eyes who had been intending to marry. Until her Hyran took it into his head that duty called him to follow the Prophet, to follow the Dragon Reborn; he would marry her when his duty was seen to. Duty had been very important to Hyran. He would have made a good and conscientious husband and father, so Nicola said. Only, whatever was in his head had not done him much good when someone split it with an axe. Nicola did not know who, or why, just that she had to get as far from the Prophet as she could. Somewhere, there had to be a place where there was no killing, where she would not always be in fear of what might be around the next corner.

Marigan, a few years older, had been plump once, but her frayed brown dress hung on her loosely now, and her blunt face looked beyond weary. Her two sons, six and seven, stared silently at the world with too-big eyes; clinging to each other, they seemed frightened of everything and everyone else, even their own mother. Marigan had dealt in cures and herbs in Samara, though she had some odd ideas about both. That was no wonder, really; a woman who offered healing with Amadicia and Whitecloaks right across the river had to keep low, and even from the first she had had to teach herself. All she had ever wanted to do was cure sickness, and she claimed to have done it well, though she had not been able to save her husband. The five years since his death had been hard, and the coming of the Prophet had certainly not helped her any. Mobs searching for Aes Sedai chased her into hiding after she had cured a man of fever and rumor had turned it into bringing him back from the dead. That was how little most people knew of Aes Sedai; death was beyond the power to Heal. Even Marigan seemed to think it was not. She did not know where she was going any more than Nicola. A village somewhere, she hoped, where she could dispense herbs again in peace.

Areina was the youngest of the three, with steady blue eyes in a face bruised purple and yellow, and not from Ghealdan at all. Her clothes would have said that if nothing else did, a short dark coat and voluminous trousers not much different from Birgitte's. They were the sum of her possessions. She would not say where she was from exactly, but she was forthcoming about the road that had led her to *Riverserpent*. About some of it; Nynaeve had to infer in places. Areina had gone to Illian meaning to bring her younger brother home before he could take the oath as a Hunter for the Horn. With thousands in the city, however, she had never found him, but somehow she had found herself taking the oath, setting out to see the world while not quite believing the

Horn of Valere existed, half hoping that somewhere she would find young Gwil and take him home. Things had been . . . difficult . . . since. Areina was not precisely reluctant to talk, but she made such an effort to put a good face on things. . . . She had been chased out of several villages, robbed once, and beaten several times. Even so, she had no intention of giving up or seeking sanctuary, or a peaceful village. The world was still out there, and Areina meant to wrestle it to the ground. Not that she put it that way, but Nynaeve knew it was what the woman meant.

Nynaeve knew very well why they touched her most, too. Each story could have been the reflection of a thread in her own life. What she did not quite understand was why she liked Areina best. It was her opinion, putting this and that together, that nearly all of Areina's troubles came from having too free a tongue, telling people exactly what she thought. It could hardly be coincidence that she was harried out of one village so quickly she had to leave her horse behind after calling the mayor a pie-faced loon and telling some village women that dry-bones kitchen sweepers had no right to question why she was on the road alone. That was what she admitted to saying. Nynaeve thought a few days of herself for example would do Areina worlds of good. And there had to be something she could do for the other two, as well. She could understand a desire for safety and peace very well.

There was an odd exchange the morning of the second day, while tempers were still tender and tongues—*some* people's tongues!—still rough. Nynaeve said something, quite mildly, about Elayne not being in her mother's palace, so she need not think Nynaeve was going to sleep shoved against the wall every night. Elayne tilted up her chin, but before she could open her mouth, Birgitte blurted, "You are the Daughter-Heir of Andor?" She hardly looked around to make sure no one was close enough to hear.

"I am." Elayne sounded more dignified than Nynaeve remembered in some time, but there was a hint of— could it be satisfaction?

Face completely blank, Birgitte simply turned away, walking up into the bow where she sat on a coil of rope, staring at the river ahead. Elayne frowned after her, then finally went to sit beside her. They sat talking softly for some time. Nynaeve would not have joined them even had she been *asked*! Whatever they discussed, Elayne seemed slightly disgruntled, as if she had expected some other result, but after that there was hardly a cross word between them.

Birgitte resumed her own name later that same day, though it was a last flare of temper that did it. With Moghedien safely behind them, she and Elayne washed the black out of their hair with pokeleaf, and Neres seeing one with red-gold curls about her shoulders and the other yellow-gold in an intricate braid, and that one with bow and quiver, muttered acridly about "Birgitte stepping out of the bloody stories." It was his misfortune that she overheard. That *was* her name, she told him sharply, and if he did not like it, she would pin his ears to either mast he chose. Blindfolded. He stalked off red-faced and shouting for lines to be tightened that could not have been made any tighter without popping.

At that point Nynaeve would not have cared whether Birgitte actually carried out the threat. Pokeleaf might have left a slight reddish cast to her own hair, yet it was close enough to its natural color almost to make her cry for joy. Unless everyone aboard came down with sore gums and toothaches, she had more than enough poke-leaf remaining. And sufficient red fennel to keep her stomach in its place. She could not help sighing in satisfaction once her hair was dry and in a proper braid again.

Of course, with Elayne channeling good winds and Neres running light or dark, thatch-roofed villages and farms sped past on either bank, marked by people waving in the day and lit windows in the night, showing no sign of the turmoil farther upriver. Broad as the misnamed craft was, it made good time, rolling along downriver.

Neres seemed torn between pleasure at his good luck at such winds and worry at moving in daylight. More than once he gazed longingly at a backwater, a tree-shrouded stream or a pool cut deep into the bank where *Riverserpent* might have been moored and hidden. Occasionally Nynaeve remarked where he could hear about how glad he must be that the people from Samara would soon be off his ship, with a comment thrown in about how well this woman was looking now that she was rested or how energetic that woman's children were. That was enough to put ideas of stopping right out of his head. It might have been easier to threaten him with the Shienarans, or Thom and Juilin, but those fellows were getting entirely too bigheaded as it was. And she certainly had no intention of arguing with a man who still would neither look at her nor talk to her.

Gray dawning of the third day saw the crew manning the sweeps again to draw them in to a dock at Boannda. It was a considerable town, larger than Samara, on a point of land where the swift River Boern, coming down from Jehannah, ran into the slower Eldar. There were even three towers inside the tall gray walls, and a building shining white beneath a red tile roof that could certainly pass for a palace, if a small one. As *Riverserpent* was lashed fast to the heavy pilings at the end of one dock—half their length across dried mud—Nynaeve wondered aloud why Neres had gone all the way to Samara when he could have unloaded his goods here.

Elayne nodded toward a stout man on the dock who wore a chain with some sort of seal hanging across his chest. There were several others like him, all with the chain and a blue coat, intently watching two other broad vessels unload at other docks. "Queen Alliandre's excisemen, I should say." Drumming his fingers on the rail, Neres was *not* looking at the men just as intently as they were at the other vessels. "Perhaps he had an arrangement with those in Samara. I don't think he wants to talk to these."

The men and women from Samara marched reluctantly up the gangplank, ignored by the excisemen. There was no custom duty on people. For the Samarans, it was the beginning of uncertainty. They had their lives ahead of them, and to begin anew, what they stood up in and what Nynaeve and Elayne had given them. Before they were halfway down the dock, still huddling together, some of the women were beginning to look as disheartened as the men. Some even began to cry. Vexation painted Elayne's face. She always wanted to take care of everyone. Nynaeve hoped Elayne did not discover that she had slipped a few more silvers to some of the women.

Not all left the ship. Areina remained, and Nicola, and Marigan, tightly clutching her sons, who gazed in anxious silence after the other children vanishing toward the town. The two lads had not said a word since Samara that Nynaeve had heard.

"I want to go with you," Nicola told Nynaeve, unconsciously wringing her hands. "I feel safe near you." Marigan nodded emphatically. Areina said nothing, but she stepped closer to the other two women, making herself part of the group even as she looked levelly at Nynaeve, defying her to send her away.

Thom shook his head slightly, and Juilin grimaced, but it was to Elayne and Birgitte that Nynaeve looked. Elayne did not hesitate in nodding, and the other woman was only a second behind. Gathering her skirts, Nynaeve marched to Neres, standing in the stern.

"I suppose I will have my ship back now," he told the air somewhere between the ship and the dock. "Not beforetime. This voyage has been the worst I ever undertook."

Nynaeve smiled broadly. For once, he did look at her before she was done. Well, he almost did.

It was not as if Neres had much choice. He could hardly appeal to the authorities in Boannda. And if he did not like the fares she offered, well, he had to sail downriver anyway. So *Riverserpent* cast off again, heading for Ebou Dar, with one stop to be made that he was not informed of until Boannda began falling astern.

"Salidar!" he growled, staring over Nynaeve's head. "Salidar's been abandoned since the Whitecloak War. It would take a fool woman to want to be ashore at Salidar."

Even smiling, Nynaeve was angry enough to embrace the Source. Neres roared, slapping at his neck and his hip at the same time. "The horseflies are very bad this time of year," she said sympathetically. Birgitte roared with laughter before they were halfway down the deck.

Standing in the bows, Nynaeve inhaled deeply as Elayne channeled to bring the wind up again and *Riverserpent* lumbered into the strong current flowing out of the Boern. She was all but eating red fennel for meals, but even if she ran out before Salidar, she would not care. Their journey was almost over. Everything she had been through was worth it, for that. Of course, she had not always thought so, and Elayne and Birgitte's rasping tongues had not been the only cause.

That first night, lying on the captain's bed in her shift while a yawning Elayne occupied the chair and Birgitte leaned against the door with her head brushing the beams, Nynaeve had used the twisted stone ring. A single rusty gimbal-mounted lamp gave light, and surprisingly, a scent of spice from the oil; maybe Neres had not liked the stench of must and mold, either. If she was ostentatious about nestling the ring between her breasts—and making sure the others knew it touched skin—well, she had cause. A few hours of superficially reasonable behavior on their parts had not made her less wary.

The Heart of the Stone was exactly as it had been every time before, pale light coming from everywhere and nowhere, the glittering crystal sword *Callandor* thrust into the floorstones beneath the great dome, rows of huge polished redstone columns running off into shadow. And that sensation of being watched that was so common in *Tel'aran'rhiod.* It was all Nynaeve could do not to flee, or set off on a frantic search through the columns. She forced herself to stand in one place beside *Callandor,* counting slowly to one thousand and pausing every hundred to call Egwene's name.

Truly, it was all she could do. The control she was so proud of vanished. Her clothes flickered with her worries about herself and Moghedien, Egwene and Rand and Lan. Between one minute and the next stout Two Rivers woolens became a muffling cloak and deep hood which became a suit of Whitecloak mail which became the red silk dress—only transparent!—which became an ever

thicker cloak which became . . . She thought her face
changed, too. Once she saw her hands, with skin darker
than Juilin's. Perhaps if Moghedien could not recognize
her . . .

"Egwene!" The last hoarse call echoed among the
columns, and Nynaeve made herself stand there shivering for one more count of one hundred. The great
chamber remained empty except for her. Wishing she
could feel more regret than haste, she stepped out of the
dream . . .

. . . and lay fingering the stone ring on its thong,
staring at the thick beams above the bed and listening to
the thousand creaks of the ship rushing downriver
through the darkness.

"Was she there?" Elayne demanded. "You were not
gone very long, but—"

"I am tired of being afraid," Nynaeve said without
taking her gaze from the beams. "I am s-so tired of being
a c-coward." The last words dissolved into tears she
could neither stop nor hide, no matter how she scrubbed
at her eyes.

Elayne was there in an instant, holding her and
smoothing her hair, and an instant later, Birgitte pressed
a cloth dampened in cool water against the back of her
neck. She cried herself out to the sound of them telling
her she was not a coward.

"If I thought Moghedien was hunting me," Birgitte
said finally, "I would run. If there was no other place to
hide than a badger's hole, I would wriggle in and curl
into a ball and sweat until she was gone. I would not
stand in front of one of Cerandin's s'redit if it charged,
either; and neither is cowardice. You must choose your
own time and your own ground, and come at her in the
way she least expects. I will take my revenge on her if
ever I can, but that is the only way I will. Anything else
would be foolish."

That was hardly what Nynaeve wanted to hear, but her
tears and their comfort made another gap in the thorny
hedges that had grown up between them.

"I will prove to you that you are no coward." Taking
the dark wooden box from the shelf where she had put it,

Elayne removed the spiral-scribed iron disc. "We will go back together."

That, Nynaeve wanted to hear even less. But there was no way to avoid it, not after they had told her she was not a coward. So back they went.

To the Stone of Tear, where they stared at *Callandor*— better than looking over your shoulder and wondering whether Moghedien was going to appear—then to the Royal Palace in Caemlyn with Elayne leading, and Emond's Field under Nynaeve's guidance. Nynaeve had seen palaces before, with their huge halls and great painted ceilings and marble floors, their gilding and fine carpets and elaborate hangings, but this was where Elayne had grown up. Seeing it, and knowing that, made her understand a little of Elayne. Of course the woman expected the world to bend itself to her; she had grown up being taught that it would, in a place where it did.

Elayne, a pale image of herself because of the *ter'angreal* she was using, was strangely quiet while they were there. But then, Nynaeve was quiet in Emond's Field. For one thing, the village was larger than she remembered, with more thatch-roofed houses and others' wooden frameworks going up. Someone was building a *very* big house just outside the village, three sprawling stories, and a stone plinth five paces high had been erected on the Green, carved all over with names. A good many she recognized; they were mostly Two Rivers names. A flagpole stood to either side of the plinth, one topped by a banner with a red wolf's head, the other one with a red eagle. Everything looked prosperous and happy—as much as she could say, with no people there—but it made no sense. What on earth were those banners? And who would be building such a house?

They flashed to the White Tower, to Elaida's study. Nothing had changed there, except that only half a dozen stools remained in the semicircle in front of Elaida's table. And the triptych of Bonwhin was gone. The painting of Rand remained, with a poorly mended tear in the canvas across Rand's face, as if someone had thrown something at it.

They rifled the papers in the lacquered box with its

golden hawks, and those on the Keeper's table in the anteroom. Documents and letters changed while they looked at them, yet they did learn a little. Elaida knew that Rand had crossed the Dragonwall into Cairhien, but of what she intended to do about it, there was no clue. An angry demand that all Aes Sedai return to the Tower immediately unless they had specific orders otherwise from her. Elaida seemed to be angry about a good deal, that so few sisters had returned after her offer of amnesty, that most of the eyes-and-ears in Tarabon were still silent, that Pedron Niall was still calling Whitecloaks back to Amadicia when she did not know why, that Davram Bashere still could not be found despite having an army with him. Fury filled every document over her seal. None of it seemed of real use or interest, except maybe about the Whitecloaks. Not that they should have any difficulty there as long as they were on *Riverserpent*.

When they returned to their bodies on the ship, Elayne was silent as she rose from the chair and replaced the disc in the box. Without thinking, Nynaeve got up to help her out of her dress. Birgitte scrambled up the ladder as they climbed into the bed together in their shifts; she intended to sleep right at the top of the ladder, she said.

Elayne channeled to extinguish the lamp. After a time lying in the dark, she said, "The palace seemed so . . . empty, Nynaeve. It felt so empty."

Nynaeve did not know what else a place was supposed to be in *Tel'aran'rhiod*. "It was the *ter'angreal* you used. You looked almost foggy to me."

"Well, I looked just fine to me." There was only a touch of asperity in Elayne's voice, though, and they settled down to sleep.

Nynaeve had remembered the other woman's elbows accurately, but they could not diminish her good mood, and neither could Elayne's complaining murmur that *she* had cold feet. She had done it. Perhaps forgetting to be afraid was not the same as not being afraid, but at least she had gone back to the World of Dreams. Perhaps one day she could find the nerve again not to be afraid.

Having begun, it was easier to go on than to stop. Every night after that they entered *Tel'aran'rhiod* together, always with a visit to the Tower to see what they could learn. There was not very much, besides an order sending an emissary to Salidar to invite the Aes Sedai there to return to the Tower. Except, the invitation—as much as Nynaeve could read before it changed to a report on screening potential novices for proper attitudes, whatever that was supposed to mean—was more a demand that those Aes Sedai submit to Elaida immediately and be thankful they were allowed to. Still, it was confirmation that they were not chasing a wild hare. The trouble with the rest of what they saw in fragments was they did not know enough to fit them together. Who *was* this Davram Bashere, and why was Elaida so frantic to find him? Why had Elaida forbidden anyone to mention the name of Mazrim Taim, the false Dragon, with a threat of stiff penalties? Why had Queen Tenobia of Saldaea and King Easar of Shienar both written letters politely but stiffly resenting White Tower meddling in their affairs? It all made Elayne murmur one of Lini's sayings: "'To know two, you must first know one.'" Nynaeve could only agree that it certainly seemed so.

Aside from the trips to Elaida's study, they worked at learning control, of themselves and their surroundings in the World of Dreams. Nynaeve did not mean to let herself be caught again as she had been by Egwene, and by the Wise Ones. Moghedien she tried not to think about. Much better to concentrate on the Wise Ones.

Of Egwene's trick of appearing in their dreams, as she had in Samara, they could puzzle out nothing; calling her did nothing except increase that uneasy feeling of being watched, and she did not make another such appearance. Trying to hold somebody else in *Tel'aran'rhiod* was incredibly frustrating, even after Elayne hit on the trick, which was to see the other as just another part of the dream. Elayne did it finally—and Nynaeve congratulated her with as good grace as she could muster—but for days Nynaeve could not. Elayne might as well have been the near mist she seemed, vanishing with a smile whenever she chose. When Nynaeve finally managed to fasten Elayne there, she felt the strain as if she were picking up a boulder.

Creating fantastical flowers or shapes by thinking of them was much more fun. The effort involved seemed related to both how large the thing was and whether it might really exist. Trees covered with wildly shaped blossoms in red and gold and purple were harder to make than a stand-mirror to examine what you had done to your dress, or what the other woman had done to it. A gleaming crystal palace rising out of the ground was harder still, and even if felt solid to the touch, it changed whenever the image in your mind wavered and vanished as soon as the image did. They quietly decided to leave animals alone after a peculiar thing—much like a horse with a horn on its nose!—chased them both up a hill before they could make it vanish. That very nearly sparked a new argument, with each of them claiming the other had made it, but by that time Elayne had recovered enough of her old self to start giggling over how they must have looked, racing up the hill with their skirts hauled up, shouting at the thing to go away. Even Elayne's stubborn refusal to admit it had been her fault could not stop Nynaeve's giggles from bubbling up, too.

Elayne alternated between the iron disc and the apparently amber plaque with its carving of a sleeping woman, but she did not really like using either *ter'angreal*. As hard as she worked with them, she did not feel as fully in *Tel'aran'rhiod* as with the ring. And each did have to be worked; it was not possible to tie the flow of Spirit, or you bounced right back out of the World of Dreams immediately. Channeling anything else at the same time seemed all but impossible, yet Elayne could not understand why. She seemed more interested in how they had been made, and not at all pleased that they did not yield their secrets as easily as the *a'dam*. Not knowing the "why" was a burr in her stocking.

Once, Nynaeve tried one of the pair, coincidentally on the night they were to meet Egwene, the night after leaving Boannda. She would not have been angry enough if not for the thing that rubbed her wrong so often. Men.

Neres began it, stumping around the deck as the sun began to sink, muttering to himself about having his cargo *stolen.* She ignored him, of course. Then Thom, making up his bed at the foot of the after mast, said quietly, "He has a point."

It was plain he did not see her in the fading lurid light, and neither did Juilin, squatting beside him. "He's a smuggler, but he did pay for those goods. Nynaeve had no right to seize them."

"A woman's flaming rights are whatever she flaming says they are." Uno laughed. "That's what women in Shienar say, anyway."

That was when they saw her and fell silent, as usual finding wisdom too late. Uno rubbed at his cheek, the one without a scar. He had removed his bandages that day, and he knew now what had been done. She thought he looked embarrassed. It was hard to tell in the fast-shifting shadows, but the other two seemed to have no expression at all.

She did nothing to them, of course, only stalked away with a firm grip on her braid. She even managed to stalk down the ladder. Elayne already had the iron disc in her hand; the dark wooden box sat open on the table. Nynaeve picked up the yellowish plaque carved inside with a sleeping woman; it felt slick and soft, not at all something that would scratch metal. With that edge of anger smoldering inside her, *saidar* was a warm glow just out of sight over her shoulder. "Maybe I can come up with some idea why this thing won't let you channel anything but dribbles."

Which was how she found herself in the Heart of the Stone, channeling a flow of Spirit into the plaque, which in *Tel'aran'rhiod* was tucked into her belt pouch. As she often did in the World of Dreams, Elayne wore a gown suitable for her mother's court, green silk embroidered in gold around the neck, with a necklace and bracelets of gold links and moonstones, but Nynaeve was surprised to discover that she herself had on something not very different, though her hair was in a braid—and its own color—instead of loose about her shoulders. Her gown was pale blue and silver, and if not so low as Luca's dresses, still lower than she thought she would have chosen. Still, she liked the way the single firedrop on its silver chain looked gleaming between her breasts. Egwene would not find it easy to bully a woman dressed so. Certainly not that that could have had anything to do with why she had donned it, even unconsciously.

Right away she saw what Elayne had meant about looking just fine; to herself, she appeared no different than the other woman, who had the twisted stone ring somehow threaded onto her necklace. Elayne, however, said she looked . . . misty. Misty was how *saidar* felt, too, except for the flow of Spirit she had begun to weave while awake. The rest was thin, and even the never-seen warmth of the True Source seemed muted. Her anger remained just strong enough for her to channel. If irritation at the men faded before the puzzle, that puzzle was its own irritant; steeling herself to confront Egwene had no part in it; she was not steeling herself at all, and there was no reason for the faint taste of boiled catfern and powdered mavinsleaf on her tongue! Yet producing a single flame, dancing in midair, one of the first things a novice was taught, seemed as difficult as throwing Lan over her shoulder. The flame looked attenuated even to her, and as soon as she tied the weave, it began to fade away. In seconds it was gone.

"Both of you?" Amys said. She and Egwene were just there, on the other side of *Callandor,* both in Aiel skirts and blouses and shawls. At least Egwene had not donned so many necklaces and bracelets. "Why do you appear so strange, Nynaeve? Have you learned to come waking?"

Nynaeve gave a little jump. She did so hate people sneaking up on her. "Egwene, how did you—" she began, smoothing her skirts, at the same time that Elayne said, "Egwene, we can't understand how you—"

Egwene broke in. "Rand and the Aiel have won a great victory at Cairhien." Out it all came in a torrent, everything she had told them in their dreams, from Sammael to the Seanchan spearhead. Each word almost tripped over the next, and she drove every one home with an intent stare.

Nynaeve exchanged confused glances with Elayne.

Surely she *had* told them. They could not have imagined it, not with every word confirmed now. Even Amys, long white hair only emphasizing the not quite Aes Sedai agelessness of her face, looked amazed at the flood.

"*Mat* killed Couladin?" Nynaeve exclaimed at one point. That had certainly not been in their dreams of her. It did not sound like Mat at all. Leading soldiers? *Mat?*

When Egwene finally trailed off, shifting her shawl and breathing a little quickly—she had barely paused for breath along the way—Elayne said weakly, "Is he well?" She sounded as if she was almost beginning to doubt her own memories.

"As well as can be expected," Amys said. "He drives himself hard, and listens to no one. Except Moiraine." Amys was not pleased.

"Aviendha is with him almost all the time," Egwene said. "She is taking good care of him for you."

Nynaeve doubted that. She did not know much about Aiel, but she suspected that if Amys said "hard," anyone else would say "murderously."

Apparently, Elayne agreed. "Then why is she letting him push himself? What is he doing?"

Quite a bit, it turned out, and clearly too much. Two hours each day practicing the sword with Lan or anyone else he could find. That made Amys' mouth tighten sourly. Two more studying the Aiel way of fighting without weapons. Egwene might find that strange, but Nynaeve was all too aware of how helpless you could be when you could not channel. Still, Rand certainly should never find himself in that position. He had become a king, or something more, surrounded by *Far Dareis Mai* guards, ordering lords and ladies about. In fact, he spent so much time ordering them, and chasing after them to make sure they did what he said, that he would not spare time for meals if the Maidens did not bring him food wherever he was. For some reason, while that seemed to irk Egwene almost as much as it did Elayne, Amys looked distinctly amused, though her face went back to Aiel stoniness once she saw Nynaeve notice. Yet another hour each day was given to a strange school he had founded, inviting not only scholars but craftsmen, from some fellow who made looking glasses to a woman who had constructed some sort of huge crossbow with pulleys that could hurl a spear a mile. He had told no one his purpose there, except maybe Moiraine, but the only answer the Aes Sedai had given Egwene was that the urge to leave something behind was strong in everyone. Moiraine did not seem to care what Rand did.

"What remains of the Shaido are retreating north," Amys said grimly, "and more slip across the Dragonwall to them every day, but Rand al'Thor seems to have forgotten them. He is sending the spears south, toward Tear. Half are gone already. Rhuarc says he has not even told the chiefs why, and I do not think Rhuarc would lie to me. Moiraine stands closer to Rand al'Thor than any except Aviendha, yet she refuses to ask him." Shaking her head, she muttered, "Though in her defense, I will say that even Aviendha has learned nothing."

"The best way to keep a secret is to tell no one," Elayne told her, which earned her a hard stare. Amys was not far behind Bair when it came to stares that made you shift your feet.

"We aren't going to reason it out here," Nynaeve said, fixing her gaze on Egwene. The other woman seemed uneasy. If there was any time to begin redressing the balance between them, it might as well be now. "What I want to know—"

"You are quite right," Egwene cut in. "We are not in Sheriam's study, where we can lounge about and chatter. What have you to tell us? Are you still with Master Luca's menagerie?"

Nynaeve's breath caught, questions flying right out of her head. There was so much to tell. And so much not to. She claimed she had followed Lanfear to the meeting between the Forsaken, and spoke only of seeing Moghedien spying. Not that she wanted to avoid telling how she had been handled by Moghedien—not really; not exactly—but Birgitte had not released them from their promise of secrecy. Of course, that meant not telling about Birgitte at all, that she was with them. It was awkward, knowing that Egwene knew Brigitte was helping them, and still having to keep pretending that

Egwene knew nothing at *all*, but Nynaeve managed despite stammering when Egwene arched her eyebrows. The Light be thanked, Elayne helped her present Samara as Galad and Masema's fault. Which it was, in truth. If either had simply sent to tell her about the ship, none of the rest would have followed.

When she finished—with Salidar—Amys said quietly, "You are certain they will support the *Car'a'carn*?"

"They must know the Prophecies of the Dragon as well as Elaida," Elayne said. "The best way to oppose her is to attach themselves to Rand, and make it clear to the world that *they* intend to support him all the way to Tarmon Gai'don." Not the slightest quaver in her voice betrayed that she was not speaking of an absolute stranger. "Otherwise, they are just rebels, with no claim to legitimacy. They need him at least as much as he needs them."

Amys nodded, but not as if she was ready to agree yet.

"I think I remember Masema," Egwene said. "Hollow eyes and a sour mouth?" Nynaeve nodded. "I can hardly imagine him as any sort of prophet, but I can see him starting a riot or a war. I'm sure Galad only did what he thought was best." Egwene's cheeks colored slightly; even the memory of Galad's face could do that. "Rand will want to know about Masema. And Salidar. If I can make him stand still long enough to listen."

"I want to know how it happens that you are both here," Amys said. She listened to their explanation, and turned the plaque over in her hand once Nynaeve fished it out. Having the *ter'angreal* touched by someone else while she was using it made Nynaeve's skin crawl. "I believe you are less here than Elayne," the Wise One said finally. "When a Dreamwalker enters the World of Dreams in her sleep, only a tiny bit of her remains with her body, just enough to keep her body alive. If she puts herself into a shallow sleep, where she can be here and also speak to those around her in the waking world, she looks as you do to one who is here fully. Perhaps it is the same. I do not know that I like it, any woman who can channel being able to enter *Tel'aran'rhiod*, even in this state." She returned the *ter'angreal* to Nynaeve.

Heaving a sigh of relief, Nynaeve hastily tucked the plaque away again. Her stomach was still fluttering.

"If you have told everything . . ." Amys paused while Nynaeve and Elayne hurriedly said that they had. The woman's blue eyes were incredibly penetrating. "Then we must go. I will admit there is more to be gained from these meetings than I first supposed, but I have much to do yet tonight." She glanced at Egwene, and they vanished as one.

Nynaeve and Elayne did not hesitate. Around them the great redstone columns changed in a blink to a small, dark-paneled room, its furnishings few, plain and sturdy. Nynaeve's anger had been wavering, and with it her hold on *saidar,* but the Mistress of Novices' study firmed both. Stubbornly defiant indeed! She hoped that Sheriam was in Salidar; it would be a pleasure to face her on an equal footing. Still, she could have wished to be somewhere else. Elayne was peering into the mirror with its flaking gilt frame, nonchalantly adjusting her hair with her hands. Only she had no need to use her hands here. She did not like being in this room either. Why had Egwene suggested meeting here? Elaida's study might not be the most comfortable place to be, but it was better than this.

A moment later, Egwene was there, on the other side of the broad table, eyes icy and hands on her hips as if she was the room's rightful occupant.

Before Nynaeve could open her mouth, Egwene said, "Have you two brainless flaptongues become witless ninnies? If I ask you to keep something to yourselves, do you immediately tell the first person you meet? Did it never occur to you that you don't have to tell everyone everything? I thought you two were good at keeping secrets." Nynaeve's cheeks grew warmer; at least she could not possibly be as scarlet as Elayne. Egwene was not quite finished. "As for how I did it, I can't teach you. You have to be a Dreamwalker. If you can touch somebody's dreams with the ring, I don't know how. And I doubt you can with that other thing. Try to keep your mind on what you're doing. Salidar may be nothing like you expect. Now, I also have things to do tonight. At least *try* to keep your wits about you!" And she was gone so suddenly the last word almost seemed to come from empty air.

Embarrassment ate at Nynaeve's anger. She *had* nearly burst out with it after Egwene asked her not to. And Birgitte: how could you keep a secret when the other woman *knew*? Embarrassment won, and *saidar* slipped away like sand through her fingers.

Nynaeve wakened with a jerk, the deep yellow *ter'angreal* firmly clutched in one hand. The gimbal-mounted lamp was turned down to a dim light. Elayne lay crowded in next to her, still asleep; the ring on its thong had slid down into the hollow of her throat.

Muttering to herself, Nynaeve clambered over the other woman to put away the plaque, then poured a little water into the washbasin to bathe her face and neck. The water was lukewarm, but it felt cool. In the shadowy light, she thought the mirror said she was still blushing. So much for redressing the balance. If only they had met anywhere else. If only she had not flapped her tongue like a brainless girl. It would have gone better if she had been using the ring, instead of being a wraith as far as the other woman was concerned. It was all Thom and Juilin's fault. And Uno's. If they had not made her angry . . . No, it was Neres' fault. He . . . She took the pitcher in both hands and washed her mouth. It was only the taste of sleep she was trying to get rid of. Nothing like boiled catfern and powdered mavinsleaf. Nothing at all.

When she turned from the washstand, Elayne was just sitting up, untying the leather cord that held the ring. "I saw you losing *saidar,* so I went by Elaida's study, but I didn't think I should stay long in case you worried. I didn't learn anything, except that Shemerin is to be arrested and reduced to Accepted." She got up and tucked the ring into the box.

"They can do that? Demote an Aes Sedai?"

"I don't know. I think Elaida is doing anything she wants. Egwene shouldn't wear those Aiel clothes. They are not very becoming."

Nynaeve let out the breath she had been holding. Obviously Elayne wanted to ignore what Egwene had said. Nynaeve was willing to let her. "No, they certainly aren't." Climbing onto the bed, she scrunched over against the wall; they took turns sleeping on the outside.

"I did not even have a chance to send a message to Rand." Elayne got in after, and the lamp winked out. The small windows let in only dribbles of moonlight. "And one to Aviendha. If she is taking care of him for me, then she ought to take care of him."

"He isn't a horse, Elayne. You don't own him."

"I never said I did. How will you feel if Lan takes up with some Cairhienin woman?"

"Don't be silly. Go to sleep." Nynaeve burrowed fiercely into her small pillow. Perhaps she should have sent word to Lan. All those noblewomen, Tairen as well as Cairhienin. Feeding a man honey instead of telling him the truth. He had better not forget who he belonged to.

Below Boannda, woods closed in tightly on both sides of the river, unbroken tangles of trees and vines. Villages and farms vanished. The Eldar might as well have run through wilderness a thousand miles from human habitation. Five days out of Samara, early afternoon found *Riverserpent* anchored in the middle of a bend in the river, while the ship's one boat ferried the remaining passengers to a beach of cracked dry mud bordered by low, forested hills. Even the tall willows and deep-rooted oaks showed some brown leaves.

"There was no need to give the man that necklace," Nynaeve said on the shore, watching the rowboat approach, crowded with four oarsmen, Juilin and the last five Shienarans. She hoped she had not been gullible; Neres had showed her his map of this stretch of the river, pointing out the mark for Salidar two miles from the water, but nothing else indicated there had ever been a village anywhere near here. The forest wall was quite unbroken. "What I paid him was quite enough."

"Not to cover his cargo," Elayne replied. "Just because he's a smuggler doesn't mean *we* have a right to take it from him." Nynaeve wondered whether she had been talking to Juilin. Probably not. It was just the law again. "Besides, yellow opals are gaudy, especially in that

setting. Anyway, it was worth it, just to see his face."
Elayne giggled abruptly. "He looked at me *this* time."
Nynaeve tried not to, but she could not help giggling too.

Thom was up near the trees, trying to amuse
Marigan's two boys by juggling colored balls produced
from his sleeves. Jaril and Seve stared at him silently,
hardly blinking, and held on to each other. Nynaeve had
not really been surprised when Marigan and Nicola
asked to accompany her. Nicola might be watching
Thom and laughing delightedly now, but she would have
spent every moment at Nynaeve's side had the latter
allowed it. Areina wanting to come had been something
of a shock, though. She was sitting off by herself on a
fallen log, watching Birgitte, who was stringing her bow.
All three women might be in for a shock when they
discovered what was in Salidar. At least Nicola would
find her sanctuary, and Marigan might even have a
chance to dispense herbs if there were not too many
Yellows about.

"Nynaeve, have you thought about . . . how we're
going to be received?"

Nynaeve looked at Elayne in astonishment. They had
crossed half the world, or near enough, and defeated the
Black Ajah twice. Well, they had had help in Tear, but
Tanchico had been all their doing. They brought news of
Elaida and the Tower she was willing to bet no one in
Salidar had. And most importantly, they could help
these sisters make contact with Rand. "Elayne, I won't
say they will greet us as heroes, but it wouldn't surprise
me if they kissed us before today is done." Rand alone
would be worth that.

Two of the barefoot sailors leaped out to hold the
rowboat against the current, and Juilin and the
Shienarans splashed ashore as the sailors scrambled back
aboard. On *Riverserpent* men were already hauling in the
anchor.

"Clear us a path, Uno," Nynaeve said. "I mean to be
there before dark." From the look of the forest, all vines
and dusty undergrowth, two miles might take that long.
If Neres had not managed to gull her. That worried her
more than anything else.

CHAPTER
50

To Teach, and Learn

Some four hours later, the sweat running down Nynaeve's face had very little to do with unseasonable heat, and she was wondering whether it might not have been better if Neres had gulled them. Or refused to carry them beyond Boannda. Late-afternoon sunlight slanted sharply through windows with mostly cracked panes. Clutching her skirts in blended irritation and unease, she tried to avoid looking at the six Aes Sedai grouped around one of the sturdy tables near the wall. Their mouths moved silently as they conferred behind a screen of *saidar*. Elayne had her chin high, her hands folded calmly at her waist, but a tightness about her eyes and the corners of her mouth spoiled her regal air. Nynaeve was not sure she wanted to know what the Aes Sedai were saying; one stunning blow after another had knocked all her high expectations into a daze. One more shock and she thought she might scream, and she did not know whether from fury or pure hysteria.

Very nearly everything except their clothes was laid out on that table, from Birgitte's silver arrow in front of stout Morvrin to the three *ter'angreal* before Sheriam, to the gilded coffers in front of dark-eyed Myrelle. Not one of the women looked pleased. Carlinya's face might have been carved from snow, even motherly Anaiya wore a stern mask, and Beonin's look of constant wide-eyed startlement had a distinctly annoyed cast. Annoyed and something more. Sometimes Beonin made as if to touch the white cloth spread neatly over the *cuendillar* seal, but her hand always stopped and retreated.

Nynaeve's eyes jerked away from the cloth. She knew exactly when things had begun to go wrong. The Warders who surrounded them in the woods had been proper, if cool—once she made Uno and the Shienarans put up their swords, anyway. And Min's warm greetings had been all laughter and hugs. But the Aes Sedai and others in the streets, caught up in their own errands, had scurried along with hardly a glance for the party being escorted in. Salidar was quite crowded, with armed men drilling in nearly every open space. The first person aside from the Warders and Min to pay any attention to them at all had been the lean Brown sister they were taken to, in what had once been the common room of this inn. She and Elayne had told the story they had agreed on to Phaedrine Sedai, or tried to. Five minutes into it, they were left standing, with strict orders not to move a foot or speak a word, even to each other. Ten more minutes, staring at one another in confusion, while all around them Accepted and white-clad novices, Warders and servants and soldiers bustled between tables where Aes Sedai pored over papers and briskly handed out orders, and then they had been hustled before Sheriam and the others so quickly Nynaeve did not think her shoes had touched the floor twice. That was when the grilling had begun, more suitable for captured prisoners than returning heroes. Nynaeve dabbed at the perspiration on her face, but as soon as she tucked the handkerchief back up her sleeve, her hands returned to their grip on her skirts.

She and Elayne were not alone standing on the colorful silk carpet. Siuan, in a plain dress of fine blue wool, might have been there by choice if Nynaeve had not known better, her face cool, utterly composed. She seemed lost in untroubled thought. Leane at least watched the Aes Sedai, yet she appeared equally confident. In fact, somehow more self-confident than

Nynaeve remembered. The copper-skinned woman
looked even more willowy, too, more supple in some
fashion. Perhaps it was her scandalous dress. That pale
green silk was every bit as high-necked as Siuan's, but it
clung to every curve of her, and the material only
managed to be opaque by a thin hair. It was their faces
that truly stunned Nynaeve, though. She had never
expected to find either alive, and certainly never looking
so very young—no more than a few years older than she
if that. They did not so much as glance at one another. In
truth, she thought she detected a distinct chill between
them.

There was another difference about them, one that
Nynaeve was just beginning to recognize. If everyone
including Min had been ginger about it, no one made any
real secret of the fact that they had been stilled. Nynaeve
could feel that lack. Perhaps it was being in a room where
all the other women could channel, or perhaps it was
knowing they had been stilled, but for the first time she
was truly conscious of the ability in Elayne and the
others. And its absence from Siuan and Leane. Something had been taken from them, cut away. It was like a
wound. Perhaps the worst wound a woman could suffer.

Curiosity overcame her. What sort of wound would it
be? What had been cut away? She might as well make use
of the waiting, and the irritation that larded itself
through her nervousness. She reached out to *saidar*. . . .

"Did anyone grant you permission to channel here,
Accepted?" Sheriam asked, and Nynaeve gave a start,
hurriedly releasing the True Source.

The green-eyed Aes Sedai led the others back to their
mismatched chairs, arranged on the carpet in a semicircle that had the four standing women as its focus. Some
of them carried things from the table. They sat staring at
Nynaeve, earlier emotion swallowed in Aes Sedai calm.
None of those ageless faces acknowledged the heat by so
much as a single bead of moisture. Finally Anaiya said in
a gently chiding voice, "You have been very long from
us, child. Whatever you have learned in the interval, you
have apparently forgotten much."

Blushing, Nynaeve curtsied. "Forgive me, Aes Sedai. I
did not mean to overstep." She hoped they thought it

was shame that heated her cheeks. She *had* been away from them a long time. Just one day ago, *she* had given the orders and people jumped when she spoke. Now she was the one expected to jump. It galled.

"You tell an interesting . . . story." Carlinya obviously believed little of it. The White sister turned Birgitte's silver arrow over in long slender hands. "And you acquired some strange possessions."

"The Panarch Amathera gave us many gifts, Aes Sedai," Elayne said. "She seemed to think we saved her throne." Even delivered in a perfectly level voice, that speech was a walk on thin ice. Nynaeve was not the only one irritated by their fall from freedom. Carlinya's smooth face tightened.

"You come with disturbing news," Sheriam said. "And some disturbing . . . things." Her slightly tilted eyes wandered to the table, to the silvery *a'dam,* and returned firmly to Elayne and Nynaeve. Since learning what it was, what it was for, most of the Aes Sedai had treated it like a live red adder. Most had.

"If the thing does what these children claim," Morvrin said absently, "we need to study it. And if Elayne really believes she can make a *ter'angreal . . ."* The Brown sister shook her head. Her real attention was on the flattened stone ring, all flecked and striped in red and blue and brown, that she held in one hand. The other two *ter'angreal* lay on her broad lap. "You say that this came from Verin Sedai? How is it this was never mentioned to us before?" That was not directed at Nynaeve or Elayne, but at Siuan.

Siuan frowned, but not the fierce frown Nynaeve remembered. It held a touch of diffidence, as if she knew she was speaking to her superiors, and so did her voice. That was another change Nynaeve could hardly believe. "Verin never told me of it. I would very much like to ask her a few questions."

"And *I* have questions about *this.*" Myrelle's olive face darkened as she unfolded a familiar paper—why had they ever kept that?—and read aloud. " 'What the bearer does is done at my order and by my authority. Obey, and keep silent, at my command. Siuan Sanche, Watcher of the Seals, Flame of Tar Valon, The Amyrlin Seat.' " She crumpled the paper and its seal in her fist. "Hardly something to be handed out to Accepted."

"At the time, I did not know who I could trust," Siuan said smoothly. The six Aes Sedai stared at her. "It was within my authority then." The six Aes Sedai did not blink. Her voice took on a thread of exasperated pleading. "You cannot call me to account for doing what I had to do when I had a perfect right to do it. When the boat's sinking, you plug the hole with what you can find."

"And why did you not tell us?" Sheriam asked quietly, but with a hint of steel. As Mistress of Novices she had never raised her voice, though sometimes you wished she would. "Three Accepted—Accepted!—sent out of the Tower chasing thirteen full sisters of the Black Ajah. Do you use babies to plug the hole in your boat, Siuan?"

"We are hardly babies," Nynaeve told her heatedly. "Several of those thirteen are dead, and we thwarted their plans twice. In Tear, we—"

Carlinya cut her off like an icy knife. "You have told us all about Tear, child. And Tanchico. And defeating Moghedien." Her mouth twisted wryly. She had already said that Nynaeve had been a fool to come within a mile of one of the Forsaken, that she was lucky to have escaped with her life. That Carlinya did not know how right she was—they certainly had not told everything—only made Nynaeve's stomach clench tighter. "You *are* children, and lucky if we decide not to spank you. Now hold your peace until you are called on to speak." Nynaeve flushed heavily, hoping they took it for embarrassment, and held her peace.

Sheriam had never taken her eyes from Siuan. "Well? Why have you never mentioned sending three children out to hunt lions?"

Siuan drew a deep breath, but folded her hands and ducked her head penitently. "There seemed no point, Aes Sedai, with so much else of importance. I have held nothing back, when there was the faintest reason for telling. Every scrap I knew of the Black Ajah, I told. I've not known where these two were or what they were up to for some time. The important thing is that they are here now, and with those three *ter'angreal*. You must realize what it means to have access to Elaida's study, to her papers, if only in bits. You'd never have known that she knows where you are until it was too late, except for that."

"We realize that," Anaiya said, eyeing Morvrin, who was still frowning at the ring. "It is just that perhaps the means of it takes us a little by surprise."

"Tel'aran'rhiod," Myrelle breathed. "Why, it has become no more than a matter for scholarly discussion in the Tower, almost a legend. And Aiel Dreamwalkers. Who would have imagined that Aiel Wise Ones could channel, much less this?"

Nynaeve wished they had been able to keep that secret—like Birgitte's true identity and a few other things they had managed to hold back—but it was difficult to keep things from slipping out when you were being questioned by women who could bore holes in stone with a look when they wanted. Well, she supposed she should be glad they had managed to hang on to what they had. Once Tel'aran'rhiod had been mentioned, and that they had entered it, a mouse would have treed cats before these women stopped asking questions.

Leane took a half-step forward, not looking at Siuan. "The important thing is that with these ter'angreal you can talk to Egwene, and through her to Moiraine. Between them, you can not only keep an eye on Rand al'Thor, you should be able to influence him even in Cairhien."

"Where he went from the Aiel Waste," Siuan said, "where I predicted he would be." If her eyes and words were directed at the Aes Sedai, her astringent tone was plainly meant for Leane, who grunted.

"Much good that did. Two Aes Sedai sent off to the Waste chasing ducks."

Oh, yes, there was very definitely a chill there.

"Enough, children," Anaiya said, very much as if they really were children and she a mother used to their petty squabbles. She eyed the other Aes Sedai meaningfully. "It will be a very good thing to be able to talk with Egwene."

"If these work as claimed," Morvrin said, bouncing

the ring on one palm and fingering the other *ter'angreal* on her lap. The woman would not believe the sky was blue without proof.

Sheriam nodded. "Yes. That will be your first duty, Elayne, Nynaeve. You will have a chance to teach Aes Sedai, showing us how to use them."

Nynaeve curtsied, baring her teeth; they could take it for a smile if they chose. Teach them? Yes, and never get near the ring, or the others, again after. Elayne's curtsy was even stiffer, her face a cool mask. Her eyes rolled toward that fool *a'dam* almost longingly.

"The letters-of-rights will be useful," Carlinya said. With all that White Ajah coolness and logic, testiness still showed in the way she clipped her words. "Gareth Bryne always wants more gold than we have, but with those, we may almost be able to satisfy him."

"Yes," Sheriam said. "And we must take most of the coin, too. There are more mouths to feed and more backs to clothe every day, here and elsewhere."

Elayne gave a gracious nod, just as if they would not take the money whatever she said, but Nynaeve simply waited. Gold and letters-of-rights and even *ter'angreal* were only a part.

"For the rest," Sheriam went on, "we are agreed that you left the Tower by command, however erroneous it was, and you cannot be held to account for it. Now that you are safely back with us, you will resume your studies."

Nynaeve only breathed out slowly. It was no more than she had expected since the questioning began. Not that she liked it, but for once no one was going to be able to accuse her of having a temper. Not when in all probability it would do no good.

Elayne, though, burst out with a sharp, "But—!" Just that, before Sheriam cut in just as sharply.

"You will resume your studies. You are both very strong, but you are not Aes Sedai yet." Those green eyes held them until she was sure they had taken it, and then she spoke again, her voice milder. Milder, but still firm. "You are returned to us, and if Salidar is not the White Tower, you may still consider it so. From what you have told us in the last hour, there is considerably more you have yet to tell." Nynaeve's breath caught, but Sheriam's eyes slid back to the *a'dam*. "A pity you did not bring the Seanchan woman with you. That, you really should have done." For some reason, Elayne blushed bright red, and looked angry at the same time. For herself, Nynaeve was only relieved it was the Seanchan the woman meant. "But Accepted cannot be called to account for not thinking as Aes Sedai," Sheriam went on. "Siuan and Leane will have many questions for you. You will cooperate with them, and answer to the best of your abilities. I trust I do not have to remind you not to take advantage of their present condition. Some Accepted, and even some novices, have thought to lay blame for events, and even take punishments into their own hands." That mild tone became cold steel. "Those young women are now extremely sorry for themselves. Need I say more?"

Nynaeve was no more hasty than Elayne to let her know she did not, which was to say they both almost stammered in their haste to get it out. Nynaeve had not thought of assigning blame—to her thinking, Aes Sedai were all to blame—but she did not want Sheriam angry with her. Realizing that fact drove the truth home bitterly; the days of freedom certainly were gone.

"Good. Now you may take the jewels the Panarch gave you, and the arrow—when there is time, you must tell me why she made you a gift like that—and go. One of the other Accepted will find you places to sleep. Proper dresses may be harder to come by, but they will be found. I expect you to put your . . . adventures . . . behind you, and fit smoothly back into your proper place." Plain although unspoken was the promise that if they did not fit back in smoothly, they would be smoothed until they did. Sheriam gave a satisfied nod when she saw they understood.

Beonin had not said a word since the shield of *saidar* was lowered, but as Nynaeve and Elayne made their curtsies, the Gray sister rose and strode to the table where their things were laid out. "And what of this?" she demanded in heavy Taraboner accents, whipping aside the white cloth that covered the seal on the Dark One's prison. For a change, her large blue-gray eyes looked more angry than startled. "Are there to be no more questions about this? Do you all mean to ignore it?" The black-and-white disc lay there, next to the washleather purse, in a dozen or more pieces, fitted back together as neatly as they could be.

"It was whole when we put it in the purse." Nynaeve paused to work moisture back into her mouth. As much as her eyes had avoided the covering cloth before, they could not leave the seal now. Leane had smirked when she saw the red dress unwrapped from around its cargo, and said . . . No, she would not run away from it, even in her head! "Why should we have thought to take special care? It's *cuendillar*!"

"We didn't look at it," Elayne said breathlessly, "or touch it more than we had to. It felt filthy, evil." It no longer did. Carlinya had made them each hold a piece, demanding to know what evil feeling they were talking about.

They had said the same things before, more than once, and no one paid them any heed now.

Sheriam rose and went to stand beside the honey-haired Gray. "We are ignoring nothing, Beonin. Asking these girls more questions will do no good. They have told us what they know."

"More questions are always good," Morvrin said, but she had stopped fiddling with the *ter'angreal* to stare at the broken seal as hard as anyone else. It might be *cuendillar*—she and Beonin had each tested it and said it was—yet she had broken one fragment with her hands.

"How many of the seven still hold?" Myrelle asked softly, as if speaking to herself. "How long until the Dark One breaks free, and the Last Battle comes?" Every Aes Sedai did some of almost everything, according to her talents and inclinations, yet each Ajah had its own reason for being. Greens—who called themselves the Battle Ajah—held themselves ready to face new Dreadlords in the Last Battle. There was almost a hint of eagerness in Myrelle's voice.

"Three," Anaiya said unsteadily. "Three still hold. If

we know everything. Let us pray that we do. Let us pray three are enough."

"Let us pray those three are stronger than this one," Morvrin muttered. *"Cuendillar* cannot be broken so, not and *be cuendillar.* It cannot."

"We will discuss this in due course," Sheriam said. "After more immediate matters that we can do something about." Taking the cloth from Beonin, she covered the broken seal once more. "Siuan, Leane, we have reached a decision concerning—" She stopped short as she turned and saw Elayne and Nynaeve. "Were you not told to go?" For all her outward calm, the turmoil inside showed in her forgetting their presence.

Nynaeve was more than ready to drop another curtsy, blurt a hurried "By your leave, Aes Sedai," and scurry for the door. Without moving a muscle, the Aes Sedai— and Siuan and Leane—watched her and Elayne go. Nynaeve felt their eyes like a shove. Elayne stepped not a whit more slowly, for all she cast another look at the *a'dam.*

Once Nynaeve had the door closed and could lean back against its unpainted wood, clutching the gilded coffer to her breasts, she took her first comfortable breath, or so it seemed, since entering the old stone inn. She did not want to think about the broken seal. Another broken seal. She would not. Those women could shear sheep with their eyes. She could almost look forward to watching their first meeting with the Wise Ones; if she was not likely to be squarely in the middle. It had been more than difficult when she first went to the Tower, learning to do as she was told by others, to bend her neck. After long months when she gave the orders—well, once she had consulted Elayne; usually—she did not know how she was going to learn to pull wool and scratch gravel all over again.

The common room, with its ill-patched plaster ceiling and cold stone fireplaces near collapsing, was the same beehive it had been when she first entered. No one gave her more than a glance now, and she gave them less. A small crowd awaited her and Elayne.

Thom and Juilin, on a rough bench against the flaking

plaster wall, had their heads together with Uno, who was squatting in front of them, long sword hilt rising over his shoulder. Areina and Nicola, both staring amazed at everything and trying not to show it, occupied another bench with Marigan, who was watching Birgitte attempt to amuse Jaril and Seve by awkwardly juggling three of Thom's colored wooden balls. Kneeling behind the boys, Min was tickling them, whispering in their ears, but they only clung to each other, silently staring with those too-big eyes.

Only two others in the entire room were not scurrying about. Two of Myrelle's three Warders happened to be leaning against the wall in conversation a few paces beyond the benches, just this side of the door back to the kitchen corridor. Croi Makin, a yellow-haired young splinter of stone from Andor with a fine profile, and Avar Hachami, hawk-nosed and square-chinned with a thick gray-streaked mustache like down-curved horns. No one would call Hachami handsome even before his dark-eyed stare made them swallow. They were not looking at Uno or Thom or anyone else, of course. It was only happenstance that they alone had nothing to do and had chosen just that spot to do it. Of course.

Birgitte dropped one of the balls when she saw Nynaeve and Elayne. "What did you tell them?" she asked quietly, barely glancing at the silver arrow in Elayne's hand. The quiver hung at her belt; but her bow was propped against the wall.

Moving closer, Nynaeve carefully did not look toward Makin and Hachami. Just as carefully she lowered her voice and was sparing with emphasis. "We told them everything they asked for."

Elayne touched Birgitte's arm. "They know you are a good friend who has helped us. You are welcome to stay here, just the same as Areina and Nicola and Marigan."

Only when some of Birgitte's tension melted did Nynaeve realize how much had been there. The blue-eyed woman scooped up the fallen yellow ball and smoothly tossed all three back to Thom, who snagged them with one hand and made them vanish in a single motion. She wore the faintest of relieved grins.

"I can't tell you how glad I am to see the pair of you," Min said for at least the fourth or fifth time. Her hair was longer than it had been, though still a dark cap around her head, and she looked different in some other way that Nynaeve could not put a finger on. Surprisingly, freshly embroidered flowers climbed the lapels of her coat; she had always worn quite plain clothes before. "A friendly face is rare around here." Her eyes flickered just a fraction toward the two Warders. "We have to settle down alone and have a long talk. I can't wait to hear what you've been up to since you left Tar Valon." Or to tell what she had been up to as well, else Nynaeve missed her guess.

"I would like very much to talk to you, too," Elayne said, quite seriously. Min looked at her, then sighed and nodded, not as eager as a moment before.

Thom and Juilin and Uno came up behind Birgitte and Min, their faces set in that way men took on when they meant to say things they thought a woman might not like to hear. Before they could open their mouths, though, a curly-haired woman in an Accepted's dress pushed between Juilin and Uno, glowering at them, and planted herself in front of Nynaeve.

Faolain's dress, with its seven bands of color at the hem for the Ajahs, was not quite as white as it should have been, and her dark face wore a scowl. "I am surprised to see you here, wilder. I thought you had gone running back to your village, and our fine Daughter-Heir to her mother."

"Are you still souring milk for a hobby, Faolain?" Elayne asked.

Nynaeve kept her face pleasant. Just barely. Twice in the Tower Faolain had been set to teach her something. To put her in her place, was her own opinion. Even when teacher and pupil were both Accepted, the teacher had the status of Aes Sedai so long as the lesson lasted, and Faolain took full advantage. The curly-haired woman had spent eight years as a novice and five more as Accepted; she was not best pleased that Nynaeve had never had to be a novice at all, or that Elayne had worn pure white for less than a year. Two lessons from Faolain, and two trips to Sheriam's study for Nynaeve, for stubbornness, temper, a list as long as her arm. She made her voice light. "I heard Siuan and Leane have been badly treated by someone. I think Sheriam means to make an example to end it once and for all." She kept her eyes steady on the other woman's, and Faolain's widened in alarm.

"I've done nothing since Sheriam—" Faolain's mouth snapped shut, and her face colored heavily. Min hid her mouth behind her hand, and Faolain jerked her head around, studying the other women, from Birgitte to Marigan. She motioned brusquely to Nicola and Areina. "You two will do, I suppose. Come with me. Now. No dawdling." They rose slowly, Areina staring warily and Nicola with fingers fretting at the waist of her dress.

Elayne stepped between them and Faolain before Nynaeve could, chin high and eyes imperious blue ice. "What do you want with them?"

"I am obeying Sheriam Sedai's orders," Faolain replied. "I myself think they are too old for first testing, but I obey orders. A sister accompanies Lord Bryne's recruiting parties, testing women even as old as Nynaeve." Her sudden smile could have come from a viper. "Shall I inform Sheriam Sedai that you disapprove, Elayne? Shall I tell her you won't let your *retainers* be tested?" Elayne's chin came down somewhat during that, but of course she could not simply back down. She needed a diversion.

Nynaeve touched Faolain's shoulder. "Have they found many?"

In spite of herself, the woman's head turned, and when she glanced back, Elayne was soothing Areina and Nicola, explaining that they would not be hurt, or forced into anything. Nynaeve would not have gone so far. When Aes Sedai found someone with the spark born in her like Elayne or Egwene, someone who would channel eventually whether she wanted to or not, they were quite open about bundling her into training whatever her wishes. They seemed more lenient about those who could be trained but would never touch *saidar* without it, and about wilders, those who had survived the one-in-four chance of teaching themselves, usually without knowing what they had done and often blocked in some way, as Nynaeve was. Supposedly they could choose to come or stay. Nynaeve had chosen to enter the Tower, but she suspected that if she had not, she still would have gone, perhaps even tied hand and foot. Aes Sedai gave women who had the smallest chance of joining them as much choice as a lamb on a feastday.

"Three," Faolain said after a moment. "All that effort, and they've found three. One a wilder." She truly did not like wilders. "I do not know why they are so eager to find new novices. The novices we have can't be raised Accepted until we regain the Tower. It is all Siuan Sanche's fault, her and Leane." A muscle in her cheek twitched, as if she realized that remark might be thought to harass the former Amyrlin and Keeper, and she seized Areina and Nicola each by an arm. "Come along. I obey orders, and if you're to be tested, you'll be tested, waste of time or no waste of time."

"A nasty woman," Min murmured, squinting after Faolain as she hurried the other across the common room. "You'd think, if there was any justice, she would have an unpleasant future ahead of her."

Nynaeve wanted to ask what Min had seen in her viewing of the curly-haired Accepted—there were a hundred questions she wanted to ask her—but Thom and the other two men planted themselves firmly in front of her and Elayne, Juilin and Uno to either side so among the three they could see in every direction. Birgitte was leading Jaril and Seve to their mother, keeping her out of it. Min knew what the men were up to, too, by the rueful look she gave them; she seemed about to say something, but in the end she only shrugged and joined Birgitte.

By Thom's face, he could have been about to comment on the weather, or ask what was for supper. Nothing important. "This place is full of dangerous fools and dreamers. They think they can depose Elaida. That's why Gareth Bryne is here. To raise an army for them."

Juilin's grin almost split his dark face in two. "Not fools. Madwomen and madmen. I don't care if Elaida was there the day Logain was born. They're mad to think they can pull down an Amyrlin sitting in the White Tower from here. We could reach Cairhien in a month, maybe."

"Ragan and a few of the others already have horses marked out for borrowing." Uno was grinning, too; it looked incredibly incongruous with that glaring red eye on his patch. "The guards are set to watch for people coming in, not going out. We can lose them in the forest. It'll be dark soon. They'll never find us." The women's donning their Great Serpent rings back by the river had had a remarkable effect on his language. Though he did seem to make up for it when he thought they could not hear.

Nynaeve looked at Elayne, who shook her head slightly. Elayne would put up with anything to be Aes Sedai. And herself? Small chance that they could influence these Aes Sedai to support Rand if they had decided to try controlling him instead. Make that no chance; she might as well be realistic. And yet . . . And yet there was Healing. She would learn nothing of it in Cairhien, but here . . . Not ten paces from her, Therva Maresis, a slender Yellow with a long nose, was methodically ticking off points on a parchment with her pen. A bald-headed Warder with a black beard stood conferring with Nisao Dachen near the door, head and shoulders above her despite being no taller than average, while Dagdara Finchey, as wide as any man in the room and taller than most, addressed a group of novices in front of one of the unlit fireplaces, briskly sending them off one by one on errands. Nisao and Dagdara were Yellow Ajah, too; it was said that Dagdara, her graying hair marking considerable age on an Aes Sedai, knew more of Healing than any two others. It was not as if Nynaeve would be able to do anything useful if she did go to Rand. Just watch him go mad. If she could progress with Healing, maybe she could find a way to hold that madness off. There was too much that Aes Sedai were willing to call hopeless and let go at that to suit her.

All of that flashed through her head in the time it took to look at Elayne and turn back to the men. "We will be staying here. Uno, if you and the others want to go to

Rand, you are free to, as far as I'm concerned. I fear I no longer have money to help you." The gold the Aes Sedai had taken was needed just as they said, but she could not help wincing at the few silvers left in her purse. These men had followed her—and Elayne, of course—for all the wrong reasons, but that did not lessen her responsibility for them. Their loyalties were to Rand; they had no reason to enter a struggle for the White Tower. With a glance at the gilded coffer, she added reluctantly, "But I do have some things you can sell along the way."

"You must go too, Thom," Elayne said. "And you, Juilin. There's no point in remaining. We have no need of you now, but Rand will." She tried to press her casket of jewels into Thom's hands, but he refused to take it.

The three men exchanged looks in that irritating way they had, Uno going so far as to roll his eye. Nynaeve thought she heard Juilin mutter something under his breath about having said they would be stubborn.

"Perhaps in a few days," Thom said.

"A few days," Juilin agreed.

Uno nodded. "I could do with a little rest if I'm going to be running from Warders halfway to Cairhien."

Nynaeve gave them her flattest stare and deliberately tugged her braid. Elayne had her chin as high as it had ever been, her blue eyes haughty enough to chip ice. Thom and the others surely knew the signs by now; their nonsense was not going to be allowed. "If you think you are still following Rand al'Thor's orders to look after us—" Elayne began in frosty tones at the same time that Nynaeve said heatedly, "You promised to do as you were told, and I mean to see—"

"Nothing like that," Thom broke in, brushing back a strand of Elayne's hair with a gnarled finger. "Nothing at all like. Can't an old man with a limp want a little rest?"

"To tell the truth," Juilin said, "I am just staying because Thom owes me money. Dice."

"Do you expect us to steal twenty horses from Warders like falling out of bed?" Uno growled. He seemed to have forgotten just offering to do exactly that.

Elayne stared, at a loss for words, and Nynaeve was having difficulty finding them herself. How far they had fallen. Not so much as a shifted foot in the three of them. The trouble was that she was torn. She had determined to send them away. She had, and not because she didn't want them around watching her curtsy and scrape right and left. Not at all. Yet with almost nothing in Salidar as she had expected, she had to admit, however reluctantly, that it would be . . . comforting . . . to know she and Elayne had more than Birgitte to depend on. Not that she would take up the offer of escape, of course—if that was what it should be called—not under any circumstances. Their presence would just be . . . comforting. Certainly not that she would let them know that. She would not have to, since they were going, whatever they thought. Rand *could* find use for them, very probably, and they would only get in the way here. Except . . .

The unpainted door opened, and Siuan stalked out, followed by Leane. They stared at each other coldly before Leane sniffed and glided away, startlingly sinuous as she vanished around Croi and Avar into the corridor that led to the kitchens. Nynaeve frowned slightly. In the midst of all that iciness there had been one instant, a brief flicker she almost missed with it right in front of her. . . .

Siuan swung toward her, then abruptly stopped short, her face going blank. Someone else had joined the small gathering.

Gareth Bryne, dented breastplate buckled over his plain buff-colored coat and steel-backed gauntlets tucked behind his sword belt, radiated command. Mostly gray hair and a bluff face gave him the appearance of a man who had seen everything, endured everything; a man who could endure anything.

Elayne smiled, nodding graciously. A far cry from her astonished stares, coming into Salidar, when she had first recognized him at the length of the street. "I will not say it is entirely good to see you, Lord Gareth. I have heard of some difficulty between Mother and you, but I am sure it can be mended. You know Mother is hasty sometimes. She will come 'round, and ask you back to your proper place in Caemlyn, you may be certain of it."

"Done is done, Elayne." Ignoring her astonishment—

Nynaeve doubted anyone who knew Elayne's rank had ever been so curt to her—he turned to Uno. "Have you thought on what I said? Shienarans are the finest heavy cavalry in the world, and I have lads who are just right for proper training."

Uno frowned, his one eye sliding to Elayne and Nynaeve. Slowly, he nodded. "I've nothing better to do. I'll ask the others."

Bryne clapped him on the shoulder. "Well enough. And you, Thom Merrilin." Thom had half turned away at the other man's approach, knuckling his mustaches and staring at the floor as if to obscure his face. Now he met Bryne's level stare with one of his own. "I once knew a fellow with a name much like yours," Bryne said. "A skilled player of a certain game."

"I once knew a fellow who looked much like you," Thom replied. "He tried hard to put me in chains. I think he'd have cut my head off if he ever laid hands on me."

"A long time ago, that would be? Men do strange things for women sometimes." Bryne glanced at Siuan and shook his head. "Will you join me for a game of stones, Master Merrilin? I sometimes find myself wishing for a man who knows the game well, the way it's played in lofty circles."

Thom's bushy white eyebrows drew down almost as far as Uno's had, but he never took his eyes from Bryne. "I might play a game or two," he said finally, "once I know the stakes. As long as you understand I don't intend to spend the rest of my life playing stones with you. I don't like staying too long in one place anymore. My feet itch, sometimes."

"So long as they don't itch in the middle of a crucial game," Bryne told him dryly. "The two of you come with me. And don't expect much sleep. Around here, everything needs doing yesterday, except what should have been done last week." Pausing, he looked at Siuan again. "My shirts came back only half clean today." With that he was leading Thom and Uno off. Siuan glared at his back, then shifted her frown to Min, and Min grimaced and darted off the way Leane had gone.

Nynaeve did not understand that last exchange at all. And the nerve of those men, thinking they could talk over her head—or under her nose, or whatever— without her understanding every word. Enough of them, anyway.

"A good thing he has no need for a thief-catcher," Juilin said, eyeing Siuan sideways, and plainly uncomfortable. He had not gotten over the shock of learning her name; Nynaeve was not sure he had taken in about her being stilled, and no longer the Amyrlin Seat. He certainly shifted his feet for *her*. "This way I can sit and talk. I've seen a lot of fellows who look like they might unwind over a mug of ale."

"He practically ignored me," Elayne said incredulously. "I don't care what the trouble is between him and Mother, he has no right. . . . Well, I will tend to Lord Gareth Bryne later. I have to talk to Min, Nynaeve."

Nynaeve started to follow as Elayne hurried toward that hall to the kitchens—Min would give straight answers—but Siuan caught her arm in an iron grip.

The Siuan Sanche who had meekly ducked her head before those Aes Sedai was gone. No one here wore the shawl. Her voice never rose; it did not need to. She fixed Juilin with a stare that had him almost jumping out of his skin. "You watch what questions you ask, thief-catcher, or you'll gut yourself for market." Those cold blue eyes shifted to Birgitte and Marigan. Marigan's mouth twisted as if she tasted something bad, and even Birgitte blinked. "You two find an Accepted named Theodrin and ask her about somewhere to sleep tonight. Those children look as if they should be in bed already. Well? Move your feet!" Before they had stirred a step— and Birgitte was moving as quickly as Marigan, maybe quicker—she rounded on Nynaeve. "You, I have questions for. You were told to cooperate, and I suggest you do if you know what's good for you."

It was like being caught in a high wind. Before Nynaeve knew it, Siuan was hurrying her up rickety steps with a railing cobbled together from unpainted wood, hustling her down a rough-floored corridor to a tiny room with two cramped beds built into the wall, one above the other. Siuan took the only stool, motioning her to sit on the lower bed. Nynaeve chose to stand, if only to show she was not going to be pushed. There was not much else in the room. A washstand with a brick propping up one leg held a chipped pitcher and basin. A few dresses hung from pegs, and what appeared to be a pallet lay rolled up in one corner. Nynaeve had fallen far in the space of a day, but Siuan had fallen farther than she could imagine. She did not think she would have too much trouble with the woman. Even if Siuan did still have the same eyes.

Siuan sniffed. "Suit yourself, then, girl. The ring. It doesn't require channeling?"

"No. You heard me tell Sheriam—"

"Anyone can use it? A woman who can't channel? A man?"

"Possibly a man." *Ter'angreal* that did not need the Power usually worked for men or women. "For any woman, yes."

"Then you are going to teach me to use it."

Nynaeve raised one eyebrow. This might be a lever to get what she wanted. If not, she had another. Maybe. "Do they know about this? All the talk was of showing them how it works. You were never mentioned."

"They don't know." Siuan did not appear shaken at all. She even smiled, and not pleasantly. "And they won't. Else they'll learn you and Elayne have been posing as full sisters since you left Tar Valon. Moiraine might be letting Egwene get away with it—if she hasn't tried it, too, I don't know a bar knot from a running hitch—but Sheriam, Carlinya . . . ? They'll have you squealing like a spawning grunter before they're done. Long before."

"That's ridiculous." Nynaeve realized she was sitting on the edge of the bed. She did not remember sitting down. Thom and Juilin would hold their tongues. No one else knew. She had to talk to Elayne. "We haven't pretended anything of the sort."

"Don't lie to me, girl. If I needed confirmation, your eyes gave it. Your stomach is turning somersaults, isn't it?"

It most certainly was. "Of course not. If I teach you

anything, it's because I want to." She was not going to let this woman bully her. The last vestige of pity winked out. "If I do, I want something in return. To study you and Leane. I want to know if stilling can be Healed."

"It can't," Siuan said flatly. "Now—"

"Anything short of death should be."

"'Should be' isn't 'is,' girl. Leane and I were promised we would be left alone. Speak to Faolain or Emara if you want to know what happens to anyone who molests us. They weren't the first or the worst, but they cried the longest."

Her other lever. Near panic had driven it right out of her head. If it existed. One glance. "What would Sheriam say if she knew you and Leane weren't ready to tear out each other's hair at all?" Siuan just looked at her. "They think you're tamed, don't they? The more you snap at anybody who can't snap back, the more they take it for proof when you leap to obey every time an Aes Sedai coughs. Was a little cringing all it took to make them forget the two of you had worked hand-in-hand for years? Or did you convince them stilling had changed everything about you, not just your face? When they find out you've been scheming behind their backs, manipulating them, you'll howl louder than any grunter. Whatever *that* is." Not so much as a blink. Siuan was not going to loose her temper and let any admissions slip out. Yet there had been something in that brief look; Nynaeve was sure of it. "I want to study you—and Leane— whenever I want. And Logain." Perhaps she could learn something there as well. Men were different; it would be like looking at the problem from another angle. Not that she would Heal him even if she discovered how. Rand's channeling was necessary. She was not about to loose another man on the world who could wield the Power. "If not, then you can forget about the ring, and *Tel'aran'rhiod.*" What was Siuan after there? Probably just to revisit something that at least seemed like being Aes Sedai. Nynaeve stamped firmly on momentarily rekindled pity. "And if you make any claims about us pretending to be Aes Sedai, then I'll have no choice but to tell about you and Leane. Elayne and I might be uncomfortable until the truth comes out, but it will, and the truth will make you weep as long as Faolain and Emara together."

Silence stretched. How did the other woman manage to look so cool? Nynaeve had always thought it had to do with being Aes Sedai. Her lips felt dry, the only part of her that did. If she was wrong, if Siuan was willing to put it to the test, she knew who would be weeping.

Finally, Siuan muttered, "I hope Moiraine has managed to keep Egwene's backbone more supple than this." Nynaeve did not understand, but she hardly had time to consider it. The next instant, the other woman was leaning forward, hand outstretched. "You keep my secrets, and I will keep yours. Teach me the ring, and you can study stilling and gentling to your heart's content."

Nynaeve barely managed to hold in a relieved sigh as she clasped the offered hand. She had done it. For the first time in what seemed forever, someone had tried to bully her and failed. She almost felt ready to face Moghedien. Almost.

Elayne caught up with Min just outside the back door of the inn and fell in beside her. Min had what looked like two or three white shirts wadded under one arm. The sun sat on the treetops, and in the fading light the stableyard had the soft look of dirt not long turned, with a huge stump that might have belonged to an oak right in the middle. The thatch-roofed stone stable had no doors, allowing a good look at men moving among filled stalls. Surprisingly, Leane was talking to a large man on the edge of the stable's shadow. Roughly dressed, he looked a blacksmith, or a brawler. What was surprising was how close Leane stood, head tilted as she stared up at him. And then she actually patted his cheek before turning away and hurrying back into the inn. The big man stared after her a moment, then melted into the shadows.

"Don't ask me what she's up to," Min said. "Strange people come to see Siuan or her, and some of the men, she . . . Well, you saw."

Elayne did not really care what Leane did. But now that she had Min alone, she did not know how to bring up what she wanted. "What are you doing?"

"Laundry," Min muttered, shifting the shirts irritably. "I can't tell you how good it is to see Siuan the mouse for once. She doesn't know whether the eagle is going to eat her or make her a pet, but she has the same choice she gives everybody else. None!"

Elayne quickened her pace to keep up as they crossed the stableyard. Whatever that was about, it gave no opening. "Did you know what Thom was going to suggest? We are staying."

"I told them you would. Not a viewing." Min's step slowed again as they started between the stable and a crumbling stone wall, down a dim alley of brush stubble and trampled weeds. "I just didn't think you would give up the chance to study again. You were always eager. Nynaeve, too, even if she won't admit it. I wish I'd been wrong. I'd go with you. At least, I . . ." She muttered something furious-sounding under her breath. "Those three you brought with you are trouble, and that *is* a viewing."

There it was. The crack she needed. But instead of asking what she had intended, she said, "You mean Marigan and Nicola and Areina? How can they be trouble?" Only a fool passed over what Min saw.

"I don't know exactly. I only caught glimpses of aura, and just out of the corner of my eye. Never when I was looking right at them, where I might have made something out. There aren't many who have auras all the time, you know. Trouble. Maybe they'll carry tales. Were you up to anything you wouldn't want the Aes Sedai to know about?"

"Certainly not," Elayne said briskly. Min looked at her sideways, and she added, "Well, nothing we didn't have to do. They can't possibly know about it anyway." This was not taking her where she wanted to go. Drawing a deep breath, she leaped off the cliff. "Min, you had a viewing about Rand and me, didn't you?" She went two steps before she realized the other woman had stopped.

"Yes." It was a wary word.

"You saw that we were going to fall in love."

"Not exactly. I saw you'd fall in love with him. I don't know what he feels for you, only that he's tied to you some way."

Elayne's mouth tightened. That was about what she had expected, but not what she wanted to hear. *"Wish" and "want" trip the feet, but "is" makes the path smoother.* That was what Lini said. You had to deal with what was, not what you wished was. "And you saw there would be someone else. Someone I'd have to . . . share . . . him with."

"Two," Min said hoarsely. "Two others. And . . . And I'm one."

Mouth already open for the next question, for a moment Elayne could only stare. "You?" she got out at last.

Min bristled. "Yes, me! Do you think I can't fall in love? I didn't want to, but I did, and that's that." She stalked past Elayne down the alleyway, and this time Elayne was slower to catch up.

It certainly explained a few things. How nervously Min had always sidestepped talking about it. The embroidery on her lapels. And unless she was imagining it, Min was wearing rouge, too. *How do I feel about it?* she wondered. She could not sort it out. "Who is the third?" she asked quietly.

"I don't know," Min mumbled. "Only that she has a temper. Not Nynaeve, thank the Light." She gave a weak laugh. "I don't think I could have survived that." Once more she gave Elayne a cautious sidelong look. "What does this mean between you and me? I like you. I never had a sister, but sometimes I feel like you. . . . I want to be your friend, Elayne, and I won't stop liking you whatever happens, but I can't stop loving him."

"I don't very much like the idea of having to share a man," Elayne said stiffly. That was certainly an understatement.

"Me, neither. Only . . . Elayne, it shames me to admit it, but I will take him any way I can get him. Not that either of us has much choice. Light, he's scrambled my whole life. Just thinking about him scrambles my brains." Min sounded as if she did not know whether to laugh or cry.

Elayne exhaled slowly. Not Min's fault. Was it better that it was Min rather than, say, Berelain or somebody else she could not abide? *"Ta'veren,"* she said. "He bends the world around him. We are chips caught in a whirlpool. But I seem to recall you and me and Egwene saying we'd never let a man come between us being friends. We will work it out somehow, Min. And when we find out who the third is . . . Well, we'll work that out, as well. Somehow." A *third!* Could *she* be Berelain? *Oh, blood and ashes!*

"Somehow," Min said bleakly. "Meanwhile, you and I are caught here in a leg trap. I know there's another, I know I can't do anything about it, but I had enough trouble reconciling myself to you, and . . . Cairhienin women aren't all like Moiraine. I saw a Cairhienin noblewoman in Baerlon once. On the surface, she made Moiraine look like Leane, but sometimes she said things, hinting. And her auras! I don't think a man in the whole town was safe alone with her, not unless he was ugly, lame, and better yet, dead."

Elayne sniffed, but she managed to make her voice light. "Never you mind about that. We have another sister, you and I, one you've never met. Aviendha is keeping a close eye on Rand, and he doesn't go ten steps without a guard of Aiel Maidens of the Spear." A Cairhienin woman? At least she had met Berelain, knew something of her. No. She was not going to fret over it like some brainless girl. A grown woman dealt with the world as it was and made the best of it. Who could it be?

They had come out into an open yard dotted with cold ashes. Huge kettles, most pitted where rust had been scrubbed away, stood against the encircling stone wall, which had been toppled in several places by trees growing up in it. Despite the shadows crossing the yard, two steaming kettles still sat on flames, and three novices, hair sweat-soaked and white skirts tied up, were hard at work on scrub boards stuck into broad washpots full of soapy water.

With a glance at the shirts under Min's arm, Elayne

embraced *saidar*. "Let me help you with those." Channeling to do assigned chores was forbidden—physical labor built character, so they said—but this could not be counted the same. If she swirled the shirts around in the water violently enough, there should be no reason to get their hands wet. "Tell me everything. Are Siuan and Leane as changed as they seem? How did you get here? Is Logain *really* here? And why are you laundering some man's shirts? Everything."

Min laughed, plainly pleased to change the subject. "'Everything' will take a week. But I'll try. First, I helped Siuan and Leane get out of the dungeon Elaida had stuck them in, and then . . ."

Making appropriate sounds of amazement, Elayne channeled Air to lift one of the boiling kettles clear of its flames. She hardly noticed the novices' incredulous stares; she was used to her own strength now, and it rarely occurred to her that she did things, without thinking, that some full Aes Sedai could not do at all. Who was the third woman? Aviendha had *better* be keeping a close eye on him.

CHAPTER
51

News Comes to Cairhien

A thin thread of blue smoke rising from the plain, short-stemmed pipe clenched in his teeth, Rand rested one hand on the balcony's stone railing and looked into the garden below. Sharp shadows were lengthening; the sun was a red ball falling through a cloudless sky. Ten days in Cairhien, and this seemed the first moment he had stood still when he was not asleep. Selande stood close by his side, pale face tilted up to watch him, not the garden. Her hair was not so elaborately done as that of a woman of higher rank, but it still added half a foot to her height. He tried to ignore her, but it was difficult to ignore a woman who insisted on pressing her firm bosom against your arm. The meeting had gone on long enough for him to want a moment's break. He had known it for a mistake as soon as Selande followed him out.

"I know a secluded pool," she said softly, "where this heat might be escaped. A sheltered pool, where nothing would disturb us." The music of Asmodean's harp drifted out through the square arches behind them. Something light, cool sounding.

Rand puffed a little more vigorously. The heat. Nothing compared to the Waste, but . . . Autumn should be coming on, yet the afternoon felt like the depths of summer. A rainless summer. Shirt-sleeved men in the garden were spreading water from buckets, doing it late to avoid evaporation, but too much was brown or dying. The weather could not be natural. The burning sun mocked him. Moiraine agreed, and Asmodean, but neither knew what to do or how, any more than he did. Sammael. Sammael he could do something about.

"Cool water," Selande murmured, "and you and I alone." She snuggled closer, though he did not see how it was possible.

He wondered when the next taunt would come. No dashing off in a temper, whatever Sammael did. Once his methodical buildup in Tear was done, then he would loose the lightning. One crushing stroke to put an end to Sammael, and add Illian to his bag at the same time. With Illian, Tear and Cairhien, plus an army of Aiel big enough to overwhelm any nation in weeks, he . . .

"Would you not like to swim? I do not swim well myself, but surely you will teach me."

Rand sighed. For a moment he wished Aviendha was there. No. The last thing he wanted was a bruised Selande running screaming with her clothes half torn off.

Hooding his eyes, he looked down at her and spoke quietly around his pipe. "I can channel." She blinked, drawing back without moving a muscle. They never understood why he would bring that up; for them it was something to be glossed over, ignored if possible. "They say I'll go mad. But I'm not mad yet. Not yet." He chuckled from deep in his chest, then cut it off abruptly, made his face blank. "Teach you to swim? I'll hold you up in the water with the Power. *Saidin* is tainted, you know. The Dark One's touch. You won't feel it, though. All around you, but you'll not feel a thing." Another chuckle, with a hint of a wheeze. Her dark eyes were as wide and round as they would go, her smile a sickly rictus. "Later, then. I want to be alone, to think about . . ." He bent as if to kiss her, and with a squeak, she dropped a curtsy so sudden that at first he thought her legs had collapsed.

Backing away, curtsying hurriedly at every other step,

she babbled about the honor of serving him, her deepest wish to serve him, all in a voice on the brink of hysteria, until she bumped into one of the square arches. A final, half-bend of her knees, and she darted inside.

With a grimace, he turned back to the railing. Frightening women. She would have made excuses had he asked her to leave him, would have taken a command as only a temporary setback unless it was to stay out of his sight, and even then. . . . Maybe word would spread this time. He had to keep a short rein on his temper; it ran away too easily of late. It was the drought he could do nothing about, the problems that sprang up like weeds wherever he looked. A few moments more alone with his pipe. Who would rule a nation when he could have easier work, such as carrying water uphill in a sieve?

Across the garden, between two of the Royal Palace's stepped towers, he had a view of Cairhien, harshly lit and shadowed, mastering the hills more than flowing over them. His crimson flag with the ancient Aes Sedai symbol hung limply above one of those two towers, a long copy of the Dragon Banner over the other. That one flew a dozen places in the city, including the tallest of the great unfinished towers, right in front of him. Shouting had done as little as orders there; neither Tairens nor Cairhienin could believe he really meant that he only wanted one, and Aiel did not care about banners one way or another.

Even now, deep inside the palace, he could hear the murmur of a city jammed to bursting. Refugees from every corner of the land, more afraid to return to their homes than they were to have the Dragon Reborn in their midst. Merchants seeping in, selling whatever people could afford to buy and buying whatever people could not afford to keep. Lords and armed men rallying to his banner, or to someone's. Hunters for the Horn thinking it must be found near him; a dozen Foregaters, or a hundred, were ready to sell it to any of them. Ogier stonemasons down from Stedding Tsofu to see if there was work for their fabled skills. Adventurers, some of whom might have been bandits a week gone, come to see what they could pick up. There had even been a hundred or so Whitecloaks, though they had galloped out as soon as it was clear the siege had been lifted. Did Pedron Niall's ingathering of the Whitecloaks concern him? Egwene gave him hints of things, but she saw matters from the White Tower, wherever she stood. The Aes Sedai point of view was not his.

At least the wagon trains full of grain were beginning to arrive from Tear with some regularity. Hungry people could riot. He wished he could have simply left it at being glad they were not so hungry anymore, but there it was. The bandits were fewer. And the civil war had not resumed. Yet. More good news. He had to make certain it stayed that way before he could leave. A hundred things to take care of before he could go after Sammael. Only Rhuarc and Bael remained of the chiefs he really trusted, those who had marched from Rhuidean with him. But if the four clans who had joined him late could not be trusted on the march to Tear, could he trust them loose in Cairhien? Indirian and the others had acknowledged him as *Car'a'carn,* but they knew him as little as he knew them. The message that morning might be a problem. Berelain, First of Mayene, was only a few hundred miles south of the city, on her way to join him with a small army; he had no idea how she had led it across Tear. Oddly, her letter had asked if Perrin was with him. No doubt she feared Rand might forget her small country if she did not remind him. It might almost be a pleasure to watch her spar with the Cairhienin, the latest in a long line of Firsts who had managed to keep Tear from swallowing their country by playing the Game of Houses. Perhaps if he put her in charge here . . . He would be taking Meilan and the other Tairens with him when the time came. If it ever came.

This was no better than what was waiting inside. Tapping the dottle from his pipe, he ground out the tabac's last sparks under his boot. No need to risk fire to the garden; it would go up like a torch. The drought. The unnatural weather. He realized he was snarling silently. First work on what he knew he could do something about. It took an effort to smooth his face before he went in.

Asmodean, as well dressed as any lord, with falls of lace at his neck, plucked a soothing melody from his harp in one corner, leaning against the dark severe paneling as if lounging at his leisure. The others who were sitting bobbed out of their chairs at Rand's appearance, and back down at his sharp gesture. Meilan, Torean and Aracome occupied carved-and-gilded chairs on one side of the deep red and gold carpet, each with a young Tairen lord at his back, mirroring the Cairhienin on the other side. Dobraine and Maringil had a young lord apiece behind them, too, each with the front of his head shaved and powdered like Dobraine's. A white-faced Selande stood at Colavaere's shoulder, and trembled when Rand looked at her.

Schooling his face, he strode down the carpet to his own chair. That chair alone was reason to control his features. It was a new gift from Colavaere and the other two, in what they imagined was the Tairen style. He must like Tairen gaudiness; he ruled Tear, had sent them here. Carved Dragons held it up, all sparkling red and gold with enamel and gilt, and great sunstones for their golden eyes. Two more made the arms, and others climbed the tall back. Countless craftsmen must have gone without sleep since his arrival to make the thing. He felt like a fool sitting on it. Asmodean's music had changed; it had a grand sound, now, a triumphal march.

And yet, there was an added wariness in those dark Cairhienin eyes watching him, a wariness reflected in the Tairens. It had been there before he went outside, too. Perhaps in attempting to curry favor they had made a mistake that was only now dawning on them. They had all tried to ignore who he was, pretend he was simply some young lord who had conquered them, who could be dealt with and manipulated. That chair—that throne—held up in front of them who and what he really was.

"Are the soldiers moving on schedule, Lord Dobraine?" The harp faded away as soon as he opened his mouth, Asmodean apparently absorbed in preening it.

The leathery man smiled grimly. "They are, my Lord Dragon." No more than that. Rand had no illusions that

Dobraine liked him more than any of the others did, or that he would not try to gain advantage where he could, but Dobraine actually seemed ready to hold to the oath he had sworn. The colorful slashes down the chest of his coat were worn from a breastplate being buckled over them.

Maringil shifted forward on his chair, whip-slender and tall for a Cairhienin, white hair almost touching his shoulders. His forehead was not shaved, and his coat, stripes nearly to his knees, bore no visible wear. "We need those men here, my Lord Dragon." Hawk's eyes blinked at the gilded throne, focused on Rand again. "There are many bandits at large in the land yet." He shifted again, so he did not have to look at the Tairens. Meilan and the other two were smiling faintly.

"I have set Aiel to hunting bandits," Rand said. They did have orders to sweep up any brigands in their path. And to not go out of their way to find them. Even Aiel could not do that and move quickly. "I'm told that three days ago, Stone Dogs killed nearly two hundred near Morelle." That was near the southernmost line claimed by Cairhien in recent years, halfway to the River Iralell. No need to let this lot know that those Aiel might be as far as the river by now. They could cover long distances faster than horses.

Maringil persisted, frowning uneasily. "There is another reason. Half of our land west of the Alguenya is in the hands of Andor." He hesitated. They all knew Rand had grown up in Andor; a dozen rumors made him a son of one Andoran House or another, even a son of Morgase herself, either cast off because he could channel or fled before he could be gentled. The slender man went on as if tiptoeing barefoot and blindfolded among daggers. "Morgase does not seem to be reaching for more as yet, but what she has already must be taken back. Her heralds have even proclaimed her right to the—" He stopped abruptly. None of them knew who Rand meant the Sun Throne for. Maybe it was Morgase.

Colavaere's dark gaze had Rand on balance scales again; she had said little today. She would not until she learned why Selande's face was so white.

Suddenly Rand was tired, of nobles balking, of all the manuevering in *Daes Dae'mar*. "Andoran claims to Cairhien will be taken care of when I am ready. Those soldiers will go to Tear. You will follow the High Lord Meilan's good example of obedience, and I'll hear no more on it." He swung toward the Tairens. "Your example is a good one, Meilan, isn't it? And yours, Aracome? If I ride out tomorrow, I won't find a thousand Defenders of the Stone camped ten miles south who were supposed to be on their way back to Tear two days ago, will I? Or two thousand armsmen from Tairen Houses?"

Those faint smiles faded with each word. Meilan became very still, dark eyes glittering, and Aracome's narrow face went pale, whether from anger or fear it was hard to say. Torean dabbed at his lumpy face with a silk handkerchief pulled from his sleeve. Rand ruled in Tear, and meant to rule; *Callandor* driven into the Heart of the Stone proved that. That was why they had not protested against his sending Cairhienin soldiers to Tear. They thought to carve new estates, perhaps kingdoms, here, far from where he ruled.

"You will not, my Lord Dragon," Meilan said finally. "Tomorrow I will ride with you so you may see for yourself."

Rand did not doubt it. A rider would be dispatched south as soon as the man could arrange it, and by tomorrow those soldiers would be far on toward Tear. It would do. For now. "I am done, then. You may leave me."

A few starts of surprise, masked so quickly they might have been imagined, and they were rising, bowing and curtsying, Selande and the young lords backing away. They had expected more. An audience with the Dragon Reborn was always long, and tortuous as they saw it, with him firmly bending them the way he meant them to go, whether it was declaring that no Tairen could claim lands in Cairhien without marrying into a Cairhienin House, or refusing to allow the expulsion of Foregaters, or making laws apply to nobles that had never applied to any but commoners before.

His eyes followed Selande for a moment. She was not

the first in the last ten days. Nor the tenth, or even the twentieth. He had been tempted, at least at first. When he rejected slender, plump promptly replaced her, as tall or dark, for Cairhienin anyway, replaced short or fair. A constant search for the woman who would please him. The Maidens turned back those who tried to sneak into his quarters at night, firmly but more gently than Aviendha had handled the one she caught. Aviendha apparently took Elayne's ownership of him with little short of deadly seriousness. Yet her Aiel sense of humor seemed to find tormenting him very satisfying; he had seen the satisfaction on her face when he groaned and hid his face as she started undressing for the night. Thus he could have resented her deadly seriousness if he had not quickly understood what was behind that string of pretty young women.

"My Lady Colavaere."

She stopped as soon as he spoke her name, cool-eyed and calm beneath her ornate tower of dark curls. Selande had no choice but to remain with her, though she was plainly as reluctant to stay as the others were to go. Meilan and Maringil bowed themselves out last, so intent on Colavaere and trying to puzzle out why she had been called to stay that they did not realize they were side by side. Their eyes were a perfect match, dark and predatory.

The dark-paneled door closed. "Selande is very pretty young woman," Rand said. "But some prefer the company of a more mature . . . more knowledgeable . . . woman. You will sup alone with me tonight, when Second Even is rung. I look forward to the pleasure." He waved her away before she could say anything, if she could have. Her face did not change, but her curtsy was a trifle unsteady. Selande looked purely amazed. And infinitely relieved.

Once the door had closed again, behind the two women, Rand threw back his head and laughed. A harsh, sardonic laugh. He was tired of the Game of Houses, so he played it without thinking. He was disgusted with himself for frightening one woman, so he frightened another. It was reason enough to laugh. Colavaere stood behind that line of young women who had been flinging themselves at him. Find a bedpartner for the Lord Dragon, a young woman whose strings she pulled, and Colavaere would have a string tied firmly to Rand. But it was some other woman she meant to bed, and perhaps even marry, the Dragon Reborn. Now she would sweat all the hours until Second Even. She had to know she was pretty, if short of beautiful, and if he rebuffed all the young women she sent, perhaps it was because he wanted one with another fifteen or so years. And she would be certain she did not dare say no to the man who held Cairhien in his fist. By tonight, she should be amenable, should stop this idiocy. Aviendha would very likely slit the throat of any woman she found in his bed; besides, he had no time for all these easily frightened doves thinking to sacrifice themselves for Cairhien and Colavaere. There were too many problems to deal with, and no time.

Light, what if Colavaere decides it's worth the sacrifice? She might. She was easily cold-blooded enough. *Then I'll have to see that it's cold with fear.* It would not be difficult. He could sense *saidin* like something just beyond the edge of sight. He could feel the taint on it. Sometimes he thought that what he felt was the taint in him, now, the dregs left by *saidin.*

He found that he was glaring at Asmodean. The man seemed to be studying him, face expressionless. The music resumed again, like water babbling over stones, soothing. So he needed soothing, did he?

The door opened without a knock, admitting Moiraine, Egwene and Aviendha together, the younger women's Aiel garb framing the Aes Sedai's pale blue. For anyone else, even Rhuarc or another chief still near the city or yet another delegation of Wise Ones, a Maiden would have entered to announce them. These three the Maidens sent on in even if he was taking a bath. Egwene glanced at "Natael" and grimaced, and the tune became lower, and for a moment intricate, perhaps a dance, before settling to what might have been the sighing of breezes. The man wore a twisted smile, directed at his harp.

"I'm surprised to see you, Egwene," Rand said. He swung his leg over the arm of the chair. "What is it—six days you've been avoiding me? Have you brought me more good news? Has Masema sacked Amador in my name? Or have these Aes Sedai you say support me turned out to be Black Ajah? You notice I don't ask *who* they are, or where. Not even how you know. I don't ask you to divulge Aes Sedai secrets, or Wise Ones' secrets, or whatever they are. Just give me the driblets you're willing to dole out, and let me worry whether what you don't care to tell me will stab me in the night."

She looked at him calmly. "You know what you need to know. And I will not tell you what you do not need to know." That was what she had said six days ago. She was as much Aes Sedai as Moiraine, for all one wore Aiel garb and the other pale blue silk.

There was nothing calm about Aviendha. She moved to stand shoulder-to-shoulder with Egwene, green eyes flashing, back so straight it might have been iron. He was half surprised Moiraine did not join them, so they could all three glare at him. Her vow of obedience left a startling amount of room, it seemed, and the three seemed to have become close since his argument with Egwene. Not that it had been much of an argument; you could not argue very well with a woman who watched with cool eyes, never raised her voice, and after one refusal to answer declined even to acknowledge your question again.

"What do you want?" he said.

"These came for you in the last hour," Moiraine said, extending two folded letters. Her voice seemed to fit Asmodean's chime-like tune.

Rand rose to take them suspiciously. "If they're for me, how did they come into your hands?" One was addressed to "Rand al'Thor" in an exact, angular hand, the other to "The Lord Dragon Reborn" in script flowing yet no less precise. The seals were unbroken. A second look made him blink. The two seals seemed to be the same red wax, and one bore the impression of the Flame of Tar Valon, the other a tower overlaid on what he recognized as the island of Tar Valon.

"Perhaps because of where they came from," Moiraine replied, "and from whom." It was no explanation, but it was as much as he would get unless he demanded more. Even then he would have to prod her through every step. She kept her vow, but in her own way. "There are no poison needles in the seals. And no traps woven."

He paused with his thumb against the Flame of Tar Valon—he had not thought of either—then broke it. Another Flame in red wax stood beside the signature, Elaida do Avriny a'Roihan in a hasty scrawl above her titles. The rest was in the angular hand.

> There can be no denial that you are the one prophesied, yet many will try to destroy you for what else you are. For the sake of the world, this cannot be allowed. Two nations have bent knee to you, and the savage Aiel as well, but the power of thrones is as dust beside the One Power. The White Tower will shelter and protect you against those who refuse to see what must be. The White Tower will see that you live to see Tarmon Gai'don. None else can do this. An escort of Aes Sedai will come to bring you to Tar Valon with the honor and respect you deserve. This I pledge to you.

"She doesn't even ask," he said wryly. He remembered Elaida well for having met her only once. A woman hard enough to make Moiraine seem a kitten. The "honor and respect" he deserved. He would wager that the escort of Aes Sedai just happened to number thirteen.

Passing Elaida's letter back to Moiraine, he opened the other. The page was covered in the same hand that had addressed it.

> With respect, I humbly beg to make myself known to the great Lord Dragon Reborn, whom the Light blesses as savior of the world.
> All the world must stand in awe of you, who has conquered Cairhien in one day as you did Tear. Yet be wary, I beseech you, for your splendor will inspire

jealousy even in those not toiled in the Shadow. Even here in the White Tower are the blind who cannot see your true radiance, which will illumine us all. Yet know that some rejoice in your coming, and will delight to serve your glory. We are not those who would steal your luster for ourselves, but rather those who would kneel to bask in your brilliance. You shall save the world, according to the Prophecies, and the world shall be yours.

To my shame, I must beg you to let no one see these words, and to destroy them when once read. I stand, naked of your protection, among some who would usurp your power, and I cannot know who around you is as faithful as I. I am told that Moiraine Damodred may be with you. She may serve you devotedly, obeying your words as law, as I will, yet I cannot know, for I remember her as a secretive woman, much given to plotting, as Cairhienin are. Yet even if you believe she is your creature, as I, I beg you to keep this missive secret, even from her. My life lies beneath your fingers, my Lord Dragon Reborn, and I am your servant.

Alviarin Freidhen

He read it through again, blinking, then handed it to Moiraine. She barely scanned the page before giving it to Egwene, who had her head over the other letter with Aviendha. Perhaps Moiraine already knew what they contained?

"A good thing you gave your oath," he said. "The way you used to be, keeping everything back, I might have been ready to suspect you by now. A good thing you're more open now." She did not react. "What do you make of it?"

"She must have heard about your swelled head," Egwene said softly. He did not think he had been meant to hear. Shaking her head, she said more loudly, "This doesn't sound like Alviarin at all."

"It is her hand," Moiraine said. "What do *you* make of it, Rand?"

"I think there's a rift in the Tower, whether Elaida

knows it or not. I assume an Aes Sedai can't write a lie more easily than she can speak one?" He did not wait for her nod. "If Alviarin had been less flowery, I might have thought they were working together to pull me in. I can't see Elaida even thinking half of what Alviarin wrote, and I can't see her having a Keeper who could write it, not if she knew."

"You are not going to do this thing," Aviendha said, Elaida's letter crumpled in her hand. It was not a question.

"I am not a fool."

"Sometimes you are not," she said grudgingly, and made it worse by raising a questioning eyebrow to Egwene, who considered for a moment, then shrugged.

"Do you see anything else?" Moiraine asked.

"I see White Tower spies," he told her dryly. "They know I hold the city." For at least two or three days after the battle, the Shaido would have stopped anything but a pigeon going north. Even a rider who knew where to change horses, no sure thing between Cairhien and Tar Valon, could not have reached the Tower in time for these letters to come back today.

Moiraine smiled. "You learn quickly. You will do well." For a moment she almost looked fond. "What will you do about it?"

"Nothing, except make sure that Elaida's 'escort' doesn't get within a mile of me." Thirteen of the weakest Aes Sedai could overwhelm him linked, and he did not think Elaida would send her weakest. "That, and be aware that the Tower knows what I do the day after I do it. Nothing more until I know more. Could Alviarin be one of your mysterious friends, Egwene?"

She hesitated, and he suddenly wondered whether she had told Moiraine any more than she had him. Was it Aes Sedai secrets she kept, or Wise Ones'? At last she said simply, "I do not know."

A rap came at the door, and Somara put her flaxen head into the room. "Matrim Cauthon has come, *Car'a'carn.* He says that you sent for him."

Four hours ago, as soon as he had learned Mat was back in the city. What would the excuse be this time? It was time to be done with excuses. "Stay," he told the women. Wise Ones made Mat almost as uneasy as Aes Sedai did; these three would put him off balance. He did not give a second thought to using them. He was going to use Mat, too. "Send him in, Somara."

Mat strolled into the room grinning, as if it was a common room. His green coat hung open, and his shirt was half unlaced, exposing the silver foxhead dangling on his sweaty chest, but the dark silk scarf was draped around his neck to hide his hanging scar in spite of the heat. "Sorry if I took too long. There were some Cairhienin who thought they knew how to play cards. Doesn't he know anything livelier?" he asked, jerking his head toward Asmodean.

"I hear," Rand said, "that every young man who can pick up a sword wants to join the Band of the Red Hand. Talmanes and Nalesean are having to turn them away in droves. And Daerid has doubled the number of his footmen."

Mat paused in lowering himself into the chair Aracome had used. "It's true. A fine lot of young . . . fellows wanting to be heroes."

"The Band of the Red Hand," Moiraine murmured. "*Shen an Calhar.* A legendary group of heroes indeed, though the men in it must have changed many times in a war that lasted well over three hundred years. It is said they were the last to fall to the Trollocs, guarding Aemon himself, when Manetheren died. Legend says a spring rose where they fell, to mark their passing, but I rather think the spring was already there."

"I wouldn't know about that." Mat touched the foxhead medallion, and his voice picked up strength. "Some fool got the name from somewhere, and they all started using it."

Moiraine glanced at the medallion dismissively. The small blue stone hanging on the forehead seemed to catch the light and glow, though the angles were wrong. "You are very brave, it seems, Mat." It was flatly said, and the silence that followed stiffened his face. "Very brave," she said finally, "to lead *Shen an Calhar* across the Alguenya and south against the Andorans. Even braver than that, for there are rumors that you went alone to scout the way, and Talmanes and Nalesean had to ride hard to catch up to you." Egwene sniffed loudly in the background. "Hardly wise for a young lord leading his men."

Mat's lip curled. "I'm no lord. I've more respect for myself than that."

"But very brave," Moiraine said as if he had not spoken. "Andoran supply wagons burned, outposts destroyed. And three battles. Three battles, and three victories. With small loss to your own men, though outnumbered." As she fingered a rip in the shoulder of his coat he sank back as far the chair would allow. "Are you drawn to the thick of battles, or are they drawn to you? I am almost surprised you came back. To hear the stories, you might have driven the Andorans back across the Erinin had you stayed."

"Do you think this is funny?" Mat snarled. "If you have something to say, say it. You can play the cat all you want, but I'm no mouse." For an instant his eyes flickered toward Egwene and Aviendha, watching with folded arms, and he fingered the silver foxhead again. He had to be wondering. It had stopped one woman's channeling from touching him. Would it stop three?

Rand only watched. Watched his friend being softened for what he meant to do to him. *Is there anything left to me but necessity?* It was a quick thought, there and gone. He would do what he must.

The Aes Sedai's voice gained a rime of crystal frost as she spoke, almost in an echo. "We all do as we must, as the Pattern decrees. For some there is less freedom than for others. It does not matter whether we choose or are chosen. What must be, must be."

Mat did not look softened at all. Wary, yes, and certainly angry, but not softened. He could have been a tomcat backed into a corner by three hounds. A tomcat who meant to go down hard. He seemed to have forgotten anyone was in the room except for himself and the three women. "You always have to push a man where you want him, don't you? Kick him there, if he won't go led by the nose. Blood and bloody ashes! Don't glare at me, Egwene, I'll speak the way I want. Burn me! All it needs is for Nynaeve to be here, yanking her braid out of her head, and Elayne staring down her nose. Well, I'm glad she isn't, to hear the news, but even if you had Nynaeve, I'd not be shoved—"

"What news?" Rand said sharply. "News Elayne shouldn't hear?"

Mat looked up at Moiraine. "You mean there's something you haven't ferreted out?"

"What news, Mat?" Rand demanded.

"Morgase is dead."

Egwene gasped, clasping both hands to her mouth below eyes like huge circles. Moiraine whispered something that might have been a prayer. Asmodean's fingers never faltered on the harp.

Rand felt as if his belly had been ripped out. *Elayne, forgive me.* And a faint echo, altered. *Ilyena, forgive me.* "Are you certain?"

"As certain as I can be without seeing the body. It seems Gaebril has been named King of Andor. And Cairhien, too, for that matter. Supposedly Morgase did it. Something about the times needing a strong man's hand or some such, as if anybody could have a stronger than Morgase herself. Only, those Andorans down south have heard rumors that she hasn't been seen in weeks. More than rumors. You tell me what it adds up to. Andor's never had a king, but now it has one, and the queen's vanished. Gaebril's the one wanted Elayne killed. I tried to tell her that, but you know how she always knows more than a mudfooted farmer. I don't think he'd balk a second at slitting a queen's throat."

Rand discovered that he was sitting in one of the chairs across from Mat, though he did not remember moving. Aviendha laid a hand on his shoulder. Concern tightened her eyes. "I am all right," he said roughly. "There's no need to send for Somara." Her face reddened, but he hardly noticed.

Elayne would never be able to forgive him. He had known that Rahvin—Gaebril—held Morgase prisoner, but he had ignored it because the Forsaken might expect him to help her. He had gone his own way, to do what they did not expect. And ended chasing Couladin instead of doing what he planned. He had known, and concentrated his attention on Sammael. Because the man taunted him. Morgase could wait while he smashed Sammael's trap and Sammael with it. And so Morgase was dead. Elayne's mother was dead. Elayne would curse him to her deathbed.

"I'll tell you one thing," Mat was going on. "There are a lot of queen's men down there. They are not so sure about fighting for a king. You find Elayne. Half of them will flock to you to put her on the—"

"Shut up!" Rand barked. He quivered so hard with fury that Egwene stepped back, and even Moiraine eyed him carefully. Aviendha's hand tightened on his shoulder, but he shook it off as he stood. Morgase dead because he had done nothing. His own hand had been on the knife as surely as Rahvin's. Elayne. "She will be avenged. Rahvin, Mat. Not Gaebril. Rahvin. I'll lay him by the heels if I never do another thing!"

"Oh, blood and bloody ashes!" Mat groaned.

"This is madness." Egwene flinched as if realizing what she had said, but she kept that firm, calm voice. "You have your hands full with Cairhien yet, not to mention the Shaido to the north and whatever it is you're planning in Tear. Do you mean to start another war, with two on your plate already and a ruined land besides?"

"Not a war. Me. I can be in Caemlyn in an hour. A raid—right, Mat?—a raid, not a war. I'll rip Rahvin's heart out." His voice was a hammer. He felt as if acid filled his veins. "I could wish I had Elaida's thirteen sisters to take with me, to smother him, and bring him to justice. Tried and hung for murder. That would be justice. But he'll just have to die however I can kill him."

"Tomorrow," Moiraine said softly.

Rand glared at her. But she was right. Tomorrow would be better. A night to let his rage cool. He needed to be cold when he faced Rahvin. Now he wanted to seize *saidin* and lay about him, destroying. Asmodean's music had changed again, to a tune that street musicians in the city had played during the civil war. You could still hear it sometimes when a Cairhienin noble passed. "The Fool Who Thought He Was King." "Get out, Natael. Get out!"

Asmodean straightened smoothly, bowing, but his face could have done for snow, and he crossed the room quickly, as if uncertain what one second more might bring. He always pushed, but perhaps this time he had pushed too far. As he opened the door, Rand spoke again.

"I will see you tonight. Or I will see you dead."

Asmodean's bow was not so graceful this time. "As my Lord Dragon commands," he said hoarsely, and hurriedly pulled the door shut with him on the other side.

The three women looked at Rand, expressionless, not blinking.

"The rest of you go, too." Mat practically bounded toward the door. "Not you. I have things to say to you yet."

Mat stopped short, sighing loudly and fiddling with his medallion. He was the only one who had moved.

"You do not have thirteen Aes Sedai," Aviendha said, "but you have two. And myself. I may not know as much as Moiraine Sedai, but I am as strong as Egwene, and I am no stranger to the dance." She meant the dance of spears, what the Aiel called battle.

"Rahvin is mine," he told her quietly. Maybe Elayne could forgive him a little if he at least avenged her mother. Probably not, but maybe he could forgive himself. A little. He forced his hands to stay at his sides, to not make fists.

"Will you draw a line on the ground for him to step over?" Egwene asked. "Put a chip on your shoulder? Have you considered that Rahvin might not be alone if he calls himself King of Andor now? Much good it will do when you appear if one of his guards puts an arrow through your heart."

He could remember wishing she would not shout at him, but it had been so much easier then. "Did you think I meant to go alone?" He had; he had never thought of anyone to guard his back, though now he could hear a small whisper, *He likes to come from behind, or at your flanks*. He could hardly think clearly at all. His anger seemed to have a life of its own, stoking the fires that kept it boiling. "But not you. This is dangerous. Moiraine can come if she wishes."

Egwene and Aviendha did not look at one another before stepping forward, but they moved as one, not stopping until they were so close even Aviendha had to tilt her head back to look up at him.

"Moiraine can come if she wishes," Egwene said.

If her voice was smooth ice, Aviendha's was molten stone. "But it is too dangerous for us."

"Have you become my father? Is your name Bran al'Vere?"

"If you have three spears, do you put two aside because they are newer made?"

"I do not want to risk you," he said stiffly.

Egwene arched her eyebrows. "Oh?" That was all.

"I am not *gai'shain* to you." Aviendha bared her teeth. "You will never choose what risks I take, Rand al'Thor. Never. Know it now."

He could . . . What? Wrap them in *saidin* and leave them? He still could not shield them. So they might well snare him in return. A fine mess, all because they wanted to be stubborn.

"You have thought of guards," Moiraine said, "but what if who is with Rahvin is Semirhage, or Graendal? Or Lanfear? These two might overwhelm one such, but could you face her and Rahvin together alone?"

There had been something in her voice when she said Lanfear's name. Was she afraid that if Lanfear was there, he might finally join her? What would he do if she was there? What could he do? "They can come," he said through clenched teeth. "Now will you go?"

"As you command," Moiraine said, but they were in no hurry about it. Aviendha and Egwene took ostentatious care in rearranging their shawls before they started for the door. Lords and ladies might dart at his word, but never them.

"You did not try to talk me out of it," he said abruptly. He meant it for Moiraine, but Egwene spoke first, though to Aviendha, and with a smile. "Stopping a man from what he wants to do is like taking a sweet from a child. Sometimes you have to do it, but sometimes it just isn't worth the trouble." Aviendha nodded.

"The Wheel weaves as the Wheel wills," was Moiraine's reply. She stood in the doorway looking more Aes Sedai than he ever remembered her, ageless, with dark eyes that seemed ready to swallow him, slight and slender yet so regal she could have commanded a roomful of queens if she could not channel a spark. That blue stone on her forehead was catching the light again. "You will do well, Rand."

He stared at the door long after it closed behind them.

It was a scuff of boots that recalled him to Mat's presence. Mat was trying to slide toward the door, moving slowly so as not to be seen.

"I need to talk to you, Mat."

Mat grimaced. Touching the foxhead like a talisman, he spun to face Rand. "If you think I'm going to put my head on the block just because those fool women did, you can forget it now. I'm no bloody hero, and I don't want to be one. Morgase was a pretty woman—I even liked her; as much as you can like a queen—but Rahvin is Rahvin, burn you, and I—"

"Shut up and listen. You have to stop running."

"Burn me if I will! This is no game I chose, and I won't—"

"I said, shut up!" Rand drove the foxhead against Mat's chest with a hard finger. "I know where you got this. I was there, remember? I cut the rope you were hanging from. I don't know exactly what got shoved into your head, but whatever it is, I need it. The clan chiefs know war, but somehow you know it too, and maybe better. I need that! So this is what you're going to do, you and the Band of the Red Hand. . . ."

"Be careful tomorrow," Moiraine said.

Egwene paused at the door to her room. "Of course we'll be careful." Her stomach was turning backflips, but she kept her voice steady. "We know how dangerous facing one of the Forsaken will be." By Aviendha's expression, they might have been talking about what was for supper. But then, she was never afraid of anything.

"Do you, now," Moiraine murmured. "Be very careful anyway, whether you think one of the Forsaken is near or not. Rand will need both of you in the days to come. You handle his temper well—though I may say your methods are unusual. He will need people who cannot be driven away or quelled by his rages, who will tell him what he must hear instead of what they think he wants to."

"You do that, Moiraine," Egwene told her.

"Of course. But he will still need you. Rest well. Tomorrow will be . . . difficult for us all." She glided away down the corridor, passing from dimness to pool of lamplight to dimness. Night was already coming to these shadowed halls, and oil was in short supply.

"Will you stay with me awhile, Aviendha?" Egwene asked. "I feel more like talking than eating."

"I must tell Amys what I have promised to do tomorrow. And I must be in Rand al'Thor's sleeping chamber when he comes."

"Elayne can never complain that you haven't watched Rand closely for her. Did you really drag the Lady Berewin down the hall by her hair?"

Aviendha's cheeks colored faintly. "Do you think these Aes Sedai in—Salidar?—will help him?"

"Be careful of that name, Aviendha. Rand cannot be allowed to find them without preparation." The way he was now, they would be more likely to gentle him, or at least send thirteen sisters of their own, than help him. She would have to stand between them in *Tel'aran'rhiod*, she and Nynaeve and Elayne, and hope those Aes Sedai had committed themselves too far to back out before they discovered how near the brink he was.

"I will be careful. Rest well. And eat well tonight. In the morning, eat nothing. It is not good to dance the spears with a full stomach."

Egwene watched her stride away before pressing her hands to her stomach. She did not think she would eat tonight or in the morning. Rahvin. And maybe Lanfear, or one of the others. Nynaeve had faced Moghedien and won. But Nynaeve was stronger than she or Aviendha, when she could channel at all. There might not be another. Rand said the Forsaken did not trust one another. She could almost wish he was wrong, or at least that he was not so certain. It was frightening when she thought she saw another man looking through his eyes, heard another man's words come out of his mouth. It should not be so; everyone was reborn as the Wheel turned. But everyone was not the Dragon Reborn. Moiraine would not talk of it. What would Rand do if Lanfear was there? Lanfear had loved Lews Therin Telamon, but what had the Dragon felt for her? How much of Rand was still Rand?

"You will work yourself into a tizzy this way," she said firmly. "You're not a child. Act like a woman."

When a serving woman brought her supper of snapbeans and potatoes and fresh baked bread, she made herself eat. It tasted like ashes.

Mat strode through the dimly lit corridors of the palace and flung open the door of the rooms that had been set aside for the young hero of the battle against the Shaido. Not that he had spent much time there; hardly any. Servants had lit two of the stand-lamps. Hero! He was no hero! What did a hero get? An Aes Sedai patting you on the head before she sent you out like a hound to do it again. A noblewoman condescending to favor you with a kiss, or laying a flower on your grave. He stalked back and forth in his anteroom, for once not pricing the flowered Illianer carpet or the chairs and chests and tables gilded and inlaid with ivory.

The stormy meeting with Rand had gone on till the sun set, him dodging, refusing, Rand following as doggedly as Hawkwing after the rout at Cole Pass. What was he to do? If he rode out again, Talmanes and Nalesean would surely follow with as many men as they could put in the saddle, expecting him to find another battle. And he probably would; that was what really put a chill on it. Much as he hated to admit it, the Aes Sedai was right. He was drawn to battle or it to him. Nobody could have tried harder to avoid one on the other side of the Alguenya.

Even Talmanes had commented on it. Until the second time his careful creeping away from one lot of Andorans took them where there was no choice but to fight another. And every time he could feel the dice rolling in his head; it was almost like a warning that a fight was just over the next hill, now.

There was always a ship, or might be, down at the docks beside the grain barges. Hard to find yourself in a battle on a ship in the middle of a river. Except the Andorans held one bank of the Alguenya for half its length or more below the city. The way his luck was running, the ship would run aground on the west bank with half the Andoran army camped there.

That left doing what Rand wanted. He could just see it.

"Good morrow, High Lord Weiramon, and all you other High Lords and Ladies. I'm a gambler, a farmboy, and I'm here to take command of your bloody army! The bloody lord Dragon Reborn will be with us as soon as he flaming takes care of one bloody little matter!"

Snatching his black-hafted spear from the corner, he hurled it the length of the room. It struck a wall hanging—a hunting scene—and the stone wall behind with a loud *clang,* then dropped to the floor, leaving the hunters neatly sliced in two. Swearing, he hurried to pick it up. The two-foot swordblade was not chipped or marred. Of course not. Aes Sedai work.

He fingered the ravens on the blade. "Will I ever be free of Aes Sedai work?"

"What was that?" Melindhra asked from the door.

He eyed her as he propped the spear against the wall, and for a change it was not spun-gold hair or clear blue eyes or a firm body that he thought of. It seemed that every Aiel went to the river sooner or later, to stare silently at so much water in one place, but Melindhra went every day, just about. "Has Kadere found ships yet?" Kadere would not be going to Tar Valon on grain barges.

"The peddler's wagons are still there. I do not know about . . . ships." She pronounced the unfamiliar word awkwardly. "Why do you wish to know?"

"I'm going away for a while. For Rand," he added hastily. Her face was too still. "I'd take you with me if I could, but you wouldn't want to leave the Maidens." A ship, or his own horse? And to where? That was the question. He could reach Tear quicker on a fast rivership than on Pips. If he was fool enough to make that choice. If he had any choice.

Melindhra's mouth tightened briefly. To his surprise, it was not over his leaving her. "So you slip back into Rand al'Thor's shadow. You have gained much honor of your own, among the Aiel as well as the wetlanders. Your honor, not honor reflected from the *Car'a'carn*."

"He can keep his honor and take it to Caemlyn or the Pit of Doom for all I care. Don't you worry. I'll find plenty of honor. I will write you about it. From Tear." Tear? He would never escape Rand, or Aes Sedai, if he made that choice.

"He is going to Caemlyn?"

Mat suppressed a wince. He was not supposed to say anything about that. Whatever he decided about the rest, he could do that much. "Just a name pulled from my pocket. Because of the Andorans down south, I suppose. I wouldn't know where he's—"

He had no warning. One instant she was just standing there, the next her foot was in his middle, driving out breath, doubling him over. Eyes bulging, he fought to keep his feet, to straighten, to think. Why? She spun like a dancer, backwards, and her other foot against the side of his head drove him staggering. Without a pause she leaped straight up, kicking out, her soft bootsole taking him hard flush in the face.

When his eyes cleared enough to see, he was on his back, halfway across the room from her. He could feel blood on his face. His head seemed stuffed with wool, and the room seemed to rock. That was when he saw her take a knife from her pouch, slim blade not much longer than her hand, gleaming in the lamplight. Winding the *shoufa* around her head in a quick motion, she raised the black veil across her face.

Groggily, he moved by instinct, without thinking. The blade came out of his sleeve, left his hand as if floating through jelly. Only then did he realize what he had done and stretch out desperately, trying to snatch it back.

The hilt bloomed between her breasts. She sagged to her knees, fell back.

Mat pushed himself up, wavering on hands and knees. He could not have stood if his life hung on it, but he crawled to her, muttering wildly. "Why? Why?"

He jerked her veil aside, and those clear blue eyes focused on him. She even smiled. He did not look at the knife-hilt. His knife-hilt. He knew where the heart was in a body. "Why, Melindhra?"

"I always liked your pretty eyes," she breathed, so faint he had to strain to hear.

"Why?"

"Some oaths are more important than others, Mat Cauthon." The slim-bladed knife came up swiftly, all her remaining strength behind it, the point driving the dangling foxhead against his chest. The silver medallion should not have stopped a blade, but the angle was just that much wrong, and some hidden flaw in the steel snapped the blade off right at the hilt just as he caught her hand. "You have the Great Lord's own luck."

"Why?" he demanded. "Burn you, why?" He knew there would be no answer. Her mouth remained open, as though she might say something more, but her eyes were already beginning to glaze.

He started to pull the veil back up, to cover her face and staring eyes, then let his hand fall. He had killed men, and Trollocs, but never a woman. Never a woman until now. Women were glad when he came into their lives. It was not boasting. Women smiled for him; even when he left them, they smiled as if they would welcome him back. That was all he ever really wanted from women; a smile, a dance, a kiss, and to be remembered fondly.

He realized his thoughts were babbling. Jerking the bladeless hilt from Melindhra's hand—it was gold-mounted jade, inlaid with golden bees—he hurled it into the marble fireplace, hoping it shattered. He wanted to cry, to howl. *I don't kill women! I kiss them, I don't . . . !*

He had to think clearly. Why? Not because he was

leaving, surely. She had hardly reacted to that. Besides, she thought he was chasing off after honor; she had always approved of that. Something she had said tugged at him, and then came back, with a chill. The Great Lord's own luck. He had heard it differently, many times. The Dark One's own luck. "A Darkfriend." A question, or certainty? He wished the thought made what he had done easier in his mind. He was going to carry her face to his grave.

Tear. He had as much as told her he was going to Tear. The dagger. Golden bees in jade. He would wager there were nine without looking. Nine golden bees on a field of green. The sign of Illian. Where Sammael ruled. Could Sammael be afraid of him? How could Sammael even know? It was only a few hours since Rand had asked Mat—told him—and he was not sure himself what he was going to do. Maybe Sammael would not take the chance? Right. One of the Forsaken, afraid of a gambler, however stuffed with other men's battle knowledge his head might be. That was ridiculous.

It all came down to this. He could believe that Melindhra had not been a Darkfriend, that she had decided to kill him on a whim, that there was no connection between a jade hilt inlaid with golden bees and his maybe going to Tear to lead an army against Illian. He could if he was a bullgoose fool. Better to err toward caution, he always said. One of the Forsaken had noticed him. He certainly was not standing in Rand's shadow now.

Sliding across the floor, he sat with his chin on his knees and his back against the door, staring at Melindhra's face, trying to decide what to do. When a servant knocked with his supper, he shouted for her to go away. Food was the last thing he wanted. What was he going to do? He wished he did not feel the dice spinning in his head.

CHAPTER
52

Choices

Laying down his razor, Rand wiped the last flecks of lather from his face and began doing up his shirtlaces. Early morning sunlight streamed through the square arches leading to his bedchamber balcony; the heavy winter curtains had been hung, but tied back to let in a breath of air. He would be presentable when he killed Rahvin. The thought loosed a bubble of rage, floating up out of his belly. He forced it back down. He would be presentable, and calm. Cold. No mistakes.

When he turned from the gilt-framed mirror, Aviendha was sitting on her rolled-up pallet against the wall, beneath a hanging portraying impossibly high gold towers. He had offered to have another bed put in the room, but she claimed mattresses were too soft for sleeping. She was watching him intently, her shift forgotten in one hand. He had been careful about not looking around from his shaving to give her time to dress, but aside from her white stockings, she wore not a stitch.

"I would not shame you in front of other men," she said abruptly.

"Shame me? What do you mean?"

She stood in one smooth motion, surprisingly pale where the sun had not touched her, slender and hard-muscled, yet with roundnesses and softnesses that haunted his dreams. This was the first time he had allowed himself to look at her openly when she flaunted herself, but she did not seem aware of it. Those big blue-green eyes were fixed on his. "I did not ask Sulin to include Enaila or Somara or Lamelle that first day. Nor did I ask them to watch you, or to do anything if you faltered. That was only their own concern."

"You just let me think they would try to carry me off like a babe if I wavered. A fine distinction."

His wry tone flew right past her. "It made you take care when you needed to."

"I see," he said dryly. "Well, I thank you for the promise not to shame me, in any case."

She smiled. "I did not say that, Rand al'Thor. I said not in front of other men. If you require it, for your own good. . . ." Her smile deepened.

"Do you mean to come like that?" He gestured irritably, taking her in from head to toe.

She had never shown the slightest embarrassment at being naked in front of him—far from it—but she glanced down at herself, then at him looking at her, and her face reddened. Suddenly she was surrounded by a flurry of dark brown wool and white *algode,* flying into her clothes so quickly that he could have thought she was channeling them on. "Have you arranged everything?" came from the middle of it. "Have you spoken to the Wise Ones? You were gone late last night. Who else comes with us? How many can you take? No wetlanders, I hope. You cannot trust them. Especially not treekillers. Can you truly carry us to Caemlyn in one hour? Is it like what I did the night . . . ? I mean to say, how will you do it? I cannot like trusting myself to things I do not know and cannot understand."

"Everything is arranged, Aviendha." Why was she babbling? And refusing to meet his eye? He had met with Rhuarc and the other chiefs still near the city; they had not truly liked his plan, but they saw it in terms of *ji'e'toh,* and none thought he had any other choice. They discussed it quickly, agreed, and then turned the talk to other things. Nothing to do with Forsaken or Illian or battle at all. Women, hunting, whether Cairhienin brandy could compare with *oosquai,* or wetlander tabac with what was grown in the Waste. For an hour he had almost forgotten what lay ahead. He hoped that the Prophecy of Rhuidean was somehow wrong, that he would not destroy those men. The Wise Ones had come to him, a delegation of more than fifty, alerted by Aviendha herself and led by Amys and Melaine and Bair; or maybe by Sorilea. With Wise Ones often it was difficult to tell who was in charge. They had not come to talk him out of anything—*ji'e'toh* again—but to make sure he understood that his obligation to Elayne did not outweigh that to the Aiel, and they had kept him in the meeting room until they were satisfied. It was that or lift them bodily out of his way to reach the door. When they wanted to be, those women were as good at ignoring shouts as Egwene had become. "We'll find out how many I can take when I try. Only Aiel." With luck, Meilan and Maringil and the rest would not know he was gone until after he went. If the Tower had spies in Cairhien, maybe the Forsaken did as well, and how could he trust people to keep secrets who could not see the sun rise without trying to use the fact in *Daes Dae'mar?*

By the time he had shrugged into a red coat embroidered in gold, a fine wool eminently suitable for a Royal Palace, in Caemlyn or Cairhien—the thought amused him, in a bleak sort of way—by that time, Aviendha was almost dressed. It was a wonder to him how she could scramble into her clothes so quickly and yet have nothing out of place. "A woman came last night while you were away."

Light! He had forgotten Colavaere. "What did you do?"

She paused in tying the laces of her blouse, eyes trying to bore a hole in his head, but her tone was offhand. "I took her back to her own chambers, where we talked for a time. There will be no more treekiller flipskirts scratching at your tent flap, Rand al'Thor."

"The very end I aimed at, Aviendha. Light! Did you hurt her badly? You can't go around beating ladies. These people cause me enough trouble without you bringing more."

She sniffed loudly and went back to her laces. "Ladies! A woman is a woman, Rand al'Thor. Unless she is a Wise One," she added judiciously. "That one sits lightly this morning, but her bruises can be hidden, and with a day's rest she will be able to leave her chambers. And she knows the right of matters, now. I told her if she caused you any bother again—*any* bother—I would come talk to her once more. A much longer talk. She will do as you say, when you say it. Her example will teach others. The treekillers understand nothing else."

Rand sighed. Not a method he would or could have chosen, but it might actually work. Or it might only make Colavaere and the others more sly from now on. Aviendha might not be worried about repercussions against herself—in fact, he would be surprised if she had even considered the possibility—but a woman who was High Seat of a powerful House was not the same as a young noblewoman of lesser rank. Whatever the effect for him, Aviendha could find herself set upon in some dark hallway and given ten times what she had given Colavaere, if not worse. "Next time, let me handle matters my way. I am the *Car'a'carn*, remember."

"You have shaving lather on your ear, Rand al'Thor."

Muttering to himself, he snatched up the striped towel and shouted, "Come!" to a rap at the door.

Asmodean entered, pale lace at the neck and cuffs of his black coat, harpcase slung on his back and a sword at his hip. It might have been winter for the coolness of his face, but his dark eyes were wary.

"What do you want, Natael?" Rand demanded. "I gave you your instructions last night."

Asmodean wet his lips and glanced once at Aviendha, who was frowning at him. "Wise instructions. I suppose I might learn something to your advantage, remaining here and watching, but the talk this morning is all of the shrieks from Lady Colavaere's apartments last night. It is said she displeased you, though no one seems to know quite how. That uncertainty is making everyone step lightly. I doubt anyone will breathe in the next few days without considering what you might make of it." Aviendha's face was a picture of insufferable self-satisfaction.

"So you want to come with me?" Rand said softly. "You want to be at my back when I face Rahvin?"

"What better place for the Lord Dragon's bard? But better yet, say under your eye. Where I can show my loyalty. I am not strong." Asmodean's grimace seemed natural enough in any man making that admission, but for an instant Rand sensed *saidin* filling the other man, felt the taint that twisted Asmodean's mouth. Just for an instant, but long enough for him to judge. If Asmodean had drawn as much as he could, he would be hard pressed to match one of the Wise Ones who could channel. "Not strong, yet perhaps I can help in some small way."

Rand wished he could see the shield Lanfear had woven. She had said it would dissipate with time, but Asmodean did not seem able to channel any more strongly now than he had the first day he was in Rand's hands. Perhaps she had lied, to give Asmodean false hope, to make Rand believe the man would grow strong enough to teach him more than he ever would. *It would be like her.* He was uncertain whether that was his thought or Lews Therin's, but he was sure it was true.

The long pause made Asmodean lick his lips again. "A day or two will not matter here. You will be back by then, or dead. Let me prove my loyalty. Perhaps I can do something. A whisker more weight on your side might shift the balance." Once more *saidin* poured into him, just for a moment. Rand felt a sensation of strain, yet it was still a feeble flow. "You know my choices. I am clinging to that tuft of grass on the cliff's lip, praying for it to hold one more heartbeat. If you fail, I am worse than dead. I must see you win and live." Suddenly eyeing Aviendha, he seemed to realize he might have said too much. His laugh was a hollow sound. "Else how can I compose the songs of the Lord Dragon's glory? A bard must have something to work with." The heat never touched Asmodean—a trick of the mind, he claimed, not the Power—but beads of sweat oozed down his forehead now.

Under his eyes, or left behind? Perhaps to run looking for a hiding place when he began wondering what was happening in Caemlyn. Asmodean would be the man he was until he died and was reborn, and perhaps even after. "Under my eyes," Rand said quietly. "And if I even suspect that where that whisker falls might displease me . . ."

"I put my trust in the Lord Dragon's mercy," Asmodean murmured, bowing. "With the Lord Dragon's permission, I will wait outside."

Rand glanced around the room as the man departed, backing away still half-bowed. His sword lay on the gilt-lined chest at the foot of the bed, Dragon-buckled sword belt wrapped around the scabbard and the Seanchan spearhead. The killing today would not be with steel, not on his part. He touched his pocket, felt the hard carved shape of the fat little man with his sword; that was the only sword he needed today. For a moment, he considered Skimming to Tear, to take back *Callandor*, or even to Rhuidean for what was hidden there. He could destroy Rahvin with either before the man knew he was there. He could destroy Caemlyn itself with either. But could he trust himself? So much power. So much of the One Power. *Saidin* hung there just out of sight. The taint seemed part of him. Rage oozed just beneath the surface, at Rahvin, at himself. If it broke loose, and he held even *Callandor* . . . What would he do? He would be invincible. With the other, he could Skim to Shayol Ghul itself, put an end to it all, end it now one way or another. One way or another. No. He was not in this alone. He could not afford anything but victory.

"The world rides on my shoulders," he murmured. Suddenly he yelped and clapped a hand to his left buttock. It felt as though a needle had stabbed him, but he did not need the goose bumps fading on his arms to tell him what had happened. "What was that for?" he growled at Aviendha.

"Just to see whether the *Lord Dragon* was still made of flesh like the rest of us mortals."

"I am," he said flatly, and seized *saidin*—all the

sweetness; all the filth—just long enough to channel briefly.

Her eyes widened, but she did not flinch, only looked at him as if nothing had occurred at all. Still, as they crossed the anteroom, she rubbed furtively at her bottom when she thought he was looking the other way. It seemed she was ordinary flesh, too. *Burn me, I thought I'd taught her a few manners.*

Pulling open the door, he stepped out and stood staring. Mat was leaning on his odd spear with that broad-brimmed hat pulled low, a little apart from Asmodean, but that was not took him aback. There were no Maidens. He should have known something was wrong when Asmodean came in unannounced. Aviendha was looking around in amazement, as if she expected to find them behind one of the tapestries.

"Melindhra tried to kill me last night," Mat said, and Rand stopped thinking about Maidens. "One minute we were talking, the next she was trying to kick my head off."

Mat told the story in short sentences. The dagger with the golden bees. His conclusions. He closed his eyes when he told how he had ended it—a simple, stark, "I killed her"—and opened them again quickly as if he saw something behind his eyelids he did not care to see.

"I'm sorry you had to do that," Rand said quietly, and Mat gave a bleak shrug.

"Better her than me. I suppose. She was a Darkfriend." He did not sound as if it made much difference.

"I will settle Sammael. Just as soon as I'm ready."

"And how many will that leave?"

"The Forsaken are not here," Aviendha snapped. "And neither are the Maidens of the Spear. Where are they? What have you done, Rand al'Thor?"

"Me? There were twenty right here when I came to bed last night, and I haven't seen one since."

"Perhaps it is because Mat . . . ." Asmodean began, and stopped when Mat looked at him, a tight-mouthed blend of pain and readiness to hit something.

"Do not be fools," Aviendha said in a firm voice. *"Far*

Dareis Mai would not claim *toh* against Mat Cauthon for this. She tried to kill him, and he killed her. Even her near-sisters would not, if she had had any. And no one would claim *toh* against Rand al'Thor for what another did unless he ordered it done. *You* have done something, Rand al'Thor, something great and dark, or they would be here."

"I've done nothing," he told her sharply. "And I don't intend to stand here discussing it. Are you dressed for the ride south, Mat?"

Mat shoved a hand into his coatpocket, fingering something. He usually kept his dice and dicecup in there. "Caemlyn. I'm tired of them sneaking up on me. I want to sneak up on one of them for a change. I just hope I get the bloody pat on the head instead of the bloody flower," he added with a grimace.

Rand did not ask him what he meant. Another *ta'veren*. Two together to twist chance perhaps. No way to tell *how*, or even *if*, but . . ."It seems like we'll be together a little longer." Mat looked more resigned than anything else.

Before they had gone far down the tapestry-lined corridor, Moiraine and Egwene met them, gliding along together as if the day held no more ahead than a walk in one of the gardens. Egwene, cool-eyed and calm, golden Great Serpent on her finger, really could have been Aes Sedai despite her Aiel clothes and shawl and the folded scarf around her temples, while Moiraine . . . Gold threads caught the light, faintly streaking Moiraine's gown of shimmering blue silk. The small blue stone on her forehead, hanging from its gold chain fastened in her waves of dark hair, shone as brightly as the large gold-set sapphires around her neck. Hardly suitable garb for what they intended, yet in his red coat, Rand could not comment.

Perhaps it was being here, where House Damodred had once held the Sun Throne, but Moiraine's graceful carriage was more regal than he remembered ever seeing it. Not even the presence of "Jasin Natael" could spoil that queenly serenity with surprise, but amazingly, she gave Mat a warm smile. "So you are going too, Mat.

Learn to trust the Pattern. Do not waste your life attempting to change what cannot be changed." From Mat's face, he might have been considering changing his mind about being there at all, but the Aes Sedai turned from him without a trace of worry. "These are for you, Rand."

"More letters?" he said. One bore his name in an elegant hand that he recognized immediately. "From you, Moiraine?" The other carried Thom Merrilin's name. Both had been sealed with blue wax, apparently with her Great Serpent ring, impressed with the image of the snake biting its own tail. "Why write me a letter? And sealed. You've never been afraid to say whatever you wanted to say to my face. If I ever forgot it, Aviendha has been reminding me that I'm only flesh and blood."

"You have changed from the boy I first saw outside the Winespring Inn." Her voice was a soft silver chiming. "You are hardly the same at all. I pray you have changed enough."

Egwene murmured something low. Rand thought it was, "I pray you have not changed too much." She was frowning at the letters as if she too wondered what was in them. So was Aviendha.

Moiraine went on more brightly, even briskly. "Seals ensure privacy. That contains things I wish you to think on; not now; when you have time for thinking. As for Thom's letter, I know no safer hands than yours in which to place it. Give it to him when you see him again. Now, there is something you must see at the docks."

"The docks?" Rand said. "Moiraine, this morning of all mornings, I've no time for—"

But she was already moving down the corridor as if sure he would follow. "I have had horses readied. Even one for you, Mat, just in case." Egwene hesitated only a moment, then followed.

Rand opened his mouth to call Moiraine back. She had sworn to obey. Whatever she had to show him, he could see it another day.

"What could an hour hurt?" Mat muttered. Perhaps he was reconsidering.

"It would not be amiss for you to be seen this

morning," Asmodean said. "Rahvin might just know of it as soon as it happens. If he has any suspicions—if he has any spies who may have listened at keyholes—it might allay them for today."

Rand looked at Aviendha. "Do you also counsel delay?"

"I counsel that you listen to Moiraine Sedai. Only fools ignore Aes Sedai."

"What could be at the docks more important than Rahvin?" he growled, then shook his head. There was a saying in the Two Rivers, not that anybody said it where women could hear. "The Creator made women to please the eye and trouble the mind." Aes Sedai were certainly no different in one respect. "One hour."

The sun was not yet high enough to lift the city wall's long shadow from the stone quay where Kadere's wagons were lined up, but he still mopped his face with a large handkerchief. It was only partly the heat that made him sweat. Great gray curtain walls stretching into the river at either end of the row of docks made the quay seem a dim box, with him caught in it. There were nothing but broad, round-bowed grain barges docked here, and the same anchored in the river waiting their turn to unload. He had considered slipping onto one when it cast off, but it meant abandoning most of what he still possessed. Yet had he thought the slow passage downriver would take him anywhere except to his death, he would have. Lanfear had not returned to his dreams, but he had the burns on his chest to remind him of her commands. Just the thought of disobeying one of the Chosen made him shiver, even with sweat rolling down his face.

If only he knew who to trust; to the extent it was possible to trust any of his fellow Darkfriends. The last of his drivers who had sworn the oaths had vanished two days ago, very likely on one of the grain barges. He still did not know which Aiel woman had slipped that note under his wagon door—"You are not alone among strangers. A way has been chosen"—though he had several possibilities in mind. The docks held almost as many Aiel as they did workmen, come to stare at the river; he had seen a few of those faces more often than seemed reasonable, and some had looked at him consideringly. A few Cairhienin had as well, and a Tairen lord. That meant nothing by itself, of course, but if he could find a few men to work with . . .

A mounted party appeared in one of the gateways, Moiraine and Rand al'Thor leading the way with the Aes Sedai's Warder as they threaded though the carts hauling grainsacks away. A wave of cheers rode with them.

"All glory to the Lord Dragon!" and "Hail the Lord Dragon!" and now and again "Glory to Lord Matrim! Glory to the Red Hand!"

For once the Aes Sedai turned down toward the tail end of the line of wagons without so much as a glance at Kadere. He was just as glad. Even if she had not been Aes Sedai, even if she had not looked at him as if she knew every black corner of his mind, he would as soon not have looked too closely at some of the things she had filled his wagons with. Yesterday evening she had made him strip the canvas off that oddly twisted redstone doorframe in the wagon just behind his. She seemed to take a perverse delight in making him help her himself with whatever she wanted to study. He would have covered the thing up again if he could bear to go near it, or could make any of his drivers do so. None with him now had seen Herid fall half through it in Rhuidean and half disappear—Herid had been the first to run away once they cleared the Jangai; the man had not been entirely right in the head after the Warder hauled him back—but they could look at it, see the way the corners did not meet properly, how you could not follow it around with your eyes without blinking and growing dizzy.

Kadere ignored the first three riders as much as the Aes Sedai had ignored him, and Mat Cauthon almost as much. The man was wearing *his* hat; he had never been able to find a replacement. The Aiel wench, Aviendha, rode up behind the young Aes Sedai's saddle, both with their skirts pushed up to show their legs. If he needed any confirmation that the Aiel woman was bedding al'Thor, he only had to see the way she looked at him; a woman who had taken a man to her bed always looked at him with that light of ownership in her eyes after. More importantly, Natael was with them. This was the first time Kadere had been this close to him since crossing the Spine of the Wall. Natael, who stood high in the Darkfriends. If he could get past the Maidens to reach Natael . . .

Suddenly Kadere blinked. Where were the Maidens? Al'Thor always had an escort of spear-wielding women. Frowning, he realized he could not see a single Maiden among the Aiel on the quay or the docks.

"Aren't you going to look at an old friend, Hadnan?"

That melodious voice jerked Kadere around, gaping at a hatchet-nosed face, dark eyes almost hidden by rolls of fat. "Keille?" It was impossible. No one survived alone in the Waste except Aiel. She *had* to be dead. But there she stood, white silk straining over her bulk, ivory combs standing tall in her dark curls.

A faint smile on her lips, she turned with a grace that still surprised him in a woman so large and lightly climbed the steps into his wagon.

For a moment he hesitated, then hurried after her. He would as soon Keille Shaogi really had died in the Waste—the woman was bossy and obnoxious; she need not think she was getting a penny of the little he had managed to salvage—but she stood as high as Jasin Natael. Perhaps she would answer a few questions. At the least, he would have someone to work with. At the worst, someone to put blame on. Power went with standing high, but so did blame for the failures of those beneath you. More than once he had fed his superiors to those still higher up in order to cover himself.

Carefully closing the door, he turned—and would have screamed if his throat had not clenched too tight for sound.

The woman who stood there wore white silk, but she was not fat. She was the most beautiful woman he had ever seen, eyes like dark, bottomless mountain pools, woven silver belting her narrow waist, silver crescents in her shimmering black hair. Kadere knew that face from his dreams.

His knees thudding to the floor shook breath loose. "Great Mistress," he said hoarsely, "how may I serve?"

Lanfear might have been looking at an insect, one she might crush beneath her slipper or might not. "By showing your obedience to my commands. I have been too busy to watch Rand al'Thor myself. Tell me what he has done, aside from conquering Cairhien, what he plans to do."

"It is difficult, Great Mistress. One such as myself cannot come close to such as he." An insect, those cool eyes said, allowed to live so long as it was useful. Kadere racked his brain for everything he had seen or heard or imagined. "He is sending Aiel south in huge numbers, Great Mistress, though I do not know why. The Tairens and Cairhienin do not seem to notice, but I don't think they can tell one Aiel from another." Neither could he. He would not dare lie to her, but if she thought he had more use than he did . . . "He has founded a school of some sort, in a city palace that belonged to a House with no survivors. . . ." At first there was no way to tell whether she liked what she was hearing, but as he went on, her face began to darken.

"What is it you want me to see, Moiraine?" Rand said impatiently, tying Jeade'en's reins to one wheel of the last wagon in line.

She was standing on tiptoe to peer over the side of the wagonbed at a pair of casks that seemed familiar. Unless he was mistaken, they held the two *cuendillar* seals, packed in wool for protection now that they were no longer unbreakable. He felt the Dark One's taint strongly here; it almost seemed to come from the casks, a faint miasma as from something rotting in a hidden place.

"It will be safe here," Moiraine murmured. Lifting her skirts gracefully, she started up the line of wagons. Lan heeled her, a half-tame wolf, the cloak hanging down his back all disturbing ripples of color and nothingness.

Rand glared. "Did she tell you what it was, Egwene?"

"Just that you had to see something. That you had to come here, anyway."

"You must trust Aes Sedai," Aviendha said, almost as levelly, but with a hint of doubt. Mat snorted.

"Well, I mean to find out now. Natael, go tell Bael I'll be with him in—"

At the other end of the line, the side of Kadere's wagon exploded, splinters scything down Aiel and townsfolk. Rand knew; he did not need goose bumps prickling his skin to know. He raced toward the wagon, after Moiraine and Lan. Time seemed to slow, everything happening at once, as if the air were jelly clinging to each moment.

Lanfear stepped out into stunned silence except for the moans and screams of the injured, something limp and pale and red-streaked hanging from her hand, dragging behind her as she walked down invisible steps. Her face was a mask carved of ice. "He told me, Lews Therin," she almost screamed, flinging the pale thing into the air. Something caught it, inflated it for a moment into a bloody, transparent statue of Hadnan Kadere; his skin, removed whole. The figure collapsed and fell as Lanfear's voice rose to a screech. "You let another woman touch you! Again!"

Moments clinging, all happening at once.

Before Lanfear reached the stones of the quay, Moiraine lifted her skirts higher and began running straight toward her. Quick as she was, Lan was quicker, ignoring her shout of, "No, Lan!" Sword coming out, long legs carried him ahead of her, color-shifting cloak waving behind as he charged. Suddenly he seemed to run into an invisible stone wall, bounce back, try to stagger forward again. One step, and as if a giant hand had smashed him aside, he flew ten paces through the air, crashing to the stones.

While he was in midair, Moiraine jerked forward, feet skidding along the pavement, until she was face to face with Lanfear. It was only for a moment. The Forsaken looked at her as though wondering what could have gotten in her way, then Moiraine was flung to one side so hard she rolled over and over until she disappeared beneath one of the wagons.

The quayside was in turmoil. Just moments since Kadere's wagon erupted, yet only the blind could not know the One Power was being wielded by the woman in white. Along the docks axes flashed, cutting ropes, freeing barges as their crews desperately fended the craft toward open water and flight. Bare-chested dockmen and dark-clothed townsfolk struggled to jump aboard. In the other direction men and women milled and screamed as they fought to pass through the gates into the city. And among them, *cadin'sor*-clad figures veiled themselves and rushed at Lanfear with spears or knives or bare hands. There could be no doubt she was the source of the attack, no doubt she fought with the Power. They ran to dance the spears regardless.

Fire rolled over them in waves. Arrows of it pierced those who came on with their clothes in flames. It was not as if Lanfear battled them, or even paid them any real mind. She might have been brushing aside gnats or bitemes. Those who fled burned as well as those who tried to fight. She moved toward Rand as if nothing else existed.

Heartbeats only.

Three steps she had taken when Rand seized the male half of the True Source, molten steel and steel-shattering ice, sweet honey and midden heap. Deep in the Void, the fight for survival was distant, the battle before him scarely less. As Moiraine vanished beneath the wagon, he channeled, pulling the heat from Lanfear's fires, sinking it into the river. Flames that a moment before engulfed human forms, vanished. In the same instant he wove the flows again, and a misty gray dome came into being, a long oval enclosing him and Lanfear and most of the wagons, an almost transparent wall that shut out all not already within. Even as he tied the weave, he was not sure what it was or where it had come from—some memory of Lews Therin's perhaps—but Lanfear's fires struck it and stopped. He could see people outside dimly, too many thrashing and flailing—he had taken the flames, not the searing of flesh; that stench still hung in the air—but none would burn now that had not already. Bodies lay inside, too, mounds of charred cloth, some stirring feebly, moaning. She did not care; her channeled flames winked out; the gnats were dispelled; she never glanced aside.

Heartbeats. He was cold in the emptiness of the Void, and if he felt sorrow for the dead and dying and scarred, the feeling was so far off it might not have been. He was cold itself. Emptiness itself. Only the rage of *saidin* filled him.

Movement to either side. Aviendha and Egwene, eyes concentrated on Lanfear. He had meant to shut them out from this. They must have raced with him. Mat and Asmodean; outside; the wall missed the final few wagons. In icy calm he channeled Air to snare Lanfear; Egwene and Aviendha could shield her while he distracted her.

Something severed his flows; they snapped back so hard that he grunted.

"One of them?" Lanfear snarled. "Which is Aviendha?" Egwene threw her head back and wailed, eyes bulging, the world's agony shrieking from her mouth. "Which?" Aviendha rose on tiptoes, shuddering, howls chasing Egwene's as they climbed higher and higher.

The thought was suddenly there in the emptiness. *Spirit woven so, with Fire and Earth. There.* Rand felt something being cut, something he could not see, and Egwene collapsed in a motionless heap, Aviendha to hands and knees, head down and swaying.

Lanfear staggered, her eyes going from the women to him, dark pools of black fire. "You are mine, Lews Therin! Mine!"

"No." Rand's voice seemed to come to his ears down a mile-long tunnel. *Distract her from the girls.* He kept moving forward, did not look back. "I was never yours, Mierin. I will always belong to Ilyena." The Void quivered with sorrow and loss. And with desperation, as he fought something besides the scouring of *saidin*. For a moment he hung balanced. *I am Rand al'Thor.* And, *Ilyena, ever and always my heart.* Balanced on a razor edge. *I am Rand al'Thor!* Other thoughts tried to well up, a fountain of them, of Ilyena, of Mierin, of what he could do to defeat her. He forced them down, even the last. If he came down on the wrong side . . . *I am Rand al'Thor!* "Your name is Lanfear, and I'll die before I love one of the Forsaken."

Something that might have been anguish crossed her face; then it was a marble mask once more. "If you are not mine," she said coldly, "then you are dead."

Agony in his chest, as if his heart was about to explode, in his head, white-hot nails driving into his brain, pain so strong that inside the Void he wanted to scream. Death was there, and he knew it. Frantically—even in the Void, frantic; emptiness shimmered, dwindled—he wove Spirit and Fire and Earth, flailing it wildly. His heart was no longer beating. Fingers of dark pain crushing the Void. Gray veil falling over his eyes. He felt his weave slice raggedly through hers. The burn of breath in empty lungs, lurch of heart beginning to pump again. He could see again, silver and black flecks floated between him and a stone-faced Lanfear still catching her balance from the rebound of her flows. The pain was there in head and chest like wounds, but the Void firmed, and bodily pain was remote.

Well that it was distant, for he had no time to recover. Forcing himself to move forward, he struck at her with Air, a club to knock her senseless. She slashed the weave, and he struck again, again, again each time that she sliced through his last weave, a furious rain of blows she somehow saw and countered, always moving closer. If he could keep her occupied for a moment more, if one of those invisible cudgels landed on her head, if he could get close enough to strike her with his fist . . . Unconscious, she would be as helpless as anyone else.

Suddenly she seemed to realize what he was doing. Still blocking his blows as easily as if she could see every one, she danced backwards until her shoulders hit the wagon behind her. And she smiled like winter's heart. "You will die slowly, and beg me to let you love me before you die," she said.

It was not at him directly that she struck this time. It was at his link to *saidin*.

Panic rang the Void like a gong at the first knife-sharp

touch, the Power diminishing as it slid deeper between him and the Source. With Spirit and Fire and Earth he cut at the knife blade; he knew where to find it; he knew where his link was, could feel that first nick. Her attempted shield vanished, reappeared, returned as fast as he could cut it, but always with that momentary ebbing of *saidin,* moments when it almost failed, leaving his counterstroke barely enough to foil her attack. Handling two weaves at once should have been easy—he could handle ten or more—but not when one was a desperate defense against something he could not know was there until it was almost too late. Not when another man's thoughts kept trying to surface inside the Void, trying to tell him how to defeat her. If he listened, it might be Lews Therin Telamon who walked away, with Rand al'Thor a voice sometimes floating in his head if that.

"I'll make *both* of those trulls watch you beg," Lanfear said. "But should I make them watch you die first, or you them?" When had she climbed into the open wagonbed? He had to watch her, watch for any hint that she was tiring, her concentration slipping. It was a vain hope. Standing beside the twisted doorframe *ter'angreal,* she looked down at him, a queen about to pass sentence, yet she could spare time for chill smiles at a dark ivory bracelet that she turned over and over in her fingers. "Which will hurt you most, Lews Therin? I want you to hurt. I want you to know pain such as no man has ever known!"

The thicker the flow to him from the Source, the harder it would be to cut. His hand tightened on his coat pocket, the fat little stone man with his sword hard against the heron branded into his palm. He drew on *saidin* as deeply as he could, till the taint floated in the emptiness with him like misting rain.

"Pain, Lews Therin."

And there was pain, the world swallowed in agony. Not heart or head this time, but everywhere, every part of him, hot needles stabbing into the Void. He almost thought he could hear a quenching hiss at each thrust, and each came deeper than the last. Her attempts to shield him did not slow; they came faster, stronger. He could not believe she was so strong. Clinging to the Void, to searing, freezing *saidin,* he defended himself wildly. He could end it, finish her. He could call down lightning, or wrap her in the fire she herself had used to kill.

Images darted through the pain. A woman in a dark merchant's dress, toppling from her horse, the fire-red sword light in his hands; she had come to kill him, with a fistful of other Darkfriends. Mat's bleak eyes; *I killed her.* A golden-haired woman lying in a ruined hallway where, it seemed, the very walls had melted and flowed. *Ilyena, forgive me!* It was a despairing cry.

He could end it. Only, he could not. He was going to die, perhaps the world would die, but he could not make himself kill another woman. Somehow it seemed the richest joke the world had ever seen.

Wiping the blood from her mouth, Moiraine crawled out from beneath the tail of the wagon and rose unsteadily to her feet, the sound of a man's laughter in her ears. In spite of herself, her eyes darted, searching for Lan, found him lying almost against the foggy gray wall of the dome that stretched overhead. He twitched, perhaps trying to find strength to rise, perhaps dying. She forced him out of her mind. He had saved her life so many times that by rights it should have belonged to him, but she had long since done what she could to see that he survived his lone war with the Shadow. Now he must live or die without her.

It was Rand laughing, on his knees on the stones of the quay. Laughing, with tears streaming down a face twisted like a man being put to the question. Moiraine felt a chill. If the madness had him, it was beyond her. She could only do what she could do. What she must do.

The sight of Lanfear hit her like a blow. Not surprise, but the shock of seeing what had been in her dreams so often since Rhuidean. Lanfear standing on the wagonbed, blazing bright as the sun with *saidar,* framed by the twisted redstone *ter'angreal* as she stared down at Rand, a pitiless smile on her lips. She was turning a bracelet in her hands. An *angreal;* unless Rand had his own *angreal,* she should be able to crush him with that. Either he did, or Lanfear was toying with him. It did not matter. Moiraine did not like that circle of carved age-dark ivory. At first glance it seemed to be an acrobat bending backwards to grip his ankles. Only a closer look would show that his wrists and ankles were bound together. She did not like it, but she had brought it out of Rhuidean. Yesterday she had taken the bracelet from a sack of odds-and-ends and left it lying there at the foot of the doorframe.

Moiraine was slight, a small woman. Her weight did not disturb the wagon at all as she pulled herself up. She winced as her dress caught on a splinter and tore, but Lanfear did not look around. The woman had dealt with every threat except Rand; he was the only corner of the world she acknowledged in the least right then.

Suppressing a small bubble of hope—she could not allow herself that luxury—Moiraine balanced upright a moment on the wagontail, then embraced the True Source and leaped at Lanfear. The Forsaken had an instant's warning, enough to turn before Moiraine struck her, clawing the bracelet away. Face to face, they toppled through the doorframe *ter'angreal.* White light swallowed everything.

CHAPTER

53

Fading Words

In the depths of a shrinking Void, Rand saw Moiraine hurtle seemingly out of nowhere to grapple with Lanfear. The attacks on him ceased as the two women plunged through the doorframe *ter'angreal* in a flash of white light that did not end; it filled the subtly twisted redstone rectangle as though trying to flood through and striking some invisible barrier. Lightnings arched silver and blue around the *ter'angreal,* more and more violently; rasping buzzes crackled through the air.

Rand staggered to his feet. The pain was not gone really, but the pressure was, bringing promise that the pain would go. His eyes could not leave the *ter'angreal. Moiraine.* Her name hung in his head, sliding across the Void.

Lan lurched by him, fixed on the wagon, leaning as if only by moving forward could he stop from falling.

More than standing was beyond Rand for the moment. He channeled, caught the Warder in flows of Air. "You . . . You can't do anything, Lan. You can't go after her."

"I know," Lan said hopelessly. Held in mid-step, he

did not struggle, only stared at the *ter'angreal* that had swallowed Moiraine. "The Light send me peace, I know."

The wagon itself had caught fire now. Rand tried to suppress the flames, but as soon as he drew the heat from one blaze the lightnings ignited another. The doorframe itself was beginning to smoke, though it was stone, a white, acrid smoke that gathered thickly under the gray dome. Even a whiff burned Rand's nostrils and made him cough; his skin prickled and stung where the smoke brushed. Hastily he untied the weave of the dome, dispelled it rather than wait for it to dissipate, and wove around the wagon a tall chimney of Air that gleamed like glass to carry the fumes high and away. Only then did he release Lan. He would not have put it past the man to follow Moiraine anyway if he could have reached the wagon. It was all in flames now, the redstone doorway as well, melting as if it were wax, but for a Warder that might not matter.

"She is gone. I cannot feel her presence." The words sounded ripped out of Lan's chest. He turned and began walking down the line of wagons without a backward glance.

Following the Warder with his eyes, Rand saw Aviendha on her knees, holding Egwene. Releasing *saidin,* he began to run down the quay. Physical pain that had been distant crashed home, but he ran, however awkwardly. Asmodean was there, too, looking around as if he expected Lanfear to leap out from behind a wagon or a toppled graincart. And Mat, squatting with his spear propped across his shoulder, fanning Egwene with his hat.

Rand skidded to a halt. "Is she . . . ?"

"I don't know," Mat said miserably.

"She still breathes." Aviendha sounded uncertain how long that would continue, but Egwene's eyes fluttered open as Amys and Bair pushed roughly past Rand with Melaine and Sorilea. The Wise Ones knelt clustered around the younger women, murmuring to themselves and each other as they examined Egwene.

"I feel . . ." Egwene began weakly, and stopped to

swallow. Her face was bloodless pale. "I . . . hurt." A
tear leaked from one eye.

"Of course you do," Sorilea said briskly. "That is what
happens when you let yourself be caught in a man's
schemes."

"She cannot go with you, Rand al'Thor." Melaine's
sun-haired beauty was openly angry, but she was not
looking at him; it could have been anger at him or anger
at what had happened.

"I . . . will be right as wellwater . . . with a little rest,"
Egwene whispered.

Bair dampened a cloth from a waterskin and laid it
across Egwene's forehead. "You will be right with a
great deal of rest. I fear you will not be meeting Nynaeve
and Elayne tonight. You will not go near *Tel'aran'rhiod*
for some days, until you are stronger again. Do not give
me that stubborn look, girl. We will watch your dreams
to make sure, if need be, and give your care to Sorilea if
you so much as think of disobeying."

"You will not disobey me more than once, Aes Sedai
or not," Sorilea said, but with a touch of sympathy at
odds with her leathery-faced grimness. Frustration was
plain in Egwene's face.

"I, at least, am well enough to do what must be done,"
Aviendha said. In truth, she looked not much less
haggard than Egwene, but she managed a defiant stare at
Rand, plainly expecting argument. Her defiance faded
somewhat when she realized the four Wise Ones were
looking at her. "I am," she muttered.

"Of course," Rand said hollowly.

"I am," she insisted. To him; she carefully avoided
meeting the Wise Ones' gaze. "Lanfear had me a moment less than she did Egwene. That was enough to make
the difference between us. I have *toh* to you, Rand
al'Thor. I do not think we would have survived many
moments more. She was very strong." Her eyes darted
down to the burning wagon. Fierce flames had already
reduced it to a shapeless charred pile inside the glassy
chimney; the redstone *ter'angreal* was no longer visible
at all. "I did not see all that happened."

"They are . . ." Rand cleared his throat. "They are
both gone. Lanfear is dead. And so is Moiraine." Egwene
began to cry, sobs shaking her in Aviendha's clasp.

Aviendha put her head down on the other woman's shoulder as if she, too, might weep.

"You are a fool, Rand al'Thor," Amys said, standing. That surprisingly youthful face beneath her headscarf and white hair was stone hard. "About this and many other things, you are a fool."

He turned away from the accusation in her eyes. Moiraine was dead. Dead because he could not bring himself to kill one of the Forsaken. He did not know whether he wanted to cry or laugh wildly; if he did either, he did not think he would be able to stop.

The dockside that had been emptying when he made the dome was filled again, though few came nearer than where that misty gray wall had stood. Wise Ones moved about aiding the burned, comforting the dying, assisted by white-robed *gai'shain* and men in the *cadin'sor*. Moans and cries stabbed at him. He had not been quick enough. Moiraine dead; no Healing for even the worst injured. Because he . . . *I could not. The Light help me, I could not!*

More Aielmen stood watching him, some only now unveiling; he still did not see one Maiden. Not only Aiel were there. Dobraine, bareheaded on a black gelding, did not take his eyes from Rand, and not far off Talmanes and Nalesean and Daerid sat their horses watching Mat almost as closely as they did Rand. People lined the top of the great city wall, outlined and cast in shadow by the rising sun, and more along the curtain walls. Two of those shadowed shapes turned away when he looked up, saw each other only twenty paces apart, and seemed to recoil. He would have wagered they were Meilan and Maringil.

Lan was back with the horses at the last wagon in the line, stroking Aldieb's white nose. Moiraine's mare.

Rand went to him. "I'm sorry, Lan. If I'd been faster, if I'd . . ." He exhaled heavily. *I couldn't kill one, so I killed the other. The Light burn me blind!* If it had, at that moment, he would not have cared.

"The Wheel weaves." Lan went to Mandarb, busied himself checking the black stallion's saddlegirth. "She was a soldier, a warrior in her way as much as I. This could have happened two hundred times these past twenty years. She knew it, and so did I. It was a good day to die." His voice was as hard as it had ever been, but those cold blue eyes were red-rimmed.

"Still, I am sorry. I should have . . ." The man would not be comforted by should-haves, and they dug at Rand's soul. "I hope you can still be my friend, Lan, after. . . . I value your counsel—and your sword-training—and I'll need both in the days to come."

"I am your friend, Rand. But I cannot stay." Lan swung up into his saddle. "Moiraine did something to me that has not been done in hundreds of years, not since the time when Aes Sedai still sometimes bonded a Warder whether he wanted it or not. She altered my bond so it passed to another when she died. Now I must find that other, become one of her Warders. I am one, already. I can feel her faintly, somewhere far to the west, and she can feel me. I must go, Rand. It is part of what Moiraine did. She said she would not allow me time to die avenging her." He gripped the reins as if holding Mandarb back, as if holding himself back from digging his spurs in. "If you ever see Nynaeve again, tell her . . ." For an instant that stone face crumpled in anguish; an instant, then it was granite again. He muttered under his breath, but Rand heard. "A clean wound heals quickest and pains shortest." Aloud, he said, "Tell her I've found someone else. Green sisters are sometimes as close to their Warders as other women are to husbands. In every way. Tell her I've gone to be a Green sister's lover, as well as her sword. These things happen. It has been a long time since I've seen her."

"I will tell her whatever you say, Lan, but I don't know that she'll believe me."

Lan bent from the saddle to catch Rand's shoulder in a hard grip. Rand remembered calling the man a half-tame wolf, but those eyes made a wolf seem a lapdog. "We are alike in many ways, you and I. There is a darkness in us. Darkness, pain, death. They radiate from us. If ever you love a woman, Rand, leave her and let her find another. It will be the best gift you can give her." Straightening, he raised one hand. "Peace favor your sword. *Tai'shar* Manetheren." The ancient salute. True blood of Manetheren.

Rand lifted his hand. "*Tai'shar* Malkier."

Lan heeled Mandarb's flanks, and the stallion leaped forward, scattering Aiel and everyone else from his path, as if to carry the last of the Malkieri wherever he was headed at a gallop the entire way.

"The last embrace of the mother welcome you home, Lan," Rand murmured, then shivered. That was part of the funeral service in Shienar, and elsewhere in the Borderlands.

They were still watching him, the Aiel, the people atop the walls. The Tower would know of today, or a version of it, as soon as a pigeon could fly there. If Rahvin did have some way of watching as well—all it took was one raven in the city, one rat here along the river—he certainly would not expect anything today. Elaida would think him weakened, perhaps more pliable, and Rahvin . . .

He realized what he was doing and winced. *Stop it! For one minute at least, stop and mourn!* He did not want all those eyes on him. Aiel fell back before him almost as readily as they had before Mandarb.

The dockmaster's slate-roofed hut was a single windowless stone room lined with shelves full of ledgers and scrolls and papers, lit by two lamps on a rough table covered with tax seals and customs stamps. Rand slammed the door behind him to shut out eyes.

Moiraine dead, Egwene injured, and Lan gone. A high price to pay for Lanfear.

"Mourn, burn you!" he growled. "She deserved that much! Don't you have any feelings left?" But mostly he felt numb. His body hurt, but under it was deadness.

Hunching his shoulders, he stuffed his hands into his pockets and felt Moiraine's letters. Slowly he drew them out. Some things he should think on, she had said. Stuffing Thom's back, he broke the seal on the other. The pages were covered thickly with Moiraine's elegant script.

These words will fade within moments after this leaves your hands—a warding attuned to you—so be careful of it. That you are reading this means that events have fallen out at the docks as I hoped. . . .

He stopped, staring, then read on quickly.

> *Since the first day I reached Rhuidean, I have known—it need not trouble you how; some secrets belong to others, and I will not betray them—that a day would come in Cairhien when news would arrive of Morgase. I did not know what that would be—if what we heard is true, the Light have mercy on her soul; she was willful and stubborn, with the temper of a lioness at times, but for all that a true, good and gracious queen—but each time that news led to the docks on the following day. There were three branches from the docks, but if you are reading this, I am gone, and so is Lanfear. . . .*

Rand's hands tightened on the pages. She had known. Known, and still she brought him here. Hurriedly he smoothed out the crumpled paper.

> *The other two paths were much worse. Down one, Lanfear killed you. Down the other, she carried you away, and when next we saw you, you called yourself Lews Therin Telamon and were her devoted lover.*
>
> *I hope that Egwene and Aviendha have survived unharmed. You see, I do not know what happens in the world after, except perhaps for one small thing which does not concern you.*
>
> *I could not tell you, for the same reason I could not tell Lan. Even given the choices, I could not be sure which you would pick. Men of the Two Rivers, it seems, retain much of storied Manetheren in them, traits shared with men of the Borderlands. It is said that a Borderlander will take a dagger's wound to avoid harm to a woman and count it fair trade. I dared not risk that you would place my life above your own, certain that somehow you could sidestep fate. Not a risk, I fear, but a foolish certainty, as today has surely proved. . . .*

"My choice, Moiraine," he muttered. "It was my choice."

A few final points.

If Lan has not already gone, tell him that what I did to him, I did for the best. He will understand one day, and I hope, bless me for it.

Trust no woman fully who is now Aes Sedai. I do not speak simply of the Black Ajah, though you must always be watchful for them. Be as suspicious of Verin as you are of Alviarin. We have made the world dance as we sang for three thousand years. That is a difficult habit to break, as I have learned while dancing to your song. You must dance free, and even the best intentioned of my sisters may well try to guide your steps as I once did.

Please deliver Thom Merrilin's letter safely when you meet him again. There is a small matter that I once told him of which I must make clear for his peace of mind.

Lastly, be wary too of Master Jasin Natael. I cannot approve wholly, but I understand. Perhaps it was the only way. Yet be careful of him. He is the same man now that he always was. Remember that always.

May the Light illumine and protect you. You will do well.

It was signed simply "Moiraine." She had almost never used her House name.

He reread the second last paragraph again closely. Somehow she had known who Asmodean was. It had to be that. Known that one of the Forsaken was right there in front of her, and never blinked once. She had known why, too, if he read it right. He would have thought in a letter that would go blank when he set it down, she could have come right out and said what she meant. Not just concerning Asmodean. About how she had learned what she had in Rhuidean—something to do with Wise Ones, or he missed his guess, and as much chance of finding out more from the letter as from them—about Aes Sedai— was there a reason she mentioned Verin? And why Alviarin instead of Elaida?—even about Thom and Lan. For some reason he did not think she had left a letter for Lan; the Warder was not the only one who believed in

clean wounds. He almost took Thom's letter out and
opened it, but she might have warded it the same way she
had his. Aes Sedai and Cairhienin, she had wrapped
herself in mystery and manipulation to the end. To the
end.

That was what he was trying to avoid with all this
blather about her keeping secrets. She had known what
would happen and come as bravely as any Aiel. Come to
her death knowing it waited. She had died because he
could not bring himself to kill Lanfear. He could not kill
one woman, so another died. His eyes fell on the last
words.

. . . You will do well.

They cut like a cold razor.

"Why do you weep here alone, Rand al'Thor? I have
heard that some wetlanders think it is shame to be seen
weeping."

He glared at Sulin, standing in the doorway. She was
fully accoutred, cased bow on her back, quiver at her
belt, round hide buckler and three spears in hand. "I'm
not. . . ." There was dampness on his cheeks. He
scrubbed it away. "It's hot in here. Makes me sweat
like a . . . What do you want? I thought you had all decided to abandon me and go back to the Three-fold
Land."

"It is not we who have abandoned you, Rand al'Thor."
Shutting the door behind her, she sat on the floor and
laid her buckler and a pair of the spears down. "You have
abandoned us." In one motion she put a foot against the
last spear between her hands, heaved, and snapped it in
two.

"What are you doing?" She tossed aside the pieces and
picked up another spear. "I said, what are you doing?"
The white-haired Maiden's face might have given even
Lan pause, but Rand bent and seized the spear between
her hands; her soft-booted foot came to rest against his
knuckles. Not lightly.

"Will you put us in skirts, and make us marry and
tend hearth? Or are we to lie beside your fire and lick
your hand when you give us a scrap of meat?" Her
muscles tensed, and the spear broke, scoring his palm
with splinters.

He snatched his freed hand back with a curse, shaking off droplets of blood. "I don't mean any such thing. I thought you understood." She took up the last spear, set her foot, and he channeled, weaving Air to hold her as she was. She only stared at him wordlessly. "Burn me, you said nothing! So I kept the Maidens out of the battle with Couladin. Not everyone fought that day. And you never said a word."

Sulin's eyes widened in incredulity. "*You* kept *us* from the dance of spears? *We* kept *you* from the dance. You were like a girl newly wed to the spear, ready to rush out and kill Couladin with never a thought for the spear you might take from behind. You are the *Car'a'carn*. You have no right to risk yourself needlessly." Her voice flattened. "Now you go to fight the Forsaken. The secret is well kept, but I have heard enough from those who lead the other societies."

"And you want to keep me out of this fight as well?" he said quietly.

"Do not be a fool, Rand al'Thor. Any could have danced the spears with Couladin; for you to risk it was the thinking of a child. None among us can face the Shadowsouled, save you."

"Then why . . . ?" He stopped; he already knew the answer. After that blood-soaked day against Couladin, he had convinced himself they would not mind. He had wanted to believe they would not.

"Those who go with you have been chosen." The words came like hurled stones. "Men from every society. Men. There are no Maidens, Rand al'Thor. *Far Dareis Mai* carries your honor, and you take ours away."

He drew a deep breath, fumbling for words. "I . . . do not like to see a woman die. I hate it, Sulin. It curdles me up inside. I could not kill a woman if my life hung on it." The pages of Moiraine's letter rustled in his hand. Dead because he could not kill Lanfear. Not always just his own life. "Sulin, I would rather go against Rahvin alone than see one of you die."

"A foolish thing. Everyone needs another to watch her back. So it is Rahvin. Even Roidan of the Thunder Walkers and Turol of the Stone Dogs held that back." She glanced at her upraised foot, held against the spear by the same flows that snared her arms. "Release me, and we will talk."

After a moment's hesitation, he unraveled the weave. He was tensed to seize her again if need be, but she only crossed her legs and sat bouncing the spear on her palms. "Sometimes I forget you were raised out of our blood, Rand al'Thor. Listen to me. I am what I am. *This* is what I am." She hefted the spear.

"Sulin—"

"Listen, Rand al'Thor. I *am* the spear. When a lover came between me and the spear, I chose the spear. Some chose the other way. Some decide they have run with the spears long enough, that they want a husband, a child. I have never wanted anything else. No chief would hesitate to send me wherever the dance is hottest. If I died there, my first-sisters would mourn me, but not a fingernail more than when our first-brother fell. A treekiller who stabbed me to the heart in my sleep would do me more honor than you do. Do you understand now?"

"I understand, but . . . ." He did understand. She did not want him to make her something other than what she was. All he had to do was be willing to watch her die. "What happens if you break the last spear?"

"If I have no honor in this life, perhaps in another." She said it as if it was just another explanation. It took him a moment to comprehend. All he had to do was be willing to watch her die.

"You don't leave me any choices, do you?" No more than Moiraine had.

"There are always choices, Rand al'Thor. You have a choice, and I have one. *Ji'e'toh* allows no other."

He wanted to snarl at her, to curse *ji'e'toh* and everyone who followed it. "Choose out your Maidens, Sulin. I don't know how many I can take, but *Far Dareis Mai* will have as many as any other society."

He stalked past her and her sudden smile. Not relief. Pleasure. Pleasure that she would have the chance to die. He should have left her wrapped up in *saidin,* left her to be dealt with somehow when he came back from Caemlyn. Slamming the door open, he strode out onto the quay—and stopped.

Enaila headed a line of Maidens, each with three spears in her hands, a line leading back from the dockmaster's door, vanishing into the nearest of the gates to the city. Some of the Aielmen on the dockside eyed them curiously, but it was obviously something between *Far Dareis Mai* and the *Car'a'carn*, and no business of any other society. Amys and three or four other Wise Ones who had once been Maidens were watching more closely. Most of the non-Aiel had gone, except for a few men nervously righting overturned grain carts and trying to look elsewhere. Enaila stepped toward Rand, then halted and smiled as Sulin came out. Not relief. Pleasure. Smiles of pleasure running back down that long line of Maidens. Smiles on those Wise Ones, too, and a sharp nod for him from Amys as if he had put an end to some idiotic behavior.

"I thought maybe they were going to go in one at a time and kiss you out of your miseries," Mat said.

Rand frowned at him, standing there leaning on his spear and grinning, wide-brimmed hat tipped back on his head. "How can you be so cheerful?" The smell of seared flesh still hung in the air, and the moans of burned men and women being cared for by Wise Ones.

"Because I'm alive," Mat snarled. "What do you want me to do, cry?" He shrugged uncomfortably. "Amys says Egwene really will be all right in a few days." He did look around then, but as though he did not want to see what he saw. "Burn me, if we're going to do this thing, let's do it. *Dovie'andi se tovya sagain.*"

"What?"

"I said, it's time to roll the dice. Did Sulin stop up your ears?"

"Time to roll the dice," Rand agreed. The flames had died inside the glassy chimney of Air, but the white smoke still rose as though flames yet consumed the *ter'angreal*. *Moiraine*. He should have . . . Done was done. The Maidens were crowding down around Sulin, as many as would fit onto the quay. Done was done, and he had to live with it. Death would be a release from what he had to live with. "Let's do it."

CHAPTER
54

To Caemlyn

F ive hundred of the Maidens behind Sulin accompanied Rand back to the Royal Palace, where Bael waited in the great court inside the front gates with Thunder Walkers and Black Eyes and Water Seekers and men from every other society, their numbers filling the courtyard and crowding back into the palace through every door down to the smallest servants' way. Some watched from lower windows, waiting their turn to come out. The surrounding stone balconies were empty. In the entire courtyard only one man waited who was not Aiel; Tairens and Cairhienin—especially Cairhienin—stayed clear when Aiel gathered. The exception stood above Bael on the wide gray steps leading into the place, Pevin, with the crimson banner hanging limply from its staff, and no more expression surrounded by Aiel than at any other time.

Aviendha, behind Rand's saddle, clung tightly to him, breasts pressed against his back, until the very moment he dismounted. There had been an exchange between her and some of the Wise Ones back at the docks that he did not think he had been supposed to hear.

"Go with the Light," Amys had said, touching Aviendha's face. "And guard him closely. You know how much depends on him."

"Much depends on you both," Bair told Aviendha, almost at the same time that Melaine said irritably, "It would be easier if you had succeeded by now."

Sorilea snorted. "Even Maidens knew how to handle men in my day."

"She has been more successful than you know," Amys told them. Aviendha shook her head; the roses-and-thorns ivory bracelet slid down her arm as she raised a hand to forestall the other woman, but Amys went on over her half-formed protests. "I have waited for her to tell us, but since she will not—" She saw him then, standing only ten feet away, with Jeade'en's reins in his hand, and cut off sharply. Aviendha turned to see what Amys was staring at; when her eyes found him, bright crimson suffused her face, then drained away so suddenly that even her sundark cheeks looked pale. The four Wise Ones fixed him with flat, unreadable gazes.

Asmodean and Mat came up behind him, leading their horses. "Do women learn that look in the cradle?" Mat muttered. "Do their mothers teach them? I'd say the mighty Car'a'carn will get his ears singed if he stays around here much longer."

Shaking his head, Rand reached up as Aviendha swung a leg over to slide down, and lifted her from the dapple's back. For a moment he held her by the waist, looking down into her clear blue-green eyes. She did not look away, and her expression never changed, but her hands tightened slowly on his forearms. What success was she supposed to have? He had thought she was set to spy on him for the Wise Ones, but if she ever asked a question about things he held back from the Wise Ones, it was in open anger at him for keeping secrets from them. Never slyly, never trying to ferret something out. Bludgeon, maybe, but never ferret. He had considered the possibility that she was like one of Colavaere's young women, but only for the brief moment it took to think of the notion. Aviendha would never let herself be used in that way. Besides, even if she had, giving him one taste of herself then denying him so much as a kiss afterward, not to mention making him chase her halfway around the world, was no way to go about it. If she was more than casual about being naked in front of him, Aiel customs were different. If his distress at it satisfied her, likely it was because she thought it was a great joke to play on him. So what was she supposed to be successful at? Plots all around him. Was everyone scheming? He could see his face in her eyes. Who had given her that silver necklace?

"I like canoodling as much as the next man," Mat said, "but don't you think there are a few too many people watching?"

Rand released Aviendha's waist and stepped back, but no more quickly than she. She bent her head, fussing with her skirt, muttering about how riding had disarrayed it, but not before he saw her cheeks redden. Well, he had not meant to embarrass her.

Scowling around the courtyard, he said, "I told you I don't know how many I can take, Bael." With the Maidens spilling back through the gates onto the ramp, there was barely room to move in the courtyard. Five hundred from each society meant six thousand Aiel; the hallways inside must be packed.

The towering Aiel chief shrugged. Like every other Aiel there, he had his *shoufa* wrapped around his head, ready to veil. No crimson headband, though it seemed at least half the others wore the black-and-white disc on their foreheads. "Every spear that can follow you, will. Will the two Aes Sedai come soon?"

"No." It was good that Aviendha kept her promise not to let him touch her again. Lanfear had tried to kill her and Egwene because she did not know which was Aviendha. How had Kadere found out to tell her? No matter. Lan was right. Women found pain—or death—when they came too close to him. "They will not be coming."

"There are stories of . . . trouble . . . by the river."

"A great victory, Bael," Rand said wearily. "And much honor earned." *But not by me.* Pevin came down past Bael to stand behind Rand's shoulder with the banner, his narrow, scarred face absolutely blank. "Does the whole palace know about this, then?" Rand asked.

"I heard," Pevin said. His jaw worked, chewing for more words. Rand had found him a replacement for his patched country coat, good red wool, and the man had had Dragons embroidered on it, one climbing either side of his chest. "That you were going. Somewhere." That seemed to exhaust his store.

Rand nodded. Rumors grew in the palace like mushrooms in the shade. But as long as Rahvin did not find out. He scanned the tile roofs and towertops. No ravens. He had not seen a raven in some time, though he heard of other men killing them. Perhaps they avoided him now. "Stand ready." He seized *saidin,* floated in emptiness, emotionless.

The gateway appeared at the foot of the steps, first a bright line that seemed to *turn,* opening into a square hole into blackness four paces wide. Not a murmur came from the Aiel. Those beyond would be able to see him as through a smoked glass, a dusky shimmering in the air, but they could as well try walking through one of the palace walls. From the side, the gateway would be invisible except to the few close enough to see what might seem a long, fine hair drawn tight.

Four paces was as large as Rand could make it. There were limits for one man by himself, Asmodean claimed; it seemed there were always limits. The amount of *saidin* you drew did not matter. The One Power had little to do with gateways, really; only the making. Beyond, was something else. A dream of a dream, Asmodean called it.

He stepped through onto what appeared to be a paving stone lifted from the courtyard, but here the gray square hung in the midst of utter darkness, with a sense that in every direction there was nothing. Nothing, forever. It was not like night. He could see himself and the stone perfectly. But everything else, everywhere else, was blackness.

It was time to see how large he could make a platform. With the thought, more stones appeared all at once, duplicating the courtyard to an inch. He imagined it

larger still. That quickly, gray stone stretched as far as he
could see. With a start, he realized that his boots were
beginning to sink into the stone under his feet; it looked
no different, yet it yielded slowly like mud, oozing up
around his boots. Hastily, he brought everything back to
a square the size of what was outside—that much stayed
solid—then began increasing it by one outer row of
stones at a time. It did not take long to realize he could
not make the platform much larger than his first attempt.
The stone still looked all right, it did not sink beneath his
feet, but the second added row felt . . . insubstantial,
like a thin shell that might crack at a wrong step. Was
that because this was as large as the thing could be made?
Or because he had not thought of it larger at first? *We all
make our limits.* The thought slid up surprisingly from
somewhere. *And we set them further out than we have any
right.*

Rand felt himself shiver. In the Void, it seemed like
feeling someone else shiver. It was well to be reminded
that Lews Therin was still inside him. He had to be
careful not to fall into a battle for self while confronting
Rahvin. If not for that, he might have . . . No. What had
happened on the quay was done; he would not make a
hash of it for breakfast.

Reducing the platform by one outer ring of square
stones, he turned. Bael was waiting out there in what
seemed a huge square doorway into daylight with the
steps beyond. At his side, Pevin looked no more perturbed by what he saw than the Aiel chief, which was to
say not at all. Pevin would carry that banner wherever
Rand went, even the Pit of Doom, and never blink. Mat
shoved back his hat to scratch his head, then jerked it
low again, muttering something about dice in his head.

"Impressive," Asmodean said quietly. "Quite impressive."

"Flatter him some other time, harper," Aviendha said.
She was the first to step through, watching Rand, not
where she put her feet. She walked all the way to him
without once so much as glancing at anything except his
face. When she reached him, though, it was to swing

away abruptly, settling her shawl over her elbows, and study the darkness. Sometimes women were stranger than anything else the Creator could possibly have made.

Bael and Pevin came right behind her; then Asmodean, one hand clutching the strap of his harpcase across his chest, the other white-knuckled on his sword hilt; and Mat, swaggering, but a trifle reluctant and grumbling as if arguing with himself. In the Old Tongue. Sulin claimed the honor to be first else, but soon a wide stream followed, not just Maidens of the Spear, but *Tain Shari*, True Bloods, and *Far Aldazar Din,* Brothers of the Eagle; Red Shields and Dawn Runners, Stone Dogs and Knife Hands, representatives of every society, crowding through.

As the numbers increased, Rand moved to the far side of the platform from the gateway. There was no need to see where he was going, really, but he wanted to. In truth, he could have remained at the other end, or gone to one side; direction here was mutable; whatever way he chose to move would take him to Caemlyn if done properly. And to the endless black of nowhere if done wrong.

Except for Bael and Sulin—and Aviendha, of course —the Aiel left a little space around him and Mat, Asmodean and Pevin. "Stay away from the edge," Rand said. The Aiel nearest him moved back all of a foot. He could not see over the forest of *shoufa*-shrouded heads. "Is it full?" he called. The thing might hold half those who wanted to go, but not many more. "Is it full?"

"Yes," a woman's voice called back finally, reluctantly —he thought it sounded like Lamelle—but there was still a milling in the gateway, Aiel sure there must be room for one more.

"Enough!" Rand shouted. "No more! Clear the gateway! Everyone stand well clear!" He did not want what had happened to the Seanchan spear to happen here to living flesh.

A pause, and then, "It is clear." It *was* Lamelle. He would have bet his last copper that Enaila and Somara were back there somewhere, too.

The gateway seemed to turn sideways, thinning until it vanished with one final flash of light.

"Blood and ashes!" Mat muttered, leaning disgustedly on his spear. "This is worse than the flaming Ways!" Which earned him a startled look from Asmodean, and a considering one from Bael. Mat did not notice; he was too busy glaring at the blackness.

There was no sense of motion, no breeze to stir the banner Pevin held. They could have been standing still. But Rand knew better; he could almost feel the place they were approaching draw nearer.

"If you come out too close to him, he will sense it." Asmodean licked his lips and avoided looking at anyone. "At least, that is what I have heard."

"I know where I am going," Rand said. Not too close. But not too far. He remembered the spot well.

No movement. Endless black, and them hanging in it. Motionless. Half an hour passed perhaps.

A slight stir ran through the Aiel.

"What is it?" Rand asked.

Murmurs came across the platform. "Someone fell," a bulky man near him said at last. Rand recognized him. Meciar. He was *Cor Darei*, a Night Spear. He wore the red headband.

"Not one of the . . ." Rand began, then caught Sulin looking at him, flat-eyed.

He turned to stare out into the darkness, anger a stain clinging to the emotionless Void. So it was not supposed to matter more to him if one of the Maidens had fallen, was it? It did. Falling forever through endless black. Would sanity crack before death came, from starvation or thirst or fear? In that fall, even an Aiel must eventually find fear strong enough to stop a heart. He almost hoped so; it must be more merciful than the other.

Burn me, what happened to all that hardness I was so proud of? A Maiden or a Stone Dog, a spear is a spear. Only, thinking it could not make it so. *I will be hard!* He would let the Maidens dance the spears where they wished. He would. And he knew he would search out the name of every one who died, that every name would be another knife-cut on his soul. *I will be hard. The Light help me, I will. The Light help me.*

Seemingly motionless, hanging in blackness.

The platform stopped. It was hard to say how he knew, when he could tell it was moving before, but he did.

He channeled, and a gateway opened in the same way it had in the courtyard in Cairhien. The angle of the sun had hardly changed, but here early-morning light shone on a paved street, and a rising slope patched brown with drought-killed grass and wildflowers, a slope topped by a stone wall two spans high or more, the stones worked rough so it seemed something natural. Above that wall he could see the golden domes of the Royal Palace of Andor, a few of the pale spires topped with banners rippling the White Lion on a breeze. On the other side of that wall was the garden where he had first met Elayne.

Blue eyes floated accusingly outside the Void, the darting memory of kisses stolen in Tear, the memory of a letter laying her heart and soul at his feet, of messages borne by Egwene professing love. What would she say if she ever learned about Aviendha, about that night together in the snow hut? Memory of another letter, icily spurning him, a queen condemning a swineherd to outer darkness. It did not matter. Lan was right. But he wanted . . . What? Who? Blue eyes, and green, and dark brown. Elayne, who maybe loved him and maybe could not make up her mind? Aviendha, who taunted him with what she would not let him touch? Min, who laughed at him, thought him a wool-headed fool? All that flashed along the boundaries of the Void. He tried to ignore it, to ignore anguished memories of another blue-eyed woman, lying dead in a palace corridor, so long ago.

He had to stand there, while Aiel dashed out behind Bael, veiling themselves, spreading left and right. It was his presence that maintained the platform; it would vanish as soon as he stepped through the gateway. Aviendha waited almost as calmly as Pevin, though she did occasionally put her head out to frown faintly in one direction or the other down the street. Asmodean fingered his sword and breathed too quickly; Rand wondered whether the man knew how to use the thing. Not that he would have to. Mat stared up the wall as though at a bad remembrance. He had entered the palace this way once, too.

The last veiled Aiel went by, and Rand motioned the others out, then followed. The gateway winked out of existence, leaving him in the middle of a long circle of wary Maidens. Aiel were running down the curving street—it followed the line of the hill; all the streets of the Inner City flowed with the land—vanishing around winding corners as they hurried to find and secure anyone who might give alarm. More were climbing the slope, and some had even begun to scale the wall, using tiny knobs and ridges for finger- and toe-holds.

Suddenly Rand stared. To his left the street bowed downward and rounded out of sight, the decline giving a view past tile-covered towers, sparkling in the morning sun with a hundred changing colors, across tile roofs all the way to one of the Inner City's many parks, its white walks and monuments forming a lion's head when seen from this angle. To his right the street rose a little before curving away, more towers topped by spires or domes of various shapes glittering above the rooftops. Aiel filled the street, fanning out quickly into side streets that spiraled away from the palace. Aiel, and not a soul else. The sun was high enough for people to be out and about their business, even this close to the palace.

Like a nightmare the wall above toppled outward in half a dozen places, Aiel and stones smashing down on those still climbing. Before those bouncing, sliding chunks of masonry reached the streets, Trollocs appeared in the openings, dropping the tree-thick battering rams they had used and drawing scythe-curved swords— more, with spiked axes and barbed spears, huge man-shapes in black mail with spikes at shoulders and elbows, huge man-faces distorted by snouts and muzzles, beaks and horns and feathers, plunging down the slope with eyeless Myrddraal like midnight serpents in their midst. All along the street howling Trollocs and silent Myrddraal poured from doorways, leaped from windows. Lightning stabbed from the cloudless sky.

Rand wove Fire and Air to meet Fire and Air, a slow-spreading shield racing lightnings' fall. Too slow. One bolt struck the shield directly above his head, shattering in a blinding glare, but others grounded themselves, and his hair lifted as the air itself seemed to hammer him down. Almost he lost the weave, almost the Void itself, but he wove what he could not see through eyes still filled with coruscating light, spread the shield against bolts from the heavens that he could at least feel hammering at it. Hammering to reach him, but that could change. Drawing *saidin* through the *angreal* in his pocket, he wove the shield until he was sure it must cover half of the Inner City, then tied it off. As he pushed himself to his feet, sight began to return, watery and painful at first. He had to move fast. Rahvin knew he was here. He had to . . .

Surprisingly little time had passed, seemingly. Rahvin had not cared how many of his own he took. Stunned Trollocs and Myrddraal on the slope were falling to spears in the hands of Maidens, many of whom moved unsteadily themselves. Some Maidens, those nearest Rand, were only now pulling themselves up from where they had been flung, and Pevin stood spraddle-legged, holding himself upright with the red banner's staff, his scarred face still blank as slate. More Trollocs boiled through the gaps in the wall above, and the din of battle filled the streets in all directions, but it might as well have been in another country so far as Rand was concerned.

There had been more than one bolt in that first volley, but not all had been aimed at him. Mat's smoking boots lay a dozen paces from where Mat himself sprawled on his back. Tendrils of smoke rose from the black haft of his spear, too, from his coat, even from the silver foxhead, hanging out of his shirt, that had not saved him from a man's channeling. Asmodean was a twisted shape of char, recognizable only from the blackened harpcase still strapped to his back. And Aviendha . . . Unmarked, she could have laid down to rest—if she could have rested staring unblinking at the sun.

Rand bent to touch her cheek. Cooling already. It felt . . . Not like flesh.

"RAAAAHVIIIIN!"

It startled him a little, that sound coming from his throat. He seemed to be sitting somewhere deep in the back of his own head, the Void around him vaster, emptier, than it had ever been before. *Saidin* raged through him. He did not care if it scoured him away. The taint seeped through everything, tarnished everything. He did not care.

Three Trollocs broke past the Maidens, great spiked axes and oddly hooked spears in hairy hands, all-too-human eyes fixing on him, standing there apparently unarmed. The one with a boar's tusked snout went down with Enaila's spear through its spine. Eagle's beak and bear's muzzle raced on toward him, one on booted feet, the other on paws.

Rand felt himself smile.

Fire burst from the two Trollocs, a flame at every pore, bursting through black mail. Even as their mouths opened to scream, a gateway opened right where they stood. Bloody halves of burning, cleanly sliced Trolloc fell, but Rand was staring through the opening. Not into blackness, but a great columned hall with lion-carved stone panels, where a large man with wings of white in his dark hair started up in surprise from a gilded throne. A dozen men, some dressed as lords, some in breast-plates, turned to see what their master was looking at.

Rand barely noticed them. "Rahvin," he said. Or someone did. He was not sure who.

Sending fire and lightning ahead of him, he stepped through and let the gateway close behind him. He was death.

Nynaeve was having no trouble maintaining the temper that allowed her to channel a flow of Spirit to the amber sleeping woman in her pouch. Even the feel of unseen eyes could not touch her through her anger this morning. Siuan stood in front of her on a Salidar street in *Tel'aran'rhiod*, a street empty save for them, a few flies, and one fox that paused to look at them curiously before trotting on.

"You must concentrate," Nynaeve barked. "You had more control than this the first time. Concentrate!"

"I *am* concentrating, you fool girl!" Siuan's plain blue wool dress was suddenly silk. The seven-striped stole of the Amyrlin Seat hung around her neck, and a golden serpent bit its own tail on her finger. Frowning at Nynaeve, she did not seem aware of the change, though she had already worn the same five times today. "If there's any difficulty, it lies in that foul-tasting brew you fed me! Faagh! I can still taste it. Like flatfish gall." Stole and ring vanished; the silk dress's high neck plunged low enough to show the twisted stone ring, dangling between her breasts on a fine gold chain.

"If you didn't insist on me teaching you when you needed something to help you sleep, you wouldn't need it." So there had been a little sheepstongue root and a few other things that were not really necessary in the mix. The woman deserved to have her tongue curdled.

"You can hardly teach me when you're teaching Sheriam and the others." The silk paled; the neck was high again, surrounded by a white lace ruff, and a cap of pearls fitted close on Siuan's hair. "Or would you rather I came after them? You claim you need *some* sleep undisturbed."

Nynaeve quivered, fists clenched at her sides. Sheriam and the others were not the worst thing stoking her anger. She and Elayne took turns bringing them to *Tel'aran'rhiod* two at a time, sometimes all six in one night, and even if she was the teacher they never let her forget she was Accepted and they Aes Sedai. One sharp word when they made a foolish mistake . . . Elayne had only been sent to scrub pots once, but Nynaeve's hands were shriveled from hot, soapy water; back where her body lay sleeping they were, anyway. But they were not the worst. Nor was the fact that she barely had a moment to spare for investigating what, if anything, could be done about stilling and gentling. Logain was more cooperative than Siuan and Leane in any case, or at least more eager. Thank the Light he understood about keeping it secret. Or thought he did; he probably believed she would Heal him eventually. No, worse than that was that Faolain had been tested and raised . . . not Aes Sedai —not without the Oath Rod, which was tight in the Tower—but to something more than Accepted. Faolain wore any dress she chose now, and if she could not wear the shawl or choose an Ajah, she had been given other authority. Nynaeve thought she had fetched more cups of water, more books—left deliberately, she was sure!—more pins and inkjars and other useless things in the last four days than she had her entire stay in the Tower. Yet even Faolain was not the worst of all. She did not even want to remember that. Her anger could have heated a house in winter.

"What's put a hook in your gills today, girl?" Siuan had on a gown like those Leane wore, only more sheer than even Leane would ever wear in public, so thin it was hard to tell what color it was. Not the first time she had had that on today, either. What was perking around in the back of the woman's mind? In the World of Dreams, things like these changes of clothing betrayed thoughts you might not even know you had. "You have been almost decent company until today," Siuan continued irritably, then paused. "Until today. I see it now. Yesterday afternoon Sheriam assigned Theodrin to begin helping you break down that block you've built up. Is that what has your shift in a twist? You don't like Theodrin telling you what to do? She's a wilder, too, girl. If anyone can help you learn to channel without eating nettles first, she—"

"And what has you so jittery you can't hold your dress still?" Theodrin—that was what really hurt. The failure. "Maybe it's something I heard last night?" Theodrin was even-tempered, good-humored, patient; she said it could not be done in one session; her own block had taken months to demolish, and she had finally realized she was channeling long before going to the Tower. Still, failure hurt, and worst of all, if anyone ever discovered that she had cried like a baby in Theodrin's comforting arms when she knew she was failing . . . "I heard you heaved Gareth Bryne's boots at his head when he told you to sit down and polish them properly—he still doesn't know Min does the polishing, does he?—so he turned you upside down and—"

Siuan's full-armed slap rung her ears. For an instant she could only stare at the other woman, eyes going wider and wider. With a wordless shriek, she tried to punch Siuan in the eye. Tried, because somehow Siuan had tangled a fist in her hair. A moment later they were down in the dirt of the street, rolling about and screaming, flailing wildly.

Grunting, Nynaeve thought she was getting the better of it even if she did not know whether she was on the top or the bottom half the time. Siuan was trying to yank her braid out by the roots with one hand while the other pounded at her ribs or anything else it could find, but she had the other woman the same way, and Siuan's yanking and punching were definitely growing weaker, and she herself was going to pound Siuan senseless in another minute, then snatch her bald. Nynaeve yelped as a toe caught her hard on the shin. The woman kicked! Nynaeve tried to knee her, but it was not easy in skirts. Kicking was not fighting fair!

Suddenly Nynaeve realized that Siuan was shaking. At first she thought the woman was crying. Then she realized it was laughter. Pushing herself up, she brushed strands of hair out of her face—her braid was all but undone—and glared down at the other woman. "What are you laughing at? Me? If you are . . . !"

"Not at you. At us." Still quivering with mirth, Siuan shoved Nynaeve off her. Siuan's hair was in wild disarray, and dust covered the plain wool dress she wore now, worn-looking and neatly darned in several places. She was barefoot, too. "Two grown women, rolling around like . . . I haven't done that since I was . . . twelve, I think. I started thinking that all we needed would be fat Cian snatching me up by an ear to tell me girls don't fight. I heard she once knocked down a drunken printer; I don't know why." Something very like giggles took her for a moment, then she quieted them and stood, brushing dust from her clothes. "If we have a disagreement, we can settle it like adult women." And in a careful tone, "Still, it might be a good idea not to discuss Gareth Bryne." She gave a start as the worn dress became a gown, red with black-and-gold embroidery around hem and swooping neckline.

Nynaeve sat there staring at her. What would she have done as Wisdom if she found two women rolling around in the dirt that way? If anything, the answer kept her anger at a simmer. Siuan still did not seem to realize that there was no need to brush away dust with your hands in *Tel'aran'rhiod*. Snatching away fingers that had been repairing her braid, Nynaeve got up quickly; before she was on her feet again, her braid hung perfect over her shoulder and her good Two Rivers woolens might have just been laundered.

"I agree," she said. She would have made any two women she caught like that sorry they had been born even before she hauled them before the Women's Circle. What was she doing lashing out with her fists like some fool man? First Cerandin—she did not want to think about that episode, but there it was—then Latelle, and now this. Was she going to get around her block by being angry all the time? Unfortunately—or perhaps fortunately—that thought did nothing for her temper. "If we have disagreements, we can . . . discuss them."

"Which I suppose means we'll shout at one another," Siuan said dryly. "Well, better that than the other."

"We would not have to shout if you—!" Drawing a deep breath, Nynaeve jerked her eyes away; this was no way to begin anew. That breath caught in her throat, and she turned her head back to Siuan so quickly it seemed she had been shaking it. She hoped it did. Just for an instant, there had been a face in a window across the street. And there was a flutter in her belly, a bubble of fear, a burn of anger at being afraid. "I think we should go back now," she said quietly.

"Go back! You said that vile concoction would put me to sleep for a good two hours, and we haven't been here much more than half that."

"Time works differently here." Had it been Moghedien? The face had vanished so quickly it could have been someone dreaming herself here for an instant. If it was Moghedien, they must not—must not on any account—let her know she had been seen. They had to get away. Bubble of fear, burn of anger. "I told you. A day in *Tel'aran'rhiod* can be an hour in the waking world, or the other way round. We—"

"I've dipped better out of the bilge in a bucket, girl.

You needn't think you can get away with shortchanging me. You'll teach me everything you teach the others, as agreed. We can go when I wake up."

There was no time. If it had been Moghedien. Siuan's dress was green silk now, and the Amyrlin's stole and her Great Serpent ring were back, but for a wonder the neckline was almost as low as anything she had worn before. The ring *ter'angreal* hung above her breasts, somehow part of a necklace of square emeralds.

Nynaeve moved without thinking. Her hand lashed out, snatched the necklace so hard it tore free from Siuan's neck. Siuan's eyes widened, but as soon as the clasp broke, she vanished, and necklace and ring melted from Nynaeve's hand. For an instant she stared at her empty fingers. What happened to someone sent out of *Tel'aran'rhiod* like that? Had she sent Siuan back to her sleeping body? Or to somewhere else? To nowhere?

Panic seized her. She was just standing there. Quick as thought she fled, the World of Dreams seeming to change around her.

She stood on a dirt street in a small village of wooden houses, none more than a single story. The White Lion of Andor waved from a tall staff, and a single stone dock stuck out into a broad river where a flock of long-billed birds flapped south low over the water. It all looked vaguely familiar, but it took her a moment to know where she was. Jurene. In Cairhien. And that river was the Erinin. It had been here that she and Egwene and Elayne had boarded the *Darter,* as badly misnamed as the *Riverserpent,* to continue their journey to Tear. That time seemed like something read in a book long ago.

Why had she jumped to Jurene? That was simple, and answered as soon as she thought of it. Jurene was the one place she knew well enough to leap to in *Tel'aran'rhiod* that she could be sure Moghedien did not know. They had been there for an hour, before Moghedien knew she existed, and she was sure neither she nor Elayne had ever mentioned it again, in *Tel'aran'rhiod* or awake.

But that left another question. The same one, in a way. Why Jurene? Why not step out of the Dream, wake up in her own bed, such as it was, if washing dishes and scrubbing floors on top of everything had not left her so weary she slept right on? *I can still step out.* Moghedien had seen her in Salidar, if that had been Moghedien. Moghedien knew Salidar now. *I can tell Sheriam.* How? Admit she was teaching Siuan? She was not supposed to have her hands on those *ter'angreal* except with Sheriam and the other Aes Sedai. How Siuan got hold of them when she wanted, Nynaeve did not know. No, she was not afraid of more hours up to her elbows in hot water. She was afraid of Moghedien. Anger burned in her belly fiercely. She wished she had some goosemint out of her scrip of herbs. *I am so . . . so* bloody *tired of being afraid.*

There was a bench in front of one of the houses, overlooking dock and river. She sat down and considered her situation from every angle. It was ridiculous. The True Source was a pale thing. She channeled a flame dancing in air above her hand. *She* might look solid—to herself, anyway—but she could see the river through that scrap of fire. She tied it off, and it faded away like mist as soon as the knot was done. How could she face Moghedien when the weakest novice in Salidar could match or better her strength? That was why she had fled here instead of leaving *Tel'aran'rhiod.* Afraid and angry at being afraid, too angry to think straight, to consider her own weakness.

She would step out of the Dream. Whatever Siuan's scheme had been, it was done; she would have to take her chances right along with Nynaeve. The thought of more hours scrubbing floors tightened her hand on her braid. Days more likely, and maybe Sheriam's switch besides. They might never let her near one of the dream *ter'angreal* again, or any *ter'angreal.* They would set Faolain over her instead of Theodrin. A finish to studying Siuan and Leane, much less Logain; maybe a finish to studying Healing.

In a fury she channeled another flame. If it was a whit stronger, she could not see it. So much for trying to crank her anger in hope it would help. "There's nothing for it but to just tell them I saw Moghedien," she muttered, yanking her braid hard enough to hurt. "Light, they *will* give me to Faolain. I'd almost rather die!"

"But you seem to enjoy running little errands for her."

That mocking voice pulled Nynaeve up off the bench like hands on her shoulders. Moghedien stood in the street all in black, shaking her head at what she saw. With all her strength Nynaeve wove a shield of Spirit and hurled it between the other woman and *saidar.* Tried to hurl it between; it was like chopping at a tree with a paper hatchet. Moghedien actually smiled before she bothered to slice Nynaeve's weave, and that as casually as brushing a biteme away from her face. Nynaeve stared at her as though poleaxed. After everything it came down to this. The One Power, useless. All the anger bubbling inside her, useless. All her plans, her hopes, useless. Moghedien did not bother to strike back. She did not even bother to channel a shield of her own. That was how much contempt she had.

"I was afraid you had seen me. I grew careless when you and Siuan started trying to kill each other. With your hands." Moghedien gave a belittling laugh. She was weaving something, lazily because there was no reason to hurry. Nyaneve did not know what it was, yet she wanted to scream. Fury seethed inside her, but fear dulled her wits, rooted her feet to the ground. "Sometimes I think you are all too ignorant even to train, you and the former *Amyrlin Seat* and all the rest. But I cannot allow you to betray me." That weave was reaching out for her. "It is time to collect you at last, it seems."

"Hold, Moghedien!" Birgitte shouted.

Nynaeve's mouth dropped open. It *was* Birgitte, as she had been, in her short white coat and wide yellow trousers, intricate golden braid pulled over her shoulder, silver arrow drawn on silver bow. It was impossible. Birgitte was no longer part of *Tel'aran'rhiod,* she was back in Salidar, making sure no one discovered Nynaeve and Siuan asleep with the sun up and began asking questions.

Moghedien was so shocked, the flows she had woven vanished. Shock lasted less than a moment, though. The gleaming arrow flew from Birgitte's bow—and evaporated. The bow evaporated. Something seemed to seize the archer, jerking her arms straight up, pulling her clear of the ground. Almost immediately she was snubbed short, pulled tight between wrists and ankles a foot above the ground.

"I should have considered the possibility of you." Moghedien turned her back on Nynaeve to move closer to Birgitte. "Do you enjoy your flesh? Without Gaidal Cain?"

Nynaeve thought of channeling. But what? A dagger that might not even penetrate the woman's skin? Fire that would not singe her skirts? Moghedien knew how useless she was; she was not even looking at her. If she stopped the flow of Spirit to the sleeping woman in amber, she would wake in Salidar, she could give warning. Her face twisted near to tears as she looked at Birgitte. The golden-haired woman hung there, staring defiantly at Moghedien. Moghedien contemplated her in return as a woodcarver would a block of wood.

There's only me, Nynaeve thought. *I might as well not be able to channel at all. There's only me.*

Lifting that first foot was like pulling it out of knee-deep mud, the second staggering step no easier. Toward Moghedien. "Don't hurt me," Nynaeve cried. "Please. Don't hurt me." A chill ran through her. Birgitte was gone. A child of perhaps three or four, in short white coat and wide yellow trousers, stood there playing with a toy-sized silver bow. Flipping her golden braid back, the child aimed the bow at Nynaeve and giggled, then stuck a finger in her mouth as though unsure whether she had done something wrong. Nynaeve sagged to her knees. It was hard work crawling in skirts, but she did not think she could have remained standing. Somehow she managed, reaching out a pleading hand and whimpering. "Please. Don't hurt me. Please. Don't hurt me." Over and over as she dragged toward the Forsaken, a broken beetle scrabbling in the dirt.

Moghedien watched silently, until at last she said, "Once I thought you were stronger than this. Now I find I truly like the sight of you on your knees. That is close enough, girl. Not that I think you have courage enough to try tearing *my* hair out. . . ." She seemed amused by the notion.

Nynaeve's hand wavered a span from Moghedien. It had to be close enough. There was only her. And *Tel'aran'rhiod.* The image formed in her head, and there it was, silver bracelet on her outstretched wrist, silver leash linking it to the silver collar around Moghedien's neck. It was not just the *a'dam* she fixed in her head, but Moghedien wearing it, Moghedien and the *a'dam,* a part of *Tel'aran'rhiod* that she held in the form she wanted. She knew something of what to expect; she had worn an *a'dam's* bracelet briefly once, in Falme. In a strange way she was aware of Moghedien in the same way she was aware of her own body, her own emotions, two sets, each distinct, but each in her own head. One thing she had only hoped, because Elayne insisted it was so. The thing was indeed a link; she could feel the Source *through* the other woman.

Moghedien's hand leaped to the collar, shock rounding her eyes. Rage and horror. Rage more than horror, at first. Nynaeve felt them almost as if they were her own. Moghedien had to know what the leash-and-collar was, yet she tried to channel anyway; at the same time Nynaeve felt a slight shifting in herself, in the *a'dam,* as the other woman tried to bend *Tel'aran'rhiod* to herself. Suppressing Moghedien's attempt was simple; the *a'dam* was a link, with her in control. Knowing that made it easy. Nynaeve did not want to channel those flows, so they were not channeled. Moghedien might as well have tried to pick up a mountain with her bare hands. Horror overwhelmed rage.

Getting to her feet, Nynaeve fastened the proper image in her mind. She did not just imagine Moghedien leashed in the *a'dam,* she *knew* Moghedien was leashed, as firmly as she knew her own name. The sense of shifting, of her skin trying to crawl, did not go away, though. "Stop that," she said sharply. The *a'dam* did not move, but it seemed to tremble unseen. She thought of blackwasp nettles lightly brushing the other woman from shoulders to knees. Moghedien shuddered, exhaled convulsively. "Stop it, I said, or I'll do worse." The shifting ceased. Moghedien watched her warily, still clutching the silver collar around her neck and with an air of being poised on her toes for flight.

Birgitte—the child who was, or had been, Birgitte—stood eyeing them curiously. Nynaeve formed the image of her as a grown woman, concentrated. The little girl put her finger back in her mouth and began studying the toy bow. Nynaeve breathed angrily. It was hard changing what someone else was already maintaining. And on top of that, Moghedien had claimed she could make changes permanent. But what she could do, she could undo. "Restore her."

"If you release me, I—"

Nynaeve thought of nettles again, and not a light brush this time. Moghedien sucked air through clenched teeth, shook like a bedsheet in a high wind.

"That," Birgitte said, "was the most frightening thing that has ever happened to me." Herself once more, she wore the short coat and wide trousers, but she had no bow or quiver. "I *was* a child, but at the same time, what was me—really me—was just some fancy floating in the back of that child's mind. And I knew it. I knew I was just going to watch what happened and play. . . ." Flipping her golden braid back over her shoulder, she gave Moghedien a hard look.

"How did you get here?" Nynaeve asked. "I am grateful, you understand, but . . . how?"

Birgitte gave Moghedien a final stony stare, then opened her coat to fish in the neck of her blouse, pulling up the twisted stone ring on a leather thong. "Siuan woke up. Just for a moment, and not all the way. Long enough to grumble about you snatching this from her. When you didn't wake right behind her, I knew something must be wrong, so I took the ring and the last of what you mixed for Siuan."

"There was hardly any left. Only the dregs."

"Enough to put me to sleep. It tastes horrible, by the way. After that, it was as easy as finding feather-dancers in Shiota. In some ways this is almost as if I were still—" Birgitte cut off with another glare for Moghedien. The silver bow reappeared in her hand, and a quiver of silver arrows at her hip, yet after one moment they vanished again. "Past is past, and the future is ahead," she said firmly. "I was not truly surprised to realize there were two of you who knew they were in *Tel'aran'rhiod.* I knew the other must be her, and when I arrived and saw the pair of you . . . It seemed as if she had already captured you, but I hoped that if I distracted her, you might come up with something."

Nynaeve felt a stab of shame. She had considered abandoning Birgitte. That was what she had almost come up with. The thought had only been there for a moment, rejected as soon as it came, but it had come. What a coward she was. Surely Birgitte never had even moments when fear almost took control of her. "I . . ." A faint taste of boiled catfern and powdered mavinsleaf. "I almost ran away," she said faintly. "I was so frightened my tongue stuck to the roof of my mouth. I almost ran away and left you."

"Oh?" Nynaeve writhed inside as Birgitte considered her. "But you did not, did you? I should have loosed before I called out, but I've never felt comfortable shooting anyone from behind. Even her. Still, it all worked out. But what do we do with her now?"

Moghedien certainly seemed to have overcome her fear. Ignoring the silver collar around her throat, she watched Nynaeve and Birgitte as though they were the prisoners, not she, and she was deliberating what to do with them. Except for an occasional twitch of her hands, as if she wanted to scratch where her skin held the memory of nettles, she appeared black-clad serenity. Only the *a'dam* let Nynaeve know there was fear in the woman, almost a gibbering, but pushed down to a muted buzz. She wished the thing let her know what Moghedien was thinking as well as feeling. Then again, she was just as glad not to be inside the mind behind those cold dark eyes.

"Before you consider anything . . . drastic," Moghedien said, "remember that I know much that would be useful to you. I have observed the other Chosen, peeked into their schemes. Is that not worth something?"

"Tell me, and I will consider whether it's worth

anything," Nynaeve said. What could she do with the woman?

"Lanfear, Graendal, Rahvin and Sammael are plotting together."

Nynaeve gave the leash a short tug, staggering her. "I know that. Tell me something new." The woman was captive here, but the *a'dam* only existed so long as they were in *Tel'aran'rhiod.*

"Do you know they are drawing Rand al'Thor to attack Sammael? But when he does, he will find the others as well, waiting to trap him between them. At least, he will find Graendal and Rahvin. I think Lanfear plays another game, one the others know nothing about."

Nynaeve exchanged worried glances with Birgitte. Rand must learn of this. He would, as soon as she and Elayne could speak to Egwene tonight. If they could manage to put their hands on the *ter'angreal* long enough.

"That is," Moghedien murmured, "if he lives long enough to find them."

Nynaeve took hold of the silvery leash where it joined the collar and pulled the Forsaken's face close to hers. Dark eyes met her gaze flatly, but she could feel anger through the *a'dam,* and fear wriggling up and being stamped down. "You listen to me. Do you think I don't know why you are pretending to be so cooperative? You think if you keep talking long enough, I will make some slip, and you can escape. You think the longer we talk, the harder I'll find it to kill you." That much was true enough. To kill somebody in cold blood, even one of the Forsaken, would be hard, maybe harder than she could manage. What was she going to do with the woman? "But you understand this. I won't allow hinting at things. If you try keeping anything back from me, I will do to you everything you ever thought of doing to me." Dread, creeping through the leash, like bone-chilling shrieks deep in Moghedien's mind. Maybe she did not know as much about *a'dam* as Nynaeve thought. Maybe she believed Nynaeve could read her thoughts if she tried. "Now if you know of some threat to Rand, something ahead of Sammael and the others, you tell me. Now!"

Words spilled from Moghedien's mouth, and her tongue flickered out to wet her lips continually. "Al'Thor means to go after Rahvin. Today. This morning. Because he thinks Rahvin killed Morgase. I don't know whether he did or not, but al'Thor believes it. But Rahvin never trusted Lanfear. He never trusted any of them. Why should he? He thought it all might be some trap set for him, so he has laid a trap of his own. He has set Wards through Caemlyn so if a man channels a spark he will know. Al'Thor will walk right into it. He almost certainly already has. I think he meant to leave Cairhien right after sunrise. I had no part of it. It was none of it my doing. I—"

Nynaeve wanted to shut her up; the fear sweat glistening on the woman's face made her sick, but if she had to listen to that pleading voice, too . . . She started to channel, wondering whether she would be strong enough to hold Moghedien's tongue, then smiled. She was linked to Moghedien, and in control. Moghedien's eyes bulged as she wove flows to stop her own mouth and tied them. Nynaeve added plugs for her ears too, before turning to Birgitte. "What do you think?"

"Elayne's heart will break. She loves her mother."

"I know that!" Nynaeve took a breath. "I will cry with her and mean every tear, but right now I must worry about Rand. I think she was telling the truth. I could almost feel it." She caught the silver leash just below her bracelet and shook it. "Maybe it's this, and maybe it was imagination. What do you believe?"

"That it's the truth. She was never very brave unless she clearly had the upper hand, or thought she could get it. And you certainly put the fear of the Light into her."

Nynaeve grimaced. Birgitte's every word put another bubble of anger in her belly. She was never very brave except when she clearly had the upper hand. That could describe herself. She had put the fear of the Light into Moghedien. She had, and she had meant every word when she said it. Boxing somebody's ears when they needed it was one thing; threatening torture, wanting to torture, even Moghedien, was something else again. And here she was trying to avoid what she knew she had to do. Never very brave except when she clearly had the upper hand. This time the bubble of anger was seeded by herself. "We have to go to Caemlyn. I do, at least. With her. I may not be able to channel strongly enough to tear paper as I am, but with the *a'dam* I can use her strength."

"You won't be able to affect anything in the waking world from *Tel'aran'rhiod,*" Birgitte said quietly.

"I know! I know, but I have to do something."

Birgitte threw back her head and laughed. "Oh, Nynaeve, it is such an embarrassment being associated with such a coward as you." Abruptly her eyes widened in surprise. "There wasn't much of your potion left. I think I am wak—" In mid-word, she was simply no longer there.

Taking a deep breath, Nynaeve untied the flows around Moghedien. Or made her do it; with the *a'dam* it was hard to tell which, really. She wished Birgitte was still there. Another pair of eyes. Someone who probably knew *Tel'aran'rhiod* better than she ever could. Someone who was brave. "We are taking a trip, Moghedien, and you are going to help me with every last scrap of you. If anything takes me by surprise . . . Suffice it to say, anything that happens to the one wearing this bracelet happens to the one wearing the collar. Only about tenfold." The sickly look on Moghedien's face said she believed. Which was just as well, since it was true.

Another deep breath, and Nynaeve began forming the image of the one place in Caemlyn she knew well enough to remember. The Royal Palace, where Elayne had taken her. Rahvin must be there. But in the waking world, not the World of Dreams. Still, she had to do something. *Tel'aran'rhiod* changed around her.

The Threads Burn

Rand stopped. A long scorch along the corridor wall marked where half a dozen costly tapestries had gone to ash. Flames licked upward on another; a number of inlaid chests and tables were only charred ruins. Not his work. Thirty paces further on, red-coated men in breastplates and helmets with barred face-guards lay contorted in death on the white floortiles, useless swords in hand. Not his work either. Rahvin had been wasteful of his own in attempting to reach Rand. He had been clever in his attacks, clever in his escapes, but from the moment he fled the throneroom he had not faced Rand for more than the instant it took to strike and flee. Rahvin was strong, perhaps as strong as Rand, and more knowledgeable, but Rand had the fat-little-man *angreal* in his pocket, and Rahvin had none.

The corridor was doubly familiar, once for having seen it before, once for having seen something similar.

I walked this way with Elayne and Gawyn the day I met Morgase. The thought slithered painfully along the boundaries of the Void. He was cold in there, without emotion. *Saidin* raged and burned, but he was icy calm.

And another thought, like a stab. *She lay on a floor like*

this, her golden hair spread as though sleeping. Ilyena Sunhair. My Ilyena.

Elaida had been there that day, too. *She Foretold the pain I'd bring. She knew the darkness in me. Some of it. Enough.*

Ilyena, I did not know what I was doing. I was mad! I am mad. Oh, Ilyena!

Elaida knew—some—but she did not tell even all of that. Better if she had told.

Oh, Light, is there no forgiveness? I did what I did in madness. Is there no mercy?

Gareth Bryne would have killed me, had he known. Morgase would have ordered my death. Morgase would be alive, perhaps. Elayne's mother alive. Aviendha alive. Mat. Moiraine. How many alive, if I had died?

I have earned my torment. I deserve the final death. Oh, Ilyena, I deserve death.

I deserve death.

Bootsteps behind him. He turned.

They came out of a broad crossing corridor not twenty paces from him, two dozen men in breastplates and helmets and the white-collared red coats of the Queen's Guards. Except that Andor had no queen now, and these men had not served her while she lived. A Myrddraal led them, pale eyeless face like something found under a rock, overlapping plates of black armor heightening the illusion of a serpent as it moved, black cloak hanging motionless however it moved. The look of the Eyeless was fear, but fear was a distant thing in the Void. They hesitated when they saw him; then the Halfman raised its black-bladed sword. Men who had not already drawn put hands to hilts.

Rand—he thought that was his name—channeled in a way he could not remember doing before.

Men and Myrddraal stiffened where they stood. White frost grew thick on them, frost that smoked as Mat's boots had smoked. The Myrddraal's upraised arm broke off with a loud crack. When it hit the floortiles, arm and sword shattered.

Rand could feel the cold—yes, that was his name; Rand—cold like a knife as he walked past and turned the way they had come. Cold, yet warmer than *saidin.*

A man and a woman crouched against the wall, servants liveried in red and white, short of their middle years and holding each other as though for protection. Seeing Rand—there was more to the name; not just Rand—the man started to rise from where he had huddled away from the Myrddraal-led band, but the woman hauled him back by his sleeve.

"Go in peace," Rand said, putting out a hand. Al'Thor. Yes, Rand al'Thor. "I'll not hurt you, but you could be hurt if you stay."

The woman's brown eyes rolled up in her head. She would have collapsed in a heap if the man had not caught her, and his narrow mouth was working rapidly, as if he was praying but could not get the words out.

Rand looked where the man was looking. His hand had stretched out of his coatsleeve far enough to bare the Dragon's golden maned head that was part of his skin. "I will not hurt you," he said, and walked on, leaving them there. He had Rahvin to corner yet. Rahvin to kill. And then?

No sound but the click of his boots on the tiles. And deep in his head, a faint voice murmuring mournfully of Ilyena and forgiveness. He strained to feel Rahvin channeling, to feel the man filled with the True Source. Nothing. *Saidin* seared his bones, froze his flesh, scoured his soul, but from without it was not easy to see until you were close. A lion in high grass, Asmodean had said once. A rabid lion. Should Asmodean count among those who should not have died? Or Lanfear? No. Not—

He had only a moment's warning to throw himself flat, a hair-thin slice of time between feeling flows suddenly woven and an arm-thick bar of white light, liquid fire, slicing through the wall, ripping across like a sword through where his chest had been. Where that bar slashed, on both sides of the hallways, wall and friezes, doors and tapestries ceased to exist. Severed wallhangings and chunks of stone and plaster broken free rained to the floor.

So much for the Forsaken fearing to use balefire. Who had told him that? Moiraine. She surely had deserved to live.

Balefire leaped from his hands, a brilliant white shaft

streaking toward where that other bar had originated. The other failed even as his punched through the wall, leaving a purple afterimage fanning across his vision. He released his own flow. Had he done it finally?

Scrambling to his feet, he channeled Air, slamming ruined doors open so hard that the remnants ripped from the hinges. Inside, the room was empty. A sitting room, with chairs arrayed before a great marble fireplace. His balefire had taken a bite out of one of the arches leading to a small courtyard with a fountain, and another from one of the fluted columns along the walk beyond.

Rahvin had not gone that way, though, and he had not died in that blast of balefire. A residue hung in the air, a fading remnant of woven *saidin*. Rand recognized it. Different from the gateway he had made to Skim to Caemlyn, or the one to Travel—he knew now that was what he had done—into the throneroom. But he had seen one like this in Tear, had made one himself.

He wove another now. A gateway, an opening at least, a hole in reality. It was not blackness on the other side. In fact, if he had not known the way was there, if he could not have seen the weave of it, he might not have known. There before him were the same arches opening onto the same courtyard and fountain, the same columned walk. For an instant the neatly rounded holes his balefire had made in arch and column wavered, filled, then were holes again. Wherever that gateway led, it was to somewhere else, a reflection of the Royal palace as once it had been a reflection of the Stone of Tear. Vaguely he regretted not talking to Asmodean about it while he had the chance, but he had never been able to speak of that day to anyone. It did not matter. On that day he had carried *Callandor,* but the *angreal* in his pocket had already proved enough to harry Rahvin.

Stepping through quickly, he loosed the weave and hurried away across the courtyard as the gateway vanished. Rahvin would have felt that gate if he was close enough and trying. The fat little stone man did not mean he could stand and wait to be attacked.

No sign of life, except for himself and one fly. That was the way it had been in Tear, too. Stand-lamps in the hallways stood unlit, with pale wicks that had never seen a flame, yet even in what should have been the dimmest hall there was light, seemingly coming from everywhere and nowhere. Sometimes those lamps moved, too, and other things as well. Between one glance and the next a tall lamp might have moved a foot, a vase in a niche an inch. Little things, as if someone had shifted them in the time his eyes were away. Wherever this was, it was a strange place.

It came to him, as he trotted along another colonnade, sensing for Rahvin, that he had not heard the voice crying over Ilyena since he channeled balefire. Perhaps he had somehow chased Lews Therin out of his head.

Good. He stopped at the edge of one of the palace gardens. The roses and whitestar bushes looked as drought bedraggled as they would have in the real palace. On some of the white spires rising above the rooftops, the White Lion banner rippled, but which spire could change in the blink of an eye. *Good, if I don't have to share my head with—*

He felt odd. Insubstantial. He raised his arm, and stared. He could see the garden through coatsleeve and arm as through a mist. A mist that was thinning. When he glanced down, he could see the walk's paving stones through himself.

No! It was not his thought. An image began to coalesce. A tall, dark-eyed man with a worry-creased face and more white in his hair than brown. *I am Lews Ther—*

I am Rand al'Thor, Rand broke in. He did not know what was happening, but the faint Dragon was beginning to fade from the misty arm held in front of his face. The arm began to look darker, the fingers on his hand longer. *I am me.* That echoed in the Void. *I am Rand al'Thor.*

He fought to picture himself in his own mind, struggled to make the image of what he saw in the mirror every day shaving, what he saw in a stand-mirror dressing. It was a frantic fight. He had never really looked at himself. The two images waxed and waned, the older dark-eyed man and the younger with blue-gray eyes. Slowly the younger image firmed, the older faded. Slowly his arm grew more solid. His arm, with the Dragon twined around it and the heron branded into his palm.

There had been times he hated those marks, but now, even enclosed within the emotionless Void, he almost grinned to see them.

Why had Lews Therin tried to take him over? To make him into Lews Therin. He was sure that was who that dark-eyed man with the suffering face had been. Why now? Because he could in this place, whatever it was? Wait. It had been Lews Therin who shouted that adamant "no." Not an attack by Lews Therin. By Rahvin, and not using the Power. If the man had been able to do this back in Caemlyn, the real Caemlyn, he would have. It had to be some ability he had gained here. And if Rahvin had gained it, perhaps he had too. The image of himself had been what held him, brought him back.

He focused on the nearest rosebush, a thing a span high, and imagined it growing thin, foggy. Obediently, it melted away to nothing, but as soon as the picture in his mind was nothing, the rosebush was suddenly back, just as it had been.

Rand nodded coldly. It had limits, then. There were always limits and rules, and he did not know them here. But he knew the Power, as much as Asmodean had taught him and he had taught himself, and *saidin* was still in him, all the sweetness of life, all the corruption of death. Rahvin had to have seen him to attack. With the Power you had to see something to affect it, or know *exactly* where it was in relation to you down to a hair. Perhaps it was different here, but he did not think so. He almost wished Lews Therin had not gone silent again. The man might know this place and its rules.

Balconies and windows overlooked the garden, in some places four stories high. Rahvin had tried to . . . unmake him. He drew on the raging torrent of *saidin* through the *angreal*. Lightnings flashed from the sky, a hundred forking silver bolts, more, stabbing at every window, every balcony. Thunder filled the garden, erupting chunks of stone. The air itself crackled, and the hair on his arms and chest tried to stand under his shirt. Even the hair on his head began to lift. He let the lightnings die. Here and there bits of shattered stone windowframe and balcony broke loose, the crash of their fall muted by the echoes of thunder still ringing in his ears.

Gaping holes peered down now where windows had. They looked like sockets in some monstrous skull, the ruined balconies like a dozen splintered mouths. If Rahvin had been at any of them, he was surely dead. Rand would not believe it until he saw the corpse. He wanted to see Rahvin dead.

Wearing a snarl he did not know was there, he stalked back into the palace. He had wanted to see Rahvin die.

Nynaeve hurled herself flat and scrambled along the hall floor as *something* slashed through the nearest wall. Moghedien slithered as fast as she, but if the woman had not, she would have hauled her by the *a'dam*. Had that been Rand, or Rahvin? She had seen bars of white fire, liquid light, like that in Tanchico, and she had no wish to be anywhere near one again. She did not know what it was, and she did not want to know. *I want to Heal, burn both of these fool men, not learn a fancy way to kill!*

She levered herself up to a crouch, peered back the way they had come. Nothing. An empty palace hallway. With a ten-foot long gash through both walls, as neat as any stoneworker could have done, and bits of tapestry lying on the floor. No sign of either man. She had not had a glimpse of either so far. Only their handiwork. Sometimes that handiwork had almost been her. A good thing that she could draw on Moghedien's anger, filter it out of the terror clawing to escape and let it seep into her. Her own was a pitiful thing that would scarcely have allowed her to sense the True Source, much less channel the flow of Spirit that kept her in *Tel'aran'rhiod*.

Moghedien was hunched over on her knees, dry retching. Nynaeve's mouth tightened. The woman had tried to remove the *a'dam* again. Her cooperation had faded quickly when they discovered Rand and Rahvin actually here in *Tel'aran'rhiod*. Well, trying to unfasten that collar when it was around your neck was its own punishment. At least Moghedien did not have anything left in her stomach this time.

"Please." Moghedien caught at Nynaeve's skirt. "I tell you, we must get away." Stark panic made her voice painful. Moghedien's clawing terror mirrored itself on her face. "They are here in the flesh. The flesh!"

"Be quiet," Nynaeve said absently. "Unless you've lied to me, that is an advantage. For me." The other woman claimed that being in the World of Dreams physically limited your control of the Dream. Or rather, she admitted it, after letting a bit of the knowledge slip. She had admitted, too, that Rahvin did not know *Tel'aran'rhiod* as well as she. Nynaeve hoped that meant he did not know it as well as *she* did. That he knew more than Rand, she did not doubt. That wool-headed man! Whatever his reason for coming after Rahvin, he should never have let the man lead him here, where he did not know the rules, where thoughts could kill.

"Why will you not understand what I tell you? Even if they had only dreamed themselves here, either would be stronger than we. Here in the flesh, they could crush us without blinking. In the flesh they can draw *saidin* more deeply than we can draw *saidar* dreaming."

"We are linked." Still not paying attention, Nynaeve gave her braid a sharp pull. No way to tell which direction they had gone. And no warning of anything until she saw them. Somehow it still seemed unfair that they could channel without her being able to see or feel the flows. A stand-lamp that had been sliced in two was suddenly whole again, then not, just as quickly. That white fire must be incredibly powerful. *Tel'aran'rhiod* usually healed itself rapidly whatever you did to it.

"You brainless fool," Moghedien sobbed, shaking Nynaeve's skirt with both hands as if wanting to shake Nynaeve. "It does not matter how brave you are. We are linked, but you contribute nothing the way you are. Not a shred. It is my strength, and your madness. They are here in the flesh, not dreaming! They are using things you have never dreamed of! They will destroy us if we stay!"

"Keep your voice down," Nynaeve snapped. "Do you want to bring one of them down on us?" She looked both ways hurriedly, but the hallway was still empty. Had that been footsteps, boots? Rand or Rahvin? One had to be approached as carefully as the other. A man in a fight for his life could strike out before he saw they were friends. Well, that she was, anyway.

"We must go," Moghedien insisted, but she did lower her voice. She got to her feet, sullen defiance twisting her mouth. Fear and anger writhed inside her, first one stronger, then the other. "Why should I help you any further? This is madness!"

"Would you rather feel the nettles again?"

Moghedien flinched, yet her dark eyes remained stubborn. "You think I will let them kill me rather than be hurt by you? You *are* mad. I will not stir from this spot until you are ready to take us away from here."

Nynaeve jerked her braid again. If Moghedien refused to walk, she would have to drag her. Not a very quick way to search, with what seemed miles of palace corridors yet to go. She should have been harsher when the woman first tried balking. In Nynaeve's place, Moghedien would have killed without hesitation, or, if she thought the other useful, woven the trick of taking someone's will, making them worship her. Nynaeve had tasted that once, in Tanchico, and even had she known how it was done, she did not think she could do it to somebody else. She despised this woman, hated her with all her being. But even if she had not needed her, she could not have killed her just standing there. The trouble was, she was afraid that Moghedien knew that too, now.

Still, a Wisdom headed the Women's Circle—even if the Circle did not always agree—and the Women's Circle dealt out punishments to women who broke the law or offended custom too deeply, and to men, too, for some transgressions. She might not have Moghedien's stomach for killing, for crushing people's minds, but. . . .

Moghedien opened her mouth, and Nynaeve filled it with a gag of Air. Or rather she made Moghedien do it; with the *a'dam* linking them, it was like channeling herself, but Moghedien knew it was her own abilities being used like a tool in Nynaeve's hand. Dark eyes glittered indignantly as Moghedien's own flows snared her arms to her sides and pulled her skirts tight around her ankles. For the rest, Nynaeve used the *a'dam*, just as with the nettles, creating the sensations she wanted the other woman to feel. Not the reality; the *feel* of reality.

Moghedien stiffened in her bonds as a leather strap seemed to strike her bottom. That was what it would feel like to her. Outrage and humiliation rolled through the leash. And contempt. Compared to her elaborate ways of hurting people, this seemed suitable for a child.

"When you are ready to cooperate again," Nynaeve said, "just nod." This could not take long. She could not just stand there while Rand and Rahvin tried to kill one another. If the wrong one died because she avoided danger by letting Moghedien keep her there . . .

Nynaeve remembered a day when she was sixteen, just after she had been judged old enough to put her hair in a braid. She had stolen a plum pudding from Corin Ayellin on a dare from Nela Thane and walked out the kitchen door right into Mistress Ayellin. Adding the aftermath, sending it along the leash in a lump, made Moghedien's eyes pop.

Grimly, Nynaeve did it again. *She won't stop me short!* Again. *I will help Rand whatever she thinks!* Again. *Even if it kills us!* Again. *Oh, Light, she could be right; Rand could kill us both before he knows it's me.* Again. *Light, I hate being afraid!* Again. *I hate her!* Again. *I hate her!* Again.

Abruptly she realized Moghedien was jerking frantically in her bonds, nodding her head so violently it seemed about to come off. For a moment, Nynaeve gaped at the other woman's tear-streaked face, then stopped what she was doing and hurriedly unraveled the flows of Air. Light, what had she done? She was not Moghedien. "I take it you won't give me any more trouble?"

"They will kill us," the other woman mumbled faintly, and nearly unintelligibly through her sobs, but at the same time she nodded a hurried acquiescence.

Deliberately, Nynaeve hardened herself. Moghedien deserved everything she had gotten and much, much more. In the Tower, one of the Forsaken would have been stilled and executed as soon as the trial could be concluded, and little evidence needed beside who she was. "Good. Now we—"

Thunder shook the entire palace, or something very much like thunder, except that the walls rattled and dust rose off the floor. Nynaeve half fell into Moghedien, and they danced trying to keep their feet. Before the upheaval had faded completely, it was replaced by a roar like some monstrous fire racing up a chimney the size of a mountain. That lasted only a moment. The silence after seemed deeper than before. No. There were boots. A man running. The sound echoed down the hallway. From the north.

Nynaeve pushed the other woman away. "Come on."

Moghedien whimpered, but did not resist being pulled down the hall. Her eyes were huge, though, and her breath came too fast. Nynaeve thought it was a good thing she had Moghedien along, and not just for access to the One Power. After all her years hiding in shadows, the Spider was such a coward she almost made Nynaeve feel brave by comparison. Almost. It was only anger at her own fear that made her able to hold on to that one flow of Spirit that kept her in *Tel'aran'rhiod*, now. Moghedien was stark terror to her bones.

Pulling Moghedien behind her by the gleaming leash, Nynaeve quickened her step. Chasing the fading sound of those other steps.

Rand stepped into the round courtyard warily. Half of the white-paved circle cut into the structure rising three stories behind him; the other half was bounded by a stone semicircle atop pale columns five paces high, sticking out into yet another garden, shaded gravel walks beneath low spreading trees. Marble benches surrounded a pool with lilypads. And fish, gold and white and red.

Suddenly the benches shifted, flowed, changed into faceless manshapes, still as white and hard-looking as the stone. He had already learned the difficulty of changing something that Rahvin had altered. Lightning danced from his fingertips, shattering stone men to shards.

The air became water. Choking, Rand struggled to swim toward the columns; he could see the garden beyond. There must be some kind of barrier to stop all the water pouring out. Before he could channel, gold and red and white shapes were darting around him, larger than the fish in the pool had been. And with teeth. They ripped at him; blood curled up in red mist. Instinctively he flailed at the fish with his hands, but the cold part of him, deep in the Void, channeled. Balefire flared, at the barrier if there was one, at any place Rahvin might be to see this courtyard. The water roiled, throwing him around violently, as it rushed in to fill the empty tunnels carved by balefire. Flickers of gold and white and red darted at him, adding new threads of crimson to the water. Tossed about, he could not see to aim his wild bolts; they flashed in every direction. No breath left. He tried to think of air, or the water being air.

Suddenly it was. He dropped hard to the paving stones among small fish flopping about, rolled over and pushed himself up. It was all air again; even his clothes were dry. The stone ring flickered between standing untouched and lying in ruins with half the columns down. Some of the trees lay tangled atop their own stumps, then stood whole, then were fallen again. The palace behind him had holes punched in white walls, even one through a high gilded dome above, and gashes slashed across windows, some with pierce-work stone screens. The damage all flickered, vanishing and reappearing. Not the slow, sometime shifts of before, but constant. Damage, then none, then some, then none, then all again.

Wincing, he pressed his hand to his side, to the old, half-healed wound. It stung as if his exertions had nearly torn it open. He stung all over, from a dozen or more bleeding bites. That had not changed. The bloody rips in his coat and breeches were still there. Had he managed to change the water back to air? Or had one of his frenzied bolts of balefire driven Rahvin off, or even killed him? It did not matter, unless it was the last.

Wiping blood out of his eyes, he studied the windows and balconies around the garden, the colonnade high on the far side. Or rather, he started to, but something else caught his eye. Below the colonnade, he could just make out the fading remnants of a weave. From there he could tell it was a gateway, but to see what kind and where it led, he had to be closer. Leaping over a jumble of worked stone that vanished while he was above it, he darted across the garden, dodging around trees fallen on the walkway. That residue was almost gone; he had to get close enough before it vanished completely.

Abruptly he fell, gravel scraping his palms as he caught

himself. He could not see anything that might have tripped him. He felt woozy, almost as if he had been hit on the head. He tried to scramble to his feet, to reach that residue. And realized his body was writhing. Long hair covered his hands; his fingers seemed to be shrinking, drawing back into his hands. They were almost paws. A trap. Rahvin had not fled. The gateway had been a trap, and he had walked into it.

Desperation clung to the Void as he struggled to cling to himself. His hands. They were hands. Almost hands. He forced himself up. His legs seemed to bend wrong. The True Source receded; the Void shrank. Streaks of panic flared beyond the emotionless emptiness. Whatever Rahvin was trying to change him to, it could not channel. *Saidin* slipping away, thinning, thin even pulled through the *angreal.* The surrounding balconies stared down at him, empty, and the colonnade. Rahvin had to be at one of those stone-screened windows, but which? He had no strength for a hundred lightning bolts this time. One burst. He could manage that. If he did it quickly. Which window? He fought to be himself, fought to draw *saidin* into him, welcomed every stain of the taint as evidence that he still held the Power. Staggering in a crooked circle, searching vainly, he roared Rahvin's name. It sounded like a beast's roar.

Pulling Moghedien behind her, Nynaeve rounded the corner. Ahead of her, a man vanished around the next turning, the sound of his boots echoing behind. She did not know how long she had been following those boots. Sometimes they had gone silent, and she had had to wait for them to start again to gain a direction. Sometimes when they stopped things happened; she had not seen any of it, but once the palace had rung like a struck bell, and another time the hair on her head had tried to stand up as the air seemed to crackle, and another . . . It did not matter. This was the first time she had caught a glimpse of the man who wore those boots. She did not think it was Rand in that black coat. The height was right, but he was too large, too heavy in the chest.

She was running before she knew it. Her stout shoes had long since become velvet slippers for silence. If she could hear him, he could hear her. Moghedien's frenzied panting was louder than their footfalls.

Nynaeve reached the turn and stopped, peeking cautiously around the corner. She held *saidar*—through Moghedien, but it was hers—ready to channel. There was no need. The hallway was empty. A door stood far down a wall with windows filled with arabesque-pierced stone, but she did not think he could have reached that. Nearer, another corridor ran off to the right. She hurried to that, looked warily again. Empty. But a staircase spiraled upward just beyond where the hallways met.

For a moment she hesitated. He had been hurrying somewhere. This corridor led back the way they had come. Would he have been running to go back? Up then.

Drawing Moghedien behind her, she climbed the steps slowly, straining to hear anything except the Forsaken's nearly hysterical breath and the blood pounding in her own ears. If she found herself face to face with him . . . She knew he was there already, somewhere ahead. Surprise had to be on her side.

At the first landing, she paused. The hallways here mirrored those below. They were just as empty, too, just as silent. Had he gone on up?

The stair quivered faintly beneath her feet as if the palace had been struck by a huge battering ram, then another. Again, as a bar of white fire punched through the top of one of the stone-screened windows, skewed wildly upward at an angle, then winked out as it started to slice into the ceiling.

Nynaeve swallowed, blinking in a vain effort to rid herself of the pale violet fan that hung across her vision in memory of the thing. That had to be Rand, trying to strike at Rahvin. If she was too close to him, Rand might catch her by accident. If he was flailing like that—it had had the look of flailing to her—he could catch her anywhere without knowing it.

The quivers had ceased. Moghedien's eyes shone with terror. By what Nynaeve felt through the *a'dam,* it was a wonder the woman was not writhing on the floor, shrieking and frothing at the mouth. Nynaeve felt a little like shrieking herself. She made herself put her foot on the next step. Up was as good a way as any. The second step was almost as hard. Slowly, though. No need to come on him too suddenly. Surprise had to be on his part. Moghedien followed like a whipped dog, shivering.

As Nynaeve climbed, she embraced *saidar* as fully as she could, as much as Moghedien could handle, to the point where the sweetness of it became almost a pain. That was the warning. More, and she would approach the point where it was more than she could take in, the point where she would still herself, burn the ability to channel right out of herself. Or perhaps out of Moghedien, under the circumstances. Or both of them. Any way at all, it would be disaster now. She held that point though, the . . . *life* . . . filling her a needle's light pressure just short of breaking skin. It was as much as she could have embraced had she been channeling on her own. She and Moghedien were much the same strength in the Power; Tanchico had proved that. Was it enough? Moghedien insisted the men were stronger. Rahvin, at least—Moghedien knew him—and it did not seem likely Rand could have survived this long unless he was just as strong. It was not fair that men should have the muscles and greater strength in the Power too. The Aes Sedai in the Tower had always said they had been equal. It just was not—

She was babbling. Taking a deep breath, she drew Moghedien behind her off the staircase. This was as high as it went.

This hall was empty. She went to where it met the crossing corridor, peeked. And there he was. A tall black-clad man, large, with wings of white in his dark hair, peering through the curving slots of one of the stone window-screens at something below. There was sweat and effort on his face, but he seemed to be smiling. A handsome face, as handsome as Galad's, but she felt no quickening of her breath for this one.

Whatever he was staring at—Rand perhaps?—had his full attention, but Nynaeve gave him no chance to notice her. It might be Rand down there. She could not tell whether Rahvin was channeling or not. She filled the corridor around him with fire from wall to wall, floor to ceiling, pouring into it all of *saidar* she held, fire so hot the stone itself smoked. The heat made her flinch back.

Rahvin screamed in the middle of the flame—it was one flame—and staggered away from her, back to where the hallway became a columned walk. A heartbeat, less, while she still flinched, and he stood, inside the flame but surrounded by clear air. Every scrap of *saidar* she could channel was going into that inferno, but he held it at bay. She could see him through the fire; it gave everything a red cast, but she could see. Smoke rose from his charred coat. His face was a seared ruin, one eye milky white. But both eyes were malevolent as he turned them on her.

No emotion reached her along the *a'dam*'s leash, only leaden dullness. Nynaeve's stomach fluttered. Moghedien had given up. Given up because death was there for them.

Fire thrust through the carved window-screens above Rand, fingers of it filling every hole, dancing toward the colonnade. As it did, the struggle within him ceased abruptly. He was himself so suddenly it was almost a shock. He had been drawing desperately at *saidin,* trying to hold onto some of it. Now it rushed into him, an avalanche of fire and ice that made his knees buckle, made the Void tremble with pain that shaved at it like a lathe.

And Rahvin stumbled backwards out onto the colonnade, face turned to something inside. Rahvin wreathed in fire, yet somehow standing as though untouched. If untouched now, it had not been so before. Only the size of the figure, the impossibility of it being anyone else, told Rand it was him. The Forsaken was a figure of char and cracked red flesh that would have strained any Healer to mend. The agony of it must have been overwhelming. Except that Rahvin would be inside the Void within that burned remnant of a man, wrapped in emptiness where the body's pain was distant and *saidin* close at hand.

Saidin raged inside Rand, and he loosed it all. Not to Heal.

"Rahvin!" he screamed, and balefire flew from his hands, molten light thicker than a man, driven by all the Power he could draw.

It struck the Forsaken, and Rahvin ceased to exist. The

Darkhounds in Rhuidean had become motes before they vanished, whatever kind of life they had had struggling to continue, or the Pattern struggling to maintain itself even for them. Before this, Rahvin simply . . . ceased.

Rand let the balefire die, pushed *saidin* away a little. Trying to blink away the purple afterimage, he stared up at the wide hole in the marble balustrade, the remains of one column a fang above it, stared at the matching hole in the palace roof. They did not flicker, as if what he had done was too strong even for this place to mend. After everything, it seemed almost too easy. Perhaps there was something up there to convince him Rahvin was really dead. He ran toward a door.

Frantically, Nynaeve threw everything into trying to close the flame tight around Rahvin once more. The thought came that she should have used lightning. She was going to die. Those horrible eyes had fixed on Moghedien, not her, but she was going to die too.

Liquid fire sliced up into the colonnade, so hot it made the fire she had made seem cool. Shock made her release her weaving, and she flung up a hand to protect her face, yet before it had raised halfway, the liquid fire was gone. So was Rahvin. She did not believe he had escaped. There had been an instant, so brief she could almost have imagined it, when that white bar touched him and he became . . . mist. Just an instant. She could have imagined. But she did not believe so. She drew a shuddering breath.

Moghedien had her face in her hands, weeping, trembling. The one emotion Nynaeve sensed through the *a'dam* was relief so powerful it drowned anything else.

Hurried boots grated on the stairs below.

Nynaeve spun, took a step toward the spiral staircase. She was surprised to realize she was drinking deeply of *saidar*, holding herself ready.

That surprise faded when Rand climbed into sight. He was not as she remembered. His features were the same, but his face was hard. Blue ice made his eyes. The bloody rips in his coat and breeches, the blood on his face, seemed to suit that face.

The way he looked, she would not be surprised if he killed Moghedien on the spot the instant he discovered who she was. Nynaeve had uses for her yet. He would recognize an *a'dam*. Without another thought she changed it, let the leash vanish, leaving only the silver bracelet on her wrist and the collar on Moghedien. A moment of panic when she comprehended what she had done, then a sigh as she realized that she still felt the other woman. It worked exactly as Elayne had said it would. Perhaps he had not seen. She was between him and Moghedien; the leash had trailed behind her.

He barely glanced at Moghedien. "I thought about those flames, coming up here. I thought it might have been you or . . . Where is this? Is this where you meet Egwene?"

Looking up at him, Nynaeve tried not to swallow. So cold, that face. "Rand, the Wise Ones say what you've done, what you are doing, is dangerous, even evil. They say you lose something of yourself if you come here in the flesh, some part of what makes you human."

"Do the Wise Ones know everything?" He brushed past her and stood staring at the colonnade. "I used to think Aes Sedai knew everything. It doesn't matter. I don't know how human the Dragon Reborn can afford to be."

"Rand, I . . ." She did not know what to say. "Here, let me Heal you at least."

He held still for her to reach up and take his head in her hands. For her part, she had to suppress a wince. His fresh wounds were not serious, only numerous—what could have bitten him; she was sure most of these were bites—but the old wound, that half-healed, never-healing wound in his side, that was a sinkhole of darkness, a well filled with what she thought the taint of *saidin* must be like. She channeled the complex flows, Air and Water, Spirit, even Fire and Earth in small amounts, that made up Healing. He did not roar and flail about. He did not even blink. He shivered. That was all. Then he took her wrists and brought her hands down from his face. She was not reluctant. His new injuries were gone, every bite and scrape and bruise, but not the old wound. Nothing had changed about that. Anything short of death should be capable of being Healed, even that. Anything!

"Is he dead?" he asked quietly. "Did you see him die?"

"He's dead, Rand. I saw."

He nodded. "But there are others still, aren't there? Other . . . Chosen."

Nynaeve felt a stabbing sliver of fear from Moghedien, but she did not glance back. "Rand, you must go. Rahvin is dead, and this place is dangerous for you as you are. You must go, and not come back here in the body."

"I will go."

He did nothing that she could see or feel—of course, she could not—but for a moment she thought the hallway behind him had . . . turned in some way. But it did not look any different. Except . . . She blinked. There was no half-gone column in the colonnade beyond him, no hole in the stone railing.

He went on as if nothing had happened. "Tell Elayne . . . . Ask her not to hate me. Ask her . . ." Pain twisted his face. For a moment she saw the boy she had known, looking as though something precious was being ripped away from him. She reached out to comfort him, and he stepped back, his face stone again, and bleak. "Lan was right. Tell Elayne to forget me, Nynaeve. Tell her I've found something else to love, and there's no room left for her. He wanted me to tell you the same thing. Lan has found someone else, too. He said for you to forget him. Better never to have been born than to love us." He stepped back again, three long steps, the hall seemed to turn dizzyingly with him in it—or part of the hall did—and he was gone.

Nynaeve stared at where he had been, and not at the fitfully flickering reappearance of the damage to the colonnade. Lan had told him to say *that*?

"A . . . remarkable man," Moghedien said softly. "A very, very dangerous man."

Nynaeve stared at her. Something new was coming through the bracelet to her. Fear was still there, but muted by . . . Expectation might have been the best way to describe it.

"I have been helpful, have I not?" Moghedien said. "Rahvin dead, Rand al'Thor saved. None of it would have been possible without me."

Nynaeve understood now. Hope more than expectation. Sooner or later Nynaeve would have to wake. The *a'dam* would vanish. Moghedien was trying to remind her of her aid—as if it had not had to be wrenched out of her—just in case Nynaeve might be steeling herself to kill before she went. "It is time for me to go, too," Nynaeve said. Moghedien's face did not alter, but fear strengthened and so did hope. A large silver cup appeared in Nynaeve's hand, apparently filled with tea. "Drink this."

Moghedien edged back. "What—?"

"Not poison. I could kill you easily enough without, if that was my aim. After all, what happens to you here is real in the waking world, too." Hope much stronger than fear now. "It will make you sleep. A deep sleep; too deep to touch *Tel'aran'rhiod*. It's called forkroot."

Moghedien took the cup slowly. "So I cannot follow you? I will not argue." She tipped back her head and swallowed until the cup was empty.

Nynaeve watched her. That much should put her down quickly. Yet a cruel streak made her speak. She knew it was cruel and did not care. Moghedien should not have any quiet rest at all. "You knew Birgitte was not dead." Moghedien's gaze narrowed slightly. "You knew who Faolain is." The other woman's eyes tried to widen, but she was already drowsy. Nynaeve could feel the forkroot's effects spreading. She concentrated on Moghedien, held there in *Tel'aran'rhiod*. No easy sleep for one of the Forsaken. "And you knew who Siuan is, that she used to be the Amyrlin Seat. I've never mentioned that in *Tel'aran'rhiod*. Never. I'll see you very shortly. In Salidar."

Moghedien's eyes rolled up her head. Nynaeve was not sure whether it was the forkroot or a faint, but it did not matter. She released the other woman, and Moghedien winked out. The silver collar rang as it hit the floortiles. Elayne would be happy about that, at least.

Nynaeve stepped out of the Dream.

*   *   *

Rand trotted along the corridors of the palace. There seemed to be less damage than he remembered, but he did not really look. He strode out into the great courtyard at the front of the palace. Blasts of Air knocked the tall gates half off their hinges. Beyond lay a huge oval plaza, and what he had been searching for. Trollocs and Myrddraal. Rahvin was dead, and the other Forsaken were elsewhere, but there were Trollocs and Myrddraal to kill in Caemlyn.

They were fighting, a milling mass of hundreds, perhaps thousands, surrounding something he could not see through their black-mailed numbers, as tall as a Myrddraal on its horse. Just barely he could make out his crimson banner deep in their midst. Some swung round to face the palace as the gates were hurled asunder.

Yet Rand stopped dead. Balls of fire rolled through the packed black-mailed mass, and burning Trollocs lay everywhere. It could not be.

Not daring to hope or think, he channeled. Shafts of balefire leaped from his hands as fast as he could weave them, narrower than his little finger, precise and cut off as soon as they struck. They were much less powerful than the one he had used against Rahvin at the end, than any he had used against Rahvin, but he could not risk one slicing through to those trapped in the center of all those Trollocs. It made little difference. The first-struck Myrddraal seemed to reverse colors, become a white-clad black shape, then it was drifting motes that vanished as its horse fled madly. Trollocs, Myrddraal, every one that turned toward him went the same, and then he began carving into the backs of those still facing the other way, so a continuous haze of sparkling dust seemed to fill the air, renewed as it evaporated.

They could not stand against that. Bestial cries of rage turned to howls of fear, and they fled in every direction except toward him. He saw one Myrddraal try to turn them and be trampled under, rider and horse, but the rest spurred their animals away.

Rand let them go. He was busy staring at the veiled Aiel bursting out of their encirclement with spears and heavy-bladed knives. It was one of them carrying the banner; Aiel did not carry banners, but this one, a bit of red headband showing beneath his *shoufa,* did. There were battles going on down some of the streets leading from the plaza, too. Aiel against Trollocs. Townsfolk against Trollocs. Even armored men in the uniform of the Queen's Guards against Trollocs. Apparently some who were willing to kill a queen could not stomach Trollocs. Rand only barely noticed, though. He was searching through the Aiel.

There. A woman in a white blouse, one hand holding up her bulky skirts as she slashed at a fleeing Trolloc with a short knife; an instant later flames enveloped the bear-snouted figure.

"Aviendha!" Rand did not know he was running until he shouted. "Aviendha!"

And there was Mat, coat torn and blood on his sword-blade spearpoint, leaning on the black shaft watching the Trollocs flee, content to let someone else do the fighting now that that was possible. And Asmodean, sword held awkwardly and trying to look every way at once in case any Trolloc decided to turn back. Rand could sense *saidin* in him, though weakly; he did not think much of Asmodean's fighting had been with that blade.

Balefire. Balefire that burned a thread out of the Pattern. The stronger that balefire was, the further back that burning went. And whatever that person had done *no longer had happened.* He did not care if his blast at Rahvin had unraveled half the Pattern. Not if this was the result.

He became aware of tears on his cheeks, and let *saidin* and the Void go. He wanted to feel this. "Aviendha!" Snatching her up, he whirled her around, with her staring down at him as if he had gone mad. He did not want to put her down, but he did. So he could hug Mat. Or try to.

Mat fended him off. "What's the matter with you? You'd think you thought we were dead. Not that we weren't, almost. Being a general has to be safer than this!"

"You're alive." Rand laughed. He brushed back

Aviendha's hair; she had lost her headscarf, and it hung loose around her neck. "I'm happy you're alive. That's all."

He took in the plaza again, and his joy faded. Nothing could extinguish it, but the bodies lying in heaps where the Aiel had made their stand lessened it. Too many of them were not big enough to be men. There was Lamelle, veil gone and half her throat as well; she would never make him soup again. Pevin, both hands clutching the wrist-thick shaft of the Trolloc spear through his chest and the first expression on his face Rand had ever seen. Surprise. Balefire had cheated death for his friends, but not for others. Too many. Too many Maidens.

Take what you can have. Rejoice in what you can save, and do not mourn your losses too long. It was not his thought, but he took it. It seemed a good way to avoid going mad before the taint on *saidin* drove him to it.

"Where did you go?" Aviendha demanded. Not angrily. If anything, she looked relieved. "One second you were there, the next you were gone."

"I had to kill Rahvin," he said quietly. She opened her mouth, but he put his fingers over it to silence her, then gently pushed her away. Take what you can have. "Leave it at that. He's dead."

Bael came limping up, *shoufa* still around his head but veil hanging down his chest. There was blood on his thigh, and on the point of his one remaining spear as well. "The Nightrunners and Shadowtwisted are running, *Car'a'carn.* Some of the wetlanders have joined the dance against them. Even some of the armored men, though they danced against us at first." Sulin was behind him, unveiled, a nasty red gash across her cheek.

"Hunt them down however long it takes," Rand said. He began walking, not sure where as long as it was away from Aviendha. "I don't want them loose on the countryside. Keep an eye on the Guards. I'll find out later which of them were Rahvin's men and which . . ." He walked on, talking and not looking back. Take what you can have.

CHAPTER

56

Glowing Embers

The high window had more than enough room for Rand to stand in it, stretching far above his head and clearing his shoulders by two feet to either side. Shirtsleeves rolled up, he stared down at one of the Royal Palace's gardens. Aviendha was trailing her hand in the fountain's redstone basin, still intrigued by so much water with no purpose but to be looked at and keep ornamental fish alive. She had been more than indignant at first, when he told her she could not go chasing Trollocs through the streets. In fact, he was not sure she would be down there now if not for a quiet escort of Maidens that Sulin did not think he had noticed. Neither was he supposed to have heard the white-haired Maiden remind her that she was *Far Dareis Mai* no longer and not yet a Wise One. Coatless, but wearing his hat against the sun, Mat was sitting on the coping of the basin, talking to her. No doubt probing for what she knew of whether the Aiel were preventing people from leaving; even if Mat did decide to accept his fate, it was unlikely he would ever stop complaining about it. Asmodean sat on a bench in the shade of a red myrtle tree, playing his harp. Rand wondered whether the man knew what had happened, or suspected. He should have no memory—for him, it never happened—but who could say what one of the Forsaken knew or could reason out?

A polite cough turned him away from the garden.

The window where he stood was a span and a half above the floor in the west wall of the throneroom, the Grand Hall where Queens of Andor had received embassies and pronounced judgment for nearly a thousand years. It was the only place he had thought he could be sure of watching Mat and Aviendha unseen and undisturbed. Rows of white columns twenty paces high marched down the sides of the hall. The light from the tall windows in the walls mingled with colored light from great windows set in the arching ceiling, windows where the White Lion alternated with portraits of early queens of the realm and scenes of great Andoran victories. Enaila and Somara did not appear impressed.

Rand let himself down by his fingertips. "Is there news from Bael?"

Enaila shrugged. "The hunt for Trollocs goes on." By her tone, the diminutive woman would have liked to be part of that. Somara's height made her seem even shorter. "Some of the city people give aid. Most hide. The city gates are held. None of the Shadowtwisted will escape, I think, but I fear some of the Nightrunners may." Myrddraal were hard to kill, and just as hard to corner. Sometimes it was easy to believe the old tales that they rode shadows and could vanish by turning sideways.

"We brought you some soup," Somara said, nodding her flaxen head toward a silver tray covered with a striped cloth, sitting on the dais that held the Lion Throne. Carved and gilded, with huge lion's paws at the ends of its legs, the throne was a massive chair at the top of four white marble stairs, with a strip of red carpet leading up to it. The Lion of Andor, picked out in moonstones on a field of rubies, would have stood above Morgase's head whenever she occupied that seat. "Aviendha says you have not eaten yet today. It is the soup Lamelle used to make for you."

"I suppose none of the servants have come back," Rand sighed. "One of the cooks, maybe? A helper?" Enaila shook her head scornfully. She would serve her time as *gai'shain* with a good grace, if it ever came to that, but the idea of anyone spending their entire life serving someone else disgusted her.

Climbing the stairs, he squatted to twitch the cloth aside. His nose twitched, too. By the smell, whichever of them had made it was no better a cook than Lamelle had been. The sound of a man's boots coming up the hall gave him an excuse to turn his back on the tray. With any luck, he would not have to eat it.

The man approaching up the long, red-and-white-tiled floor was certainly no Andorman, in his short gray coat and those baggy trousers stuffed into boots turned down at the knee. Slender and only a head taller than Enaila, he had a hooked beak of a nose and dark tilted eyes. Gray streaked his black hair and a thick mustache like down-curved horns around his wide mouth. He paused to make a leg and bow slightly, handling the curved sword at his hip gracefully despite the fact that incongruously he carried two silver goblets in one hand and a sealed pottery jar in the other.

"Forgive my intrusion," he said, "but there was no one to announce me." His clothes might be plain and even travel-worn, but he had what appeared to be an ivory rod capped with a golden wolf's head thrust behind his sword belt. "I am Davram Bashere, Marshal-General of Saldaea. I am here to speak with the Lord Dragon, who rumors in the city say is here in the Royal Palace. I assume that I address him?" For an instant his eyes went to the glittering Dragons twining red-and-gold around Rand's arms.

"I am Rand al'Thor, Lord Bashere. The Dragon Reborn." Enaila and Somara had moved between Rand and the man, each with a hand on the hilt of her long-bladed knife, poised to veil. "I am surprised to find a Saldaean lord in Caemlyn, much less wanting to speak to me."

"In truth, I rode to Caemlyn to speak to Morgase, but I was put off by Lord Gaebril's toadies—King Gaebril, I should say? Or does he still live?" Bashere's tone said he doubted it, and did not care one way or the other. He did not pause. "Many in the city say Morgase is dead, as well."

"They're both dead," Rand said bleakly. He sat down on the throne, his head resting against the moonstone Lion of Andor. The throne had been sized for women. "I killed Gaebril, but not before he killed Morgase."

Bashere quirked an eyebrow. "Should I hail King Rand of Andor, then?"

Rand leaned forward angrily. "Andor has always had a queen, and it still does. Elayne was Daughter-Heir. With her mother dead, she is queen. Maybe she has to be crowned first—I don't know the law—but she is queen as far as I am concerned. I am the Dragon Reborn. That is as much as I want, and more. What is it you want of me, Lord Bashere?"

If his anger disturbed Bashere at all, the man gave no outward sign. Those tilted eyes watched Rand carefully, but not uneasily. "The White Tower allowed Mazrim Taim to escape. The false Dragon." He paused, then went on when Rand said nothing. "Queen Tenobia did not want Saldaea troubled again, so I was sent to hunt him down once more and put an end to him. I have followed him south for many weeks. You need not fear I've brought a foreign army into Andor. Except for an escort of ten, the rest I left camped in Braem Wood, well north of any border Andor has claimed in two hundred years. But Taim is in Andor. I am sure of it."

Rand leaned back again, hesitating. "You cannot have him, Lord Bashere."

"May I ask why not, my Lord Dragon? If you wish to use Aiel to hunt him, I have no objection. My men will remain in Braem Wood until I return."

This part of his plan he had not meant to reveal so soon. Delay could be costly, but he had intended to have a firm hold on the nations first. Yet it might as well begin now. "I am announcing an amnesty. I can channel, Lord Bashere. Why should another man be hunted down and killed or gentled because he can do what I can? I will announce that any man who can touch the True Source, any man who wants to learn, can come to me and have my protection. The Last Battle is coming, Lord Bashere. There may not be time for any of us to go mad before, and I would not waste one man for the risk anyway. When the Trollocs came out of the Blight in the Trolloc Wars, they marched with Dreadlords, men and women who wielded the Power for the Shadow. We will face that again at Tarmon Gai'don. I don't know how many Aes Sedai will be at my side, but I won't turn away any man who channels if he will march with me. Mazrim Taim is mine, Lord Bashere, not yours."

"I see." It was flatly said. "You have taken Caemlyn. I hear that Tear is yours, and Cairhien soon will be if it is not already. Do you mean to conquer the world with your Aiel and your army of men channeling the One Power?"

"If I must." Rand said it just as levelly. "I'll welcome any ruler as an ally who welcomes me, but so far all I've seen is maneuvering for power, or outright hostility. Lord Bashere, there's anarchy in Tarabon and Arad Doman, and not far from it in Cairhien. Amadicia is eyeing Altara. The Seanchan—you may have heard rumors of them in Saldaea; the worst are likely true— the Seanchan on the other side of the world eyeing us all. Men fighting their own petty battles with Tarmon Gai'don on the horizon. We need peace. Time before the Trollocs come, before the Dark One breaks free, time to ready ourselves. If the only way I can find time and peace for the world is to impose it, I will. I don't want to, but I will."

"I have read *The Karaethon Cycle*," Bashere said. Putting the goblets under his arm for a moment, he broke the wax seal on the jar and filled them with wine. "More importantly, Queen Tenobia has read the Prophecies, too. I cannot speak for Kandor, or Arafel, or Shienar. I believe they will come to you—not a child in the Borderlands but knows the Shadow waits in the Blight to descend on us—but I cannot speak for them." Enaila eyed the goblet he handed her suspiciously, but she climbed the stairs to hand it to Rand. "In truth," Bashere continued, "I cannot even speak for Saldaea.

Tenobia rules; I am only her general. But I think once I send a fast rider to her with a message, the return will be that Saldaea marches with the Dragon Reborn. In the meanwhile, I offer you my services, and those of nine thousand Saldaean horse."

Rand swirled the goblet, staring down into the dark red wine. Sammael in Illian, and other Forsaken the Light alone knew where. Seanchan waiting across the Aryth Ocean, and men here ready to leap for their own advantage and profit whatever it cost the world. "Peace is far off yet," he said softly. "It will be blood and death for some time to come."

"It always is," Bashere replied quietly, and Rand did not know which statement he was speaking to. Perhaps both.

Tucking his harp under his arm, Asmodean drifted away from Mat and Aviendha. He enjoyed playing, but not for a pair who did not listen, much less appreciate. He was not sure what had happened that morning, and not sure he wanted to be sure. Too many Aiel had expressed surprise at seeing him, had claimed they had seen him dead; he did not want details. There was a long gash down the wall in front of him. He knew what made that sharp edge, that surface as slick as ice, smoother than any hand could have polished in a hundred years.

Idly—but with a shiver, too—he wondered whether being reborn in this fashion made him a new man. He did not think so. Immortality was gone. That was a gift of the Great Lord; he used that name in his head, whatever al'Thor demanded on his tongue. That was proof enough that he was himself. Immortality gone— he knew it must be imagination, yet sometimes he thought he could feel time dragging at him, pulling him toward a grave he had never thought to meet—and drawing the little of *saidin* he could was like drinking sewage. He was hardly sorry Lanfear was dead. Rahvin either, but Lanfear especially, for what she had done to him. He would laugh when each of the others died, too, and most for the last. It was not that he had been reborn as a new man at all, but he would cling to that tuft of grass on the cliff's brink as long as he could. The roots would give way eventually, the long fall would come, but until then he was still alive.

He pulled open a small door, intending to find his way to the pantry. There should be some decent wine. One step, and he stopped, the blood draining from his face. "You? No!" The word still hung in the air when death took him.

Morgase blotted sweat from her face, then tucked the handkerchief back up her sleeve and readjusted her somewhat ragged straw hat. At least she had managed to acquire a decent riding dress, though even fine gray wool was still uncomfortable in this heat. Actually, Tallanvor had acquired it. Letting her horse walk, she eyed the tall young man, riding up ahead through the trees. Basel Gill's roundness emphasized how tall and fit Tallanvor was. He had handed the dress to her saying it suited her better than the itchy thing she had fled the palace in, looking down at her, never blinking, never speaking a word of respect. Of course, she herself had decided it was not safe for anyone to know who she was, especially after discovering Gareth Bryne gone from Kore Springs; why did the man have to be off chasing barnburners when she needed him? No matter; she would do as well without him. But there was something disturbing in Tallanvor's eyes when he called her simply Morgase.

Sighing, she glanced back over her shoulder. Hulking Lamgwin rode watching the forest, Breane at his side watching him as much as anything else. Her army had not grown a whit since Caemlyn. Too many had heard of nobles exiled for no cause and unjust laws in the capital to do more than scoff at the most casual mention of stirring a hand in support of their rightful ruler. She doubted that even knowing who spoke to them would have made a difference. So here she rode through Altara, keeping to forest as much as possible because there seemed to be parties of armed men everywhere, rode through the forest with a scar-faced street tough, a besotted refugee Cairhienin noblewoman, a stout innkeeper who could hardly keep from kneeling whenever she glanced at him, and a young soldier who sometimes looked at her as though she had on one of those dresses she had worn for Gaebril. And Lini, of course. There was no forgetting Lini.

As if thinking of her had been a summons, the old nurse heeled her horse closer. "Better to keep your eyes ahead," she said quietly. "'A young lion charges quickest, and when you least expect it.'"

"You think Tallanvor is dangerous?" Morgase said sharply, and Lini gave her a sidelong, considering look.

"Only the way any man can be dangerous. A fine figure of man, don't you think? More than tall enough. Strong hands, I should think. 'There's no point letting honey age too long before you eat it.'"

"Lini," Morgase said warningly. The old woman had been going on this way too often of late. Tallanvor was a handsome man, his hands did look strong, and he had a well-turned calf, but he was young, and she was his queen. The last thing she needed was to start looking at him as a man instead of her subject and soldier. She was about to tell Lini that—and that the woman had lost her wits if she thought she was going to take up with any man ten years her junior; he had to be that—but Tallanvor and Gill were turning back. "You hold your tongue, Lini. If you put foolish ideas into that young man's head, I will leave you somewhere." Lini's snort would have earned the highest noble in Andor time in a cell to meditate. If she still had her throne, it would.

"Are you sure you want to do this, girl? 'It's too late to change your mind after you've jumped off the cliff.'"

"I will find my allies where I can find them," Morgase told her stiffly.

Tallanvor reined up, sitting tall in his saddle. Sweat rolled down his face, but he seemed to ignore the heat. Master Gill tugged at the neck of his disc-covered jerkin as though he wished he could have it off.

"The wood gives way to farms just ahead," Tallanvor said, "but it isn't likely anyone will recognize you here." Morgase met his gaze levelly; day by day it was becoming increasingly hard to look away when he was looking at her. "Another ten miles should take us to Cormaed. If that fellow in Sehar was not lying, there will be a ferry, and we can be on the Amadicia side before dark. Are you certain you want to do this, Morgase?"

The way he said her name . . . No. She was letting Lini's ridiculous fancies take hold of her. It was the accursed heat. "I have made up my mind, young Tallanvor," she said coolly, "and I do not expect you to question me when I have done so."

She heeled her mount hard, letting the horse's leap forward break their gazes apart, letting it shove past him. He could catch up to her. She would find her allies where she found them. She would have her throne back, and woe to Gaebril or *any* man who thought he could sit on it in her place.

And the Glory of the Light did shine upon him.
And the Peace of the Light did he give men.
Binding nations to him. Making one of many.
Yet the shards of hearts did give wounds.
And what was once did come again
    —in fire and in storm
splitting all in twain.
For his peace . . .
    —for his peace . . .
. . . was the peace . . .
. . . was the peace . . .
. . . of the sword.
And the Glory of the Light did shine upon him.

    —from *"Glory of the Dragon"*
       composed by Meane sol Ahelle, the Fourth
       Age

The End
of the Fifth Book of
The Wheel of Time

GLOSSARY

A Note on Dates in This Glossary. The Toman Calendar (devised by Toma dur Ahmid) was adopted approximately two centuries after the death of the last male Aes Sedai, recording years After the Breaking of the World (AB). So many records were destroyed in the Trolloc Wars that at their end there was argument about the exact year under the old system. A new calendar, proposed by Tiam of Gazar, celebrated freedom from the Trolloc threat and recorded each year as a Free Year (FY). The Gazaran Calendar gained wide acceptance within twenty years after the Wars' end. Artur Hawkwing attempted to establish a new calendar based on the founding of his empire (FF, From the Founding), but only historians now refer to it. After the death and destruction of the War of the Hundred Years, a third calendar was devised by Uren din Jubai Soaring Gull, a scholar of the Sea Folk, and promulgated by the Panarch Farede of Tarabon. The Farede Calendar, dating from the arbitrarily decided end of the War of the Hundred Years and recording years of the New Era (NE), is currently in use.

Accepted: Young women in training to be Aes Sedai who have reached a certain level of power and passed certain tests. It normally takes five to ten years to be raised from novice to Accepted. Somewhat less confined by rules than novices, they are allowed to choose their own areas of study, within limits. Accepted wear a Great Serpent ring on the third finger of the left hand. When an Accepted is raised Aes Sedai, which usually takes another five to ten years, she chooses her Ajah, gains the right to wear the shawl, and may wear the ring on any finger or not at all if circumstances warrant. *See also* Aes Sedai.

a'dam (AYE-dam): A Seanchan device for controlling a woman who can channel, consisting of a collar and bracelet linked by a leash, all of silvery metal. It has no effect on a woman who cannot channel. *See also damane*; Seanchan; *sul'dam.*

Aes Sedai (EYEZ seh-DEYE): Wielders of the One Power. Since the Time of Madness, all are women. Widely distrusted and feared, even hated. Blamed by many for the Breaking of the World, and thought to meddle in the affairs of nations. At the same time, few rulers are without an Aes Sedai advisor, even where such a connection must be secret. After some years of channeling the One Power, Aes Sedai take on an ageless quality, so that one old enough to be a grandmother may show no signs of age except perhaps a few gray hairs. *See also* Ajah; Amyrlin Seat; Time of Madness.

Age of Legends: Age ended by the War of the Shadow and the Breaking of the World. A time when Aes Sedai performed wonders now only dreamed of. *See also* Breaking of the World; War of the Shadow; Wheel of Time.

Aiel (eye-EEL): The people of the Aiel Waste. Fierce and hardy. They veil their faces before they kill. Deadly warriors with weapons or bare hands, they will not touch a sword, nor ride a horse unless pressed. Their pipers play them into battle with the music of dances. Aiel call battle "the dance," and "the dance of spears." They are divided into twelve clans: the Chareen, the Codarra, the Daryne, the Goshien, the Miagoma, the

Nakai, the Reyn, the Shaarad, the Shaido, the Shiande, the Taardad, and the Tomanelle. Sometimes they speak of a thirteenth clan, the Clan That Is Not, the Jenn, who were the builders of Rhuidean. *See also* Aiel warrior societies; Aiel Waste; Rhuidean.

Aiel kinship terms: Aiel relationships of blood are expressed in complex ways which outsiders consider unwieldy, but which Aiel consider precise. A few examples must suffice to demonstrate, as an entire volume would be needed for a full explanation. First-brother and first-sister have the same mother. Second-brother and second-sister refer to the children of one's mother's first-sister or first-brother, and sister-mothers and sister-fathers are first-sisters and first-brothers of one's mother. Greatfather or greatmother refers to the father or mother of one's own mother, while the parents of one's father are second greatfather or second greatmother; one is closer blood kin to one's mother than father. Beyond this the complications grow and are thickened by such factors as the ability of close friends to adopt each other as first-brother or first-sister. When it is also considered that Aiel women who are close friends sometimes marry the same man, thus becoming sister-wives and married to each other as well as to him, the convolutions become even more apparent.

Aiel War: (976–78 NE) When King Laman (LAY-mahn) of Cairhien cut down *Avendoraldera,* four clans of the Aiel crossed the Spine of the World. They looted and burned the capital city of Cairhien as well as many other cities and towns, and the conflict extended into Andor and Tear. By the conventional view, the Aiel were finally defeated at the Battle of the Shining Walls, before Tar Valon; in fact, Laman was killed in that battle, and having done what they came for, the Aiel recrossed the Spine. *See also Avendoraldera;* Cairhien; Spine of the World.

Aiel warrior societies: Aiel warriors are all members of one of twelve societies. These are Black Eyes *(Seia Doon),* Brothers of the Eagle *(Far Aldazar Din),* Dawn Runners *(Rahien Sorei),* Knife Hands *(Sovin Nai),* Maidens of the Spear *(Far Dareis Mai),* Mountain

Dancers *(Hama N'dore)*, Night Spears *(Cor Darei)*, Red Shields *(Aethan Dor)*, Stone Dogs *(Shae'en M'taal)*, Thunder Walkers *(Sha'mad Conde)*, True Bloods *(Tain Shari)*, and Water Seekers *(Duadhe Mahdi'in)*. Each has its own customs, and sometimes specific duties. For example, Red Shields act as police, and Stone Dogs are often used as rearguards during retreats, while Maidens are often scouts. Aiel clans frequently raid and battle one another, but members of the same society will not fight each other even if their clans do so. Thus there are always lines of contact between the clans, even during open warfare. *See also* Aiel; Aiel Waste; *Far Dareis Mai.*

Aiel Waste: Harsh, rugged and all-but-waterless land east of the Spine of the World. Called the Three-fold Land by the Aiel. Few outsiders enter; the Aiel consider themselves at war with all other peoples and do not welcome strangers. Only peddlers, gleemen, and the Tuatha'an are allowed safe entry, although Aiel avoid all contact with the Tuatha'an, whom they call "the Lost Ones." No maps of the Waste itself are known to exist.

Ajah (AH-jah): Societies among the Aes Sédai, seven in number and designated by colors: Blue, Red, White, Green, Brown, Yellow and Gray. All Aes Sedai except the Amyrlin Seat belong to one. Each follows a specific philosophy of the use of the One Power and the purposes of the Aes Sedai. The Red Ajah bends its energies to finding men who can channel, and to gentling them. The Brown forsakes the mundane world and dedicates itself to seeking knowledge, while the White, largely eschewing both the world and the value of worldly knowledge, devotes itself to questions of philosophy and truth. The Green Ajah (called the Battle Ajah during the Trolloc Wars) holds itself ready for Tarmon Gai'don, the Yellow concentrates on the study of Healing, and Blue sisters involve themselves with causes and justice. The Gray are mediators, seeking harmony and consensus. Rumors of a Black Ajah, dedicated to serving the Dark One, are officially denied.

Alviarin Freidhen (ahl-vee-AH-rihn FREYE-dhehn): An Aes Sedai of the White Ajah, now raised to Keeper of the Chronicles, second only to the Amyrlin Seat among Aes Sedai. A woman of cold logic and colder ambition.

Amadicia (ah-mah-DEE-cee-ah): a nation lying south of the Mountains of Mist, between Tarabon and Altara. Its capital Amador (AH-mah-door) is the home of the Children of the Light, whose Lord Captain Commander has, in fact if not in name, more power than the king. Anyone with the ability to channel is outlawed in Amadicia; by law they are to be imprisoned or exiled, but in actuality are often killed while "resisting arrest." The banner of Amadicia is a six-pointed silver star overlaid on a red thistle on a field of blue. *See also* channel; Children of the Light.

Amyrlin Seat (AHM-ehr-lin SEAT): (1) Leader of the Aes Sedai. Elected for life by the Hall of the Tower, which consists of three representatives (called Sitters, as in "a Sitter for the Green") from each Ajah. The Amyrlin Seat has, theoretically, supreme authority among the Aes Sedai, and ranks as the equal of a king or queen. A slightly less formal usage is "the Amyrlin." (2) The throne on which the leader of the Aes Sedai sits.

Amys (ah-MEESE): Wise One of Cold Rocks Hold, and a dreamwalker. An Aiel of the Nine Valleys sept of the Taardad Aiel. Wife of Rhuarc, sister-wife to Lian (lee-AHN), who is roofmistress of Cold Rocks Hold. Amys is sister-mother to Aviendha.

Andor (AN-door): A wealthy land which stretches from the Mountains of Mist to the River Erinin, at least on a map, though the queen's control has not reached further west than the River Manetherendrelle in several generations. *See also* Daughter-Heir.

angreal **(anh-gree-AHL):** Remnants of the Age of Legends that allow anyone capable of channeling to handle a greater amount of the Power than is safe or even possible unaided. Some were made for use by women, others by men. Rumors of *angreal* usable by both men and women have never been confirmed.

Their making is no longer known, and few remain in existence. *See also* channel; *sa'angreal; ter'angreal.*

Arad Doman (AH-rad do-MAHN): Nation on the Aryth Ocean. Presently racked by civil war and simultaneously by wars against those who have declared for the Dragon Reborn and against Tarabon. Most Domani merchants are women, and according to the saying, to "let a man trade with a Domani" is to do something extremely foolish. Domani women are famous—or infamous—for their beauty, seductiveness, and scandalous clothes.

Artur Hawkwing: Legendary king, Artur Paendrag Tanreall (AHR-tuhr PAY-ehn-DRAG tahn-REE-ahl). Ruled FY 943–94. United all lands west of the Spine of the World. Sent armies across the Aryth Ocean (FY 992), but contact with these was lost at his death, which set off the War of the Hundred Years. His sign was a golden hawk in flight. *See also* War of the Hundred Years.

Avendesora **(AH-vehn-deh-SO-rah):** In the Old Tongue, "the Tree of Life." Mentioned in many stories and legends, which give various locations. Its true location is known to only a few.

Avendoraldera **(AH-ven-doh-ral-DEH-rah):** Tree grown in the city of Cairhien from a sapling of *Avendesora,* a gift from the Aiel in 566 NE, although no written record shows any connection between the Aiel and *Avendesora. See* Aiel War.

Aviendha (ah-vee-EHN-dah): A woman of the Nine Valleys sept of the Taardad Aiel, in training to be a Wise One. She fears nothing, except her fate.

Bair (BAYR): A Wise One of the Haido sept of the Shaarad Aiel. A dreamwalker.

Berelain 'sur Paendrag (BEH-reh-lain suhr PAY-ehn-DRAG): First of Mayene, Blessed of the Light, Defender of the Waves, High Seat of House Paeron (pay-eh-ROHN). A beautiful and willful young woman, and a skillful ruler. *See also* Mayene.

Birgitte (ber-GEET-teh): Hero of legend and story, renowned for her beauty almost as much as for her bravery and skill at archery. Supposedly carried a silver bow and silver arrows with which she never missed. One of the heroes to be called back when the Horn of Valere is sounded. Always linked with the hero-swordsman Gaidal Cain. Except for her beauty and skill with a bow, she is little like the stories of her. *See also* Cain, Gaidal; Horn of Valere.

Blight, the: *See* Great Blight.

Borderlands: The nations bordering the Great Blight: Saldaea, Arafel, Kandor, and Shienar. Their history is one of unending raids and war against Trollocs and Myrddraal. *See also* Great Blight.

Breaking of the World: During the Time of Madness, male Aes Sedai who had gone insane changed the face of the earth. They leveled mountain ranges and raised new mountains, lifted dry land where seas had been and made oceans cover once dry land. Much of the world was completely depopulated, the survivors scattered like dust on the wind. This destruction is remembered in stories, legends, and history as the Breaking of the World. *See also* Time of Madness.

Breane Taborwin (bree-AN tah-BOR-wihn): Formerly a high-ranking lady of Cairhien, now a penniless refugee who has found happiness with the sort of man she once had servants flog out of her sight.

cadin'sor **(KAH-dihn-sohr):** Garb of Aiel warriors; coat and breeches in browns and grays that fade into rock or shadow, along with soft, laced knee-high boots. In the Old Tongue, "working clothes."

Caemlyn (KAYM-lihn): The capital city of Andor. *See* Andor.

Cairhien (KEYE-ree-EHN): Both a nation along the Spine of the World and the capital city of that nation. The city was burned and looted during the Aiel War, as were many other towns and villages. The abandonment of farmland near the Spine of the World after the war made necessary the importation of grain. The assassination of King Galldrian (998 NE) resulted in war for succession to the Sun Throne, disrupting grain shipments and bringing famine. The banner of

Cairhien is a many-rayed golden sun rising on a field of sky blue. *See also* Aiel War.

Callandor (CAH-lahn-DOOR): The Sword That Is Not a Sword, the Sword That Cannot Be Touched. Crystal sword once held in the Stone of Tear. A powerful male *sa'angreal*. Its removal from the chamber called the Heart of the Stone was, along with the fall of the Stone, a major sign of the Dragon's Rebirth and the approach of Tarmon Gai'don. Replaced in the Heart, driven into the stone, by Rand al'Thor. *See also* Dragon Reborn; *sa'angreal;* Stone of Tear.

channel (verb): To control the flow of the One Power. *See also* One Power.

Children of the Light: Society of strict ascetic beliefs, owing allegiance to no nation and dedicated to the defeat of the Dark One and the destruction of all Darkfriends. Founded during the War of the Hundred Years to proselytize against an increase in Darkfriends, they evolved during the war into a completely military society. Extremely rigid in beliefs, and certain that only they know the truth and the right. Consider Aes Sedai and any who support them to be Darkfriends. Known disparagingly as Whitecloaks. Their sign is a golden sunburst on a field of white.

Colavaere (COH-lah-veer) of House Saighan (sye-GHAN): A high-ranking lady of Cairhien, manipulative and scheming, which is to describe Cairhienin nobility in general, who has had so much power that she sometimes forgets her own vulnerability to a greater.

Couladin (COO-lah-dihn): An ambitious man of the Domai sept of the Shaido Aiel. His warrior society is *Seia Doon,* the Black Eyes.

cuendillar (CWAIN-deh-yar): An indestructible substance created during the Age of Legends. Any force used in an attempt to break it is absorbed, making *cuendillar* stronger. Also called heartstone.

damane (dah-MAH-nee): In the Old Tongue, literally: "leashed one." Seanchan term for women who can channel and are, as they see it, properly controlled by use of *a'dam*. Women who can channel but are not yet *damane* are called *marath'damane,* literally, "those who must be leashed." *See also a'dam;* Seanchan; *sul'dam.*

Darkfriends: Adherents of the Dark One. They believe they will gain great power and rewards, even immortality, when he is freed.

Dark One: Most common name, used in every land, for Shai'tan (SHAY-ih-TAN). The source of evil, antithesis of the Creator. Imprisoned by the Creator in Shayol Ghul at the moment of Creation. An attempt to free him brought about the War of the Shadow, the tainting of *saidin,* the Breaking of the World, and the end of the Age of Legends.

Dark One, naming the: Saying the true name of the Dark One (Shai'tan) draws his attention, bringing ill fortune at best, disaster at worst. For that reason many euphemisms are used, among them the Dark One, Father of Lies, Sightblinder, Lord of the Grave, Shepherd of the Night, Heartsbane, Soulsbane, Heartfang, Old Grim, Grassburner and Leafblighter. Darkfriends call him the Great Lord of the Dark. Someone who seems to be inviting ill fortune is often said to be "naming the Dark One."

Daughter-Heir: Title of the heir to the Lion Throne of Andor. Without a surviving daughter, the throne goes to the nearest female blood relation of the Queen. Dissension over exactly who was nearest by blood has several times led to power struggles, the latest being "the Succession"—so called in Andor and "the Third War of Andoran Succession" elsewhere—which brought Morgase of House Trakand to the throne.

Dobraine (doh-BRAIN) of House Taborwin (tah-BOHR-wihn): A high-ranking lord of Cairhien who believes in keeping the letter of his oaths.

Dragon, false: Name given to various men who have claimed to be the Dragon Reborn. Some began wars that involved many nations. Over the centuries most were unable to channel, but a few could. All, however, either disappeared or were captured or killed without fulfilling any of the Prophecies of the Dragon. Among those who could channel, the most powerful were Raolin Darksbane (active 335–36 AB), Yurian Stonebow (*circa* 1300–1308 AB), Davian (FY 351), Guaire Amalasan (FY 939–43), Logain (997 NE), and Mazrim Taim (998 NE). *See also* Dragon Reborn.

Dragon, Prophecies of the: Little known except among the well-educated and seldom spoken of, the Prophecies, given in *The Karaethon Cycle* (ka-REE-ah-thon), foretell that the Dark One will be freed again, and that Lews Therin Telamon, the Dragon, will be Reborn to fight Tarmon Gai'don, the Last Battle against the Shadow. He will, say the Prophecies, save the world—and Break it again. *See also* Dragon, the.

Dragon, the: Name by which Lews Therin Telamon was known during the War of the Shadow, some three thousand or more years ago. In the madness that overtook all male Aes Sedai, Lews Therin killed everyone who carried any of his blood, as well as everyone he loved, thus earning the name Kinslayer. *See also* Dragon, Prophecies of the; Dragon Reborn.

Dragon Reborn: According to the Prophecies of the Dragon, the man who is the Rebirth of Lews Therin Kinslayer. *See also* Dragon, false; Dragon, Prophecies of the; Dragon, the.

Dragonwall: *See* Spine of the World.

Dreadlords: Men and women able to channel, who went over to the Shadow during the Trolloc Wars, acting as generals over armies of Trollocs, Myrddraal and Darkfriends. Occasionally confused with the Forsaken by the less well educated.

Dreamer: *See* Talents.

dreamwalker: Aiel name for a woman able to enter *Tel'aran'rhiod*. *See also* Tel'aran'rhiod.

Egwene al'Vere (eh-GWAIN al-VEER): A young woman from Emond's Field, in the Two Rivers district of Andor. Now one of the Accepted, she is in training with Aiel dreamwalkers, and is possibly a Dreamer. *See also* dreamwalker; Talents.

Elaida do Avriny a'Roihan (eh-LY-da doh AHV-rih-nee ah-ROY-han): An Aes Sedai, formerly of the Red Ajah, now raised to the Amyrlin Seat. Once advisor to

Queen Morgase of Andor. She sometimes has the Foretelling.

Elayne (ee-LAIN) of House Trakand (trah-KAND): Queen Morgase's daughter, the Daughter-Heir to the Throne of Andor. Now one of the Accepted. Her sign is a golden lily. *See also:* Daughter-Heir.

Enaila (eh-NYE-lah): A Maiden of the Spear. Of the Jarra sept of the Chareen Aiel. Touchy concerning her height, she has a remarkable attitude toward Rand al'Thor considering that she is no more than a year older than he.

Faile (fah-EEL): In the Old Tongue, means "falcon." Name assumed by Zarine Bashere (zah-REEN bah-SHEER), a young woman from Saldaea.

Faolain Orande (FOW-lain oh-RAN-deh): An Accepted who does not like wilders.

***Far Dareis Mai* (FAHR DAH-rize MY):** In the Old Tongue, literally, "Of the Spear Maidens." Aiel warrior society which, unlike any other, admits women and only women. A Maiden may not marry and remain in the society, nor may she fight while carrying a child. Any child born to a Maiden is given to another woman to raise, in such a way that no one knows the child's mother. ("You may belong to no man, nor may any man belong to you, nor any child. The spear is your lover, your child, and your life.") *See also* Aiel; Aiel warrior societies.

Five Powers: There are threads to the One Power, named according to the sorts of things that can be done using them—Earth, Air (sometimes called Wind), Fire, Water, and Spirit, which are called the Five Powers. A wielder of the Power will have a greater strength with one, or possibly two but rarely more, and lesser with the others. In the Age of Legends, Spirit was found equally in men and in women, but great ability with Earth and/or Fire occurred much more often among men, ability with Water and/or Air among women. Despite exceptions, it was so often so that Earth and Fire came to be regarded as male Powers, Air and Water as female.

Flame of Tar Valon: Symbol of Tar Valon, the Amyrlin

Seat, and the Aes Sedai. A stylized representation of a flame; a white teardrop, point upwards.

Forsaken, the: Name given to thirteen of the most powerful Aes Sedai of the Age of Legends, thus among the most powerful ever known, who went over to the Dark One during the War of the Shadow in return for the promise of immortality. Their own name for themselves was "the Chosen." According to both legend and fragmentary records, they were imprisoned along with the Dark One when his prison was re-sealed. The names given to them are still used to frighten children. They were: Aginor (AGH-ih-nohr), Asmodean (ahs-MOH-dee-an), Balthamel (BAAL-thah-mell), Be'lal (BEH-lahl), Demandred (DEE-man-drehd), Graendal (GREHN-dahl), Ishamael (ih-SHAH-may-EHL), Lanfear (LAN-feer), Mesaana (meh-SAH-nah), Moghedien (moh-GHEH-dee-ehn), Rahvin (RAAV-ihn), Sammael (SAHM-may-EHL), and Semirhage (SEH-mih-RHAHG).

Gaidal Cain (GAY-dahl KAIN): Hero-swordsman of legend and story, always linked to Birgitte and said to be as handsome as she was beautiful. One of the heroes supposed to be called back when the Horn of Valere is sounded. *See also* Birgitte; Horn of Valere.

Gaidin (GYE-deen): In the Old Tongue, "Brother to Battles." A title used by Aes Sedai for the Warders. *See also* Warder.

gai'shain **(GYE-shain):** In the Old Tongue, "Pledged to Peace in Battle." An Aiel taken prisoner by other Aiel during raid or battle is required by *ji'e'toh* to serve his or her captor humbly and obediently for one year and a day, touching no weapon and doing no violence. A Wise One, a blacksmith, a child or a woman with a child under the age of ten may not be made *gai'shain*.

Galad (gah-LAHD): Lord Galadedrid Damodred (gah-LAHD-eh-drihd DAHM-oh-drehd): Called Galad. Half-brother to Elayne and Gawyn, sharing the same father, Taringail (TAH-rihn-gail) Damodred. His sign is a winged silver sword, point down.

Game of Houses: Name given the scheming, plots, and

manipulations for advantage by noble Houses. Great value is given to subtlety, to aiming at one thing while seeming to aim at another, and to achieving ends with the least visible effort. Also known as the Great Game, and sometimes by its name in the Old Tongue: *Da'es Daemar* (DAH-ess day-MAR).

Gareth Bryne (GAH-rehth BRIHN): Once Captain-General of the Queen's Guards in Andor. Exiled by Queen Morgase. Considered one of the greatest generals living. The sigil of House Bryne is a wild bull, the rose crown of Andor around its neck. Gareth Bryne's personal sigil is three golden stars, each of five rays.

Gawyn (GAH-wihn) of House Trakand (trah-KAND): Queen Morgase's son, and Elayne's brother, who will be First Prince of the Sword when Elayne ascends to the throne. His sign is a white boar.

gentling: The act, performed by Aes Sedai, of shutting off a male who can channel from the One Power. Necessary because any man who channels will go insane from the taint on *saidin* and almost certainly do horrible things with the Power in his madness before the taint kills him. One who has been gentled can still sense the True Source, but cannot touch it. Whatever madness has come before gentling is arrested but not cured, and if it is done soon enough death can be averted. A man who is gentled, however, inevitably gives up wanting to live; those who do not succeed in committing suicide usually die anyway within a year or two. *See also* One Power; stilling.

gleeman: A traveling storyteller, musician, juggler, tumbler, and all-around entertainer. Known by their trademark cloaks of many-colored patches, gleemen perform mainly in the villages and smaller towns.

Great Blight: A region in the far north, entirely corrupted by the Dark One. A haunt of Trollocs, Myrddraal, and other creatures of the Shadow.

Great Lord of the Dark: Name by which Darkfriends refer to the Dark One, claiming that to speak his true name would be blasphemous.

Great Serpent: A symbol for time and eternity, ancient before the Age of Legends began, consisting of a serpent eating its own tail. A ring in the shape of the Great Serpent is awarded to women who have been raised to the Accepted among the Aes Sedai.

High Lords of Tear: Acting as a council, the High Lords are historically the rulers of the nation of Tear, which has neither king nor queen. Their numbers are not fixed, and have varied from as many as twenty to as few as six. Not to be confused with the Lords of the Land, who are lesser Tairen lords.

Horn of Valere (vah-LEER): The legendary object of the Great Hunt of the Horn, it can call back dead heroes from the grave to fight against the Shadow. A new Hunt of the Horn has been called, and sworn Hunters for the Horn can now be found in many nations.

Illian (IHL-lee-an): A great port on the Sea of Storms, capital city of the nation of the same name.

Isendre (ih-SEHN-dreh): A beautiful and greedy woman who angered the wrong woman and for once in her life told the truth when she denied stealing.

ji'e'toh **(jih-eh-toh):** In the Old Tongue, "honor and obligation" or "honor and duty." The complex code by which Aiel live, and which would take a shelf of volumes to explain. By way of small example, there are many paths to gain honor in battle. The smallest is to kill, for anyone can kill. The greatest is to touch an armed and living enemy without causing harm. Somewhere in the middle is to make an enemy *gai'shain.* For another example, shame, which also has many levels in *ji'e'toh,* is considered on many of those levels to be worse than pain, injury or even death. For a third, there are, again, many degrees of *toh,* or obligation, but even the smallest of these must be met in full. *Toh* outweighs other considerations to the extent that an Aiel will often accept shame, if necessary, to fulfill an obligation that might seem minor to an outlander. *See also gai'shain.*

Juilin Sandar (JUY-lihn sahn-DAHR): A thief-catcher from Tear.

Kadere, Hadnan (kah-DEER, HAHD-nahn): A supposed peddler who regrets ever having entered the Aiel Waste.

Lamgwin Dorn (lam-GWIHN DOHRN): A street tough and brawler who is loyal to his queen.

Lan (LAN); al'Lan Mandragoran (AHL-LAN man-DRAG-or-an): A Warder, bonded to Moiraine. Uncrowned King of Malkier, Dai Shan (Battle Lord), and the last surviving Malkieri lord. *See also* Warder; Moiraine; Malkier.

Lanfear (LAN-feer): In the Old Tongue, "Daughter of the Night." One of the Forsaken. Unlike the others, she chose this name herself. Said to have loved Lews Therin Telamon, and to have hated his wife, Ilyena. *See also* Forsaken; Dragon, the.

Leane Sharif (lee-AHN-eh shah-REEF): Once an Aes Sedai of the Blue Ajah, and Keeper of the Chronicles. Now deposed and stilled, seeking to rediscover who she is. *See also* Ajah.

Length, units of: 10 inches = 1 foot; 3 feet = 1 pace; 2 paces = 1 span; 1000 spans = 1 mile; 4 miles = 1 league.

Lews Therin Telamon; Lews Therin Kinslayer: *See* Dragon, the.

Liandrin (lee-AHN-drihn): An Aes Sedai formerly of the Red Ajah, from Tarabon. Now known to be of the Black Ajah.

Lini (LIHN-nee): Childhood nurse to the Lady Elayne, and before her to Elayne's mother, Morgase, as well as to Morgase's mother. A woman of vast inner strength, considerable perception, and a great many sayings.

Logain (loh-GAIN): A man who once claimed to be the Dragon Reborn, now gentled. *See also* Dragon, false.

Lugard (LOO-gahrd): Nominally the capital of Murandy, though that country is a quilt of loyalties to towns and individual lords and ladies, and whoever sits on the throne seldom has any real control over even the city. Lugard is a major trade center, and a byword for thievery, licentiousness and general disrepute.

Macura, Ronde (mah-CURE-ah, rohn-deh): A seamstress in Amadicia who tried to serve too many masters and mistresses without knowing who they all were.

Maighande (mye-GHAN-deh): One of the greatest battles of the Trolloc Wars. The victory of humankind here began the long push that finally drove the Trollocs back to the Great Blight. *See also* Great Blight; Trolloc Wars.

Malkier (mahl-KEER): A nation, once one of the Borderlands, now consumed by the Blight. The sign of Malkier was a golden crane in flight.

Manetheren (mahn-EHTH-ehr-ehn): One of the Ten Nations that made the Second Covenant. Also the capital city of that nation. Both city and nation were utterly destroyed in the Trolloc Wars. *See also* Trolloc Wars.

Mat Cauthon: A young man, from Emond's Field in the Two Rivers district of Andor, who is *ta'veren* and also extremely lucky. Full name: Matrim (MAT-trim) Cauthon.

Mayene (may-EHN): City-state on the Sea of Storms, hemmed in and historically oppressed by Tear. The ruler of Mayene is styled "the First"; Firsts claim to be descendants of Artur Hawkwing. The banner of Mayene is a golden hawk in flight on a field of blue.

Mazrim Taim (MAHZ-rihm tah-EEM): A false Dragon who raised havoc in Saldaea until he was defeated and captured. Not only able to channel, but supposedly of great strength. *See also* Dragon, false.

Meilan (MYE-lan) of House Mendiana (mehn-dee-AH-nah): A High Lord of Tear. A competent general, but a man of ambitions and hates. *See also* High Lords of Tear.

Melaine (meh-LAYN): A Wise One of the Jhirad sept of Goshien Aiel. A dreamwalker. *See also* dreamwalker.

Melindhra (meh-LIHN-dhrah): A Maiden of the Spear, of the Jumai sept of the Shaido Aiel. A woman of divided loyalties. *See also* Aiel warrior societies.

Min (MIN): A young woman with the ability to read things about people in the auras and images she sometimes sees surrounding them.

Moiraine (mwah-RAIN): An Aes Sedai of the Blue Ajah. Born in Cairhein, of House Damodred, though not in line of succession to the throne, and raised in the Royal Palace. Rarely uses her House name, and keeps her association with it as secret as possible.

Morgase (moor-GAYZ): By the Grace of the Light, Queen of Andor, Defender of the Realm, Protector of the People, High Seat of House Trakand. Her sign is three golden keys. The sign of House Trakand is a silver keystone.

Myrddraal (MUHRD-draal): Creatures of the Dark One, commanders of the Trollocs. Twisted offspring of Trollocs in which the human stock used to create the Trollocs has resurfaced, but tainted by the evil that made the Trollocs. They have no eyes, but can see like eagles in light or dark. They have certain powers stemming from the Dark One, including the ability to cause paralyzing fear with a look, and to vanish wherever there are shadows. Among Myrddraal's known weaknesses is that they are reluctant to cross running water. Mirrors reflect them only mistily. In different lands they are known by many names, among them Halfman, the Eyeless, Shadowman, Lurk, Fetch, and Fade.

Natael, Jasin (nah-TAYL, JAY-sihn): Name used by Asmodean, one of the Forsaken.

Niall, Pedron (NEYE-awl, PAY-drohn): Lord Captain Commander of the Children of the Light. *See also* Children of the Light.

Nynaeve al'Meara (NIGH-neev al-MEER-ah): A woman once the Wisdom of Emond's Field, in the Two Rivers district of Andor. Now one of the Accepted.

Oaths, Three: The oaths taken by an Accepted on being raised to Aes Sedai. Spoken while holding the Oath Rod, a *ter'angreal* that makes oaths binding. They are: (1) To speak no word that is not true. (2) To make no weapon with which one man may kill another. (3) Never to use the One Power as a weapon except against Shadowspawn, or in the last extreme of defense of her own life, or that of her Warder or another Aes Sedai. The second oath was the first adopted after the War of the Shadow. The first oath, while held to the letter, is often circumvented by careful speaking. It is believed that the last two are inviolable.

Ogier (OH-gehr): (1) A non-human race, characterized by great height (ten feet is average for adult males), broad, almost snout-like noses, and long, tufted ears. They live in areas called *stedding,* which they rarely leave, and they typically have little contact with humankind. Knowledge of them among humans is sparse, and many believe Ogier to be only legends, though they are wondrous stonemasons and built most of the great cities constructed after the Breaking.

Old Tongue: The language spoken during the Age of Legends. It is generally expected that nobles and the educated will have learned to speak it, but most know only a few words. Translation is often difficult, as it is a language capable of many subtly different meanings. *See also* Age of Legends.

One Power: The power drawn from the True Source. The vast majority of people are completely unable to learn to channel the One Power. A very small number can be taught to channel, and an even tinier number have the ability inborn. These few have no need to be taught; eventually they will channel whether they want to or not, often without even realizing what they are doing. This inborn ability usually manifests itself in late adolescence or early adulthood. If control is not taught, or self-learned (extremely difficult, with a success rate of only one in four), death is certain. Since the Time of Madness, no man has been able to channel the Power without eventually going completely, horribly mad, and then, even if he has learned some control, dying from a wasting sickness that causes the sufferer to rot alive, a sickness caused, as is the madness, by the Dark One's taint on *saidin. See also* Aes Sedai; channel; Five Powers; Time of Madness; True Source.

Pattern of an Age: The Wheel of Time weaves the threads of human lives into the Pattern of an Age, often called simply the Pattern, which forms the substance of reality for that Age. *See also ta'veren.*

Rand al'Thor (RAND al-THOR): A young man from Emond's Field, in the Two Rivers district of Andor, who is *ta'veren.* Once a shepherd. Now proclaimed as the Dragon Reborn, and also as He Who Comes With the Dawn, prophecied to unite the Aiel and break them. It also seems likely that he is the Coramoor, or Chosen One, sought by the Sea Folk. *See also* Aiel; Dragon Reborn.

Rhuarc (RHOURK): An Aiel, clan chief of the Taardad Aiel.

Rhuidean (RHUY-dee-ahn): A great city, the only one in the Aiel Waste and totally unknown to the outside world. Abandoned for nearly three thousand years. Once men among the Aiel were allowed to enter Rhuidean only once, in order to be tested, inside a great *ter'angreal,* for fitness to become clan chief (only one in three survived), and women only twice, for testing in that same *ter'angreal* and again to become Wise Ones, though with a considerably higher survival rate. Now the city is inhabited again, by Aiel, and a great lake occupies one end of the valley of Rhuidean, fed by an underground ocean of fresh water and in turn feeding the only river in the Waste.

sa'angreal (SAH-ahn-GREE-ahl): Remnants of the Age of Legends that allow channeling much more of the One Power than is otherwise possible or safe. A *sa'angreal* is similar to, but more powerful than, an *angreal.* The amount of the Power that can be wielded with a *sa'angreal* compares to the amount that can be handled with an *angreal* as the Power wielded with the aid of an *angreal* does to the amount that can be handled unaided. The making of them is no longer known. As with *angreal,* there are male and female *sa'angreal.* Only a handful remain, far fewer even than *angreal.*

saidar (sah-ih-DAHR); saidin (sah-ih-DEEN): *See* True Source.

Seanchan (SHAWN-CHAN): (1) Descendants of the armies Artur Hawkwing sent across the Aryth Ocean, who conquered the lands there. They believe that any woman who can channel must be controlled for the safety of everyone else, and any man who can channel must be killed for the same reason. (2) The land from which the Seanchan come.

Seekers for Truth: A police/spy organization of the Seanchan Imperial Throne. Although most Seekers are property of the Imperial family, they have wide powers. Even one of the Blood (a Seanchan noble) can be arrested for failure to answer any question put by a Seeker, or for failure to cooperate fully with a Seeker, this last defined by the Seekers themselves, subject only to review by the Empress.

Shayol Ghul (SHAY-ol GHOOL): A mountain in the Blasted Lands, beyond the Great Blight. Site of the Dark One's prison.

Siuan Sanche (SWAHN SAHN-chay): Daughter of a Tairen fisherman, according to Tairen law she was put on a ship to Tar Valon before the second sunset after discovery that she had the potential to channel. Once Aes Sedai of the Blue Ajah and later Amyrlin Seat, she was deposed and stilled. Now seeking to avoid the fate she fears.

Spine of the World: A towering mountain range, with few passes, which separates the Aiel Waste from the lands to the west. Also called the Dragonwall.

stilling: The act, performed by Aes Sedai, of shutting off a woman who can channel from the One Power. A woman who has been stilled can sense the True Source, but not touch it. So seldom has it been done that novices are required to learn the names and crimes of all women who have suffered it. Officially, stilling is the result of trial and sentence for a crime. When it happens accidentally, it is called being burned out. In practice, the term "stilling" is often used for both. Women who have been stilled, however it occurred, seldom survive long; they seem to simply give up and die.

Stone of Tear: A great fortress in the city of Tear, said to have been made with the One Power soon after the Breaking of the World. Attacked and besieged unsuccessfully countless times, it fell in a single night to the Dragon Reborn and a few hundred Aiel, thus fulfilling two parts of the Prophecies of the Dragon. *See also* Dragon, Prophecies of the.

sul'dam (SOOL-dam): Literally, "leash holder." Seanchan term for a woman with the ability to control, by means of an *a'dam,* a woman who can channel. A fairly honored position among the Seanchan. What is known only to a few is that *sul'dam* are in fact those women who could be taught to channel. *See also a'dam; damane;* Seanchan.

Talents: Abilities in the use of the One Power in specific areas. The best known is Healing. Some, such as Traveling, the ability to shift from one place to another without crossing the intervening space, have been lost to the Aes Sedai of today. Others, such as Foretelling (the ability to foretell future events, but in a general way), are now found rarely. Another Talent long thought lost is Dreaming, which involves, among other things, interpreting the Dreamer's dreams to foretell future events in more specific fashion than Foretelling does. Some Dreamers had the ability to enter *Tel'aran'rhiod,* the World of Dreams, and (it is said) even other people's dreams. The last acknowledged Dreamer was Corianin Nedeal (coh-ree-AHN-ihn neh-dee-AHL), who died in 526 NE, but there is now another, known to but a few. *See also Tel'aran'rhiod.*

Tallanvor, Martyn (TAL-lahn-vohr, mahr-TEEN): Guardsman-Lieutenant of the Queen's Guards who loves his queen more than life or honor.

ta'maral'ailen (tah-MAHR-ahl-EYE-lehn): In the Old Tongue, "Web of Destiny." A great change in the Pattern of an Age, centered around one or more people who are *ta'veren. See also* Pattern of an Age; *ta'veren.*

Tanchico (tan-CHEE-coh): Capital city of Tarabon. *See* Tarabon.

Tarabon (TAH-rah-BON): Nation on the Aryth Ocean.

Once a great trading nation, a source of rugs, dyes and fireworks produced by the Guild of Illuminators, among other things. Little news has come out of Tarabon since the land became racked by anarchy and civil war compounded by simultaneous wars against Arad Doman and the Dragonsworn, people who have sworn to follow the Dragon Reborn.

Tarmon Gai'don (TAHR-mohn GAY-dohn): The Last Battle. *See also* Dragon, Prophecies of the; Horn of Valere.

ta'veren **(tah-VEER-ehn):** A person around whom the Wheel of Time weaves all surrounding life-threads, perhaps ALL life-threads, to form a Web of Destiny. *See also* Pattern of an Age; *ta'maral'ailen.*

Tear (TEER): A nation on the Sea of Storms. Also the capital city of that nation, a great seaport. The banner of Tear is three white crescent moons slanting across a field half red, half gold. *See also* Stone of Tear.

Telamon, Lews Therin (TEHL-ah-mon, LOOZ THEH-rihn): *See* Dragon, the.

Tel'aran'rhiod **(tel-AYE-rahn-rhee-ODD):** In the Old Tongue, "the Unseen World," or "the World of Dreams." A world glimpsed in dreams which was believed by the ancients to permeate and surround all other possible worlds. Many can touch *Tel'aran'rhiod* for a few moments in their dreams, but few have ever had the ability to enter it at will, though some *ter'angreal* have recently been discovered to confer that ability. Unlike other dreams, what happens to living things in the World of Dreams is real; a wound taken there will still exist on awakening, and one who dies there does not wake at all. *See also ter'angreal.*

ter'angreal **(TEER-ahn-GREE-ahl):** Remnants of the Age of Legends that use the One Power. Unlike *angreal* and *sa'angreal,* each *ter'angreal* was made to do a particular thing. Some *ter'angreal* are used by Aes Sedai, but the original purposes of many are unknown. Some require channeling, while others may be used by anyone. Some will kill or destroy the ability to channel of any woman who uses them. Like *angreal* and *sa'angreal,* the making of them has been lost since the Breaking of the World. *See also angreal; sa'angreal.*

Thom Merrilin (TOM MER-rih-lihn): A not-so-simple gleeman and traveler. *See also* gleeman.

Time of Madness: The years after the Dark One's counterstroke tainted the male half of the True Source, when male Aes Sedai went mad and Broke the World. The exact duration of this period is unknown, but it is believed to have lasted nearly one hundred years. It ended completely only with the death of the last male Aes Sedai. *See also* One Power; True Source.

Trollocs (TRAHL-lohks): Creatures of the Dark One, created during the War of the Shadow. Huge of stature, they are a twisted blend of animal and human stock. Divided into tribe-like bands, among them the Dha'vol, the Ko'bal, and the Dhai'mon. Vicious by nature, they kill for the pure pleasure of killing. Deceitful in the extreme, they cannot be trusted unless coerced by fear.

Trolloc Wars: A series of wars, beginning about 1000 AB and lasting more than three hundred years, during which Trolloc armies ravaged the world. Eventually the Trollocs were driven back into the Great Blight, but some nations ceased to exist, and others that survived were almost depopulated. All records of the time are fragmentary.

True Source: The driving force of the universe, which turns the Wheel of Time. Divided into a male half (*saidin*) and a female half (*saidar*), which work at the same time with and against each other. Only a man can draw on *saidin,* only a woman on *saidar.* Since the beginning of the Time of Madness, *saidin* has been tainted by the Dark One's touch. *See also* One Power.

Verin Mathwin (VEH-rihn MATH-wihn): Aes Sedai of the Brown Ajah, last known to be in the Two Rivers purportedly seeking girls who could be taught to channel. *See also* Ajah.

Warder: A warrior bonded to an Aes Sedai. The bonding is a thing of the One Power: by it he gains such gifts as quick healing, the ability to go long periods without food, water, or rest, and the ability to sense the taint of the Dark One at a distance. So long as a Warder lives, the Aes Sedai to whom he is bonded knows he is alive however far away he is, and when he dies she will know the moment and manner of his death. While most Ajahs believe an Aes Sedai may have one Warder bonded to her at a time, the Red Ajah refuses to bond any Warders at all, and the Green Ajah believes an Aes Sedai may bond as many as she wishes. Ethically the Warder must accede to the bonding voluntarily, but it has been known to be done against the Warder's will. What the Aes Sedai gain from the bonding is a closely held secret. *See also* Aes Sedai.

War of Power: *See* War of the Shadow.

War of the Hundred Years (FY 994–FY 1117): A series of overlapping wars among constantly shifting alliances, precipitated by the death of Artur Hawkwing and the resulting struggle for his empire. The War of the Hundred Years depopulated large parts of the lands between the Aryth Ocean and the Aiel Waste, from the Sea of Storms to the Great Blight. So great was the destruction that only fragmentary records of the time remain. The empire of Artur Hawkwing was pulled apart, and the nations of the present day were formed. *See also* Hawkwing, Artur.

War of the Shadow: Also known as the War of Power. Began shortly after the attempt to free the Dark One, and soon involved the whole world. In a world where even the memory of war had been forgotten, every facet of war was rediscovered, often twisted by the Dark One's touch on the world, and the One Power was used as a weapon. The war was ended by the resealing of the Dark One into his prison in a strike led by Lews Therin Telamon, the Dragon, and one hundred male Aes Sedai called the Hundred Companions. The Dark One's counterstroke tainted *saidin* and drove Lews Therin and the Hundred Companions insane, thus beginning the Time of Madness. *See also* Dragon, the; One Power, the; Time of Madness, the.

Weight, units of: 10 ounces = 1 pound; 10 pounds = 1 stone; 10 stone = 1 hundredweight; 10 hundredweight = 1 ton.

Wheel of Time, the: Time is a wheel with seven spokes, each spoke an Age. As the Wheel turns, Ages come and go, each leaving memories that fade to legend, then to myth, and are forgotten by the time that Age comes again. The Pattern of an Age is slightly different each time an Age comes, and each time it is subject to greater change.

Whitecloaks: *See* Children of the Light.

wilder: A woman who has learned to channel the One Power on her own, surviving the crisis as only one in four does. Such women usually build barriers against knowing what it is they are doing, but if these can be broken down, wilders are among the most powerful of channelers. The term is often used in derogatory fashion.

Wisdom: In villages, a woman chosen by the Women's Circle for her knowledge of such things as healing and foretelling the weather, as well as common good sense. Generally considered the equal of the Mayor, and in some villages his superior. She is chosen for life, and it is very rare for a Wisdom to be removed from office before her death. Depending on the land, she may instead have another title, such as Guide, Healer, Wise Woman, or Seeker.

Wise One: Among the Aiel, Wise Ones are women chosen by other Wise Ones and trained in healing, herbs and other things, much like Wisdoms. Usually there is a single Wise One to each clan or sept hold. They have great authority and responsibility, as well as great influence with sept and clan chiefs, though these men often accuse them of meddling. Wise Ones stand outside all feuds and battles, and according to *ji'e'toh* may not be harmed or impeded in any way. Some Wise Ones have the ability to channel, but they do not advertise this. Three Wise Ones now living are dreamwalkers, with the ability to enter *Tel'aran'rhiod* and to speak to other people in their dreams, among other things. *See also* dreamwalker; *ji'e'toh; Tel'aran'rhiod.*

About the Author

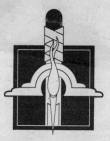

Robert Jordan was born in 1948 in Charleston, South Carolina, where he lived with his wife, Harriet, in a house built in 1797. He taught himself to read when he was four with the incidental aid of a twelve-year-older brother, and was tackling Mark Twain and Jules Verne by five. He graduated from The Citadel, the Military College of South Carolina, with a degree in physics. He served two tours in Vietnam with the U.S. Army; among his decorations are the Distinguished Flying Cross, the Bronze Star with "V," and two Vietnamese Crosses of Gallantry. A history buff, he also wrote dance and theater criticism. He enjoyed the outdoor sports of hunting, fishing, and sailing, and the indoor sports of poker, chess, pool, and pipe collecting. He died on September 16, 2007.

TOR
BOOKS The Best in Fantasy

Robert Jordan • *The Wheel of Tim*

Book One: *The Eye of the World*
0-812-51181-6 • $6.99 ($8.99 CAN) / in hardcover: 0-312-85009-3 • $27.95

"Jordan writes with the stark vision of light and darkness, and some-times childish sense of wonder, that permeates J.R.R. Tolkien works. His style is undebatably his own." —*Pittsburgh Press*

Book Two: *The Great Hunt*
0-812-51772-5 • $7.99 ($9.99 CAN) / in hardcover: 0-312-85140-5 • $27.95

"Those who like fantasy can rejoice. This is the genuine article."
—John Lee, author of *The Unicorn Solution*

Book Three: *The Dragon Reborn*
0-812-51371-1 • $7.99 ($9.99 CAN) / in hardcover: 0-312-85248-7 • $27.95

"One of *the* books to read this year." —*Science Fiction Review*

Book Four: *The Shadow Rising*
0-812-51373-8 • $7.99 ($9.99 CAN) / in hardcover: 0-312-85431-5 • $27.95 ($39.95 CAN)

"Complex, exciting. One of the best yet."
—*The Post and Courier* (Charleston, SC)

Book Five: *The Fires of Heaven*
0-812-55030-7 • $7.99 ($9.99 CAN) / in hardcover: 0-312-85427-7 • $25.95 ($29.95 CAN)

"This volume, indeed the whole saga, surpasses all but a few of peers." —*ALA Booklist*

Book Six: *Lord of Chaos*
0-812-51375-4 • $7.99 ($9.99 CAN) / in hardcover: 0-312-85428-5 • $27.95 ($39.95 CAN)

"A great read....Some surprising new developments....I can't rec mend starting anywhere but at the beginning, but the volu only get richer as they go along." —*Locus*

Book Seven: *A Crown of Swords*
0-812-55028-5 • $7.99 ($9.99 CAN) ! in hardcover: 0-312-85767-5 • $27.95 ($34.95 CAN)

"Jordan's preeminent saga [has] remained remarkably rich....Will n disappoint." —*ALA Booklist*

All these books are available in both hardcover and paperback. not see them on display, ask your bookseller to order them fc